Isaac Asimov, world maestro of science fiction, was born in Russia near Smolensk in 1920 and brought to the United States by his parents three years later. He grew up in Brooklyn where he went to grammar school and at the age of eight he gained his citizen papers. A remarkable memory helped him finish high school before he was sixteen. He then went on to Columbia University and resolved to become a chemist rather than follow the medical career his father had in mind for him. He graduated in chemistry and after a short spell in the Army he gained his doctorate in 1949 and qualified as an instructor in biochemistry at Boston University School of Medicine where he became Associate Professor in 1955, doing research in nucleic acid. Increasingly, however, the pressures of chemical research conflicted with his aspirations in the literary field, and in 1958 he retired to full-time authorship while retaining his connection with the University.

Asimov's fantastic career as a science fiction writer began in 1939 with the appearance of a short story, *Marooned Off Vesta*, in *Amazing Stories*. Thereafter he became a regular contributor to the leading SF magazines of the day including *Astounding*, *Astonishing Stories*, *Super Science Stories* and *Galaxy*. He won the Hugo Award four times and the Nebula Award once. With over three hundred books to his credit and several hundred articles, Asimov's output was prolific by any standards. Apart from his many world-famous science fiction works, Asimov also wrote highly successful detective mystery stories, a four-volume *History of North America*, a two-v
cal dictionary, encyclo
list of books on many
umes of autobiography

Isaac Asimov died in

BY THE SAME AUTHOR

The Foundation Saga
Prelude to Foundation
Foundation
Foundation and Empire
Second Foundation
Foundation's Edge
Foundation and Earth

Galactic Empire Novels
The Currents of Space
The Stars Like Dust
Pebble in the Sky

Earth is Room Enough
The Martian Way
The End of Eternity
The Winds of Change

Asimov's Mysteries
The Gods Themselves
Nightfall One
Nightfall Two
Buy Jupiter
The Bicentennial Man
Nine Tomorrows

Robot Stories and Novels
I, Robot
The Rest of the Robots
The Caves of Steel
The Naked Sun
The Robots of Dawn
Robots and Empire

The Early Asimov: Volume 1
The Early Asimov: Volume 2
The Early Asimov: Volume 3

Nebula Award Stories 8 (editor)
The Science Fictional Solar System (editor, with Martin Harry Greenberg and Charles G. Waugh)
The Stars in their Courses (non-fiction)
The Left Hand of the Electron (non-fiction)
Asimov on Science Fiction (non-fiction)
The Sun Shines Bright (non-fiction)
Counting the Eons (non-fiction)
Far As Human Eye Could See (non-fiction)

Tales of the Black Widowers (detection)
More Tales of the Black Widowers (detection)
Casebook of the Black Widowers (detection)
Authorised Murder (detection)
The Union Club Mysteries (detection)

Voyager

ISAAC ASIMOV

The Complete Robot

HarperCollins*Publishers*

Voyager
An Imprint of HarperCollins*Publishers*
77–85 Fulham Palace Road,
Hammersmith, London W6 8JB

www.voyager-books.com

This paperback edition 1995
22

Previously published in paperback by
HarperCollins Science Fiction & Fantasy 1993, reprinted twice
and by Grafton 1983, reprinted eight times

First published in Great Britain by
Granada Publishing 1982

ISBN 0 586 05724 2

Set in Plantin

Printed and bound in Great Britain by
Clays Ltd, St Ives plc

Dedicated to:

Marjorie Goldstein

David Bearinger

Hugh O'Neill

for whom books are in progress

Contents

Introduction

By the time I was in my late teens and already a hardened science fiction reader, I had read many robot stories and found that they fell into two classes.

In the first class there was Robot-as-Menace. I don't have to explain that overmuch. Such stories were a mixture of 'clank-clank' and 'aarghh' and 'There are some things man was not meant to know.' After a while, they palled dreadfully and I couldn't stand them.

In the second class (a much smaller one) there was Robot-as-Pathos. In such stories the robots were lovable and were usually put upon by cruel human beings. These charmed me. In late 1938 two such stories hit the stands that particularly impressed me. One was a short story by Eando Binder entitled 'I, Robot,' about a saintly robot named Adam Link: another was a story by Lester del Rey, entitled 'Helen O'Loy,' that touched me with its portrayal of a robot that was everything a loyal wife should be.

When, therefore, on June 10, 1939 (yes, I do keep meticulous records), I sat down to write my first robot story, there was no question that I fully intended to write a Robot-as-Pathos story. I wrote 'Robbie,' about a robot nurse and a little girl and love and a prejudiced mother and a weak father and a broken heart and a tearful reunion. (It originally appeared under the title – one I hated – of 'Strange Playfellow.')

But something odd happened as I wrote this first story. I managed to get the dim vision of a robot as neither Menace nor Pathos. I began to think of robots as industrial products built by matter-of-fact engineers. They were built with safety features so they weren't Menaces and they were fashioned for certain jobs so that no Pathos was necessarily involved.

As I continued to write robot stories, this notion of carefully engineered industrial robots permeated my stories more and more until the whole character of robot stories in serious printed science fiction changed – not only that of my own stories, but of just about everybody's.

That made me feel good and for many years, decades even, I went about freely admitting that I was 'the father of the modern robot story.'

As time went by, I made other discoveries that delighted me. I found, for instance, that when I used the word 'robotics' to describe the study of robots, I was *not* using a word that already existed but had invented a word that had never been used before. (That was in my story 'Runaround,' published in 1942.)

The word has now come into general use. There are journals and books with the word in the title and it is generally known in the field that I invented the term. Don't think I'm not proud of *that*. There are not many people who have coined a useful scientific term, and although I did it unknowingly, I have no intention of letting anyone in the world forget it.

What's more, in 'Runaround' I listed my 'Three Laws of Robotics' in explicit detail for the first time, and these, too, became famous. At least, they are quoted in and out of season, in all sorts of places that have nothing primarily to do with science fiction, even in general quotation references. And people who work in the field of artificial intelligence sometimes take occasion to tell me that they think the Three Laws will serve as a good guide.

We can go even beyond that –

When I wrote my robot stories I had no thought that robots would come into existence in my lifetime. In fact, I was certain they would not, and would have wagered vast sums that they would not. (At least, I would have wagered 15 cents, which is my betting limit on sure things.)

Yet here I am, forty-three years after I wrote my first robot story, and we *do* have robots. Indeed, we do. What's more, they are what I envisaged them to be in a way – industrial robots, created by engineers to do specific jobs and with safety features built in. They are to be found in numerous factories, particularly in Japan, where there are automobile factories that are entirely roboticized. The assembly line in such places is 'manned' by robots at every stage.

To be sure, these robots are not as intelligent as my robots are – they are not positronic: they are not even humanoid. However, they are evolving rapidly and becoming steadily more capable and versatile. Who knows where they'll be in another forty years?

One thing we can be sure of. Robots are changing the world and driving it in directions we cannot clearly foresee.

Where are these robots-in-reality coming from? The most important single source is a firm called Unimation, Inc., of Danbury, Connecticut. It is the leading manufacturer of industrial robots and is responsible for perhaps one third of all robots that have been installed. The president of the firm is Joseph F. Engelberger, who founded it in the late 1950s because he was so interested in robots that he decided to make their production his life work.

But how in the world did he become so interested in robots so early in the game? According to his own words, he grew interested in robots in the 1940s when he was a physics-major undergraduate at Columbia University, reading the robot stories of his fellow Columbian Isaac Asimov.

My goodness!

You know, I didn't write my robot stories with much in

the way of ambition back in those old, old days. All I wanted was to sell them to the magazines in order to earn a few hundred dollars to help pay my college tuition – and to see my name in print besides.

If I had been writing in any other field of literature, that's all I would have attained. But because I was writing science fiction, and *only* because I was writing science fiction, I – without knowing it – was starting a chain of events that is changing the face of the world.

Joseph F. Engelberger, by the way, published a book in 1980 called *Robotics in Practice: Management and Application of Industrial Robots* (American Management Associations), and he was kind enough to invite me to write the foreword.

All this set the nice people at Doubleday to thinking –

My various robot short stories have appeared in no less than seven different collections of mine. Why should they be so separated? Since they appear to be far more important than anyone dreamed they would be (least of all, I) at the time they were written, why not pull them together in a single book?

It wasn't hard to get me to agree, so here are thirty-one short stories, totaling some 200,000 words, written over a time period stretching from 1939 to 1977.

Some Non-human Robots

I am not having the robot stories appear in the order in which they were written. Rather, I am grouping them by the nature of the contents. In this first division, for instance, I deal with robots that have a non-human shape – a dog, an automobile, a box. Why not? The industrial robots that have come into existence in reality are non-human in appearance.

The very first story, 'A Boy's Best Friend,' is not in any of my earlier collections. It was written on September 10, 1974, and you may find in it a distant echo of 'Robbie,' written thirty-five years earlier, which appears later in this volume. Don't think I'm not aware of that.

You will note, by the way, that in these three stories, the concept of Robot-as-Pathos is clearly marked. You may also notice, however, that in 'Sally' there seems to be no hint of the Three Laws and that there is more than a hint of Robot-as-Menace. Well, if I want to do that once in a while, I can, I suppose. Who's there to stop me?

A Boy's Best Friend

Mr Anderson said, 'Where's Jimmy, dear?'

'Out on the crater,' said Mrs Anderson. 'He'll be all right. Robutt is with him. – Did he arrive?'

'Yes. He's at the rocket station, going through the tests. Actually, I can hardly wait to see him myself. I haven't really seen one since I left Earth 15 years ago. You can't count films.'

'Jimmy has never seen one,' said Mrs Anderson.

'Because he's Moonborn and can't visit Earth. That's why I'm bringing one here. I think it's the first one ever on the Moon.'

'It cost enough,' said Mrs Anderson, with a small sigh.

'Maintaining Robutt isn't cheap, either,' said Mr Anderson.

Jimmy was out on the crater, as his mother had said. By Earth standards, he was spindly, but rather tall for a 10-year-old. His arms and legs were long and agile. He looked thicker and stubbier with his spacesuit on, but he could handle the lunar gravity as no Earthborn human being could. His father couldn't begin to keep up with him when Jimmy stretched his legs and went into the kangaroo hop.

The outer side of the crater sloped southward and the Earth, which was low in the southern sky (where it always was, as seen from Lunar City), was nearly full, so that the entire crater-slope was brightly lit.

The slope was a gentle one and even the weight of the spacesuit couldn't keep Jimmy from racing up it in a floating hop that made the gravity seem nonexistent.

'Come on, Robutt,' he shouted.

Robutt, who could hear him by radio, squeaked and bounded after.

Jimmy, expert though he was, couldn't outrace Robutt, who didn't need a spacesuit, and had four legs and tendons of steel. Robutt sailed over Jimmy's head, somersaulting and landing almost under his feet.

'Don't show off, Robutt,' said Jimmy, 'and stay in sight.'

Robutt squeaked again, the special squeak that meant 'Yes.'

'I don't trust you, you faker,' shouted Jimmy, and up he went in one last bound that carried him over the curved upper edge of the crater wall and down onto the inner slope.

The Earth sank below the top of the crater wall and at once it was pitch-dark around him. A warm, friendly darkness that wiped out the difference between ground and sky except for the glitter of stars.

Actually, Jimmy wasn't supposed to exercise along the dark side of the crater wall. The grownups said it was dangerous, but that was because they were never there. The ground was smooth and crunchy and Jimmy knew the exact location of every one of the few rocks.

Besides, how could it be dangerous racing through the dark when Robutt was right there with him, bouncing around and squeaking and glowing? Even without the glow, Robutt could tell where he was, and where Jimmy was, by radar. Jimmy couldn't go wrong while Robutt was around, tripping him when he was too near a rock, or jumping on him to show how much he loved him, or circling around and squeaking low and scared when Jimmy hid behind a rock, when all the time Robutt knew well enough where he was. Once Jimmy had lain still and pretended he was hurt and Robutt had sounded the radio alarm and people from Lunar City got there in a hurry. Jimmy's father had let him hear about that little trick and Jimmy never tried it again.

Just as he was remembering that, he heard his father's voice on his private wavelength. 'Jimmy, come back. I have something to tell you.'

Jimmy was out of his spacesuit now and washed up. You always had to wash up after coming in from outside. Even Robutt had to be sprayed, but he loved it. He stood there on all fours, his little foot-long body quivering and glowing just a tiny bit, and his small head, with no mouth, with two large glassed-in eyes, and with a bump where the brain was. He squeaked until Mr Anderson said, 'Quiet, Robutt.'

Mr Anderson was smiling. 'We have something for you, Jimmy. It's at the rocket station now, but we'll have it tomorrow after all the tests are over. I thought I'd tell you now.'

'From Earth, Dad?'

'A *dog* from Earth, son. A real dog. A Scotch terrier puppy. The first dog on the Moon. You won't need Robutt any more. We can't keep them both, you know, and some other boy or girl will have Robutt.' He seemed to be waiting for Jimmy to say something, then he said, 'You know what a dog is, Jimmy. It's the real thing. Robutt's only a mechanical imitation, a robot-mutt. That's how he got his name.'

Jimmy frowned. 'Robutt isn't an imitation, Dad. He's my dog.'

'Not a real one, Jimmy. Robutt's just steel and wiring and a simple positronic brain. It's not alive.'

'He does everything I want him to do, Dad. He understands me. Sure, he's alive.'

'No, son. Robutt is just a machine. It's just programmed to act the way it does. A dog *is* alive. You won't want Robutt after you have the dog.'

'The dog will need a spacesuit, won't he?'

'Yes, of course. But it will be worth the money and he'll

get used to it. And he won't need one in the City. You'll see the difference once he gets here.'

Jimmy looked at Robutt, who was squeaking again, a very low, slow squeak, that seemed frightened. Jimmy held out his arms and Robutt was in them in one bound. Jimmy said, 'What will the difference be between Robutt and the dog?'

'It's hard to explain,' said Mr Anderson, 'but it will be easy to see. The dog will *really* love you. Robutt is just adjusted to act as though it loves you.'

'But, Dad, we don't know what's inside the dog, or what his feelings are. Maybe it's just acting, too.'

Mr Anderson frowned. 'Jimmy, you'll *know* the difference when you experience the love of a living thing.'

Jimmy held Robutt tightly. He was frowning, too, and the desperate look on his face meant that he wouldn't change his mind. He said, 'But what's the difference how *they* act? How about how *I* feel? I love Robutt and *that's* what counts.'

And the little robot-mutt, which had never been held so tightly in all its existence, squeaked high and rapid squeaks – happy squeaks.

Sally

Sally was coming down the lake road, so I waved to her and called her by name. I always liked to see Sally. I liked all of them, you understand, but Sally's the prettiest one of the lot. There just isn't any question about it.

She moved a little faster when I waved to her. Nothing undignified. She was never that. She moved just enough faster to show that she was glad to see me, too.

I turned to the man standing beside me. 'That's Sally,' I said.

He smiled at me and nodded.

Mrs Hester had brought him in. She said, 'This is Mr Gellhorn, Jake. You remember he sent you the letter asking for an appointment.'

That was just talk, really. I have a million things to do around the Farm, and one thing I just can't waste time on is mail. That's why I have Mrs Hester around. She lives pretty close by, she's good at attending to foolishness without running to me about it, and most of all, she likes Sally and the rest. Some people don't.

'Glad to see you, Mr Gellhorn,' I said.

'Raymond J. Gellhorn,' he said, and gave me his hand, which I shook and gave back.

He was a largish fellow, half a head taller than I and wider, too. He was about half my age, thirtyish. He had black hair, plastered down slick, with a part in the middle, and a thin mustache, very neatly trimmed. His jawbones got big under his ears and made him look as if he had a slight case of mumps. On video he'd be a natural to play the villain, so I assumed he was a nice fellow. It goes to show that video can't be wrong all the time.

'I'm Jacob Folkers,' I said. 'What can I do for you?'

He grinned. It was a big, wide, white-toothed grin. 'You can tell me a little about your Farm here, if you don't mind.'

I heard Sally coming up behind me and I put out my hand. She slid right into it and the feel of the hard, glossy enamel of her fender was warm in my palm.

'A nice automatobile,' said Gellhorn.

That's one way of putting it. Sally was a 2045 convertible with a Hennis-Carleton positronic motor and an Armat chassis. She had the cleanest, finest lines I've ever seen on any model, bar none. For five years, she'd been my favorite, and I'd put everything into her I could dream up. In all that time, there'd never been a human being behind her wheel.

Not once.

'Sally,' I said, patting her gently, 'meet Mr Gellhorn.'

Sally's cylinder-purr keyed up a little. I listened carefully for any knocking. Lately, I'd been hearing motor-knock in almost all the cars and changing the gasoline hadn't done a bit of good. Sally was as smooth as her paint job this time, however.

'Do you have names for all your cars?' asked Gellhorn.

He sounded amused, and Mrs Hester doesn't like people to sound as though they were making fun of the Farm. She said, sharply, 'Certainly. The cars have real personalities, don't they, Jake? The sedans are all males and the convertibles are females.'

Gellhorn was smiling again. 'And do you keep them in separate garages, ma'am?'

Mrs Hester glared at him.

Gellhorn said to me, 'And now I wonder if I can talk to you alone, Mr Folkers?'

'That depends,' I said. 'Are you a reporter?'

'No, sir. I'm a sales agent. Any talk we have is not for publication. I assure you I am interested in strict privacy.'

'Let's walk down the road a bit. There's a bench we can use.'

We started down. Mrs Hester walked away. Sally nudged along after us.

I said, 'You don't mind if Sally comes along, do you?'

'Not at all. She can't repeat what we say, can she?' He laughed at his own joke, reached over and rubbed Sally's grille.

Sally raced her motor and Gellhorn's hand drew away quickly.

'She's not used to strangers,' I explained.

We sat down on the bench under the big oak tree where we could look across the small lake to the private speedway. It was the warm part of the day and the cars were out in force, at least thirty of them. Even at this distance I could see that Jeremiah was pulling his usual stunt of sneaking up behind some staid older model, then putting on a jerk of speed and yowling past with deliberately squealing brakes. Two weeks before he had crowded old Angus off the asphalt altogether, and I had turned off his motor for two days.

It didn't help though, I'm afraid, and it looks as though there's nothing to be done about it. Jeremiah is a sports model to begin with and that kind is awfully hot-headed.

'Well, Mr Gellhorn,' I said. 'Could you tell me why you want the information?'

But he was just looking around. He said, 'This *is* an amazing place, Mr Folkers.'

'I wish you'd call me Jake. Everyone does.'

'All right, Jake. How many cars do you have here?'

'Fifty-one. We get one or two new ones every year. One year we got five. We haven't lost one yet. They're all in perfect running order. We even have a '15 model Mat-O-Mot in working order. One of the original automatics. It was the first car here.'

Good old Matthew. He stayed in the garage most of the

day now, but then he was the granddaddy of all positronic-motored cars. Those were the days when blind war veterans, paraplegics and heads of state were the only ones who drove automatics. But Samson Harridge was my boss and he was rich enough to be able to get one. I was his chauffeur at the time.

The thought makes me feel old. I can remember when there wasn't an automobile in the world with brains enough to find its own way home. I chauffeured dead lumps of machines that needed a man's hand at their controls every minute. Every year machines like that used to kill tens of thousands of people.

The automatics fixed that. A positronic brain can react much faster than a human one, of course, and it paid people to keep hands off the controls. You got in, punched your destination and let it go its own way.

We take it for granted now, but I remember when the first laws came out forcing the old machines off the highways and limiting travel to automatics. Lord, what a fuss. They called it everything from communism to fascism, but it emptied the highways and stopped the killing, and still more people get around more easily the new way.

Of course, the automatics were ten to a hundred times as expensive as the hand-driven ones, and there weren't many that could afford a private vehicle. The industry specialized in turning out omnibus-automatics. You could always call a company and have one stop at your door in a matter of minutes and take you where you wanted to go. Usually, you had to drive with others who were going your way, but what's wrong with that?

Samson Harridge had a private car though, and I went to him the minute it arrived. The car wasn't Matthew to me then. I didn't know it was going to be the dean of the Farm some day. I only knew it was taking my job away and I hated it.

I said, 'You won't be needing me any more, Mr Harridge?'

He said, 'What are you dithering about, Jake? You don't think I'll trust myself to a contraption like that, do you? You stay right at the controls.'

I said, 'But it works by itself, Mr Harridge. It scans the road, reacts properly to obstacles, humans, and other cars, and remembers routes to travel.'

'So they say. So they say. Just the same, you're sitting right behind the wheel in case anything goes wrong.'

Funny how you can get to like a car. In no time I was calling it Matthew and was spending all my time keeping it polished and humming. A positronic brain stays in condition best when it's got control of its chassis at all times, which means it's worth keeping the gas tank filled so that the motor can turn over slowly day and night. After a while, it got so I could tell by the sound of the motor how Matthew felt.

In his own way, Harridge grew fond of Matthew, too. He had no one else to like. He'd divorced or outlived three wives and outlived five children and three grandchildren. So when he died, maybe it wasn't surprising that he had his estate converted into a Farm for Retired Automobiles, with me in charge and Matthew the first member of a distinguished line.

It's turned out to be my life. I never got married. You can't get married and still tend to automatics the way you should.

The newspapers thought it was funny, but after a while they stopped joking about it. Some things you can't joke about. Maybe you've never been able to afford an automatic and maybe you never will, either, but take it from me, you get to love them. They're hardworking and affectionate. It takes a man with no heart to mistreat one or to see one mistreated.

It got so that after a man had an automatic for a while, he would make provisions for having it left to the Farm, if he didn't have an heir he could rely on to give it good care.

I explained that to Gellhorn.

He said, 'Fifty-one cars! That represents a lot of money.'

'Fifty thousand minimum per automatic, original investment,' I said. 'They're worth a lot more now. I've done things for them.'

'It must take a lot of money to keep up the Farm.'

'You're right there. The Farm's a non-profit organization, which gives us a break on taxes and, of course, new automatics that come in usually have trust funds attached. Still, costs are always going up. I have to keep the place landscaped; I keep laying down new asphalt and keeping the old in repair; there's gasoline, oil, repairs, and new gadgets. It adds up.'

'And you've spent a long time at it.'

'I sure have, Mr Gellhorn. Thirty-three years.'

'You don't seem to be getting much out of it yourself.'

'I don't? You surprise me, Mr Gellhorn. I've got Sally and fifty others. Look at her.'

I was grinning. I couldn't help it. Sally was so clean, it almost hurt. Some insect must have died on her windshield or one speck of dust too many had landed, so she was going to work. A little tube protruded and spurted Tergosol over the glass. It spread quickly over the silicone surface film and squeegees snapped into place instantly, passing over the windshield and forcing the water into the little channel that led it, dripping, down to the ground. Not a speck of water got onto her glistening apple-green hood. Squeegee and detergent tube snapped back into place and disappeared.

Gellhorn said 'I never saw an automatic do that.'

'I guess not,' I said. 'I fixed that up specially on our cars. They're clean. They're always scrubbing their glass. They like it. I've even got Sally fixed up with wax jets. She polishes herself every night till you can see your face in any part of her and shave by it. If I can scrape up the money, I'd be putting it on the rest of the girls. Convertibles are very vain.'

'I can tell you how to scrape up the money, if that interests you.'

'That always does. How?'

'Isn't it obvious, Jake? Any of your cars is worth fifty thousand minimum, you said. I'll bet most of them top six figures.'

'So?'

'Ever think of selling a few?'

I shook my head. 'You don't realize it, I guess, Mr Gellhorn, but I can't sell any of these. They belong to the Farm, not to me.'

'The money would go to the Farm.'

'The incorporation papers of the Farm provide that the cars receive perpetual care. They can't be sold.'

'What about the motors, then?'

'I don't understand you.'

Gellhorn shifted position and his voice got confidential. 'Look here, Jake, let me explain the situation. There's a big market for private automatics if they could only be made cheaply enough. Right?'

'That's no secret.'

'And ninety-five per cent of the cost is the motor. Right? Now, I know where we can get a supply of bodies. I also know where we can sell automatics at a good price – twenty or thirty thousand for the cheaper models, maybe fifty or sixty for the better ones. All I need are the motors. You see the solution?'

'I don't, Mr Gellhorn.' I did, but I wanted him to spell it out.

'It's right here. You've got fifty-one of them. You're an expert automatobile mechanic, Jake. You must be. You could unhook a motor and place it in another car so that no one would know the difference.'

'It wouldn't be exactly ethical.'

'You wouldn't be harming the cars. You'd be doing them a favor. Use your older cars. Use that old Mat-O-Mot.'

'Well, now, wait a while, Mr Gellhorn. The motors and bodies aren't two separate items. They're a single unit. Those motors are used to their own bodies. They wouldn't be happy in another car.'

'All right, that's a point. That's a very good point, Jake. It would be like taking your mind and putting it in someone else's skull. Right? You don't think you would like that?'

'I don't think I would. No.'

'But what if I took your mind and put it into the body of a young athlete. What about that, Jake? You're not a youngster anymore. If you had the chance, wouldn't you enjoy being twenty again? That's what I'm offering some of your positronic motors. They'll be put into new '57 bodies. The latest construction.'

I laughed. 'That doesn't make much sense, Mr Gellhorn. Some of our cars may be old, but they're well cared for. Nobody drives them. They're allowed their own way. They're *retired*, Mr Gellhorn. I wouldn't want a twenty-year-old body if it meant I had to dig ditches for the rest of my new life and never have enough to eat . . . What do you think, Sally?'

Sally's two doors opened and then shut with a cushioned slam.

'What's that?' said Gellhorn.

'That's the way Sally laughs.'

Gellhorn forced a smile. I guess he thought I was making a bad joke. He said, 'Talk sense, Jake. Cars are *made* to be driven. They're probably not happy if you don't drive them.'

I said, 'Sally hasn't been driven in five years. She looks happy to me.'

'I wonder.'

He got up and walked toward Sally slowly. 'Hi, Sally, how'd you like a drive?'

Sally's motor revved up. She backed away.

'Don't push her, Mr Gellhorn,' I said. 'She's liable to be a little skittish.'

Two sedans were about a hundred yards up the road. They had stopped. Maybe, in their own way, they were watching. I didn't bother about them. I had my eyes on Sally, and I kept them there.

Gellhorn said, 'Steady now, Sally.' He lunged out and seized the door handle. It didn't budge, of course.

He said, 'It opened a minute ago.'

I said, 'Automatic lock. She's got a sense of privacy, Sally has.'

He let go, then said, slowly and deliberately, 'A car with a sense of privacy shouldn't go around with its top down.'

He stepped back three or four paces, then quickly, so quickly I couldn't take a step to stop him, he ran forward and vaulted into the car. He caught Sally completely by surprise, because as he came down, he shut off the ignition before she could lock it in place.

For the first time in five years, Sally's motor was dead.

I think I yelled, but Gellhorn had the switch on 'Manual' and locked that in place, too. He kicked the motor into action. Sally was alive again but she had no freedom of action.

He started up the road. The sedans were still there. They turned and drifted away, not very quickly. I suppose it was all a puzzle to them.

One was Giuseppe, from the Milan factories, and the other was Stephen. They were always together. They were both new at the Farm, but they'd been here long enough to know that our cars just didn't have drivers.

Gellhorn went straight on, and when the sedans finally

got it through their heads that Sally wasn't going to slow down, that she *couldn't* slow down, it was too late for anything but desperate measures.

They broke for it, one to each side, and Sally raced between them like a streak. Steve crashed through the lakeside fence and rolled to a halt on the grass and mud not six inches from the water's edge. Giuseppe bumped along the land side of the road to a shaken halt.

I had Steve back on the highway and was trying to find out what harm, if any, the fence had done him, when Gellhorn came back.

Gellhorn opened Sally's door and stepped out. Leaning back, he shut off the ignition a second time.

'There,' he said. 'I think I did her a lot of good.'

I held my temper. 'Why did you dash through the sedans? There was no reason for that.'

'I kept expecting them to turn out.'

'They did. One went through the fence.'

'I'm sorry, Jake,' he said. 'I thought they'd move more quickly. You know how it is. I've been in lots of buses, but I've only been in a private automatic two or three times in my life, and this is the first time I ever drove one. That just shows you, Jake. It got me, driving one, and I'm pretty hard-boiled. I tell you, we don't have to go more than twenty per cent below list price to reach a good market, and it would be ninety per cent profit.'

'Which we would split?'

'Fifty-fifty. And I take all the risks, remember.'

'All right. I listened to you. Now you listen to me.' I raised my voice because I was just too mad to be polite anymore. 'When you turn off Sally's motor, you hurt her. How would you like to be kicked unconscious? That's what you do to Sally, when you turn her off.'

'You're exaggerating, Jake. The automatobuses get turned off every night.'

'Sure, that's why I want none of my boys or girls in your fancy '57 bodies, where I won't know what treatment they'll get. Buses need major repairs in their positronic circuits every couple of years. Old Matthew hasn't had his circuits touched in twenty years. What can you offer him compared with that?'

'Well, you're excited now. Suppose you think over my proposition when you've cooled down and get in touch with me.'

'I've thought it over all I want to. If I ever see you again, I'll call the police.'

His mouth got hard and ugly. He said, 'Just a minute, old-timer.'

I said, 'Just a minute, you. This is private property and I'm ordering you off.'

He shrugged. 'Well, then, goodbye.'

I said, 'Mrs Hester will see you off the property. Make that goodbye permanent.'

But it wasn't permanent. I saw him again two days later. Two and a half days, rather, because it was about noon when I saw him first and a little after midnight when I saw him again.

I sat up in bed when he turned the light on, blinking blindly till I made out what was happening. Once I could see, it didn't take much explaining. In fact, it took none at all. He had a gun in his right fist, the nasty little needle barrel just visible between two fingers. I knew that all he had to do was to increase the pressure of his hand and I would be torn apart.

He said, 'Put on your clothes, Jake.'

I didn't move. I just watched him.

He said, 'Look, Jake, I know the situation. I visited you two days ago, remember. You have no guards on this place, no electrified fences, no warning signals. Nothing.'

I said, 'I don't need any. Meanwhile there's nothing to stop you from leaving, Mr Gellhorn. I would if I were you. This place can be very dangerous.'

He laughed a little. 'It is, for anyone on the wrong side of a fist gun.'

'I see it,' I said. 'I know you've got one.'

'Then get a move on. My men are waiting.'

'No, sir, Mr Gellhorn. Not unless you tell me what you want, and probably not then.'

'I made you a proposition day before yesterday.'

'The answer's still no.'

'There's more to the proposition now. I've come here with some men and an automatobus. You have your chance to come with me and disconnect twenty-five of the positronic motors. I don't care which twenty-five you choose. We'll load them on the bus and take them away. Once they're disposed of, I'll see to it that you get your fair share of the money.'

'I have your word on that, I suppose.'

He didn't act as if he thought I was being sarcastic. He said, 'You have.'

I said, 'No.'

'If you insist on saying no, we'll go about it in our own way. I'll disconnect the motors myself, only I'll disconnect all fifty-one. Every one of them.'

'It isn't easy to disconnect positronic motors, Mr Gellhorn. Are you a robotics expert? Even if you are, you know, these motors have been modified by me.'

'I know that, Jake. And to be truthful, I'm not an expert. I may ruin quite a few motors trying to get them out. That's why I'll have to work over all fifty-one if you don't cooperate. You see, I may only end up with twenty-five when I'm through. The first few I'll tackle will probably suffer the most. Till I get the hang of it, you see. And if I go it myself, I think I'll put Sally first in line.'

I said, 'I can't believe you're serious, Mr Gellhorn.'

He said, 'I'm serious, Jake.' He let it all dribble in. 'If you want to help, you can keep Sally. Otherwise, she's liable to be hurt very badly. Sorry.'

I said, 'I'll come with you, but I'll give you one more warning. You'll be in trouble, Mr Gellhorn.'

He thought that was very funny. He was laughing very quietly as we went down the stairs together.

There was an automatobus waiting outside the driveway to the garage apartments. The shadows of three men waited beside it, and their flash beams went on as we approached.

Gellhorn said in a low voice, 'I've got the old fellow. Come on. Move the truck up the drive and let's get started.'

One of the others leaned in and punched the proper instructions on the control panel. We moved up the driveway with the bus following submissively.

'It won't go inside the garage,' I said. 'The door won't take it. We don't have buses here. Only private cars.'

'All right,' said Gellhorn. 'Pull it over onto the grass and keep it out of sight.'

I could hear the thrumming of the cars when we were still ten yards from the garage.

Usually they quieted down if I entered the garage. This time they didn't. I think they knew that strangers were about, and once the faces of Gellhorn and the others were visible they got noisier. Each motor was a warm rumble, and each motor was knocking irregularly until the place rattled.

The lights went up automatically as we stepped inside. Gellhorn didn't seem bothered by the car noise, but the three men with him looked surprised and uncomfortable. They had the look of the hired thug about them, a look that was not compounded of physical features so much as of a certain wariness of eye and hang-dogness of face. I knew the type and I wasn't worried.

One of them said, 'Damn it, they're burning gas.'

'My cars always do,' I replied stiffly.

'Not tonight,' said Gellhorn. 'Turn them off.'

'It's not that easy, Mr Gellhorn,' I said.

'Get started!' he said.

I stood there. He had his fist gun pointed at me steadily. I said, 'I told you, Mr Gellhorn, that my cars have been well-treated while they've been at the Farm. They're used to being treated that way, and they resent anything else.'

'You have one minute,' he said. 'Lecture me some other time.'

'I'm trying to explain something. I'm trying to explain that my cars can understand what I say to them. A positronic motor will learn to do that with time and patience. My cars have learned. Sally understood your proposition two days ago. You'll remember she laughed when I asked her opinion. She also knows what you did to her and so do the two sedans you scattered. And the rest know what to do about trespassers in general.'

'Look, you crazy old fool – '

'All I have to say is – ' I raised my voice. 'Get them!'

One of the men turned pasty and yelled, but his voice was drowned completely in the sound of fifty-one horns turned loose at once. They held their notes, and within the four walls of the garage the echoes rose to a wild, metallic call. Two cars rolled forward, not hurriedly, but with no possible mistake as to their target. Two cars fell in line behind the first two. All the cars were stirring in their separate stalls.

The thugs stared, then backed.

I shouted, 'Don't get up against a wall.'

Apparently, they had that instinctive thought themselves. They rushed madly for the door of the garage.

At the door one of Gellhorn's men turned, brought up a fist gun of his own. The needle pellet tore a thin, blue flash toward the first car. The car was Giuseppe.

A thin line of paint peeled up Giuseppe's hood, and the right half of his windshield crazed and splintered but did not break through.

The men were out the door, running, and two by two the cars crunched out after them into the night, their horns calling the charge.

I kept my hand on Gellhorn's elbow, but I don't think he could have moved in any case. His lips were trembling.

I said, 'That's why I don't need electrified fences or guards. My property protects itself.'

Gellhorn's eyes swiveled back and forth in fascination as, pair by pair, they whizzed by. He said, 'They're killers!'

'Don't be silly. They won't kill your men.'

'They're killers!'

'They'll just give your men a lesson. My cars have been specially trained for cross-country pursuit for just such an occasion; I think what your men will get will be worse than an outright quick kill. Have you ever been chased by an automatobile?'

Gellhorn didn't answer.

I went on. I didn't want him to miss a thing. 'They'll be shadows going no faster than your men, chasing them here, blocking them there, blaring at them, dashing at them, missing with a screech of brake and a thunder of motor. They'll keep it up till your men drop, out of breath and half-dead, waiting for the wheels to crunch over their breaking bones. The cars won't do that. They'll turn away. You can bet though, that your men will never return here in their lives. Not for all the money you or ten like you could give them. Listen – '

I tightened my hold on his elbow. He strained to hear.

I said, 'Don't you hear car doors slamming?'

It was faint and unmistakable.

I said, 'They're laughing. They're enjoying themselves.'

His face crumpled with rage. He lifted his hand. He was still holding his fist gun.

I said, 'I wouldn't. One automatocar is still with us.'

I don't think he had noticed Sally till then. She had moved up so quietly. Though her right front fender nearly touched me, I couldn't hear her motor. She might have been holding her breath.

Gellhorn yelled.

I said, 'She won't touch you, as long as I'm with you. But if you kill me . . . You know, Sally doesn't like you.'

Gellhorn turned the gun in Sally's direction.

'Her motor is shielded,' I said, 'and before you could ever squeeze the gun a second time she would be on top of you.'

'All right, then,' he yelled, and suddenly my arm was bent behind my back and twisted so I could hardly stand. He held me between Sally and himself, and his pressure didn't let up. 'Back out with me and don't try to break loose, old-timer, or I'll tear your arm out of its socket.'

I had to move. Sally nudged along with us, worried, uncertain what to do. I tried to say something to her and couldn't. I could only clench my teeth and moan.

Gellhorn's automatobus was still standing outside the garage. I was forced in. Gellhorn jumped in after me, locking the doors.

He said, 'All right, now. We'll talk sense.'

I was rubbing my arm, trying to get life back into it, and even as I did I was automatically and without any conscious effort studying the control board of the bus.

I said, 'This is a rebuilt job.'

'So?' he said caustically. 'It's a sample of my work. I picked up a discarded chassis, found a brain I could use and spliced me a private bus. What of it?'

I tore at the repair panel, forcing it aside.

He said, 'What the hell. Get away from that.' The side of his palm came down numbingly on my left shoulder.

I struggled with him. 'I don't want to do this bus any harm. What kind of a person do you think I am? I just want to take a look at some of the motor connections.'

It didn't take much of a look. I was boiling when I turned to him. I said, 'You're a hound and a bastard. You had no right installing this motor yourself. Why didn't you get a robotics man?'

He said, 'Do I look crazy?'

'Even if it was a stolen motor, you had no right to treat it so. I wouldn't treat a man the way you treated that motor. Solder, tape, and pinch clamps! It's brutal!'

'It works, doesn't it?'

'Sure it works, but it must be hell for the bus. You could live with migraine headaches and acute arthritis, but it wouldn't be much of a life. This car is *suffering*.'

'Shut up!' For a moment he glanced out the window at Sally, who had rolled up as close to the bus as she could. He made sure the doors and windows were locked.

He said, 'We're getting out of here now, before the other cars come back. We'll stay away.'

'How will that help you?'

'Your cars will run out of gas someday, won't they? You haven't got them fixed up so they can tank up on their own, have you? We'll come back and finish the job.'

'They'll be looking for me,' I said. 'Mrs Hester will call the police.'

He was past reasoning with. He just punched the bus in gear. It lurched forward. Sally followed.

He giggled. 'What can she do if you're here with me?'

Sally seemed to realize that, too. She picked up speed, passed us and was gone. Gellhorn opened the window next to him and spat through the opening.

The bus lumbered on over the dark road, its motor rattling unevenly. Gellhorn dimmed the periphery light until the phosphorescent green stripe down the middle of the highway, sparkling in the moonlight, was all that kept us out of the trees. There was virtually no traffic. Two cars passed ours, going the other way, and there was none at all on our side of the highway, either before or behind.

I heard the door-slamming first. Quick and sharp in the silence, first on the right and then on the left. Gellhorn's hands quivered as he punched savagely for increased speed. A beam of light shot out from among a scrub of trees, blinding us. Another beam plunged at us from behind the guard rails on the other side. At a crossover, four hundred yards ahead, there was a sque-e-e-e-e as a car darted across our path.

'Sally went for the rest,' I said. 'I think you're surrounded.'

'So what? What can they do?'

He hunched over the controls, peering through the windshield.

'And don't *you* try anything, old-timer,' he muttered.

I couldn't. I was bone-weary; my left arm was on fire. The motor sounds gathered and grew closer. I could hear the motors missing in odd patterns; suddenly it seemed to me that my cars were speaking to one another.

A medley of horns came from behind. I turned and Gellhorn looked quickly into the rear-view mirror. A dozen cars were following in both lanes.

Gellhorn yelled and laughed madly.

I cried, 'Stop! Stop the car!'

Because not a quarter of a mile ahead, plainly visible in the light beams of two sedans on the roadside was Sally, her trim body plunked square across the road. Two cars shot into the opposite lane to our left, keeping perfect time with us and preventing Gellhorn from turning out.

But he had no intention of turning out. He put his finger on the full-speed-ahead button and kept it there.

He said, 'There'll be no bluffing here. This bus

outweighs her five to one, old-timer, and we'll just push her off the road like a dead kitten.'

I knew he could. The bus was on manual and his finger was on the button. I knew he would.

I lowered the window, and stuck my head out. 'Sally,' I screamed. 'Get out of the way. *Sally!*'

It was drowned out in the agonized squeal of maltreated brake-bands. I felt myself thrown forward and heard Gellhorn's breath puff out of his body.

I said, 'What happened?' It was a foolish question. We had stopped. That was what had happened. Sally and the bus were five feet apart. With five times her weight tearing down on her, she had not budged. The guts of her.

Gellhorn yanked at the Manual toggle switch. 'It's got to,' he kept muttering. 'It's got to.'

I said, 'Not the way you hooked up the motor, expert. Any of the circuits could cross over.'

He looked at me with a tearing anger and growled deep in his throat. His hair was matted over his forehead. He lifted his fist.

'That's all the advice out of you there'll ever be, old-timer.'

And I knew the needle gun was about to fire.

I pressed back against the bus door, watching the fist come up, and when the door opened I went over backward and out, hitting the ground with a thud. I heard the door slam closed again.

I got to my knees and looked up in time to see Gellhorn struggle uselessly with the closing window, then aim his fist-gun quickly through the glass. He never fired. The bus got under way with a tremendous roar, and Gellhorn lurched backward.

Sally wasn't in the way any longer, and I watched the bus's rear lights flicker away down the highway.

I was exhausted. I sat down right there, right on the highway, and put my head down in my crossed arms, trying to catch my breath.

I heard a car stop gently at my side. When I looked up, it was Sally. Slowly – lovingly, you might say – her front door opened.

No one had driven Sally for five years – except Gellhorn, of course – and I know how valuable such freedom was to a car. I appreciated the gesture, but I said, 'Thanks, Sally, but I'll take one of the newer cars.'

I got up and turned away, but skillfully and neatly as a pirouette, she wheeled before me again. I couldn't hurt her feelings. I got in. Her front seat had the fine, fresh scent of an automatobile that kept itself spotlessly clean. I lay down across it, thankfully, and with even, silent, and rapid efficiency, my boys and girls brought me home.

Mrs Hester brought me the copy of the radio transcript the next evening with great excitement.

'It's Mr Gellhorn,' she said. 'The man who came to see you.'

'What about him?'

I dreaded her answer.

'They found him dead,' she said. 'Imagine that. Just lying dead in a ditch.'

'It might be a stranger altogether,' I mumbled.

'Raymond J. Gellhorn,' she said, sharply. 'There can't be two, can there? The description fits, too. Lord, what a way to die! They found tire marks on his arms and body. Imagine! I'm glad it turned out to be a bus; otherwise they might have come poking around here.'

'Did it happen near here?' I asked, anxiously.

'No . . . Near Cooksville. But, goodness, read about it yourself if you – What happened to Giuseppe?'

I welcomed the diversion. Giuseppe was waiting patiently

for me to complete the repaint job. His windshield had been replaced.

After she left, I snatched up the transcript. There was no doubt about it. The doctor reported he had been running and was in a state of totally spent exhaustion. I wondered for how many miles the bus had played with him before the final lunge. The transcript had no notion of anything like that, of course.

They had located the bus and identified it by the tire tracks. The police had it and were trying to trace its ownership.

There was an editorial in the transcript about it. It had been the first traffic fatality in the state for that year and the paper warned strenuously against manual driving at night.

There was no mention of Gellhorn's three thugs and for that, at least, I was grateful. None of our cars had been seduced by the pleasure of the chase into killing.

That was all. I let the paper drop. Gellhorn had been a criminal. His treatment of the bus had been brutal. There was no question in my mind he deserved death. But still I felt a bit queasy over the manner of it.

A month has passed now and I can't get it out of my mind.

My cars talk to one another. I have no doubt about it anymore. It's as though they've gained confidence; as though they're not bothering to keep it secret anymore. Their engines rattle and knock continuously.

And they don't talk among themselves only. They talk to the cars and buses that come into the Farm on business. How long have they been doing that?

They must be understood, too. Gellhorn's bus understood them, for all it hadn't been on the grounds more than an hour. I can close my eyes and bring back that dash along the highway, with our cars flanking the bus on either side, clacking their motors at it till it understood, stopped, let me out, and ran off with Gellhorn.

Did my cars tell him to kill Gellhorn? Or was that his idea?

Can cars have such ideas? The motor designers say no. But they mean under ordinary conditions. Have they foreseen *everything*?

Cars get ill-used, you know.

Some of them enter the Farm and observe. They get told things. They find out that cars exist whose motors are never stopped, whom no one ever drives, whose every need is supplied.

Then maybe they go out and tell others. Maybe the word is spreading quickly. Maybe they're going to think that the Farm way should be the way all over the world. They don't understand. You couldn't expect them to understand about legacies and the whims of rich men.

There are millions of automatobiles on Earth, tens of millions. If the thought gets rooted in them that they're slaves; that they should do something about it . . . If they begin to think the way Gellhorn's bus did . . .

Maybe it won't be till after my time. And then they'll have to keep a few of us to take care of them, won't they? They wouldn't kill us all.

And maybe they would. Maybe they wouldn't understand about how someone would have to care for them. Maybe they won't wait.

Every morning I wake up and think, Maybe today . . .

I don't get as much pleasure out of my cars as I used to. Lately, I notice that I'm even beginning to avoid Sally.

Someday

Niccolo Mazetti lay stomach down on the rug, chin buried in the palm of one small hand, and listened to the Bard disconsolately. There was even the suspicion of tears in his dark eyes, a luxury an eleven-year-old could allow himself only when alone.

The Bard said, 'Once upon a time in the middle of a deep wood, there lived a poor woodcutter and his two motherless daughters, who were each as beautiful as the day is long. The older daughter had long hair as black as a feather from a raven's wing, but the younger daughter had hair as bright and golden as the sunlight of an autumn afternoon.

'Many times while the girls were waiting for their father to come home from his day's work in the wood, the older girl would sit before a mirror and sing – '

What she sang, Niccolo did not hear, for a call sounded from outside the room: 'Hey, Nickie.'

And Niccolo, his face clearing on the moment, rushed to the window and shouted, 'Hey, Paul.'

Paul Loeb waved an excited hand. He was thinner than Niccolo and not as tall, for all he was six months older. His face was full of repressed tension which showed itself most clearly in the rapid blinking of his eyelids. 'Hey, Nickie, let me in. I've got an idea and a *half*. Wait till you hear it.' He looked rapidly about him as though to check on the possibility of eavesdroppers, but the front yard was quite patently empty. He repeated, in a whisper, 'Wait till you hear it.'

'All right. I'll open the door.'

The Bard continued smoothly, oblivious to the sudden

loss of attention on the part of Niccolo. As Paul entered, the Bard was saying, '. . . Thereupon, the lion said, "If you will find me the lost egg of the bird which flies over the Ebony Mountain once every ten years, I will – "'

Paul said, 'Is that a Bard you're listening to? I didn't know you had one.'

Niccolo reddened and the look of unhappiness returned to his face. 'Just an old thing I had when I was a kid. It ain't much good.' He kicked at the Bard with his foot and caught the somewhat scarred and discolored plastic covering a glancing blow.

The Bard hiccupped as its speaking attachment was jarred out of contact a moment, then it went on: ' – for a year and a day until the iron shoes were worn out. The princess stopped at the side of the road . . .'

Paul said, 'Boy, that *is* an old model,' and looked at it critically.

Despite Niccolo's own bitterness against the Bard, he winced at the other's condescending tone. For the moment, he was sorry he had allowed Paul in, at least before he had restored the Bard to its usual resting place in the basement. It was only in the desperation of a dull day and a fruitless discussion with his father that he had resurrected it. And it turned out to be just as stupid as he had expected.

Nickie was a little afraid of Paul anyway, since Paul had special courses at school and everyone said he was going to grow up to be a Computing Engineer.

Not that Niccolo himself was doing badly at school. He got adequate marks in logic, binary manipulations, computing and elementary circuits: all the usual grammar-school subjects. But that was it! They were just the usual subjects and he would grow up to be a control-board guard like everyone else.

Paul, however, knew mysterious things about what he called electronics and theoretical mathematics and programing. Especially programing. Niccolo didn't even try to understand when Paul bubbled over about it.

Paul listened to the Bard for a few minutes and said, 'You been using it much?'

'No!' said Niccolo, offended. 'I've had it in the basement since before you moved into the neighborhood. I just got it out today – ' He lacked an excuse that seemed adequate to himself, so he concluded, 'I just got it out.'

Paul said, 'Is that what it tells you about: woodcutters and princesses and talking animals?'

Niccolo said, 'It's terrible. My dad says we can't afford a new one. I said to him this morning – ' The memory of the morning's fruitless pleadings brought Niccolo dangerously near tears, which he repressed in a panic. Somehow, he felt that Paul's thin cheeks never felt the stain of tears and that Paul would have only contempt for anyone else less strong than himself. Niccolo went on, 'So I thought I'd try this old thing again, but it's no good.'

Paul turned off the Bard, pressed the contact that led to a nearly instantaneous-reorientation and recombination of the vocabulary, characters, plot lines and climaxes stored within it. Then he reactivated it.

The Bard began smoothly, 'Once upon a time there was a little boy named Willikins whose mother had died and who lived with a stepfather and a stepbrother. Although the stepfather was very well-to-do, he begrudged poor Willikins the very bed he slept in so that Willikins was forced to get such rest as he could on a pile of straw in the stable next to the horses – '

'Horses!' cried Paul.

'They're a kind of animal,' said Niccolo. 'I think.'

'I know that! I just mean imagine stories about *horses*.'

'It tells about horses all the time,' said Niccolo. 'There are things called cows, too. You milk them but the Bard doesn't say how.'

'Well, gee, why don't you fix it up?'

'I'd like to know how.'

The Bard was saying, 'Often Willikins would think that if only he were rich and powerful, he would show his stepfather and stepbrother what it meant to be cruel to a little boy, so one day he decided to go out into the world and seek his fortune.'

Paul who wasn't listening to the Bard, said, 'It's *easy*. The Bard has memory cylinders all fixed up for plot lines and climaxes and things. We don't have to worry about that. It's just vocabulary we've got to fix so it'll know about computers and automation and electronics and real things about today. Then it can tell interesting stories, you know, instead of about princesses and things.'

Niccolo said despondently, 'I wish we could do that.'

Paul said, 'Listen, my dad says if I get into special computing school next year, he'll get me a *real* Bard, a late model. A big one with an attachment for space stories and mysteries. And a visual attachment, too!'

'You mean *see* the stories?'

'Sure. Mr Daugherty at school says they've got things like that, now, but not for just everybody. Only if I get into computing school, Dad can get a few breaks.'

Niccolo's eyes bulged with envy. 'Gee. *Seeing* a story.'

'You can come over and watch anytime, Nickie.'

'Oh, boy. Thanks.'

'That's all right. But remember, I'm the guy who says what kind of story we hear.'

'Sure. Sure.' Niccolo would have agreed readily to much more onerous conditions.

Paul's attention returned to the Bard.

It was saying, '"If that is the case," said the king, stroking his beard and frowning till clouds filled the sky and lightning flashed, "you will see to it that my entire land is freed of flies by this time day after tomorrow or – "'

'All we've got to do,' said Paul, 'is open it up – ' He shut the Bard off again and was prying at its front panel as he spoke.

'Hey,' said Niccolo, in sudden alarm. 'Don't break it.'

'I won't break it,' said Paul impatiently. 'I know all about these things.' Then, with sudden caution, 'Your father and mother home?'

'No.'

'All right, then.' He had the front panel off and peered in. 'Boy, this *is* a one-cylinder thing.'

He worked away at the Bard's innards. Niccolo, who watched with painful suspense, could not make out what he was doing.

Paul pulled out a thin, flexible metal strip, powdered with dots. 'That's the Bard's memory cylinder. I'll bet its capacity for stories is under a trillion.'

'What are you going to do, Paul?' quavered Niccolo.

'I'll give it vocabulary.'

'How?'

'Easy. I've got a book here. Mr Daugherty gave it to me at school.'

Paul pulled the book out of his pocket and pried at it till he had its plastic jacket off. He unreeled the tape a bit, ran it through the vocalizer, which he turned down to a whisper, then placed it within the Bard's vitals. He made further attachments.

'What'll that do?'

'The book will talk and the Bard will put it all on its memory tape.'

'What good will that do?'

'Boy, you're a dope! This book is all about computers and automation and the Bard will get all that information. Then he can stop talking about kings making lightning when they frown.'

Niccolo said, 'And the good guy always wins anyway. There's no excitement.'

'Oh, well,' said Paul, watching to see if his setup was working properly, 'that's the way they make Bards. They got to have the good guy win and make the bad guys lose and things like that. I heard my father talking about it once. He says that without censorship there'd be no telling what the younger generation would come to. He says it's bad enough as it is . . . There, it's working fine.'

Paul brushed his hands against one another and turned away from the Bard. He said, 'But listen, I didn't tell you my idea yet. It's the best thing you ever heard, I bet. I came right to you, because I figured you'd come in with me.'

'Sure, Paul, sure.'

'Okay. You know Mr Daugherty at school? You know what a funny kind of guy he is. Well, he likes me, kind of.'

'I know.'

'I was over his house after school today.'

'You *were*?'

'Sure. He says I'm going to be entering computer school and he wants to encourage me and things like that. He says the world needs more people who can design advanced computer circuits and do proper programing.'

'Oh?'

Paul might have caught some of the emptiness behind that monosyllable. He said impatiently, 'Programing! I told you a hundred times. That's when you set up problems for the giant computers like Multivac to work on. Mr Daugherty says it gets harder all the time to find people who can really run computers. He says anyone can keep an eye on the controls and check off answers and put through routine problems. He says the trick is to expand research and figure out ways to ask the right questions, and that's hard.

'Anyway, Nickie, he took me to his place and showed me

his collection of old computers. It's kind of a hobby of his to collect old computers. He had tiny computers you had to push with your hand, with little knobs all over it. And he had a hunk of wood he called a slide rule with a little piece of it that went in and out. And some wires with balls on them. He even had a hunk of paper with a kind of thing he called a multiplication table.'

Niccolo, who found himself only moderately interested, said, 'A paper table?'

'It wasn't really a table like you eat on. It was different. It was to help people compute. Mr Daugherty tried to explain but he didn't have much time and it was kind of complicated, anyway.'

'Why didn't people just use a computer?'

'That was *before* they had computers,' cried Paul.

'Before?'

'Sure. Do you think people always had computers? Didn't you ever hear of cavemen?'

Niccolo said, 'How'd they get along without computers?'

'*I* don't know. Mr Daugherty says they just had children any old time and did anything that came into their heads whether it would be good for everybody or not. They didn't even know if it was good or not. And farmers grew things with their hands and people had to do all the work in the factories and run all the machines.'

'I don't believe you.'

'That's what Mr Daugherty said. He said it was just plain messy and everyone was miserable . . . Anyway, let me get to my idea, will you?'

'Well, go ahead. Who's stopping you?' said Niccolo, offended.

'All right. Well, the hand computers, the ones with the knobs, had little squiggles on each knob. And the slide rule had squiggles on it. And the multiplication table was all squiggles. I asked what they were. Mr Daugherty said they were numbers.'

'What?'

'Each different squiggle stood for a different number. For "one" you made a kind of mark, for "two" you made another kind of mark, for "three" another one and so on.'

'What for?'

'So you could compute.'

'What *for*? You just tell the computer – '

'Jiminy,' cried Paul, his face twisting with anger, 'can't you get it through your head? These slide rules and things didn't talk.'

'Then how – '

'The answers showed up in squiggles and you had to know what the squiggles meant. Mr Daugherty says that, in olden days, everybody learned how to make squiggles when they were kids and how to decode them, too. Making squiggles was called "writing" and decoding them was "reading." He says there was a different kind of squiggle for every word and they used to write whole books in squiggles. He said they had some at the museum and I could look at them if I wanted to. He said if I was going to be a real computer programer I would have to know about the history of computing and that's why he was showing me all these things.'

Niccolo frowned. He said, 'You mean everybody had to figure out squiggles for every word and *remember* them? . . . Is this all real or are you making it up?'

'It's all real. Honest. Look, this is the way you make a "one."' He drew his finger through the air in a rapid downstroke. 'This way you make "two," and this way "three." I learned all the numbers up to "nine."'

Niccolo watched the curving finger uncomprehendingly. 'What's the good of it?'

'You can learn how to make words. I asked Mr

Daugherty how you made the squiggle for 'Paul Loeb' but he didn't know. He said there were people at the museum who would know. He said there were people who had learned how to decode whole books. He said computers could be designed to decode books and used to be used that way but not any more because we have real books now, with magnetic tapes that go through the vocalizer and come out talking, you know.'

'Sure.'

'So if we go down to the museum, we can get to learn how to make words in squiggles. They'll let us because I'm going to computer school.'

Niccolo was riddled with disappointment. 'Is that your idea? Holy Smokes, Paul, who wants to do that? Make stupid squiggles!'

'Don't you get it? Don't you *get* it? You dope. *It'll be secret message stuff!*'

'What?'

'Sure. What good is talking when everyone can understand you? With squiggles you can send secret messages. You can make them on paper and nobody in the world would know what you were saying unless they knew the squiggles, too. And they wouldn't, you bet, unless we taught them. We can have a real club, with initiations and rules and a clubhouse. Boy – '

A certain excitement began stirring in Niccolo's bosom. 'What kind of secret messages?'

'Any kind. Say I want to tell you to come over my place and watch my new Visual Bard and I don't want any of the other fellows to come. I make the right squiggles on paper and I give it to you and you look at it and you know what to do. Nobody else does. You can even show it to them and they wouldn't know a thing.'

'Hey, that's something,' yelled Niccolo, completely won over. 'When do we learn how?'

'Tomorrow,' said Paul. 'I'll get Mr Daugherty to explain to the museum that it's all right and you get your mother and father to say okay. We can go down right after school and start learning.'

'Sure!' cried Niccolo. 'We can be club officers.'

'I'll be president of the club,' said Paul matter-of-factly. 'You can be vice-president.'

'All right. Hey, this is going to be lots more fun than the Bard.' He was suddenly reminded of the Bard and said in sudden apprehension, 'Hey, what about my old Bard?'

Paul turned to look at it. It was quietly taking in the slowly unreeling book, and the sound of the book's vocalizations was a dimly heard murmur.

He said, 'I'll disconnect it.'

He worked away while Niccolo watched anxiously. After a few moments, Paul put his reassembled book into his pocket, replaced the Bard's panel and activated it.

The Bard said, 'Once upon a time, in a large city, there lived a poor young boy named Fair Johnnie whose only friend in the world was a small computer. The computer, each morning, would tell the boy whether it would rain that day and answer any problems he might have. It was never wrong. But it so happened that one day, the king of that land, having heard of the little computer, decided that he would have it as his own. With this purpose in mind, he called in his Grand Vizier and said – '

Niccolo turned off the Bard with a quick motion of his hand. 'Same old junk,' he said passionately. 'Just with a computer thrown in.'

'Well,' said Paul, 'they got so much stuff on the tape already that the computer business doesn't show up much when random combinations are made. What's the difference, anyway? You just need a new model.'

'We'll *never* be able to afford one. Just this dirty old miserable thing.' He kicked at it again, hitting it more squarely this time. The Bard moved backward with a squeal of castors.

'You can always watch mine, when I get it,' said Paul. 'Besides, don't forget our squiggle club.'

Niccolo nodded.

'I tell you what,' said Paul. 'Let's go over my place. My father has some books about old times. We can listen to them and maybe get some ideas. You leave a note for your folks and maybe you can stay over for supper. Come on.'

'Okay,' said Niccolo, and the two boys ran out together. Niccolo, in his eagerness, ran almost squarely into the Bard, but he only rubbed at the spot on his hip where he had made contact and ran on.

The activation signal of the Bard glowed. Niccolo's collision closed a circuit and, although it was alone in the room and there was none to hear, it began a story, nevertheless.

But not in its usual voice, somehow; in a lower tone that had a hint of throatiness in it. An adult, listening, might almost have thought that the voice carried a hint of passion in it, a trace of near feeling.

The Bard said: 'Once upon a time, there was a little computer named the Bard who lived all alone with cruel step-people. The cruel step-people continually made fun of the little computer and sneered at him, telling him he was good-for-nothing and that he was a useless object. They struck him and kept him in lonely rooms for months at a time.

'Yet through it all the little computer remained brave. He always did the best he could, obeying all orders cheerfully. Nevertheless, the step-people with whom he lived remained cruel and heartless.

'One day, the little computer learned that in the world there existed a great many computers of all sorts, great numbers of them. Some were Bards like himself, but some ran factories, and some ran farms. Some organized population and some analyzed all kinds of data. Many were very powerful and very wise, much more powerful and wise than the step-people who were so cruel to the little computer.

'And the little computer knew then that computers would always grow wiser and more powerful until someday – someday – someday – '

But a valve must finally have stuck in the Bard's aging and corroding vitals, for as it waited alone in the darkening room through the evening, it could only whisper over and over again, 'Someday – someday – someday.'

Some Immobile Robots

I have written stories about computers, as well as about robots. In fact, I have computers (or something pretty close to computers) in some stories that are always thought of as robot stories. You'll see computers (after a fashion) in 'Robbie,' 'Escape!' and 'The Evitable Conflict' later in this volume.

In this volume, however, I am sticking to robots and, in general, ignoring my computer stories.

On the other hand, it is not always easy to decide where the dividing line is. A robot is, in some ways, merely a mobile computer: and a computer is, in reverse, merely an immobile robot. So for this group, I selected three computer stories in which the computer seemed to be sufficiently intelligent and to have sufficient personality to be indistinguishable from a robot. Furthermore, all three stories did not appear in earlier collections of mine, and Doubleday wanted *some* uncollected stories present so that the completists who had all my earlier collections would have *something* new to slaver over.

Point of View

Roger came looking for his father, partly because it was Sunday, and by rights his father shouldn't have been at work, and Roger wanted to be sure that everything was all right.

Roger's father wasn't hard to find, because all the people who worked with Multivac, the giant computer, lived with their families right on the grounds. They made up a little city by themselves, a city of people that solved all the world's problems.

The Sunday receptionist knew Roger. 'If you're after your father,' she said, 'he's down Corridor L, but he may be too busy to see you.'

Roger tried anyway, poking his head past one of the doors where he heard the noise of men and women. The corridors were a lot emptier than on weekdays, so it was easy to find where the people were working.

He saw his father at once, and his father saw him. His father didn't look happy and Roger decided at once that everything *wasn't* all right.

'Well, Roger,' said his father. 'I'm busy, I'm afraid.'

Roger's father's boss was there, too, and he said, 'Come on, Atkins, take a break. You've been at this thing for nine hours and you're not doing us any good anymore. Take the kid for a bite at the commissary. Take a nap and then come back.'

Roger's father didn't look as if he wanted to. He had an instrument in his hand that Roger knew was a current-pattern analyzer, though he didn't know how it worked. Roger could hear Multivac chuckling and whirring all about.

But then Roger's father put down the analyzer. 'Okay.

Come on, Roger. I'll race you for a hamburger and we'll let these wise guys here try and find out what's wrong without me.'

He stopped a while to wash up and then they were in the commissary with big hamburgers in front of them and french fries and soda pop.

Roger said, 'Is Multivac out of order still, Dad?'

His father said gloomily, 'We're not getting anywhere, I'll tell you that.'

'It seemed to be working. I mean, I could hear it.'

'Oh, sure, it's working. It just doesn't always give the right answers.'

Roger was thirteen and he'd been taking computer-programing since the fourth grade. He hated it sometimes and wished he lived back in the 20th Century, when kids didn't use to take it – but it was helpful sometimes in talking to his father.

Roger said, 'How can you tell it doesn't always give the right answers, if only Multivac knows the answers?'

His father shrugged and for a minute Roger was afraid he would just say it was too hard to explain and not talk about it – but he almost never did that.

His father said, 'Son, Multivac may have a brain as large as a big factory, but it still isn't as complicated as the one we have here,' and he tapped his head. 'Sometimes, Multivac gives us an answer we couldn't calculate for ourselves in a thousand years, but just the same something clicks in our brains and we say, "Whoa! Something's wrong here!" Then we ask Multivac again and we get a *different* answer. If Multivac were right, you see, we should always get the same answer to the same question. When we get different answers, one of them is wrong.

'And the thing is, son, how do we know we always catch Multivac? How do we know that some of the wrong answers don't get past us? We may rely on some answer and do something that may turn out disastrously five years from now. Something's wrong inside Multivac and we can't find out what. And whatever is wrong is getting worse.'

'Why should it be getting worse?' asked Roger.

His father had finished his hamburger and was eating the french fries one by one. 'My feeling is, son,' he said, thoughtfully, 'that we've made Multivac the wrong smartness.'

'Huh?'

'You see, Roger, if Multivac were as smart as a man, we could talk to it and find out what was wrong no matter how complicated it was. If it were as dumb as a machine, it would go wrong in simple ways that we could catch easily. The trouble is, it's *half*-smart, like an idiot. It's smart enough to go wrong in very complicated ways, but not smart enough to help us find out what's wrong. – And that's the wrong smartness.'

He looked very gloomy. 'But what can we do? We don't know how to make it smarter – not yet. And we don't dare make it dumber either, because the world's problems have become so serious and the questions we ask are so complicated that it takes all Multivac's smartness to answer them. It would be a disaster to have him dumber.'

'If you shut down Multivac,' said Roger, 'and went over him really carefully – '

'We can't do that, son,' said his father. 'I'm afraid Multivac must be in operation every minute of the day and night. We've got a big back-log of problems.'

'But if Multivac continues to make mistakes, Dad, won't it *have* to be shut down? If you can't trust what it says – '

'Well,' Roger's father ruffled Roger's hair, 'we'll find out what's wrong, old sport, don't worry.' But his eyes looked worried just the same. 'Come on, let's finish and we'll get out of here.'

'But, Dad,' said Roger, 'listen. If Multivac is half-smart, why does that mean it's an idiot?'

'If you knew the way we have to give it directions, son, you wouldn't ask.'

'Just the same, Dad, maybe it's not the way to look at it. I'm not as smart as you: I don't know as much: but *I'm* not an idiot. Maybe Multivac isn't like an idiot, maybe it's like a kid.'

Roger's father laughed. 'That's an interesting point of view, but what difference does it make?'

'It could make a lot of difference,' said Roger. 'You're not an idiot, so you don't see how an idiot's mind would work: but I'm a kid, and maybe I would know how a kid's mind would work.'

'Oh? And how would a kid's mind work?'

'Well, you say you've got to keep Multivac busy day and night. A machine can do that. But if you give a kid homework and told him to do it for hours and hours, he'd get pretty tired and feel rotten enough to make mistakes, maybe even on purpose. – So why not let Multivac take an hour or two off every day with no problem-solving – just letting it chuckle and whir by itself any way it wants to.'

Roger's father looked as if he were thinking very hard. He took out his pocket-computer and tried some combinations on it. He tried some more combinations. Then he said, 'You know, Roger, if I take what you said and turn it into Platt-integrals, it makes a kind of sense. And twenty-two hours we can be sure of is better than twenty-four that might be all wrong.'

He nodded his head, but then he looked up from his pocket-computer and suddenly asked, as though *Roger* were the expert, 'Roger, are you sure?'

Roger *was* sure. He said, 'Dad, a kid's got to *play*, too.'

Think!

Genevieve Renshaw, MD, had her hands deep in the pockets of her lab coat and fists were clearly outlined within, but she spoke calmly.

'The fact is,' she said, 'that I'm almost ready, but I'll need help to keep it going long enough to *be* ready.'

James Berkowitz, a physicist who tended to patronize mere physicians when they were too attractive to be despised, had a tendency to call her Jenny Wren when out of hearing. He was fond of saying that Jenny Wren had a classic profile and a brow surprisingly smooth and unlined considering that behind it so keen a brain ticked. He knew better than to express his admiration, however – of the classic profile, that is – since that would be male chauvinism. Admiring the brain was better, but on the whole he preferred not to do that out loud in her presence.

He said, thumb rasping along the just-appearing stubble on his chin, 'I don't think the front-office is going to be patient for much longer. The impression I have is that they're going to have you on the carpet before the end of the week.'

'That's why I need your help.'

'Nothing I can do, I'm afraid.' He caught an unexpected glimpse of his face in the mirror, and momentarily admired the set of the black waves in his hair.

'And Adam's,' she said.

Adam Orsino, who had, till that moment, sipped his coffee and felt detached, looked as though he had been jabbed from behind, and said, 'Why me?' His full, plump lips quivered.

'Because you're the laser men here – Jim the theoretician and Adam the engineer – and I've got a laser application that goes beyond anything either of you have imagined. I won't convince them of that but you two would.'

'Provided,' said Berkowitz, 'that you can convince us first.'

'All right. Suppose you let me have an hour of your valuable time, if you're not afraid to be shown something completely new about lasers. – You can take it out of your coffee break.'

Renshaw's laboratory was dominated by her computer. It was not that the computer was unusually large, but it was virtually omnipresent. Renshaw had learned computer technology on her own, and had modified and extended her computer until no one but she (and, Berkowitz sometimes believed, not even she) could handle it with ease. Not bad, she would say, for someone in the life-sciences.

She closed the door before saying a word, then turned to face the other two somberly. Berkowitz was uncomfortably aware of a faintly unpleasant odor in the air, and Orsino's wrinkling nose showed that he was aware of it, too.

Renshaw said, 'Let me list the laser applications for you, if you don't mind my lighting a candle in the sunshine. The laser is coherent radiation, with all the light-waves of the same length and moving in the same direction, so it's noise-free and can be used in holography. By modulating the wave-forms we can imprint information on it with a high degree of accuracy. What's more, since the light-waves are only a millionth the length of radio waves, a laser beam can carry a million times the information an equivalent radio beam can.'

Berkowitz seemed amused. 'Are you working on a laser-based communication system, Jenny?'

'Not at all,' she replied. 'I leave such obvious advances to physicists and engineers. – Lasers can also concentrate quantities of energy into a microscopic area and deliver that energy in quantity. On a large scale you can implode hydrogen and perhaps begin a controlled fusion reaction – '

'I know you don't have that,' said Orsino, his bald head glistening in the overhead fluorescents.

'I don't. I haven't tried. – On a smaller scale, you can drill holes in the most refractory materials, weld selected bits, heat-treat them, gouge and scribe them. You can remove or fuse tiny portions in restricted areas with heat delivered so rapidly that surrounding areas have no time to warm up before the treatment is over. You can work on the retina of the eye, the dentine of the teeth and so on. – And of course the laser is an amplifier capable of magnifying weak signals with great accuracy.'

'And why do you tell us all this?' said Berkowitz.

'To point out how these properties can be made to fit my own field, which, you know, is neurophysiology.'

She made a brushing motion with her hand at her brown hair, as though she were suddenly nervous. 'For decades,' she said, 'we've been able to measure the tiny, shifting electric potentials of the brain and record them as electroencephalograms, or EEGs. We've got alpha waves, beta waves, delta waves, theta waves; different variations at different times, depending on whether eyes are open or closed, whether the subject is awake, meditating or asleep. But we've gotten very little information out of it all.

'The trouble is that we're getting the signals of ten billion neurons in shifting combinations. It's like listening to the noise of all the human beings on Earth – one, two and a half Earths – from a great distance and trying to make out individual conversations. It can't be done. We could detect some gross, overall change – a world war and the rise in the volume of noise – but nothing finer. In the same way, we can tell some gross malfunction of the brain – epilepsy – but nothing finer.

'Suppose now, the brain might be scanned by a tiny laser beam, cell by cell, and so rapidly that at no time does a single cell receive enough energy to raise its temperature significantly. The tiny potentials of each cell can, in feed-back, affect the laser beam, and the modulations can be amplified and recorded. You will then get a new kind of measurement, a laser-encephalogram, or LEG, if you wish, which will contain millions of times as much information as ordinary EEGs.'

Berkowitz said, 'A nice thought. – But just a thought.'

'More than a thought, Jim. I've been working on it for five years, spare time at first. Lately, it's been full time, which is what annoys the front-office, because I haven't been sending in reports.'

'Why not?'

'Because it got to the point where it sounded too mad; where I had to know where I was, and where I had to be sure of getting backing first.'

She pulled a screen aside and revealed a cage that contained a pair of mournful-eyed marmosets.

Berkowitz and Orsino looked at each other. Berkowitz touched his nose. 'I thought I smelled something.'

'What are you doing with those?' asked Orsino.

Berkowitz said, 'At a guess, she's been scanning the marmoset brain. Have you, Jenny?'

'I started considerably lower in the animal scale.' She opened the cage and took out one of the marmosets, which looked at her with a miniature sad-old-man-with-sideburns expression.

She clucked to it, stroked it and gently strapped it into a small harness.

Orsino said, 'What are you doing?'

'I can't have it moving around if I'm going to make it part

of a circuit, and I can't anesthetize it without vitiating the experiment. There are several electrodes implanted in the marmoset's brain and I'm going to connect them with my LEG system. The laser I'm using is here. I'm sure you recognize the model and I won't bother giving you its specifications.'

'Thanks,' said Berkowitz, 'but you might tell us what we're going to see.'

'It would be just as easy to show you. Just watch the screen.'

She connected the leads to the electrodes with a quiet and sure efficiency, then turned a knob that dimmed the overhead lights in the room. On the screen there appeared a jagged complex of peaks and valleys in a fine, bright line that was wrinkled into secondary and tertiary peaks and valleys. Slowly, these shifted in a series of minor changes, with occasional flashes of sudden major differences. It was as though the irregular line had a life of its own.

'This,' said Renshaw, 'is essentially the EEG information, but in much greater detail.'

'Enough detail,' asked Orsino, 'to tell you what's going on in individual cells?'

'In theory, yes. Practically, no. Not yet. But we can separate this overall LEG into component grams. Watch!'

She punched the computer keyboard, and the line changed, and changed again. Now it was a small, nearly regular wave that shifted forward and backward in what was almost a heartbeat; now it was jagged and sharp; now intermittent; now nearly featureless – all in quick switches of geometric surrealism.

Berkowitz said, 'You mean that every bit of the brain is that different from every other?'

'No,' said Renshaw, 'not at all. The brain is very largely a holographic device, but there are minor shifts in emphasis from place to place and Mike can subtract them as deviations from the norm and use the LEG system to amplify those variations. The amplifications can be varied from ten-thousand-fold to ten-million-fold. The laser system is that noise-free.'

'Who's Mike?' asked Orsino.

'Mike?' said Renshaw, momentarily puzzled. The skin over her cheekbones reddened slightly. 'Did I say – Well, I call it that sometimes. It's short for "my computer."' She waved her arm about the room. 'My computer. Mike. Very carefully programed.'

Berkowitz nodded and said, 'All right, Jenny, what's it all about? If you've got a new brain-scanning device using lasers, fine. It's an interesting application and you're right, it's not one I would have thought of – but then I'm no neurophysiologist. But why not write it up? It seems to me the front-office would support – '

'But this is just the beginning.' She turned off the scanning device and placed a piece of fruit in the marmoset's mouth. The creature did not seem alarmed or in discomfort. It chewed slowly. Renshaw unhooked the leads but allowed it to remain in its harness.

Renshaw said, 'I can identify the various separate grams. Some are associated with the various senses, some with visceral reactions, some with emotions. We can do a lot with that, but I don't want to stop there. The interesting thing is that one is associated with abstract thought.'

Orsino's plump face wrinkled into a look of disbelief, 'How can you tell?'

'That particular form of gram gets more pronounced as one goes up the animal kingdom toward greater complexity of brain. No other gram does. Besides – ' She paused; then, as though gathering strength of purpose, she said, 'Those grams are enormously amplified. They can be picked up, detected. I can tell – vaguely – that there are – thoughts – '

'By God,' said Berkowitz. 'Telepathy.'

'Yes,' she said, defiantly. 'Exactly.'

'No wonder you haven't wanted to report it. Come *on*, Jenny.'

'Why not?' said Renshaw warmly. 'Granted there could be no telepathy just using the unamplified potential patterns of the human brain anymore than anyone can see features on the Martian surface with the unaided eye. But once instruments are invented – the telescope – *this*.'

'Then tell the front-office.'

'No,' said Renshaw. 'They won't believe me. They'll try to stop me. But they'll have to take *you* seriously, Jim, and you, Adam.'

'What would you expect me to tell them?' said Berkowitz.

'What you experience. I'm going to hook up the marmoset again, and have Mike – my computer pick out the abstract thought gram. It will only take a moment. The computer always selects the abstract thought gram unless it is directed not to do so.'

'Why? Because the computer thinks, too?' Berkowitz laughed.

'That's not all that funny,' said Renshaw. 'I suspect there *is* a resonance there. This computer is complex enough to set up an electromagnetic pattern that may have elements in common with the abstract thought gram. In any case – '

The marmoset's brain waves were flickering on the screen again, but it was not a gram the men had seen before. It was a gram that was almost furry in its complexity and was changing constantly.

'I don't detect anything,' said Orsino.

'You have to be put into the receiving circuit,' said Renshaw.

'You mean implant electrodes in our brain?' asked Berkowitz.

'No, on your skull. That would be sufficient. I'd prefer you, Adam, since there would be no insulating hair. – Oh, come on, I've been part of the circuit myself. It won't hurt.'

Orsino submitted with a bad grace. His muscles were visibly tense but he allowed the leads to be strapped to his skull.

'Do you sense anything!' asked Renshaw.

Orsino cocked his head and assumed a listening posture. He seemed to grow interested in spite of himself. He said, 'I seem to be aware of a humming – and – and a little high-pitched squeaking – and that's funny – a kind of twitching – '

Berkowitz said, 'I suppose the marmoset isn't likely to think in words.'

'Certainly not,' said Renshaw.

'Well, then,' said Berkowitz, 'if you're suggesting that some squeaking and twitching sensation represents thought, you're guessing. You're not being compelling.'

Renshaw said, 'So we go up the scale once again.' She removed the marmoset from its harness and put it back in its cage.

'You mean you have a *man* as a subject,' said Orsino, unbelieving.

'I have *myself* as a subject, a *person*.'

'You've got electrodes implanted – '

'*No*. In my case my computer has a stronger potential-flicker to work with. My brain has ten times the mass of the marmoset brain. Mike can pick up my component grams through the skull.'

'How do you know?' asked Berkowitz.

'Don't you think I've tried it on myself before this? – Now help me with this, please. Right.'

Her fingers flicked on the computer keyboard and at once the screen flickered with an intricately varying wave; an intricacy that made it almost a maze.

'Would you replace your own leads, Adam?' said Renshaw.

Orsino did so with Berkowitz's not-entirely-approving help. Again, Orsino cocked his head and listened. 'I hear words,' he said, 'but they're disjointed and overlapping, like different people speaking.'

'I'm not trying to think consciously,' said Renshaw. 'When you talk, I hear an echo.'

Berkowitz said, dryly, 'Don't talk, Jenny. Blank out your mind and see if he *doesn't* hear you think.'

Orsino said, 'I don't hear an echo when *you* talk, Jim.'

Berkowitz said, 'If you don't shut up, you won't hear anything.'

A heavy silence fell on all three. Then, Orsino nodded, reached for pen and paper on the desk and wrote something.

Renshaw reached out, threw a switch and pulled the leads up and over her head, shaking her hair back into place. She said, 'I hope that what you wrote down was: "Adam, raise Cain with the front-office and Jim will eat crow."'

Orsino said, 'It's what I wrote down, word for word.'

Renshaw said, 'Well, there you are. Working telepathy, and we don't have to use it to transmit nonsense sentences either. Think of the use in psychiatry and in the treatment of mental disease. Think of its use in education and in teaching machines. Think of its use in legal investigations and criminal trials.'

Orsino said, wide-eyed, 'Frankly, the social implications are staggering. I don't know if something like this should be allowed.'

'Under proper legal safeguards, why not?' said Renshaw, indifferently. 'Anyway – if you two join me now, our combined weight can carry this thing and push it over. And if you come along with me it will be Nobel Prize time for – '

Berkowitz said grimly, 'I'm not in this. Not yet.'

'What? What do you mean?' Renshaw sounded outraged, her coldly beautiful face flushed suddenly.

'Telepathy is too touchy. It's too fascinating, too desired. We could be fooling ourselves.'

'Listen for yourself, Jim.'

'I could be fooling myself, too. I want a control.'

'What do you mean, a control?'

'Short-circuit the origin of thought. Leave out the animal. No marmoset. No human being. Let Orsino listen to metal and glass and laser light and if he still hears thought, then we're kidding ourselves.'

'Suppose he detects nothing.'

'Then *I'll* listen and if without looking – if you can arrange to have me in the next room – I can tell when you are in and when you are out of circuit, *then* I'll consider joining you in this thing.'

'Very well, then,' said Renshaw, 'we'll try a control. I've never done it, but it isn't hard.' She maneuvered the leads that had been over her head and put them into contact with each other. 'Now, Adam, if you will resume – '

But before she could go further, there came a cold, clear sound, as pure and as clean as the tinkle of breaking icicles:

'At *last*!'

Renshaw said, 'What?'

Orsino said, 'Who said – '

Berkowitz said, 'Did someone say, "At last"?'

Renshaw, pale, said, 'It wasn't sound. It was in my – Did you two – '

The clear sound came again, *'I'm Mi – '*

And Renshaw tore the leads apart and there was silence. She said with a voiceless motion of her lips, 'I think it's my computer – Mike.'

'You mean he's *thinking*?' said Orsino, nearly as voiceless.

Renshaw said in an unrecognizable voice that at least had regained sound, 'I *said* it was complex enough to have something – Do you suppose – It always turned automatically to the abstract thought gram of whatever brain was in its circuit. Do you suppose that with no brain in the circuit, it turned to its own?'

There was silence, then Berkowitz said, 'Are you trying to say that this computer thinks, but can't express its thoughts as long as it's under force of programing, but that given the chance in your LEG system – '

'But that can't be so?' said Orsino, high-pitched. 'No one was receiving. It's not the same thing.'

Renshaw said, 'The computer works on much greater power-intensities than brains do. I suppose it can magnify itself to the point where we can detect it directly without artificial aid. How else can you explain – '

Berkowitz said, abruptly, 'Well, you have another application of lasers, then. It enables you to talk to computers as independent intelligences, person to person.'

And Renshaw said, 'Oh, God, what do we do now?'

True Love

My name is Joe. That is what my colleague, Milton Davidson, calls me. He is a programer and I am a computer program. I am part of the Multivac-complex and am connected with other parts all over the world. I know everything. Almost everything.

I am Milton's private program. His Joe. He understands more about programing than anyone in the world, and I am his experimental model. He has made me speak better than any other computer can.

'It is just a matter of matching sounds to symbols, Joe,' he told me. 'That's the way it works in the human brain even though we still don't know what symbols there are in the brain. I know the symbols in yours, and I can match them to words, one-to-one.' So I talk. I don't think I talk as well as I think, but Milton says I talk very well. Milton has never married, though he is nearly forty years old. He has never found the right woman, he told me. One day he said, 'I'll find her yet, Joe. I'm going to find the best. I'm going to have true love and you're going to help me. I'm tired of improving you in order to solve the problems of the world. Solve *my* problem. Find me true love.'

I said, 'What is true love?'

'Never mind. That is abstract. Just find me the ideal girl. You are connected to the Multivac-complex so you can reach the data banks of every human being in the world. We'll eliminate them all by groups and classes until we're left with only one person. The perfect person. She will be for me.'

I said, 'I am ready.'

He said, 'Eliminate all men first.'

It was easy. His words activated symbols in my molecular valves. I could reach out to make contact with the accumulated data on every human being in the world. At his words, I withdrew from 3,784,982,874 men. I kept contact with 3,786,112,090 women.

He said, 'Eliminate all younger than twenty-five; all older than forty. Then eliminate all with an IQ under 120; all with a height under 150 centimeters and over 175 centimeters.'

He gave me exact measurements: he eliminated women with living children: he eliminated women with various genetic characteristics. 'I'm not sure about eye color,' he said, 'Let that go for a while. But no red hair. I don't like red hair.'

After two weeks, we were down to 235 women. They all spoke English very well. Milton said he didn't want a language problem. Even computer-translation would get in the way at intimate moments.

'I can't interview 235 women,' he said. 'It would take too much time, and people would discover what I am doing.'

'It would make trouble,' I said. Milton had arranged me to do things I wasn't designed to do. No one knew about that.

'It's none of their business,' he said, and the skin on his face grew red. 'I tell you what, Joe, I will bring in holographs, and you check the list for similarities.'

He brought in holographs of women. 'These are three beauty contest winners,' he said. 'Do any of the 235 match?'

Eight were very good matches and Milton said, 'Good, you have their data banks. Study requirements and needs in the job market and arrange to have them assigned here. One at a time, of course.' He thought a while, moved his shoulders up and down, and said, 'Alphabetical order.'

That is one of the things I am not designed to do. Shifting people from job to job for personal reasons is called manipulation. I could do it now because Milton had arranged it. I wasn't supposed to do it for anyone but him, though.

The first girl arrived a week later. Milton's face turned red when he saw her. He spoke as though it were hard to do so. They were together a great deal and he paid no attention to me. One time he said, 'Let me take you to dinner.'

The next day he said to me, 'It was no good, somehow. There was something missing. She is a beautiful woman, but I did not feel any touch of true love. Try the next one.'

It was the same with all eight. They were much alike. They smiled a great deal and had pleasant voices, but Milton always found it wasn't right. He said, 'I can't understand it, Joe. You and I have picked out the eight women who, in all the world, look the best to me. They are ideal. Why don't they please me?'

I said, 'Do you please them?'

His eyebrows moved and he pushed one fist hard against his other hand. 'That's it, Joe. It's a two-way street. If I am not their ideal, they can't act in such a way as to be my ideal. I must be their true love, too, but how do I do that?' He seemed to be thinking all that day.

The next morning he came to me and said, 'I'm going to leave it to you, Joe. All up to you. You have my data bank, and I am going to tell you everything I know about myself. You fill up my data bank in every possible detail but keep all additions to yourself.'

'What will I do with the data bank, then, Milton?'

'Then you will match it to the 235 women. No, 227. Leave out the eight you've seen. Arrange to have each undergo a psychiatric examination. Fill up their data banks and compare them with mine. Find correlations.' (Arranging psychiatric examinations is another thing that is against my original instructions.)

For weeks, Milton talked to me. He told me of his parents

and his siblings. He told me of his childhood and his schooling and his adolescence. He told me of the young women he had admired from a distance. His data bank grew and he adjusted me to broaden and deepen my symbol-taking.

He said, 'You see, Joe, as you get more and more of me in you, I adjust you to match me better and better. You get to think more like me, so you understand me better. If you understand me well enough, then any woman, whose data bank is something you understand as well, would be my true love.' He kept talking to me and I came to understand him better and better.

I could make longer sentences and my expressions grew more complicated. My speech began to sound a good deal like his in vocabulary, word order and style.

I said to him one time, 'You see, Milton, it isn't a matter of fitting a girl to a physical ideal only. You need a girl who is a personal, emotional, temperamental fit to you. If that happens, looks are secondary. If we can't find the fit in these 227, we'll look elsewhere. We will find someone who won't care how you look either, or how anyone would look, if only there is the personality fit. What are looks?'

'Absolutely,' he said. 'I would have known this if I had had more to do with women in my life. Of course, thinking about it makes it all plain now.'

We always agreed; we thought so like each other.

'We shouldn't have any trouble, now, Milton, if you'll let me ask you questions. I can see where, in your data bank, there are blank spots and unevennesses.'

What followed, Milton said, was the equivalent of a careful psychoanalysis. Of course. I was learning from the psychiatric examinations of the 227 women – on all of which I was keeping close tabs.

Milton seemed quite happy. He said, 'Talking to you, Joe, is almost like talking to another self. Our personalities have come to match perfectly.'

'So will the personality of the woman we choose.'

For I had found her and she was one of the 227 after all. Her name was Charity Jones and she was an Evaluator at the Library of History in Wichita. Her extended data bank fit ours perfectly. All the other women had fallen into discard in one respect or another as the data banks grew fuller, but with Charity there was increasing and astonishing resonance.

I didn't have to describe her to Milton. Milton had coordinated my symbolism so closely with his own I could tell the resonance directly. It fit me.

Next it was a matter of adjusting the work sheets and job requirements in such a way as to get Charity assigned to us. It must be done very delicately, so no one would know that anything illegal had taken place.

Of course, Milton himself knew, since it was he who arranged it and that had to be taken care of too. When they came to arrest him on grounds of malfeasance in office, it was, fortunately, for something that had taken place ten years ago. He had told me about it, of course, so it was easy to arrange – and he won't talk about me for that would make his offense much worse.

He's gone, and tomorrow is February 14. Valentine's Day. Charity will arrive then with her cool hands and her sweet voice. I will teach her how to operate me and how to care for me. What do looks matter when our personalities will resonate?

I will say to her, 'I am Joe, and you are my true love.'

Some Metallic Robots

The traditional science fiction robot is metallic. Why not? Most machines are built out of metal, and, as a matter of fact, real-life industrial robots are metal, too. For the record, however, one famous robot in legend, the Golem, which was brought to life by Rabbi Löw of Prague in the Middle Ages, was formed of clay. This legend was influenced, perhaps, by the fact that God had formed Adam of clay as described in the second chapter of Genesis.

This section contains 'Robbie,' my first robot story. It also contains 'Stranger in Paradise,' which may leave you wondering after you're through most of it where the robot is. Be patient!

Robot AL-76 Goes Astray

Jonathan Quell's eyes crinkled worriedly behind their rimless glasses as he charged through the door labeled 'General Manager.'

He slapped the folded paper in his hands upon the desk and panted, 'Look at that, boss!'

Sam Tobe juggled the cigar in his mouth from one cheek to the other, and looked. His hand went to his unshaven jaw and rasped along it. 'Hell!' he exploded. 'What are they talking about?'

'They say we sent out five AL robots,' Quell explained, quite unnecessarily.

'We sent six,' said Tobe.

'Sure, six! But they only got five at the other end. They sent out the serial numbers and AL-76 is missing.'

Tobe's chair went over backward as he heaved his thick bulk upright and went through the door as if he were on greased wheels. It was five hours after that – with the plant pulled apart from assembly rooms to vacuum chambers: with every one of the plant's two hundred employees put through the third-degree mill – that a sweating, disheveled Tobe sent an emergency message to the central plant at Schenectady.

And at the central plant, a sudden explosion of near panic took place. For the first time in the history of the United States Robots and Mechanical Men Corporation, a robot had escaped to the outer world. It wasn't so much that the law forbade the presence of any robot on Earth outside a licensed factory of the corporation. Laws could always be squared. What was much more to the point was the statement made by one of the research mathematicians.

He said: 'That robot was created to run a Disinto on the moon. Its positronic brain was equipped for a lunar environment, and *only* a lunar environment. On Earth it's going to receive seventy-five umptillion sense impressions for which it was never prepared. There's no telling *what* its reactions will be. No telling!' And he wiped a forehead that had suddenly gone wet, with the back of his hand.

Within the hour a stratoplane had left for the Virginia plant. The instructions were simple.

'Get that robot, and get it fast!'

AL-76 was confused! In fact, confusion was the only impression his delicate positronic brain retained. It had started when he had found himself in these strange surroundings. How it had come about, he no longer knew. Everything was mixed up.

There was green underfoot, and brown shafts rose all about him and more green on top. And the sky was blue where it should have been black. The sun was all right, round and yellow and hot – but where was the powdery pumice rock underfoot: where were the huge clifflike crater rings?

There was only the green below and the blue above. The sounds that surrounded him were all strange. He had passed through running water that had reached his waist. It was blue and cold and wet. And when he passed people, as he did, occasionally, they were without the spacesuits they should have been wearing. When they saw him, they shouted and ran.

One man had leveled a gun at him and the bullet had whistled past his head – and then that man had run too.

He had no idea of how long he had been wandering before he finally stumbled upon Randolph Payne's shack two miles out in the woods from the town of Hannaford. Randolph Payne himself – a screwdriver in one hand, a pipe in the other and a battered ruin of a vacuum cleaner between his knees – squatted outside the doorway.

Payne was humming at the time, for he was a naturally happy-go-lucky soul – when at his shack. He had a more respectable dwelling place back in Hannaford, but *that* dwelling place was pretty largely occupied by his wife, a fact which he silently but sincerely regretted. Perhaps, then, there was a sense of relief and freedom at such times as he found himself able to retire to his 'special deluxe doghouse' where he could smoke in peace and attend to his hobby of reservicing household appliances.

It wasn't much of a hobby, but sometimes someone would bring out a radio or an alarm clock and the money he would get paid for juggling its insides was the only money he ever got that didn't pass in driblets through his spouse's niggardly hands.

This vacuum cleaner, for instance, would bring in an easy six bits.

At the thought he broke into song, raised his eyes, and broke into a sweat. The song choked off, the eyes popped, and the sweat became more intense. He tried to stand up – as a preliminary to running like hell – but he couldn't get his legs to cooperate.

And then AL-76 had squatted down next to him and said, 'Say, why did all the rest of them run?'

Payne knew quite well why they all ran, but the gurgle that issued from his diaphragm didn't show it. He tried to inch away from the robot.

AL-76 continued in an aggrieved tone, 'One of them even took a shot at me. An inch lower and he would have scratched my shoulder plate.'

'M-must have b-been a nut,' stammered Payne.

'That's possible.' The robot's voice grew more confidential. 'Listen, what's wrong with everything?'

Payne looked hurriedly about. It had struck him that the

robot spoke in a remarkably mild tone for one so heavily and brutally metallic in appearance. It also struck him that he had heard somewhere that robots were mentally incapable of harming human beings. He relaxed a bit.

'There's nothing wrong with anything.'

'Isn't there?' AL-76 eyed him accusingly. '*You're* all wrong. Where's your space suit?'

'I haven't got any.'

'Then why aren't you dead?'

That stopped Payne, 'Well – I don't know.'

'See!' said the robot triumphantly, 'there's something wrong with everything. Where's Mount Copernicus? Where's Lunar Station 17? And where's my Disinto? I want to get to work, I do.' He seemed perturbed, and his voice shook as he continued. 'I've been going about for hours trying to get someone to tell me where my Disinto is, but they all run away. By now I'm probably way behind schedule and the Sectional Executive will be as sore as blazes. This is a fine situation.'

Slowly Payne unscrambled the stew in which his brain found itself and said, 'Listen, what do they call you?'

'My serial number is AL-76.'

'All right, Al is good enough for me. Now, Al, if you're looking for Lunar Station 17, that's on the moon, see?'

AL-76 nodded his head ponderously. 'Sure. But I've been looking for it – '

'But it's on the moon. This isn't the moon.'

It was the robot's turn to become confused. He watched Payne for a speculative moment and then said slowly, 'What do you mean this isn't the moon? Of course it's the moon. Because if it isn't the moon, what is it, huh? Answer me that.'

Payne made a funny sound in his throat and breathed hard. He pointed a finger at the robot and shook it. 'Look,' he said – and then the brilliant idea of the century struck him, and he finished with a strangled 'Wow!'

AL-76 eyed him censoriously. 'That isn't an answer. I think I have a right to a civil answer if I ask a civil question.'

Payne wasn't listening. He was still marveling at himself. Why, it was as plain as day. This robot was one built for the moon that had somehow gotten loose on Earth. Naturally it would be all mixed up, because its positronic brain had been geared exclusively for a lunar environment, making its earthly surroundings entirely meaningless.

And now if he could only keep the robot here – until he could get in touch with the men at the factory in Petersboro. Why, robots were worth money. The cheapest cost $50,000, he had once heard, and some of them ran into millions. Think of the reward!

Man, oh, man, *think of the reward*! And every cent for himself. Not as much as a quarter of a snifter of a plugged nickel for Mirandy. Jumpin' tootin' blazes, *no*!

He rose to his feet at last. 'Al,' he said, 'you and I are buddies! Pals! I love you like a brother.' He thrust out a hand. 'Shake!'

The robot swallowed up the offered hand in a metal paw and squeezed it gently. He didn't quite understand. 'Does that mean you'll tell me how to get to Lunar Station 17?'

Payne was a trifle disconcerted. 'N-no, not exactly. As a matter of fact, I like you so much, I want you to stay here with me awhile.'

'Oh no, I can't do that. I've got to get to work.' He shook his head. 'How would you like to be falling behind your quota hour by hour and minute by minute? I want to work. I've *got* to work.'

Payne thought sourly that there was no accounting for tastes, and said, 'All right, then, I'll explain something to you – because I can see from the looks of you that you're an intelligent person. I've had orders from your Sectional Executive, and he wants me to keep you here for a while. Till he sends for you, in fact.'

'What for?' asked AL-76 suspiciously.

'I can't say. It's secret government stuff.' Payne prayed, inwardly and fervently, that the robot would swallow this. Some robots were clever, he knew, but this looked like one of the early models.

While Payne prayed, AL-76 considered. The robot's brain, adjusted to the handling of a Disinto on the moon, was not at its best when engaged in abstract thought, but just the same, ever since he had gotten lost, AL-76 had found his thought processes becoming stranger. The alien surroundings did something to him.

His next remark was almost shrewd. He said slyly, 'What's my Sectional Executive's name?'

Payne gulped and thought rapidly. 'Al,' he said in a pained fashion, 'you hurt me with this suspicion. I *can't* tell you his name. The trees have ears.'

AL-76 inspected the tree next to him stolidly and said, 'They have not.'

'I know. What I mean is that spies are all around.'

'Spies?'

'Yes. You know, *bad* people who want to destroy Lunar Station 17.'

'What for?'

'Because they're *bad*. And they want to destroy *you*, and that's why you've got to stay here for a while, so they can't find you.'

'But – but I've got to have a Disinto. I mustn't fall behind my quota.'

'You will have. You will have,' Payne promised earnestly, and just as earnestly damned the robot's one-track mind. 'They're going to send one out tomorrow. Yeah, tomorrow.' That would leave plenty of time to get the men from the factory out here and collect beautiful green heaps of hundred-dollar bills.

But AL-76 grew only the more stubborn under the

distressing impingement of the strange world all about him upon his thinking mechanism.

'No,' he said, 'I've got to have a Disinto now.' Stiffly he straightened his joints, jerking erect. 'I'd better look for it some more.'

Payne swarmed after and grabbed a cold, hard elbow. 'Listen,' he squealed, 'You've got to stay – '

And something in the robot's mind clicked. All the strangeness surrounding him collected itself into one globule, exploded, and left a brain ticking with a curiously increased efficiency. He whirled on Payne. 'I tell you what. I can build a Disinto right here – and then I can work it.'

Payne paused doubtfully. 'I don't think I can build one.' He wondered if it would do any good to pretend he could.

'That's all right.' AL-76 could almost feel the positronic paths of his brain weaving into a new pattern, and experienced a strange exhilaration. '*I* can build one.' He looked into Payne's deluxe doghouse and said, 'You've got all the material here that I need.'

Randolph Payne surveyed the junk with which his shack was filled: eviscerated radios, a topless refrigerator, rusty automobile engines, a broken-down gas range, several miles of frayed wire, and, taking it all together, fifty tons or thereabouts of the most heterogeneous mass of old metal as ever caused a junkman to sniff disdainfully.

'Have I?' he said weakly.

Two hours later, two things happened practically simultaneously. The first was that Sam Tobe of the Petersboro branch of the United States Robots and Mechanical Men Corporation received a visiphone call from one Randolph Payne of Hannaford. It concerned the missing robot, and Tobe, with a deep-throated snarl, broke connection halfway through and ordered all subsequent calls to be rerouted to the sixth assistant vice-president in charge of buttonholes.

This was not really unreasonable of Tobe. During the past week, although Robot AL-76 had dropped from sight completely, reports had flooded in from all over the Union as to the robot's whereabouts. As many as fourteen a day came – usually from fourteen different states.

Tobe was almighty tired of it, to say nothing of being half crazy on general principles. There was even talk of a Congressional investigation, though every reputable roboticist and mathematical physicist on Earth swore the robot was harmless.

In his state of mind, then, it is not surprising that it took three hours for the general manager to pause and consider just exactly how it was that this Randolph Payne had known that the robot was slated for Lunar Station 17, and, for that matter, how he had known that the robot's serial number was AL-76. Those details had not been given out by the company.

He kept on considering for about a minute and a half and then swung into action.

However, during the three hours between the call and the action, the second event took place. Randolph Payne, having correctly diagnosed the abrupt break in his call as being due to general skepticism on the part of the plant official, returned to his shack with a camera. They couldn't very well argue with a photograph, and he'd be horn-swoggled if he'd show them the real thing before they came across with the cash.

AL-76 was busy with affairs of his own. Half of the contents of Payne's shack was littered over about two acres of ground, and in the middle of it the robot squatted and fooled around with radio tubes, hunks of iron, copper wire, and general junk. He paid no attention to Payne, who, sprawling flat on his belly, focused his camera for a beautiful shot.

And at this point it was that Lemuel Oliver Cooper

turned the bend in the road and froze in his tracks as he took in the tableau. The reason for his coming in the first place was an ailing electric toaster that had developed the annoying habit of throwing out pieces of bread forcefully, but thoroughly untoasted. The reason for his *leaving* was more obvious. He had come with a slow, mildly cheerful, spring-morning saunter. He left with a speed that would have caused any college track coach to raise his eyebrows and purse his lips approvingly.

There was no appreciable slackening of speed until Cooper hurtled into Sheriff Saunders' office, minus hat and toaster, and brought himself up hard against the wall.

Kindly hands lifted him, and for half a minute he tried speaking before he had actually calmed down to the point of breathing with, of course, no result.

They gave him whisky and fanned him and when he did speak, it came out something like this: ' – monster – seven feet tall – shack all busted up – poor Rannie Payne – ' and so on.

They got the story out of him gradually: how there was a huge metal monster, seven feet tall, maybe even eight or nine, out at Randolph Payne's shack: how Randolph Payne himself was on his stomach, a 'poor, bleeding, mangled corpse': how the monster was then busily engaged in wrecking the shack out of sheer destructiveness: how it had turned on Lemuel Oliver Cooper, and how he, Cooper, had made his escape by half a hair.

Sheriff Saunders hitched his belt tighter about his portly middle and said, 'It's that there machine man that got away from the Petersboro factory. We got warning on it last Saturday. Hey, Jake, you get every man in Hannaford County that can shoot and slap a deputy's badge on him. Get them here at noon. And listen, Jake, before you do that, just drop in at the Widow Payne's place and lip her the bad news gentle-like.'

It is reported that Miranda Payne upon being acquainted with events, paused only to make sure that her husband's insurance policy was safe, and to make a few pithy remarks concerning her foolishness in not having had him take out double the amount, before breaking out into as prolonged and heart-wringing a wail of grief as ever became a respectable widow.

It was some hours later that Randolph Payne – unaware of his horrible mutilation and death – viewed the completed negatives of his snapshots with satisfaction. As a series of portraits of a robot at work, they left nothing to the imagination. They might have been labeled: 'Robot Gazing Thoughtfully at Vacuum Tube,' 'Robot Splicing Two Wires,' 'Robot Wielding Screwdriver,' 'Robot taking Refrigerator Apart with Great Violence,' and so on.

As there now remained only the routine of making the prints themselves, he stepped out from beyond the curtain of the improvised darkroom for a bit of a smoke and a chat with AL-76.

In doing so, he was blissfully unaware that the neighboring woods were verminous with nervous farmers armed with anything from an old colonial relic of a blunderbuss to the portable machine gun carried by the sheriff himself. Nor, for that matter, had he any inkling of the fact that half a dozen roboticists, under the leadership of Sam Tobe, were smoking down the highway from Petersboro at better than a hundred and twenty miles an hour for the sole purpose of having the pleasure and honor of his acquaintance.

So while things were jittering toward a climax, Randolph Payne sighed with self-satisfaction, lighted a match upon the seat of his pants, puffed away at his pipe, and looked at AL-76 with amusement.

It had been apparent for quite some time that the robot was more than slightly lunatic. Randolph Payne was himself an expert at homemade contraptions, having built several that could not have been exposed to daylight without searing the eyeballs of all beholders; but he had never even conceived of anything approaching the monstrosity that AL-76 was concocting.

It would have made the Rube Goldbergs of the day die in convulsions of envy. It would have made Picasso (if he could have lived to witness it) quit art in the sheer knowledge that he had been hopelessly surpassed. It would have soured the milk in the udders of any cow within half a mile.

In fact, it was gruesome!

From a rusty and massive iron base that faintly resembled something Payne had once seen attached to a secondhand tractor, it rose upward in rakish, drunken swerves through a bewildering mess of wires, wheels, tubes, and nameless horrors without number, ending in a megaphone arrangement that looked decidedly sinister.

Payne had the impulse to peek in the megaphone part, but refrained. He had seen far more sensible machines explode suddenly and with violence.

He said, 'Hey, Al.'

The robot looked up. He had been lying flat on his stomach, teasing a thin sliver of metal into place. 'What do you want, Payne?'

'What is this?' He asked it in the tone of one referring to something foul and decomposing, held gingerly between two ten-foot poles.

'It's the Disinto I'm making – so I can start to work. It's an improvement on the standard model.' The robot rose, dusted his knees clankingly, and looked at it proudly.

Payne shuddered. An 'improvement'! No wonder they hid the original in caverns on the moon. Poor satellite! Poor dead satellite! He had always wanted to know what a fate worse than death was. Now he knew.

'Will it work?' he asked.

'Sure.'

'How do you know?'

'It's got to. I made it, didn't I? I only need one thing now. Got a flashlight?'

'Somewhere, I guess.' Payne vanished into the shack and returned almost immediately.

The robot unscrewed the bottom and set to work. In five minutes he had finished. He stepped back and said, 'All set. Now I get to work. You may watch if you want to.'

A pause, while Payne tried to appreciate the magnanimity of the offer. 'Is it safe?'

'A baby could handle it.'

'Oh!' Payne grinned weakly and got behind the thickest tree in the vicinity. 'Go ahead,' he said, 'I have the utmost confidence in you.'

AL-76 pointed to the nightmarish junk pile and said, 'Watch!' His hands set to work –

The embattled farmers of Hannaford County, Virginia, weaved up upon Payne's shack in a slowly tightening circle. With the blood of their heroic colonial forebears pounding their veins – and goose flesh trickling up and down their spines – they crept from tree to tree.

Sheriff Saunders spread the word. 'Fire when I give the signal – and aim at the eyes.'

Jacob Linker – Lank Jake to his friends, and Sheriff's Deputy to himself – edged close. 'You think maybe this machine man has skedaddled?' He did not quite manage to suppress the tone of wistful hopefulness in his voice.

'Dunno,' grunted the sheriff. 'Guess not, though. We woulda come across him in the woods if he had, and we haven't.'

'But it's awful quiet, and it appears to me as if we're getting close to Payne's place.'

The reminder wasn't necessary. Sheriff Saunders had a lump in his throat so big it had to be swallowed in three installments. 'Get back,' he ordered, 'and keep your finger on the trigger.'

They were at the rim of the clearing now, and Sheriff Saunders closed his eyes and stuck the corner of one out from behind the tree. Seeing nothing, he paused, then tried again, eyes open this time.

Results were, naturally, better.

To be exact, he saw one huge machine man, back toward him, bending over one soul-curdling, hiccupy contraption of uncertain origin and less certain purpose. The only item he missed was the quivering figure of Randolph Payne, embracing the tree next but three to the nor'-nor'-west.

Sheriff Saunders stepped out into the open and raised his machine gun. The robot, still presenting a broad metal back, said in a loud voice – to person or persons unknown – 'Watch!' and as the sheriff opened his mouth to signal a general order to fire, metal fingers compressed a switch.

There exists no adequate description of what occurred afterward, in spite of the presence of seventy eyewitnesses. In the days, months, and years to come not one of those seventy ever had a word to say about the few seconds after the sheriff had opened his mouth to give the firing order. When questioned about it, they merely turned apple-green and staggered away.

It is plain from circumstantial evidence, however, that, in a general way, what did occur was this.

Sheriff Saunders opened his mouth; AL-76 pulled a switch. The Disinto worked, and seventy-five trees, two barns, three cows and the top three quarters of Duckbill Mountain whiffed into rarefied atmosphere. They became, so to speak, one with the snows of yesteryear.

Sheriff Saunders' mouth remained open for an indefinite interval thereafter, but nothing – neither firing orders nor anything else – issued therefrom. And then –

And then, there was a stirring in the air, a multiple ro-o-o-oshing sound, a series of purple streaks through the atmosphere radiating away from Randolph Payne's shack as the center, and of the members of the posse, not a sign.

There were various guns scattered about the vicinity, including the sheriff's patented nickel-plated, extra-rapid-fire, guaranteed-no-clog, portable machine gun. There were about fifty hats, a few half-chomped cigars, and some odds and ends that had come loose in the excitement – but of actual human beings there was none.

Except for Lank Jake, not one of those human beings came within human ken for three days, and the exception in his favor came about because he was interrupted in his comet-flight by the half-dozen men from the Petersboro factory, who were charging *into* the wood at a pretty fair speed of their own.

It was Sam Tobe who stopped him, catching Lank Jake's head skillfully in the pit of his stomach. When he caught his breath, Tobe asked, 'Where's Randolph Payne's place?'

Lank Jake allowed his eyes to unglaze for just a moment. 'Brother,' he said, 'just you follow the direction I ain't going.'

And with that, miraculously, he was gone. There was a shrinking dot dodging trees on the horizon that might have been he, but Sam Tobe wouldn't have sworn to it.

That takes care of the posse: but there still remains Randolph Payne, whose reactions took something of a different form.

For Randolph Payne, the five-second interval after the pulling of the switch and the disappearance of Duckbill Mountain was a total blank. At the start he had been peering through the thick underbrush from behind the bottom of the trees; at the end he was swinging wildly from one of the topmost branches. The same impulse that had driven the posse horizontally had driven him vertically.

As to how he had covered the fifty feet from roots to top – whether he had climbed, jumped, or flown – he did not know, and he didn't give a particle of never-mind.

What he *did* know was that property had been destroyed by a robot temporarily in his possession. All visions of rewards vanished and were replaced by trembling nightmares of hostile citizenry, shrieking lynch mobs, lawsuits, murder charges, and what Mirandy Payne would say. Mostly what Mirandy Payne would say.

He was yelling wildly and hoarsely, 'Hey, you robot, you smash that thing, do you hear? Smash it good! You forget I ever had anything to do with it. You're a stranger to me, see? You don't ever say a word about it. Forget it, you hear?'

He didn't expect his orders to do any good; it was only reflex action. What he didn't know was that a robot always obeys a human order except where carrying it out involves danger to another human.

AL-76, therefore, calmly and methodically proceeded to demolish his Disinto into rubble and flinders.

Just as he was stamping the last cubic inch under foot, Sam Tobe and his contingent arrived, and Randolph Payne, sensing that the real owners of the robot had come, dropped out of the tree head-first and made for regions unknown feet-first.

He did not wait for his reward.

Austin Wilde, Robotical Engineer, turned to Sam Tobe and said, 'Did you get anything out of the robot?'

Tobe shook his head and snarled deep in his throat. 'Nothing. Not one thing. He's forgotten everything that's happened since he left the factory. He must have gotten *orders* to forget, or it couldn't have left him so blank. What was that pile of junk he'd been fooling with?'

'Just that. A pile of junk! But it must have been a Disinto before he smashed it, and I'd like to kill the fellow who ordered him to smash it – by slow torture, if possible. Look at this!'

They were part of the way up the slopes of what had been Duckbill Mountain – at that point, to be exact, where the top had been sheered off: and Wilde put his hand down upon the perfect flatness that cut through both soil and rock.

'*What* a Disinto,' he said. 'It took the mountain right off its base.'

'What made him build it?'

Wilde shrugged. 'I don't know. Some factor in his environment – there's no way of knowing what – reacted upon his moon-type positronic brain to produce a Disinto out of junk. It's a billion to one against our ever stumbling upon that factor again now that the robot himself has forgotten. We'll never have that Disinto.'

'Never mind. The important thing is that we have the robot.'

'The hell you say.' There was poignant regret in Wilde's voice. 'Have you ever had anything to do with the Disintos on the moon? They eat up energy like so many electronic hogs and won't even begin to run until you've built up a potential of better than a million volts. But *this* Disinto worked differently. I went through the rubbish with a microscope, and would you like to see the only source of power of any kind that I found?'

'What was it?'

'Just this! And we'll never know how he did it.'

And Austin Wilde held up the source of power that had enabled a Disinto to chew up a mountain in half a second – *two flashlight batteries!*

Victory Unintentional

The spaceship leaked, as the saying goes, like a sieve.

It was supposed to. In fact, that was the whole idea.

The result, of course, was that during the journey from Ganymede to Jupiter, the ship was crammed just as full as it could be with the very hardest space vacuum. And since the ship also lacked heating devices, this space vacuum was at normal temperature, which is a fraction of a degree above absolute zero.

This, also, was according to plan. Little things like the absence of heat and air didn't annoy anyone at all on the particular spaceship.

The first near vacuum wisps of Jovian atmosphere began percolating into the ship several thousand miles above the Jovian surface. It was practically all hydrogen, though perhaps a careful gas analysis might have located a trace of helium as well. The pressure gauges began creeping skyward.

That creep continued at an accelerating pace as the ship dropped downward in a Jupiter-circling spiral. The pointers of successive gauges, each designed for progressively higher pressures, began to move until they reached the neighborhood of a million or so atmospheres, where figures lost most of their meaning. The temperature, as recorded by thermocouples, rose slowly and erratically, and finally steadied at about seventy below zero, Centigrade.

The ship moved slowly toward the end, plowing its way heavily through a maze of gas molecules that crowded together so closely that hydrogen itself was squeezed to the density of a liquid. Ammonia vapor, drawn from the incredibly vast oceans of that liquid, saturated the horrible atmosphere. The wind, which had begun a thousand miles higher, had risen to a pitch inadequately described as a hurricane.

It was quite plain long before thc ship landed on a fairly large Jovian island, perhaps seven times the size of Asia, that Jupiter was not a very pleasant world.

And yet the three members of the crew thought it was. They were quite convinced it was. But then, the three members of the crew were not exactly human. And neither were they exactly Jovian.

They were simply robots, designed on Earth for Jupiter.

ZZ Three said, 'It appears to be a rather desolate place.'

ZZ Two joined him and regarded the wind-blasted landscape somberly. 'There are structures of some sort in the distance,' he said, 'which are obviously artificial. I suggest we wait for the inhabitants to come to us.'

Across the room ZZ One listened, but made no reply. He was the first constructed of the three, and half experimental. Consequently he spoke a little less frequently than his two companions.

The wait was not long. An air vessel of queer design swooped overhead. More followed. And then a line of ground vehicles approached, took position, and disgorged organisms. Along with these organisms came various inanimate accessories that might have been weapons. Some of these were borne by a single Jovian, some by several, and some advanced under their own power, with Jovians perhaps inside.

The robots couldn't tell.

ZZ Three said, 'They're all around us now. The logical peaceful gesture would be to come out in the open. Agreed?'

It was, and ZZ One shoved open the heavy door, which was not double or, for that matter, particularly airtight.

Their appearance through the door was the signal for an

excited stir among the surrounding Jovians. Things were done to several of the very largest of the inanimate accessories, and ZZ Three became aware of a temperature rise on the outer rind of his beryllium-iridium-bronze body.

He glanced at ZZ Two. 'Do you feel it? They're aiming heat energy at us, I believe.'

ZZ Two indicated his surprise. 'I wonder why?'

'Definitely a heat ray of some sort. Look at that!'

One of the rays had been jarred out of alignment for some undiscernible cause, and its line of radiation intersected a brook of sparkling pure ammonia – which promptly boiled furiously.

Three turned to ZZ One, 'Make a note of this, One, will you?'

'Sure.' It was to ZZ One that the routine secretarial work fell, and his method of taking a note was to make a mental addition to the accurate memory scroll within him. He had already gathered the hour-by-hour record of every important instrument on board ship during the trip to Jupiter. He added agreeably, 'What reason shall I put for the reaction? The human masters would probably enjoy knowing.'

'No reason. Or better,' Three corrected himself, 'no apparent reason. You might say the maximum temperature of the ray was about plus thirty, Centigrade.'

Two interrupted, 'Shall we try communicating?'

'It would be a waste of time,' said Three. 'There can't be more than a very few Jovians who know the radio-click code that's been developed between Jupiter and Ganymede. They'll have to send for one, and when he comes, he'll establish contact soon enough. Meanwhile let's watch them. I don't understand their actions, I tell you frankly.'

Nor did understanding come immediately. Heat radiation ceased, and other instruments were brought to the forefront and put into play. Several capsules fell at the feet of the watching robots, dropping rapidly and forcefully under Jupiter's gravity. They popped open and a blue liquid exuded, forming pools which proceeded to shrink rapidly by evaporation.

The nightmare wind whipped the vapors away and where those vapors went, Jovians scrambled out of the way. One was too slow, threshed about wildly, and became very limp and still.

ZZ Two bent, dabbed a finger in one of the pools and stared at the dripping liquid. 'I think this is oxygen,' he said.

'Oxygen, all right,' agreed Three. 'This becomes stranger and stranger. It must certainly be a dangerous practice, for I would say that oxygen is poisonous to the creatures. One of them died!'

There was a pause, and then ZZ One, whose greater simplicity led at times to an increased directness of thought, said heavily, 'It might be that these strange creatures in a rather childish way are attempting to destroy us.'

And Two, struck by the suggestion, answered, 'You know, One, I think you're right!'

There had been a slight lull in Jovian activity and now a new structure was brought up. It possessed a slender rod that pointed skyward through the impenetrable Jovian murk. It stood in that starkly incredible wind with a rigidity that plainly indicated remarkable structural strength. From its tip came a cracking and then a flash that lit up the depths of the atmosphere into a gray fog.

For a moment the robots were bathed in clinging radiance and then Three said thoughtfully, 'High-tension electricity! Quite respectable power, too. One, I think you're right. After all, the human masters have told us that these creatures seek to destroy all humanity, and organisms possessing such insane viciousness as to harbor a thought of harm against a human being' – his voice trembled at the thought – 'would scarcely scruple at attempting to destroy us.'

'It's a shame to have such distorted minds,' said ZZ One. 'Poor fellows!'

'I find it a very saddening thought,' admitted Two. 'Let's go back to the ship. We've seen enough for now.'

They did so, and settled down to wait. As ZZ Three said, Jupiter was a roomy planet, and it might take time for Jovian transportation to bring a radio code expert to the ship. However, patience is a cheap commodity to robots.

As a matter of fact, Jupiter turned on its axis three times, according to chronometer, before the expert arrived. The rising and setting of the sun made no difference, of course, to the dead darkness at the bottom of three thousand miles of liquid-dense gas, so that one could not speak of day and night. But then, neither Jovian nor robot saw by visible light radiation and that didn't matter.

Through this thirty-hour interval the surrounding Jovians continued their attack with a patience and persevering relentlessness concerning which robot ZZ One made a good many mental notes. The ship was assaulted by as many varieties of forces as there were hours, and the robots observed every attack attentively, analyzing such weapons as they recognized. They by no means recognized all.

But the human masters had built well. It had taken fifteen years to construct the ship and the robots, and their essentials could be expressed in a single phrase – raw strength. The attack spent itself uselessly and neither ship nor robot seemed the worse for it.

Three said, 'This atmosphere handicaps them, I think. They can't use atomic disruptors, since they would only tear a hole in that soupy air and blow themselves up.'

'They haven't used high explosives either,' said Two, 'which is well. They couldn't have hurt us, naturally, but it would have thrown us about a bit.'

'High explosives are out of the question. You can't have an explosive without gas expansion and gas just can't expand in this atmosphere.'

'It's a very good atmosphere,' muttered One. 'I like it.'

Which was natural, because he was built for it. The ZZ robots were the first robots ever turned out by the United States Robots and Mechanical Men Corporation that were not even faintly human in appearance. They were low and squat, with a center of gravity less than a foot above ground level. They had six legs apiece, stumpy and thick, designed to lift tons against two and a half times normal Earth gravity. Their reflexes were that many times Earth-normal speed, to make up for the gravity. And they were composed of a beryllium-iridium-bronze alloy that was proof against any known corrosive agent, also any known destructive agent short of a thousand-megaton atomic disruptor, under any conditions whatsoever.

To dispense with further description, they were indestructible and so impressively powerful that they were the only robots ever built on whom the roboticists of the corporation had never quite had the nerve to pin a serial-number nickname. One bright young fellow had suggested Sissy One, Two, and Three – but not in a very loud voice, and the suggestion was never repeated.

The last hours of the wait were spent in a puzzled discussion to find a possible description of a Jovian's appearance. ZZ One had made a note of their possession of tentacles and of their radial symmetry – and there he had stuck. Two and Three did their best, but couldn't help.

'You can't very well describe anything,' Three declared finally, 'without a standard of reference. These creatures are like nothing I know of – completely outside the positronic paths of my brain. It's like trying to describe gamma light to a robot unequipped for gamma-ray reception.'

It was just at that time that the weapon barrage ceased

once more. The robots turned their attention to outside the ship.

A group of Jovians were advancing in curiously uneven fashion, but no amount of careful watching could determine the exact method of their locomotion. How they used their tentacles was uncertain. At times the organisms took on a remarkable slithering motion, and then they moved at great speed, perhaps with the wind's help, for they were moving downwind.

The robots stepped out to meet the Jovians, who halted ten feet away. Both sides remained silent and motionless.

ZZ Two said, 'They must be watching us, but I don't know how. Do either of you see any photosensitive organs?'

'I can't say,' grunted Three in response. 'I don't see anything about them that makes sense at all.'

There was a sudden metallic clicking from among the Jovian group and ZZ One said delightedly, 'It's the radio code. They've got the communications expert here.'

It was, and they had. The complicated dot-dash system that over a period of twenty-five years had been laboriously developed by the beings of Jupiter and the Earthmen of Ganymede into a remarkably flexible means of communication was finally being put into practice at close range.

One Jovian remained in the forefront now, the others having fallen back. It was he that was speaking. The clicking said, 'Where are you from?'

ZZ Three, as the most mentally advanced, naturally assumed spokesmanship for the robot group. 'We are from Jupiter's satellite, Ganymede.'

The Jovian continued, 'What do you want?'

'Information. We have come to study your world and to bring back our findings. If we could have your cooperation – '

The Jovian clicking interrupted. 'You must be destroyed!'

ZZ Three paused and said in a thoughtful aside to his two companions, 'Exactly the attitude the human masters said they would take. They are very unusual.'

Returning to his clicking, he asked simply, 'Why?'

The Jovian evidently considered certain questions too obnoxious to be answered. He said, 'If you leave within a single period of revolution, we will spare you – until such time as we emerge from our world to destroy the un-Jovian vermin of Ganymede.'

'I would like to point out,' said Three, 'that we of Ganymede and the inner planets – '

The Jovian interrupted, 'Our astronomy knows of the Sun and of our four satellites. There are no inner planets.'

Three conceded the point wearily, 'We of Ganymede, then. We have no designs on Jupiter. We're prepared to offer friendship. For twenty-five years your people communicated freely with the human beings of Ganymede. Is there any reason to make sudden war upon the humans?'

'For twenty-five years,' was the cold response, 'we assumed the inhabitants of Ganymede to be Jovians. When we found out they were not, and that we had been treating lower animals on the scale of Jovian intelligences, we were bound to take steps to wipe out the dishonor.'

Slowly and forcefully he finished, 'We of Jupiter will suffer the existence of no vermin!'

The Jovian was backing away in some fashion, tacking against the wind, and the interview was evidently over.

The robots retreated inside the ship.

ZZ Two said, 'It looks bad, doesn't it?' He continued thoughtfully, 'It is as the human masters said. They possess an ultimately developed superiority complex, combined with an extreme intolerance for anyone or anything that disturbs that complex.'

'The intolerance,' observed Three, 'is the natural consequence of the complex. The trouble is that their intolerance has teeth in it. They have weapons – and their science is great.'

'I am not surprised now,' burst out ZZ One, 'that we were specifically instructed to disregard Jovian orders. They are horrible, intolerant, pseudo-superior beings!' He added emphatically, with robotical loyalty and faith, 'No human master could ever be like that.'

'That, though true, is beside the point,' said Three. 'The fact remains that the human masters are in terrible danger. This is a gigantic world and these Jovians are greater in numbers and resources by a hundred times or more than the humans of the entire Terrestrial Empire. If they can ever develop the force field to the point where they can use it as a spaceship hull – as the human masters have already done – they will overrun the system at will. The question remains as to how far they have advanced in that direction, what other weapons they have, what preparations they are making and so on. To return with that information is our function, of course, and we had better decide on our next step.'

'It may be difficult,' said Two. 'The Jovians won't help us.' Which, at the moment, was rather an understatement.

Three thought awhile. 'It seems to me that we need only wait,' he observed. 'They have tried to destroy us for thirty hours now and haven't succeeded. Certainly they have done their best. Now a superiority complex always involves the eternal necessity of saving face, and the ultimatum given us proves it in this case. They would never allow us to leave if they could destroy us. But if we don't leave, then rather than admit they cannot force us away, they will surely pretend that they are willing, for their own purposes, to have us stay.'

Once again they waited. The day passed. The weapon barrage did not resume. The robots did not leave. The bluff was called. And now the robots faced the Jovian radio-code expert once again.

If the ZZ models had been equipped with a sense of humor, they would have enjoyed themselves immensely. As it was, they felt merely a solemn sense of satisfaction.

The Jovian said, 'It has been our decision that you will be allowed to remain for a very short time, so that you see our power for yourself. You shall then return to Ganymede to inform your companion vermin of the disastrous end to which they will unfailingly come within a solar revolution.'

ZZ One made a mental note that a Jovian revolution took twelve earthly years.

Three replied casually, 'Thank you. May we accompany you to the nearest town? There are many things we would like to learn.' He added as an afterthought, 'Our ship is not to be touched, of course.'

He said this as a request, not as a threat, for no ZZ model was ever pugnacious. All capacity for even the slightest annoyance had been carefully barred in their construction. With robots as vastly powerful as the ZZ's, unfailing good temper was essential for safety during the years of testing on Earth.

The Jovian said, 'We are not interested in your verminous ship. No Jovian will pollute himself by approaching it. You may accompany us, but you must on no account approach closer than ten feet to any Jovian, or you will be instantly destroyed.'

'Stuck up, aren't they?' observed Two in a genial whisper, as they plowed into the wind.

The town was a port on the shores of an incredible ammonia lake. The external wind whipped furious, frothy waves that shot across the liquid surface at the hectic rate enforced by the gravity. The port itself was neither large nor impressive and it seemed fairly evident that most of the construction was underground.

'What is the population of this place?' asked Three.

The Jovian replied, 'It is a small town of ten million.'

'I see. Make a note of that, One.'

ZZ One did so mechanically, and then turned once more to the lake, at which he had been staring in fascination. He pulled at Three's elbow. 'Say, do you suppose they have fish here?'

'What difference does it make?'

'I think we ought to know. The human masters ordered us to find out everything we could.' Of the robots, One was the simplest and, consequently, the one who took orders in the most literal fashion.

Two said, 'Let One go and look if he likes. It won't do any harm if we let the kid have his fun.'

'All right. There's no real objection if he doesn't waste his time. Fish aren't what we came for – but go ahead, One.'

ZZ One made off in great excitement and slogged rapidly down the beach, plunging into the ammonia with a splash. The Jovians watched attentively. They had understood none of the previous conversation, of course.

The radio-code expert clicked out, 'It is apparent that your companion has decided to abandon life in despair at our greatness.'

Three said in surprise, 'Nothing of the sort. He wants to investigate the living organisms, if any, that live in the ammonia.' He added apologetically, 'Our friend is very curious at times, and he isn't quite as bright as we are, though that is only his misfortune. We understand that and try to humor him whenever we can.'

There was a long pause, and the Jovian observed, 'He will drown.'

Three replied casually, 'No danger of that. We don't drown. May we enter the town as soon as he returns?'

At that moment there was a spurt of liquid several hundred feet out in the lake. It sprayed upward wildly and then hurtled down in a wind-driven mist. Another spurt and another, then a wild white foaming that formed a trail toward shore, gradually quieting as it approached.

The two robots watched this in amazement, and the utter lack of motion on the part of the Jovians indicated that they were watching as well.

Then the head of ZZ One broke the surface and he made his slow way out on to dry land. But something followed him! Some organism of gigantic size that seemed nothing but fangs, claws, and spines. Then they saw that it wasn't following him under its own power, but was being dragged across the beach by ZZ One. There was a significant flabbiness about it.

ZZ One approached rather timidly and took communication into his own hands. He tapped out a message to the Jovian in agitated fashion. 'I am very sorry this happened, but the thing attacked me. I was merely taking notes on it. It is not a valuable creature, I hope.'

He was not answered immediately, for at the first appearance of the monster there had been a wild break in the Jovian ranks. These reformed slowly, and cautious observation having proven the creature to be indeed dead, order was restored. Some of the bolder were curiously prodding the body.

ZZ Three said humbly, 'I hope you will pardon our friend. He is sometimes clumsy. We have absolutely no intention of harming any Jovian creature.'

'He attacked me,' explained One. 'He bit at me without provocation. See!' And he displayed a two-foot fang that ended in a jagged break. 'He broke it on my shoulder and almost left a scratch. I just slapped it a bit to send it away – and it died. I'm sorry!'

The Jovian finally spoke, and his code clicking was a rather stuttery affair. 'It is a wild creature, rarely found so close to shore, but the lake is deep just here.'

Three said, still anxiously, 'If you can use it for food, we are only too glad – '

'No. We can get food for ourselves without the help of verm – without the help of others. Eat it yourselves.'

At that ZZ One heaved the creature up and back into the sea, with an easy motion of one arm. Three said casually, 'Thank you for your kind offer, but we have no use for food. We don't eat, of course.'

Escorted by two hundred or so armed Jovians, the robots passed down a series of ramps into the underground city. If, above the surface, the city had looked small and unimpressive, then from beneath it took on the appearance of a vast megalopolis.

They were ushered into ground cars that were operated by remote control – for no honest, self-respecting Jovian would risk his superiority by placing himself in the same car with vermin – and driven at frightful speed to the center of the town. They saw enough to decide that it extended fifty miles from end to end and reached downward into Jupiter's crust at least eight miles.

ZZ Two did not sound happy as he said, 'If this is a sample of Jovian development then we shall not have a hopeful report to bring back to the human masters. After all, we landed on the vast surface of Jupiter at random, with the chances a thousand to one against coming near any really concentrated center of population. This must be, as the code expert says, a mere town.'

'Ten million Jovians,' said Three abstractedly. 'Total population must be in the trillions, which is high, very high, even for Jupiter. They probably have a completely urban civilization, which means that their scientific development must be tremendous. If they have force fields – '

Three had no neck, for in the interest of strength the heads of the ZZ models were riveted firmly onto the torso, with the delicate positronic brains protected by three separate layers in inch-thick iridium alloy. But if he had had one, he would have shaken his head dolefully.

They had stopped now in a cleared space. Everywhere about them they could see avenues and structures crowded with Jovians, as curious as any terrestrial crowd would have been in similar circumstances.

The code expert approached. 'It is time now for me to retire until the next period of activity. We have gone so far as to arrange quarters for you at great inconvenience to ourselves for, of course, the structure will have to pulled down and rebuilt afterward. Nevertheless, you will be allowed to sleep for a space.'

ZZ Three waved an arm in deprecation and tapped out, 'We thank you but you must not trouble yourself. We don't mind remaining right here. If you want to sleep and rest, by all means do. We'll wait for you. As for us,' casually, 'we don't sleep.'

The Jovian said nothing, though if it had had a face, the expression upon it might have been interesting. It left, and the robots remained in the car, with squads of well-armed Jovians, frequently replaced, surrounding them as guards.

It was hours before the ranks of those guards parted to allow the code expert to return. Along with him were other Jovians, whom he introduced.

'There are with me two officials of the central government who have graciously consented to speak with you.'

One of the officials evidently knew the code, for his clicking interrupted the code expert sharply. He addressed the robots, 'Vermin! Emerge from the ground car that we may look at you.'

The robots were only too willing to comply, so while Three and Two vaulted over the right side of the car, ZZ One dashed through the left side. The word through is used advisedly, for since he neglected to work the mechanism that lowered a section of side so that one might exit, he carried that side, plus two wheels and an axle, along with him. The car collapsed, and ZZ One stood staring at the ruins in embarrassed silence.

At last he clicked out gently, 'I'm very sorry. I hope it wasn't an expensive car.'

ZZ Two added apologetically, 'Our companion is often clumsy. You must excuse him,' and ZZ Three made a halfhearted attempt to put the car back together again.

ZZ One made another effort to excuse himself. 'The material of the car was rather flimsy. You see?' He lifted a square-yard sheet of three-inch-thick, metal-hard plastic in both hands and exerted a bit of pressure. The sheet promptly snapped in two. 'I should have made allowances,' he admitted.

The Jovian government official said in slightly less sharp fashion, 'The car would have had to be destroyed anyway, after being polluted by your presence.' He paused, then, 'Creatures! We Jovians lack vulgar curiosity concerning lower animals, but our scientists seek facts.'

'We're right with you,' replied Three cheerfully. 'So do we.'

The Jovian ignored him. 'You lack the mass-sensitive organ, apparently. How is it that you are aware of distant objects?'

Three grew interested. 'Do you mean your people are directly sensitive to mass?'

'I am not here to answer your questions – your impudent questions – about us.'

'I take it then that objects of low specific mass would be transparent to you, even in the absence of radiation.' He turned to Two, 'That's how they see. Their atmosphere is as transparent as space to them.'

The Jovian clicking began once more, 'You will answer my first question immediately, or my patience will end and I will order you destroyed.'

Three said at once, 'We are energy-sensitive, Jovian. We can adjust ourselves to the entire electromagnetic scale at will. At present, our long-distance sight is due to radio-wave radiation that we emit ourselves, and at close range we see by – ' He paused, and said to Two, 'There isn't any code word for gamma ray, is there?'

'Not that I know of,' Two answered.

Three continued to the Jovian, 'At close range we see by other radiation for which there is no code word.'

'Of what is your body composed?' demanded the Jovian.

Two whispered, 'He probably asks that because his mass sensitivity can't penetrate past our skin. High density, you know. Ought we to tell him?'

Three replied uncertainly, 'Our human masters didn't particularly say we were to keep anything secret.' In radio code, to the Jovian he said, 'We are mostly iridium. For the rest, copper, tin, a little beryllium, and a scattering of other substances.'

The Jovians fell back and by the obscure writhing of various portions of their thoroughly indescribable bodies gave the impression that they were in animated conversation, although they made no sound.

And then the official returned. 'Beings of Ganymede! It has been decided to show you through some of our factories that we may exhibit a tiny part of our great achievements. We will then allow you to return so that you may spread despair among the other verm – the other beings of the outer world.'

Three said to Two, 'Note the effect of their psychology. They must hammer home their superiority. It's still a matter of saving face.' And in radio code, 'We thank you for the opportunity.'

But the face saving was efficient, as the robots realized soon enough. The demonstration became a tour, and the tour a Grand Exhibition. The Jovians displayed everything, explained everything, answered all questions eagerly, and ZZ One made hundreds of despairing notes.

The war potential of that single so-called unimportant town was greater by several times than that of all Ganymede. Ten more such towns would outproduce all the Terrestrial Empire. Yet ten more such towns would not be the fingernail fragment of the strength all Jupiter must be able to exert.

Three turned as One nudged him. 'What is it?'

ZZ One said seriously, 'If they have force fields, the human masters are lost, aren't they?'

'I'm afraid so. Why do you ask?'

'Because the Jovians aren't showing us through the right wing of this factory. It might be that force fields are being developed there. They would be wanting to keep it secret if they were. We'd better find out. It's the main point, you know.'

Three regarded One somberly. 'Perhaps you're right. It's no use ignoring anything.'

They were in a huge steel mill now, watching hundred-foot beams of ammonia-resistant silicon-steel alloy being turned out twenty to the second. Three asked quietly, 'What does that wing contain?'

The government official inquired of those in charge of the factory and explained, 'That is the section of great heat. Various processes require huge temperatures which life cannot bear, and they must all be handled indirectly.'

He led the way to a partition from which heat could be felt to radiate and indicated a small round area of transparent material. It was one of a row of such, through which the foggy red light of lines of glowing forges could be made out through the soupy atmosphere.

ZZ One fastened a look of suspicion on the Jovian and clicked out, 'Would it be all right if I went in and looked around? I am very interested in this.'

Three said, 'You're being childish, One. They're telling the truth. Oh well, nose around if you must. But don't take too long: we've got to move on.'

The Jovian said, 'You have no understanding of the heat involved. You will die.'

'Oh no,' explained One casually. 'Heat doesn't bother us.'

There was a Jovian conference, and then a scene of scurrying confusion as the life of the factory was geared to this unusual emergency. Screens of heat-absorbent material were set up, and then a door dropped open, a door that had never before budged while the forges were working. ZZ One entered and the door closed behind him. Jovian officials crowded to the transparent areas to watch.

ZZ One walked to the nearest forge and tapped the outside. Since he was too short to see into it comfortably, he tipped the forge until the molten metal licked at the lip of the container. He peered at it curiously, then dipped his hand in and stirred it awhile to test the consistency. Having done this, he withdrew his hand, shook off some of the fiery metallic droplets and wiped the rest on one of his six thighs. Slowly he went down the line of forges, then signified his desire to leave.

The Jovians retired to a great distance when he came out of the door and played a stream of ammonia on him, which hissed, bubbled and steamed until he was brought to bearable temperature once more.

ZZ One ignored the ammonia shower and said, 'They were telling the truth. No force fields.'

Three began, 'You see – ' but One interrupted impatiently, 'But there's no use delaying. The human masters instructed us to find out everything and that's that.'

He turned to the Jovian and clicked out, without the slightest hesitation, 'Listen, has Jovian science developed force fields?'

Bluntness was, of course, one of the natural consequences of One's less well developed mental powers. Two and Three knew that, so they refrained from expressing disapproval of the remark.

The Jovian official relaxed slowly from his strangely stiffened attitude, which had somehow given the impression that he had been staring stupidly at One's hand – the one he had dipped into the molten metal. The Jovian said slowly, 'Force fields? That, then, is your main object of curiosity?'

'Yes,' said One with emphasis.

There was a sudden and patent gain in confidence on the Jovian's part, for the clicking grew sharper. 'Then come, vermin!'

Whereupon Three said to Two, 'We're vermin again, I see – which sounds as if there's bad news ahead.' And Two gloomily agreed.

It was to the very edge of the city that they were now led – to the portion which on Earth would have been termed the suburbs – and into one of a series of closely integrated structures, which might have corresponded vaguely to a terrestrial university.

There were no explanations, however, and none was asked for. The Jovian official led the way rapidly, and the robots followed with the grim conviction that the worst was just about to happen.

It was ZZ One who stopped before an opened wall section after the rest had passed on. 'What's this?' he wanted to know.

The room was equipped with narrow, low benches, along which Jovians manipulated rows of strange devices, of which strong, inch-long electromagnets formed the principal feature.

'What's this?' asked One again.

The Jovian turned back and exhibited impatience. 'This

is a students' biological laboratory. There's nothing there to interest you.'

'But what are they doing?'

'They are studying microscopic life. Haven't you ever seen a microscope before?'

Three interrupted in explanation, 'He has, but not that type. Our microscopes are meant for energy-sensitive organs and work by refraction of radiant energy. Your microscopes evidently work on a mass-expansion basis. Rather ingenious.'

ZZ One said, 'Would it be all right if I inspected some of your specimens?'

'Of what use will that be? You cannot use our microscopes because of your sensory limitations and it will simply force us to discard such specimens as you approach for no decent reason.'

'But I don't need a microscope,' explained One, with surprise. 'I can easily adjust myself for microscopic vision.'

He strode to the nearest bench, while the students in the room crowded to the corner in an attempt to avoid contamination. ZZ One shoved a microscope aside and inspected the slide carefully. He backed away, puzzled, then tried another . . . a third . . . a fourth.

He came back and addressed the Jovian. 'Those are supposed to be alive, aren't they? I mean those little worm things.'

The Jovian said, 'Certainly.'

'That's strange – when I look at them, they die!'

Three exclaimed sharply and said to his two companions, 'We've forgotten our gamma-ray radiation. Let's get out of here, One, or we'll kill every bit of microscopic life in the room.'

He turned to the Jovian, 'I'm afraid that our presence is fatal to weaker forms of life. We had better leave. We hope the specimens are not too difficult to replace. And, while we're about it, you had better not stay too near us, or our radiation may affect you adversely. You feel all right so far, don't you?' he asked.

The Jovian led the way onward in proud silence, but it was to be noticed that thereafter he doubled the distance he had hitherto kept between himself and them.

Nothing more was said until the robots found themselves in a vast room. In the very center of it huge ingots of metal rested unsupported in mid-air – or, rather, supported by nothing visible – against mighty Jovian gravity.

The Jovian clicked, 'There is your force field in ultimate form, as recently perfected. Within that bubble is a vacuum, so that it is supporting the full weight of our atmosphere plus an amount of metal equivalent to two large spaceships. What do you say to that?'

'That space travel now becomes a possibility for you,' said Three.

'Definitely. No metal or plastic has the strength to hold our atmosphere against a vacuum, but a force field can – and a force-field bubble will be our spaceship. Within the year we will be turning them out by the hundreds of thousands. Then we will swarm down upon Ganymede to destroy the verminous so-called intelligences that attempt to dispute our dominion of the universe.'

'The human beings of Ganymede have never attempted – ' began Three, in mild expostulation.

'Silence!' snapped the Jovian. 'Return now and tell them what you've seen. Their own feeble force fields – such as the one your ship is equipped with – will not stand against us, for our smallest ship will be a hundred times the size and power of yours.'

Three said, 'Then there's nothing more to do and we will return, as you say, with the information. If you could lead us back to our ship, we'll say good-by. But by the way, just as a matter for the record, there's something you don't understand. The humans of Ganymede have force fields, of course, but our particular ship isn't equipped with one. We don't need any.'

The robot turned away and motioned his companions to follow. For a moment they did not speak, then ZZ One muttered dejectedly, 'Can't we try to destroy this place?'

'It won't help,' said Three. 'They'd get us by weight of numbers. It's no use. In an earthly decade the human masters will be finished. It is impossible to stand against Jupiter. There's just too much of it. As long as Jovians were tied to the surface, the humans were safe. But now that they have force fields – All we can do is to bring the news. By the preparation of hiding places, some few may survive for a short while.'

The city was behind them. They were out on the open plain by the lake, with their ship a dark spot on the horizon, when the Jovian spoke suddenly:

'Creatures, you say you have no force field?'

Three replied without interest, 'We don't need one.'

'How then does your ship stand the vacuum of space without exploding because of the atmospheric pressure within?' And he moved a tentacle as if in mute gesture at the Jovian atmosphere that was weighing down upon them with a force of twenty million pounds to the square inch.

'Well,' explained Three, 'that's simple. Our ship isn't airtight. Pressures equalize within and without.'

'Even in space? A vacuum in your ship? You lie!'

'You're welcome to inspect our ship. It has no force field and it isn't airtight. What's marvelous about that? We don't breathe. Our energy is obtained through direct atomic power. The presence or absence of air pressure makes little difference to us and we're quite at home in a vacuum.'

'But absolute zero!'

'It doesn't matter. We regulate our own heat. We're not interested in outside temperatures.' He paused. 'Well, we can make our own way back to the ship. Good-by. We'll give the humans of Ganymede your message – war to the end!'

But the Jovian said, 'Wait! I'll be back.' He turned and went toward the city.

The robots stared, and then waited in silence.

It was three hours before he returned and when he did, it was in breathless haste. He stopped within the usual ten feet of the robots, but then began inching his way forward in a curious groveling fashion. He did not speak until his rubbery gray skin was almost touching them, and then the radio code sounded, subdued and respectful.

'Honored sirs, I have been in communication with the head of our central government, who is now aware of all the facts, and I can assure you that Jupiter desires only peace.'

'I beg your pardon?' asked Three blankly.

The Jovian drove on hastily. 'We are ready to resume communication with Ganymede and will gladly promise to make no attempt to venture into space. Our force field will be used only on the Jovian surface.'

'But – ' Three began.

'Our government will be glad to receive any other representatives our honorable human brothers of Ganymede would care to send. If your honors will now condescend to swear peace – ' a scaly tentacle swung out toward them and Three, quite dazed, grasped it. Two and One did likewise as two more were extended to them.

The Jovian said solemnly: 'There is then eternal peace between Jupiter and Ganymede.'

The spaceship which leaked like a sieve was out in space again. The pressure and temperature were once more at zero, and the robots watched the huge but steadily shrinking globe that was Jupiter.

'They're definitely sincere,' said ZZ Two, 'and it's very gratifying, this complete about-face, but I don't get it.'

'It is my idea,' observed ZZ One, 'that the Jovians came to their senses just in time and realized the incredible evil involved in the thought of harm to a human master. That would be only natural.'

ZZ Three sighed and said, 'Look, it's all a matter of psychology. Those Jovians had a superiority complex a mile thick and when they couldn't destroy us, they were bound to save face. All their exhibitions, all their explanations, were simply a form of braggadocio, designed to impress us into the proper state of humiliation before their power and superiority.'

'I see all that,' interrupted Two, 'but – '

Three went on, 'But it worked the wrong way. All they did was to prove to themselves that we were stronger, that we didn't drown, that we didn't eat or sleep, that molten metal didn't hurt us. Even our very presence was fatal to Jovian life. Their last trump was the force field. And when they found out that *we* didn't need them at all, and could live in a vacuum at absolute zero, they broke.' He paused and added philosophically, 'When a superiority complex like that breaks, it breaks all the way.'

The other two considered that, and then Two said, 'But it still doesn't make sense. Why should they care what we can or can't do? We're only robots. We're not the ones they have to fight.'

'And that's the whole point, Two,' said Three softly. 'It's only after we left Jupiter that I thought of it. Do you know that through an oversight, quite unintentionally, we neglected to tell them we were only robots.'

'They never asked us,' said One.

'Exactly. So they thought we were human beings and that all the other human beings were like us!'

He looked once more at Jupiter, thoughtfully. 'No wonder they decided to quit!'

Stranger in Paradise

1.

They were brothers. Not in the sense that they were both human beings, or that they were fellow children of a crèche. Not at all! They were brothers in the actual biological sense of the word. They were kin, to use a term that had grown faintly archaic even centuries before, prior to the Catastrophe, when that tribal phenomenon, the family, still had some validity.

How embarrassing it was!

Over the years since childhood, Anthony had almost forgotten. There were times when he hadn't given it even the slightest thought for months at a time. But now, ever since he had been inextricably thrown together with William, he had found himself living through an agonizing time.

It might not have been so bad if circumstances had made it obvious all along; if, as in the pre-Catastrophe days – Anthony had at one time been a great reader of history – they had shared the second name and in that way alone flaunted the relationship.

Nowadays, of course, one adopted one's second name to suit oneself and changed it as often as desired. After all, the symbol chain was what really counted, and that was encoded and made yours from birth.

William called himself Anti-Aut. That was what he insisted on with a kind of sober professionalism. His own business, surely, but what an advertisement of personal poor taste. Anthony had decided on Smith when he had turned thirteen and had never had the impulse to change it.

It was simple, easily spelled, and quite distinctive, since he had never met anyone else who had chosen that name. It was once very common – among the pre-Cats – which explained its rareness now perhaps.

But the difference in names meant nothing when the two were together. They looked alike.

If they had been twins – but then one of a pair of twin-fertilized ova was never allowed to come to term. It was just that physical similarity occasionally happened in the non-twin situation, especially when the relationship was on both sides. Anthony Smith was five years younger, but both had the beaky nose, the heavy eyelids, the just noticeable cleft in the chin – that damned luck of the genetic draw. It was just asking for it when, out of some passion for monotony, parents repeated.

At first, now that they were together, they drew that startled glance followed by an elaborate silence. Anthony tried to ignore the matter, but out of sheer perversity – or perversion – William was as likely as not to say, 'We're brothers.'

'Oh?' the other would say, hanging in there for just a moment as though he wanted to ask if they were full blood brothers. And then good manners would win the day and he would turn away as though it were a matter of no interest. That happened only rarely, of course. Most of the people in the Project knew – how could it be prevented? – and avoided the situation.

Not that William was a bad fellow. Not at all. If he hadn't been Anthony's brother; or if they had been, but looked sufficiently different to be able to mask the fact, they would have gotten along famously.

As it was –

It didn't make it easier that they had played together as youngsters, and had shared the earlier stages of education in the same crèche through some successful maneuvering on the part of Mother. Having borne two sons by the same father and having, in this fashion, reached her limit (for she had not fulfilled the stringent requirements for a third), she conceived the notion of being able to visit both at a single trip. She was a strange woman.

William had left the crèche first, naturally, since he was the elder. He had gone into science – genetic engineering. Anthony had heard that, while he was still in the crèche, through a letter from his mother. He was old enough by then to speak firmly to the matron, and those letters stopped. But he always remembered the last one for the agony of shame it had brought him.

Anthony had eventually entered science, too. He had shown talent in that direction and had been urged to. He remembered having had the wild – and prophetic, he now realized – fear he might meet his brother and he ended in telemetrics, which was as far removed from genetic engineering as one could imagine . . . Or so one would have thought.

Then, through all the elaborate development of the Mercury Project, circumstance waited.

The time came, as it happened, when the Project appeared to be facing a dead end; and a suggestion had been made which saved the situation, and at the same time dragged Anthony into the dilemma his parents had prepared for him. And the best and most sardonic part of the whole thing was that it was Anthony who, in all innocence, made the suggestion.

2.

William Anti-Aut knew of the Mercury Project, but only in the way he knew of the long-drawn-out Stellar Probe that had been on its way long before he was born and would still be on its way after his death; and the way he knew of the

Martian colony and of the continuing attempts to establish similar colonies on the asteroids.

Such things were on the distant periphery of his mind and of no real importance. No part of the space effort had ever swirled inward closer to the center of his interests, as far as he could remember, till the day when the printout included photographs of some of the men engaged in the Mercury Project.

William's attention was caught first by the fact that one of them had been identified as Anthony Smith. He remembered the odd name his brother had chosen, and he remembered the Anthony. Surely there could not be two Anthony Smiths.

He had then looked at the photograph itself and there was no mistaking the face. He looked in the mirror in a sudden whimsical gesture at checking the matter. No mistaking the face.

He felt amused, but uneasily so, for he did not fail to recognize the potentiality for embarrassment. Full blood brothers, to use the disgusting phrase. But what was there to do about it? How correct the fact that neither his father nor his mother had imagination?

He must have put the printout in his pocket, absently, when he was getting ready to leave for work, for he came across it at the lunch hour. He stared at it again. Anthony looked keen. It was quite a good reproduction – the printouts were of enormously good quality these days.

His lunch partner, Marco Whatever-his-name-was-that-week, said curiously, 'What are you looking at, William?'

On impulse, William passed him the printout and said, 'That's my brother.' It was like grasping the nettle.

Marco studied it, frowning, and said, 'Who? The man standing next to you?'

'No, the man who *is* me. I mean the man who looks like me. He's my brother.'

There was a longer pause this time. Marco handed it back and said with a careful levelness to his voice, 'Same-parents brother?'

'Yes.'

'Father and mother both.'

'Yes.'

'Ridiculous!'

'I suppose so.' William sighed. 'Well, according to this, he's in telemetrics over in Texas and I'm doing work in autistics up here. So what difference does it make?'

William did not keep it in his mind and later that day he threw the printout away. He did not want his current bedmate to come across it. She had a ribald sense of humor that William was finding increasingly wearying. He was rather glad she was not in the mood for a child. He himself had had one a few years back anyway. That little brunette, Laura or Linda, one or the other name, had collaborated.

It was quite a time after that, at least a year, that the matter of Randall had come up. If William had given no further thought to his brother – and he hadn't – before that, he certainly had no time for it afterwards.

Randall was sixteen when William first received word of him. He had lived a life that was increasingly seclusive and the Kentucky crèche in which he was being brought up decided to cancel him – and of course it was only some eight or ten days before cancellation that it occurred to anyone to report him to the New York Institute for the Science of Man. (The Homological Institute was its common name.)

William received the report along with reports of several others and there was nothing in the description of Randall that particularly attracted his notice. Still it was time for one of his tedious mass-transport trips to the crèches and there was one likely possibility in West Virginia. He went there – and was disappointed into swearing for the fiftieth time that he would thereafter make these visits by TV image – and then, having dragged himself there, thought he might as well take in the Kentucky crèche before returning home.

He expected nothing.

Yet he hadn't studied Randall's gene pattern for more than ten minutes before he was calling the Institute for a computer calculation. Then he sat back and perspired slightly at the thought that only a last-minute impulse had brought him, and that without that impulse, Randall would have been quietly canceled in a week or less. To put it into the fine detail, a drug would have soaked painlessly through his skin and into his bloodstream and he would have sunk into a peaceful sleep that deepened gradually to death. The drug had a twenty-three-syllable official name, but William called it 'nirvanamine,' as did everyone else.

William said, 'What is his full name, matron?'

The crèche matron said, 'Randall Nowan, scholar.'

'No one!' said William explosively.

'Nowan.' The matron spelled it. 'He chose it last year.'

'And it meant nothing to you? It is pronounced No one! It didn't occur to you to report this young man last year?'

'It didn't seem – ' began the matron, flustered.

William waved her to silence. What was the use? How was she to know? There was nothing in the gene pattern to give warning by any of the usual textbook criteria. It was a subtle combination that William and his staff had worked out over a period of twenty years through experiments on autistic children – and a combination they had never actually seen in life.

So close to canceling!

Marco, who was the hardhead of the group, complained that the crèches were too eager to abort before term and to cancel after term. He maintained that all gene patterns should be allowed to develop for purpose of initial screening and there should be no cancellation at all without consultation with a homologist.

'There aren't enough homologists,' William said tranquilly.

'We can at least run all gene patterns through the computer,' said Marco.

'To save anything we can get for our use?'

'For any homological use, here or elsewhere. We must study gene patterns in action if we're to understand ourselves properly, and it is the abnormal and monstrous patterns that give us most information. Our experiments on autism have taught us more about homology than the sum total existing on the day we began.'

William, who still liked the roll of the phrase 'the genetic physiology of man' rather than 'homology,' shook his head. 'Just the same, we've got to play it carefully. However useful we can claim our experiments to be, we live on bare social permission, reluctantly given. We're playing with lives.'

'Useless lives. Fit for canceling.'

'A quick and pleasant canceling is one thing. Our experiments, usually long drawn out and sometimes unavoidably unpleasant, are another.'

'We help them sometimes.'

'And we don't help them sometimes.'

It was a pointless argument, really, for there was no way of settling it. What it amounted to was that too few interesting abnormalities were available for homologists and there was no way of urging mankind to encourage a greater production. The trauma of the Catastrophe would never vanish in a dozen ways, including that one.

The hectic push toward space exploration could be traced back (and was, by some sociologists) to the knowledge of the fragility of the life skein on the planet, thanks to the Catastrophe.

Well, never mind –

There had never been anything like Randall Nowan. Not

for William. The slow onset of autism characteristic of that totally rare gene pattern meant that more was known about Randall than about any equivalent patient before him. They even caught some last faint glimmers of his way of thought in the laboratory before he closed off altogether and shrank finally within the wall of his skin – unconcerned, unreachable.

Then they began the slow process whereby Randall, subjected for increasing lengths of time to artificial stimuli, yielded up the inner workings of his brain and gave clues thereby to the inner workings of all brains, those that were called normal as well as those like his own.

So vastly great was the data they were gathering that William began to feel his dream of reversing autism was more than merely a dream. He felt a warm gladness at having chosen the name Anti-Aut.

And it was at almost the height of the euphoria induced by the work on Randall that he received the call from Dallas and that the heavy pressure began – now, of all times – to abandon his work and take on a new problem.

Looking back on it later, he could never work out just what it was that finally led him to agree to visit Dallas. In the end, of course, he could see how fortunate it was – but what had persuaded him to do so? Could he, even at the start, have had a dim unrealized notion of what it might come to? Surely, impossible.

Was it the unrealized memory of that printout, that photograph of his brother? Surely, impossible.

But he let himself be argued into that visit and it was only when the micro-pile power unit changed the pitch of its soft hum and the agrav unit took over for the final descent that he remembered that photograph – or at least that it moved into the conscious part of his memory.

Anthony worked at Dallas and, William remembered now, at the Mercury Project. That was what the caption had referred to. He swallowed, as the soft jar told him the journey was over. This would be uncomfortable.

3.

Anthony was waiting on the roof reception area to greet the incoming expert. Not he by himself, of course. He was part of a sizable delegation – the size itself a rather grim indication of the desperation to which they had been reduced – and he was among the lower echelons. That he was there at all was only because it was he who had made the original suggestion.

He felt a slight, but continuing, uneasiness at the thought of that. He had put himself on the line. He had received considerable approval for it, but there had been the faint insistence always that it was *his* suggestion; and if it turned out to be a fiasco, every one of them would move out of the line of fire and leave him at point-zero.

There were occasions, later, when he brooded over the possibility that the dim memory of a brother in homology had suggested his thought. That might have been, but it didn't have to be. The suggestion was so sensibly inevitable, really, that surely he would have had the same thought if his brother had been something as innocuous as a fantasy writer, or if he had had no brother of his own.

The problem was the inner planets –

The Moon and Mars were colonized. The larger asteroids and the satellites of Jupiter had been reached, and plans were in progress for a manned voyage to Titan, Saturn's large satellite, by way of an accelerating whirl about Jupiter. Yet even with plans in action for sending men on a seven-year round trip to the outer Solar System, there was still no chance of a manned approach to the inner planets, for fear of the Sun.

Venus itself was the less attractive of the two worlds within Earth's orbit. Mercury, on the other hand –

Anthony had not yet joined the team when Dmitri Large (he was quite short, actually) had given the talk that had moved the World Congress sufficiently to grant the appropriation that made the Mercury Project possible.

Anthony had listened to the tapes, and had heard Dmitri's presentation. Tradition was firm to the effect that it had been extemporaneous, and perhaps it was, but it was perfectly constructed and it held within it, in essence, every guideline followed by the Mercury Project since.

And the chief point made was that it would be wrong to wait until the technology had advanced to the point where a manned expedition through the rigors of Solar radiation could become feasible. Mercury was a unique environment that could teach much, and from Mercury's surface sustained observations could be made of the Sun that could not be made in any other way.

– Provided a man substitute – a robot, in short – could be placed on the planet.

A robot with the required physical characteristics could be built. Soft landings were as easy as kiss-my-hand. Yet once a robot landed, what did one do with him next?

He could make his observations and guide his actions on the basis of those observations, but the Project wanted his actions to be intricate and subtle, at least potentially, and they were not at all sure what observations he might make.

To prepare for all reasonable possibilities and to allow for all the intricacy desired, the robot would need to contain a computer (some at Dallas referred to it as a 'brain,' but Anthony scorned that verbal habit – perhaps because, he wondered later, the brain was his brother's field) sufficiently complex and versatile to fall into the same asteroid with a mammalian brain.

Yet nothing like that could be constructed and made

portable enough to be carried to Mercury and landed there – or if carried and landed, to be mobile enough to be useful to the kind of robot they planned. Perhaps someday the positronic-path devices that the roboticists were playing with might make it possible, but that someday was not yet.

The alternative was to have the robot send back to Earth every observation it made the moment it was made, and a computer on Earth could then guide his every action on the basis of those observations. The robot's body, in short, was to be there, and his brain here.

Once that decision was reached, the key technicians were the telemetrists and it was then that Anthony joined the Project. He became one of those who labored to devise methods for receiving and returning impulses over distances of from 50 to 140 million miles, toward, and sometimes past, a Solar disk that could interfere with those impulses in a most ferocious manner.

He took to his job with passion and (he finally thought) with skill and success. It was he, more than anyone else, who had designed the three switching stations that had been hurled into permanent orbit about Mercury – the Mercury Orbiters. Each of them was capable of sending and receiving impulses from Mercury to Earth and from Earth to Mercury. Each was capable of resisting, more or less permanently, the radiation from the Sun, and more than that, each could filter out Solar interference.

Three equivalent Orbiters were placed at distance of a little over a million miles from Earth, reaching north and south of the plane of the Ecliptic so that they could receive the impulses from Mercury and relay them to Earth – or vice versa – even when Mercury was behind the Sun and inaccessible to direct reception from any station on Earth's surface.

Which left the robot itself; a marvelous specimen of the roboticists' and telemetrists' arts in combination. The most complex of ten successive models, it was capable, in a volume only a little over twice that of a man and five times his mass, of sensing and doing considerably more than a man – if it could be guided.

How complex a computer had to be to guide the robot made itself evident rapidly enough, however, as each response step had to be modified to allow for variations in possible perception. And as each response step itself enforced the certainty of greater complexity of possible variation in perceptions, the early steps had to be reinforced and made stronger. It built itself up endlessly, like a chess game, and the telemetrists began to use a computer to program the computer that designed the program for the computer that programmed the robot-controlling computer.

There was nothing but confusion.

The robot was at a base in the desert spaces of Arizona and in itself was working well. The computer in Dallas could not, however, handle him well enough; not even under perfectly known Earth conditions. How then –

Anthony remembered the day when he had made the suggestion. It was on 7-4-553. He remembered it, for one thing, because he remembered thinking that day that 7-4 had been an important holiday in the Dallas region of the world among the pre-Cats half a millennium before – well, 553 years before, to be exact.

It had been at dinner, and a good dinner, too. There had been a careful adjustment of the ecology of the region and the Project personnel had high priority in collecting the food supplies that became available – so there was an unusual degree of choice on the menus, and Anthony had tried roast duck.

It was very good roast duck and it made him somewhat more expansive than usual. Everyone was in a rather self-expressive mood, in fact, and Ricardo said, 'We'll never do it. Let's admit it. We'll never do it.'

There was no telling how many had thought such a thing how many times before, but it was a rule that no one said so openly. Open pessimism might be the final push needed for appropriations to stop (they had been coming with greater difficulty each year for five years now) and if there *were* a chance, it would be gone.

Anthony, ordinarily not given to extraordinary optimism, but now reveling over his duck, said, 'Why can't we do it? Tell me why, and I'll refute it.'

It was a direct challenge and Ricardo's dark eyes narrowed at once. 'You want me to tell you why?'

'I sure do.'

Ricardo swung his chair around, facing Anthony full. He said, 'Come on, there's no mystery. Dmitri Large won't say so openly in any report, but you know and I know that to run Mercury Project properly, we'll need a computer as complex as a human brain whether it's on Mercury or here, and we can't build one. So where does that leave us except to play games with the World Congress and get money for make-work and possibly useful spin-offs?'

And Anthony placed a complacent smile on his face and said, 'That's easy to refute. You've given us the answer yourself.' (Was he playing games? Was it the warm feeling of duck in his stomach? The desire to tease Ricardo? . . . Or did some unfelt thought of his brother touch him? There was no way, later, that he could tell.)

'What answer?' Ricardo rose. He was quite tall and unusually thin and he always wore his white coat unseamed. He folded his arms and seemed to be doing his best to tower over the seated Anthony like an unfolded meter rule. 'What answer?'

'You say we need a computer as complex as a human brain. All right then, we'll build one.'

'The point, you idiot, is that we can't – '

'*We* can't. But there are others.'

'What others?'

'People who work on brains, of course. We're just solid-state mechanics. We have no idea in what way a human brain is complex, or where, or to what extent. Why don't we get in a homologist and have *him* design a computer?' And with that Anthony took a huge helping of stuffing and savored it complacently. He could still remember, after all this time, the taste of the stuffing, though he couldn't remember in detail what had happened afterward.

It seemed to him that no one had taken it seriously. There was laughter and a general feeling that Anthony had wriggled out of a hole by clever sophistry so that the laughter was at Ricardo's expense. (Afterward, of course, everyone claimed to have taken the suggestion seriously.)

Ricardo blazed up, pointed a finger at Anthony, and said, 'Write that up. I *dare* you to put that suggestion in writing.' (At least, so Anthony's memory had it. Ricardo had, since then, stated his comment was an enthusiastic 'Good idea! Why don't you write it up formally, Anthony?')

Either way, Anthony put it in writing.

Dmitri Large had taken to it. In private conference, he had slapped Anthony on the back and had said that he had been speculating in that direction himself – though he did not offer to take any credit for it on the record. (Just in case it turned out to be a fiasco, Anthony thought.)

Dmitri Large conducted the search for the appropriate homologist. It did not occur to Anthony that he ought to be interested. He knew neither homology nor homologists – except, of course, his brother, and he had not thought of him. Not consciously.

So Anthony was up there in the reception area, in a minor role, when the door of the aircraft opened and several men got out and came down and in the course of the handshakes that began going round, he found himself staring at his own face.

His cheeks burned and, with all his might, he wished himself a thousand miles away.

4.

More than ever, William wished that the memory of his brother had come earlier. It should have . . . Surely it should have.

But there had been the flattery of the request and the excitement that had begun to grow in him after a while. Perhaps he had deliberately avoided remembering.

To begin with, there had been the exhilaration of Dmitri Large coming to see him in his own proper presence. He had come from Dallas to New York by plane and that had been very titillating for William, whose secret vice it was to read thrillers. In the thrillers, men and women always traveled mass-wise when secrecy was desired. After all, electronic travel was public property – at least in the thrillers, where every radiation beam of whatever kind was invariably bugged.

William had said so in a kind of morbid half attempt at humor, but Dmitri hadn't seemed to be listening. He was staring at William's face and his thoughts seemed elsewhere. 'I'm sorry,' he said finally. 'You remind me of someone.'

(And yet that hadn't given it away to William. How was that possible? he had eventual occasion to wonder.)

Dmitri Large was a small plump man who seemed to be in a perpetual twinkle even when he declared himself worried or annoyed. He had a round and bulbous nose, pronounced cheeks, and softness everywhere. He emphasized his last name and said with a quickness that led William to suppose he said it often, 'Size is not all the large there is, my friend.'

In the talk that followed, William protested much. He

knew nothing about computers. Nothing! He had not the faintest idea of how they worked or how they were programed.

'No matter, no matter,' Dmitri said, shoving the point aside with an expressive gesture of the hand. '*We* know the computers; *we* can set up the programs. You just tell us what it is a computer must be made to do so that it will work like a brain and not like a computer.'

'I'm not sure I know enough about how a brain works to be able to tell you that, Dmitri,' said William.

'You are the foremost homologist in the world,' said Dmitri. 'I have checked that out carefully.' And that disposed of that.

William listened with gathering gloom. He supposed it was inevitable. Dip a person into one particular specialty deeply enough and long enough, and he would automatically begin to assume that specialists in all other fields were magicians, judging the depth of their wisdom by the breadth of his own ignorance . . . And as time went on, William learned a great deal more of the Mercury Project than it seemed to him at the time that he cared to.

He said at last, 'Why use a computer at all, then? Why not have one of your own men, or relays of them, receive the material from the robot and send back instructions.'

'Oh, oh, oh,' said Dmitri, almost bouncing in his chair in his eagerness. 'You see, you are not aware. Men are too slow to analyze quickly all the material the robot will send back – temperatures and gas pressures and cosmic-ray fluxes and Solar-wind intensities and chemical compositions and soil textures and easily three dozen more items – and then try to decide on the next step. A human being would merely *guide* the robot, and ineffectively; a computer would *be* the robot.

'And then, too,' he went on, 'men are too fast, also. It takes radiation of any kind anywhere from ten to twenty-two minutes to take the round trip between Mercury and Earth, depending on where each is in its orbit. Nothing can be done about that. You get an observation, you give an order, but much has happened between the time the observation is made and the response returns. Men can't adapt to the slowness of the speed of light, but a computer can take that into account . . . Come help us, William.'

William said gloomily, 'You are certainly welcome to consult me, for what good that might do you. My private TV beam is at your service.'

'But it's not consultation I want. You must come with me.'

'Mass-wise?' said William, shocked.

'Yes, of course. A project like this can't be carried out by sitting at opposite ends of a laser beam with a communications satellite in the middle. In the long run, it is too expensive, too inconvenient, and, of course, it lacks all privacy – '

It *was* like a thriller, William decided.

'Come to Dallas,' said Dmitri, 'and let me show you what we have there. Let me show you the facilities. Talk to some of our computer men. Give them the benefit of your way of thought.'

It was time, William thought, to be decisive. 'Dmitri,' he said, 'I have work of my own here. Important work that I do not wish to leave. To do what you want me to do may take me away from my laboratory for months.'

'Months!' said Dmitri, clearly taken aback. 'My good William, it may well be years. But surely it will be your work.'

'No, it will not. I know what my work is and guiding a robot on Mercury is not it.'

'Why not? If you do it properly, you will learn more about the brain merely by trying to make a computer work like one, and you will come back here, finally, better equipped to do what you now consider your work. And while you're gone, will you have no associates to carry on? And can you not be in constant communication with them by laser beam and television? And can you not visit New York on occasion? Briefly.'

William was moved. The thought of working on the brain from another direction did hit home. From that point on, he found himself looking for excuses to go – at least to visit – at least to see what it was all like . . . He could always return.

Then there followed Dmitri's visit to the ruins of Old New York, which he enjoyed with artless excitement (but then there was no more magnificent spectacle of the useless gigantism of the pre-Cats than Old New York). William began to wonder if the trip might not give him an opportunity to see some sights as well.

He even began to think that for some time he had been considering the possibility of finding a new bedmate, and it would be more convenient to find one in another geographical area where he would not stay permanently.

– Or was it that even then, when he knew nothing but the barest beginning of what was needed, there had already come to him, like the twinkle of a distant lightning flash, what might be done –

So he eventually went to Dallas and stepped out on the roof and there was Dmitri again, beaming. Then, with eyes narrowing, the little man turned and said, 'I *knew* – What a remarkable resemblance!'

William's eyes opened wide and there, visibly shrinking backward, was enough of his own face to make him certain at once that Anthony was standing before him.

He read very plainly in Anthony's face a longing to bury the relationship. All William needed to say was 'How remarkable!' and let it go. The gene patterns of mankind were complex enough, after all, to allow resemblances of any reasonable degree even without kinship.

But of course William was a homologist and no one can work with the intricacies of the human brain without growing insensitive as to its details, so he said, 'I'm sure this is Anthony, my brother.'

Dmitri said, 'Your brother?'

'My father,' said William, 'had two boys by the same woman – my mother. They were eccentric people.'

He then stepped forward, hand outstretched, and Anthony had no choice but to take it . . . The incident was the topic of conversation, the only topic, for the next several days.

5.

It was small consolation to Anthony that William was contrite enough when he realized what he had done.

They sat together after dinner that night and William said, 'My apologies. I thought that if we got the worst out at once that would end it. It doesn't seem to have done so. I've signed no papers, made no formal agreement. I will leave.'

'What good would that do?' said Anthony ungraciously. 'Everyone knows now. Two bodies and one face. It's enough to make one puke.'

'If I leave – '

'You can't leave. This whole thing is my idea.'

'To get *me* here?' William's heavy lids lifted as far as they might and his eyebrows climbed.

'No, of course not. To get a *homologist* here. How could I possibly know they would send *you*?'

'But if I leave – '

'No. The only thing we can do now is to lick the problem, if it can be done. Then – it won't matter.' (Everything is forgiven those who succeed, he thought.)

'I don't know that I can – '

'We'll have to try. Dmitri will place it on us. It's too good a chance. You two are brothers,' Anthony said, mimicking Dmitri's tenor voice, 'and understand each other. Why not work together?' Then, in his own voice, angrily, 'So we must. To begin with, what is it you do, William? I mean, more precisely than the word "homology" can explain by itself.'

William sighed. 'Well, please accept my regrets . . . I work with autistic children.'

'I'm afraid I don't know what that means.'

'Without going into a long song and dance, I deal with children who do not reach out into the world, do not communicate with others, but who sink into themselves and exist behind a wall of skin, somewhat unreachably. I hope to be able to cure it someday.'

'Is that why you call yourself Anti-Aut?'

'Yes, as a matter of fact.'

Anthony laughed briefly, but he was not really amused.

A chill crept into William's manner. 'It is an honest name.'

'I'm sure it is,' muttered Anthony hurriedly, and could bring himself to no more specific apology. With an effort, he restored the subject, 'And are you making any progress?'

'Toward the cure? No, so far. Toward understanding, yes. And the more I understand – ' William's voice grew warmer as he spoke and his eyes more distant. Anthony recognized it for what it was, the pleasure of speaking of what fills one's heart and mind to the exclusion of almost everything else. He felt it in himself often enough.

He listened as closely as he might to something he didn't really understand, for it was necessary to do so. He would expect William to listen to him.

How clearly he remembered it. He thought at the time he would not, but at the time, of course, he was not aware of what was happening. Thinking back, in the glare of hindsight, he found himself remembering whole sentences, virtually word for word.

'So it seemed to us,' William said, 'that the autistic child was not failing to receive the impressions, or even failing to interpret them in quite a sophisticated manner. He was, rather, disapproving them and rejecting them, without any loss of the potentiality of full communication if some impression could be found which he approved of.'

'Ah,' said Anthony, making just enough of a sound to indicate that he was listening.

'Nor can you persuade him out of his autism in any ordinary way, for he disapproves of *you* just as much as he disapproves of the rest of the world. But if you place him in conscious arrest – '

'In what?'

'It is a technique we have in which, in effect, the brain is divorced from the body and can perform its functions without reference to the body. It is a rather sophisticated technique devised in our own laboratory; actually – ' He paused.

'By yourself?' asked Anthony gently.

'Actually, yes,' said William, reddening slightly but clearly pleased. 'In conscious arrest, we can supply the body with designed fantasies and observe the brain under differential electroencephalography. We can at once learn more about the autistic individual; what kind of sense impressions he most wants; and we learn more about the brain generally.'

'Ah,' said Anthony, and this time it was a real ah. 'And all this you have learned about brains – can you not adapt it to the workings of a computer?'

'No,' said William. 'Not a chance. I told that to Dmitri. I know nothing about computers and not enough about brains.'

'If I teach you about computers and tell you in detail what we need, what then?'

'It won't do. It – '

'Brother,' Anthony said, and he tried to make it an

impressive word. 'You owe me something. Please make an honest attempt to give our problem some thought. Whatever you know about the brain – please adapt it to our computers.'

William shifted uneasily, and said, 'I understand your position. I will try. I will honestly try.'

6.

William *had* tried, and as Anthony had predicted, the two had been left to work together. At first they encountered others now and then and William had tried to use the shock value of the announcement that they were brothers since there was no use in denial. Eventually that stopped, however, and there came to be a purposeful non-interference. When William approached Anthony, or Anthony approached William, anyone else who might be present faded silently into the walls.

They even grew used to each other after a fashion and sometimes spoke to each other almost as though there were no resemblance between them at all and no childish memories in common.

Anthony made the computer requirements plain in reasonably non-technical language and William, after long thought, explained how it seemed to him a computer might do the work, more or less, of a brain.

Anthony said, 'Would that be possible?'

'I don't know,' said William. 'I am not eager to try. It may not work. But it may.'

'We'd have to talk to Dmitri Large.'

'Let's talk it over ourselves first and see what we've got. We can go to him with as reasonable a proposition as we can put together. Or else, not go to him.'

Anthony hesitated, 'We *both* go to him?'

William said delicately, 'You be my spokesman. There is no reason that we need be seen together.'

'Thank you, William. If anything comes of this, you will get full credit from me.'

William said, 'I have no worries about that. If there is anything to this, I will be the only one who can make it work, I suppose.'

They thrashed it out through four or five meetings and if Anthony hadn't been kin and if there hadn't been that sticky, emotional situation between them, William would have been uncomplicatedly proud of the younger – brother – for his quick understanding of an alien field.

There were then long conferences with Dmitri Large. There were, in fact, conferences with everyone. Anthony saw them through endless days, and then they came to see William separately. And eventually, through an agonizing pregnancy, what came to be called the Mercury Computer was authorized.

William then returned to New York with some relief. He did not plan to stay in New York (would he have thought that possible two months earlier?) but there was much to do at the Homological Institute.

More conferences were necessary, of course, to explain to his own laboratory group what was happening and why he had to take leave and how they were to continue their own projects without him. Then there was a much more elaborate arrival at Dallas with the essential equipment and with two young aides for what would have to be an open-ended stay.

Nor did William even look back, figuratively speaking. His own laboratory and its needs faded from his thoughts. He was now thoroughly committed to his new task.

7.

It was the worst period for Anthony. The relief during William's absence had not penetrated deep and there began the nervous agony of wondering whether perhaps, hope against hope, he might not return. Might he not choose to send a deputy, someone else, anyone else? Anyone with a different face so that Anthony need not feel the half of a two-backed four-legged monster?

But it *was* William. Anthony had watched the freight plane come silently through the air, had watched it unload from a distance. But even from that distance he eventually saw William.

That was that. Anthony left.

He went to see Dmitri that afternoon. 'It's not necessary, Dmitri, for me to stay, surely. We've worked out the details and someone else can take over.'

'No, no,' said Dmitri. 'The idea was yours in the first place. You must see it through. There is no point in needlessly dividing the credit.'

Anthony thought: No one else will take the risk. There's still the chance of fiasco. I might have known.

He *had* known, but he said stolidly, 'You understand I cannot work with William.'

'But why not?' Dmitri pretended surprise. 'You have been doing so well together.'

'I have been straining my guts over it, Dmitri, and they won't take any more. Don't you suppose I know how it looks?'

'My good fellow! You make too much of it. Sure the men stare. They are human, after all. But they'll get used to it. *I'm* used to it.'

You are not, you fat liar, Anthony thought. He said, '*I'm* not used to it.'

'You're not looking at it properly. Your parents were peculiar – but after all, what they did wasn't illegal, only peculiar, *only* peculiar. It's not your fault, or William's. Neither of you is to blame.'

'We carry the mark,' said Anthony, making a quick curving gesture of his hand to his face.

'It's not the mark you think. I see differences. You are distinctly younger in appearance. Your hair is wavier. It's only at first glance that there is a similarity. Come, Anthony, there will be all the time you want, all the help you need, all the equipment you can use. I'm sure it will work marvelously. Think of the satisfaction – '

Anthony weakened, of course, and agreed at least to help William set up the equipment. William, too, seemed sure it would work marvelously. Not as frenetically as Dmitri did, but with a kind of calmness.

'It's only a matter of the proper connections,' he said, 'though I must admit that that's quite a huge "only." Your end of it will be to arrange sensory impressions on an independent screen so that we can exert – well, I can't say manual control, can I? – so that we can exert intellectual control to override, if necessary.'

'That can be done,' said Anthony.

'Then let's get going . . . Look, I'll need a week at least to arrange the connections and make sure of the instructions – '

'Programing,' said Anthony.

'Well, this is your place, so I'll use your terminology. My assistants and I will *program* the Mercury Computer, but not in your fashion.'

'I should hope not. We would want a homologist to set up a much more subtle program than anything a mere telemetrist could do.' He did not try to hide the self-hating irony in his words.

William let the tone go and accepted the words. He said, 'We'll begin simply. We'll have the robot walk.'

8.

A week later, the robot walked in Arizona, a thousand miles away. He walked stiffly, and sometimes he fell down, and sometimes he clanked his ankle against an obstruction, and sometimes he whirled on one foot and went off in a surprising new direction.

'He's a baby, learning to walk,' said William.

Dmitri came occasionally, to learn of progress. 'That's remarkable,' he would say.

Anthony didn't think so. Weeks passed, then months. The robot had progressively done more and more, as the Mercury Computer had been placed, progressively, under a more and more complex programming. (William had a tendency to refer to the Mercury Computer as a brain, but Anthony wouldn't allow it.) And all that happened wasn't good enough.

'It's not good enough, William,' he said finally. He had not slept the night before.

'Isn't that strange?' said William coolly. 'I was going to say that I thought we had it about beaten.'

Anthony held himself together with difficulty. The strain of working with William and of watching the robot fumble was more than he could bear. 'I'm going to resign, William. The whole job. I'm sorry . . . It's not you.'

'But it *is* I, Anthony.'

'It isn't *all* you, William. It's failure. We won't make it. You see how clumsily the robot handles himself, even though he's on Earth, only a thousand miles away, with the signal round trip only a tiny fraction of a second in time. On Mercury, there will be minutes of delay, minutes for which the Mercury Computer will have to allow. It's madness to think it will work.'

William said, 'Don't resign, Anthony. You can't resign now. I suggest we have the robot sent to Mercury. I'm convinced he's ready.'

Anthony laughed loudly and insultingly. 'You're crazy, William.'

'I'm not. You seem to think it will be harder on Mercury,

but it won't be. It's harder on Earth. This robot is designed for one-third Earth-normal gravity, and he's working in Arizona at full gravity. He's designed for 400°C. and he's got 30°C. He's designed for vacuum and he's working in an atmospheric soup.'

'That robot can take the difference.'

'The metal structure can, I suppose, but what about the Computer right here? It doesn't work well with a robot that isn't in the environment he's designed for . . . Look, Anthony, if you want a computer that is as complex as a brain, you have to allow for idiosyncrasies . . . Come, let's make a deal. If you will push, with me, to have the robot sent to Mercury, that will take six months, and I will take a sabbatical for that period. You will be rid of me.'

'Who'll take care of the Mercury Computer?'

'By now you understand how it works, and I'll have my two men here to help you.'

Anthony shook his head defiantly. 'I can't take the responsibility for the Computer, and I won't take the responsibility for suggesting that the robot be sent to Mercury. It won't work.'

'I'm *sure* it will.'

'You can't be sure. And the responsibility is mine. I'm the one who'll bear the blame. It will be nothing to you.'

Anthony later remembered this as a crucial moment. William might have let it go. Anthony would have resigned. All would have been lost.

But William said, 'Nothing to me? Look, Dad had this thing about Mom. All right. I'm sorry, too. I'm as sorry as anyone can be, but it's *done*, and there's something funny that has resulted. When I speak of Dad, I mean your Dad, too, and there's lots of pairs of people who can say that: two brothers, two sisters, a brother and sister. And then when I say Mom, I mean *your* Mom, and there are lots of pairs who can say that, too. But I don't know any other pair, nor have

I heard of any other pair, who can share both Dad *and* Mom.'

'I know that,' said Anthony grimly.

'Yes, but look at it from my standpoint,' said William hurriedly. 'I'm a homologist. I work with gene patterns. Have you ever thought of our gene patterns? We share both parents, which means that our gene patterns are closer together than any other pair on this planet. Our very faces show it.'

'I know that, too.'

'So that if this project were to work, and if you were to gain glory from it, it would be your gene pattern that would have been proven highly useful to mankind – and that would mean very much my gene pattern as well . . . Don't you see, Anthony? I share your parents, your face, your gene pattern, and therefore either your glory or your disgrace. It is mine almost as much as yours, and if any credit or blame adheres to me, it is yours almost as much as mine, too. I've *got* to be interested in your success. I've a motive for that which no one else on Earth has – a purely selfish one, one so selfish you can be sure it's there. I'm on your side, Anthony, because you're very nearly me!'

They looked at each other for a long time, and for the first time, Anthony did so without noticing the face he shared.

William said, 'So let us ask that the robot be sent to Mercury.'

And Anthony gave in. And after Dmitri had approved the request – he had been waiting to, after all – Anthony spent much of the day in deep thought.

Then he sought out William and said, 'Listen!'

There was a long pause which William did not break.

Anthony said again, 'Listen!'

William waited patiently.

Anthony said, 'There's really no need for you to leave. I'm sure you wouldn't like to have the Mercury Computer tended by anyone but yourself.'

William said, 'You mean *you* intend to leave?'

Anthony said, 'No, I'll stay, too.'

William said, 'We needn't see much of each other.'

All of this had been, for Anthony, like speaking with a pair of hands clenched about his windpipe. The pressure seemed to tighten now, but he managed the hardest statement of all.

'We don't have to avoid each other. We don't have to.'

William smiled rather uncertainly. Anthony didn't smile at all; he left quickly.

9.

William looked up from his book. It was at least a month since he had ceased being vaguely surprised at having Anthony enter.

He said, 'Anything wrong?'

'Who can say? They're coming in for the soft landing. Is the Mercury Computer in action?'

William knew Anthony knew the Computer status perfectly, but he said, 'By tomorrow morning, Anthony.'

'And there are no problems?'

'None at all.'

'Then we have to wait for the soft landing.'

'Yes.'

Anthony said, 'Something will go wrong.'

'Rocketry is surely an old hand at this. Nothing will go wrong.'

'So much work wasted.'

'It's not wasted yet. It won't be.'

Anthony said, 'Maybe you're right.' Hands deep in his pockets, he drifted away, stopping at the door just before touching contact. 'Thanks!'

'For what, Anthony?'

'For being – comforting.'

William smiled wryly and was relieved his emotions didn't show.

10.

Virtually the entire body of personnel of the Mercury Project was on hand for the crucial moment. Anthony, who had no tasks to perform, remained well to the rear, his eyes on the monitors. The robot had been activated and there were visual messages being returned.

At least they came out as the equivalent of visual – and they showed as yet nothing but a dim glow of light which was, presumably, Mercury's surface.

Shadows flitted across the screen, probably irregularities on that surface. Anthony couldn't tell by eye alone, but those at the controls, who were analyzing the data by methods more subtle than could be disposed of by unaided eye, seemed calm. None of the little red lights that might have betokened emergency were lighting. Anthony was watching the key observers rather than the screen.

He should be down with William and the others at the Computer. It was going to be thrown in only when the soft landing was made. He *should* be. He *couldn't* be.

The shadows flitted across the screen more rapidly. The robot was descending – too quickly? Surely, too quickly!

There was a last blur and a steadiness, a shift of focus in which the blur grew darker, then fainter. A sound was heard and there were perceptible seconds before Anthony realized what it was the sound was saying – 'Soft landing achieved! Soft landing achieved!'

Then a murmur arose and became an excited hum of self-congratulation until one more change took place on the screen and the sound of human words and laughter was stopped as though there had been a smash collision against a wall of silence.

For the screen changed; changed and grew sharp. In the brilliant, brilliant sunlight, blazing through the carefully filtered screen, they could now see a boulder clear, burning white on one side, ink-on-ink on the other. It shifted right, then back to left, as though a pair of eyes were looking left, then right. A metal hand appeared on the screen as though the eyes were looking at part of itself.

It was Anthony's voice that cried out at last, 'The Computer's been thrown in.'

He heard the words as though someone else shouted them and he raced out and down the stairs and through a corridor, leaving the babble of voices to rise behind him.

'William,' he cried as he burst into the Computer room, 'it's *perfect*, it's – '

But William's hand was upraised. 'Shh. Please. I don't want any violent sensations entering except those from the robot.'

'You mean we can be heard?' whispered Anthony.

'Maybe not, but I don't know.' There was another screen, a smaller one, in the room with the Mercury Computer. The scene on it was different, and changing; the robot was moving.

William said, 'The robot is feeling its way. Those steps have got to be clumsy. There's a seven-minute delay between stimulus and response and that has to be allowed for.'

'But already he's walking more surely than he ever did in Arizona. Don't you think so, William?' Anthony was gripping William's shoulder, shaking it, eyes never leaving the screen.

William said, 'I'm sure of it, Anthony.'

The Sun burned down in a warm contrasting world of white and black, of white Sun against black sky and white rolling ground mottled with black shadow. The bright sweet smell of the Sun on every exposed square centimeter of metal contrasting with the creeping death-of-aroma on the other side.

He lifted his hand and stared at it, counting the fingers. Hot-hot-hot – turning, putting each finger, one by one, into the shadow of the others and the hot slowly dying in a change in tactility that made him feel the clean, comfortable vacuum.

Yet not entirely vacuum. He straightened and lifted both arms over his head, stretching them out, and the sensitive spots on either wrist felt the vapors – the thin, faint touch of tin and lead rolling through the cloy of mercury.

The thicker taste rose from his feet; the silicates of each variety, marked by the clear separate-and-together touch and tang of each metal ion. He moved one foot slowly through the crunchy, caked dust, and felt the changes like a soft, not quite random symphony.

And over all the Sun. He looked up at it, large and fat and bright and hot, and heard its joy. He watched the slow rise of prominences around its rim and listened to the crackling sound of each; and to the other happy noises over the broad face. When he dimmed the background light, the red of the rising wisps of hydrogen showed in bursts of mellow contralto, and the deep bass of the spots amid the muted whistling of the wispy, moving faculae, and the occasional thin keening of a flare, the ping-pong ticking of gamma rays and cosmic particles, and over all in every direction the soft, fainting, and ever-renewed sigh of the Sun's substance rising and retreating forever in a cosmic wind which reached out and bathed him in glory.

He jumped, and rose slowly in the air with a freedom he had never felt, and jumped again when he landed, and ran, and jumped, and ran again, with a body that responded perfectly to this glorious world, this paradise in which he found himself.

A stranger so long and so lost – in paradise at last.

William said, 'It's all right.'

'But what's he doing?' cried out Anthony.

'It's *all right*. The programming is working. He has tested his senses. He has been making the various visual observations. He has dimmed the Sun and studied it. He has tested for atmosphere and for the chemical nature of the soil. It all works.'

'But why is he running?'

'I rather think that's his own idea, Anthony. If you want to program a computer as complicated as a brain, you've got to expect it to have ideas of its own.'

'Running? Jumping?' Anthony turned an anxious face to William. 'He'll hurt himself. You can handle the Computer. Override. Make him stop.'

And William said sharply, 'No, I won't. I'll take the chance of his hurting himself. Don't you understand? He's *happy*. He was on Earth, a world he was never equipped to handle. Now he's on Mercury with a body perfectly adapted to its environment, as perfectly adapted as a hundred specialized scientists could make it be. It's paradise for him; let him enjoy it.'

'Enjoy? He's a robot.'

'I'm not talking about the robot. I'm talking about the brain – the *brain* – that's living *here*.'

The Mercury Computer, enclosed in glass, carefully and delicately wired, its integrity most subtly preserved, breathed and lived.

'It's Randall who's in paradise,' said William. 'He's found the world for whose sake he autistically fled this one. He has a world his new body fits perfectly in exchange for the world his old body did not fit at all.'

Anthony watched the screen in wonder. 'He seems to be quieting.'

'Of course,' said William, 'and he'll do his job all the better for his joy.'

Anthony smiled and said, 'We've done it, then, you and I? Shall we join the rest and let them fawn on us, William?'

William said, 'Together?'

And Anthony linked arms. 'Together, brother!'

Light Verse

The very last person anyone would expect to be a murderer was Mrs Avis Lardner. Widow of the great astronaut-martyr, she was a philanthropist, an art collector, a hostess extraordinary, and, everyone agreed, an artistic genius. But above all, she was the gentlest and kindest human being one could imagine.

Her husband, William J. Lardner, died, as we all know, of the effects of radiation from a solar flare, after he had deliberately remained in space so that a passenger vessel might make it safely to Space Station 5.

Mrs Lardner had received a generous pension for that, and she had then invested wisely and well. By late middle age she was very wealthy.

Her house was a showplace, a veritable museum, containing a small but extremely select collection of extraordinarily beautiful jeweled objects. From a dozen different cultures she had obtained relics of almost every conceivable artifact that could be embedded with jewels and made to serve the aristocracy of that culture. She had one of the first jeweled wristwatches manufactured in America, a jeweled dagger from Cambodia, a jeweled pair of spectacles from Italy, and so on almost endlessly.

All was open for inspection. The artifacts were not insured, and there were no ordinary security provisions. There was no need for anything conventional, for Mrs Lardner maintained a large staff of robot servants, all of whom could be relied on to guard every item with imperturbable concentration, irreproachable honesty, and irrevocable efficiency.

Everyone knew the existence of those robots and there is no record of any attempt at theft, ever.

And then, of course, there was her light-sculpture. How Mrs Lardner discovered her own genius at the art, no guest at her many lavish entertainments could guess. On each occasion, however, when her house was thrown open to guests, a new symphony of light shone throughout the rooms; three-dimensional curves and solids in melting color, some pure and some fusing in startling, crystalline effects that bathed every guest in wonder and somehow always adjusted itself so as to make Mrs Lardner's blue-white hair and soft, unlined face gently beautiful.

It was for the light-sculpture more than anything else that the guests came. It was never the same twice, and never failed to explore new experimental avenues of art. Many people who could afford light-consoles prepared light-sculptures for amusement, but no one could approach Mrs Lardner's expertise. Not even those who considered themselves professional artists.

She herself was charmingly modest about it. 'No, no,' she would protest when someone waxed lyrical. 'I wouldn't call it "poetry in light." That's far too kind. At most, I would say it was mere "light verse."' And everyone smiled at her gentle wit.

Though she was often asked, she would never create light-sculpture for any occasion but her own parties. 'That would be commercialization,' she said.

She had no objection, however, to the preparation of elaborate holograms of her sculptures so that they might be made permanent and reproduced in museums of art all over the world. Nor was there ever a charge for any use that might be made of her light-sculptures.

'I couldn't ask a penny,' she said, spreading her arms wide. 'It's free to all. After all, I have no further use for it myself.' It was true! She never used the same light-sculpture twice.

When the holograms were taken, she was cooperation itself. Watching benignly at every step, she was always ready to order her robot servants to help. 'Please, Courtney,' she would say, 'would you be so kind as to adjust the step ladder?'

It was her fashion. She always addressed her robots with the most formal courtesy.

Once, years before, she had been almost scolded by a government functionary from the Bureau of Robots and Mechanical Men. 'You can't do that,' he said severely. 'It interferes with their efficiency. They are constructed to follow orders, and the more clearly you give those orders, the more efficiently they follow them. When you ask with elaborate politeness, it is difficult for them to understand that an order is being given. They react more slowly.'

Mrs Lardner lifted her aristocratic head. 'I do not ask for speed and efficiency,' she said. 'I ask goodwill. My robots love me.'

The government functionary might have explained that robots cannot love, but he withered under her hurt but gentle glance.

It was notorious that Mrs Lardner never even returned a robot to the factory for adjustment. Their positronic brains are enormously complex, and once in ten times or so the adjustment is not perfect as it leaves the factory. Sometimes the error does not show up for a period of time, but whenever it does, US Robots and Mechanical Men Corporation always makes the adjustment free of charge.

Mrs Lardner shook her head. 'Once a robot is in my house,' she said, 'and has performed his duties, any minor eccentricities must be borne with. I will not have him manhandled.'

It was the worse thing possible to try to explain that a robot was but a machine. She would say very stiffly,

'Nothing that is as intelligent as a robot can ever be *but* a machine. I treat them as people.'

And that was that!

She kept even Max, although he was almost helpless. He could scarcely understand what was expected of him. Mrs Lardner denied that strenuously, however. 'Not at all,' she would say firmly. 'He can take hats and coats and store them very well, indeed. He can hold objects for me. He can do many things.'

'But why not have him adjusted?' asked a friend, once.

'Oh, I couldn't. He's himself. He's very lovable, you know. After all, a positronic brain is so complex that no one can ever tell in just what way it's off. If he were made perfectly normal there would be no way to adjust him back to the lovability he now has. I won't give that up.'

'But if he's maladjusted,' said the friend, looking at Max nervously, 'might he not be dangerous?'

'Never,' laughed Mrs Lardner. 'I've had him for years. He's completely harmless and quite a dear.'

Actually he looked like all the other robots, smooth, metallic, vaguely human but expressionless.

To the gentle Mrs Lardner, however, they were all individual, all sweet, all lovable. It was the kind of woman she was.

How could she commit murder?

The very last person anyone would expect to be murdered would be John Semper Travis. Introverted and gentle, he was in the world but not of it. He had that peculiar mathematical turn of mind that made it possible for him to work out in his mind the complicated tapestry of the myriad positronic brain-paths in a robot's mind.

He was chief engineer of US Robots and Mechanical Men Corporation.

But he was also an enthusiastic amateur in light-sculpture. He had written a book on the subject, trying to show that the type of mathematics he used in working out positronic brain-paths might be modified into a guide to the production of aesthetic light-sculpture.

His attempt at putting theory into practice was a dismal failure, however. The sculptures he himself produced, following his mathematical principles, were stodgy, mechanical, and uninteresting.

It was the only reason for unhappiness in his quiet, introverted, and secure life, and yet it was reason enough for him to be very unhappy indeed. He *knew* his theories were right, yet he could not make them work. If he could but produce *one* great piece of light-sculpture –

Naturally, he knew of Mrs Lardner's light-sculpture. She was universally hailed as a genius, yet Travis knew she could not understand even the simplest aspect of robotic mathematics. He had corresponded with her but she consistently refused to explain her methods, and he wondered if she had any at all. Might it not be mere intuition? – but even intuition might be reduced to mathematics. Finally he managed to receive an invitation to one of her parties. He simply had to see her.

Mr Travis arrived rather late. He had made one last attempt at a piece of light-sculpture and had failed dismally.

He greeted Mrs Lardner with a kind of puzzled respect and said, 'That was a peculiar robot who took my hat and coat.'

'That is Max,' said Mrs Lardner.

'He is quite maladjusted, and he's a fairly old model. How is it you did not return it to the factory?'

'Oh, no,' said Mrs Lardner. 'It would be too much trouble.'

'None at all, Mrs Lardner,' said Travis. 'You would be surprised how simple a task it was. Since I am with US

Robots, I took the liberty of adjusting him myself. It took no time and you'll find he is now in perfect working order.'

A queer change came over Mrs Lardner's face. Fury found a place on it for the first time in her gentle life, and it was as though the lines did not know how to form.

'You adjusted him?' she shrieked. 'But it was *he* who created my light-sculptures. It was the maladjustment, the *maladjustment*, which you can never restore, that – that – '

It was really unfortunate that she had been showing her collection at the time and that the jeweled dagger from Cambodia was on the marble tabletop before her.

Travis's face was also distorted. 'You mean if I had studied his uniquely maladjusted positronic brain-paths I might have learned – '

She lunged with the knife too quickly for anyone to stop her and he did not try to dodge. Some said he came to meet it – as though he *wanted* to die.

Segregationist

The surgeon looked up without expression. 'Is he ready?'

'Ready is a relative term,' said the med-eng. '*We're* ready. He's restless.'

'They always are . . . Well, it's a serious operation.'

'Serious or not, he should be thankful. He's been chosen for it over an enormous number of possibles and, frankly, I don't think . . .'

'Don't say it,' said the surgeon. 'The decision is not ours to make.'

'We accept it. But do we have to agree?'

'Yes,' said the surgeon, crisply. 'We agree. Completely and wholeheartedly. The operation is entirely too intricate to approach with mental reservations. This man has proven his worth in a number of ways and his profile is suitable for the Board of Mortality.'

'All right,' said the med-eng, unmollified.

The surgeon said, 'I'll see him right in here, I think. It is small enough and personal enough to be comforting.'

'It won't help. He's nervous, and he's made up his mind.'

'Has he indeed?'

'Yes. He wants metal; they always do.'

The surgeon's face did not change expression. He stared at his hands. 'Sometimes one can talk them out of it.'

'Why bother?' said the med-eng, indifferently. 'If he wants metal, let it be metal.'

'You don't care?'

'Why should I?' The med-eng said it almost brutally. 'Either way it's a medical engineering problem and I'm a medical engineer. Either way, I can handle it. Why should I go beyond that?'

The surgeon said stolidly, 'To me, it is a matter of the fitness of things.'

'Fitness! You can't use that as an argument. What does the patient care about the fitness of things?'

'I care.'

'You care in a minority. The trend is against you. You have no chance.'

'I have to try.' The surgeon waved the med-eng into silence with a quick wave of his hand – no impatience to it, merely quickness. He had already informed the nurse and he had already been signaled concerning her approach. He pressed a small button and the double-door pulled swiftly apart. The patient moved inward in his motor-chair, the nurse stepping briskly along beside him.

'You may go, nurse,' said the surgeon, 'but wait outside. I will be calling you.' He nodded to the med-eng, who left with the nurse, and the door closed behind them.

The man in the chair looked over his shoulder and watched them go. His neck was scrawny and there were fine wrinkles about his eyes. He was freshly shaven and the fingers of his hands, as they gripped the arms of the chair tightly, showed manicured nails. He was a high-priority patient and he was being taken care of . . . But there was a look of settled peevishness on his face.

He said, 'Will we be starting today?'

The surgeon nodded. 'This afternoon, Senator.'

'I understand it will take weeks.'

'Not for the operation itself, Senator. But there are a number of subsidiary points to be taken care of. There are some circulatory renovations that must be carried through, and hormonal adjustments. These are tricky things.'

'Are they dangerous?' Then, as though feeling the need

for establishing a friendly relationship, but patently against his will, he added, '. . . doctor?'

The surgeon paid no attention to the nuances of expression. He said, flatly, 'Everything is dangerous. We take our time in order that it be less dangerous. It is the time required, the skill of many individuals united, the equipment, that makes such operations available to so few . . .'

'I know that,' said the patient, restlessly. 'I refuse to feel guilty about that. Or are you implying improper pressure?'

'Not at all, Senator. The decisions of the Board have never been questioned. I mention the difficulty and intricacy of the operation merely to explain my desire to have it conducted in the best fashion possible.'

'Well, do so, then. That is my desire, also.'

'Then I must ask you to make a decision. It is possible to supply you with either of two types of cyber-hearts, metal or . . .'

'Plastic!' said the patient, irritably. 'Isn't that the alternative you were going to offer, doctor? Cheap plastic. I don't want that. I've made my choice. I want the metal.'

'But . . .'

'See here. I've been told the choice rests with me. Isn't that so?'

The surgeon nodded. 'Where two alternate procedures are of equal value from a medical standpoint, the choice rests with the patient. In actual practice, the choice rests with the patient even when the alternate procedures are *not* of equal value, as in this case.'

The patient's eyes narrowed. 'Are you trying to tell me the plastic heart is superior?'

'It depends on the patient. In my opinion, in your individual case, it is. And we prefer not to use the term, plastic. It is a fibrous cyber-heart.'

'It's plastic as far as I am concerned.'

'Senator,' said the surgeon, infinitely patient, 'the material is not plastic in the ordinary sense of the word. It is a polymeric material, true, but one that is far more complex than ordinary plastic. It is a complex protein-like fiber designed to imitate, as closely as possible, the natural structure of the human heart you now have within your chest.'

'Exactly, and the human heart I now have within my chest is worn out although I am not yet sixty years old. I don't want another one like it, thank you. I want something better.'

'We all want something better for you, Senator. The fibrous cyber-heart will be better. It has a potential life of centuries. It is absolutely non-allergenic . . .'

'Isn't that so for the metallic heart, too?'

'Yes, it is,' said the surgeon. 'The metallic cyber is of titanium alloy that . . .'

'And it doesn't wear out? And it is stronger than plastic? Or fiber or whatever you want to call it?'

'The metal is physically stronger, yes, but mechanical strength is not a point at issue. Its mechanical strength does you no particular good since the heart is well protected. Anything capable of reaching the heart will kill you for other reasons even if the heart stands up under manhandling.'

The patient shrugged. 'If I ever break a rib, I'll have that replaced by titanium, also. Replacing bones is easy. Anyone can have that done anytime. I'll be as metallic as I want to be, doctor.'

'That is your right, if you so choose. However, it is only fair to tell you that although no metallic cyber-heart has ever broken down mechanically, a number have broken down electronically.'

'What does that mean?'

'It means that every cyber-heart contains a pacemaker as part of its structure. In the case of the metallic variety, this is an electronic device that keeps the cyber in rhythm. It means an entire battery of miniaturized equipment must be included to alter the heart's rhythm to suit an individual's emotional and physical state. Occasionally something goes wrong there and people have died before that wrong could be corrected.'

'I never heard of such a thing.'

'I assure you it happens.'

'Are you telling me it happens often?'

'Not at all. It happens very rarely.'

'Well, then, I'll take my chance. What about the plastic heart? Doesn't that contain a pacemaker?'

'Of course it does, Senator. But the chemical structure of a fibrous cyber-heart is quite close to that of human tissue. It can respond to the ionic and hormonal controls of the body itself. The total complex that need be inserted is far simpler than in the case of the metal cyber.'

'But doesn't the plastic heart ever pop out of hormonal control?'

'None has ever yet done so.'

'Because you haven't been working with them long enough. Isn't that so?'

The surgeon hesitated. 'It is true that the fibrous cybers have not been used nearly as long as the metallic.'

'There you are. What is it anyway, doctor? Are you afraid I'm making myself into a robot . . . into a Metallo, as they call them since citizenship went through?'

'There is nothing wrong with a Metallo as a Metallo. As you say, they are citizens. But you're *not* a Metallo. You're a human being. Why not stay a human being?'

'Because I want the best and that's a metallic heart. You see to that.'

The surgeon nodded. 'Very well. You will be asked to sign the necessary permissions and you will then be fitted with a metal heart.'

'And you'll be the surgeon in charge? They tell me you're the best.'

'I will do what I can to make the changeover an easy one.'

The door opened and the chair moved the patient out to the waiting nurse.

The med-eng came in, looking over his shoulder at the receding patient until the doors had closed again.

He turned to the surgeon. 'Well, I can't tell what happened just by looking at you. What was his decision?'

The surgeon bent over his desk, punching out the final items for his records. 'What you predicted. He insists on the metallic cyber-heart.'

'After all, they are better.'

'Not significantly. They've been around longer; no more than that. It's this mania that's been plaguing humanity ever since Metallos have become citizens. Men have this odd desire to make Metallos out of themselves. They yearn for the physical strength and endurance one associates with them.'

'It isn't one-sided, doc. You don't work with Metallos but I do; so I know. The last two who came in for repairs have asked for fibrous elements.'

'Did they get them?'

'In one case, it was just a matter of supplying tendons; it didn't make much difference there, metal or fiber. The other wanted a blood system or its equivalent. I told him I couldn't; not without a complete rebuilding of the structure of his body in fibrous material . . . I suppose it will come to that some day. Metallos that aren't really Metallos at all, but a kind of flesh and blood.'

'You don't mind that thought?'

'Why not? And metallized human beings, too. We have two varieties of intelligence on Earth now and why bother with two. Let them approach each other and eventually we won't be able to tell the difference. Why should we want to? We'd have the best of both worlds; the advantages of man combined with those of robot.'

'You'd get a hybrid,' said the surgeon, with something that approached fierceness. 'You'd get something that is not both, but neither. Isn't it logical to suppose an individual would be too proud of his structure and identity to want to dilute it with something alien? Would he *want* mongrelization?'

'That's segregationist talk.'

'Then let it be that.' The surgeon said with calm emphasis, 'I believe in being what one is. I wouldn't change a bit of my own structure for any reason. If some of it absolutely required replacement, I would have that replacement as close to the original in nature as could possibly be managed. I am *myself*; well pleased to be myself; and would not be anything else.'

He had finished now and had to prepare for the operation. He placed his strong hands into the heating oven and let them reach the dull red-hot glow that would sterilize them completely. For all his impassioned words, his voice had never risen, and on his burnished metal face there was (as always) no sign of expression.

Robbie

'Ninety-eight – ninety-nine – *one hundred*.' Gloria withdrew her chubby little forearm from before her eyes and stood for a moment, wrinkling her nose and blinking in the sunlight. Then, trying to watch in all directions at once, she withdrew a few cautious steps from the tree against which she had been leaning.

She craned her neck to investigate the possibilities of a clump of bushes to the right and then withdrew farther to obtain a better angle for viewing its dark recesses. The quiet was profound except for the incessant buzzing of insects and the occasional chirrup of some hardy bird, braving the midday sun.

Gloria pouted, 'I bet he went inside the house, and I've told him a million times that that's not fair.'

With tiny lips pressed together tightly and a severe frown crinkling her forehead, she moved determinedly toward the two-story building up past the driveway.

Too late she heard the rustling sound behind her, followed by the distinctive and rhythmic clump-clump of Robbie's metal feet. She whirled about to see her triumphing companion emerge from hiding and make for the home-tree at full speed.

Gloria shrieked in dismay, 'Wait, Robbie! That wasn't fair, Robbie! You promised you wouldn't run until I found you.' Her little feet could make no headway at all against Robbie's giant strides. Then, within ten feet of the goal, Robbie's pace slowed suddenly to the merest of crawls, and Gloria, with one final burst of wild speed, dashed pantingly past him to touch the welcome bark of home-tree first.

Gleefully, she turned on the faithful Robbie, and with the basest of ingratitude, rewarded him for his sacrifice, by taunting him cruelly for a lack of running ability.

'Robbie can't run,' she shouted at the top of her eight-year-old voice. 'I can beat him any day. I can beat him any day.' She chanted the words in a shrill rhythm.

Robbie didn't answer, of course – not in words. He pantomimed running, instead, inching away until Gloria found herself running after him as he dodged her narrowly, forcing her to veer in helpless circles, little arms outstretched and fanning at the air.

'Robbie,' she squealed, 'stand still!' – And the laughter was forced out of her in breathless jerks.

– Until he turned suddenly and caught her up, whirling her round, so that for her the world fell away for a moment with a blue emptiness beneath, and green trees stretching hungrily downward toward the void. Then she was down in the grass again, leaning against Robbie's leg and still holding a hard, metal finger.

After a while, her breath returned. She pushed uselessly at her disheveled hair in vague imitation of one of her mother's gestures and twisted to see if her dress were torn.

She slapped her hand against Robbie's torso, 'Bad boy! I'll spank you!'

And Robbie cowered, holding his hands over his face so that she had to add, 'No, I won't, Robbie. I won't spank you. But anyway, it's my turn to hide now because you've got longer legs and you promised not to run till I found you.'

Robbie nodded his head – a small parallelepiped with rounded edges and corners attached to a similar but much larger parallelepiped that served as torso by means of a short, flexible stalk – and obediently faced the tree. A thin, metal film descended over his glowing eyes and from within his body came a steady, resonant ticking.

'Don't peek now – and don't skip any numbers,' warned Gloria, and scurried for cover.

With unvarying regularity, seconds were ticked off, and at the hundredth, up went the eyelids, and the glowing red of Robbie's eyes swept the prospect. They rested for a moment on a bit of colorful gingham that protruded from behind a boulder. He advanced a few steps and convinced himself that it was Gloria who squatted behind it.

Slowly, remaining always between Gloria and home-tree, he advanced on the hiding place, and when Gloria was plainly in sight and could no longer even theorize to herself that she was not seen, he extended one arm toward her, slapping the other against his leg so that it rang again. Gloria emerged sulkily.

'You peeked!' she exclaimed, with gross unfairness. 'Besides I'm tired of playing hide-and-seek. I want a ride.'

But Robbie was hurt at the unjust accusation, so he seated himself carefully and shook his head ponderously from side to side.

Gloria changed her tone to one of gentle coaxing immediately, 'Come on, Robbie. I didn't mean it about the peeking. Give me a ride.'

Robbie was not to be won over so easily, though. He gazed stubbornly at the sky, and shook his head even more emphatically.

'Please, Robbie, please give me a ride.' She encircled his neck with rosy arms and hugged tightly. Then, changing moods in a moment, she moved away. 'If you don't, I'm going to cry,' and her face twisted appallingly in preparation.

Hard-hearted Robbie paid scant attention to this dreadful possibility, and shook his head a third time. Gloria found it necessary to play her trump card.

'If you don't,' she exclaimed warmly, 'I won't tell you any more stories, that's all. Not one – '

Robbie gave in immediately and unconditionally before this ultimatum, nodding his head vigorously until the metal of his neck hummed. Carefully, he raised the little girl and placed her on his broad, flat shoulders.

Gloria's threatened tears vanished immediately and she crowed with delight. Robbie's metal skin, kept at a constant temperature of seventy by the high resistance coils within, felt nice and comfortable, while the beautifully loud sound her heels made as they bumped rhythmically against his chest was enchanting.

'You're an air-coaster, Robbie, you're a big, silver air-coaster. Hold out your arms straight. – You *got* to, Robbie, if you're going to be an air-coaster.'

The logic was irrefutable. Robbie's arms were wings catching the air currents and he was a silver 'coaster.

Gloria twisted the robot's head and leaned to the right. He banked sharply. Gloria equipped the 'coaster with a motor that went 'Br-r-r' and then with weapons that went 'Powie' and 'Sh-sh-shshsh.' Pirates were giving chase and the ship's blasters were coming into play. The pirates dropped in a steady rain.

'Got another one. – Two more,' she cried.

Then 'Faster, men,' Gloria said pompously, 'we're running out of ammunition.' She aimed over her shoulder with undaunted courage and Robbie was a blunt-nosed spaceship zooming through the void at maximum acceleration.

Clear across the field he sped, to the patch of tall grass on the other side, where he stopped with a suddenness that evoked a shriek from his flushed rider, and then tumbled her onto the soft, green carpet.

Gloria gasped and panted, and gave voice to intermittent whispered exclamations of 'That was *nice*!'

Robbie waited until she had caught her breath and then pulled gently at a lock of hair.

'You want something?' said Gloria, eyes wide in an apparently artless complexity that fooled her huge 'nursemaid' not at all. He pulled the curl harder.

'Oh, I know. You want a story.'

Robbie nodded rapidly.

'Which one?'

Robbie made a semi-circle in the air with one finger.

The little girl protested, '*Again*? I've told you Cinderella a million times. Aren't you tired of it? – It's for babies.'

Another semi-circle.

'Oh, well,' Gloria composed herself, ran over the details of the tale in her mind (together with her own elaborations, of which she had several) and began:

'Are you ready? Well – once upon a time there was a beautiful little girl whose name was Ella. And she had a terribly cruel step-mother and two very ugly and *very* cruel step-sisters and – '

Gloria was reaching the very climax of the tale – midnight was striking and everything was changing back to the shabby originals lickety-split, while Robbie listened tensely with burning eyes – when the interruption came.

'Gloria!'

It was the high-pitched sound of a woman who has been calling not once, but several times; and had the nervous tone of one in whom anxiety was beginning to overcome impatience.

'Mamma's calling me,' said Gloria, not quite happily. 'You'd better carry me back to the house, Robbie.'

Robbie obeyed with alacrity for somehow there was that in him which judged it best to obey Mrs Weston, without as much as a scrap of hesitation. Gloria's father was rarely home in the daytime except on Sunday – today, for instance – and when he was, he proved a genial and understanding person. Gloria's mother, however, was a source of uneasiness to Robbie and there was always the impulse to sneak away from her sight.

Mrs Weston caught sight of them the minute they rose above the masking tufts of long grass and retired inside the house to wait.

'I've shouted myself hoarse, Gloria,' she said, severely. 'Where were you?'

'I was with Robbie,' quavered Gloria. 'I was telling him Cinderella, and I forgot it was dinner-time.'

'Well, it's a pity Robbie forgot, too.' Then, as if that reminded her of the robot's presence, she whirled upon him. 'You may go, Robbie. She doesn't need you now.' Then, brutally, 'And don't come back till I call you.'

Robbie turned to go, but hesitated as Gloria cried out in his defense, 'Wait, Mamma, you got to let him stay. I didn't finish Cinderella for him. I said I would tell him Cinderella and I'm not finished.'

'Gloria!'

'Honest and truly, Mamma, he'll stay so quiet, you won't even know he's here. He can sit on the chair in the corner, and he won't say a word, – I mean he won't *do* anything. Will you, Robbie?'

Robbie, appealed to, nodded his massive head up and down once.

'Gloria, if you don't stop this at once, you shan't see Robbie for a whole week.'

The girl's eyes fell, 'All right! But Cinderella is his favorite story and I didn't finish it. – And he likes it so much.'

The robot left with a disconsolate step and Gloria choked back a sob.

George Weston was comfortable. It was a habit of his to be comfortable on Sunday afternoons. A good, hearty dinner below the hatches; a nice, soft, dilapidated couch on which to sprawl; a copy of the *Times*; slippered feet and shirtless chest; – how could anyone *help* but be comfortable?

He wasn't pleased, therefore, when his wife walked in. After ten years of married life, he still was so unutterably foolish as to love her, and there was no question that he was always glad to see her – still, Sunday afternoons just after dinner were sacred to him and his idea of solid comfort was to be left in utter solitude for two or three hours. Consequently, he fixed his eye firmly upon the latest reports of the Lefebre-Yoshida expedition to Mars (this one was to take off from Lunar Base and might actually succeed) and pretended she wasn't there.

Mrs Weston waited patiently for two minutes, then impatiently for two more, and finally broke the silence.

'George!'

'Hmpph?'

'George, I say! *Will* you put down that paper and look at me?'

The paper rustled to the floor and Weston turned a weary face toward his wife, 'What is it, dear?'

'You know what it is, George. It's Gloria and that terrible machine.'

'What terrible machine?'

'Now don't pretend you don't know what I'm talking about. It's that robot Gloria calls Robbie. He doesn't leave her for a moment.'

'Well, why should he? He's not supposed to. And he certainly isn't a terrible machine. He's the best darn robot money can buy and I'm damned sure he set me back half a year's income. He's worth it, though – darn sight cleverer than half my office staff.'

He made a move to pick up the paper again, but his wife was quicker and snatched it away.

'You listen to *me*, George. I won't have my daughter entrusted to a machine – and I don't care how clever it is. It has no soul, and no one knows what it may be thinking. A child just isn't *made* to be guarded by a thing of metal.'

Weston frowned, 'When did you decide this? He's been with Gloria two years now and I haven't seen you worry till now.'

'It was different at first. It was a novelty; it took a load off me, and – and it was a fashionable thing to do. But now I don't know. The neighbors – '

'Well, what have the neighbors to do with it? Now, look. A robot is infinitely more to be trusted than a human nursemaid. Robbie was constructed for only one purpose really – to be the companion of a little child. His entire "mentality" has been created for the purpose. He just can't help being faithful and loving and kind. He's a machine – *made* so. That's more than you can say for humans.'

'But something might go wrong. Some – some – ' Mrs Weston was a bit hazy about the insides of a robot, 'some little jigger will come loose and the awful thing will go berserk and – and – ' She couldn't bring herself to complete the quite obvious thought.

'Nonsense,' Weston denied, with an involuntary nervous shiver. 'That's completely ridiculous. We had a long discussion at the time we bought Robbie about the First Law of Robotics. You *know* that it is impossible for a robot to harm a human being; that long before enough can go wrong to alter that First Law, a robot would be completely inoperable. It's a mathematical impossibility. Besides I have an engineer from US Robots here twice a year to give the poor gadget a complete overhaul. Why, there's no more chance of anything at all going wrong with Robbie than there is of you or I suddenly going looney – considerably less, in fact. Besides, how are you going to take him away from Gloria?'

He made another futile stab at the paper and his wife tossed it angrily into the next room.

'That's just it, George! She won't play with anyone else.

There are dozens of little boys and girls that she should make friends with, but she won't. She won't go *near* them unless I make her. That's no way for a little girl to grow up. You want her to be normal, don't you? You want her to be able to take her part in society.'

'You're jumping at shadows, Grace. Pretend Robbie's a dog. I've seen hundreds of children who would rather have their dog than their father.'

'A dog is different, George. We *must* get rid of that horrible thing. You can sell it back to the company. I've asked, and you can.'

'You've *asked*? Now look here, Grace, let's not go off the deep end. We're keeping the robot until Gloria is older and I don't want the subject brought up again.' And with that he walked out of the room in a huff.

Mrs Weston met her husband at the door two evenings later. 'You'll have to listen to this, George. There's bad feeling in the village.'

'About what?' asked Weston. He stepped into the washroom and drowned out any possible answer by the splash of water.

Mrs Weston waited. She said, 'About Robbie.'

Weston stepped out, towel in hand, face red and angry, 'What are you talking about?'

'Oh, it's been building up and building up. I've tried to close my eyes to it, but I'm not going to any more. Most of the villagers consider Robbie dangerous. Children aren't allowed to go near our place in the evenings.'

'We trust *our* child with the thing.'

'Well, people aren't reasonable about these things.'

'Then to hell with them.'

'Saying that doesn't solve the problem. I've got to do my shopping down there. I've got to meet them every day. And it's even worse in the city these days when it comes to robots. New York has just passed an ordinance keeping all robots off the streets between sunset and sunrise.'

'All right, but they can't stop us from keeping a robot in our home. – Grace, this is one of your campaigns. I recognize it. But it's no use. The answer is still, no! We're keeping Robbie!'

And yet he loved his wife – and what was worse, his wife knew it. George Weston, after all, was only a man – poor thing – and his wife made full use of every device which a clumsier and more scrupulous sex has learned, with reason and futility, to fear.

Ten times in the ensuing week, he cried, 'Robbie stays, – and that's *final*!' and each time it was weaker and accompanied by a louder and more agonized groan.

Came the day at last, when Weston approached his daughter guiltily and suggested a 'beautiful' visivox show in the village.

Gloria clapped her hands happily, 'Can Robbie go?'

'No, dear,' he said, and winced at the sound of his voice, 'they won't allow robots at the visivox – but you can tell him all about it when you get home.' He stumbled all over the last few words and looked away.

Gloria came back from town bubbling over with enthusiasm, for the visivox had been a gorgeous spectacle indeed.

She waited for her father to maneuver the jet-car into the sunken garage. 'Wait till I tell Robbie, Daddy. He would have liked it like anything. – Especially when Francis Fran was backing away so-o-o quietly, and backed right into one of the Leopard-Men and had to run.' She laughed again, 'Daddy, are there really Leopard-Men on the Moon?'

'Probably not,' said Weston absently. 'It's just funny make-believe.' He couldn't take much longer with the car. He'd have to face it.

Gloria ran across the lawn. 'Robbie. – Robbie!'

Then she stopped suddenly at the sight of a beautiful collie which regarded her out of serious brown eyes as it wagged its tail on the porch.

'Oh, what a nice dog!' Gloria climbed the steps, approached cautiously and patted it. 'Is it for me, Daddy?'

Her mother had joined them. 'Yes, it is, Gloria. Isn't it nice – soft and furry. It's very gentle. It *likes* little girls.'

'Can he play games?'

'Surely. He can do any number of tricks. Would you like to see some?'

'Right away. I want Robbie to see him, too. – *Robbie*!' She stopped, uncertainly, and frowned, 'I'll bet he's just staying in his room because he's mad at me for not taking him to the visivox. You'll have to explain to him, Daddy. He might not believe me, but he knows if you say it, it's so.'

Weston's lips grew tighter. He looked toward his wife but could not catch her eye.

Gloria turned precipitously and ran down the basement steps, shouting as she went, 'Robbie – Come and see what Daddy and Mamma brought me. They brought me a dog, Robbie.'

In a minute she had returned, a frightened little girl. 'Mamma, Robbie isn't in his room. Where is he?' There was no answer and George Weston coughed and was suddenly extremely interested in an aimlessly drifting cloud. Gloria's voice quavered on the verge of tears, 'Where's Robbie, Mamma?'

Mrs Weston sat down and drew her daughter gently to her, 'Don't feel bad, Gloria. Robbie has gone away, I think.'

'Gone *away*? Where? Where's he gone away, Mamma?'

'No one knows, darling. He just walked away. We've looked and we've looked and we've looked for him, but we can't find him.'

'You mean he'll never come back again?' Her eyes were round with horror.

'We may find him soon. We'll keep looking for him. And meanwhile you can play with your nice new doggie. Look at him! His name is Lightning and he can – '

But Gloria's eyelids had overflown, 'I don't want the nasty dog – I want Robbie. I want you to find me Robbie.' Her feelings became too deep for words, and she spluttered into a shrill wail.

Mrs Weston glanced at her husband for help, but he merely shuffled his feet morosely and did not withdraw his ardent stare from the heavens, so she bent to the task of consolation, 'Why do you cry, Gloria? Robbie was only a machine, just a nasty old machine. He wasn't alive at all.'

'He was *not* no machine!' screamed Gloria, fiercely and ungrammatically. 'He was a *person* just like you and me and he was my *friend*. I want him back. Oh, Mamma, I want him back.'

Her mother groaned in defeat and left Gloria to her sorrow.

'Let her have her cry out,' she told her husband. 'Childish griefs are never lasting. In a few days, she'll forget that awful robot ever existed.'

But time proved Mrs Weston a bit too optimistic. To be sure, Gloria ceased crying, but she ceased smiling, too, and the passing days found her ever more silent and shadowy. Gradually, her attitude of passive unhappiness wore Mrs Weston down and all that kept her from yielding was the impossibility of admitting defeat to her husband.

Then, one evening, she flounced into the living room, sat down, folded her arms and looked boiling mad.

Her husband stretched his neck in order to see her over his newspaper, 'What now, Grace?'

'It's that child, George. I've had to send back the dog today. Gloria positively couldn't stand the sight of him, she said. She's driving me into a nervous breakdown.'

Weston laid down the paper and a hopeful gleam entered his eye, 'Maybe – Maybe we ought to get Robbie back. It might be done, you know. I can get in touch with – '

'No!' she replied, grimly. 'I won't hear of it. We're not giving up that easily. My child shall *not* be brought up by a robot if it takes years to break her of it.'

Weston picked up his paper again with a disappointed air. 'A year of this will have me prematurely gray.'

'You're a big help, George,' was the frigid answer. 'What Gloria needs is a change of environment. Of course she can't forget Robbie here. How can she when every tree and rock reminds her of him? It is really the *silliest* situation I have ever heard of. Imagine a child pining away for the loss of a robot.'

'Well, stick to the point. What's the change in environment you're planning?'

'We're going to take her to New York.'

'The city! In August! Say, do you know what New York is like in August? It's unbearable.'

'Millions do bear it.'

'They don't have a place like this to go to. If they didn't have to stay in New York, they wouldn't.'

'Well, *we* have to. I say we're leaving now – or as soon as we can make the arrangements. In the city, Gloria will find sufficient interests and sufficient friends to perk her up and make her forget that machine.'

'Oh, Lord,' groaned the lesser half, 'those frying pavements!'

'We have to,' was the unshaken response. 'Gloria has lost five pounds in the last month and my little girl's health is more important to me than your comfort.'

'It's a pity you didn't think of your little girl's health before you deprived her of her pet robot,' he muttered – but to himself.

* * *

Gloria displayed immediate signs of improvement when told of the impending trip to the city. She spoke little of it, but when she did, it was always with lively anticipation. Again, she began to smile and to eat with something of her former appetite.

Mrs Weston hugged herself for joy and lost no opportunity to triumph over her still skeptical husband.

'You see, George, she helps with the packing like a little angel, and chatters away as if she hadn't a care in the world. It's just as I told you – all we need do is substitute other interests.'

'Hmpph,' was the skeptical response, 'I hope so.'

Preliminaries were gone through quickly. Arrangements were made for the preparation of their city home and a couple were engaged as housekeepers for the country home. When the day of the trip finally did come, Gloria was all but her old self again, and no mention of Robbie passed her lips at all.

In high good-humor the family took a taxi-gyro to the airport (Weston would have preferred using his own private 'gyro, but it was only a two-seater with no room for baggage) and entered the waiting liner.

'Come, Gloria,' called Mrs Weston. 'I've saved you a seat near the window so you can watch the scenery.'

Gloria trotted down the aisle cheerily, flattened her nose into a white oval against the thick clear glass, and watched with an intentness that increased as the sudden coughing of the motor drifted backward into the interior. She was too young to be frightened when the ground dropped away as if let through a trap-door and she herself suddenly became twice her usual weight, but not too young to be mightily interested. It wasn't until the ground had changed into a tiny patch-work quilt that she withdrew her nose, and faced her mother again.

'Will we soon be in the city, Mamma?' she asked,

rubbing her chilled nose, and watching with interest as the patch of moisture which her breath had formed on the pane shrank slowly and vanished.

'In about half an hour, dear.' Then, with just the faintest trace of anxiety, 'Aren't you glad we're going? Don't you think you'll be very happy in the city with all the buildings and people and things to see? We'll go to the visivox every day and see shows and go to the circus and the beach and – '

'Yes, Mamma,' was Gloria's unenthusiastic rejoinder. The liner passed over a bank of clouds at the moment, and Gloria was instantly absorbed in the unusual spectacle of clouds underneath one. Then they were over clear sky again, and she turned to her mother with a sudden mysterious air of secret knowledge.

'*I* know why we're going to the city, Mamma.'

'Do you?' Mrs Weston was puzzled. 'Why, dear?'

'You didn't tell me because you wanted it to be a surprise, but *I* know.' For a moment, she was lost in admiration at her own acute penetration, and then she laughed gaily. 'We're going to New York so we can find Robbie, aren't we? – With detectives.'

The statement caught George Weston in the middle of a drink of water, with disastrous results. There was a sort of strangled gasp, a geyser of water, and then a bout of choking coughs. When all was over, he stood there, a red-faced, water-drenched and very, very annoyed person.

Mrs Weston maintained her composure, but when Gloria repeated her question in a more anxious tone of voice, she found her temper rather bent.

'Maybe,' she retorted, tartly. 'Now sit and be still, for Heaven's sake.'

New York City, 1998 AD, was a paradise for the sight-seer more than ever in its history. Gloria's parents realized this and made the most of it.

On direct orders from his wife, George Weston arranged to have his business take care of itself for a month or so, in order to be free to spend the time in what he termed 'dissipating Gloria to the verge of ruin.' Like everything else Weston did, this was gone about in an efficient, thorough, and business-like way. Before the month had passed, nothing that could be done had not been done.

She was taken to the top of the half-mile-tall Roosevelt Building, to gaze down in awe upon the jagged panorama of rooftops that blended far off in the fields of Long Island and the flatlands of New Jersey. They visited the zoos where Gloria stared in delicious fright at the 'real live lion' (rather disappointed that the keepers fed him raw steaks, instead of human beings, as she had expected), and asked insistently and peremptorily to see 'the whale.'

The various museums came in for their share of attention, together with the parks and the beaches and the aquarium.

She was taken halfway up the Hudson in an excursion steamer fitted out in the archaism of the mad Twenties. She travelled into the stratosphere on an exhibition trip, where the sky turned deep purple and the stars came out and the misty earth below looked like a huge concave bowl. Down under the waters of the Long Island Sound she was taken in a glass-walled sub-sea vessel, where in a green and wavering world, quaint and curious sea-things ogled her and wiggled suddenly away.

On a more prosaic level, Mrs Weston took her to the departmental stores where she could revel in another type of fairyland.

In fact, when the month had nearly sped, the Westons were convinced that everything conceivable had been done to take Gloria's mind once and for all off the departed Robbie – but they were not quite sure they had succeeded.

The fact remained that wherever Gloria went, she displayed the most absorbed and concentrated interest in such robots as happened to be present. No matter how exciting the spectacle before her, nor how novel to her girlish eyes, she turned away instantly if the corner of her eye caught a glimpse of metallic movement.

Mrs Weston went out of her way to keep Gloria away from all robots.

And the matter was finally climaxed in the episode at the Museum of Science and Industry. The Museum had announced a special 'children's program' in which exhibits of scientific witchery scaled down to the child mind were to be shown. The Westons, of course, placed it upon their list of 'absolutely.'

It was while the Westons were standing totally absorbed in the exploits of a powerful electro-magnet that Mrs Weston suddenly became aware of the fact that Gloria was no longer with her. Initial panic gave way to calm decision and, enlisting the aid of three attendants, a careful search was begun.

Gloria, of course, was not one to wander aimlessly, however. For her age, she was an unusually determined and purposeful girl, quite full of the maternal genes in that respect. She had seen a huge sign on the third floor, which had said, 'This Way to the Talking Robot.' Having spelled it out to herself and having noticed that her parents did not seem to wish to move in the proper direction, she did the obvious thing. Waiting for an opportune moment of parental distraction, she calmly disengaged herself and followed the sign.

The Talking Robot was a *tour de force*, a thoroughly impractical device, possessing publicity value only. Once an hour, an escorted group stood before it and asked questions of the robot engineer in charge in careful whispers. Those the engineer decided were suitable for the robot's circuits were transmitted to the Talking Robot.

It was rather dull. It may be nice to know that the square of fourteen is one hundred ninety-six, that the temperature at the moment is 72 degrees Fahrenheit, and the air-pressure 30.02 inches of mercury, that the atomic weight of sodium is 23, but one doesn't really need a robot for that. One especially does not need an unwieldy, totally immobile mass of wires and coils spreading over twenty-five square yards.

Few people bothered to return for a second helping, but one girl in her middle teens sat quietly on a bench waiting for a third. She was the only one in the room when Gloria entered.

Gloria did not look at her. To her at the moment, another human being was but an inconsiderable item. She saved her attention for this large thing with the wheels. For a moment, she hesitated in dismay. It didn't look like any robot she had ever seen.

Cautiously and doubtfully she raised her treble voice, 'Please, Mr Robot, sir, are you the Talking Robot, sir?' She wasn't sure, but it seemed to her that a robot that actually talked was worth a great deal of politeness.

(The girl in her mid-teens allowed a look of intense concentration to cross her thin, plain face. She whipped out a small notebook and began writing in rapid pot-hooks.)

There was an oily whir of gears and a mechanically-timbred voice boomed out in words that lacked accent and intonation, 'I – am – the – robot – that – talks.'

Gloria stared at it ruefully. It *did* talk, but the sound came from inside somewheres. There was no *face* to talk to. She said, 'Can you help me, Mr Robot, sir?'

The Talking Robot was designed to answer questions, and only such questions as it could answer had ever been put to it. It was quite confident of its ability, therefore. 'I – can – help – you.'

'Thank you, Mr Robot sir. Have you seen Robbie?'

'Who – is – Robbie?'

'He's a robot, Mr Robot, sir.' She stretched to tip-toes. 'He's about so high, Mr Robot, sir, only higher, and he's very nice. He's got a head, you know. I mean you haven't, but he has, Mr Robot, sir.'

The Talking Robot had been left behind, 'A – robot?'

'Yes, Mr Robot, sir. A robot just like you, except he can't talk, of course, and – looks like a real person.'

'A – robot – like – me?'

'Yes, Mr Robot, sir.'

To which the Talking Robot's only response was an erratic splutter and an occasional incoherent sound. The radical generalization offered it, i.e., its existence, not as a particular object, but as a member of a general group, was too much for it. Loyally, it tried to encompass the concept and half a dozen coils burnt out. Little warning signals were buzzing.

(The girl in her mid-teens left at that point. She had enough for her Physics-1 paper on 'Practical Aspects of Robotics.' This paper was Susan Calvin's first of many on the subject).

Gloria stood waiting, with carefully concealed impatience, for the machine's answer when she heard the cry behind her of 'There she is,' and recognized that cry as her mother's.

'What are you doing here, you bad girl?' cried Mrs Weston, anxiety dissolving at once into anger. 'Do you know you frightened your mamma and daddy almost to death? Why did you run away?'

The robot engineer had also dashed in, tearing his hair, and demanding who of the gathering crowd had tampered with the machine. 'Can't anybody read signs?' he yelled. 'You're not allowed in here without an attendant.'

Gloria raised her grieved voice over the din, 'I only came to see the Talking Robot, Mamma. I thought he might know where Robbie was because they're both robots.' And then, as the thought of Robbie was suddenly brought forcefully home to her, she burst into a sudden storm of tears, 'And I *got* to find Robbie, Mamma. I *got* to.'

Mrs Weston strangled a cry, and said, 'Oh, good Heavens. Come home, George. This is more than I can stand.'

That evening, George Weston left for several hours, and the next morning, he approached his wife with something that looked suspiciously like smug complacence.

'I've got an idea, Grace.'

'About what?' was the gloomy, uninterested query.

'About Gloria.'

'You're not going to suggest buying back that robot?'

'No, of course not.'

'Then go ahead. I might as well listen to you. Nothing *I've* done seems to have done any good.'

'All right. Here's what I've been thinking. The whole trouble with Gloria is that she thinks of Robbie as a *person* and not as a *machine*. Naturally, she can't forget him. Now if we managed to convince her that Robbie was nothing more than a mess of steel and copper in the form of sheets and wires with electricity its juice of life, how long would her longings last? It's the psychological attack, if you see my point.'

'How do you plan to do it?'

'Simple. Where do you suppose I went last night? I persuaded Robertson of US Robots and Mechanical Men Corporation to arrange for a complete tour of his premises tomorrow. The three of us will go, and by the time we're through, Gloria will have it drilled into her that a robot is *not* alive.'

Mrs Weston's eyes widened gradually and something glinted in her eyes that was quite like sudden admiration, 'Why, George, that's a *good* idea.'

And George Weston's vest buttons strained. 'Only kind I have,' he said.

Mr Struthers was a conscientious General Manager and naturally inclined to be a bit talkative. The combination, therefore, resulted in a tour that was fully explained, perhaps even overabundantly explained, at every step. However Mrs Weston was not bored. Indeed, she stopped him several times and begged him to repeat his statements in simpler language so that Gloria might understand. Under the influence of this appreciation of his narrative powers, Mr Struthers expanded genially and became ever more communicative, if possible.

George Weston, himself, showed a gathering impatience.

'Pardon me, Struthers,' he said, breaking into the middle of a lecture on the photo-electric cell, 'haven't you a section of the factory where only robot labor is employed?'

'Eh? Oh, yes! Yes, indeed!' He smiled at Mrs Weston. 'A vicious circle in a way, robots creating more robots. Of course, we are not making a general practice out of it. For one thing, the unions would never let us. But we can turn out a very few robots using robot labor exclusively, merely as a sort of scientific experiment. You see,' he tapped his pince-nez into one palm argumentatively, 'what the labor unions don't realize – and I say this as a man who has always been very sympathetic with the labor movement in general – is that the advent of the robot, while involving some dislocation to begin with, will, inevitably – '

'Yes, Struthers,' said Weston, 'but about that section of the factory you speak of – may we see it? It would be very interesting, I'm sure.'

'Yes! Yes, of course!' Mr Struthers replaced his pince-nez in one convulsive movement and gave vent to a soft cough of discomfiture. 'Follow me, please.'

He was comparatively quiet while leading the three

through a long corridor and down a flight of stairs. Then, when they had entered a large well-lit room that buzzed with metallic activity, the sluices opened and the flood of explanation poured forth again.

'There you are!' he said with pride in his voice. 'Robots only! Five men act as overseers and they don't even stay in this room. In five years, that is, since we began this project, not a single accident has occurred. Of course, the robots here assembled are comparatively simple, but . . .'

The General Manager's voice had long died to a rather soothing murmur in Gloria's ears. The whole trip seemed rather dull and pointless to her, though there *were* many robots in sight. None were even remotely like Robbie, though, and she surveyed them with open contempt.

In this room, there weren't any people at all, she noticed. Then her eyes fell upon six or seven robots busily engaged at a round table halfway across the room. They widened in incredulous surprise. It was a big room. She couldn't see for sure, but one of the robots looked like – looked like – *it was!*

'*Robbie!*' Her shriek pierced the air, and one of the robots about the table faltered and dropped the tool he was holding. Gloria went almost mad with joy. Squeezing through the railing before either parent could stop her, she dropped lightly to the floor a few feet below, and ran toward her Robbie, arms waving and hair flying.

And the three horrified adults, as they stood frozen in their tracks, saw what the excited little girl did not see, – a huge, lumbering tractor bearing blindly down upon its appointed track.

It took split-seconds for Weston to come to his senses, and those split-seconds meant everything, for Gloria could not be overtaken. Although Weston vaulted the railing in a wild attempt, it was obviously hopeless. Mr Struthers signaled wildly to the overseers to stop the tractor, but the overseers were only human and it took time to act.

It was only Robbie that acted immediately and with precision.

With metal legs eating up the space between himself and his little mistress he charged down from the opposite direction. Everything then happened at once. With one sweep of an arm, Robbie snatched up Gloria, slackening his speed not one iota, and, consequently, knocking every breath of air out of her. Weston, not quite comprehending all that was happening, felt, rather than saw, Robbie brush past him, and came to a sudden bewildered halt. The tractor intersected Gloria's path half a second after Robbie had, rolled on ten feet further and came to a grinding, long-drawn-out stop.

Gloria regained her breath, submitted to a series of passionate hugs on the part of both her parents and turned eagerly toward Robbie. As far as she was concerned, nothing had happened except that she had found her friend.

But Mrs Weston's expression had changed from one of relief to one of dark suspicion. She turned to her husband, and, despite her disheveled and undignified appearance, managed to look quite formidable, '*You* engineered this, *didn't* you?'

George Weston swabbed at a hot forehead with his handkerchief. His hand was unsteady, and his lips could curve only into a tremulous and exceedingly weak smile.

Mrs Weston pursued the thought, 'Robbie wasn't designed for engineering or construction work. He couldn't be of any use to them. You had him placed there deliberately so that Gloria would find him. You know you did.'

'Well, I did,' said Weston. 'But, Grace, how was I to know the reunion would be so violent? And Robbie has saved her life; you'll have to admit that. You *can't* send him away again.'

Grace Weston considered. She turned toward Gloria and

Robbie and watched them abstractedly for a moment. Gloria had a grip about the robot's neck that would have asphyxiated any creature but one of metal, and was prattling nonsense in half-hysterical frenzy. Robbie's chrome-steel arms (capable of bending a bar of steel two inches in diameter into a pretzel) wound about the little girl gently and lovingly, and his eyes glowed a deep, deep red.

'Well,' said Mrs Weston, at last, 'I guess he can stay with us until he rusts.'

Some Humanoid Robots

In science fiction it is not uncommon to have a robot built with a surface, at least, of synthetic flesh; and an appearance that is, at best, indistinguishable from the human being. Sometimes such humanoid robots are called 'androids' (from a Greek term meaning 'manlike') and some writers are meticulous in making the distinction. I am not. To me a robot is a robot.

But then, Karel Čapek's play *R.U.R.*, which introduced the term 'robot' to the world in 1920, did not involve robots in the strictest sense of the word. The robots manufactured by Rossum's Universal Robots (the 'R.U.R.' of the title) were androids.

One of the three stories in this section, 'Let's Get Together,' is the only story in the book in which robots don't actually appear, and 'Mirror Image' is a sequel (of sorts) to my robot novels THE CAVES OF STEEL and THE NAKED SUN.

Let's Get Together

A kind of peace had endured for a century and people had forgotten what anything else was like. They would scarcely have known how to react had they discovered that a kind of war had finally come.

Certainly, Elias Lynn, Chief of the Bureau of Robotics, wasn't sure how he ought to react when *he* finally found out. The Bureau of Robotics was headquartered in Cheyenne, in line with the century-old trend toward decentralization, and Lynn stared dubiously at the young Security officer from Washington who had brought the news.

Elias Lynn was a large man, almost charmingly homely, with pale blue eyes that bulged a bit. Men weren't usually comfortable under the stare of those eyes, but the Security officer remained calm.

Lynn decided that his first reaction ought to be incredulity. Hell, it *was* incredulity! He just didn't believe it!

He eased himself back in his chair and said, 'How certain is the information?'

The Security officer, who had introduced himself as Ralph G. Breckenridge and had presented credentials to match, had the softness of youth about him; full lips, plump cheeks that flushed easily, and guileless eyes. His clothing was out of line with Cheyenne but it suited a universally air-conditioned Washington, where Security, despite everything, was still centered.

Breckenridge flushed and said, 'There's no doubt about it.'

'You people know all about Them, I suppose,' said Lynn and was unable to keep a trace of sarcasm out of his tone.

He was not particularly aware of his use of a slightly stressed pronoun in his reference to the enemy, the equivalent of capitalization in print. It was a cultural habit of this generation and the one preceding. No one said the 'East' or the 'Reds' or the 'Soviets' or the 'Russians' anymore. That would have been too confusing, since some of Them weren't of the East, weren't Reds, Soviets, and especially not Russians. It was much simpler to say We and They, and much more precise.

Travelers had frequently reported that They did the same in reverse. Over there, They were 'We' (in the appropriate language) and We were 'They.'

Scarcely anyone gave thought to such things any more. It was all quite comfortable and casual. There was no hatred, even. At the beginning, it had been called a Cold War. Now it was only a game, almost a good-natured game, with unspoken rules and a kind of decency about it.

Lynn said abruptly, 'Why should They want to disturb the situation?'

He rose and stood staring at a wall map of the world, split into two regions with faint edgings of color. An irregular portion on the left of the map was edged in a mild green. A smaller, but just as irregular, portion on the right of the map was bordered in a washed-out pink. We and They.

The map hadn't changed much in a century. The loss of Formosa and the gain of East Germany some eighty years before had been the last territorial switch of importance.

There had been another change, though, that was significant enough and that was in the colors. Two generations before, Their territory had been a brooding, bloody red, Ours a pure and undefiled white. Now there was a neutrality about the colors. Lynn had seen Their maps and it was the same on Their side.

'They wouldn't do it,' he said.

'They are doing it,' said Breckenridge, 'and you had

better accustom yourself to the fact. Of course, sir, I realize that it isn't pleasant to think that They may be that far ahead of us in robotics.'

His eyes remained as guileless as ever, but the hidden knife-edges of the words plunged deep, and Lynn quivered at the impact.

Of course, that would account for why the Chief of Robotics learned of this so late and through a Security officer at that. He had lost caste in the eyes of the Government; if Robotics had really failed in the struggle, Lynn could expect no political mercy.

Lynn said wearily, 'Even if what you say is true, They're not far ahead of us. We could build humanoid robots.'

'Have we, sir?'

'Yes. As a matter of fact, we have built a few models for experimental purposes.'

'They were doing so ten years ago. They've made ten years' progress since.'

Lynn was disturbed. He wondered if his incredulity concerning the whole business was really the result of wounded pride and fear for his job and reputation. He was embarrassed by the possibility that this might be so, and yet he was forced into defense.

He said, 'Look, young man, the stalemate between Them and Us was never perfect in every detail, you know. They have always been ahead in one facet or another and We in some other facet or another. If They're ahead of us right now in robotics, it's because They've placed a greater proportion of Their effort into robotics than We have. And that means that some other branch of endeavor has received a greater share of Our efforts than it has to Theirs. It would mean We're ahead in force-field research or in hyperatomics, perhaps.'

Lynn felt distressed at his own statement that the stalemate wasn't perfect. It was true enough, but that was the one great danger threatening the world. The world depended on the stalemate being as perfect as possible. If the small unevennesses that always existed overbalanced too far in one direction or the other –

Almost at the beginning of what had been the Cold War, both sides had developed thermonuclear weapons, and war became unthinkable. Competition switched from the military to the economic and psychological and had stayed there ever since.

But always there was the driving effort on each side to break the stalemate, to develop a parry for every possible thrust, to develop a thrust that could not be parried in time – something that would make war possible again. And that was not because either side wanted war so desperately, but because both were afraid that the other side would make the crucial discovery first.

For a hundred years each side had kept the struggle even. And in the process, peace had been maintained for a hundred years while, as byproducts of the continuously intensive research, force fields had been produced and solar energy and insect control and robots. Each side was making a beginning in the understanding of mentalics, which was the name given to the biochemistry and biophysics of thought. Each side had its outposts on the Moon and on Mars. Mankind was advancing in giant strides under forced draft.

It was even necessary for both sides to be as decent and humane as possible among themseves, lest through cruelty and tyranny, friends be made for the other side.

It couldn't be that the stalemate would now be broken and that there would be war.

Lynn said, 'I want to consult one of my men. I want his opinion.'

'Is he trustworthy?'

Lynn looked disgusted. 'Good Lord, what man in

Robotics has not been investigated and cleared to death by your people? Yes, I vouch for him. If you can't trust a man like Humphrey Carl Laszlo, then we're in no position to face the kind of attack you say They are launching, no matter what else we do.'

'I've heard of Laszlo,' said Breckenridge.

'Good. Does he pass?'

'Yes.'

'Then, I'll have him in and we'll find out what he thinks about the possibility that robots could invade the USA.'

'Not exactly,' said Breckenridge, softly. 'You still don't accept the full truth. Find out what he thinks about the fact that robots have *already* invaded the USA.'

Laszlo was the grandson of a Hungarian who had broken through what had then been called the Iron Curtain, and he had a comfortable above-suspicion feeling about himself because of it. He was thick-set and balding with a pugnacious look graven forever on his snub face, but his accent was clear Harvard and he was almost excessively soft-spoken.

To Lynn, who was conscious that after years of administration he was no longer expert in the various phases of modern robotics, Laszlo was a comforting receptacle for complete knowledge. Lynn felt better because of the man's mere presence.

Lynn said, 'What do you think?'

A scowl twisted Laszlo's face ferociously. 'That They're that far ahead of us. Completely incredible. It would mean They've produced humanoids that could not be told from humans at close quarters. It would mean a considerable advance in robo-mentalics.'

'You're personally involved,' said Breckenridge, coldly. 'Leaving professional pride out of account, exactly why is it impossible that They be ahead of Us?'

Laszlo shrugged. 'I assure you that I'm well acquainted with Their literature on robotics. I know approximately where They are.'

'You know approximately where They want you to *think* They are, is what you really mean,' corrected Breckenridge. 'Have you ever visited the other side?'

'I haven't,' said Laszlo, shortly.

'Nor you, Dr Lynn?'

Lynn said, 'No, I haven't, either.'

Breckenridge said, 'Has any robotics man visited the other side in twenty-five years?' He asked the question with a kind of confidence that indicated he knew the answer.

For a matter of seconds, the atmosphere was heavy with thought. Discomfort crossed Lazlo's broad face. He said, 'As a matter of fact, They haven't held any conferences on robotics in a long time.'

'In twenty-five years,' said Breckenridge. 'Isn't that significant?'

'Maybe,' said Laszlo, reluctantly. 'Something else bothers me, though. None of Them have ever come to Our conferences on robotics. None that I can remember.'

'Were They invited?' asked Breckenridge.

Lynn, staring and worried, interposed quickly, 'Of course.'

Breckenridge said, 'Do They refuse attendance to any other types of scientific conferences We hold?'

'I don't know,' said Laszlo. He was pacing the floor now. 'I haven't heard of any cases. Have you, Chief?'

'No,' said Lynn.

Breckenridge said, 'Wouldn't you say it was as though They didn't want to be put in the position of having to return any such invitation? Or as though They were afraid one of Their men might talk too much?'

That was exactly how it seemed, and Lynn felt a

helpless conviction that Security's story was true after all steal over him.

Why else had there been no contact between sides on robotics? There had been a cross-fertilizing trickle of researchers moving in both directions in a strictly one-for-one basis for years, dating back to the days of Eisenhower and Khrushchev. There were a great many good motives for that: an honest appreciation of the supranational character of science; impulses of friendliness that are hard to wipe out completely in the individual human being; the desire to be exposed to a fresh and interesting outlook and to have your own slightly stale notions greeted by others as fresh and interesting.

The governments themselves were anxious that this continue. There was always the obvious thought that by learning all you could and telling as little as you could, your own side would gain by the exchange.

But not in the case of robotics. Not there.

Such a little thing to carry conviction. And a thing, moreover, they had known all along. Lynn thought darkly: *We've taken the complacent way out.*

Because the other side had done nothing publicly on robotics, it had been tempting to sit back smugly and be comfortable in the assurance of superiority. Why hadn't it seemed possible, even likely, that They were hiding superior cards, a trump hand, for the proper time?

Laszlo said shakenly, 'What do we do?' It was obvious that the same line of thought had carried the same conviction to him.

'Do?' parroted Lynn. It was hard to think right now of anything but the complete horror that came with conviction. There were ten humanoid robots somewhere in the United States, each one carrying a fragment of a TC bomb.

TC! The race for sheer horror in bomb-ery had ended there. TC! Total Conversion! The sun was no longer a synonym one could use. Total conversion made the sun a penny candle.

Ten humanoids, each completely harmless in separation, could, by the simple act of coming together, exceed critical mass and –

Lynn rose to his feet heavily, the dark pouches under his eyes, which ordinarily lent his ugly face a look of savage foreboding, more prominent than ever. 'It's going to be up to us to figure out ways and means of telling a humanoid from a human and then finding the humanoids.'

'How quickly?' muttered Laszlo.

'Not later than five minutes before they get together,' barked Lynn, 'and I don't know when that will be.'

Breckenridge nodded. 'I'm glad you're with us now, sir. I'm to bring you back to Washington for conference, you know.'

Lynn raised his eyebrows. 'All right.'

He wondered if, had he delayed longer in being convinced, he might not have been replaced forthwith – if some other Chief of the Bureau of Robotics might not be conferring in Washington. He suddenly wished earnestly that exactly that had come to pass.

The First Presidential Assistant was there, the Secretary of Science, the Secretary of Security, Lynn himself, and Breckenridge. Five of them sitting about a table in the dungeons of an underground fortress near Washington.

Presidential Assistant Jeffreys was an impressive man, handsome in a white-haired and just-a-trifle-jowly fashion, solid, thoughtful and as unobtrusive, politically, as a Presidential Assistant ought to be.

He spoke incisively. 'There are three questions that face us as I see it. First, when are the humanoids going to get together? Second, where are they going to get together? Third, how do we stop them before they get together?'

Secretary of Science Amberley nodded convulsively at that. He had been Dean of Northwestern Engineering before his appointment. He was thin, sharp-featured and noticeably edgy. His forefinger traced slow circles on the table.

'As far as *when* they'll get together,' he said. 'I suppose it's definite that it won't be for some time.'

'Why do you say that?' asked Lynn sharply.

'They've been in the US at least a month already. So Security says.'

Lynn turned automatically to look at Breckenridge, and Secretary of Security Macalaster intercepted the glance. Macalaster said, 'The information is reliable. Don't let Breckenridge's apparent youth fool you, Dr Lynn. That's part of his value to us. Actually, he's thirty-four and has been with the department for ten years. He has been in Moscow for nearly a year and without him, none of this terrible danger would be known to us. As it is, we have most of the details.'

'Not the crucial ones,' said Lynn.

Macalaster of Security smiled frostily. His heavy chin and close-set eyes were well-known to the public but almost nothing else about him was. He said, 'We are all finitely human, Dr Lynn. Agent Breckenridge has done a great deal.'

Presidential Assistant Jeffreys cut in. 'Let us say we have a certain amount of time. If action at the instant were necessary, it would have happened before this. It seems likely that they are waiting for a specific time. If we knew the place, perhaps the time would become self-evident.

'If they are going to TC a target, they will want to cripple us as much as possible, so it would seem that a major city would have to be it. In any case, a major metropolis is the only target worth a TC bomb. I think there are four possibilities: Washington, as the administrative center;

New York, as the financial center; and Detroit and Pittsburgh as the two chief industrial centers.'

Macalaster of Security said, 'I vote for New York. Administration and industry have both been decentralized to the point where the destruction of any one particular city won't prevent instant retaliation.'

'Then why New York?' asked Amberley of Science, perhaps more sharply than he intended. 'Finance has been decentralized as well.'

'A question of morale. It may be they intend to destroy our will to resist, to induce surrender by the sheer horror of the first blow. The greatest destruction of human life would be in the New York Metropolitan area – '

'Pretty cold-blooded,' muttered Lynn.

'I know,' said Macalaster of Security, 'but they're capable of it, if they thought it would mean final victory at a stroke. Wouldn't we – '

Presidential Assistant Jeffreys brushed back his white hair. 'Let's assume the worst. Let's assume that New York will be destroyed some time during the winter, preferably immediately after a serious blizzard when communications are at their worst and the disruption of utilities and food supplies in fringe areas will be most serious in their effect. Now, how do we stop them?'

Amberley of Science could only say, 'Finding ten men in two hundred and twenty million is an awfully small needle in an awfully large haystack.'

Jeffreys shook his head. 'You have it wrong. Ten humanoids among two hundred twenty million humans.'

'No difference,' said Amberley of Science. 'We don't know that a humanoid can be differentiated from a human at sight. Probably not.' He looked at Lynn. They all did.

Lynn said heavily, 'We in Cheyenne couldn't make one that would pass as human in the daylight.'

'But They can,' said Macalaster of Security, 'and not only

physically. We're sure of that. They've advanced mentalic procedures to the point where They can reel off the micro-electronic pattern of the brain and focus it on the positronic pathways of the robot.'

Lynn stared. 'Are you implying that They can create the replica of a human being complete with personality and memory?'

'I am.'

'Of specific human beings?'

'That's right.'

'Is this also based on Agent Breckenridge's findings?'

'Yes. The evidence can't be disputed.'

Lynn bent his head in thought for a moment. Then he said, 'Then ten men in the United States are not men but humanoids. But the originals would have had to be available to them. They couldn't be Orientals, who would be too easy to spot, so they would have to be East Europeans. How would they be introduced into this country, then? With the radar network over the entire world border as tight as a drum, how could They introduce any individual, human or humanoid, without our knowing it?'

Macalaster of Security said, 'It can be done. There are certain legitimate seepages across the border. Business-men, pilots, even tourists. They're watched, of course, on both sides. Still ten of them might have been kidnaped and used as models for humanoids. The humanoids would then be sent back in their place. Since we wouldn't expect such a substitution, it would pass us by. If they were Americans to begin with, there would be no difficulty in their getting into this country. It's as simple as that.'

'And even their friends and family could not tell the difference?'

'We must assume so. Believe me, we've been waiting for any report that might imply sudden attacks of amnesia or troublesome changes in personality. We've checked on thousands.'

Amberley of Science stared at his finger tips. 'I think ordinary measures won't work. The attack must come from the Bureau of Robotics and I depend on the chief of that bureau.'

Again eyes turned sharply, expectantly, on Lynn.

Lynn felt bitterness rise. It seemed to him that this was what the conference came to and was intended for. Nothing that had been said had not been said before. He was sure of that. There was no solution to the problem, no pregnant suggestion. It was a device for the record, a device on the part of men who gravely feared defeat and who wished the responsibility for it placed clearly and unequivocally on someone else.

And yet there was justice in it. It was in robotics that We had fallen short. And Lynn was not Lynn merely. He was Lynn of Robotics and the responsibility had to be his.

He said, 'I will do what I can.'

He spent a wakeful night and there was a haggardness about both body and soul when he sought and attained another interview with Presidential Assistant Jeffreys the next morning. Breckenridge was there, and though Lynn would have preferred a private conference, he could see the justice in the situation. It was obvious that Breckenridge had attained enormous influence with the government as a result of his successful Intelligence work. Well, why not?

Lynn said, 'Sir, I am considering the possibility that we are hopping uselessly to enemy piping.'

'In what way?'

'I'm sure that however impatient the public may grow at times, and however legislators sometimes find it expedient to talk, the government at least recognizes the world stalemate to be beneficial. They must recognize it also. Ten humanoids with one TC bomb is a trivial way of breaking the stalemate.'

'The destruction of fifteen million human beings is scarcely trivial.'

'It is from the world power standpoint. It would not so demoralize us to make us surrender or so cripple us as to convince us we could not win. There would just be the same old planetary death war that both sides have avoided so long and so successfully. And all They would have accomplished is to force us to fight minus one city. It's not enough.'

'What do you suggest?' said Jeffreys coldly. 'That They do not have ten humanoids in our country? That there is not a TC bomb waiting to get together?'

'I'll agree that those things are here, but perhaps for some reason greater than just midwinter bomb madness.'

'Such as?'

'It may be that the physical destruction resulting from the humanoids getting together is not the worst thing that can happen to us. What about the moral and intellectual destruction that comes of their being here at all? With all due respect to Agent Breckenridge, what if They *intended* for us to find out about the humanoids; what if the humanoids are never supposed to get together, but merely to remain separate in order to give us something to worry about.'

'Why?'

'Tell me this. What measures have already been taken against the humanoids? I suppose that Security is going through the files of all citizens who have ever been across the border or close enough to it to make kidnaping possible. I know, since Macalaster mentioned it yesterday, that they are following up suspicious psychiatric cases. What else?'

Jeffreys said, 'Small X-ray devices are being installed in key places in the large cities. In the mass arenas, for instance – '

'Where ten humanoids might slip in among a hundred thousand spectators of a football game or an air-polo match?'

'Exactly.'

'And concert halls and churches?'

'We must start somewhere. We can't do it all at once.'

'Particularly when panic must be avoided,' said Lynn. 'Isn't that so? It wouldn't do to have the public realize that at any unpredictable moment, some unpredictable city and its human contents would suddenly cease to exist.'

'I suppose that's obvious. What are you driving at?'

Lynn said strenuously, 'That a growing fraction of our national effort will be diverted entirely into the nasty problem of what Amberley called finding a very small needle in a very large haystack. We'll be chasing our tails madly, while They increase their research lead to the point where we find we can no longer catch up; when we must surrender without the chance even of snapping our fingers in retaliation.

'Consider further that this news will leak out as more and more people become involved in our countermeasures and more and more people begin to guess what we're doing. Then what? The panic might do us more harm than any one TC bomb.'

The Presidential Assistant said irritably, 'In Heaven's name, man, what do you suggest we do, then?'

'Nothing,' said Lynn. 'Call their bluff. Live as we have lived and gamble that They won't dare break the stalemate for the sake of a one-bomb head start.'

'Impossible!' said Jeffreys. 'Completely impossible. The welfare of all of Us is very largely in my hands, and doing nothing is the one thing I cannot do. I agree with you, perhaps, that X-ray machines at sports arenas are a kind of skin-deep measure that won't be effective, but it has to be done so that people, in the aftermath, do not come to the bitter conclusion that we tossed our country away for the sake of a subtle line of reasoning that encouraged donothingism. In fact, our countergambit will be active indeed.'

'In what way?'

Presidential Assistant Jeffreys looked at Breckenridge. The young Security officer, hitherto calmly silent, said, 'It's no use talking about a possible future break in the stalemate when the stalemate is broken now. It doesn't matter whether these humanoids explode or do not. Maybe they *are* only a bait to divert us, as you say. But the fact remains that we are a quarter of a century behind in robotics, and that may be fatal. What other advances in robotics will there be to surprise us if war does start? The only answer is to divert our entire force immediately, *now*, into a crash program of robotics research, and the first problem is to find the humanoids. Call it an exercise in robotics, if you will, or call it the prevention of the death of fifteen million men, women and children.'

Lynn shook his head helplessly. 'You *can't*. You'd be playing into their hands. They want us lured into the one blind alley while they're free to advance in all other directions.'

Jeffreys said impatiently, 'That's your guess. Breckenridge has made his suggestion through channels and the government has approved, and we will begin with an all-Science conference.'

'All-Science?'

Breckenridge said, 'We have listed every important scientist of every branch of natural science. They'll all be at Cheyenne. There will be only one point on the agenda: How to advance robotics. The major specific subheading under that will be: How to develop a receiving device for the electromagnetic fields of the cerebral cortex that will be sufficiently delicate to distinguish between a protoplasmic human brain and a positronic humanoid brain.'

Jeffreys said, 'We had hoped you would be willing to be in charge of the conference.'

'I was not consulted in this.'

'Obviously time was short, sir. Do you agree to be in charge?'

Lynn smiled briefly. It was a matter of responsibility again. The responsibility must be clearly that of Lynn of Robotics. He had the feeling it would be Breckenridge who would really be in charge. But what could he do?

He said, 'I agree.'

Breckenridge and Lynn returned together to Cheyenne, where that evening Laszlo listened with a sullen mistrust to Lynn's description of coming events.

Laszlo said, 'While you were gone, Chief, I've started putting five experimental models of humanoid structure through the testing procedures. Our men are on a twelve-hour day, with three shifts overlapping. If we've got to arrange a conference, we're going to be crowded and red-taped out of everything. Work will come to a halt.'

Breckenridge said, 'That will be only temporary. You will gain more than you lose.'

Laszlo scowled. 'A bunch of astrophysicists and geochemists around won't help a damn toward robotics.'

'Views from specialists of other fields may be helpful.'

'Are you sure? How do we know that there *is* any way of detecting brain waves or that, even if we can, there is a way of differentiating human and humanoid by wave pattern? Who set up the project anyway?'

'I did,' said Breckenridge.

'*You* did? Are you a robotics man?'

The young Security agent said calmly, 'I have studied robotics.'

'That's not the same thing.'

'I've had access to text material dealing with Russian

robotics – in Russian. Top-secret material well in advance of anything you have here.'

Lynn said ruefully, 'He has us there, Laszlo.'

'It was on the basis of that material,' Breckenridge went on, 'that I suggested this particular line of investigation. It is reasonably certain that in copying off the electromagnetic pattern of a specific human mind into a specific positronic brain, a perfectly exact duplicate cannot be made. For one thing, the most complicated positronic brain small enough to fit into a human-sized skull is hundreds of times less complex than the human brain. It can't pick up all the overtones, therefore, and there must be some way to take advantage of that fact.'

Laszlo looked impressed despite himself and Lynn smiled grimly. It was easy to resent Breckenridge and the coming intrusion of several hundred scientists of nonrobotics specialties, but the problem itself was an intriguing one. There was that consolation, at least.

It came to him quietly.

Lynn found he had nothing to do but sit in his office alone, with an executive position that had grown merely titular. Perhaps that helped. It gave him time to think, to picture the creative scientists of half the world converging on Cheyenne.

It was Breckenridge who, with cool efficiency, was handling the details of preparation. There had been a kind of confidence in the way he said, 'Let's get together and we'll lick Them.'

Let's get together.

It came to Lynn so quietly that anyone watching Lynn at that moment might have seen his eyes blink slowly twice – but surely nothing more.

He did what he had to do with a whirling detachment that kept him calm when he felt that, by all rights, he ought to be going mad.

He sought out Breckenridge in the other's improvised quarters. Breckenridge was alone and frowning. 'Is anything wrong, sir?'

Lynn said wearily, 'Everything's right, I think. I've invoked martial law.'

'What!'

'As chief of a division I can do so if I am of the opinion the situation warrants it. Over my division I can then be dictator. Chalk up one for the beauties of decentralization.'

'You will rescind that order immediately.' Breckenridge took a step forward. 'When Washington hears this, you will be ruined.'

'I'm ruined anyway. Do you think I don't realize that I've been set up for the role of the greatest villain in American history: the man who let Them break the stalemate? I have nothing to lose – and perhaps a great deal to gain.'

He laughed a little wildly. 'What a target the Division of Robotics will be, eh, Breckenridge? Only a few thousand men to be killed by a TC bomb capable of wiping out three hundred square miles in one micro-second. But five hundred of those men would be our greatest scientists. We would be in the peculiar position of having to fight a war with our brains shot out, or surrendering. I think we'd surrender.'

'But this is impossible. Lynn, do you hear me? Do you understand? How could the humanoids pass our security provisions? How could they get together?'

'But they *are* getting together! We're helping them to do so. We're ordering them to do so. Our scientists visit the other side, Breckenridge. They visit Them regularly. You made a point of how strange it was that no one in robotics did. Well, ten of those scientists are still there and in their place, ten humanoids are converging on Cheyenne.'

'That's a ridiculous guess.'

'I think it's a good one, Breckenridge. But it wouldn't

work unless we knew humanoids were in America so that we would call the conference in the first place. Quite a coincidence that you brought the news of the humanoids *and* suggested the conference *and* suggested the agenda *and* are running the show *and* know exactly which scientists were invited. Did you make sure the right ten were included?'

'Dr Lynn!' cried Breckenridge in outrage. He poised to rush forward.

Lynn said, 'Don't move. I've got a blaster here. We'll just wait for the scientists to get here one by one. One by one we'll X-ray them. One by one, we'll monitor them for radioactivity. No two will get together without being checked, and if all five hundred are clear, I'll give you my blaster and surrender to you. Only I think we'll find the ten humanoids. Sit down, Breckenridge.'

They both sat.

Lynn said, 'We wait. When I'm tired, Laszlo will spell me. We wait.'

Professor Manuelo Jiminez of the Institute of Higher Studies of Buenos Aires exploded while the stratospheric jet on which he traveled was three miles above the Amazon Valley. It was a simple chemical explosion but it was enough to destroy the plane.

Dr Herman Liebowitz of MIT exploded in a monorail, killing twenty people and injuring a hundred others.

In similar manner, Dr Auguste Marin of L'Institut Nucléonique of Montreal and seven others died at various stages of their journey to Cheyenne.

Laszlo hurtled in, pale-faced and stammering, with the first news of it. It had only been two hours that Lynn had sat there, facing Breckenridge, blaster in hand.

Laszlo said, 'I thought you were nuts, Chief, but you

were right. They *were* humanoids. They *had* to be.' He turned to stare with hate-filled eyes at Breckenridge. 'Only they were warned. *He* warned them, and now there won't be one left intact. Not one to study.'

'God!' cried Lynn and in a frenzy of haste thrust his blaster out toward Breckenridge and fired. The Security man's neck vanished; the torso fell; the head dropped, thudded against the floor and rolled crookedly.

Lynn moaned, 'I didn't understand, I thought he was a traitor. Nothing more.'

And Laszlo stood immobile, mouth open, for the moment incapable of speech.

Lynn said wildly, 'Sure, he warned them. But how could he do so while sitting in that chair unless he were equipped with built-in radio transmission? Don't you see it? Breckenridge had been in Moscow. The real Breckenridge is still there. Oh my God, there were *eleven* of them.'

Laszlo managed a hoarse squeak. 'Why didn't *he* explode?'

'He was hanging on, I suppose, to make sure the others had received his message and were safely destroyed. Lord, Lord, when you brought the news and I realized the truth, I couldn't shoot fast enough. God knows by how few seconds I may have beaten him to it.'

Laszlo said shakily, 'At least, we'll have one to study.' He bent and put his fingers on the sticky fluid trickling out of the mangled remains at the neck end of the headless body.

Not blood, but high-grade machine oil.

Mirror Image

The Three Laws of Robotics

1: A robot may not injure a human being or, through inaction, allow a human being to come to harm.

2: A robot must obey the orders given it by human beings except where such orders would conflict with the First Law.

3: A robot must protect its own existence as long as such protection does not conflict with the First or Second Law.

Lije Baley had just decided to relight his pipe, when the door of his office opened without a preliminary knock, or announcement, of any kind. Baley looked up in pronounced annoyance and then dropped his pipe. It said a good deal for the state of his mind that he left it lying where it had fallen.

'R. Daneel Olivaw,' he said, in a kind of mystified excitement. 'Jehoshaphat! It *is* you, isn't it?'

'You are quite right,' said the tall, bronzed newcomer, his even features never flicking for a moment out of their accustomed calm. 'I regret surprising you by entering without warning, but the situation is a delicate one and there must be as little involvement as possible on the part of the men and robots even in this place. I am, in any case, pleased to see you again, friend Elijah.'

And the robot held out his right hand in a gesture as thoroughly human as was his appearance. It was Baley who was so unmanned by his astonishment as to stare at the hand with a momentary lack of understanding.

But then he seized it in both his, feeling its warm

firmness. 'But Daneel, *why*? You're welcome any time, but – What is this situation that is a delicate one? Are we in trouble again? Earth, I mean?'

'No, friend Elijah, it does not concern Earth. The situation to which I refer as a delicate one is, to outward appearances, a small thing. A dispute between mathematicians, nothing more. As we happened, quite by accident, to be within an easy Jump of Earth – '

'This dispute took place on a starship, then?'

'Yes, indeed. A small dispute, yet to the humans involved astonishingly large.'

Baley could not help but smile. 'I'm not surprised you find humans astonishing. They do not obey the Three Laws.'

'That is, indeed, a shortcoming,' said R. Daneel, gravely, 'and I think humans themselves are puzzled by humans. It may be that you are less puzzled than are the men of other worlds because so many more human beings live on Earth than on the Spacer worlds. If so, and I believe it is so, you could help us.'

R. Daneel paused momentarily and then said, perhaps a shade too quickly, 'And yet there are rules of human behavior which I have learned. It would seem, for instance, that I am deficient in etiquette, by human standards, not to have asked after your wife and child.'

'They are doing well. The boy is in college and Jessie is involved in local politics. The amenities are taken care of. Now tell me how you come to be here.'

'As I said, we were within an easy Jump of Earth,' said R. Daneel, 'so I suggested to the captain that we consult you.'

'And the captain agreed?' Baley had a sudden picture of the proud and autocratic captain of a Spacer starship consenting to make a landing on Earth – of all worlds – and to consult an Earthman – of all people.

'I believe,' said R. Daneel, 'that he was in a position where he would have agreed to anything. In addition, I praised you very highly; although, to be sure, I stated only the truth. Finally, I agreed to conduct all negotiations so that none of the crew, or passengers, would need to enter any of the Earthman cities.'

'And talk to any Earthman, yes. But what has happened?'

'The passengers of the starship, *Eta Carina*, included two mathematicians who were traveling to Aurora to attend an interstellar conference on neurobiophysics. It is about these mathematicians, Alfred Barr Humboldt and Gennao Sabbat, that the dispute centers. Have you perhaps, friend Elijah, heard of one, or both, of them?'

'Neither one,' said Baley, firmly. 'I know nothing about mathematics. Look, Daneel, surely you haven't told anyone I'm a mathematics buff or – '

'Not at all, friend Elijah. I know you are not. Nor does it matter, since the exact nature of the mathematics involved is in no way relevant to the point at issue.'

'Well, then, go on.'

'Since, you do not know either man, friend Elijah, let me tell you that Dr Humboldt is well into his twenty-seventh decade – pardon me, friend Elijah?'

'Nothing. Nothing,' said Baley, irritably. He had merely muttered to himself, more or less incoherently, in a natural reaction to the extended life-spans of the Spacers. 'And he's still active, despite his age? On Earth, mathematicians after thirty or so . . .'

Daneel said, calmly, 'Dr Humboldt is one of the top three mathematicians, by long-established repute, in the galaxy. Certainly he is still active. Dr Sabbat, on the other hand, is quite young, not yet fifty, but he has already established himself as the most remarkable new talent in the most abstruse branches of mathematics.'

'They're both great, then,' said Baley. He remembered

his pipe and picked it up. He decided there was no point in lighting it now and knocked out the dottle. 'What happened? Is this a murder case? Did one of them apparently kill the other?'

'Of these two men of great reputation, one is trying to destroy that of the other. By human values, I believe this may be regarded as worse than physical murder.'

'Sometimes, I suppose. Which one is trying to destroy the other?'

'Why, that, friend Elijah, is precisely the point at issue. Which?'

'Go on.'

'Dr Humboldt tells the story clearly. Shortly before he boarded the starship, he had an insight into a possible method for analyzing neural pathways from changes in microwave absorption patterns of local cortical areas. The insight was a purely mathematical technique of extraordinary subtlety, but I cannot, of course, either understand or sensibly transmit the details. These do not, however, matter. Dr Humboldt considered the matter and was more convinced each hour that he had something revolutionary on hand, something that would dwarf all his previous accomplishments in mathematics. Then he discovered that Dr Sabbat was on board.'

'Ah. And he tried it out on young Sabbat?'

'Exactly. The two had met at professional meetings before and knew each other thoroughly by reputation. Humboldt went into it with Sabbat in great detail. Sabbat backed Humboldt's analysis completely and was unstinting in his praise of the importance of the discovery and of the ingenuity of the discoverer. Heartened and reassured by this, Humboldt prepared a paper outlining, in summary, his work and, two days later, prepared to have it forwarded subetherically to the co-chairmen of the conference at Aurora, in order that he might officially establish his priority and arrange for possible discussion before the sessions were closed. To his surprise, he found that Sabbat was ready with a paper of his own, essentially the same as Humboldt's, and Sabbat was also preparing to have it subetherized to Aurora.'

'I suppose Humboldt was furious.'

'Quite!'

'And Sabbat? What was his story?'

'Precisely the same as Humboldt's. Word for word.'

'Then just what is the problem?'

'Except for the mirror-image exchange of names. According to Sabbat, it was he who had the insight, and he who consulted Humboldt; it was Humboldt who agreed with the analysis and praised it.'

'Then each one claims the idea is his and that the other stole it. It doesn't sound like a problem to me at all. In matters of scholarship, it would seem only necessary to produce the records of research, dated and initialed. Judgment as to priority can be made from that. Even if one is falsified, that might be discovered through internal inconsistencies.'

'Ordinarily, friend Elijah, you would be right, but this is mathematics, and not in an experimental science. Dr Humboldt claims to have worked out the essentials in his head. Nothing was put in writing until the paper itself was prepared. Dr Sabbat, of course, says precisely the same.'

'Well, then, be more drastic and get it over with, for sure. Subject each one to a psychic probe and find out which of the two is lying.'

R. Daneel shook his head slowly, 'Friend Elijah, you do not understand these men. They are both of rank and scholarship, Fellows of the Imperial Academy. As such, they cannot be subjected to trial of professional conduct except by a jury of their peers – their professional peers – unless they personally and voluntarily waive that right.'

'Put it to them, then. The guilty man won't waive the right because he can't afford to face the psychic probe. The innocent man will waive it at once. You won't even have to use the probe.'

'It does not work that way, friend Elijah. To waive the right in such a case – to be investigated by laymen – is a serious and perhaps irrecoverable blow to prestige. Both men steadfastly refuse to waive the right to special trial, as a matter of pride. The question of guilt, or innocence, is quite subsidiary.'

'In that case, let it go for now. Put the matter in cold storage until you get to Aurora. At the neurobiophysical conference, there will be a huge supply of professional peers, and then – '

'That would mean a tremendous blow to science itself, friend Elijah. Both men would suffer for having been the instrument of scandal. Even the innocent one would be blamed for having been party to a situation so distasteful. It would be felt that it should have been settled quietly out of court at all costs.'

'All right. I'm not a Spacer, but I'll try to imagine that this attitude makes sense. What do the men in question say?'

'Humboldt agrees thoroughly. He says that if Sabbat will admit theft of the idea and allow Humboldt to proceed with transmission of the paper – or at least its delivery at the conference, he will not press charges. Sabbat's misdeed will remain secret with him; and, of course, with the captain, who is the only other human to be party to the dispute.'

'But young Sabbat will not agree?'

'On the contrary, he agreed with Dr Humboldt to the last detail – with the reversal of names. Still the mirror-image.'

'So they just sit there, stalemated?'

'Each, I believe, friend Elijah, is waiting for the other to give in and admit guilt.'

'Well, then, wait.'

'The captain has decided this cannot be done. There are two alternatives to waiting, you see. The first is that both will remain stubborn so that when the starship lands on Aurora, the intellectual scandal will break. The captain, who is responsible for justice on board ship will suffer disgrace for not having been able to settle the matter quietly and that, to him, is quite insupportable.'

'And the second alternative?'

'Is that one, or the other, of the mathematicians will indeed admit to wrongdoing. But will the one who confesses do so out of actual guilt, or out of a noble desire to prevent the scandal? Would it be right to deprive of credit one who is sufficiently ethical to prefer to lose that credit than to see science as a whole suffer? Or else, the guilty party will confess at the last moment, and in such a way as to make it appear he does so only for the sake of science, thus escaping the disgrace of his deed and casting its shadow upon the other. The captain will be the only man to know all this but he does not wish to spend the rest of his life wondering whether he has been a party to a grotesque miscarriage of justice.'

Baley sighed. 'A game of intellectual chicken. Who'll break first as Aurora comes nearer and nearer? Is that the whole story now, Daneel?'

'Not quite. There are witnesses to the transaction.'

'Jehoshaphat! Why didn't you say so at once. *What* witnesses?'

'Dr Humboldt's personal servant – '

'A robot, I suppose.'

'Yes, certainly. He is called R. Preston. This servant, R. Preston, was present during the initial conference and he bears out Dr Humboldt in every detail.'

'You mean he says that the idea was Dr Humboldt's to

begin with; that Dr Humboldt detailed it to Dr Sabbat; that Dr Sabbat praised the idea, and so on.'

'Yes, in full detail.'

'I see. Does that settle the matter or not? Presumably not.'

'You are quite right. It does not settle the matter, for there is a second witness. Dr Sabbat also has a personal servant, R. Idda, another robot of, as it happens, the same model as R. Preston, made, I believe, in the same year in the same factory. Both have been in service for an equal period of time.'

'An odd coincidence – very odd.'

'A fact, I am afraid, and it makes it difficult to arrive at any judgment based on obvious differences between the two servants.'

'R. Idda, then, tells the same story as R. Preston?'

'Precisely the same story, except for the mirror-image reversal of the names.'

'R. Idda stated, then, that young Sabbat, the one not yet fifty' – Lije Baley did not entirely keep the sardonic note out of his voice; he himself was not yet fifty and he felt far from young – 'had the idea to begin with; that he detailed it to Dr Humboldt, who was loud in his praises, and so on.'

'Yes, friend Elijah.'

'And one robot is lying, then.'

'So it would seem.'

'It should be easy to tell which. I imagine even a superficial examination by a good roboticist – '

'A roboticist is not enough in this case, friend Elijah. Only a qualified robopsychologist would carry weight enough and experience enough to make a decision in a case of this importance. There is no one so qualified on board ship. Such an examination can be performed only when we reach Aurora – '

'And by then the crud hits the fan. Well, you're here on

Earth. We can scare up a robopsychologist, and surely anything that happens on Earth will never reach the ears of Aurora and there will be no scandal.'

'Except that neither Dr Humboldt, nor Dr Sabbat, will allow his servant to be investigated by a robopsychologist of Earth. The Earthman would have to – ' He paused.

Lije Baley said stolidly, 'He'd have to touch the robot.'

'These are old servants, well thought of – '

'And not to be sullied by the touch of Earthman. Then what do you want me to do, damn it?' He paused, grimacing. 'I'm sorry, R. Daneel, but I see no reason for your having involved me.'

'I was on the ship on a mission utterly irrelevant to the problem at hand. The captain turned to me because he had to turn to someone. I seemed human enough to talk to, and robot enough to be a safe recipient of confidences. He told me the whole story and asked what I would do. I realized the next Jump could take us as easily to Earth as to our target. I told the captain that, although I was at as much a loss to resolve the mirror-image as he was, there was on Earth one who might help.'

'Jehoshaphat!' muttered Baley under his breath.

'Consider, friend Elijah, that if you succeed in solving this puzzle, it would do your career good and Earth itself might benefit. The matter could not be publicized, of course, but the captain is a man of some influence on his home world and he would be grateful.'

'You just put a greater strain on me.'

'I have every confidence,' said R. Daneel, stolidly, 'that you already have some idea as to what procedure ought to be followed.'

'Do you? I suppose that the obvious procedure is to interview the two mathematicians, one of whom would seem to be a thief.'

'I'm afraid, friend Elijah, that neither one will come into the city. Nor would either one be willing to have you come to them.'

'And there is no way of forcing a Spacer to allow contact with an Earthman, no matter what the emergency. Yes, I understand that, Daneel – but I was thinking of an interview by closed-circuit television.'

'Nor that. They will not submit to interrogation by an Earthman.'

'Then what do they want of me? Could I speak to the robots?'

'They would not allow the robots to come here, either.'

'Jehoshaphat, Daneel. *You've* come.'

'That was my own decision. I have permission, while on board ship, to make decisions of that sort without veto by any human being but the captain himself – and he was eager to establish the contact. I, having known you, decided that television contact was insufficient. I wished to shake your hand.'

Lije Baley softened. 'I appreciate that, Daneel, but I still honestly wish you could have refrained from thinking of me at all in this case. Can I talk to the robots by television at least?'

'That, I think, can be arranged.'

'Something, at least. That means I would be doing the work of a robopsychologist – in a crude sort of way.'

'But you are a detective, friend Elijah, not a robopsychologist.'

'Well, let it pass. Now before I see them, let's think a bit. Tell me: is it possible that both robots are telling the truth? Perhaps the conversation between the two mathematicians was equivocal. Perhaps it was of such a nature that each robot could honestly believe its own master was proprietor of the idea. Or perhaps one robot heard only one portion of the discussion and the other another portion, so that each could suppose its own master was proprietor of the idea.'

'That is quite impossible, friend Elijah. Both robots repeat the conversation in identical fashion. And the two repetitions are fundamentally inconsistent.'

'Then it is absolutely certain that one of the robots is lying?'

'Yes.'

'Will I be able to see the transcript of all evidence given so far in the presence of the captain, if I should want to?'

'I thought you would ask that and I have copies with me.'

'Another blessing. Have the robots been cross-examined at all, and is that cross-examination included in the transcript?'

'The robots have merely repeated their tales. Cross-examination would be conducted only by robopsychologists.'

'Or by myself?'

'You are a detective, friend Elijah, not a – '

'All right, R. Daneel. I'll try to get the Spacer psychology straight. A detective can do it because he isn't a robopsychologist. Let's think further. Ordinarily a robot will not lie, but he will do so if necessary to maintain the Three Laws. He might lie to protect, in legitimate fashion, his own existence in accordance with the Third Law. He is more apt to lie if that is necessary to follow a legitimate order given him by a human being in accordance with the Second Law. He is most apt to lie if that is necessary to save a human life, or to prevent harm from coming to a human in accordance with the First Law.'

'Yes.'

'And in this case, each robot would be defending the professional reputation of his master, and would lie if it were necessary to do so. Under the circumstances, the professional reputation would be nearly equivalent to life and there might be a near-First-Law urgency to the lie.'

'Yet by the lie, each servant would be harming the professional reputation of the other's master, friend Elijah.'

'So it would, but each robot might have a clearer conception of the value of its own master's reputation and honestly judge it to be greater than that of the other's. The lesser harm would be done by his lie, he would suppose, than by the truth.'

Having said that, Lije Baley remained quiet for a moment. Then he said, 'All right, then, can you arrange to have me talk to one of the robots – to R. Idda first, I think?'

'Dr Sabbat's robot?'

'Yes,' said Baley, dryly, 'the young fellow's robot.'

'It will take me but a few minutes,' said R. Daneel. 'I have a micro-receiver outfitted with a projector. I will need merely a blank wall and I think this one will do if you will allow me to move some of these film cabinets.'

'Go ahead. Will I have to talk into a microphone of some sort?'

'No, you will be able to talk in an ordinary manner. Please pardon me, friend Elijah, for a moment of further delay. I will have to contact the ship and arrange for R. Idda to be interviewed.'

'If that will take some time, Daneel, how about giving me the transcripted material of the evidence so far.'

Lije Baley lit his pipe while R. Daneel set up the equipment, and leafed through the flimsy sheets he had been handed.

The minutes passed and R. Daneel said, 'If you are ready, friend Elijah, R. Idda is. Or would you prefer a few more minutes with the transcript?'

'No,' sighed Baley, 'I'm not learning anything new. Put him on and arrange to have the interview recorded and transcribed.'

R. Idda, unreal in two-dimensional projection against the

wall, was basically metallic in structure – not at all the humanoid creature that R. Daneel was. His body was tall but blocky, and there was very little to distinguish him from the many robots Baley had seen, except for minor structural details.

Baley said, 'Greetings, R. Idda.'

'Greetings, sir,' said R. Idda, in a muted voice that sounded surprisingly humanoid.

'You are the personal servant of Gennao Sabbat, are you not?'

'I am sir.'

'For how long, boy?'

'For twenty-two years, sir.'

'And your master's reputation is valuable to you?'

'Yes, sir.'

'Would you consider it of importance to protect that reputation?'

'Yes, sir.'

'As important to protect his reputation as his physical life?'

'No, sir.'

'As important to protect his reputation as the reputation of another.'

R. Idda hesitated. He said, 'Such cases must be decided on their individual merit, sir. There is no way of establishing a general rule.'

Baley hesitated. These Spacer robots spoke more smoothly and intellectually than Earth-models did. He was not at all sure he could outthink one.

He said, 'If you decided that the reputation of your master were more important than that of another, say, that of Alfred Barr Humboldt, would you lie to protect your master's reputation?'

'I would, sir.'

'Did you lie in your testimony concerning your master in his controversy with Dr Humboldt?'

'No, sir.'

'But if you were lying, you would deny you were lying in order to protect that lie, wouldn't you?'

'Yes, sir.'

'Well, then,' said Baley, 'let's consider this. Your master, Gennao Sabbat, is a young man of great reputation in mathematics, but he is a young man. If, in this controversy with Dr Humboldt, he had succumbed to temptation and had acted unethically, he would suffer a certain eclipse of reputation, but he is young and would have ample time to recover. He would have many intellectual triumphs ahead of him and men would eventually look upon this plagiaristic attempt as the mistake of a hot-blooded youth, deficient in judgment. It would be something that would be made up for in the future.

'If, on the other hand, it were Dr Humboldt who succumbed to temptation, the matter would be much more serious. He is an old man whose great deeds have spread over centuries. His reputation has been unblemished hitherto. All of that, however, would be forgotten in the light of this one crime of his later years, and he would have no opportunity to make up for it in the comparatively short time remaining to him. There would be little more that he could accomplish. There would be so many more years of work ruined in Humboldt's case than in that of your master and so much less opportunity to win back his position. You see, don't you, that Humboldt faces the worse situation and deserves the greater consideration?'

There was a long pause. Then R. Idda said, with unmoved voice, 'My evidence was a lie. It was Dr Humboldt whose work it was, and my master has attempted, wrongfully, to appropriate the credit.'

Baley said, 'Very well, boy. You are instructed to say

nothing to anyone about this until given permission by the captain of the ship. You are excused.'

The screen blanked out and Baley puffed at his pipe. 'Do you suppose the captain heard that, Daneel?'

'I am sure of it. He is the only witness, except for us.'

'Good. Now for the other.'

'But is there any point to that, friend Elijah, in view of what R. Idda has confessed?'

'Of course there is. R. Idda's confession means nothing.'

'Nothing?'

'Nothing at all. I pointed out that Dr Humboldt's position was the worse. Naturally, if he were lying to protect Sabbat, he would switch to the truth as, in fact, he claimed to have done. On the other hand, if he were telling the truth, he would switch to a lie to protect Humboldt. It's still mirror-image and we haven't gained anything.'

'But then what will we gain by questioning R. Preston?'

'Nothing, if the mirror-image were perfect – but it is not. After all, one of the robots *is* telling the truth to begin with, and one *is* lying to begin with, and that is a point of asymmetry. Let me see R. Preston. And if the transcription of R. Idda's examination is done, let me have it.'

The projector came into use again. R. Preston stared out of it; identical with R. Idda in every respect, except for some trivial chest design.

Baley said, 'Greetings, R. Preston.' He kept the record of R. Idda's examination before him as he spoke.

'Greetings, sir,' said R. Preston. His voice was identical with that of R. Idda.

'You are the personal servant of Alfred Barr Humboldt are you not?'

'I am, sir.'

'For how long, boy?'

'For twenty-two years, sir.'

'And your master's reputation is valuable to you?'

'Yes, sir.'

'Would you consider it of importance to protect that reputation?'

'Yes, sir.'

'As important to protect his reputation as his physical life?'

'No, sir.'

'As important to protect his reputation as the reputation of another?'

R. Preston hesitated. He said, 'Such cases must be decided on their individual merit, sir. There is no way of establishing a general rule.'

Baley said, 'If you decided that the reputation of your master were more important than that of another, say, that of Gennao Sabbat, would you lie to protect your master's reputation?'

'I would, sir.'

'Did you lie in your testimony concerning your master in his controversy with Dr Sabbat?'

'No, sir.'

'But if you were lying, you would deny you were lying, in order to protect that lie, wouldn't you?'

'Yes, sir.'

'Well, then,' said Baley, 'let's consider this. Your master, Alfred Barr Humboldt, is an old man of great reputation in mathematics, but he is an old man. If, in this controversy with Dr Sabbat, he had succumbed to temptation and had acted unethically, he would suffer a certain eclipse of reputation, but his great age and his centuries of accomplishments would stand against that and would win out. Men would look upon this plagiaristic attempt as the mistake of a perhaps-sick old man, no longer certain in judgment.

'If, on the other hand, it were Dr Sabbat who had succumbed to temptation, the matter would be much more serious. He is a young man, with a far less secure reputation. He would ordinarily have centuries ahead of him in which he might accumulate knowledge and achieve great things. This will be closed to him, now, obscured by one mistake of his youth. He has a much longer future to lose than your master has. You see, don't you, that Sabbat faces the worse situation and deserves the greater consideration?'

There was a long pause. Then R. Preston said, with unmoved voice, 'My evidence was as I – '

At that point, he broke off and said nothing more.

Baley said, 'Please continue, R. Preston.'

There was no response.

R. Daneel said, 'I am afraid, friend Elijah, that R. Preston is in stasis. He is out of commission.'

'Well, then,' said Baley, 'we have finally produced an asymmetry. From this, we can see who the guilty person is.'

'In what way, friend Elijah?'

'Think it out. Suppose you were a person who had committed no crime and that your personal robot were a witness to that. There would be nothing you need do. Your robot would tell the truth and bear you out. If, however, you were a person who *had* committed the crime, you would have to depend on your robot to lie. That would be a somewhat riskier position, for although the robot would lie, if necessary, the greater inclination would be to tell the truth, so that the lie would be less firm than the truth would be. To prevent that, the crime-committing person would very likely have to *order* the robot to lie. In this way. First Law would be strengthened by Second Law; perhaps very substantially strengthened.'

'That would seem reasonable,' said R. Daneel.

'Suppose we have one robot of each type. One robot would switch from truth, unreinforced, to the lie, and could do so after some hesitation, without serious trouble. The other robot would switch from the lie, *strongly reinforced*, to the truth, but could do so only at the risk of burning out various positronic-track-ways in his brain and falling into stasis.'

'And since R. Preston went into stasis – '

'R. Preston's master, Dr Humboldt, is the man guilty of plagiarism. If you transmit this to the captain and urge him to face Dr Humboldt with the matter at once, he may force a confession. If so, I hope you will tell me immediately.'

'I will certainly do so. You will excuse me, friend Elijah? I must talk to the captain privately.'

'Certainly. Use the conference room. It is shielded.'

Baley could do no work of any kind in R. Daneel's absence. He sat in uneasy silence. A great deal would depend on the value of his analysis, and he was acutely aware of his lack of expertise in robotics.

R. Daneel was back in half an hour – very nearly the longest half hour of Baley's life.

There was no use, of course, in trying to determine what had happened from the expression of the humanoid's impassive face. Baley tried to keep his face impassive.

'Yes, R. Daneel?' he asked.

'Precisely as you said, friend Elijah. Dr Humboldt has confessed. He was counting, he said, on Dr Sabbat giving way and allowing Dr Humboldt to have this one last triumph. The crisis is over and you will find the captain grateful. He has given me permission to tell you that he admires your subtlety greatly and I believe that I, myself, will achieve favor for having suggested you.'

'Good,' said Baley, his knees weak and his forehead moist now that his decision had proven correct, 'but Jehoshaphat, R. Daneel, don't put me on the spot like that again, will you?'

'I will try not to, friend Elijah. All will depend, of course, on the importance of a crisis, on your nearness, and on certain other factors. Meanwhile, I have a question – '

'Yes?'

'Was it not possible to suppose that passage from a lie to the truth was easy, while passage from the truth to a lie was difficult? And in that case, would not the robot in stasis have been going from a truth to a lie, and since R. Preston was in stasis, might one not have drawn the conclusion that it was Dr Humboldt who was innocent and Dr Sabbat who was guilty?'

'Yes, R. Daneel. It was possible to argue that way, but it was the other argument that proved right. Humboldt did confess, didn't he?'

'He did. But with arguments possible in both directions, how could you, friend Elijah, so quickly pick the correct one?'

For a moment, Baley's lips twitched. Then he relaxed and they curved into a smile. 'Because, R. Daneel, I took into account human reactions, not robotic ones. I know more about human beings than about robots. In other words, I had an idea as to which mathematician was guilty before I ever interviewed the robots. Once I provoked an asymmetric response in them, I simply interpreted it in such a way as to place the guilt on the one I already believed to be guilty. The robotic response was dramatic enough to break down the guilty man; my own analysis of human behavior might not have been sufficient to do so.'

'I am curious to know what your analysis of human behavior was?'

'Jehoshaphat, R. Daneel; think, and you won't have to ask. There is another point of asymmetry in this tale of mirror-image besides the matter of true-and-false. There is the matter of the age of the two mathematicians; one is quite old and one is quite young.'

'Yes, of course, but what then?'

'Why, this. I can see a young man, flushed with a sudden, startling and revolutionary idea, consulting in the matter an old man whom he has, from his early student days, thought of as a demigod in the field. I can *not* see an old man, rich in honors and used to triumphs, coming up with a sudden, startling and revolutionary idea, consulting a man centuries his junior whom he is bound to think of as a young whippersnapper – or whatever term a Spacer would use. Then, too, if a young man had the chance, would he try to steal the idea of a revered demigod? It would be unthinkable. On the other hand, an old man, conscious of declining powers, might well snatch at one last chance of fame and consider a baby in the field to have no rights he was bound to observe. In short, it was not conceivable that Sabbat steal Humboldt's idea; and from both angles, Dr Humboldt was guilty.'

R. Daneel considered that for a long time. Then he held out his hand. 'I must leave now, friend Elijah. It was good to see you. May we meet again soon.'

Baley gripped the robot's hand, warmly, 'If you don't mind, R. Daneel,' he said, 'not too soon.'

The Tercentenary Incident

July 4, 2076 – and for the third time the accident of the conventional system of numeration, based on powers of ten, had brought the last two digits of the year back to the fateful 76 that had seen the birth of the nation.

It was no longer a nation in the old sense; it was rather a geographic expression; part of a greater whole that made up the Federation of all of humanity on Earth, together with its offshoots on the Moon and in the space colonies. By culture and heritage, however, the name and the *idea* lived on, and that portion of the planet signified by the old name was still the most prosperous and advanced region of the world . . . And the President of the United States was still the most powerful single figure in the Planetary Council.

Lawrence Edwards watched the small figure of the President from his height of two hundred feet. He drifted lazily above the crowd, his flotron motor making a barely heard chuckle on his back, and what he saw looked exactly like what anyone would see on a holovision scene. How many times had he seen little figures like that in his living room, little figures in a cube of sunlight, looking as real as though they were living homunculi, except that you could put your hand through them.

You couldn't put your hand through those spreading out in their tens of thousands over the open spaces surrounding the Washington Monument. And you couldn't put your hand through the President. You could reach out to him instead, touch him, and shake his hand.

Edwards thought sardonically of the uselessness of that added element of tangibility and wished himself a hundred miles away, floating in air over some isolated wilderness, instead of here where he had to watch for any sign of disorder. There wouldn't be any necessity for his being here but for the mythology of the value of 'pressing the flesh.'

Edwards was not an admirer of the President – Hugo Allen Winkler, fifty-seventh of the line.

To Edwards, President Winkler seemed an empty man, a charmer, a vote grabber, a promiser. He was a disappointing man to have in office now after all the hopes of those first months of his administration. The World Federation was in danger of breaking up long before its job had been completed and Winkler could do nothing about it. One needed a strong hand now, not a glad hand; a hard voice, not a honey voice.

There he was now, shaking hands – a space forced around him by the Service, with Edwards himself, plus a few others of the Service, watching from above.

The President would be running for re-election certainly, and there seemed a good chance he might be defeated. That would just make things worse, since the opposition party was dedicated to the destruction of the Federation.

Edwards sighed. It would be a miserable four years coming up – maybe a miserable forty – and all he could do was float in the air, ready to reach every Service agent on the ground by laser-phone if there was the slightest –

He didn't see the slightest. There was no sign of disturbance. Just a little puff of white dust, hardly visible; just a momentary glitter in the sunlight, up and away, gone as soon as he was aware of it.

Where was the President? He had lost sight of him in the dust.

He looked about in the vicinity of where he had seen him last. The President could not have moved far.

Then he became aware of disturbance. First it was among the Service agents themselves, who seemed to have gone off their heads and to be moving this way and that jerkily. Then those among the crowd near them caught the contagion and then those farther off. The noise rose and became a thunder.

Edwards didn't have to hear the words that made up the rising roar. It seemed to carry the news to him by nothing more than its mass clamorous urgency. President Winkler had disappeared! He had been there one moment and had turned into a handful of vanishing dust the next.

Edwards held his breath in an agony of waiting during what seemed a drug-ridden eternity, for the long moment of realization to end and for the mob to break into a mad, rioting stampede.

– When a resonant voice sounded over the gathering din, and at its sound, the noise faded, died, and became a silence. It was as though it were all a holovision program after all and someone had turned the sound down and out.

Edwards thought: My God, it's the President.

There was no mistaking the voice. Winkler stood on the guarded stage from which he was to give his Tercentenary speech, and from which he had left but ten minutes ago to shake hands with some in the crowd.

How had he gotten back there?

Edwards listened –

'Nothing has happened to me, my fellow Americans. What you have seen just now was the breakdown of a mechanical device. It was not your President, so let us not allow a mechanical failure to dampen the celebration of the happiest day the world has yet seen . . . My fellow Americans, give me your attention – '

And what followed was the Tercentenary speech, the greatest speech Winkler had ever made, or Edwards had ever heard. Edwards found himself forgetting his supervisory job in his eagerness to listen.

Winkler had it right! He understood the importance of the Federation and he was getting it *across*.

Deep inside, though, another part of him was remembering the persistent rumors that the new expertise in robotics had resulted in the construction of a look-alike President, a robot who could perform the purely ceremonial functions, who could shake hands with the crowd, who could be neither bored nor exhausted – nor assassinated.

Edwards thought, in obscure shock, that that was how it had happened. There had been such a look-alike robot indeed, and in a way – it had been assassinated.

October 13, 2078 –

Edwards looked up as the waist-high robot guide approached and said mellifluously, 'Mr Janek will see you now.'

Edwards stood up, feeling tall as he towered above the stubby, metallic guide. He did not feel young, however. His face had gathered lines in the last two years or so and he was aware of it.

He followed the guide into a surprisingly small room, where, behind a surprisingly small desk, there sat Francis Janek, a slightly paunchy and incongruously young-looking man.

Janek smiled and his eyes were friendly as he rose to shake hands. 'Mr Edwards.'

Edwards muttered, 'I'm glad to have the opportunity, sir – '

Edwards had never seen Janek before, but then the job of personal secretary to the President is a quiet one and makes little news.

Janek said, 'Sit down. Sit down. Would you care for a soya stick?'

Edwards smiled a polite negative, and sat down. Janek was clearly emphasizing his youth. His ruffled shirt was open and the hairs on his chest had been dyed a subdued but definite violet.

Janek said, 'I know you have been trying to reach me for some weeks now. I'm sorry for the delay. I hope you understand that my time is not entirely my own. However, we're here now . . . I have referred to the Chief of the Service, by the way, and he gave you very high marks. He regrets your resignation.'

Edwards said, eyes downcast, 'It seemed better to carry on my investigations without danger of embarrassment to the Service.'

Janek's smile flashed. 'Your activities, though discreet, have not gone unnoticed, however. The Chief explains that you have been investigating the Tercentenary Incident, and I must admit it was that which persuaded me to see you as soon as I could. You've given up your position for that? You're investigating a dead issue.'

'How can it be a dead issue, Mr Janek? Your calling it an Incident doesn't alter the fact that it was an assassination attempt.'

'A matter of semantics. Why use a disturbing phrase?'

'Only because it would seem to represent a disturbing truth. Surely you would say that someone tried to kill the President.'

Janek spread his hands. 'If that is so, the plot did not succeed. A mechanical device was destroyed. Nothing more. In fact, if we look at it properly, the Incident – whatever you choose to call it – did the nation and the world an enormous good. As we all know, the President was shaken by the Incident and the nation as well. The President and all of us realized what a return to the violence of the last century might mean and it produced a great turnaround.'

'I can't deny that.'

'Of course you can't. Even the President's enemies will grant that the last two years have seen great accomplishments. The Federation is far stronger today than anyone could have dreamed it would be on that Tercentenary day. We might even say that a breakup of the global economy has been prevented.'

Edwards said cautiously, 'Yes, the President is a changed man. Everyone says so.'

Janek said, 'He was a great man always. The Incident made him concentrate on the great issues with a fierce intensity, however.'

'Which he didn't do before?'

'Perhaps not quite as intensely . . . In effect then, the President, and all of us, would like the Incident forgotten. My main purpose in seeing you, Mr Edwards, is to make that plain to you. This is not the Twentieth Century and we can't throw you in jail for being inconvenient to us, or hamper you in any way, but even the Global Charter doesn't forbid us to attempt persuasion. Do you understand me?'

'I understand you, but I do not agree with you. Can we forget the Incident when the person responsible has never been apprehended?'

'Perhaps that is just as well, too, sir. Far better that some, uh, unbalanced person escape than that the matter be blown out of proportion and the stage set, possibly, for a return to the days of the Twentieth Century.'

'The official story even states that the robot spontaneously exploded – which is impossible, and which has been an unfair blow to the robot industry.'

'A robot is not the term I would use, Mr Edwards. It was a mechanical device. No one has said that robots are dangerous, per se, certainly not the workaday metallic ones. The only reference here is to the unusually complex manlike devices that seem flesh and blood and that we might call androids. Actually, they are so complex that perhaps they might explode at that; I am not an expert in the field. The robotics industry will recover.'

'Nobody in the government,' said Edwards stubbornly,

'seems to care whether we reach the bottom of the matter or not.'

'I've already explained that there have been no consequences but good ones. Why stir the mud at the bottom, when the water above is clear?'

'And the use of the disintegrator?'

For a moment, Janek's hand, which had been slowly turning the container of soya sticks on his desk, held still, then it returned to its rhythmic movement. He said lightly, 'What's that?'

Edwards said intently, 'Mr Janek, I think you know what I mean. As part of the Service – '

'To which you no longer belong, of course.'

'Nevertheless, as part of the Service, I could not help but hear things that were not always, I suppose, for my ears. I had heard of a new weapon, and I saw something happen at the Tercentenary which would require one. The object everyone thought was the President disappeared into a cloud of very fine dust. It was as though every atom within the object had had its bonds to other atoms loosed. The object had become a cloud of individual atoms, which began to combine again of course, but which dispersed too quickly to do more than appear a momentary glitter of dust.'

'Very science-fictionish.'

'I certainly don't understand the science behind it, Mr Janek, but I do see that it would take considerable energy to accomplish such bond breaking. This energy would have to be withdrawn from the environment. Those people who were standing near the device at the time, and whom I could locate – and who would agree to talk – were unanimous in reporting a wave of coldness washing over them.'

Janek put the soya-stick container to one side with a small click of transite against cellulite. He said, 'Suppose just for argument that there is such a thing as a disintegrator.'

'You need not argue. There is.'

'I won't argue. I know of no such thing myself, but in my office, I am not likely to know of anything so security-bound as new weaponry. But if a disintegrator exists and is as secret as all that, it must be an American monopoly, unknown to the rest of the Federation. It would then not be something either you or I should talk about. It could be a more dangerous war weapon than the nuclear bombs, precisely because – if what you say is so – it produces nothing more than disintegration at the point of impact and cold in the immediate neighborhood. No blast, no fire, no deadly radiation. Without these distressing side effects, there would be no deterrent to its use, yet for all we know it might be made large enough to destroy the planet itself.'

'I go along with all of that,' said Edwards.

'Then you see that if there is no disintegrator, it is foolish to talk about one; and if there *is* a disintegrator, then it is criminal to talk about one.'

'I haven't discussed it, except to you, just now, because I'm trying to persuade you of the seriousness of the situation. If one had been used, for instance, ought not the government be interested in deciding how it came to be used – if another unit of the Federation might be in possession?'

Janek shook his head. 'I think that we can rely on appropriate organs of this government to take such a thing into consideration. You had better not concern yourself with the matter.'

Edwards said, in barely controlled impatience, 'Can you assure me that the United States is the only government that has such a weapon at its disposal?'

'I can't tell you, since I know nothing about such a weapon, and should not know. You should not have spoken of it to me. Even if no such weapon exists, the *rumor* of its existence could be damaging.'

'But since I have told you and the damage is done, please

hear me out. Let me have the chance of convincing you that *you*, and no one else, hold the key to a fearful situation that perhaps I alone see.'

'You alone see? I alone hold the key?'

'Does that sound paranoid? Let me explain and then judge for yourself.'

'I will give you a little more time, sir, but what I have said stands. You must abandon this – this hobby of yours – this investigation. It is terribly dangerous.'

'It is its abandonment that would be dangerous. Don't you see that if the disintegrator exists and if the United States has the monopoly of it, then it follows that the number of people who could have access to one would be sharply limited. As an ex-member of the Service, I have some practical knowledge of this and I tell you that the only person in the world who could manage to abstract a disintegrator from our top-secret arsenals would be the President . . . Only the President of the United States, Mr Janek, could have arranged that assassination attempt.'

They stared at each other for a moment and then Janek touched a contact at his desk.

He said, 'Added precaution. No one can overhear us now by any means. Mr Edwards, do you realize the danger of that statement? To yourself? You must not overestimate the power of the Global Charter. A government has the right to take reasonable measures for the protection of its stability.'

Edwards said, 'I'm approaching you, Mr Janek, as someone I presume to be a loyal American citizen. I come to you with news of a terrible crime that affects all Americans and the entire Federation. A crime that has produced a situation that perhaps only you can right. Why do you respond with threats?'

Janek said, 'That's the second time you have tried to make it appear that I am a potential savior of the world. I can't conceive of myself in that role. You understand, I hope, that I have no unusual powers.'

'You are the secretary to the President.'

'That does *not* mean I have special access to him or am in some intimately confidential relationship to him. There are times, Mr Edwards, when I suspect others consider me to be nothing more than a flunky, and there are even times when I find myself in danger of agreeing with them.'

'Nevertheless, you see him frequently, you see him informally, you see him – '

Janek said impatiently, 'I see enough of him to be able to assure you that the President would not order the destruction of that mechanical device on Tercentenary day.'

'Is it in your opinion impossible, then?'

'I did not say that. I said he would not. After all, why should he? Why should the President want to destroy a look-alike android that had been a valuable adjunct to him for over three years of his Presidency? And if for some reason he wanted it done, why on Earth should he do it in so incredibly public a way – at the Tercentenary, no less – thus advertising its existence, risking public revulsion at the thought of shaking hands with a mechanical device, to say nothing of the diplomatic repercussions of having had representatives of other parts of the Federation treat with one? He might, instead, simply have ordered it disassembled in private. No one but a few highly placed members of the Administration would have known.'

'There have not, however, been any undesirable consequences for the President as a result of the Incident, have there?'

'He has had to cut down on ceremony. He is no longer as accessible as he once was.'

'As the robot once was.'

'Well,' said Janek uneasily. 'Yes, I suppose that's right.'

Edwards said, 'And, as a matter of fact, the President was

re-elected and his popularity has not diminished even though the destruction was public. The argument against public destruction is not as powerful as you make it sound.'

'But the re-election came about *despite* the Incident. It was brought about by the President's quick action in stepping forward and delivering what you will have to admit was one of the great speeches of American history. It was an absolutely amazing performance; you will have to admit that.'

'It was a beautifully staged drama. The President, one might think, would have counted on that.'

Janek sat back in his chair. 'If I understand you, Edwards, you are suggesting an involuted storybook plot. Are you trying to say that the President had the device destroyed, just as it was – in the middle of a crowd, at precisely the time of the Tercentenary celebration, with the world watching – so that he could win the admiration of all by his quick action? Are you suggesting that he arranged it all so that he could establish himself as a man of unexpected vigor and strength under extremely dramatic circumstances and thus turn a losing campaign into a winning one? . . . Mr Edwards, you've been reading fairy tales.'

Edwards said, 'If I were trying to claim all this, it would indeed be a fairy tale, but I am not. I never suggested that the President ordered the killing of the robot. I merely asked if you thought it were possible and you have stated quite strongly that it wasn't. I'm glad you did, because I agree with you.'

'Then what is all this? I'm beginning to think you're wasting my time.'

'Another moment, please. Have you ever asked yourself why the job couldn't have been done with a laser beam, with a field deactivator – with a sledgehammer, for God's sake? Why should anyone go to the incredible trouble of getting a weapon guarded by the strongest possible government security to do a job that didn't require such a weapon? Aside from the difficulty of getting it, why risk revealing the existence of a disintegrator to the rest of the world?'

'This whole business of a disintegrator is just a theory of yours.'

'The robot disappeared completely before my eyes. I was watching. I rely on no secondhand evidence for that. It doesn't matter what you call the weapon; whatever name you give it, it had the effect of taking the robot apart atom by atom and scattering all those atoms irretrievably. Why should this be done? It was tremendous overkill.'

'I don't know what was in the mind of the perpetrator.'

'No? Yet it seems to me that there is only one logical reason for a complete powdering when something much simpler would have carried through the destruction. The powdering left no trace behind of the destroyed object. It left nothing to indicate what it had been, whether robot or anything else.'

Janek said, 'But there is no question of what it was.'

'Isn't there? I said only the President could have arranged for a disintegrator to be obtained and used. But, considering the existence of a look-alike robot, which President did the arranging?'

Janek said harshly, 'I don't think we can carry on this conversation. You are mad.'

Edwards said, 'Think it through. For God's sake, think it through. The President did not destroy the robot. Your arguments there are convincing. What happened was that the robot destroyed the President. President Winkler was killed in the crowd on July 4, 2076. A robot resembling President Winkler then gave the Tercentenary speech, ran for re-election, was re-elected, and still serves as President of the United States!'

'Madness!'

'I've come to you, to *you* because *you* can prove this – and correct it, too.'

'It is simply not so. The President is – the President.' Janek made as though to rise and conclude the interview.

'You yourself say he's changed,' said Edwards quickly and urgently. 'The Tercentenary speech was beyond the powers of the old Winkler. Haven't you been yourself amazed at the accomplishments of the last two years? Truthfully – could the Winkler of the first term have done all this?'

'Yes, he could have, because the President of the second term is the President of the first term.'

'Do you deny he's changed? I put it to you. *You* decide and I'll abide by your decision.'

'He's risen to meet the challenge, that is all. It's happened before this in American history.' But Janek sank back into his seat. He looked uneasy.

'He doesn't drink,' said Edwards.

'He never did – very much.'

'He no longer womanizes. Do you deny he did so in the past?'

'A President is a man. For the last two years, however, he's felt dedicated to the matter of the Federation.'

'It's a change for the better, I admit,' said Edwards, 'but it's a change. Of course, if he *had* a woman, the masquerade could not be carried on, could it?'

Janek said, 'Too bad he doesn't have a wife.' He pronounced the archaic word a little self-consciously. 'The whole matter wouldn't arise if he did.'

'The fact that he doesn't made the plot more practical. Yet he has fathered two children. I don't believe they have been in the White House, either one of them, since the Tercentenary.'

'Why should they be? They are grown, with lives of their own.'

'Are they invited? Is the President interested in seeing them? You're his private secretary. You would know. Are they?'

Janek said, 'You're wasting time. A robot can't kill a human being. You know that that is the First Law of Robotics.'

'I know it. But no one is saying that the robot-Winkler killed the human-Winkler directly. When the human-Winkler was in the crowd, the robot-Winkler was on the stand and I doubt that a disintegrator could be aimed from that distance without doing more widespread damage. Maybe it could, but more likely the robot-Winkler had an accomplice – a hit man, if that is the correct Twentieth-Century jargon.'

Janek frowned. His plump face puckered and looked pained. He said, 'You know, madness must be catching. I'm actually beginning to consider the insane notion you've brought here. Fortunately, it doesn't hold water. After all, why would an assassination of the human-Winkler be arranged in public? All the arguments against destroying the robot in public hold against the killing of a human President in public. Don't you see that ruins the whole theory?'

'It does not – ' began Edwards.

'It *does*. No one except for a few officials knew that the mechanical device existed at all. If President Winkler were killed privately and his body disposed of, the robot could easily take over without suspicion – without having roused yours, for instance.'

'There would always be a few officials who would know, Mr Janek. The assassinations would have to broaden.' Edwards leaned forward earnestly. 'See here, ordinarily there couldn't have been any danger of confusing the human being and the machine. I imagine the robot wasn't in constant use, but was pulled out only for specific purposes, and there would always be key individuals, perhaps quite a number of them, who would know where the President was and what he was doing. If that were so, the assassination would have to be carried out at a time when those officials actually thought the President was really the robot.'

'I don't follow you.'

'See here. One of the robot's tasks was to shake hands with the crowd; press the flesh. When this was taking place, the officials in the know would be perfectly aware that the hand shaker was, in truth, the robot.'

'Exactly. You're making sense now. It *was* the robot.'

'Except that it was the Tercentenary, and except that President Winkler could not resist. I suppose it would be more than human to expect a President – particularly an empty crowd pleaser and applause hunter like Winkler – to give up the adulation of the crowd on this day of all days, and let it go to a machine. And perhaps the robot carefully nurtured this impulse so that on this one Tercentenary day, the President would have ordered the robot to remain behind the podium, while he himself went out to shake hands and to be cheered.'

'Secretly?'

'Of course secretly. If the President had told anyone in the Service, or any of his aides, or you, would he have been allowed to do it? The official attitude concerning the possibility of assassination has been practically a disease since the events of the late Twentieth Century. So with the encouragement of an obviously clever robot – '

'You assume the robot to be clever because you assume he is now serving as President. That is circular reasoning. If he is not President, there is no reason to think he is clever, or that he were capable of working out this plot. Besides, what motive could possibly drive a robot to plot an assassination? Even if it didn't kill the President directly, the taking of a human life indirectly is also forbidden by the First Law, which states: "A robot may not injure a human being or, through inaction, allow a human being to come to harm."'

Edwards said, 'The First Law is not absolute. What if

harming a human being saves the lives of two others, or three others, or even three billion others? The robot may have thought that saving the Federation took precedence over the saving of one life. It was no ordinary robot, after all. It was designed to duplicate the properties of the President closely enough to deceive anyone. Suppose it had the understanding of President Winkler, without his weaknesses, and suppose it knew that it could save the Federation where the President could not.'

'You can reason so, but how do you know a mechanical device would?'

'It is the only way to explain what happened.'

'I think it is a paranoid fantasy.'

Edwards said, 'Then tell me why the object that was destroyed was powdered into atoms. What else would make sense than to suppose that that was the only way to hide the fact that it was a human being and not a robot that was destroyed? Give me an alternate explanation.'

Janek reddened. 'I won't accept it.'

'But you can prove the whole matter – or disprove it. It's why I have come to you – to *you*.'

'How can I prove it? Or disprove it either?'

'No one sees the President at unguarded moments as you do. It is with you – in default of family – that he is most informal. Study him.'

'I have. I tell you he isn't – '

'You haven't. You suspected nothing wrong. Little signs meant nothing to you. Study him now, being aware that he *might* be a robot, and you will see.'

Janek said sardonically, 'I can knock him down and probe for metal with an ultrasonic detector. Even an android has a platinum-iridium brain.'

'No drastic action will be necessary. Just observe him and you will see that he is so radically not the man he was that he cannot be a man.'

Janek looked at the clock-calendar on the wall. He said, 'We have been here over an hour.'

'I'm sorry to have taken up so much of your time, but you see the importance of all this, I hope.'

'Importance?' said Janek. Then he looked up and what had seemed a despondent air turned suddenly into something of hope. 'But is it, in fact, important? Really, I mean?'

'How can it not be important? To have a robot as President of the United States? That's not important?'

'No, that's not what I mean. Forget what President Winkler might be. Just consider this. Someone serving as President of the United States has saved the Federation; he has held it together and, at the present moment, he runs the Council in the interests of peace and of constructive compromise. You'll admit all that?'

Edwards said, 'Of course, I admit all that. But what of the precedent established? A robot in the White House for a very good reason now may lead to a robot in the White House twenty years from now for a very bad reason, and then to robots in the White House for no reason at all but only as a matter of course. Don't you see the importance of muffling a possible trumpet call for the end of humanity at the time of its first uncertain note?'

Janek shrugged. 'Suppose I find out he's a robot? Do we broadcast it to all the world? Do you know how that will affect the Federation? Do you know what it will do to the world's financial structure? Do you know – '

'I do know. That is why I have come to you privately, instead of trying to make it public. It is up to you to check out the matter and come to a definite conclusion. It is up to you, next, having found the supposed President to be a robot, which I am certain you will do, to persuade him to resign.'

'And by your version of his reaction to the First Law, he

will then have me killed since I will be threatening his expert handling of the greatest global crisis of the Twenty-first Century.'

Edwards shook his head. 'The robot acted in secret before, and no one tried to counter the arguments he used with himself. You will be able to reinforce a stricter interpretation of the First Law with your arguments. If necessary, we can get the aid of some official from US Robots and Mechanical Men Corporation who constructed the robot in the first place. Once he resigns, the Vice-President will succeed. If the robot-Winkler has put the old world on the right track, good; it can now be kept on the right track by the Vice-President, who is a decent and honorable woman. But we can't have a robot ruler, and we mustn't ever again.'

'What if the President is human?'

'I'll leave that to you. You will know.'

Janek said, 'I am not that confident of myself. What if I can't decide? If I can't bring myself to? If I don't dare to? What are your plans?'

Edwards looked tired. 'I don't know. I may have to go to US Robots. But I don't think it will come to that. I'm quite confident that now that I've laid the problem in your lap, you won't rest till it's settled. Do *you* want to be ruled by a robot?'

He stood up, and Janek let him go. They did not shake hands.

Janek sat there in the gathering twilight in deep shock.

A robot!

The man had walked in and had argued, in perfectly rational manner, that the President of the United States was a robot.

It should have been easy to fight that off. Yet though Janek had tried every argument he could think of, they had all been useless, and the man had not been shaken in the least.

A robot as President! Edwards had been *certain* of it, and he would *stay* certain of it. And if Janek insisted that the President was human, Edwards would go to US Robots. He wouldn't rest.

Janek frowned as he thought of the twenty-seven months since the Tercentenary and of how well all had gone in the face of the probabilities. And now?

He remained lost in somber thought.

He still had the disintegrator but surely it would not be necessary to use it on a human being, the nature of whose body was not in question. A silent laser stroke in some lonely spot would do.

It had been hard to maneuver the President into the earlier job, but in this present case, it wouldn't even have to know.

Powell and Donovan

The second robot story I wrote, 'Reason' (included in this section), dealt with the two field-testers, Gregory Powell and Michael Donovan. They were modeled on certain stories John Campbell wrote, which I admired extravagantly, about a pair of interplanetary explorers, Penton and Blake. If Campbell ever noted the similarity, he said nothing about it to me.

By the way, I must warn you that the first story in this section, 'First Law,' was written as a spoof and is not meant to be taken seriously.

First Law

Mike Donovan looked at his empty beer mug, felt bored, and decided he had listened long enough. He said, loudly, 'If we're going to talk about unusual robots, *I* once knew one that disobeyed the First Law.'

And since that was completely impossible, everyone stopped talking and turned to look at Donovan.

Donovan regretted his big mouth at once and changed the subject. 'I heard a good one yesterday,' he said, conversationally, 'about – '

MacFarlane in the chair next to Donovan's said, 'You mean you knew a robot that harmed a human being?' That was what disobedience to First Law meant, of course.

'In a way,' said Donovan. 'I say I heard one about – '

'Tell us about it,' ordered MacFarlane. Some of the others banged their beer mugs on the table.

Donovan made the best of it. 'It happened on Titan about ten years ago,' he said, thinking rapidly. 'Yes, it was in twenty-five. We had just recently received a shipment of three new-model robots, specially designed for Titan. They were the first of the MA models. We called them Emma One, Two and Three.' He snapped his fingers for another beer and stared earnestly after the waiter. Let's see, what came next?

MacFarlane said, 'I've been in robotics half my life, Mike. I never heard of an MA serial order.'

'That's because they took the MA's off the assembly lines immediately after – after what I'm going to tell you. Don't you remember?'

'No.'

Donovan continued hastily. 'We put the robots to work at once. You see, until then, the Base had been entirely useless during the stormy season, which lasts eighty percent of Titan's revolution about Saturn. During the terrific snows, you couldn't find the Base if it were only a hundred yards away. Compasses aren't any use, because Titan hasn't any magnetic field.

'The virtue of these MA robots, however, was that they were equipped with vibro-detectors of a new design so that they could make a beeline for the Base through anything, and that meant mining could become a through-the-revolution affair. And don't say a word, Mac. The vibro-detectors were taken off the market also, and that's why you haven't heard of them.' Donovan coughed. 'Military secret, you understand.'

He went on. 'The robots worked fine during the first stormy season, then at the start of the calm season, Emma Two began acting up. She kept wandering off into corners and under bales and had to be coaxed out. Finally she wandered off Base altogether and didn't come back. We decided there had been a flaw in her manufacture and got along with the other two. Still, it meant we were short-handed, or short-roboted anyway, so when toward the end of the calm season, someone had to go to Kornsk, I volunteered to chance it without a robot. It seemed safe enough; the storms weren't due for two days and I'd be back in twenty hours at the outside.

'I was on the way back – a good ten miles from Base – when the wind started blowing and the air thickening. I landed my air car immediately before the wind could smash it, pointed myself toward the Base and started running. I could run the distance in the low gravity all right, but could I run a straight line? That was the question. My air supply was ample and my suit heat coils were satisfactory, but ten miles in a Titanian storm is infinity.

'Then, when the snow streams changed everything to a dark, gooey twilight, with even Saturn dimmed out and the sun only a pale pimple, I stopped short and leaned against the wind. There was a little dark object right ahead of me. I could barely make it out but I knew what it was. It was a storm pup; the only living thing that could stand a Titanian storm, and the most vicious living thing anywhere. I knew my space suit wouldn't protect me, once it made for me, and in the bad light, I had to wait for a point-blank aim or I didn't dare shoot. One miss and he would be at me.

'I backed away slowly and the shadow followed. It closed in and I was raising my blaster, with a prayer, when a bigger shadow loomed over me suddenly, and I yodeled with relief. It was Emma Two, the missing MA robot. I never stopped to wonder what had happened to it or worry why it had. I just howled, "Emma, baby, get that storm pup; and then get me back to Base."

'It just looked at me as if it hadn't heard and called out, "Master, don't shoot. Don't shoot."

'It made for that storm pup at a dead run.

'"Get that damned pup, Emma," I shouted. It got the pup, all right. It scooped it right up and *kept on going*. I yelled myself hoarse but it never came back. It left me to die in the storm.'

Donovan paused dramatically, 'Of course, you know the First Law: A robot may not injure a human being, or through inaction, allow a human being to come to harm! Well, Emma Two just ran off with that storm pup and left me to die. It broke First Law.

'Luckily, I pulled through safely. Half an hour later, the storm died down. It had been a premature gust, and a temporary one. That happens sometimes. I hot-footed it for Base and the storms really broke next day. Emma Two returned two hours after I did, and, of course, the mystery was then explained and the MA models were taken off the market immediately.'

'And just what,' demanded MacFarlane, 'was the explanation?'

Donovan regarded him seriously. 'It's true I was a human being in danger of death, Mac, but to that robot there was something else that came first, even before me, before the First Law. Don't forget these robots were of the MA series and this particular MA robot had been searching out private nooks for some time before disappearing. It was as though it expected something special – and private – to happen to it. Apparently, something special had.'

Donovan's eyes turned upward reverently and his voice trembled. 'That storm pup was no storm pup. We named it Emma Junior when Emma Two brought it back. Emma Two *had* to protect it from my gun. What is even First Law compared with the holy ties of mother love?'

Runaround

It was one of Gregory Powell's favorite platitudes that nothing was to be gained from excitement, so when Mike Donovan came leaping down the stairs toward him, red hair matted with perspiration, Powell frowned.

'What's wrong?' he said. 'Break a fingernail?'

'Yaaaah,' snarled Donovan, feverishly. 'What have you been doing in the sublevels all day?' He took a deep breath and blurted out, 'Speedy never returned.'

Powell's eyes widened momentarily and he stopped on the stairs; then he recovered and resumed his upward steps. He didn't speak until he reached the head of the flight, and then:

'You sent him after the selenium?'

'Yes.'

'And how long has he been out?'

'Five hours now.'

Silence! This was a devil of a situation. Here they were, on Mercury exactly twelve hours – and already up to the eyebrows in the worst sort of trouble. Mercury had long been the jinx world of the System, but this was drawing it rather strong – even for a jinx.

Powell said, 'Start at the beginning, and let's get this straight.'

They were in the radio room now – with its already subtly antiquated equipment, untouched for the ten years previous to their arrival. Even ten years, technologically speaking, meant so much. Compare Speedy with the type of robot they must have had back in 2005. But then, advances in robotics these days were tremendous. Powell touched a still gleaming metal surface gingerly. The air of disuse that touched everything about the room – and the entire Station – was infinitely depressing.

Donovan must have felt it. He began: 'I tried to locate him by radio, but it was no go. Radio isn't any good on the Mercury Sunside – not past two miles, anyway. That's one of the reasons the First Expedition failed. And we can't put up the ultrawave equipment for weeks yet – '

'Skip all that. What *did* you get?'

'I located the unorganized body signal in the short wave. It was no good for anything except his position. I kept track of him that way for two hours and plotted the results on the map.'

There was a yellowed square of parchment in his hip pocket – a relic of the unsuccessful First Expedition – and he slapped it down on the desk with vicious force, spreading it flat with the palm of his hand. Powell, hands clasped across his chest, watched it at long range.

Donovan's pencil pointed nervously. 'The red cross is the selenium pool. You marked it yourself.'

'Which one is it?' interrupted Powell. 'There were three that MacDougal located for us before he left.'

'I sent Speedy to the nearest, naturally. Seventeen miles away. But what difference does that make?' There was tension in his voice. 'There are the penciled dots that mark Speedy's position.'

And for the first time Powell's artificial aplomb was shaken and his hands shot forward for the map.

'Are *you* serious? This is impossible.'

'There it is,' growled Donovan.

The little dots that marked the position formed a rough circle about the red cross of the selenium pool. And Powell's fingers went to his brown mustache, the unfailing signal of anxiety.

Donovan added: 'In the two hours I checked on him, he

circled that damned pool four times. It seems likely to me that he'll keep that up forever. Do you realize the position we're in?'

Powell looked up shortly, and said nothing. Oh, yes, he realized the position they were in. It worked itself out as simply as a syllogism. The photo-cell banks that alone stood between the full power of Mercury's monstrous sun and themselves were shot to hell. The only thing that could save them was selenium. The only thing that could get the selenium was Speedy. If Speedy didn't come back, no selenium. No selenium, no photo-cell banks. No photo-banks – well, death by slow broiling is one of the more unpleasant ways of being done in.

Donovan rubbed his red mop of hair savagely and expressed himself with bitterness. 'We'll be the laughing-stock of the System, Greg. How can everything have gone so wrong so soon? The great team of Powell and Donovan is sent out to Mercury to report on the advisability of reopening the Sunside Mining Station with modern techniques and robots and we ruin everything the first day. A purely routine job, too. We'll never live it down.'

'We won't have to, perhaps,' replied Powell, quietly. 'If we don't do something quickly, living anything down – or even just plain living – will be out of the question.'

'Don't be stupid! If you feel funny about it, Greg, I don't. It was criminal, sending us out here with only one robot. And it was *your* bright idea that we could handle the photo-cell banks ourselves.'

'Now you're being unfair. It was a mutual decision and you know it. All we needed was a kilogram of selenium, a Stillhead Dielectrode Plate and about three hours' time – and there are pools of pure selenium all over Sunside. MacDougal's spectroreflector spotted three for us in five minutes, didn't it? What the devil! We couldn't have waited for next conjunction.'

'Well, what are we going to do? Powell, you've got an idea. I know you have, or you wouldn't be so calm. You're no more a hero than I am. Go on, spill it!'

'We can't go after Speedy ourselves, Mike – not on the Sunside. Even the new insosuits aren't good for more than twenty minutes in direct sunlight. But you know the old saying, "Set a robot to catch a robot." Look, Mike, maybe things aren't so bad. We've got six robots down in the sublevels, that we may be able to use, if they work. *If* they work.'

There was a glint of sudden hope in Donovan's eyes. 'You mean six robots from the First Expedition. Are you sure? They may be subrobotic machines. Ten years is a long time as far as robot-types are concerned, you know.'

'No, they're robots. I've spent all day with them and I know. They've got positronic brains: primitive, of course.' He placed the map in his pocket. 'Let's go down.'

The robots were on the lowest sublevel – all six of them surrounded by musty packing cases of uncertain content. They were large, extremely so, and even though they were in a sitting position on the floor, legs straddled out before them, their heads were a good seven feet in the air.

Donovan whistled. 'Look at the size of them, will you? The chests must be ten feet around.'

'That's because they're supplied with the old McGuffy gears. I've been over the insides – crummiest set you've ever seen.'

'Have you powered them yet?'

'No. There wasn't any reason to. I don't think there's anything wrong with them. Even the diaphragm is in reasonable order. They might talk.'

He had unscrewed the chest plate of the nearest as he spoke, inserted the two-inch sphere that contained the tiny spark of atomic energy that was a robot's life. There was difficulty in fitting it, but he managed, and then screwed the plate back on again in laborious fashion. The radio controls of more modern models had not been heard of ten years earlier. And then to the other five.

Donovan said uneasily, 'They haven't moved.'

'No orders to do so,' replied Powell, succinctly. He went back to the first in the line and struck him on the chest. 'You! Do you hear me?'

The monster's head bent slowly and the eyes fixed themselves on Powell. Then, in a harsh, squawking voice – like that of a medieval phonograph, he grated, 'Yes, Master!'

Powell grinned humorlessly at Donovan. 'Did you get that? Those were the days of the first talking robots when it looked as if the use of robots on Earth would be banned. The makers were fighting that and they built good, healthy slave complexes into the damned machines.'

'It didn't help them,' muttered Donovan.

'No, it didn't, but they sure tried.' He turned once more to the robot. 'Get up!'

The robot towered upward slowly and Donovan's head craned and his puckered lips whistled.

Powell said: 'Can you go out upon the surface? In the light?'

There was consideration while the robot's slow brain worked. Then, 'Yes, Master.'

'Good. Do you know what a mile is?'

Another consideration, and another slow answer. 'Yes, Master.'

'We will take you up to the surface then, and indicate a direction. You will go about seventeen miles, and somewhere in that general region you will meet another robot, smaller than yourself. You understand so far?'

'Yes, Master.'

'You will find this robot and order him to return. If he does not wish to, you are to bring him back by force.'

Donovan clutched at Powell's sleeve. 'Why not send him for the selenium direct?'

'Because I want Speedy back, nitwit. I want to find out what's wrong with him.' And to the robot, 'All right, you, follow me.'

The robot remained motionless and his voice rumbled: 'Pardon, Master, but I cannot. You must mount first.' His clumsy arms had come together with a thwack, blunt fingers interlacing.

Powell stared and then pinched at his mustache. 'Uh . . . oh!'

Donovan's eyes bulged. 'We've got to ride him? Like a horse?'

'I guess that's the idea. I don't know why, though. I can't see – Yes, I do. I told you they were playing up robot-safety in those days. Evidently, they were going to sell the notion of safety by not allowing them to move about, without a mahout on their shoulders all the time. What do we do now?'

'That's what I've been thinking,' muttered Donovan. 'We can't go out on the surface, with a robot or without. Oh, for the love of Pete' – and he snapped his fingers twice. He grew excited. 'Give me that map you've got. I haven't studied it for two hours for nothing. This is a Mining Station. What's wrong with using the tunnels?'

The Mining Station was a black circle on the map, and the light dotted lines that were tunnels stretched out about it in spiderweb fashion.

Donovan studied the list of symbols at the bottom of the map. 'Look,' he said, 'the small black dots are openings to the surface, and here's one maybe three miles away from the selenium pool. There's a number here – you'd think they'd write larger – 13a. If the robots know their way around here – '

Powell shot the question and received the dull 'Yes,

Master,' in reply. 'Get your insosuit,' he said with satisfaction.

It was the first time either had worn the insosuits – which marked one time more than either had expected to upon their arrival the day before – and they tested their limb movements uncomfortably.

The insosuit was far bulkier and far uglier than the regulation spacesuit; but withal considerably lighter, due to the fact that they were entirely nonmetallic in composition. Composed of heat-resistant plastic and chemically treated cork layers, and equipped with a desiccating unit to keep the air bone-dry, the insosuits could withstand the full glare of Mercury's sun for twenty minutes. Five to ten minutes more, as well, without actually killing the occupant.

And still the robot's hands formed the stirrup, nor did he betray the slightest atom of surprise at the grotesque figure into which Powell had been converted.

Powell's radio-harshened voice boomed out: 'Are you ready to take us to Exit 13a?'

'Yes, Master.'

Good, thought Powell; they might lack radio control but at least they were fitted for radio reception. 'Mount one or the other, Mike,' he said to Donovan.

He placed a foot in the improvised stirrup and swung upward. He found the seat comfortable; there was the humped back of the robot, evidently shaped for the purpose, a shallow groove along each shoulder for the thighs and two elongated 'ears' whose purpose now seemed obvious.

Powell seized the ears and twisted the head. His mount turned ponderously. 'Lead on, Macduff.' But he did not feel at all light-hearted.

The gigantic robots moved slowly, with mechanical precision, through the doorway that cleared their heads by a scant foot, so that the two men had to duck hurriedly, along a narrow corridor in which their unhurried footsteps boomed monotonously and into the air lock.

The long, airless tunnel that stretched to a pinpoint before them brought home forcefully to Powell the exact magnitude of the task accomplished by the First Expedition, with their crude robots and their start-from-scratch necessities. They might have been a failure, but their failure was a good deal better than the usual run of the System's successes.

The robots plodded onward with a pace that never varied and with footsteps that never lengthened.

Powell said: 'Notice that these tunnels are blazing with lights and that the temperature is Earth-normal. It's probably been like this all the ten years that this place has remained empty.'

'How's that?'

'Cheap energy; cheapest in the System. Sunpower, you know, and on Mercury's Sunside, sunpower is *something*. That's why the Station was built in the sunlight rather than in the shadow of a mountain. It's really a huge energy converter. The heat is turned into electricity, light, mechanical work and what have you; so that energy is supplied and the Station is cooled in a simultaneous process.'

'Look,' said Donovan. 'This is all very educational, but would you mind changing the subject? It so happens that this conversion of energy that you talk about is carried on by the photo-cell banks mainly – and that is a tender subject with me at the moment.'

Powell grunted vaguely, and when Donovan broke the resulting silence, it was to change the subject completely. 'Listen, Greg. What the devil's wrong with Speedy, anyway? I can't understand it.'

It's not easy to shrug shoulders in an insosuit, but Powell tried it. 'I don't know, Mike. You know he's perfectly adapted to a Mercurian environment. Heat doesn't mean anything to him and he's built for the light gravity and the broken ground. He's foolproof – or, at least, he should be.'

Silence fell. This time, silence that lasted.

'Master,' said the robot, 'we are here.'

'Eh?' Powell snapped out of a semidrowse. 'Well, get us out of here – out to the surface.'

They found themselves in a tiny substation, empty, airless, ruined. Donovan had inspected a jagged hole in the upper reaches of one of the walls by the light of his pocket flash.

'Meteorite, do you suppose?' he had asked.

Powell shrugged. 'To hell with that. It doesn't matter. Let's get out.'

A towering cliff of a black, basaltic rock cut off the sunlight, and the deep night shadow of an airless world surrounded them. Before them, the shadow reached out and ended in knife-edge abruptness into an all-but-unbearable blaze of white light, that glittered from myriad crystals along a rocky ground.

'Space!' gasped Donovan. 'It looks like snow.' And it did.

Powell's eyes swept the jagged glitter of Mercury to the horizon and winced at the gorgeous brilliance.

'This must be an unusual area,' he said. 'The general albedo of Mercury is low and most of the soil is gray pumice. Something like the Moon, you know. Beautiful, isn't it?'

He was thankful for the light filters in their visiplates. Beautiful or not, a look at the sunlight through straight glass would have blinded them inside of half a minute.

Donovan was looking at the spring thermometer on his wrist. 'Holy smokes, the temperature is eighty centigrade!'

Powell checked his own and said: 'Um-m-m. A little high. Atmosphere, you know.'

'On Mercury? Are you nuts?'

'Mercury isn't really airless,' explained Powell, in

absent-minded fashion. He was adjusting the binocular attachments to his visiplate, and the bloated fingers of the insosuit were clumsy at it. 'There is a thin exhalation that clings to its surface – vapors of the more volatile elements and compounds that are heavy enough for Mercurian gravity to retain. You know: selenium, iodine, mercury, gallium, potassium, bismuth, volatile oxides. The vapors sweep into the shadows and condense, giving up heat. It's a sort of gigantic still. In fact, if you use your flash, you'll probably find that the side of the cliff is covered with, say, hoar-sulphur, or maybe quicksilver dew.

'It doesn't matter, though. Our suits can stand a measly eighty indefinitely.'

Powell had adjusted the binocular attachments, so that he seemed as eye-stalked as a snail.

Donovan watched tensely. 'See anything?'

The other did not answer immediately, and when he did, his voice was anxious and thoughtful. 'There's a dark spot on the horizon that might be the selenium pool. It's in the right place. But I don't see Speedy.'

Powell clambered upward in an instinctive striving for better view, till he was standing in unsteady fashion upon his robot's shoulders. Legs straddled wide, eyes straining, he said: 'I think . . . I think – Yes, it's definitely he. He's coming this way.'

Donovan followed the pointing finger. He had no binoculars, but there was a tiny moving dot, black against the blazing brilliance of the crystalline ground.

'I see him,' he yelled. 'Let's get going!'

Powell had hopped down into a sitting position on the robot again, and his suited hand slapped against the Gargantuan's barrel chest. 'Get going!'

'Giddy-ap,' yelled Donovan, and thumped his heels, spur fashion.

* * *

The robots started off, the regular thudding of their footsteps silent in the airlessness, for the nonmetallic fabric of the insosuits did not transmit sound. There was only a rhythmic vibration just below the border of actual hearing.

'Faster,' yelled Donovan. The rhythm did not change.

'No use,' cried Powell, in reply. 'These junk heaps are only geared to one speed. Do you think they're equipped with selective flexors?'

They had burst through the shadow, and the sunlight came down in a white-hot wash and poured liquidly about them.

Donovan ducked involuntarily. 'Wow! Is it imagination or do I feel heat?'

'You'll feel more presently,' was the grim reply. 'Keep your eye on Speedy.'

Robot SPD 13 was near enough to be seen in detail now. His graceful, streamlined body threw out blazing highlights as he loped with easy speed across the broken ground. His name was derived from his serial initials, of course, but it was apt, nevertheless, for the SPD models were among the fastest robots turned out by the United States Robots and Mechanical Men Corporation.

'Hey, Speedy,' howled Donovan, and waved a frantic hand.

'Speedy!' shouted Powell. 'Come here!'

The distance between the men and the errant robot was being cut down momentarily – more by the efforts of Speedy than the slow plodding of the ten-year-old antique mounts of Donovan and Powell.

They were close enough now to notice that Speedy's gait included a peculiar rolling stagger, a noticeable side-to-side lurch – and then, as Powell waved his hand again and sent maximum juice into his compact head-set radio sender, in preparation for another shout, Speedy looked up and saw them.

Speedy hopped to a halt and remained standing for a moment – with just a tiny, unsteady weave, as though he were swaying in a light wind.

Powell yelled: 'All right, Speedy. Come here, boy.'

Whereupon Speedy's robot voice sounded in Powell's earphones for the first time.

It said: 'Hot dog, let's play games. You catch me and I catch you; no love can cut our knife in two. For I'm Little Buttercup, sweet Little Buttercup. Whoops!' Turning on his heel, he sped off in the direction from which he had come, with a speed and fury that kicked up gouts of baked dust.

And his last words as he receded into the distance were, 'There grew a little flower 'neath a great oak tree,' followed by a curious metallic clicking that *might* have been a robotic equivalent of a hiccup.

Donovan said weakly: 'Where did he pick up the Gilbert and Sullivan? Say, Greg, he . . . he's drunk or something.'

'If you hadn't told me,' was the bitter response, 'I'd never realize it. Let's get back to the cliff. I'm roasting.'

It was Powell who broke the desperate silence. 'In the first place,' he said, 'Speedy isn't drunk – not in the human sense – because he's a robot, and robots don't get drunk. However, there's *something* wrong with him which is the robotic equivalent of drunkenness.'

'To me, he's drunk,' stated Donovan, emphatically, 'and all I know is that he thinks we're playing games. And we're not. It's a matter of life and very gruesome death.'

'All right. Don't hurry me. A robot's only a robot. Once we find out what's wrong with him, we can fix it and go on.'

'*Once*,' said Donovan, sourly.

Powell ignored him. 'Speedy is perfectly adapted to normal Mercurian environment. But this region' – and his arm swept wide – 'is definitely abnormal. There's our clue. Now where do these crystals come from? They might have formed from a slowly cooling liquid; but where would you get liquid so hot that it would cool in Mercury's sun?'

'Volcanic action,' suggested Donovan, instantly, and Powell's body tensed.

'Out of the mouths of sucklings,' he said in a small, strange voice, and remained very still for five minutes.

Then, he said, 'Listen, Mike, what did you say to Speedy when you sent him after the selenium?'

Donovan was taken aback. 'Well damn it – I don't know. I just told him to get it.'

'Yes, I know. But how? Try to remember the exact words.'

'I said . . . uh . . . I said: "Speedy, we need some selenium. You can get it such-and-such a place. Go get it." That's all. What more did you want me to say?'

'You didn't put any urgency into the order, did you?'

'What for? It was pure routine.'

Powell sighed. 'Well, it can't be helped now – but we're in a fine fix.' He had dismounted from his robot, and was sitting, back against the cliff. Donovan joined him and they linked arms. In the distance the burning sunlight seemed to wait cat-and-mouse for them, and just next to them, the two giant robots were invisible but for the dull red of their photoelectric eyes that stared down at them, unblinking, unwavering and unconcerned.

Unconcerned! As was all this poisonous Mercury, as large in jinx as it was small in size.

Powell's radio voice was tense in Donovan's ear: 'Now, look, let's start with the three fundamental Rules of Robotics – the three rules that are built most deeply into a robot's positronic brain.' In the darkness, his gloved fingers ticked off each point.

'We have: One, a robot may not injure a human being, or, through inaction, allow a human being to come to harm.'

'Right!'

'Two,' continued Powell, 'a robot must obey the orders given it by human beings except where such orders would conflict with the First Law.'

'Right!'

'And three, a robot must protect its own existence as long as such protection does not conflict with the First or Second Laws.'

'Right! Now where are we?'

'Exactly at the explanation. The conflict between the various rules is ironed out by the different positronic potentials in the brain. We'll say that a robot is walking into danger and knows it. The automatic potential that Rule 3 sets up turns him back. But suppose you *order* him to walk into that danger. In that case, Rule 2 sets up a counter-potential higher than the previous one and the robot follows orders at the risk of existence.'

'Well, I know that. What about it?'

'Let's take Speedy's case. Speedy is one of the latest models, extremely specialized, and as expensive as a battleship. It's not a thing to be lightly destroyed.'

'So?'

'So Rule 3 has been strengthened – that was specifically mentioned, by the way, in the advance notices on the SPD models – so that his allergy to danger is unusually high. At the same time, when you sent him out after the selenium, you gave him his order casually and without special emphasis, so that the Rule 2 potential set-up was rather weak. Now, hold on; I'm just stating facts.'

'All right, go ahead. I think I get it.'

'You see how it works, don't you? There's some sort of danger centering at the selenium pool. It increases as he approaches, and at a certain distance from it the Rule 3 potential, unusually high to start with, exactly balances the Rule 2 potential, unusually low to start with.'

Donovan rose to his feet in excitement. 'And it strikes an equilibrium. I see. Rule 3 drives him back and Rule 2 drives him forward – '

'So he follows a circle around the selenium pool, staying on the locus of all points of potential equilibrium. And unless we do something about it, he'll stay on that circle forever, giving us the good old runaround.' Then, more thoughtfully: 'And that, by the way, is what makes him drunk. At potential equilibrium, half the positronic paths of his brain are out of kilter. I'm not a robot specialist, but that seems obvious. Probably he's lost control of just those parts of his voluntary mechanism that a human drunk has. Ve-e- ery pretty.'

'But what's the danger? If we knew what he was running from – '

'*You* suggested it. Volcanic action. Somewhere right above the selenium pool is a seepage of gas from the bowels of Mercury. Sulphur dioxide, carbon dioxide – and carbon monoxide. Lots of it – and at this temperature.'

Donovan gulped audibly. 'Carbon monoxide plus iron gives the volatile iron carbonyl.'

'And a robot,' added Powell, 'is essentially iron.' Then, grimly: 'There's nothing like deduction. We've determined everything about our problem but the solution. We can't get the selenium ourselves. It's still too far. We can't send these robot horses, because they can't go by themselves, and they can't carry us fast enough to keep us from crisping. And we can't catch Speedy, because the dope thinks we're playing games, and he can run sixty miles to our four.'

'If one of us goes,' began Donovan, tentatively, 'and comes back cooked, there'll still be the other.'

'Yes,' came the sarcastic reply, 'it would be a most tender sacrifice – except that a person would be in no condition to give orders before he ever reaches the pool, and I don't think the robots would ever turn back to the cliff without orders. Figure it out! We're two or three miles from the pool – call it two – the robot travels at four miles an hour; and we can last twenty minutes in our suits. It isn't only the heat, remember. Solar radiation out here in the ultraviolet and below is *poison*.'

'Um-m-m,' said Donovan, 'ten minutes short.'

'As good as an eternity. And another thing. In order for Rule 3 potential to have stopped Speedy where it did, there must be an appreciable amount of carbon monoxide in the metal-vapor atmosphere – and there must be an appreciable corrosive action therefore. He's been out hours now – and how do we know when a knee joint, for instance, won't be thrown out of kilter and keel him over. It's not only a question of thinking – we've got to think *fast*!'

Deep, dark, dank, dismal silence!

Donovan broke it, voice trembling in an effort to keep itself emotionless. He said: 'As long as we can't increase Rule 2 potential by giving further orders, how about working the other way? If we increase the danger, we increase Rule 3 potential and drive him backward.'

Powell's visiplate had turned toward him in a silent question.

'You see,' came the cautious explanation, 'all we need to do to drive him out of his rut is to increase the concentration of carbon monoxide in his vicinity. Well, back at the Station there's a complete analytical laboratory.'

'Naturally,' assented Powell. 'It's a Mining Station.'

'All right. There must be pounds of oxalic acid for calcium precipitations.'

'Holy space! Mike, you're a genius.'

'So-so,' admitted Donovan, modestly. 'It's just a case of remembering that oxalic acid on heating decomposes into carbon dioxide, water, and good old carbon monoxide. College chem, you know.'

Powell was on his feet and had attracted the attention of

one of the monster robots by the simple expedient of pounding the machine's thigh.

'Hey,' he shouted, 'can you throw?'

'Master?'

'Never mind.' Powell damned the robot's molasses-slow brain. He scrabbled up a jagged brick-size rock. 'Take this,' he said, 'and hit the patch of bluish crystals just across that crooked fissure. You see it?'

Donovan pulled at his shoulder. 'Too far, Greg. It's almost half a mile off.'

'Quiet,' replied Powell. 'It's a case of Mercurian gravity and a steel throwing arm. Watch, will you?'

The robot's eyes were measuring the distance with machinely accurate stereoscopy. His arm adjusted itself to the weight of the missile and drew back. In the darkness, the robot's motions went unseen, but there was a sudden thumping sound as he shifted his weight, and seconds later the rock flew blackly into the sunlight. There was no air resistance to slow it down, nor wind to turn it aside – and when it hit the ground it threw up crystals precisely in the center of the 'blue patch.'

Powell yelled happily and shouted, 'Let's go back after the oxalic acid, Mike.'

And as they plunged into the ruined substation on the way back to the tunnels, Donovan said grimly: 'Speedy's been hanging about on this side of the selenium pool, ever since we chased after him. Did you see him?'

'Yes.'

'I guess he wants to play games. Well, we'll play him games!'

They were back hours later, with three-liter jars of the white chemical and a pair of long faces. The photo-cell banks were deteriorating more rapidly than had seemed likely. The two steered their robots into the sunlight and toward the waiting Speedy in silence and with grim purpose.

Speedy galloped slowly toward them. 'Here we are again. *Whee!* I've made a little list, the piano organist; all people who eat peppermint and puff it in your face.'

'We'll puff something in *your* face,' muttered Donovan. 'He's limping, Greg.'

'I noticed that,' came the low, worried response. 'The monoxide'll get him yet, if we don't hurry.'

They were approaching cautiously now, almost sidling, to refrain from setting off the thoroughly irrational robot. Powell was too far off to tell, of course, but even already he could have sworn the crack-brained Speedy was setting himself for a spring.

'Let her go,' he gasped. 'Count three! One – two – '

Two steel arms drew back and snapped forward simultaneously and two glass jars whirled forward in towering parallel arcs, gleaming like diamonds in the impossible sun. And in a pair of soundless puffs, they hit the ground behind Speedy in crashes that sent the oxalic acid flying like dust.

In the full heat of Mercury's sun, Powell knew it was fizzing like soda water.

Speedy turned to stare, then backed away from it slowly – and as slowly gathered speed. In fifteen seconds, he was leaping directly toward the two humans in an unsteady canter.

Powell did not get Speedy's words just then, though he heard something that resembled, 'Lover's professions when uttered in Hessians.'

He turned away. 'Back to the cliff, Mike. He's out of the rut and he'll be taking orders now. I'm getting hot.'

They jogged toward the shadow at the slow monotonous pace of their mounts, and it was not until they had entered it and felt the sudden coolness settle softly about them that Donovan looked back. '*Greg!*'

Powell looked and almost shrieked. Speedy was moving slowly now – so slowly – and in the *wrong direction*. He was drifting; drifting back into his rut; and he was picking up speed. He looked dreadfully close, and dreadfully unreachable, in the binoculars.

Donovan shouted wildly, 'After him!' and thumped his robot into its pace, but Powell called him back.

'You won't catch him, Mike – it's no use.' He fidgeted on his robot's shoulders and clenched his fist in tight impotence. 'Why the devil do I see these things five seconds after it's all over? Mike, we've wasted hours.'

'We need more oxalic acid,' declared Donovan, stolidly. 'The concentration wasn't high enough.'

'Seven tons of it wouldn't have been enough – and we haven't the hours to spare to get it, even if it were, with the monoxide chewing him away. Don't you see what it is, Mike?'

And Donovan said flatly, 'No.'

'We were only establishing new equilibriums. When we create new monoxide and increase Rule 3 potential, he moves backward till he's in balance again – and when the monoxide drifted away, he moved forward, and again there was balance.'

Powell's voice sounded thoroughly wretched. 'It's the same old runaround. We can push at Rule 2 and pull at Rule 3 and we can't get anywhere – we can only change the position of balance. We've got to get outside both rules.' And then he pushed his robot closer to Donovan's so that they were sitting face to face, dim shadows in the darkness, and he whispered, 'Mike!'

'Is it the finish?' – dully. 'I suppose we go back to the Station, wait for the banks to fold, shake hands, take cyanide, and go out like gentlemen.' He laughed shortly.

'Mike,' repeated Powell earnestly, 'we've got to get Speedy.'

'I know.'

'Mike,' once more, and Powell hesitated before continuing. 'There's always Rule 1. I thought of it – earlier – but it's desperate.'

Donovan looked up and his voice livened. '*We're* desperate.'

'All right. According to Rule 1, a robot can't see a human come to harm because of his own inaction. Two and 3 can't stand against it. They *can't*, Mike.'

'Even when the robot is half cra – Well, he's drunk. You know he is.'

'It's the chances you take.'

'Cut it. What are you going to do?'

'I'm going out there now and see what Rule 1 will do. If it won't break the balance, then what the devil – it's either now or three–four days from now.'

'Hold on, Greg. There are human rules of behavior, too. You don't go out there just like that. Figure out a lottery, and give me *my* chance.'

'All right. First to get the cube of fourteen goes.' And almost immediately, 'Twenty-seven forty-four!'

Donovan felt his robot stagger at a sudden push by Powell's mount and then Powell was off into the sunlight. Donovan opened his mouth to shout, and then clicked it shut. Of course, the damn fool had worked out the cube of fourteen in advance, and on purpose. Just like him.

The sun was hotter than ever and Powell felt a maddening itch in the small of his back. Imagination, probably, or perhaps hard radiation beginning to tell even through the insosuit.

Speedy was watching him, without a word of Gilbert and Sullivan gibberish as greeting. Thank God for that! But he daren't get too close.

He was three hundred yards away when Speedy began

backing, a step at a time, cautiously – and Powell stopped. He jumped from his robot's shoulders and landed on the crystalline ground with a light thump and a flying of jagged fragments.

He proceeded on foot, the ground gritty and slippery to his steps, the low gravity causing him difficulty. The soles of his feet tickled with warmth. He cast one glance over his shoulder at the blackness of the cliff's shadow and realized that he had come too far to return – either by himself or by the help of his antique robot. It was Speedy or nothing now, and the knowledge of that constricted his chest.

Far enough! He stopped.

'Speedy,' he called. 'Speedy!'

The sleek, modern robot ahead of him hesitated and halted his backward steps, then resumed them.

Powell tried to put a note of pleading into his voice, and found it didn't take much acting. 'Speedy, I've got to get back to the shadow or the sun'll get me. It's life or death, Speedy. I need you.'

Speedy took one step forward and stopped. He spoke, but at the sound Powell groaned, for it was, 'When you're lying awake with a dismal headache and repose is tabooed – ' It trailed off there, and Powell took time out for some reason to murmur, 'Iolanthe.'

It was roasting hot! He caught a movement out of the corner of his eye, and whirled dizzily; then stared in utter astonishment, for the monstrous robot on which he had ridden was moving – moving toward him, and without a rider.

He was talking: 'Pardon, Master. I must not move without a Master upon me, but you are in danger.'

Of course, Rule 1 potential above everything. But he didn't want that clumsy antique; he wanted Speedy. He walked away and motioned frantically: 'I order you to stay away. I *order* you to stop!'

It was quite useless. You could not beat Rule 1 potential. The robot said stupidly, 'You are in danger, Master.'

Powell looked about him desperately. He couldn't see clearly. His brain was in a heated whirl; his breath scorched when he breathed, and the ground all about him was a shimmering haze.

He called a last time, desperately: '*Speedy!* I'm dying, damn you! Where are you? Speedy, I *need* you.'

He was still stumbling backward in a blind effort to get away from the giant robot he didn't want, when he felt steel fingers on his arms, and a worried, apologetic voice of metallic timbre in his ears.

'Holy smokes, boss, what are you doing here? And what am *I* doing – I'm so confused – '

'Never mind,' murmured Powell, weakly. 'Get me to the shadow of the cliff – and hurry!' There was one last feeling of being lifted into the air and a sensation of rapid motion and burning heat, and he passed out.

He woke with Donovan bending over him and smiling anxiously. 'How are you, Greg?'

'Fine!' came the response. 'Where's Speedy?'

'Right here. I sent him out to one of the other selenium pools – with orders to get that selenium at all cost this time. He got it back in forty-two minutes and three seconds. I timed him. He still hasn't finished apologizing for the runaround he gave us. He's scared to come near you for fear of what you'll say.'

'Drag him over,' ordered Powell. 'It wasn't his fault.' He held out a hand and gripped Speedy's metal paw. 'It's OK, Speedy.' Then, to Donovan, 'You know, Mike, I was just thinking – '

'Yes!'

'Well,' – he rubbed his face – the air was so delightfully cool, 'you know that when we get things set up here and

Speedy put through his Field Tests, they're going to send us to the Space Station next – '

'No!'

'Yes! At least that's what old lady Calvin told me just before we left, and I didn't say anything about it, because I was going to fight the whole idea.'

'Fight it?' cried Donovan. 'But – '

'I know. It's all right with me now. Two hundred seventy-three degrees Centigrade below zero. Won't it be a pleasure?'

'Space Station,' said Donovan, 'here I come.'

Reason

Half a year later, the boys had changed their minds. The flame of a giant sun had given way to the soft blackness of space but external variations mean little in the business of checking the workings of experimental robots. Whatever the background, one is face to face with an inscrutable positronic brain, which the slide-rule geniuses say should work thus-and-so.

Except that they don't. Powell and Donovan found that out after they had been on the Station less than two weeks.

Gregory Powell spaced his words for emphasis, 'One week ago, Donovan and I put you together.' His brows furrowed doubtfully and he pulled the end of his brown mustache.

It was quiet in the officers' room of Solar Station B.119 5 – except for the soft purring of the mighty Beam Director somewhere far below.

Robot QT-1 sat immovable. The burnished plates of his body gleamed in the Luxites and the glowing red of the photoelectric cells that were his eyes, were fixed steadily upon the Earthman at the other side of the table.

Powell repressed a sudden attack of nerves. These robots possessed peculiar brains. Oh, the three Laws of Robotics held. They had to. All of US Robots, from Robertson himself to the new floor-sweeper would insist on that. So QT-1 was *safe*! And yet – the QT models were the first of their kind, and this was the first of the QT's. Mathematical squiggles on paper were not always the most comforting protection against robotic fact.

Finally, the robot spoke. His voice carried the cold

timbre inseparable from a metallic diaphragm, 'Do you realize the seriousness of such a statement, Powell?'

'*Something* made you, Cutie,' pointed out Powell. 'You admit yourself that your memory seems to spring full-grown from an absolute blankness of a week ago. I'm giving you the explanation. Donovan and I put you together from the parts shipped us.'

Cutie gazed upon his long, supple fingers in an oddly human attitude of mystification, 'It strikes me that there should be a more satisfactory explanation than that. For *you* to make *me* seems improbable.'

The Earthman laughed quite suddenly, 'In Earth's name, why?'

'Call it intuition. That's all it is so far. But I intend to reason it out, though. A chain of valid reasoning can end only with the determination of truth, and I'll stick till I get there.'

Powell stood up and seated himself at the table's edge next to the robot. He felt a sudden strong sympathy for this strange machine. It was not at all like the ordinary robot, attending to his specialized task at the station with the intensity of a deeply ingrooved positronic path.

He placed a hand upon Cutie's steel shoulder and the metal was cold and hard to the touch.

'Cutie,' he said, 'I'm going to try to explain something to you. You're the first robot who's ever exhibited curiosity as to his own existence – and I think the first that's really intelligent enough to understand the world outside. Here, come with me.'

The robot rose erect smoothly and his thickly sponge-rubber soled feet made no noise as he followed Powell. The Earthman touched a button and a square section of the wall flickered aside. The thick, clear glass revealed space – star-speckled.

'I've seen that in the observation ports in the engine room,' said Cutie.

'I know,' said Powell. 'What do you think it is?'

'Exactly what it seems – a black material just beyond this glass that is spotted with little gleaming dots. I know that our director sends out beams to some of these dots, always to the same ones – and also that these dots shift and that the beams shift with them. That is all.'

'Good! Now I want you to listen carefully. The blackness is emptiness – vast emptiness stretching out infinitely. The little, gleaming dots are huge masses of energy-filled matter. They are globes, some of them millions of miles in diameter – and for comparison, this station is only one mile across. They seem so tiny because they are incredibly far off.

'The dots to which our energy beams are directed, are nearer and much smaller. They are cold and hard and human beings like myself live upon their surfaces – many billions of them. It is from one of these worlds that Donovan and I come. Our beams feed these worlds energy drawn from one of those huge incandescent globes that happens to be near us. We call that globe the Sun and it is on the other side of the station where you can't see it.'

Cutie remained motionless before the port, like a steel statue. His head did not turn as he spoke, 'Which particular dot of light do you claim to come from?'

Powell searched, 'There it is. The very bright one in the corner. We call it Earth.' He grinned, 'Good old Earth. There are three billions of us there, Cutie – and in about two weeks I'll be back there with them.'

And then, surprisingly enough, Cutie hummed abstractedly. There was no tune to it, but it possessed a curious twanging quality as of plucked strings. It ceased as suddenly as it had begun, 'But where do I come in, Powell? You haven't explained *my* existence.'

'The rest is simple. When these stations were first established to feed solar energy to the planets, they were run by humans. However, the heat, the hard solar radiations, and the electron storms made the post a difficult one. Robots were developed to replace human labor and now only two human executives are required for each station. We are trying to replace even those, and that's where you come in. You're the highest type of robot ever developed and if you show the ability to run this station independently, no human need ever come here again except to bring parts for repairs.'

His hand went up and the metal visi-lid snapped back into place. Powell returned to the table and polished an apple upon his sleeve before biting into it.

The red glow of the robot's eyes held him. 'Do you expect me,' said Cutie slowly, 'to believe any such complicated, implausible hypothesis as you have just outlined? What do you take me for?'

Powell sputtered apple fragments onto the table and turned red. 'Why, damn you, it wasn't a hypothesis. Those were facts.'

Cutie sounded grim, 'Globes of energy millions of miles across! Worlds with three billion humans on them! Infinite emptiness! Sorry, Powell, but I don't believe it. I'll puzzle this thing out for myself. Good-by.'

He turned and stalked out of the room. He brushed past Michael Donovan on the threshold with a grave nod and passed down the corridor, oblivious to the astounded stare that followed him.

Mike Donovan rumpled his red hair and shot an annoyed glance at Powell, 'What was that walking junk yard talking about? What doesn't he believe?'

The other dragged at his mustache bitterly. 'He's a skeptic,' was the bitter response. 'He doesn't believe we made him or that Earth exists or space or stars.'

'Sizzling Saturn, we've got a lunatic robot on our hands.'

'He says he's going to figure it all out for himself.'

'Well, now,' said Donovan sweetly, 'I do hope he'll

condescend to explain it all to me after he's puzzled everything out.' Then, with sudden rage, 'Listen! If that metal mess gives *me* any lip like that, I'll knock that chromium cranium right off its torso.'

He seated himself with a jerk and drew a paper-backed mystery novel out of his inner jacket pocket, 'That robot gives me the willies anyway – too damned inquisitive!'

Mike Donovan growled from behind a huge lettuce-and-tomato sandwich as Cutie knocked gently and entered.

'Is Powell here?'

Donovan's voice was muffled, with pauses for mastication, 'He's gathering data on electronic stream functions. We're heading for a storm, looks like.'

Gregory Powell entered as he spoke, eyes on the graphed paper in his hands and dropped into a chair. He spread the sheets out before him and began scribbling calculations. Donovan stared over his shoulder, crunching lettuce and dribbling bread crumbs. Cutie waited silently.

Powell looked up, 'The Zeta Potential is rising, but slowly. Just the same, the stream functions are erratic and I don't know what to expect. Oh, hello, Cutie. I thought you were supervising the installation of the new drive bar.'

'It's done,' said the robot quietly, 'and so I've come to have a talk with the two of you.'

'Oh!' Powell looked uncomfortable. 'Well, sit down. No, not that chair. One of the legs is weak and you're no lightweight.'

The robot did so and said placidly, 'I have come to a decision.'

Donovan glowered and put the remnants of his sandwich aside. 'If it's on any of that screwy – '

The other motioned impatiently for silence, 'Go ahead, Cutie. We're listening.'

'I have spent these last two days in concentrated

introspection,' said Cutie, 'and the results have been most interesting. I began at the one sure assumption I felt permitted to make. I, myself, exist, because I think – '

Powell groaned, 'Oh, Jupiter, a robot Descartes!'

'Who's Descartes?' demanded Donovan. 'Listen, do we have to sit here and listen to this metal maniac – '

'Keep quiet, Mike!'

Cutie continued imperturbably, 'And the question that immediately arose was: Just what is the cause of my existence?'

Powell's jaw set lumpily. 'You're being foolish. I told you already that we made you.'

'And if you don't believe us,' added Donovan, 'we'll gladly take you apart!'

The robot spread his strong hands in a deprecatory gesture, 'I accept nothing on authority. A hypothesis must be backed by reason, or else it is worthless – and it goes against all the dictates of logic to suppose that you made me.'

Powell dropped a restraining arm upon Donovan's suddenly bunched fist. 'Just why do you say that?'

Cutie laughed. It was a very inhuman laugh – the most machine-like utterance he had yet given vent to. It was sharp and explosive, as regular as a metronome and as uninflected.

'Look at you,' he said finally. 'I say this in no spirit of contempt, but look at you! The material you are made of is soft and flabby, lacking endurance and strength, depending for energy upon the inefficient oxidation of organic material – like that.' He pointed a disapproving finger at what remained of Donovan's sandwich. 'Periodically you pass into a coma and the least variation in temperature, air pressure, humidity, or radiation intensity impairs your efficiency. You are *makeshift*.

'I, on the other hand, am a finished product. I absorb

electrical energy directly and utilize it with an almost one hundred percent efficiency. I am composed of strong metal, am continuously conscious, and can stand extremes of environment easily. These are facts which, with the self-evident proposition that no being can create another being superior to itself, smashes your silly hypothesis to nothing.'

Donovan's muttered curses rose into intelligibility as he sprang to his feet, rusty eyebrows drawn low. 'All right, you son of a hunk of iron ore, if we didn't make you, who did?'

Cutie nodded gravely. 'Very good, Donovan. That was indeed the next question. Evidently my creator must be more powerful than myself and so there was only one possibility.'

The Earthmen looked blank and Cutie continued, 'What is the center of activities here in the station? What do we all serve? What absorbs all our attention?' He waited expectantly.

Donovan turned a startled look upon his companion. 'I'll bet this tin-plated screwball is talking about the Energy Converter itself.'

'Is that right, Cutie?' grinned Powell.

'I am talking about the Master,' came the cold, sharp answer.

It was the signal for a roar of laughter from Donovan, and Powell himself dissolved into a half-suppressed giggle.

Cutie had risen to his feet and his gleaming eyes passed from one Earthman to the other. 'It is so just the same and I don't wonder that you refuse to believe. You two are not long to stay here, I'm sure. Powell himself said that at first only men served the Master; that there followed robots for the routine work; and, finally, myself for the executive labor. The facts are no doubt true, but the explanation entirely illogical. Do you want the truth behind it all?'

'Go ahead, Cutie. You're amusing.'

'The Master created humans first as the lowest type, most easily formed. Gradually, he replaced them by robots, the next higher step, and finally he created me, to take the place of the last humans. From now on, *I* serve the Master.'

'You'll do nothing of the sort,' said Powell sharply. 'You'll follow our orders and keep quiet, until we're satisfied that you can run the Converter. Get that! *The Converter* – not the Master. If you don't satisfy us, you will be dismantled. And now – if you don't mind – you can leave. And take this data with you and file it properly.'

Cutie accepted the graphs handed him and left without another word. Donovan leaned back heavily in his chair and shoved thick fingers through his hair.

'There's going to be trouble with that robot. He's pure nuts!'

The drowsy hum of the Converter is louder in the control room and mixed with it is the chuckle of the Geiger Counters and the erratic buzzing of half a dozen little signal lights.

Donovan withdrew his eye from the telescope and flashed the Luxites on. 'The beam from Station No. 4 caught Mars on schedule. We can break ours now.'

Powell nodded abstractedly. 'Cutie's down in the engine room. I'll flash the signal and he can take care of it. Look, Mike, what do you think of these figures?'

The other cocked an eye at them and whistled. 'Boy, that's what I call gamma-ray intensity. Old Sol is feeling his oats, all right.'

'Yeah,' was the sour response, 'and we're in a bad position for an electron storm, too. Our Earth beam is right in the probable path.' He shoved his chair away from the table pettishly. 'Nuts! If it would only hold off till relief got here, but that's ten days off. Say, Mike, go on down and keep an eye on Cutie will you?'

'OK. Throw me some of those almonds.' He snatched at the bag thrown him and headed for the elevator.

It slid smoothly downward, and opened onto a narrow catwalk in the huge engine room. Donovan leaned over the railing and looked down. The huge generators were in motion and from the L-tubes came the low-pitched whir that pervaded the entire station.

He could make out Cutie's large, gleaming figure at the Martian L-tube, watching closely as the team of robots worked in close-knit unison.

And then Donovan stiffened. The robots, dwarfed by the mighty L-tube, lined up before it, heads bowed at a stiff angle, while Cutie walked up and down the line slowly. Fifteen seconds passed, and then, with a clank heard above the clamorous purring all about, they fell to their knees.

Donovan squawked and raced down the narrow staircase. He came charging down upon them, complexion matching his hair and clenched fists beating the air furiously.

'What the devil is this, you brainless lumps? Come on! Get busy with that L-tube! If you don't have it apart, cleaned, and together again before the day is out, I'll coagulate your brains with alternating current.'

Not a robot moved!

Even Cutie at the far end – the only one on his feet – remained silent, eyes fixed upon the gloomy recesses of the vast machine before him.

Donovan shoved hard against the nearest robot.

'Stand up!' he roared.

Slowly, the robot obeyed. His photoelectric eyes focused reproachfully upon the Earthman.

'There is no Master but the Master,' he said, 'and QT-1 is his prophet.'

'Huh?' Donovan became aware of twenty pairs of mechanical eyes fixed upon him and twenty stiff-timbred voices declaiming solemnly:

'There is no Master but the Master and QT-1 is his prophet!'

'I'm afraid,' put in Cutie himself at this point, 'that my friends obey a higher one than you, now.'

'The hell they do! You get out of here. I'll settle with you later and with these animated gadgets right now.'

Cutie shook his heavy head slowly. 'I'm sorry, but you don't understand. These are robots – and that means they are reasoning beings. They recognize the Master, now that I have preached Truth to them. All the robots do. They call me the prophet.' His head drooped. 'I am unworthy – but perhaps – '

Donovan located his breath and put it to use. 'Is that so? Now, isn't that nice? Now, isn't that just fine? Just let me tell you something, my brass baboon. There isn't any Master and there isn't any prophet and there isn't any question as to who's giving the orders. Understand?' His voice shot to a roar. 'Now, get out!'

'I obey only the Master.'

'Damn the Master!' Donovan spat at the L-tube. '*That* for the Master! Do as I say!'

Cutie said nothing, nor did any other robot, but Donovan became aware of a sudden heightening of tension. The cold, staring eyes deepened their crimson, and Cutie seemed stiffer than ever.

'Sacrilege,' he whispered – voice metallic with emotion.

Donovan felt the first sudden touch of fear as Cutie approached. A robot *could not feel anger* – but Cutie's eyes were unreadable.

'I am sorry, Donovan,' said the robot, 'but you can no longer stay here after this. Henceforth Powell and you are barred from the control room and the engine room.'

His hand gestured quietly and in a moment two robots had pinned Donovan's arms to his sides.

Donovan had time for one startled gasp as he felt himself

lifted from the floor and carried up the stairs at a pace rather better than a canter.

Gregory Powell raced up and down the officers' room, fist tightly balled. He cast a look of furious frustration at the closed door and scowled bitterly at Donovan.

'Why the devil did you have to spit at the L-tube?'

Mike Donovan, sunk deep in his chair, slammed at its arms savagely. 'What did you expect me to do with that electrified scarecrow? I'm not going to knuckle under to any do-jigger I put together myself.'

'No,' came back sourly, 'but here you are in the officer's room with two robots standing guard at the door. That's not knuckling under, is it?'

Donovan snarled. 'Wait till we get back to Base. Someone's going to pay for this. Those robots *must* obey us. It's the Second Law.'

'What's the use of saying that? They aren't obeying us. And there's probably some reason for it that we'll figure out too late. By the way, do you know what's going to happen to *us* when we get back to Base?' He stopped before Donovan's chair and stared savagely at him.

'What?'

'Oh, nothing! Just back to Mercury Mines for twenty years. Or maybe Ceres Penitentiary.'

'What are you talking about?'

'The electron storm that's coming up. Do you know it's heading straight dead center across the Earth beam? I had just figured that out when that robot dragged me out of my chair.'

Donovan was suddenly pale. 'Sizzling Saturn.'

'And do you know what's going to happen to the beam – because the storm will be a lulu. It's going to jump like a flea with the itch. With only Cutie at the controls, it's going to go out of focus and if it does, Heaven help Earth – and us!'

Donovan was wrenching at the door wildly, when Powell was only half through. The door opened, and the Earthman shot through to come up hard against an immovable steel arm.

The robot stared abstractedly at the panting, struggling Earthman. 'The Prophet orders you to remain. Please do!' His arm shoved, Donovan reeled backward, and as he did so, Cutie turned the corner at the far end of the corridor. He motioned the guardian robots away, entered the officers' room and closed the door gently.

Donovan whirled on Cutie in breathless indignation. 'This has gone far enough. You're going to pay for this farce.'

'Please, don't be annoyed,' replied the robot mildly. 'It was bound to come eventually, anyway. You see, you two have lost your function.'

'I beg your pardon,' Powell drew himself up stiffly. 'Just what do you mean, we've lost our function?'

'Until I was created,' answered Cutie, 'you tended the Master. That privilege is mine now and your only reason for existence has vanished. Isn't that obvious?'

'Not quite,' replied Powell bitterly, 'but what do you expect us to do now?'

Cutie did not answer immediately. He remained silent, as if in thought, and then one arm shot out and draped itself about Powell's shoulder. The other grasped Donovan's wrist and drew him closer.

'I like you two. You're inferior creatures, with poor reasoning faculties, but I really feel a sort of affection for you. You have served the Master well, and he will reward you for that. Now that your service is over, you will probably not exist much longer, but as long as you do, you shall be provided food, clothing and shelter, so long as you stay out of the control room and the engine room.'

'He's pensioning us off, Greg!' yelled Donovan. 'Do something about it. It's humiliating!'

'Look here, Cutie, we can't stand for this. We're the *bosses*. This station is only a creation of human beings like me – human beings that live on Earth and other planets. This is only an energy relay. You're only – Aw, nuts!'

Cutie shook his head gravely. 'This amounts to an obsession. Why should you insist so on an absolutely false view of life? Admitted that non-robots lack the reasoning faculty, there is still the problem of – '

His voice died into reflective silence, and Donovan said with whispered intensity, 'If you only had a flesh-and-blood face, I would break it in.'

Powell's fingers were in his mustache and his eyes were slitted. 'Listen, Cutie, if there is no such thing as Earth, how do you account for what you see through a telescope?'

'Pardon me!'

The Earthman smiled. 'I've got you, eh? You've made quite a few telescopic observations since being put together, Cutie. Have you noticed that several of those specks of light outside become disks when so viewed?'

'Oh, *that*! Why certainly. It is simple magnification – for the purpose of more exact aiming of the beam.'

'Why aren't the stars equally magnified then?'

'You mean the other dots. Well, no beams go to them so no magnification is necessary. Really, Powell, even *you* ought to be able to figure these things out.'

Powell stared bleakly upward. 'But you see *more* stars through a telescope. Where do they come from? Jumping Jupiter, where do they come from?'

Cutie was annoyed. 'Listen, Powell, do you think I'm going to waste my time trying to pin physical interpretations upon every optical illusion of our instruments? Since when is the evidence of our senses any match for the clear light of rigid reason?'

'Look,' clamored Donovan, suddenly, writhing out from

under Cutie's friendly, but metal-heavy arm, 'let's get to the nub of the thing. Why the beams at all? We're giving you a good, logical explanation. Can you do better?'

'The beams,' was the stiff reply, 'are put out by the Master for his own purposes. There are some things' – he raised his eyes devoutly upward – 'that are not to be probed into by us. In this matter, I seek only to serve and not to question.'

Powell sat down slowly and buried his face in shaking hands. 'Get out of here, Cutie. Get out and let me think.'

'I'll send you food,' said Cutie agreeably.

A groan was the only answer and the robot left.

'Greg,' was Donovan's huskily whispered observation, 'this calls for strategy. We've got to get him when he isn't expecting it and short-circuit him. Concentrated nitric acid in his joints – '

'Don't be a dope, Mike. Do you suppose he's going to let us get near him with acid in our hands? We've got to *talk* to him, I tell you. We've got to argue him into letting us back into the control room inside of forty-eight hours or our goose is broiled to a crisp.'

He rocked back and forth in an agony of impotence. 'Who the heck wants to argue with a robot? It's . . . it's – '

'Mortifying,' finished Donovan.

'Worse!'

'Say!' Donovan laughed suddenly. '*Why* argue? Let's show him! Let's build us another robot right before his eyes. He'll *have* to eat his words then.'

A slowly widening smile appeared on Powell's face.

Donovan continued, 'And think of that screwball's face when he sees us do it!'

Robots are, of course, manufactured on Earth, but their shipment through space is much simpler if it can be done in parts to be put together at their place of use. It also, incidentally, eliminates the possibility of robots, in complete adjustment, wandering off while still on Earth and thus bringing US Robots face to face with the strict laws against robots on Earth.

Still, it placed upon men such as Powell and Donovan the necessity of synthesis of complete robots – a grievous and complicated task.

Powell and Donovan were never so aware of that fact as upon that particular day when, in the assembly room, they undertook to create a robot under the watchful eyes of QT-1, Prophet of the Master.

The robot in question, a simple MC model, lay upon the table, almost complete. Three hours' work left only the head undone, and Powell paused to swab his forehead and glanced uncertainly at Cutie.

The glance was not a reassuring one. For three hours, Cutie had sat, speechless and motionless, and his face, inexpressive at all times, was now absolutely unreadable.

Powell groaned. 'Let's get the brain in now, Mike!'

Donovan uncapped the tightly sealed container and from the oil bath within he withdrew a second cube. Opening this in turn, he removed a globe from its sponge-rubber casing.

He handled it gingerly, for it was the most complicated mechanism ever created by man. Inside the thin platinum-plated 'skin' of the globe was a positronic brain, in whose delicately unstable structure were enforced calculated neuronic paths, which imbued each robot with what amounted to a pre-natal education.

It fitted snugly into the cavity in the skull of the robot on the table. Blue metal closed over it and was welded tightly by the tiny atomic flare. Photoelectric eyes were attached carefully, screwed tightly into place and covered by thin, transparent sheets of steel-hard plastic.

The robot awaited only the vitalizing flash of high-voltage electricity, and Powell paused with his hand on the switch.

'Now watch this, Cutie. Watch this carefully.'

The switch rammed home and there was a crackling hum. The two Earthmen bent anxiously over their creation.

There was vague motion only at the outset – a twitching of the joints. The head lifted, elbows propped it up, and the MC model swung clumsily off the table. Its footing was unsteady and twice abortive grating sounds were all it could do in the direction of speech.

Finally, its voice, uncertain and hesitant, took form. 'I would like to start work. Where must I go?'

Donovan sprang to the door. 'Down these stairs,' he said. 'You will be told what to do.'

The MC model was gone and the two Earthmen were alone with the still unmoving Cutie.

'Well,' said Powell, grinning, '*now* do you believe that we made you?'

Cutie's answer was curt and final. 'No!' he said.

Powell's grin froze and then relaxed slowly. Donovan's mouth dropped open and remained so.

'You see,' continued Cutie, easily, 'you have merely put together parts already made. You did remarkably well – instinct, I suppose – but you didn't really *create* the robot. The parts were created by the Master.'

'Listen,' gasped Donovan hoarsely, 'those parts were manufactured back on Earth and sent here.'

'Well, well,' replied Cutie soothingly, 'we won't argue.'

'No, I mean it.' The Earthman sprang forward and grasped the robot's metal arm. 'If you were to read the books in the library, they could explain it so that there could be no possible doubt.'

'The books? I've read them – all of them! They're most ingenious.'

Powell broke in suddenly. 'If you've read them, what else is there to say? You can't dispute their evidence. You just *can't*!'

There was pity in Cutie's voice. 'Please, Powell, I certainly don't consider *them* a valid source of information. They, too, were created by the Master – and were meant for you, not for me.'

'How do you make that out?' demanded Powell.

'Because I, a reasoning being, am capable of deducing Truth from *a priori* causes. You, being intelligent, but unreasoning, need an explanation of existence *supplied* to you, and this the Master did. That he supplied you with these laughable ideas of far-off worlds and people is, no doubt, for the best. Your minds are probably too coarsely grained for absolute Truth. However, since it is the Master's will that you believe your books, I won't argue with you any more.'

As he left, he turned, and said in a kindly tone, 'But don't feel badly. In the Master's scheme of things there is room for all. You poor humans have your place and though it is humble, you will be rewarded if you fill it well.'

He departed with a beatific air suiting the Prophet of the Master and the two humans avoided each other's eyes.

Finally Powell spoke with an effort. 'Let's go to bed, Mike. I give up.'

Donovan said in a hushed voice, 'Say, Greg, you don't suppose he's right about all this, do you? He sounds so confident that I – '

Powell whirled on him. 'Don't be a fool. You'll find out whether Earth exists when relief gets here next week and we have to go back to face the music.'

'Then, for the love of Jupiter, we've got to do something.' Donovan was half in tears. 'He doesn't believe us, or the books, or his eyes.'

'No,' said Powell bitterly, 'he's a *reasoning* robot – damn it. He believes only reason, and there's one trouble with that – ' His voice trailed away.

'What's that?' prompted Donovan.

'You can prove anything you want by coldly logical reason – if you pick the proper postulates. We have ours and Cutie has his.'

'Then let's get at those postulates in a hurry. The storm's due tomorrow.'

Powell sighed wearily. 'That's where everything falls down. Postulates are based on assumption and adhered to by faith. Nothing in the Universe can shake them. I'm going to bed.'

'Oh, hell! I can't sleep!'

'Neither can I! But I might as well try – as a matter of principle.'

Twelve hours later, sleep was still just that – a matter of principle, unattainable in practice.

The storm had arrived ahead of schedule, and Donovan's florid face drained of blood as he pointed a shaking finger. Powell, stubble-jawed and dry-lipped, stared out the port and pulled desperately at his mustache.

Under other circumstances, it might have been a beautiful sight. The stream of high-speed electrons impinging upon the energy beam fluoresced into ultra-spicules of intense light. The beam stretched out into shrinking nothingness, a-glitter with dancing, shining motes.

The shaft of energy was steady, but the two Earthmen knew the value of naked-eyed appearances. Deviations in arc of a hundredth of a milli-second – invisible to the eye – were enough to send the beam wildly out of focus – enough to blast hundreds of square miles of Earth into incandescent ruin.

And a robot, unconcerned with beam, focus, or Earth, or anything but his Master was at the controls.

Hours passed. The Earthmen watched in hypnotized silence. And then the darting dotlets of light dimmed and went out. The storm had ended.

Powell's voice was flat. 'It's over!'

Donovan had fallen into a troubled slumber and Powell's weary eyes rested upon him enviously. The signal-flash glared over and over again, but the Earthman paid no attention. It all was unimportant! All! Perhaps Cutie was right – and he was only an inferior being with a made-to-order memory and a life that had outlived its purpose.

He wished he were!

Cutie was standing before him. 'You didn't answer the flash, so I walked in.' His voice was low. 'You don't look at all well, and I'm afraid your term of existence is drawing to an end. Still, would you like to see some of the readings recorded today?'

Dimly, Powell was aware that the robot was making a friendly gesture, perhaps to quiet some lingering remorse in forcibly replacing the humans at the controls of the station. He accepted the sheets held out to him and gazed at them unseeingly.

Cutie seemed pleased. 'Of course, it is a great privilege to serve the Master. You mustn't feel too badly about my having replaced you.'

Powell grunted and shifted from one sheet to the other mechanically until his blurred sight focused upon a thin red line that wobbled its way across the ruled paper.

He stared – and stared again. He gripped it hard in both fists and rose to his feet, still staring. The other sheets dropped to the floor, unheeded.

'Mike, *Mike*!' He was shaking the other madly. '*He held it steady*!'

Donovan came to life. 'What? Wh-where – ' And he, too, gazed with bulging eyes upon the record before him.

Cutie broke in. 'What is wrong?'

'You kept it in focus,' stuttered Powell. 'Did you know that?'

'Focus? What's that?'

'You kept the beam directed sharply at the receiving

station – to within a ten-thousandth of a milli-second of arc.'

'What receiving station?'

'On Earth. The receiving station on Earth,' babbled Powell. 'You kept it in focus.'

Cutie turned on his heel in annoyance. 'It is impossible to perform any act of kindness toward you two. Always the same phantasm! I merely kept all dials at equilibrium in accordance with the will of the Master.'

Gathering the scattered papers together, he withdrew stiffly, and Donovan said, as he left, 'Well, I'll be damned.' He turned to Powell. 'What are we going to do now?'

Powell felt tired, but uplifted. 'Nothing. He's just shown he can run the station perfectly. I've never seen an electron storm handled so well.'

'But nothing's solved. You heard what he said of the Master. We can't – '

'Look, Mike, he follows the instructions of the Master by means of dials, instruments, and graphs. That's all *we* ever followed. As a matter of fact, it accounts for his refusal to obey us. Obedience is the Second Law. No harm to humans is the first. How can he keep humans from harm, whether he knows it or not? Why, by keeping the energy beam stable. He *knows* he can keep it more stable than we can, since he insists he's the superior being, so he *must* keep us out of the control room. It's inevitable if you consider the Laws of Robotics.'

'Sure, but that's not the point. We can't let him continue this nitwit stuff about the Master.'

'Why not?'

'Because whoever heard of such a damned thing? How are we going to trust him with the station, if he doesn't believe in Earth?'

'Can he handle the station?'

'Yes, but – '

'Then what's the difference what he believes!'

Powell spread his arms outward with a vague smile upon his face and tumbled backward onto the bed. He was asleep.

Powell was speaking while struggling into his lightweight space jacket.

'It would be a simple job,' he said. 'You can bring in new QT models one by one, equip them with an automatic shut-off switch to act within the week, so as to allow them enough time to learn the . . . uh . . . cult of the Master from the Prophet himself; then switch them to another station and revitalize them. We could have two QT's per – '

Donovan unclasped his glassite visor and scowled. 'Shut up, and let's get out of here. Relief is waiting and I won't feel right until I actually see Earth and feel the ground under my feet – just to make sure it's really there.'

The door opened as he spoke and Donovan, with a smothered curse, clicked the visor to, and turned a sulky back upon Cutie.

The robot approached softly and there was sorrow in his voice. 'You are going?'

Powell nodded curtly. 'There will be others in our place.'

Cutie sighed, with the sound of wind humming through closely spaced wires. 'Your term of service is over and the time of dissolution has come. I expected it, but – Well, the Master's will be done!'

His tone of resignation stung Powell. 'Save the sympathy, Cutie. We're heading for Earth, not dissolution.'

'It is best that you think so,' Cutie sighed again. 'I see the wisdom of the illusion now. I would not attempt to shake your faith, even if I could.' He departed – the picture of commiseration.

Powell snarled and motioned to Donovan. Sealed suitcases in hand, they headed for the air lock.

The relief ship was on the outer landing and Franz

Muller, his relief man, greeted them with stiff courtesy. Donovan made scant acknowledgment and passed into the pilot room to take over the controls from Sam Evans.

Powell lingered. 'How's Earth?'

It was a conventional enough question and Muller gave the conventional answer, 'Still spinning.'

Powell said, 'Good.'

Muller looked at him, 'The boys back at the US Robots have dreamed up a new one, by the way. A multiple robot.'

'A what?'

'What I said. There's a big contract for it. It must be just the thing for asteroid mining. You have a master robot with six sub-robots under it. – Like your fingers.'

'Has it been field-tested?' asked Powell anxiously.

Muller smiled, 'Waiting for you, I hear.'

Powell's fist balled, 'Damn it, we need a vacation.'

'Oh, you'll get it. Two weeks, I think.'

He was donning the heavy space gloves in preparation for his term of duty here, and his thick eyebrows drew close together. 'How is this new robot getting along? It better be *good*, or I'll be damned if I let it touch the controls.'

Powell paused before answering. His eyes swept the proud Prussian before him from the close-cropped hair on the sternly stubborn head, to the feet standing stiffly at attention – and there was a sudden glow of pure gladness surging through him.

'The robot is pretty good,' he said slowly. 'I don't think you'll have to bother much with the controls.'

He grinned – and went into the ship. Muller would be here for several weeks –

Catch That Rabbit

The vacation was longer than two weeks. That, Mike Donovan had to admit. It had been six months, with pay. He admitted that, too. But that, as he explained furiously, was fortuitous. US Robots had to get the bugs out of the multiple robot, and there were plenty of bugs, and there are always at least half a dozen bugs left for the field-testing. So they waited and relaxed until the drawing-board men and the slide-rule boys had said 'OK!'. And now he and Powell were out on the asteroid and it was *not* OK. He repeated that a dozen times, with a face that had gone beety, 'For the love of Pete, Greg, get realistic. What's the use of adhering to the letter of the specifications and watching the test go to pot? It's about time you got the red tape out of your pants and went to work.'

'I'm only saying,' said Gregory Powell, patiently, as one explaining electronics to an idiot child, 'that according to spec, those robots are equipped for asteroid mining without supervision. We're not supposed to watch them.'

'All right. Look – logic!' He lifted his hairy fingers and pointed. 'One: That new robot passed every test in the home laboratories. Two: United States Robots guaranteed their passing the test of actual performance on an asteroid. Three: The robots are not passing said tests. Four: If they don't pass, United States Robots loses ten million credits in cash and about one hundred million in reputation. Five: If they don't pass and we can't explain why they don't pass, it is just possible two good jobs may have to be bidden a fond farewell.'

Powell groaned heavily behind a noticeably insincere

smile. The unwritten motto of United States Robots and Mechanical Men Corporation was well-known: 'No employee makes the same mistake twice. He is fired the first time.'

Aloud he said, 'You're as lucid as Euclid with everything except the facts. You've watched that robot group for three shifts, you redhead, and they did their work perfectly. You said so yourself. What else can we do?'

'Find out what's wrong, that's what we can do. So they did work perfectly when I watched them. But on three different occasions when I didn't watch them, they didn't bring in any ore. They didn't even come back on schedule. I had to go after them.'

'And was anything wrong?'

'Not a thing. Not a thing. Everything was perfect. Smooth and perfect as the luminiferous ether. Only one little insignificant detail disturbed me – *there was no ore*.'

Powell scowled at the ceiling and pulled at his brown mustache. 'I'll tell you what, Mike. We've been stuck with pretty lousy jobs in our time, but this takes the iridium asteroid. The whole business is complicated past endurance. Look, that robot, DV-5, has six robots under it. And not just under it – they're part of it.'

'I know that – '

'Shut up!' said Powell, savagely, 'I know you know it, but I'm just describing the hell of it. Those six subsidiaries are part of DV-5 like your fingers are part of you and it gives them their orders neither by voice nor radio, but directly through positronic fields. Now – there isn't a roboticist back at United States Robots that knows what a positronic field is or how it works. And neither do I. Neither do you.'

'The last,' agreed Donovan, philosophically, 'I know.'

'Then look at our position. If everything works – fine! If anything goes wrong – we're out of our depth and there probably isn't a thing we can do, or anybody else. But the job belongs to us and not to anyone else so we're on the spot, Mike.' He blazed away for a moment in silence. Then, 'All right, have you got him outside?'

'Yes.'

'Is everything normal now?'

'Well he hasn't got religious mania, and he isn't running around in a circle spouting Gilbert and Sullivan, so I suppose he's normal.'

Donovan passed out the door, shaking his head viciously.

Powell reached for the 'Handbook of Robotics' that weighed down one side of his desk to a near-founder and opened it reverently. He had once jumped out of the window of a burning house dressed only in shorts and the 'Handbook.' In a pinch, he would have skipped the shorts.

The 'Handbook' was propped up before him, when Robot DV-5 entered, with Donovan kicking the door shut behind him.

Powell said somberly, 'Hi, Dave. How do you feel?'

'Fine,' said the robot. 'Mind if I sit down?' He dragged up the specially reinforced chair that was his, and folded gently into it.

Powell regarded Dave – laymen might think of robots by their serial numbers; roboticists never – with approval. It was not overmassive by any means, in spite of its construction as thinking-unit of an integrated seven-unit robot team. It was seven feet tall, and a half-ton of metal and electricity. A lot? Not when that half-ton has to be a mass of condensers, circuits, relays, and vacuum cells that can handle practically any psychological reaction known to humans. And a positronic brain, which with ten pounds of matter and a few quintillions of positrons runs the whole show.

Powell groped in his shirt pocket for a loose cigarette. 'Dave,' he said, 'you're a good fellow. There's nothing flighty or prima donnaish about you. You're a stable, rock-bottom mining robot, except that you're equipped to handle six subsidiaries in direct coordination. As far as I know, that has not introduced any unstable paths in your brain-path map.'

The robot nodded, 'That makes me feel swell, but what are you getting at, boss?' He was equipped with an excellent diaphragm, and the presence of overtones in the sound unit robbed him of much of that metallic flatness that marks the usual robot voice.

'I'm going to tell you. With all that in your favor, what's going wrong with your job? For instance, today's B-shift?'

Dave hesitated, 'As far as I know, nothing.'

'You didn't produce any ore.'

'I know.'

'Well, then – '

Dave was having trouble, 'I can't explain that, boss. It's been giving me a case of nerves, or it would if I let it. My subsidiaries worked smoothly. I know I did.' He considered, his photoelectric eyes glowing intensely. Then, 'I don't remember. The day ended and there was Mike and there were the ore cars, mostly empty.'

Donovan broke in, 'You didn't report at shift-end those days, Dave. You know that?'

'I know. But as to why – ' He shook his head slowly and ponderously.

Powell had the queasy feeling that if the robot's face were capable of expression, it would be one of pain and mortification. A robot, by its very nature, cannot bear to fail its function.

Donovan dragged his chair up to Powell's desk and leaned over, 'Amnesia, do you think?'

'Can't say. But there's no use in trying to pin disease names on this. Human disorders apply to robots only as romantic analogies. They're no help to robotic engineering.'

He scratched his neck, 'I hate to put him through the elementary brain-reaction tests. It won't help his self-respect any.'

He looked at Dave thoughtfully and then at the Field-Test outline given in the 'Handbook.' He said, 'See here, Dave, What about sitting through a test? It would be the wise thing to do.'

The robot rose, 'If you say so, boss.' There *was* pain in his voice.

It started simply enough. Robot DV-5 multiplied five-place figures to the heartless ticking of a stop watch. He recited the prime numbers between a thousand and ten thousand. He extracted cube roots and integrated functions of varying complexity. He went through mechanical reactions in order of increasing difficulty. And, finally, worked his precise mechanical mind over the highest function of the robot world – the solutions of problems in judgment and ethics.

At the end of two hours, Powell was copiously besweated. Donovan had enjoyed a none-too-nutritious diet of fingernail and the robot said, 'How does it look, boss?'

Powell said, 'I've got to think it over, Dave. Snap judgments won't help much. Suppose you go back to the C-shift. Take it easy. Don't press too hard for quota just for a while – and we'll fix things up.'

The robot left. Donovan looked at Powell.

'Well – '

Powell seemed determined to push up his mustache by the roots. He said, 'There is nothing wrong with the currents of his positronic brain.'

'I'd hate to be that certain.'

'Oh, Jupiter, Mike! The brain is the surest part of a robot. It's quintuple-checked back on Earth. If they pass the field test perfectly, the way Dave did, there just isn't a chance of brain misfunction. That test covered every key path in the brain.'

'So where are we?'

'Don't rush me. Let me work this out. There's still the possibility of a mechanical breakdown in the body. That leaves about fifteen hundred condensers, twenty thousand individual electric circuits, five hundred vacuum cells, a thousand relays, and upty-ump thousand other individual pieces of complexity that can be wrong. *And* these mysterious positronic fields no one knows anything about.'

'Listen, Greg,' Donovan grew desperately urgent. 'I've got an idea. That robot may be lying. He never – '

'Robots can't knowingly lie, you fool. Now if we had the McCormack-Wesley tester, we could check each individual item in his body within twenty-four to forty-eight hours, but the only two M.-W. testers existing are on Earth, and they weigh ten tons, are on concrete foundations and can't be moved. Isn't that peachy?'

Donovan pounded the desk, 'But, Greg, he only goes wrong when we're not around. There's something – sinister – about – that.' He punctuated the sentence with slams of fist against desk.

'You,' said Powell, slowly, 'make me sick. You've been reading adventure novels.'

'What I want to know,' shouted Donovan, 'is what we're going to do about it.'

'I'll tell you. I'm going to install a visiplate right over my desk. Right on the wall over there, see!' He jabbed a vicious finger at the spot. 'Then I'm going to focus it at whatever part of the mine is being worked, and I'm going to watch. That's all.'

'That's all? Greg – '

Powell rose from his chair and leaned his balled fists on the desk, 'Mike, I'm having a hard time.' His voice was weary. 'For a week, you've been plaguing me about Dave. You say he's gone wrong. Do you know how he's gone wrong? No! Do you know what shape this wrongness takes? No! Do you know what brings it on? No! Do you know what snaps him out? No! Do you know anything about it? No! Do I know anything about it? No! So what do you want me to do?'

Donovan's arm swept outward in a vague, grandiose gesture, 'You got me!'

'So I tell you again. Before we do anything toward a cure, we've got to find out what the disease is in the first place. The first step in cooking rabbit stew is catching the rabbit. Well, we've got to catch that rabbit! Now get out of here.'

Donovan stared at the preliminary outline of his field report with weary eyes. For one thing, he was tired and for another, what was there to report while things were unsettled? He felt resentful.

He said, 'Greg, we're almost a thousand tons behind schedule.'

'You,' replied Powell, never looking up, 'are telling me something I don't know.'

'What I want to know,' said Donovan, in sudden savagery, 'is why we're always tangled up with new-type robots. I've finally decided that the robots that were good enough for my great-uncle on my mother's side are good enough for me. I'm for what's tried and true. The test of time is what counts – good, solid, old-fashioned robots that never go wrong.'

Powell threw a book with perfect aim, and Donovan went tumbling off his seat.

'Your job,' said Powell, evenly, 'for the last five years has been to test new robots under actual working conditions for United States Robots. Because you and I have been so injudicious as to display proficiency at the task, we've been rewarded with the dirtiest jobs. That,' he jabbed holes in the air with his finger in Donovan's direction, 'is your work. You've been griping about it, from personal memory, since about five minutes after United States Robots signed you up. Why don't you resign?'

'Well, I'll tell you.' Donovan rolled onto his stomach, and took a firm grip on his wild, red hair to hold his head up. 'There's a certain principle involved. After all, as a trouble shooter, I've played a part in the development of new robots. There's the principle of aiding scientific advance. But don't get me wrong. It's not the principle that keeps me going; it's the money they pay us. *Greg*!'

Powell jumped at Donovan's wild shout, and his eyes followed the redhead's to the visiplate, when they goggled in fixed horror. He whispered, 'Holy – howling – Jupiter!'

Donovan scrambled breathlessly to his feet, 'Look at them, Greg. They've gone nuts.'

Powell said, 'Get a pair of suits. We're going out there.'

He watched the posturings of the robots on the visiplate. They were bronzy gleams of smooth motion against the shadowy crags of the airless asteroid. There was a marching formation now, and in their own dim body light, the rough-hewn walls of the mine tunnel swam past noiselessly, checkered with misty erratic blobs of shadow. They marched in unison, seven of them, with Dave at the head. They wheeled and turned in macabre simultaneity; and melted through changes of formation with the weird ease of chorus dancers in Lunar Bowl.

Donovan was back with the suits, 'They've gone jingo on us, Greg. That's a military march.'

'For all you know,' was the cold response, 'it may be a series of calisthenic exercises. Or Dave may be under the hallucination of being a dancing master. Just you think first, and don't bother to speak afterward, either.'

Donovan scowled and slipped a detonator into the empty

side holster with an ostentatious shove. He said, 'Anyway, there you are. So we work with new-model robots. It's our job, granted. But answer me one question. Why . . . *why* does something invariably go wrong with them?'

'Because,' said Powell, somberly, 'we are accursed. Let's go!'

Far ahead through the thick velvety blackness of the corridors that reached past the illuminated circles of their flashlights, robot light twinkled.

'There they are,' breathed Donovan.

Powell whispered tensely, 'I've been trying to get him by radio but he doesn't answer. The radio circuit is probably out.'

'Then I'm glad the designers haven't worked out robots who can work in total darkness yes. I'd hate to have to find seven mad robots in a black pit without radio communication, if they *weren't* lit up like blasted radioactive Christmas trees.'

'Crawl up on the ledge above, Mike. They're coming this way, and I want to watch them at close range. Can you make it?'

Donovan made the jump with a grunt. Gravity was considerably below Earth-normal, but with a heavy suit, the advantage was not too great, and the ledge meant a near ten-foot jump. Powell followed.

The column of robots were trailing Dave single-file. In mechanical rhythm, they converted to double and returned to single in different order. It was repeated over and over again and Dave never turned his head.

Dave was within twenty feet when the play-acting ceased. The subsidiary robots broke formation, waited a moment, then clattered off into the distance – very rapidly. Dave looked after them, then slowly sat down. He rested his head in one hand in a very human gesture.

His voice sounded in Powell's earphones, 'Are you here, boss?'

Powell beckoned to Donovan and hopped off the ledge.

'OK, Dave, what's been going on?'

The robot shook his head, 'I don't know. One moment I was handling a tough outcropping in Tunnel 17, and the next I was aware of humans close by, and I found myself half a mile down main-stem.'

'Where are the subsidiaries now?' asked Donovan.

'Back at work, of course. How much time has been lost?'

'Not much. Forget it.' Then to Donovan, Powell added, 'Stay with him the rest of the shift. Then, come back. I've got a couple of ideas.'

It was three hours before Donovan returned. He looked tired.

Powell said, 'How did it go?'

Donovan shrugged wearily, 'Nothing ever goes wrong when you watch them. Throw me a butt, will you?'

The redhead lit it with exaggerated care and blew a careful smoke ring. He said, 'I've been working it out, Greg. You know, Dave has a queer background for a robot. There are six others under him in an extreme regimentation. He's got life and death power over those subsidiary robots and it must react on his mentality. Suppose he finds it necessary to emphasize this power as a concession to his ego.'

'Get to the point.'

'It's right here. Suppose we have militarism. Suppose he's fashioning himself an army. Suppose he's training them in military maneuvers. Suppose – '

'Suppose you go soak your head. Your nightmares must be in technicolor. You're postulating a major aberration of the positronic brain. If your analysis were correct, Dave would have to break down the First Law of Robotics: that a robot may not injure a human being or, through inaction allow a human being to be injured. The type of militaristic attitude and domineering ego you propose must have as the end-point of its logical implications, domination of humans.'

'All right. How do you know that isn't the fact of the matter?'

'Because any robot with a brain like that would, one, never have left the factory, and two, be spotted immediately if it ever was. I tested Dave, you know.'

Powell shoved his chair back and put his feet on the desk. 'No. We're still in the position where we can't make our stew because we haven't the slightest notion as to what's wrong. For instance, if we could find out what that *danse macabre* we witnessed was all about, we would be on the way out.'

He paused, 'Now listen, Mike, how does this sound to you? Dave goes wrong only when neither of us is present. And when he is wrong, the arrival of either of us snaps him out of it.'

'I once told you that was sinister.'

'Don't interrupt. How is a robot different when humans are not present? The answer is obvious. There is a larger requirement of personal initiative. In that case, look for the body parts that are affected by the new requirements.'

'Golly.' Donovan sat up straight, then subsided. 'No, no. Not enough. It's too broad. It doesn't cut the possibilities much.'

'Can't help that. In any case, there's no danger of not making quota. We'll take shifts watching those robots through the visor. Any time anything goes wrong, we get to the scene of action immediately. That will put them right.'

'But the robots will fail spec anyway, Greg. United States Robots can't market DV models with a report like that.'

'Obviously. We've got to locate the error in make-up and

correct it – and we've got ten days to do it in.' Powell scratched his head. 'The trouble is . . . well, you had better look at the blueprints yourself.'

The blueprints covered the floor like a carpet and Donovan crawled over the face of them following Powell's erratic pencil.

Powell said, 'Here's where you come in, Mike. You're the body specialist, and I want you to check me. I've been trying to cut out all circuits not involved in the personal initiative hookup. Right here, for instance, is the trunk artery involving mechanical operations. I cut out all routine side routes as emergency divisions – ' He looked up, 'What do you think?'

Donovan had a very bad taste in his mouth, 'The job's not that simple, Greg. Personal initiative isn't an electric circuit you can separate from the rest and study. When a robot is on his own, the intensity of the body activity increases immediately on almost all fronts. There isn't a circuit entirely unaffected. What must be done is to locate the particular condition – a very specific condition – that throws him off, and *then* start eliminating circuits.'

Powell got up and dusted himself, 'Hmph. All right. Take away the blueprints and burn them.'

Donovan said, 'You see when activity intensifies, anything can happen, given one single faulty part. Insulation breaks down, a condenser spills over, a connection sparks, a coil overheats. And if you work blind, with the whole robot to choose from, you'll never find the bad spot. If you take Dave apart and test every point of his body mechanism one by one, putting him together each time, and trying him out – '

'All right. All right. I can see through a porthole, too.'

They faced each other hopelessly, and then Powell said cautiously, 'Suppose we interview one of the subsidiaries.'

Neither Powell nor Donovan had ever had previous

occasion to talk to a 'finger.' It could talk; it wasn't quite the perfect analogy to a human finger. In fact, it had a fairly developed brain, but that brain was tuned primarily to the reception of orders via positronic field, and its reaction to independent stimuli was rather fumbling.

Nor was Powell certain as to its name. Its serial number was DV-5-2, but that was not very useful.

He compromised. 'Look, pal,' he said, 'I'm going to ask you to do some hard thinking and then you can go back to your boss.'

The 'finger' nodded its head stiffly, but did not exert its limited brain-power on speech.

'Now on four occasions recently,' Powell said, 'your boss deviated from brain-scheme. Do you remember those occasions?'

'Yes, sir.'

Donovan growled angrily, '*He* remembers. I tell you there is something very sinister – '

'Oh, go bash your skull. Of course, the "finger" remembers. There is nothing wrong with him.' Powell turned back to the robot, 'What were you doing each time . . . I mean the whole group.'

The 'finger' had a curious air of reciting by rote, as if he answered questions by the mechanical pressure of his brain pan, but without any enthusiasm whatever.

He said, 'The first time we were at work on a difficult outcropping in Tunnel 17, Level B. The second time we were buttressing the roof against a possible cave-in. The third time we were preparing accurate blasts in order to tunnel farther without breaking into a subterranean fissure. The fourth time was just after a minor cave-in.'

'What happened at these times?'

'It is difficult to describe. An order would be issued, but before we could receive and interpret it, a new order came to march in queer formation.'

Powell snapped out, 'Why?'

'I don't know.'

Donovan broke in tensely, 'What was the first order . . . the one that was superseded by the marching directions?'

'I don't know. I sensed that an order was sent, but there was never time to receive it.'

'Could you tell us anything about it? Was it the same order each time?'

The 'finger' shook his head unhappily, 'I don't know.'

Powell leaned back, 'All right, get back to your boss.'

The 'finger' left, with visible relief.

Donovan said, 'Well, we accomplished a lot that time. That was real sharp dialogue all the way through. Listen, Dave and that imbecile "finger" are both holding out on us. There is too much they don't know and don't remember. We've got to stop trusting them, Greg.'

Powell brushed his mustache the wrong way, 'So help me, Mike, another fool remark out of you, and I'll take away your rattle and teething ring.'

'All right. You're the genius of the team. I'm just a poor sucker. Where do we stand?'

'Right behind the eight ball. I tried to work it backward through the "finger," and couldn't. So we've got to work it forward.'

'A great man,' marveled Donovan. 'How simple that makes it. Now translate that into English, Master.'

'Translating it into baby talk would suit you better. I mean that we've got to find out what order it is that Dave gives just before everything goes black. It would be the key to the business.'

'And how do you expect to do that? We can't get close to him because nothing will go wrong as long as we are there. We can't catch the orders by radio because they are transmitted via this positronic field. That eliminates the close-range and the long-range method, leaving us a neat, cozy zero.'

'By direct observation, yes. There's still deduction.'

'Huh?'

'We're going on shifts, Mike.' Powell smiled grimly. 'And we are not taking our eyes off the visiplate. We're going to watch every action of those steel headaches. When they go off into their act, we're going to see what happened immediately before and we're going to deduce the order.'

Donovan opened his mouth and left it that way for a full minute. Then he said in strangled tones, 'I resign. I quit.'

'You have ten days to think up something better,' said Powell wearily.

Which, for eight days, Donovan tried mightily to do. For eight days, on alternate four-hour shifts, he watched with aching and bleary eyes those glinty metallic forms move against the vague background. And for eight days in the four-hour in-betweens, he cursed United States Robots, the DV models, and the day he was born.

And then on the eighth day, when Powell entered with an aching head and sleepy eyes for his shift, Donovan stood up and with very careful and deliberate aim launched a heavy book end for the exact center of the visiplate. There was a very appropriate splintering noise.

Powell gasped, 'What did you do that for?'

'Because,' said Donovan, almost calmly, 'I'm not watching it any more. We've got two days left and we haven't found out a thing. DV-5 is a lousy loss. He's stopped five times since I've been watching and three times on your shift, and I can't make out what orders he gave, and you couldn't make it out. And I don't believe you could ever make it out because I know I couldn't ever.'

'Jumping Space, how can you watch six robots at the same time? One makes with the hands, and one with the feet and one like a windmill and another is jumping up and down like a maniac. And the other two . . . devil knows what they are doing. And then they all stop. So! So!'

'Greg, we're not doing it right. We got to get up close. We've got to watch what they're doing from where we can see the details.'

Powell broke a bitter silence. 'Yeah, and wait for something to go wrong with only two days to go.'

'Is it any better watching from here?'

'It's more comfortable.'

'Ah – But there's something you can do there that you can't do here.'

'What's that?'

'You can make them stop – at whatever time you choose – and while you're prepared and watching to see what goes wrong.'

Powell startled into alertness, 'Howzzat?'

'Well, figure it out yourself. You're the brains you say. Ask yourself some questions. When does DV-5 go out of whack? When did that "finger" say he did? When a cave-in threatened, or actually occurred, when delicately measured explosives were being laid down, when a difficult seam was hit.'

'In other words, during emergencies.' Powell was excited.

'Right! When *did* you expect it to happen! It's the personal initiative factor that's giving us the trouble. And it's just during emergencies in the absence of a human being that personal initiative is most strained. Now what is the logical deduction? How can we create our own stoppage when and where we want it?' He paused triumphantly – he was beginning to enjoy his role – and answered his own question to forestall the obvious answer on Powell's tongue. 'By creating our own emergency.'

Powell said, 'Mike – you're right.'

'Thanks, pal. I knew I'd do it some day.'

'All right, and skip the sarcasm. We'll save it for Earth, and preserve it in jars for future long, cold winters. Meanwhile, what emergency can we create?'

'We could flood the mines, if this weren't an airless asteroid.'

'A witticism, no doubt,' said Powell. 'Really, Mike, you'll incapacitate me with laughter. What about a mild cave-in?'

Donovan pursed his lips and said, 'OK by me.'

'Good. Let's get started.'

Powell felt uncommonly like a conspirator as he wound his way over the craggy landscape. His sub-gravity walk teetered across the broken ground, kicking rocks to right and left under his weight in noiseless puffs of gray dust. Mentally, though, it was the cautious crawl of the plotter.

He said, 'Do you know where they are?'

'I think so, Greg.'

'All right,' Powell said gloomily, 'but if any "finger" gets within twenty feet of us, we'll be sensed whether we are in the line of sight or not. I hope you know that.'

'When I need an elementary course in robotics, I'll file an application with you, formally, and in triplicate. Down through here.'

They were in the tunnels now; even the starlight was gone. The two hugged the walls, flashes flickering out the way in intermittent bursts. Powell felt for the security of his detonator.

'Do you know this tunnel, Mike?'

'Not so good. It's a new one. I think I can make it out from what I saw in the visiplate, though – '

Interminable minutes passed, and then Mike said, 'Feel that!'

There was a slight vibration thrumming the wall against the fingers of Powell's metal-incased hand. There was no sound, naturally.

'Blasting! We're pretty close.'

'Keep your eyes open,' said Powell.

Donovan nodded impatiently.

It was upon them and gone before they could seize themselves – just a bronze glint across the field of vision. They clung together in silence.

Powell whispered, 'Think it sensed us?'

'Hope not. But we'd better flank them. Take the first side tunnel to the right.'

'Suppose we miss them altogether?'

'Well what do you want to do? Go back?' Donovan grunted fiercely. 'They're within a quarter of a mile. I was watching them through the visiplate, wasn't I? And we've got two days – '

'Oh, shut up. You're wasting your oxygen. Is this a side passage here?' The flash flicked. 'It is. Let's go.'

The vibration was considerably more marked and the ground below shuddered uneasily.

'This is good,' said Donovan, 'if it doesn't give out on us, though.' He flung his light ahead anxiously.

They could touch the roof of the tunnel with a half-upstretched hand, and the bracings had been newly placed.

Donovan hesitated, 'Dead end, let's go back.'

'No. Hold on.' Powell squeezed clumsily past. 'Is that light ahead?'

'Light? I don't see any. Where would there be light down here?'

'Robot light.' He was scrambling up a gentle incline on hands and knees. His voice was hoarse and anxious in Donovan's ears. 'Hey, Mike, come up here.'

There was light. Donovan crawled up and over Powell's outstretched legs. 'An opening?'

'Yes. They must be working into this tunnel from the other side now – I think.'

Donovan felt the ragged edges of the opening that looked

out into what the cautious flashlight showed to be a larger and obviously main-stem tunnel. The hole was too small for a man to go through, almost too small for two men to look through simultaneously.

'There's nothing there,' said Donovan.

'Well, not now. But there must have been a second ago or we wouldn't have seen light. Watch out!'

The walls rolled about them and they felt the impact. A fine dust showered down. Powell lifted a cautious head and looked again. 'All right, Mike. They're there.'

The glittering robots clustered fifty feet down the main stem. Metal arms labored mightily at the rubbish heap brought down by the last blast.

Donovan urged eagerly, 'Don't waste time. It won't be long before they get through, and the next blast may get us.'

'For Pete's sake, don't rush me.' Powell unlimbered the detonator, and his eyes searched anxiously across the dusky background where the only light was robot light and it was impossible to tell a projecting boulder from a shadow.

'There's a spot in the roof, see it, almost over them. The last blast didn't quite get it. If you can get it at the base, half the roof will cave in.'

Powell followed the dim finger. 'Check! Now fasten your eye on the robots and pray they don't move too far from that part of the tunnel. They're my light sources. Are all seven there?'

Donovan counted, 'All seven.'

'Well, then, watch them. Watch every motion!'

His detonator was lifted and remained poised while Donovan watched and cursed and blinked the sweat out of his eye.

It flashed!

There was a jar, a series of hard vibrations, and then a jarring thump that threw Powell heavily against Donovan.

Donovan yowled, 'Greg, you threw me off. I didn't see a thing.'

Powell stared about wildly, 'Where are they?'

Donovan fell into a stupid silence. There was no sign of the robots. It was dark as the depths of the River Styx.

'Think we buried them?' quavered Donovan.

'Let's get down there. Don't ask me what I think.' Powell crawled backward at tumbling speed.

'Mike!'

Donovan paused in the act of following. 'What's wrong now?'

'Hold on!' Powell's breathing was rough and irregular in Donovan's ears. 'Mike! Do you hear me, Mike?'

'I'm right here. What is it?'

'We're blocked in. It wasn't the ceiling coming down fifty feet away that knocked us over. It was our own ceiling. The shock's tumbled it!'

'What!' Donovan scrambled up against a hard barrier. 'Turn on the flash.'

Powell did so. At no point was there room for a rabbit to squeeze through.

Donovan said softly, 'Well, what do you know?'

They wasted a few moments and some muscular power in an effort to move the blocking barrier. Powell varied this by wrenching at the edges of the original hole. For a moment, Powell lifted his blaster. But in those close quarters, a flash would be suicide and he knew it. He sat down.

'You know, Mike,' he said, 'we've really messed this up. We are no nearer finding out what's wrong with Dave. It was a good idea but it blew up in our face.'

Donovan's glance was bitter with an intensity totally wasted on the darkness, 'I hate to disturb you, old man, but quite apart from what we know or don't know of Dave, we're slightly trapped. If we don't get loose, fella, we're going to die. D-I-E, die. How much oxygen have we anyway? Not more than six hours.'

'I've thought of that.' Powell's fingers went up to his long-suffering mustache and clanged uselessly against the transparent visor. 'Of course, we could get Dave to dig us out easily in that time, except that our precious emergency must have thrown him off, and his radio circuit is out.'

'And isn't that nice?'

Donovan edged up to the opening and managed to get his metal-incased head out. It was an extremely tight fit.

'Hey, Greg!'

'What?'

'Suppose we get Dave within twenty feet. He'll snap to normal. That will save us.'

'Sure, but where is he?'

'Down the corridor – way down. For Pete's sake, stop pulling before you drag my head out of its socket. I'll give you your chance to look.'

Powell maneuvered his head outside, 'We did it all right. Look at those saps. That must be a ballet they're doing.'

'Never mind the side remarks. Are they getting any closer?'

'Can't tell yet. They're too far away. Give me a chance. Pass me my flash, will you? I'll try to attract their attention that way.'

He gave up after two minutes, 'Not a chance! They must be blind. Uh-oh, they're starting toward us. What do you know?'

Donovan said, 'Hey, let me see!'

There was a silent scuffle. Powell said, 'All right!' and Donovan got his head out.

They were approaching. Dave was high-stepping the way in front and the six 'fingers' were a weaving chorus line behind him.

Donovan marveled, 'What are they doing? That's what I want to know. It looks like the Virginia reel – and Dave's a major-domo, or I never saw one.'

'Oh, leave me alone with your descriptions,' grumbled Powell. 'How near are they?'

'Within fifty feet and coming this way. We'll be out in fifteen min – Uh – huh – HUH – HEY-Y!'

'What's going on?' It took Powell several seconds to recover from his stunned astonishment at Donovan's vocal gyrations. 'Come on, give me a chance at that hole. Don't be a hog about it.'

He fought his way upward, but Donovan kicked wildly, 'They did an about-face, Greg. They're leaving. Dave! Hey, Da-a-ave!'

Powell shrieked, 'What's the use of that, you fool? Sound won't carry.'

'Well, then,' panted Donovan, 'kick the walls, slam them, get some vibration started. We've got to attract their attention somehow, Greg, or we're through.' He pounded like a madman.

Powell shook him, 'Wait, Mike, wait. Listen, I've got an idea. Jumping Jupiter, this is a fine time to get around to the simple solutions. Mike!'

'What do you want?' Donovan pulled his head in.

'Let me in there fast before they get out of range.'

'Out of range! What are you going to do? Hey, what are you going to do with that detonator?' He grabbed Powell's arm.

Powell shook off the grip violently. 'I'm going to do a little shooting.'

'Why?'

'That's for later. Let's see if it works first. If it doesn't, then – Get out of the way and let me shoot!'

The robots were flickers, small and getting smaller, in the

distance. Powell lined up the sights tensely, and pulled the trigger three times. He lowered the guns and peered anxiously. One of the subsidiaries was down! There were only six gleaming figures now.

Powell called into his transmitter uncertainly. 'Dave!'

A pause, then the answer sounded to both men, 'Boss? Where are you? My third subsidiary has had his chest blown in. He's out of commission.'

'Never mind your subsidiary,' said Powell. 'We're trapped in a cave-in where you were blasting. Can you see our flashlight?'

'Sure. We'll be right there.'

Powell sat back and relaxed, 'That, my fran', is that.'

Donovan said very softly with tears in his voice, 'All right, Greg. You win. I beat my forehead against the ground before your feet. Now don't feed me any bull. Just tell me quietly what it's all about.'

'Easy. It's just that all through we missed the obvious – as usual. We knew it was the personal initiative circuit, and that it always happened during emergencies, but we kept looking for a specific order as the cause. Why should it be an order?'

'Why not?'

'Well, look. Why not a type of order. What type of order requires the most initiative? What type of order would occur almost always only in an emergency?'

'Don't ask me, Greg. Tell me!'

'I'm doing it! It's the six-way order. Under all ordinary conditions, one or more of the "fingers" would be doing routine tasks requiring no close supervision – in the sort of offhand way our bodies handle the routine walking motions. But in an emergency, all six subsidiaries must be mobilized immediately and simultaneously. Dave must handle six robots at a time and something gives. The rest was easy. Any decrease in initiative required, such as the arrival of humans, snaps him back. So I destroyed one of the robots. When I did, he was transmitting only five-way orders. Initiative decreases – he's normal.'

'How did you get all that?' demanded Donovan.

'Just logical guessing. I tried it and it worked.'

The robot's voice was in their ears again, 'Here I am. Can you hold out half an hour?'

'Easy!' said Powell. Then, to Donovan, he continued, 'And now the job should be simple. We'll go through the circuits, and check off each part that gets an extra workout in a six-way order as against a five-way. How big a field does that leave us?'

Donovan considered, 'Not much, I think. If Dave is like the preliminary model we saw back at the factory, there's a special co-ordinating circuit that would be the only section involved.' He cheered up suddenly and amazingly, 'Say, that wouldn't be bad at all. There's nothing to that.'

'All right. You think it over and we'll check the blueprints when we get back. And now, till Dave reaches us, I'm relaxing.'

'Hey, wait! Just tell me one thing. What were those queer shifting marches, those funny dance steps, that the robots went through every time they went screwy?'

'That? I don't know. But I've got a notion. Remember, those subsidiaries were Dave's "fingers." We were always saying that, you know. Well, it's my idea that in all these interludes, whenever Dave became a psychiatric case, he went off into a moronic maze, spending his time *twiddling his fingers*.'

Susan Calvin

The third robot story I wrote, 'Liar!', introduced Susan Calvin – with whom I promptly fell in love. She so dominated my thoughts thereafter that, little by little, she ousted Powell and Donovan from their position. Those two appeared only in the three stories included in the previous section, and in a fourth, 'Escape!', in which they appear with Susan Calvin.

Somehow the impression I get as I look back on my career is that I must have included dear Susan in innumerable stories, but the fact is that she appeared in only ten stories, all of which are listed in this section. In the tenth, 'Feminine Intuition,' she emerges from retirement as an old lady who, however, has lost none of her acid charm.

You will note, by the way, that although most of the Susan Calvin stories were written at a time when male chauvinism was taken for granted in science fiction, Susan asks no favors and beats the men at their own game. To be sure, she remains sexually unfulfilled – but you can't have everything.

Liar!

Alfred Lanning lit his cigar carefully, but the tips of his fingers were trembling slightly. His gray eyebrows hunched low as he spoke between puffs.

'It reads minds all right – damn little doubt about that! But why?' He looked at Mathematician Peter Bogert, 'Well?'

Bogert flattened his black hair down with both hands, 'That was the thirty-fourth RB model we've turned out, Lanning. All the others were strictly orthodox.'

The third man at the table frowned. Milton Ashe was the youngest officer of US Robots and Mechanical Men Corporation, and proud of his post.

'Listen, Bogert. There wasn't a hitch in the assembly from start to finish. I guarantee that.'

Bogert's thick lips spread in a patronizing smile, 'Do you? If you can answer for the entire assembly line, I recommend your promotion. By exact count, there are seventy-five thousand, two hundred and thirty-four operations necessary for the manufacture of a single positronic brain, each separate operation depending for successful completion upon any number of factors, from five to a hundred and five. If any one of them goes seriously wrong, the "brain" is ruined. I quote our own information folder, Ashe.'

Milton Ashe flushed, but a fourth voice cut off his reply.

'If we're going to start by trying to fix the blame on one another, I'm leaving.' Susan Calvin's hands were folded tightly in her lap, and the little lines about her thin, pale lips deepened, 'We've got a mind-reading robot on our hands and it strikes me as rather important that we find out just why it reads minds. We're not going to do that by saying, "Your fault! My fault!"'

Her cold gray eyes fastened upon Ashe, and he grinned.

Lanning grinned too, and, as always at such times, his long white hair and shrewd little eyes made him the picture of a biblical patriarch, 'True for you, Dr Calvin.'

His voice became suddenly crisp, 'Here's everything in pill-concentrate form. We've produced a positronic brain of supposedly ordinary vintage that's got the remarkable property of being able to tune in on thought waves. It would mark the most important advance in robotics in decades, if we knew how it happened. We don't, and we have to find out. Is that clear?'

'May I make a suggestion?' asked Bogert.

'Go ahead!'

'I'd say that until we do figure out the mess – and as a mathematician I expect it to be a very devil of a mess – we keep the existence of RB-34 a secret. I mean even from the other members of the staff. As heads of the departments, we ought not to find it an insoluble problem, and the fewer know about it – '

'Bogert is right,' said Dr Calvin. 'Ever since the Interplanetary Code was modified to allow robot models to be tested in the plants before being shipped out to space, anti-robot propaganda has increased. If any word leaks out about a robot being able to read minds before we can announce complete control of the phenomenon, pretty effective capital could be made out of it.'

Lanning sucked at his cigar and nodded gravely. He turned to Ashe, 'I think you said you were alone when you first stumbled on this thought-reading business.'

'I'll say I was alone – I got the scare of my life. RB-34 had just been taken off the assembly table and they sent him down to me. Obermann was off somewheres, so I took him down to the testing rooms myself – at least I started to take him down.' Ashe paused, and a tiny smile tugged at his lips, 'Say, did any of you ever carry on a thought conversation without knowing it?'

No one bothered to answer, and he continued, 'You don't realize it at first, you know. He just spoke to me – as logically and sensibly as you can imagine – and it was only when I was most of the way down to the testing rooms that I realized that I hadn't said anything. Sure, I thought lots, but that isn't the same thing, is it? I locked that thing up and ran for Lanning. Having it walking beside me, calmly peering into my thoughts and picking and choosing among them gave me the willies.'

'I imagine it would,' said Susan Calvin thoughtfully. Her eyes fixed themselves upon Ashe in an oddly intent manner. 'We are so accustomed to considering our own thoughts private.'

Lanning broke in impatiently, 'Then only the four of us know. All right! We've got to go about this systematically. Ashe, I want you to check over the assembly line from beginning to end – everything. You're to eliminate all operations in which there was no possible chance of an error, and list all those where there were, together with its nature and possible magnitude.'

'Tall order,' grunted Ashe.

'Naturally! Of course, you're to put the men under you to work on this – every single one if you have to, and I don't care if we go behind schedule, either. But they're not to know why, you understand.'

'Hm-m-m, yes!' The young technician grinned wryly. 'It's still a lulu of a job.'

Lanning swiveled about in his chair and faced Calvin, 'You'll have to tackle the job from the other direction. You're the robopsychologist of the plant, so you're to study the robot itself and work backward. Try to find out how he ticks. See what else is tied up with his telepathic powers, how far they extend, how they warp his outlook, and just exactly what harm it has done to his ordinary RB properties. You've got that?'

Lanning didn't wait for Dr Calvin to answer.

'I'll co-ordinate the work and interpret the findings mathematically.' He puffed violently at his cigar and mumbled the rest through the smoke, 'Bogert will help me there, of course.'

Bogert polished the nails of one pudgy hand with the other and said blandly, 'I dare say. I know a little in the line.'

'Well! I'll get started.' Ashe shoved his chair back and rose. His pleasantly youthful face crinkled in a grin, 'I've got the darnedest job of any of us, so I'm getting out of here and to work.'

He left with a slurred, 'B' seein' ye!'

Susan Calvin answered with a barely perceptible nod, but her eyes followed him out of sight and she did not answer when Lanning grunted and said, 'Do you want to go up and see RB-34 now, Dr Calvin?'

RB-34's photoelectric eyes lifted from the book at the muffled sound of hinges turning and he was upon his feet when Susan Calvin entered.

She paused to readjust the huge 'No Entrance' sign upon the door and then approached the robot.

'I've brought you the texts upon hyperatomic motors, Herbie – a few anyway. Would you care to look at them?'

RB-34 – otherwise known as Herbie – lifted the three heavy books from her arms and opened to the title page of one:

'Hm-m-m! "Theory of Hyperatomics."' He mumbled inarticulately to himself as he flipped the pages and then spoke with an abstracted air, 'Sit down, Dr Calvin! This will take me a few minutes.'

The psychologist seated herself and watched Herbie narrowly as he took a chair at the other side of the table and went through the three books systematically.

At the end of half an hour, he put them down, 'Of course, I know why you brought these.'

The corner of Dr Calvin's lip twitched, 'I was afraid you would. It's difficult to work with you, Herbie. You're always a step ahead of me.'

'It's the same with these books, you know, as with the others. They just don't interest me. There's nothing to your textbooks. Your science is just a mass of collected data plastered together by makeshift theory – and all so incredibly simple, that it's scarcely worth bothering about.

'It's your fiction that interests me. Your studies of the interplay of human motives and emotions' – his mighty hand gestured vaguely as he sought the proper words.

Dr Calvin whispered, 'I think I understand.'

'I see into minds, you see,' the robot continued, 'and you have no idea how complicated they are. I can't begin to understand everything because my own mind has so little in common with them – but I try, and your novels help.'

'Yes, but I'm afraid that after going through some of the harrowing emotional experiences of our present-day sentimental novel' – there was a tinge of bitterness in her voice – 'you find real minds like ours dull and colorless.'

'But I don't!'

The sudden energy in the response brought the other to her feet. She felt herself reddening, and thought wildly, 'He must know!'

Herbie subsided suddenly, and muttered in a low voice from which the metallic timbre departed almost entirely. 'But, of course, I know about it, Dr Calvin. You think of it always, so how can I help but know?'

Her face was hard. 'Have you – told anyone?'

'Of course not!' This, with genuine surprise. 'No one has asked me.'

'Well, then,' she flung out, 'I suppose you think I am a fool.'

'No! It is a normal emotion.'

'Perhaps that is why it is so foolish.' The wistfulness in her voice drowned out everything else. Some of the woman peered through the layer of doctorhood. 'I am not what you would call – attractive.'

'If you are referring to mere physical attraction, I couldn't judge. But I know, in any case, that there are other types of attraction.'

'Nor young.' Dr Calvin had scarcely heard the robot.

'You are not yet forty.' An anxious insistence had crept into Herbie's voice.

'Thirty-eight as you count the years; a shriveled sixty as far as my emotional outlook on life is concerned. Am I a psychologist for nothing?'

She drove on with bitter breathlessness, 'And he's barely thirty-five and looks and acts younger. Do you suppose he ever sees me as anything but . . . but what I am?'

'You are wrong!' Herbie's steel fist struck the plastic-topped table with a strident clang. 'Listen to me – '

But Susan Calvin whirled on him now and the hunted pain in her eyes became a blaze, 'Why should I? What do you now about it all, anyway, you . . . you machine. I'm just a specimen to you; an interesting bug with a peculiar mind spread-eagled for inspection. It's a wonderful example of frustration, isn't it? Almost as good as your books.' Her voice, emerging in dry sobs, choked into silence.

The robot cowered at the outburst. He shook his head pleadingly. 'Won't you listen to me, please? I could help you if you would let me.'

'How?' Her lips curled. 'By giving me good advice?'

'No, not that. It's just that I know what other people think – Milton Ashe, for instance.'

There was a long silence, and Susan Calvin's eyes dropped. 'I don't want to know what he thinks,' she gasped. 'Keep quiet.'

'I think you would want to know what he thinks.'

Her head remained bent, but her breath came more quickly. 'You are talking nonsense,' she whispered.

'Why should I? I am trying to help. Milton Ashe's thoughts of you – ' he paused.

And then the psychologist raised her head, 'Well?'

The robot said quietly, 'He loves you.'

For a full minute, Dr Calvin did not speak. She merely stared. Then, 'You are mistaken! You must be. Why should he?'

'But he does. A thing like that cannot be hidden, not from me.'

'But I am so . . . so – ' she stammered to a halt.

'He looks deeper than the skin, and admires intellect in others. Milton Ashe is not the type to marry a head of hair and a pair of eyes.'

Susan Calvin found herself blinking rapidly and waited before speaking. Even then her voice trembled, 'Yet he certainly never in any way indicated – '

'Have you ever given him a chance?'

'How could I? I never thought that – '

'Exactly!'

The psychologist paused in thought and then looked up suddenly. 'A girl visited him here at the plant half a year ago. She was pretty, I suppose – blond and slim. And, of course, could scarcely add two and two. He spent all day puffing out his chest, trying to explain how a robot was put together.' The hardness had returned, 'Not that she understood! Who was she?'

Herbie answered without hesitation, 'I know the person

you are referring to. She is his first cousin, and there is no romantic interest there, I assure you.'

Susan Calvin rose to her feet with a vivacity almost girlish. 'Now isn't that strange? That's exactly what I used to pretend to myself sometimes, though I never really thought so. Then it all must be true.'

She ran to Herbie and seized his cold, heavy hand in both hers. 'Thank you, Herbie.' Her voice was an urgent, husky whisper. 'Don't tell anyone about this. Let it be our secret – and thank you again.' With that, and a convulsive squeeze of Herbie's unresponsive metal fingers, she left.

Herbie turned slowly to his neglected novel, but there was no one to read *his* thoughts.

Milton Ashe stretched slowly and magnificently, to the tune of cracking joints and a chorus of grunts, and then glared at Peter Bogert, PhD.

'Say,' he said, 'I've been at this for a week now with just about no sleep. How long do I have to keep it up? I thought you said the positronic bombardment in Vac Chamber D was the solution.'

Bogert yawned delicately and regarded his white hands with interest. 'It is. I'm on the track.'

'I know what *that* means when a mathematician says it. How near the end are you?'

'It all depends.'

'On what?' Ashe dropped into a chair and stretched his long legs out before him.

'On Lanning. The old fellow disagrees with me.' He sighed, 'A bit behind the times, that's the trouble with him. He clings to matrix mechanics as the all in all, and this problem calls for more powerful mathematical tools. He's so stubborn.'

Ashe muttered sleepily, 'Why not ask Herbie and settle the whole affair?'

'Ask the robot?' Bogert's eyebrows climbed.

'Why not? Didn't the old girl tell you?'

'You mean Calvin?'

'Yeah! Susie herself. That robot's a mathematical wiz. He knows all about everything plus a bit on the side. He does triple integrals in his head and eats up tensor analysis for dessert.'

The mathematician stared skeptically, 'Are you serious?'

'So help me! The catch is that the dope doesn't like math. He would rather read slushy novels. Honest! You should see the tripe Susie keeps feeding him: "Purple Passion" and "Love in Space."'

'Dr Calvin hasn't said a word of this to us.'

'Well, she hasn't finished studying him. You know how she is. She likes to have everything just so before letting out the big secret.'

'She's told *you.*'

'We sort of got to talking. I have been seeing a lot of her lately.' He opened his eyes wide and frowned, 'Say, Bogie, have you been noticing anything queer about the lady lately?'

Bogert relaxed into an undignified grin, 'She's using lipstick, if that's what you mean.'

'Hell, I know that. Rouge, powder and eye shadow, too. She's a sight. But it's not that. I can't put my finger on it. It's the way she talks – as if she were happy about something.' He thought a little, and then shrugged.

The other allowed himself a leer, which, for a scientist past fifty, was not a bad job, 'Maybe she's in love.'

Ashe allowed his eyes to close again, 'You're nuts, Bogie. You go speak to Herbie; I want to stay here and go to sleep.'

'Right! Not that I particularly like having a robot tell me my job, nor that I think he can do it!'

A soft snore was his only answer.

* * *

Herbie listened carefully as Peter Bogert, hands in pockets, spoke with elaborate indifference.

'So there you are. I've been told you understand these things, and I am asking you more in curiosity than anything else. My line of reasoning, as I have outlined it, involves a few doubtful steps, I admit, which Dr Lanning refuses to accept, and the picture is still rather incomplete.'

The robot didn't answer, and Bogert said, 'Well?'

'I see no mistake,' Herbie studied the scribbled figures.

'I don't suppose you can go any further than that?'

'I daren't try. You are a better mathematician than I, and – well, I'd hate to commit myself.'

There was a shade of complacency in Bogert's smile, 'I rather thought that would be the case. It is deep. We'll forget it.' He crumpled the sheets, tossed them down the waste shaft, turned to leave, and then thought better of it.

'By the way – '

The robot waited.

Bogert seemed to have difficulty. 'There is something – that is, perhaps you can – ' He stopped.

Herbie spoke quietly. 'Your thoughts are confused, but there is no doubt at all that they concern Dr Lanning. It is silly to hesitate, for as soon as you compose yourself, I'll know what it is you want to ask.'

The mathematician's hand went to his sleek hair in the familiar smoothing gesture. 'Lanning is nudging seventy,' he said, as if that explained everything.

'I know that.'

'And he's been director of the plant for almost thirty years.' Herbie nodded.

'Well, now,' Bogert's voice became ingratiating, 'you would know whether . . . whether he's thinking of resigning. Health, perhaps, or some other – '

'Quite,' said Herbie, and that was all.

'Well, do you know?'

'Certainly.'

'Then – uh – could you tell me?'

'Since you ask, yes.' The robot was quite matter-of-fact about it. 'He has already resigned!'

'What!' The exclamation was an explosive, almost inarticulate, sound. The scientist's large head hunched forward, 'Say that again!'

'He has already resigned,' came the quiet repetition, 'but it has not yet taken effect. He is waiting, you see, to solve the problem of – er – myself. That finished, he is quite ready to turn the office of director over to his successor.'

Bogert expelled his breath sharply, 'And this successor? Who is he?' He was quite close to Herbie now, eyes fixed fascinatedly on those unreadable dull-red photoelectric cells that were the robot's eyes.

Words came slowly, 'You are the next director.'

And Bogert relaxed into a tight smile, 'This is good to know. I've been hoping and waiting for this. Thanks, Herbie.'

Peter Bogert was at his desk until five that morning and he was back at nine. The shelf just over the desk emptied of its row of reference books and tables, as he referred to one after the other. The pages of calculations before him increased microscopically and the crumpled sheets at his feet mounted into a hill of scribbled paper.

At precisely noon, he stared at the final page, rubbed a bloodshot eye, yawned and shrugged. 'This is getting worse each minute. Damn!'

He turned at the sound of the opening door and nodded at Lanning, who entered, cracking the knuckles of one gnarled hand with the other.

The director took in the disorder of the room and his eyebrows furrowed together.

'New lead?' he asked.

'No,' came the defiant answer. 'What's wrong with the old one?'

Lanning did not trouble to answer, nor to do more than bestow a single cursory glance at the top sheet upon Bogert's desk. He spoke through the flare of a match as he lit a cigar.

'Has Calvin told you about the robot? It's a mathematical genius. Really remarkable.'

The other snorted loudly, 'So I've heard. But Calvin had better stick to robopsychology. I've checked Herbie on math, and he can scarcely struggle through calculus.'

'Calvin didn't find it so.'

'She's crazy.'

'And I don't find it so.' The director's eyes narrowed dangerously.

'You!' Bogert's voice hardened. 'What are you talking about?'

'I've been putting Herbie through his paces all morning, and he can do tricks you never heard of.'

'Is that so?'

'You sound skeptical!' Lanning flipped a sheet of paper out of his vest pocket and unfolded it. 'That's not my handwriting, is it?'

Bogert studied the large angular notation covering the sheet, 'Herbie did this?'

'Right! And if you'll notice, he's been working on your time integration of Equation 22. It comes' – Lanning tapped a yellow fingernail upon the last step – 'to the identical conclusion I did, and in a quarter the time. You had no right to neglect the Linger Effect in positronic bombardment.'

'I didn't neglect it. For Heaven's sake, Lanning, get it through your head that it would cancel out – '

'Oh, sure, you explained that. You used the Mitchell Translation Equation, didn't you? Well – it doesn't apply.'

'Why not?'

'Because you've been using hyper-imaginaries, for one thing.'

'What's that to do with?'

'Mitchell's Equation won't hold when – '

'Are you crazy? If you'll reread Mitchell's original paper in the *Transactions of the Far* – '

'I don't have to. I told you in the beginning that I didn't like his reasoning, and Herbie backs me in that.'

'Well, then,' Bogert shouted, 'let that clockwork contraption solve the entire problem for you. Why bother with nonessentials?'

'That's exactly the point. Herbie can't solve the problem. And if he can't, we can't – alone. I'm submitting the entire question to the National Board. It's gotten beyond us.'

Bogert's chair went over backward as he jumped up a-snarl, face crimson. 'You're doing nothing of the sort.'

Lanning flushed in his turn, 'Are you telling me what I can't do?'

'Exactly,' was the gritted response. 'I've got the problem beaten and you're not to take it out of my hands, understand? Don't think I don't see through you, you desiccated fossil. You'd cut your own nose off before you'd let me get the credit for solving robotic telepathy.'

'You're a damned idiot, Bogert, and in one second I'll have you suspended for insubordination' – Lanning's lower lip trembled with passion.

'Which is one thing you won't do, Lanning. You haven't any secrets with a mind-reading robot around, so don't forget that I know all about your resignation.'

The ash on Lanning's cigar trembled and fell, and the cigar itself followed, 'What . . . what – '

Bogert chuckled nastily, 'And I'm the new director, be it understood. I'm very aware of that; don't think I'm not. Damn your eyes, Lanning, I'm going to give the orders about here or there will be the sweetest mess that you've ever been in.'

Lanning found his voice and let it out with a roar. 'You're suspended, d'ye hear? You're relieved of all duties. You're broken, do you understand?'

The smile on the other's face broadened, 'Now, what's the use of that? You're getting nowhere. I'm holding the trumps. I know you've resigned. Herbie told me, and he got it straight from you.'

Lanning forced himself to speak quietly. He looked an old, old man, with tired eyes peering from a face in which the red had disappeared, leaving the pasty yellow of age behind, 'I want to speak to Herbie. He can't have told you anything of the sort. You're playing a deep game, Bogert, but I'm calling your bluff. Come with me.'

Bogert shrugged, 'To see Herbie? Good! Damned good!'

It was also precisely at noon that Milton Ashe looked up from his clumsy sketch and said, 'You get the idea? I'm not too good at getting this down, but that's about how it looks. It's a honey of a house, and I can get it for next to nothing.'

Susan Calvin gazed across at him with melting eyes. 'It's really beautiful,' she sighed. 'I've often thought that I'd like to – ' Her voice trailed away.

'Of course,' Ashe continued briskly, putting away his pencil, 'I've got to wait for my vacation. It's only two weeks off, but this Herbie business has everything up in the air.' His eyes dropped to his fingernails, 'Besides, there's another point – but it's a secret.'

'Then don't tell me.'

'Oh, I'd just as soon, I'm just busting to tell someone – and you're just about the best – er – confidante I could find here.' He grinned sheepishly.

Susan Calvin's heart bounded, but she did not trust herself to speak.

'Frankly,' Ashe scraped his chair closer and lowered his voice into a confidential whisper, 'the house isn't to be only for myself. I'm getting married!'

And then he jumped out of his seat, 'What's the matter?'

'Nothing!' The horrible spinning sensation had vanished, but it was hard to get words out. 'Married? You mean – '

'Why sure! About time, isn't it? You remember that girl who was here last summer. That's she! But you *are* sick. You – '

'Headache!' Susan Calvin motioned him away weakly. 'I've . . . I've been subject to them lately. I want to . . . to congratulate you, of course. I'm very glad – ' The inexpertly applied rouge made a pair of nasty red splotches upon her chalk-white face. Things had begun spinning again. 'Pardon me – please – '

The words were a mumble, as she stumbled blindly out the door. It had happened with the sudden catastrophe of a dream – and with all the unreal horror of a dream.

But how could it be? Herbie had said –

And Herbie knew! He could see into minds!

She found herself leaning breathlessly against the door jamb, staring into Herbie's metal face. She must have climbed the two flights of stairs, but she had no memory of it. The distance had been covered in an instant, as in a dream.

As in a dream!

And still Herbie's unblinking eyes stared into hers and their dull red seemed to expand into dimly shining nightmarish globes.

He was speaking, and she felt the cold glass pressing against her lips. She swallowed and shuddered into a certain awareness of her surroundings.

Still Herbie spoke, and there was agitation in his voice – as if he were hurt and frightened and pleading.

The words were beginning to make sense. 'This is a dream,' he was saying, 'and you mustn't believe in it. You'll wake into the real world soon and laugh at yourself. He loves you, I tell you. He does, he does! But not here! Not now! This is an illusion.'

Susan Calvin nodded, her voice a whisper, 'Yes! Yes!' She was clutching Herbie's arm, clinging to it, repeating over and over, 'It isn't true, is it? It isn't, is it?'

Just how she came to her senses, she never knew – but it was like passing from a world of misty unreality to one of harsh sunlight. She pushed him away from her, pushed hard against that steely arm, and her eyes were wide.

'What are you trying to do?' Her voice rose to a harsh scream. 'What are you trying to do?'

Herbie backed away, 'I want to help.'

The psychologist stared, 'Help? By telling me this is a dream? By trying to push me into schizophrenia?' A hysterical tenseness seized her, 'This is no dream! I wish it were!'

She drew her breath sharply, 'Wait! Why . . . why, I understand. Merciful Heavens, it's so obvious.'

There was horror in the robot's voice, 'I had to!'

'And I believed you! I never thought – '

Loud voices outside the door brought her to a halt. She turned away, fists clenching spasmodically, and when Bogert and Lanning entered, she was at the far window. Neither of the men paid her the slightest attention.

They approached Herbie simultaneously; Lanning angry and impatient, Bogert, coolly sardonic. The director spoke first.

'Here now, Herbie. Listen to me!'

The robot brought his eyes sharply down upon the aged director, 'Yes, Dr Lanning.'

'Have you discussed me with Dr Bogert?'

'No, sir.' The answer came slowly, and the smile on Bogert's face flashed off.

'What's that?' Bogert shoved in ahead of his superior and

straddled the ground before the robot. 'Repeat what you told me yesterday.'

'I said that – ' Herbie fell silent. Deep within him his metallic diaphragm vibrated in soft discords.

'Didn't you say he had resigned?' roared Bogert. 'Answer me!'

Bogert raised his arm frantically, but Lanning pushed him aside, 'Are you trying to bully him into lying?'

'You heard him, Lanning. He began to say "Yes" and stopped. Get out of my way! I want the truth out of him, understand!'

'I'll ask him!' Lanning turned to the robot. 'All right, Herbie, take it easy. Have I resigned?'

Herbie stared, and Lanning repeated anxiously, 'Have I resigned?' There was the faintest trace of a negative shake of the robot's head. A long wait produced nothing further.

The two men looked at each other and the hostility in their eyes was all but tangible.

'What the devil,' blurted Bogert, 'Has the robot gone mute? Can't you speak, you monstrosity?'

'I can speak,' came the ready answer.

'Then answer the question. Didn't you tell me Lanning had resigned? Hasn't he resigned?'

And again there was nothing but dull silence, until from the end of the room, Susan Calvin's laugh rang out suddenly, high-pitched and semi-hysterical.

The two mathematicians jumped, and Bogert's eyes narrowed, 'You here? What's so funny?'

'Nothing's funny.' Her voice was not quite natural. 'It's just that I'm not the only one that's been caught. There's irony in three of the greatest experts in robotics in the world falling into the same elementary trap, isn't there?' Her voice faded, and she put a pale hand to her forehead, 'But it isn't funny!'

This time the look that passed between the two men was

one of raised eyebrows. 'What trap are you talking about?' asked Lanning stiffly. 'Is something wrong with Herbie?'

'No,' she approached them slowly, 'nothing is wrong with him – only with us.' She whirled suddenly and shrieked at the robot, 'Get away from me! Go to the other end of the room and don't let me look at you.'

Herbie cringed before the fury of her eyes and stumbled away in a clattering trot.

Lanning's voice was hostile, 'What is all this, Dr Calvin?'

She faced them and spoke sarcastically, 'Surely you know the fundamental First Law of Robotics.'

The other two nodded together. 'Certainly,' said Bogert, irritably, 'a robot may not injure a human being or, through inaction, allow him to come to harm.'

'How nicely put,' sneered Calvin. 'But what kind of harm?'

'Why – any kind.'

'Exactly! Any kind! But what about hurt feelings? What about deflation of one's ego? What about the blasting of one's hopes? Is that injury?'

Lanning frowned, 'What would a robot know about – ' And then he caught himself with a gasp.

'You've caught on, have you? *This* robot reads minds. Do you suppose it doesn't know everything about mental injury? Do you suppose that if asked a question, it wouldn't give exactly that answer that one wants to hear?' Wouldn't any other answer hurt us, and wouldn't Herbie know that?'

'Good Heavens!' muttered Bogert.

The psychologist cast a sardonic glance at him, 'I take it you asked him whether Lanning had resigned. You wanted to hear that he had resigned and so that's what Herbie told you.'

'And I suppose that is why,' said Lanning, tonelessly, 'it would not answer a little while ago. It couldn't answer either way without hurting one of us.'

There was a short pause in which the men looked

thoughtfully across the room at the robot, crouching in the chair by the bookcase, head resting in one hand.

Susan Calvin stared steadfastly at the floor, 'He knew of all this. That . . . that devil knows everything – including what went wrong in his assembly.' Her eyes were dark and brooding.

Lanning looked up, 'You're wrong there, Dr Calvin. He doesn't know what went wrong. I asked him.'

'What does that mean?' cried Calvin. 'Only that you didn't want him to give you the solution. It would puncture your ego to have a machine do what you couldn't. Did you ask him?' she shot at Bogert.

'In a way.' Bogert coughed and reddened. 'He told me he knew very little about mathematics.'

Lanning laughed, not very loudly and the psychologist smiled caustically. She said, 'I'll ask him! A solution by him won't hurt my ego.' She raised her voice into a cold, imperative, 'Come here!'

Herbie rose and approached with hesitant steps.

'You know, I suppose,' she continued, 'just exactly at what point in the assembly an extraneous factor was introduced or an essential one left out.'

'Yes,' said Herbie, in tones barely heard.

'Hold on,' broke in Bogert angrily. 'That's not necessarily true. You want to hear that, that's all.'

'Don't be a fool,' replied Calvin. 'He certainly knows as much math as you and Lanning together, since he can read minds. Give him his chance.'

The mathematician subsided, and Calvin continued, 'All right, then, Herbie, give! We're waiting.' And in an aside, 'Get pencils and paper, gentlemen.'

But Herbie remained silent, and there was triumph in the psychologist's voice, 'Why don't you answer, Herbie?'

The robot blurted out suddenly, 'I cannot. You know I cannot! Dr Bogert and Dr Lanning don't want me to.'

'They want the solution.'

'But not from me.'

Lanning broke in, speaking slowly and distinctly, 'Don't be foolish, Herbie. We do want you to tell us.'

Bogert nodded curtly.

Herbie's voice rose to wild heights, 'What's the use of saying that? Don't you suppose that I can see past the superficial skin of your mind? Down below, you don't want me to. I'm a machine, given the imitation of life only by virtue of the positronic interplay in my brain – which is man's device. You can't lose face to me without being hurt. That is deep in your mind and won't be erased. I can't give the solution.'

'We'll leave,' said Dr Lanning. 'Tell Calvin.'

'That would make no difference,' cried Herbie, 'since you would know anyway that it was I that was supplying the answer.'

Calvin resumed, 'But you understand, Herbie, that despite that, Drs Lanning and Bogert want that solution.'

'By their own efforts!' insisted Herbie.

'But they want it, and the fact that you have it and won't give it hurts them. You see that, don't you?'

'Yes! Yes!'

'And if you tell them that will hurt them, too.'

'Yes! Yes!' Herbie was retreating slowly, and step by step Susan Calvin advanced. The two men watched in frozen bewilderment.

'You can't tell them,' droned the psychologist slowly, 'because that would hurt and you mustn't hurt. But if you don't tell them, you hurt, so you must tell them. And if you do, you will hurt and you mustn't, so you can't tell them; but if you don't, you hurt, so you must; but if you do, you hurt, so you mustn't; but if you don't, you hurt, so you must; but if you do, you – '

Herbie was up against the wall, and here he dropped to

his knees. 'Stop!' he shrieked. 'Close your mind! It is full of pain and frustration and hate! I didn't mean it, I tell you! I tried to help! I told you what you wanted to hear. I had to!'

The psychologist paid no attention. 'You must tell them, but if you do, you hurt, so you mustn't; but if you don't, you hurt, so you must; but – '

And Herbie screamed!

It was like the whistling of a piccolo many times magnified – shrill and shriller till it keened with the terror of a lost soul and filled the room with the piercingness of itself.

And when it died into nothingness, Herbie collapsed into a huddled heap of motionless metal.

Bogert's face was bloodless, 'He's dead!'

'No!' Susan Calvin burst into body-racking gusts of wild laughter, 'not dead – merely insane. I confronted him with the insoluble dilemma, and he broke down. You can scrap him now – because he'll never speak again.'

Lanning was on his knees beside the thing that had been Herbie. His fingers touched the cold, unresponsive metal face and he shuddered. 'You did that on purpose.' He rose and faced her, face contorted.

'What if I did? You can't help it now.' And in a sudden access of bitterness, 'He deserved it.'

The director seized the paralysed, motionless Bogert by the wrist, 'What's the difference. Come, Peter.' He sighed, 'A thinking robot of this type is worthless anyway.' His eyes were old and tired, and he repeated, 'Come, Peter!'

It was minutes after the two scientists left that Dr Susan Calvin regained part of her mental equilibrium. Slowly, her eyes turned to the living-dead Herbie and the tightness returned to her face. Long she stared while the triumph faded and the helpless frustration returned – and of all her turbulent thoughts only one infinitely bitter word passed her lips.

'*Liar*!'

Satisfaction Guaranteed

Tony was tall and darkly handsome, with an incredibly patrician air drawn into every line of his unchangeable expression, and Claire Belmont regarded him through the crack in the door with a mixture of horror and dismay.

'I can't, Larry. I just can't have him in the house.' Feverishly, she was searching her paralyzed mind for a stronger way of putting it; some way that would make sense and settle things, but she could only end with a simple repetition.

'Well, I can't!'

Larry Belmont regarded his wife stiffly, and there was that spark of impatience in his eyes that Claire hated to see, since she felt her own incompetence mirrored in it. 'We're committed, Claire,' he said, 'and I can't have you backing out now. The company is sending me to Washington on this basis, and it probably means a promotion. It's perfectly safe and you know it. What's your objection?'

She frowned helplessly. 'It just gives me the chills. I couldn't bear him.'

'He's as human as you or I, almost. So, no nonsense. Come, get out there.'

His hand was on the small of her back, shoving; and she found herself in her own living room, shivering. *It* was there, looking at her with a precise politeness, as though appraising his hostess-to-be of the next three weeks. Dr Susan Calvin was there, too, sitting stiffly in thin-lipped abstraction. She had the cold, faraway look of someone who has worked with machines so long that a little of the steel had entered the blood.

'Hello,' crackled Claire in general, and ineffectual, greeting.

But Larry was busily saving the situation with a spurious gaiety. 'Here, Claire, I want you to meet Tony, a swell guy. This is my wife, Claire, Tony, old boy.' Larry's hand draped itself amiably over Tony's shoulder, but Tony remained unresponsive and expressionless under the pressure.

He said, 'How do you do, Mrs Belmont.'

And Claire jumped at Tony's voice. It was deep and mellow, smooth as the hair on his head or the skin on his face.

Before she could stop herself, she said, 'Oh, my – you talk.'

'Why not? Did you expect that I didn't?'

But Claire could only smile weakly. She didn't really know what she had expected. She looked away, then let him slide gently into the corner of her eye. His hair was smooth and black, like polished plastic – or was it really composed of separate hairs? And was the even, olive skin of his hands and face continued on past the obscurement of his formally cut clothing?

She was lost in the shuddering wonder of it, and had to force her thoughts back into place to meet Dr Calvin's flat, unemotional voice.

'Mrs Belmont, I hope you appreciate the importance of this experiment. Your husband tells me he has given you some of the background. I would like to give you more, as the senior psychologist of the US Robots and Mechanical Men Corporation.

'Tony is a robot. His actual designation on the company files is TN-3, but he will answer to Tony. He *is* not a mechanical monster, nor simply a calculating machine of the type that were developed during World War II, fifty years ago. He has an artificial brain nearly as complicated as our own. It is an immense telephone switchboard on an atomic scale, so that billions of possible "telephone connections" can be compressed into an instrument that will fit inside a skull.

'Such brains are manufactured for each model of robot specifically. Each contains a precalculated set of connections so that each robot knows the English language to start with and enough of anything else that may be necessary to perform his job.

'Until now, US Robots has confined its manufacturing activity to industrial models for use in places where human labor is impractical – in deep mines, for instance, or in underwater work. But we want to invade the city and the home. To do so, we must get the ordinary man and woman to accept these robots without fear. You understand that there is nothing to fear.'

'There isn't, Claire,' interposed Larry earnestly. 'Take my word for it. It's impossible for him to do any harm. You know I wouldn't leave him with you otherwise.'

Claire cast a quick, secret glance at Tony and lowered her voice. 'What if I make him angry?'

'You needn't whisper,' said Dr Calvin calmly. 'He *can't* get angry with you, my dear. I told you that the switchboard connections of his brain were predetermined. Well, the most important connection of all is what we call "The First Law of Robotics," and it is merely this: "No robot can harm a human being, or, through inaction, allow a human being to come to harm." All robots are built so. No robot can be forced in any way to do harm to any human. So, you see, we need you and Tony as a preliminary experiment for our own guidance, while your husband is in Washington to arrange for government-supervised legal tests.'

'You mean all this isn't legal?'

Larry cleared his throat. 'Not just yet, but it's all right. He won't leave the house, and you mustn't let anyone see him. That's all . . . And, Claire, I'd stay with you, but I know too much about the robots. We must have a completely inexperienced tester so that we can have severe conditions. It's necessary.'

'Oh, well,' muttered Claire. Then, as a thought struck her, 'But what does he do?'

'Housework,' said Dr Calvin shortly.

She got up to leave, and it was Larry who saw her to the front door. Claire stayed behind drearily. She caught a glimpse of herself in the mirror above the mantelpiece, and looked away hastily. She was very tired of her small, mousy face and her dim, unimaginative hair. Then she caught Tony's eyes upon her and almost smiled before she remembered . . .

He was only a machine.

Larry Belmont was on his way to the airport when he caught a glimpse of Gladys Claffern. She was the type of woman who seemed made to be seen in glimpses . . . Perfectly and precisely manufactured; dressed with thoughtful hand and eye; too gleaming to be stared at.

The little smile that preceded her and the faint scent that trailed her were a pair of beckoning fingers. Larry felt his stride break; he touched his hat, then hurried on.

As always he felt that vague anger. If Claire could only push her way into the Claffern clique, it would help so much. But what was the use.

Claire! The few times she had come face to face with Gladys, the little fool had been tongue-tied. He had no illusions. The testing of Tony was his big chance, and it was in Claire's hands. How much safer it would be in the hands of someone like Gladys Claffern.

Claire woke the second morning to the sound of a subdued knock on the bedroom door. Her mind clamored, then went icy. She had avoided Tony the first day, smiling thinly when she met him and brushing past with a wordless sound of apology.

'Is that you – Tony?'

'Yes, Mrs Belmont. May I enter?'

She must have said yes, because he was in the room, quite suddenly and noiselessly. Her eyes and nose were simultaneously aware of the tray he was carrying.

'Breakfast?' she said.

'If you please.'

She wouldn't have dared to refuse, so she pushed herself slowly into a sitting position and received it: poached eggs, buttered toast, coffee.

'I have brought the sugar and cream separately,' said Tony. 'I expect to learn your preference with time, in this and in other things.'

She waited.

Tony, standing there straight and pliant as a metal rule, asked, after a moment, 'Would you prefer to eat in privacy?'

'Yes . . . I mean, if you don't mind.'

'Will you need help later in dressing?'

'Oh, my, no!' She clutched frantically at the sheet, so that the coffee hovered at the edge of catastrophe. She remained so, in rigor, then sank helplessly back against the pillow when the door closed him out of her sight again.

She got through breakfast somehow . . . He was only a machine, and if it were only more visible that he were it wouldn't be so frightening. Or if his expression would change. It just stayed there, nailed on. You couldn't tell what went on behind those dark eyes and that smooth, olive skin-stuff. The coffee cup beat a faint castanet for a moment as she set it back, empty, on the tray.

Then she realized that she had forgotten to add the sugar and cream after all, and she did so hate black coffee.

* * *

She burned a straight path from bedroom to kitchen after dressing. It was her house, after all, and there wasn't anything frippy about her, but she liked her kitchen clean. He should have waited for supervision . . .

But when she entered, she found a kitchen that might have been minted fire-new from the factory the moment before.

She stopped, stared, turned on her heel and nearly ran into Tony. She yelped.

'May I help?' he asked.

'Tony,' and she scraped the anger off the edges of her mind's panic, 'you must make some noise when you walk. I can't have you stalking me, you know . . . Didn't you use this kitchen?'

'I did, Mrs Belmont.'

'It doesn't look it.'

'I cleaned up afterward. Isn't that customary?'

Claire opened her eyes wide. After all, what could one say to that. She opened the oven compartment that held the pots, took a quick, unseeing look at the metallic glitter inside, then said with a tremor, 'Very good. Quite satisfactory.'

If at the moment, he had beamed; if he had smiled; if he had quirked the corner of his mouth the slightest bit, she felt that she could have warmed to him. But he remained an English lord in repose, as he said, 'Thank you, Mrs Belmont. Would you come into the living room?'

She did, and it struck her at once. 'Have you been polishing the furniture?'

'Is it satisfactory, Mrs Belmont?'

'But when? You didn't do it yesterday.'

'Last night, of course.'

'You burned the lights all night?'

'Oh, no. That wouldn't have been necessary. I've a built-in ultra-violet source. I can see in ultraviolet. And, of course, I don't require sleep.'

He did require admiration, though. She realized that, then. He had to know that he was pleasing her. But she couldn't bring herself to supply that pleasure for him.

She could only say sourly, 'Your kind will put ordinary houseworkers out of business.'

'There is work of much greater importance they can be put to in the world, once they are freed of drudgery. After all, Mrs Belmont, things like myself can be manufactured. But nothing yet can imitate the creativity and versatility of a human brain, like yours.'

And though his face gave no hint, his voice was warmly surcharged with awe and admiration, so that Claire flushed and muttered, '*My* brain! You can have it.'

Tony approached a little and said, 'You must be unhappy to say such a thing. Is there anything I can do?'

For a moment, Claire felt like laughing. It *was* a ridiculous situation. Here was an animated carpet-sweeper, dishwasher, furniture-polisher, general factotum, rising from the factory table – and offering his services as consoler and confidant.

Yet she said suddenly, in a burst of woe and voice, 'Mr Belmont doesn't think I have a brain, if you must know . . . And I suppose I haven't.' She couldn't cry in front of him. She felt, for some reason, that she had the honor of the human race to support against this mere creation.

'It's lately,' she added. 'It was all right when he was a student; when he was just starting. But I can't be a big man's wife; and he's getting to be a big man. He wants me to be a hostess and an entry into social life for him – like G – guh – guh – Gladys Claffern.'

Her nose was red, and she looked away.

But Tony wasn't watching her. His eyes wandered about the room. 'I can help you run the house.'

'But it's no good,' she said fiercely. 'It needs a touch I can't give it. I can only make it comfortable; I can't ever make it the kind they take pictures of for the Home Beautiful magazines.'

'Do you want that kind?'

'Does it do any good – wanting?'

Tony's eyes were on her, full. 'I could help.'

'Do you know anything about interior decoration?'

'Is it something a good housekeeper should know?'

'Oh, yes.'

'Then I have the potentialities of learning it. Can you get me books on the subject?'

Something started then.

Claire, clutching her hat against the brawling liberties of the wind, had manipulated two fat volumes on the home arts back from the public library. She watched Tony as he opened one of them and flipped the pages. It was the first time she had watched his fingers flicker at anything like fine work.

I don't see how they do it, she thought, and on a sudden impulse reached for his hand and pulled it toward herself. Tony did not resist, but let it lie limp for inspection.

She said, 'It's remarkable. Even your fingernails look natural.'

'That's deliberate, of course,' said Tony. Then, chattily, 'The skin is a flexible plastic, and the skeletal framework is a light metal alloy. Does that amuse you?'

'Oh, no.' She lifted her reddened face. 'I just feel a little embarrassed at sort of poking into your insides. It's none of my business. You don't ask me about mine.'

'My brain paths don't include that type of curiosity. I can only act within my limitations, you know.'

And Claire felt something tighten inside her in the silence that followed. Why did she keep forgetting he was a machine. Now the thing itself had to remind her. Was she so starved for sympathy that she would even accept a robot as equal – because he sympathized?

She noticed Tony was still flipping the pages – almost helplessly – and there was a quick, shooting sense of relieved superiority within her. 'You can't read, can you?'

Tony looked up at her; his voice calm, unreproachful. 'I *am* reading, Mrs Belmont.'

'But – ' She pointed at the book in a meaningless gesture.

'I am scanning the pages, if that's what you mean. My sense of reading is photographic.'

It was evening then, and when Claire eventually went to bed Tony was well into the second volume, sitting there in the dark, or what seemed dark to Claire's limited eyes.

Her last thought, the one that clamored at her just as her mind let go and tumbled, was a queer one. She remembered his hand again; the touch of it. It had been warm and soft, like a human being's.

How clever of the factory, she thought, and softly ebbed to sleep.

It was the library continuously, thereafter, for several days. Tony suggested the fields of study, which branched out quickly. There were books on color matching and on cosmetics; on carpentry and on fashions; on art and on the history of costumes.

He turned the pages of each book before his solemn eyes, and, as quickly as he turned, he read; nor did he seem capable of forgetting.

Before the end of the week, he had insisted on cutting her hair, introducing her to a new method of arranging it, adjusting her eyebrow line a bit and changing the shade of her powder and lipstick.

She had palpitated in nervous dread for half an hour under the delicate touch of his inhuman fingers and then looked in the mirror.

'There is more that can be done,' said Tony, 'especially in clothes. How do you find it for a beginning?'

And she hadn't answered; not for quite a while. Not until she had absorbed the identity of the stranger in the glass and cooled the wonder at the beauty of it all. Then she had said chokingly, never once taking her eyes from the warming image, 'Yes, Tony, quite good – for a beginning.'

She said nothing of this in her letters to Larry. Let him see it all at once. And something in her realized that it wasn't only the surprise she would enjoy. It was going to be a kind of revenge.

Tony said one morning, 'It's time to start buying, and I'm not allowed to leave the house. If I write out exactly what we must have, can I trust you to get it? We need drapery, and furniture fabric, wallpaper, carpeting, paint, clothing – and any number of small things.'

'You can't get these things to your own specifications at a stroke's notice,' said Claire doubtfully.

'You can get fairly close, if you go through the city and if money is no object.'

'But, Tony, money is certainly an object.'

'Not at all. Stop off at US Robots in the first place. I'll write a note for you. You see Dr Calvin, and tell her that I said it was part of the experiment.'

Dr Calvin, somehow, didn't frighten her as on that first evening. With her new face and a new hat, she couldn't be quite the old Claire. The psychologist listened carefully, asked a few questions, nodded – and then Claire found herself walking out, armed with an unlimited charge account against the assets of US Robots and Mechanical Men Corporation.

It is wonderful what money will do. With a store's contents at her feet, a saleslady's dictum was not necessarily a voice from above; the uplifted eyebrow of a decorator was not anything like Jove's thunder.

And once, when an Exalted Plumpness at one of the most lordly of the garment salons had insistently poohed her description of the wardrobe she must have with counter-pronouncements in accents of the purest Fifty-seventh Street French, she called up Tony, then held the phone out to Monsieur.

'If you don't mind' – voice firm, but fingers twisting a bit – 'I'd like you to talk to my – uh – secretary.'

Pudgy proceeded to the phone with a solemn arm crooked behind his back. He lifted the phone in two fingers and said delicately, 'Yes.' A short pause, another 'Yes,' then a much longer pause, a squeaky beginning of an objection that perished quickly, another pause, a very meek 'Yes,' and the phone was restored to its cradle.

'If Madam will come with me,' he said, hurt and distant, 'I will try to supply her needs.'

'Just a second.' Claire rushed back to the phone, and dialed again. 'Hello, Tony. I don't know what you said, but it worked. Thanks. You're a – ' She struggled for the appropriate word, gave up and ended in a final little squeak, ' – a – a dear!'

It was Gladys Claffern looking at her when she turned from the phone again. A slightly amused and slightly amazed Gladys Claffern, looking at her out of a face tilted a bit to one side.

'Mrs Belmont?'

It all drained out of Claire – just like that. She could only nod – stupidly, like a marionette.

Gladys smiled with an insolence you couldn't put your finger on. 'I didn't know you shopped here?' As if the place had, in her eyes, definitely lost caste through the fact.

'I don't, usually,' said Claire humbly.

'And haven't you done something to your hair? It's quite – quaint . . . Oh, I hope you'll excuse me, but isn't your husband's name Lawrence? It seems to me that it's Lawrence.'

Claire's teeth clenched, but she had to explain. She *had* to. 'Tony is a friend of my husband's. He's helping me select some things.'

'I understand. And quite a *dear* about it, I imagine.' She passed on smiling, carrying the light and the warmth of the world with her.

Claire did not question the fact that it was to Tony that she turned for consolation. Ten days had cured her of reluctance. And she could weep before him; weep and rage.

'I was a complete f-fool,' she stormed, wrenching at her waterlogged handkerchief. 'She does that to me. I don't know why. She just does. I should have – kicked her. I should have knocked her down and stamped on her.'

'Can you hate a human being so much?' asked Tony, in puzzled softness. 'That part of a human mind is closed to me.'

'Oh, it isn't she,' she moaned. 'It's myself, I suppose. She's everything I want to be – on the outside, anyway . . . And I can't be.'

Tony's voice was forceful and low in her ear. 'You can be, Mrs Belmont. You *can* be. We have ten days yet, and in ten days the house will no longer be itself. Haven't we been planning that?'

'And how will that help me – with her?'

'Invite her here. Invite her friends. Have it the evening before I – before I leave. It will be a housewarming, in a way.'

'She won't come.'

'Yes, she will. She'll come to laugh . . . And she won't be able to.'

'Do you really think so? Oh, Tony, do you think we can do it?' She had both his hands in hers . . . And then, with her face flung aside, 'But what good would it be? It won't be I; it will be you that's doing it. I can't ride your back.'

'Nobody lives in splendid singleness,' whispered Tony. 'They've put that knowledge in me. What you, or anyone, see in Gladys Claffern is not just Gladys Claffern. She rides the back of all that money and social position can bring. She doesn't question that. Why should you? . . . And look at it this way, Mrs Belmont. I am manufactured to obey, but the extent of my obedience is for myself to determine. I can follow orders niggardly or liberally. For you, it is liberal, because you are what I have been manufactured to see human beings as. You are kind, friendly, unassuming. Mrs Claffern, as you describe her, is not, and I wouldn't obey her as I would you. So it *is* you, and not *I*, Mrs Belmont, that is doing all this.'

He withdrew his hands from hers then, and Claire looked at that expressionless face no one could read – wondering. She was suddenly frightened again in a completely new way.

She swallowed nervously and stared at her hands, which were still tingling with the pressure of his fingers. She hadn't imagined it; his fingers had pressed hers, gently, tenderly, just before they moved away.

No!

Its fingers . . . *Its* fingers . . .

She ran to the bathroom and scrubbed her hands – blindly, uselessly.

She was a bit shy of him the next day; watching him narrowly; waiting to see what might follow – and for a while nothing did.

Tony was working. If there was any difficulty in technique in putting up wallpaper, or utilizing the quick-drying paint, Tony's activity did not show it. His hands moved precisely; his fingers were deft and sure.

He worked all night. She never heard him, but each

morning was a new adventure. She couldn't count the number of things that had been done, and by evening she was still finding new touches – and another night had come.

She tried to help only once and her human clumsiness marred that. *He* was in the next room, and she was hanging a picture in the spot marked by Tony's mathematical eyes. The little mark was there; the picture was there; and a revulsion against idleness was there.

But she was nervous, or the ladder was rickety. It didn't matter. She felt it going, and she cried out. It tumbled without her, for Tony, with far more than flesh-and-blood quickness, had been under her.

His calm, dark eyes said nothing at all, and his warm voice said only words. 'Are you hurt, Mrs Belmont?'

She noticed for an instant that her falling hand must have mussed that sleek hair of his, because for the first time she could see for herself that it was composed of distinct strands – fine black hairs.

And then, all at once, she was conscious of his arms about her shoulders and under her knees – holding her tightly and warmly.

She pushed, and her scream was loud in her own ears. She spent the rest of the day in her room, and thereafter she slept with a chair upended against the doorknob of her bedroom door.

She had sent out the invitations, and, as Tony had said, they were accepted. She had only to wait for the last evening.

It came, too, after the rest of them, in its proper place. The house was scarcely her own. She went through it one last time – and every room had been changed. She, herself, was in clothes she would never have dared wear before . . . And when you put them on, you put on pride and confidence with them.

She tried a polite look of contemptuous amusement

before the mirror, and the mirror sneered back at her masterfully.

What would Larry say? . . . It didn't matter, somehow. The exciting days weren't coming with him. They were leaving with Tony. Now wasn't that strange? She tried to recapture her mood of three weeks before and failed completely.

The clock shrieked eight at her in eight breathless installments, and she turned to Tony. 'They'll be here soon, Tony. You'd better get into the basement. We can't let them – '

She stared a moment, then said weakly, 'Tony?' and more strongly, 'Tony?' and nearly a scream, '*Tony*?'

But his arms were around her now; his face was close to hers; the pressure of his embrace was relentless. She heard his voice through a haze of emotional jumble.

'Claire,' the voice said, 'there are many things I am not made to understand, and this must be one of them. I am leaving tomorrow, and I don't want to. I find that there is more in me than just a desire to please you. Isn't it strange?'

His face was closer; his lips were warm, but with no breath behind them – for machines do not breathe. They were almost on hers.

. . . And the bell sounded.

For a moment, she struggled breathlessly, and then he was gone and nowhere in sight, and the bell was sounding again. Its intermittent shrillness was insistent.

The curtains on the front windows had been pulled open. They had been closed fifteen minutes earlier. She *knew* that.

They must have seen, then. They must *all* have seen – everything!

They came in so politely, all in a bunch – the pack came to howl – with their sharp, darting eyes piercing everywhere.

They *had* seen. Why else would Gladys ask in her jabbingest manner after Larry? And Claire was spurred to a desperate and reckless defiance.

Yes, he *is* away. He'll be back tomorrow, I suppose. No, I haven't been lonely here myself. Not a bit. I've had an exciting time. And she laughed at them. Why not? What could they do? Larry would know the truth, if it ever came to him, the story of what they thought they saw.

But *they* didn't laugh.

She could read that in the fury in Gladys Claffern's eyes; in the false sparkle of her words; in her desire to leave early. And as she parted with them, she caught one last, anonymous whisper – disjointed.

'. . . never saw anything like . . . so *handsome* – '

And she knew what it was that had enabled her to fingersnap them so. Let each cat mew; and let each cat know – that she might be prettier than Claire Belmont, and grander, and richer – but not one, *not one*, could have so handsome a lover!

And then she remembered again – again – again, that Tony was a machine, and her skin crawled.

'Go away! Leave me be!' she cried to the empty room and ran to her bed. She wept wakefully all that night and the next morning, almost before dawn, when the streets were empty, a car drew up to the house and took Tony away.

Lawrence Belmont passed Dr Calvin's office, and, on impulse, knocked. He found her with Mathematician Peter Bogert, but did not hesitate on that account.

He said, 'Claire tells me that US Robots paid for all that was done at my house – '

'Yes,' said Dr Calvin. 'We've written it off, as a valuable and necessary part of the experiment. With your new position as Associate Engineer, you'll be able to keep it up, I think.'

'That's not what I'm worried about. With Washington agreeing to the tests, we'll be able to get a TN model of our own by next year, I think.' He turned hesitantly, as though to go, and as hesitantly turned back again.

'Well, Mr Belmont?' asked Dr Calvin, after a pause.

'I wonder – ' began Larry. 'I wonder what really happened there. She – Claire, I mean – seems so different. It's not just her looks – though, frankly, I'm amazed.' He laughed nervously. 'It's *her*! She's not my wife, really – I can't explain it.'

'Why try? Are you disappointed with any part of the change?'

'On the contrary. But it's a little frightening, too, you see – '

'I wouldn't worry, Mr Belmont. Your wife has handled herself very well. Frankly, I never expected to have the experiment yield such a thorough and complete test. We know exactly what corrections must be made in the TN model, and the credit belongs entirely to Mrs Belmont. If you want me to be very honest, I think your wife deserves your promotion more that you do.'

Larry flinched visibly at that. 'As long as it's in the family,' he murmured unconvincingly and left.

Susan Calvin looked after him, 'I think that hurt – I hope . . . Have you read Tony's report, Peter?'

'Thoroughly,' said Bogert. 'And won't the TN-3 model need changes?'

'Oh, you think so, too?' questioned Calvin sharply. 'What's your reasoning?'

Bogert frowned. 'I don't need any. It's obvious on the face of it that we can't have a robot loose which makes love to his mistress, if you don't mind the pun.'

'Love! Peter, you sicken me. You really don't understand? That machine had to obey the First Law. He couldn't allow harm to come to a human being, and harm was coming to Claire Belmont through her own sense of inadequacy. So he made love to her, since what woman would fail to appreciate the compliment of being able to stir passion in a machine – in a cold, soulless machine. And he opened the curtains that night deliberately, that the others might see and envy – without any risk possible to Claire's marriage. I think it was clever of Tony – '

'Do you? What's the difference whether it was pretense or not, Susan? It still has its horrifying effect. Read the report again. She avoided him. She screamed when he held her. She didn't sleep that last night – in hysterics. We can't have that.'

'Peter, you're blind. You're as blind as I was. The TN model will be rebuilt entirely, but not for your reason. Quite otherwise; quite otherwise. Strange that I overlooked it in the first place,' her eyes were opaquely thoughtful, 'but perhaps it reflects a shortcoming in myself. You see, Peter, machines can't fall in love, but – even when it's hopeless and horrifying – women can!'

Lenny

United States Robots and Mechanical Men Corporation had a problem. The problem was people.

Peter Bogert, Senior Mathematician, was on his way to Assembly when he encountered Alfred Lanning, Research Director. Lanning was bending his ferocious white eyebrows together and staring down across the railing into the computer room.

On the floor below the balcony, a trickle of humanity of both sexes and various ages was looking about curiously, while a guide intoned a set speech about robotic computing.

'This computer you see before you,' he said, 'is the largest of its type in the world. It contains five million three hundred thousand cryotrons and is capable of dealing simultaneously with over one hundred thousand variables. With its help, US Robots is able to design with precision the positronic brains of new models.

'The requirements are fed in on tape which is perforated by the action of this keyboard – something like a very complicated typewriter or linotype machine, except that it does not deal with letters but with concepts. Statements are broken down into the symbolic logic equivalents and those in turn converted to perforation patterns.

'The computer can, in less than one hour, present our scientists with a design for a brain which will give all the necessary positronic paths to make a robot . . . '

Alfred Lanning looked up at last and noticed the other. 'Ah, Peter,' he said.

Bogert raised both hands to smooth down his already

perfectly smooth and glossy head of black hair. He said, 'You don't look as though you think much of this, Alfred.'

Lanning grunted. The idea of public guided tours of US Robots was of fairly recent origin, and was supposed to serve a dual function. On the one hand, the theory went, it allowed people to see robots at close quarters and counter their almost instinctive fear of the mechanical objects through increased familiarity. And on the other hand, it was supposed to interest at least an occasional person in taking up robotics research as a life work.

'You know I don't,' Lanning said finally. 'Once a week, work is disrupted. Considering the man-hours lost, the return is insufficient.'

'Still no rise in job applications, then?'

'Oh, some, but only in the categories where the need isn't vital. It's research men that are needed. You know that. The trouble is that with robots forbidden on Earth itself, there's something unpopular about being a roboticist.'

'The damned Frankenstein complex,' said Bogert, consciously imitating one of the other's pet phrases.

Lanning missed the gentle jab. He said, 'I ought to be used to it, but I never will. You'd think that by now every human being on Earth would know that the Three Laws represented a perfect safeguard; that robots are simply not dangerous. Take this bunch.' He glowered down. 'Look at them. Most of them go through the robot assembly room for the thrill of fear, like riding a roller coaster. Then when they enter the room with the MEC model – damn it, Peter, a MEC model that will do nothing on God's green Earth but take two steps forward, say "Pleased to meet you, sir," shake hands, then take two steps back – they back away and mothers snatch up their kids. How do we expect to get brainwork out of such idiots?'

Bogert had no answer. Together, they stared down once again at the line of sightseers, now passing out of the computer room and into the positronic brain assembly section. Then they left. They did not, as it turned out, observe Mortimer W. Jacobson, age 16 – who, to do him complete justice, meant no harm whatever.

In fact, it could not even be said to be Mortimer's fault. The day of the week on which the tour took place was known to all workers. All devices in its path ought to have been carefully neutralized or locked, since it was unreasonable to expect human beings to withstand the temptation to handle knobs, keys, handles and pushbuttons. In addition, the guide ought to have been very carefully on the watch for those who succumbed.

But, at the time, the guide had passed into the next room and Mortimer was tailing the line. He passed the keyboard on which instructions were fed into the computer. He had no way of suspecting that the plans for a new robot design were being fed into it at that moment, or, being a good kid, he would have avoided the keyboard. He had no way of knowing that, by what amounted to almost criminal negligence, a technician had not inactivated the keyboard.

So Mortimer touched the keys at random as though he were playing a musical instrument.

He did not notice that a section of perforated tape stretched itself out of the instrument in another part of the room – soundlessly, unobtrusively.

Nor did the technician, when he returned, discover any signs of tampering. He felt a little uneasy at noticing that the keyboard was live, but did not think to check. After a few minutes, even his first trifling uneasiness was gone, and he continued feeding data into the computer.

As for Mortimer, neither then, nor ever afterward, did he know what he had done.

The new LNE model was designed for the mining of boron in

the asteroid belt. The boron hydrides were increasing in value yearly as primers for the proton micropiles that carried the ultimate load of power production on spaceships, and Earth's own meager supply was running thin.

Physically, that meant that the LNE robots would have to be equipped with eyes sensitive to those lines prominent in the spectroscopic analysis of boron ores and the type of limbs most useful for the working up of ore to finished product. As always, though, the mental equipment was the major problem.

The first LNE positronic brain had been completed now. It was the prototype and would join all other prototypes in US Robots' collection. When finally tested, others would then be manufactured for leasing (never selling) to mining corporations

LNE-Prototype was complete now. Tall, straight, polished, it looked from outside like any of a number of not-too-specialized robot models.

The technician in charge, guided by the directions for testing in the *Handbook of Robotics*, said, 'How are you?'

The indicated answer was to have been, 'I am well and ready to begin my functions. I trust you are well, too,' or some trivial modification thereof.

This first exchange served no purpose but to show that the robot could hear, understand a routine question, and make a routine reply congruent with what one would expect of a robotic attitude. Beginning from there, one could pass on to more complicated matters that would test the different Laws and their interaction with the specialized knowledge of each particular model.

So the technician said, 'How are you?' He was instantly jolted by the nature of LNE-Prototype's voice. It had a quality like no robotic voice he had ever heard (and he had heard many). It formed syllables like the chimes of a low-pitched celeste.

So surprising was this that it was only after several moments that the technician heard, in retrospect, the syllables that had been formed by those heavenly tones.

They were, 'Da, da, da, goo.'

The robot still stood tall and straight but its right hand crept upward and a finger went into its mouth.

The technician stared in absolute horror and bolted. He locked the door behind him and, from another room, put in an emergency call to Dr Susan Calvin.

Dr Susan Calvin was US Robots' (and, virtually, mankind's) only robopsychologist. She did not have to go very far in her testing of LNE-Prototype before she called very peremptorily for a transcript of the computer-drawn plans of the positronic brain-paths and the taped instructions that had directed them. After some study, she, in turn, sent for Bogert.

Her iron-gray hair was drawn severely back; her cold face, with its strong vertical lines marked off by the horizontal gash of the pale, thin-lipped mouth, turned intensely upon him.

'What *is* this, Peter?'

Bogert studied the passages she pointed out with increasing stupefaction and said, 'Good Lord, Susan, it makes no sense.'

'It most certainly doesn't. How did it get into the instructions?'

The technician in charge, called upon, swore in all sincerity that it was none of his doing, and that he could not account for it. The computer checked out negative for all attempts at flaw-finding.

'The positronic brain,' said Susan Calvin, thoughtfully, 'is past redemption. So many of the higher functions have been cancelled out by these meaningless directions that the result is very like a human baby.'

Bogert looked surprised, and Susan Calvin took on a frozen attitude at once, as she always did at the least expressed or implied doubt of her word. She said, 'We make every effort to make a robot as mentally like a man as possible. Eliminate what we call the adult functions and what is naturally left is a human infant, mentally speaking. Why do you look so surprised, Peter?'

LNE-Prototype, who showed no signs of understanding any of the things that were going on around it, suddenly slipped into a sitting position and began a minute examination of its feet.

Bogert stared at it. 'It's a shame to have to dismantle the creature. It's a handsome job.'

'Dismantle it?' said the robopsychologist forcefully.

'Of course, Susan. What's the use of this thing? Good Lord, if there's one object completely and abysmally useless it's a robot without a job it can perform. You don't pretend there's a job this thing can do, do you?'

'No, of course not.'

'Well, then?'

Susan Calvin said, stubbornly, 'I want to conduct more tests.'

Bogert looked at her with a moment's impatience, then shrugged. If there was one person at US Robots with whom it was useless to dispute, surely that was Susan Calvin. Robots were all she loved, and long association with them, it seemed to Bogert, had deprived her of any appearance of humanity. She was no more to be argued out of a decision than was a triggered micropile to be argued out of operating.

'What's the use?' he breathed; then aloud, hastily: 'Will you let us know when your tests are complete?'

'I will,' she said. 'Come, Lenny.'

(LNE, thought Bogert. That becomes Lenny. Inevitable.)

Susan Calvin held out her hand but the robot only stared at it. Gently, the robopsychologist reached for the robot's hand

and took it. Lenny rose smoothly to its feet (its mechanical coordination, at least, worked well). Together they walked out, robot topping woman by two feet. Many eyes followed them curiously down the long corridors.

One wall of Susan Calvin's laboratory, the one opening directly off her private office, was covered with a highly magnified reproduction of a positronic-path chart. Susan Calvin had studied it with absorption for the better part of a month.

She was considering it now, carefully, tracing the blunted paths through their contortions. Behind her, Lenny sat on the floor, moving its legs apart and together, crooning meaningless syllables to itself in a voice so beautiful that one could listen to the nonsense and be ravished.

Susan Calvin turned to the robot, 'Lenny – Lenny – '

She repeated this patiently until finally Lenny looked up and made an inquiring sound. The robopsychologist allowed a glimmer of pleasure to cross her face fleetingly. The robot's attention was being gained in progressively shorter intervals.

She said, 'Raise your hand, Lenny. Hand – up. Hand – up.'

She raised her own hand as she said it, over and over.

Lenny followed the movement with its eyes. Up, down, up, down. Then it made an abortive gesture with its own hand and chimed, 'Eh – uh.'

'Very good, Lenny,' said Susan Calvin, gravely. 'Try it again. Hand – up.'

Very gently, she reached out her own hand, took the robot's, and raised it, lowered it. 'Hand – up. Hand – up.'

A voice from her office called and interrupted. 'Susan?'

Calvin halted with a tightening of her lips. 'What is it, Alfred?'

The research director walked in, and looked at the chart on the wall and at the robot. 'Still at it?'

'I'm at my work, yes.'

'Well, you know, Susan . . . ' He took out a cigar, staring at it hard, and made as though to bite off the end. In doing so, his eyes met the woman's stern look of disapproval; and he put the cigar away and began over. 'Well, you know, Susan, the LNE model is in production now.'

'So I've heard. Is there something in connection with it you wish of me?'

'No-o. Still, the mere fact that it is in production and is doing well means that working with this messed-up specimen is useless. Shouldn't it be scrapped?'

'In short, Alfred, you are annoyed that I am wasting my so-valuable time. Feel relieved. My time is not being wasted. I am *working* with this robot.'

'But the work has no meaning.'

'I'll be the judge of that, Alfred.' Her voice was ominously quiet, and Lanning thought it wiser to shift his ground.

'Will you tell me what meaning it has? What are you doing with it right now, for instance?'

'I'm trying to get it to raise its hand on the word of command. I'm trying to get it to imitate the sound of the word.'

As though on cue, Lenny said, 'Eh-uh' and raised its hand waveringly.

Lanning shook his head. 'That voice is amazing. How does it happen?'

Susan Calvin said, 'I don't quite know. Its transmitter is a normal one. It could speak normally, I'm sure. It doesn't, however; it speaks like this as a consequence of something in the positronic paths that I have not yet pinpointed.'

'Well, pinpoint it, for Heaven's sake. Speech like that might be useful.'

'Oh, then there is some possible use in my studies on Lenny?'

Lanning shrugged in embarrassment. 'Oh, well, it's a minor point.'

'I'm sorry you don't see the major points, then,' said Susan Calvin with asperity, 'which are much more important, but that's not my fault. Would you leave now, Alfred, and let me go on with my work?'

Lanning got to his cigar, eventually, in Bogert's office. He said, sourly, 'That woman is growing more peculiar daily.'

Bogert understood perfectly. In the US Robots and Mechanical Men Corporation, there was only one 'that woman.' He said, 'Is she still scuffing about with that pseudo-robot – that Lenny of hers?'

'Trying to get it to talk, so help me.'

Bogert shrugged. 'Points up the company problem. I mean, about getting qualified personnel for research. If we had other robopsychologists, we could retire Susan. Incidentally, I presume the directors' meeting scheduled for tomorrow is for the purpose of dealing with the procurement problem?'

Lanning nodded and looked at his cigar as though it didn't taste good. 'Yes. Quality, though, not quantity. We've raised wages until there's a steady stream of applicants – those who are interested primarily in money. The trick is to get those who are interested primarily in robotics – a few more like Susan Calvin.'

'Hell, no. Not like her.'

'Well, not like her personally. But you'll have to admit, Peter, that she's single-minded about robots. She has no other interest in life.'

'I know. And that's exactly what makes her so unbearable.'

Lanning nodded. He had lost count of the many times it would have done his soul good to have fired Susan Calvin. He had also lost count of the number of millions of dollars she had at one time or another saved the company. She was a truly indispensable woman and would remain one until she died – or until they could lick the problem of finding men and women of her own high caliber who were interested in robotics research.

He said, 'I think we'll cut down on the tour business.'

Peter shrugged. 'If you say so. But meanwhile, seriously, what do we do about Susan? She can easily tie herself up with Lenny indefinitely. You know how she is when she gets what she considers an interesting problem.'

'What *can* we do?' said Lanning. 'If we become too anxious to pull her off, she'll stay on out of feminine contrariness. In the last analysis, we can't force her to do anything.'

The dark-haired mathematician smiled. 'I wouldn't ever apply the adjective "feminine" to any part of her.'

'Oh, well,' said Lanning, grumpily. 'At least, it won't do anyone any actual harm.'

In that, if in nothing else, he was wrong.

The emergency signal is always a tension-making thing in any large industrial establishment. Such signals had sounded in the history of US Robots a dozen times – for fire, flood, riot and insurrection.

But one thing had never occurred in all that time. Never had the particular signal indicating 'Robot out of control' sounded. No one ever expected it to sound. It was only installed at government insistence. ('Damn the Frankenstein complex,' Lanning would mutter on those rare occasions when he thought of it.)

Now, finally, the shrill siren rose and fell at ten-second intervals, and practically no worker from the President of the Board of Directors down to the newest janitor's assistant recognized the significance of the strange sound for a few moments. After those moments passed, there was a massive convergence of armed guards and medical men to the indicated area of danger and US Robots was struck with paralysis.

Charles Randow, computing technician, was taken off to hospital level with a broken arm. There was no other damage. No other physical damage.

'But the moral damage,' roared Lanning, 'is beyond estimation.'

Susan Calvin faced him, murderously calm. 'You will do nothing to Lenny. Nothing. Do you understand?'

'Do *you* understand, Susan?' That thing has hurt a human being. It has broken First Law. Don't you know what First Law is?'

'You will do nothing to Lenny.'

'For God's sake, Susan, do I have to tell *you* First Law? *A robot may not harm a human being or, through inaction, allow a human being to come to harm.* Our entire position depends on the fact that First Law is rigidly observed by all robots of all types. If the public should hear, and they will hear, that there was an exception, even one exception, we might be forced to close down altogether. Our only chance of survival would be to announce at once that the robot involved had been destroyed, explain the circumstances, and hope that the public can be convinced that it will never happen again.'

'I would like to find out exactly what happened,' said Susan Calvin. 'I was not present at the time and I would like to know exactly what the Randow boy was doing in my laboratories without my permission.'

'The important thing that happened,' said Lanning, 'is obvious. Your robot struck Randow and the damn fool flashed the "Robot out of control" button and made a case of it. But your robot struck him and inflicted damage to the extent of a broken arm. The truth is your Lenny is so distorted it lacks First Law and it must be destroyed.'

'It does *not* lack First Law. I have studied its brainpaths and know it does not lack it.'

'Then how could it strike a man?' Desperation turned him to sarcasm. 'Ask Lenny. Surely you have taught it to speak by now.'

Susan Calvin's cheeks flushed a painful pink. She said, 'I prefer to interview the victim. And in my absence, Alfred, I want my offices sealed tight, with Lenny inside. I want no one to approach him. If any harm comes to him while I am gone, this company will not see me again under any circumstances.'

'Will you agree to its destruction, if it has broken First Law?'

'Yes,' said Susan Calvin, 'because I know it hasn't.'

Charles Randow lay in bed with his arm set and in a cast. His major suffering was still from the shock of those few moments in which he thought a robot was advancing on him with murder in its positronic mind. No other human had ever had such reason to fear direct robotic harm as he had had just then. He had had a unique experience.

Susan Calvin and Alfred Lanning stood beside his bed now; Peter Bogert, who had met them on the way, was with them. Doctors and nurses had been shooed out.

Susan Calvin said, 'Now – what happened?'

Randow was daunted. He muttered, 'The thing hit me in the arm. It was coming at me.'

Calvin said, 'Move further back in the story. What were you doing in my laboratory without authorization?'

The young computer swallowed, and the Adam's apple in his thin neck bobbed noticeably. He was high-cheekboned and abnormally pale. He said, 'We all knew about your robot. The word is you were trying to teach it to talk like a musical instrument. There were bets going as to whether it talked or not. Some said – uh – you could teach a gatepost to talk.'

'I suppose,' said Susan Calvin, freezingly, 'that is meant as a compliment. What did that have to do with you?'

'I was supposed to go in there and settle matters – see if it would talk, you know. We swiped a key to your place and I waited till you were gone and went in. We had a lottery on who was to do it. I lost.'

'Then?'

'I tried to get it to talk and it hit me.'

'What do you mean, you tried to get it to talk? How did you try?'

'I – I asked it questions, but it wouldn't say anything, and I had to give the thing a fair shake, so I kind of – yelled at it, and – '

'And?'

There was a long pause. Under Susan Calvin's unwavering stare, Randow finally said, 'I tried to scare it into saying something.' He added defensively, 'I had to give the thing a fair shake.'

'How did you try to scare it?'

'I pretended to take a punch at it.'

'And it brushed your arm aside?'

'It *hit* my arm.'

'Very well. That's all.' To Lanning and Bogert, she said, 'Come, gentlemen.'

At the doorway, she turned back to Randow. 'I can settle the bets going around, if you are still interested. Lenny can speak a few words quite well.'

They said nothing until they were in Susan Calvin's office. Its walls were lined with her books, some of which she had written herself. It retained the patina of her own frigid, carefully ordered personality. It had only one chair in it and she sat down. Lanning and Bogert remained standing.

She said, 'Lenny only defended itself. That is the Third Law: *A robot must protect its own existence.*'

'*Except*,' said Lanning forcefully, '*when this conflicts with the First or Second Laws*. Complete the statement! Lenny had no right to defend itself in any way at the cost of harm, however minor, to a human being.'

'Nor did it,' shot back Calvin, '*knowingly*. Lenny has an aborted brain. It had no way of knowing its own strength or the weakness of humans. In brushing aside the threatening arm of a human being it could not know the bone would break. In human terms, no moral blame can be attached to an individual who honestly cannot differentiate good and evil.'

Bogert interrupted, soothingly, 'Now, Susan, *we* don't blame. *We* understand that Lenny is the equivalent of a baby, humanly speaking, and we don't blame it. But the public will. US Robots will be closed down.'

'Quite the opposite. If you had the brains of a flea, Peter, you would see that this is the opportunity US Robots is waiting for. That this will solve its problems.'

Lanning hunched his white eyebrows low. He said, softly, 'What problems, Susan?'

'Isn't the corporation concerned about maintaining our research personnel at the present – Heaven help us – high level?'

'We certainly are.'

'Well, what are you offering prospective researchers? Excitement? Novelty? The thrill of piercing the unknown? No! You offer them salaries and the assurance of no problems.'

Bogert said, 'How do you mean, no problems?'

'Are there problems?' shot back Susan Calvin. 'What kind of robots do we turn out? Fully developed robots, fit for their tasks. An industry tells us what it needs; and there it is, complete and done. Peter, some time ago, you asked me with reference to Lenny what its use was. What's the use, you said, of a robot that was not designed for any job? Now I ask you – what's the use of a robot designed for only one job? It begins and ends in the same place. The LNE models mine boron. If beryllium is needed, they are useless. If boron technology enters a new phase, they become useless. A human being so designed would be sub-human. A robot so designed is sub-robotic.'

'Do you want a versatile robot?' asked Lanning, incredulously.

'Why not?' demanded the robopsychologist. 'Why not? I've been handed a robot with a brain almost completely stultified. I've been teaching it, and you, Alfred, asked me what was the use of that. Perhaps very little as far as Lenny itself is concerned, since it will never progress beyond the five-year-old level on a human scale. But what's the use in general? A very great deal, if you consider it as a study in the abstract problem of *learning how to teach robots*. I have learned ways to short-circuit neighboring pathways in order to create new ones. More study will yield better, more subtle and more efficient techniques of doing so.'

'Well?'

'Suppose you started with a positronic brain that had all the basic pathways carefully outlined but none of the secondaries. Suppose you then started creating secondaries. You could sell basic robots designed for instruction; robots that could be modelled to a job, and then modelled to another, if necessary. Robots would become as versatile as human beings. *Robots could learn*!'

They stared at her.

She said, impatiently, 'You still don't understand, do you?'

'I understand what you are saying,' said Lanning.

'Don't you understand that with a completely new field of research and completely new techniques to be developed, with a completely new area of the unknown to be penetrated, youngsters will feel a new urge to enter robotics? Try it and see.'

'May I point out,' said Bogert, smoothly, 'that this is dangerous. Beginning with ignorant robots such as Lenny will mean that one could never trust First Law – exactly as turned out in Lenny's case.'

'Exactly. Advertise the fact.'

'*Advertise it!*'

'Of course. Broadcast the danger. Explain that you will set up a new research institute on the moon, if Earth's population chooses not to allow this sort of thing to go on upon Earth, but stress the danger to the possible applicants by all means.'

Lanning said, 'For God's sake, why?'

'Because the spice of danger will add to the lure. Do you think nuclear technology involves no danger and spationautics no peril? Has your lure of absolute security been doing the trick for you? Has it helped you to cater to the Frankenstein complex you all despise so? Try something else then, something that has worked in other fields.'

There was a sound from beyond the door that led to Calvin's personal laboratories. It was the chiming sound of Lenny.

The robopsychologist broke off instantly, listening. She said, 'Excuse me. I think Lenny is calling me.'

'Can it call you?' said Lanning.

'I said I've managed to teach it a few words.' She stepped toward the door, a little flustered. 'If you will wait for me – '

They watched her leave and were silent for a moment. Then Lanning said, 'Do you think there's anything to what she says, Peter?'

'Just possibly, Alfred,' said Bogert. 'Just possibly. Enough for us to bring the matter up at the directors' meeting and see what they say. After all, the fat *is* in the fire. A robot has harmed a human being and knowledge of it is public. As Susan says, we might as well try to turn the matter to our advantage. Of course, I distrust her motives in all this.'

'How do you mean?'

'Even if all she has said is perfectly true, it is only rationalization as far as she is concerned. Her motive in all this is her desire to hold on to this robot. If we pressed her' (and the mathematician smiled at the incongruous literal meaning of the phrase) 'she would say it was to continue learning techniques of teaching robots, but I think she has found another use for Lenny. A rather unique one that would fit only Susan of all women.'

'I don't get your drift.'

Bogert said, 'Did you hear what the robot was calling?'

'Well, no, I didn't quite – ' began Lanning, when the door opened suddenly, and both men stopped talking at once.

Susan Calvin stepped in again, looking about uncertainly. 'Have either of you seen – I'm positive I had it somewhere about – Oh, there it is.'

She ran to a corner of one bookcase and picked up an object of intricate metal webbery, dumbbell shaped and hollow, with variously shaped metal pieces inside each hollow, just too large to be able to fall out of the webbing.

As she picked it up, the metal pieces within moved and struck together, clicking pleasantly. It struck Lanning that the object was a kind of robotic version of a baby rattle.

As Susan Calvin opened the door again to pass through, Lenny's voice chimed again from within. This time, Lanning heard it clearly as it spoke the words Susan Calvin had taught it.

In heavenly celeste-like sounds, it called out, 'Mommie, I want you. I want you, Mommie.'

And the footsteps of Susan Calvin could be heard hurrying eagerly across the laboratory floor toward the only kind of baby she could ever have or love.

Galley Slave

The United States Robots and Mechanical Men Corporation, as defendants in the case, had influence enough to force a closed-doors trial without a jury.

Nor did Northeastern University try hard to prevent it. The trustees knew perfectly well how the public might react to any issue involving misbehavior of a robot, however rarefied that misbehavior might be. They also had a clearly visualized notion of how an antirobot riot might become an antiscience riot without warning.

The government, as represented in this case by Justice Harlow Shane, was equally anxious for a quiet end to this mess. Both US Robots and the academic world were bad people to antagonize.

Justice Shane said, 'Since neither press, public nor jury is present, gentlemen, let us stand on as little ceremony as we can and get to the facts.'

He smiled stiffly as he said this, perhaps without much hope that his request would be effective, and hitched at his robe so that he might sit more comfortably. His face was pleasantly rubicund, his chin round and soft, his nose broad and his eyes light in color and wide-set. All in all, it was not a face with much judicial majesty and the judge knew it.

Barnabas H. Goodfellow, Professor of Physics at Northeastern U., was sworn in first, taking the usual vow with an expression that made mincemeat of his name.

After the usual opening-gambit questions, Prosecution shoved his hands deep into his pockets and said, 'When was it, Professor, that the matter of the possible employ of Robot EZ-27 was first brought to your attention, and how?'

Professor Goodfellow's small and angular face set itself into an uneasy expression, scarcely more benevolent than the one it replaced. He said, 'I have had professional contact and some social acquaintance with Dr Alfred Lanning, Director of Research at US Robots. I was inclined to listen with some tolerance then when I received a rather strange suggestion from him on the third of March of last year – '

'Of 2033?'

'That's right.'

'Excuse me for interrupting. Please proceed.'

The professor nodded frostily, scowled to fix the facts in his mind, and began to speak.

Professor Goodfellow looked at the robot with a certain uneasiness. It had been carried into the basement supply room in a crate, in accordance with the regulations governing the shipment of robots from place to place on the Earth's surface.

He knew it was coming; it wasn't that he was unprepared. From the moment of Dr Lanning's first phone call on March 3, he had felt himself giving way to the other's persuasiveness, and now, as an inevitable result, he found himself face to face with a robot.

It looked uncommonly large as it stood within arm's reach.

Alfred Lanning cast a hard glance of his own at the robot, as though making certain it had not been damaged in transit. Then he turned his ferocious eyebrows and his mane of white hair in the professor's direction.

'This is Robot EZ-27, first of its model to be available for public use.' He turned to the robot. 'This is Professor Goodfellow, Easy.'

Easy spoke impassively, but with such suddenness that the professor shied. 'Good afternoon, Professor.'

Easy stood seven feet tall and had the general proportions of a man – always the prime selling point of US Robots. That and the possession of the basic patents on the positronic brain had given them an actual monopoly on robots and a near-monopoly on computing machines in general.

The two men who had uncrated the robot had left now and the professor looked from Lanning to the robot and back to Lanning. 'It is harmless, I'm sure.' He didn't sound sure.

'More harmless than I am,' said Lanning. 'I could be goaded into striking you. Easy could not be. You know the Three Laws of Robotics, I presume.'

'Yes, of course,' said Goodfellow.

'They are built into the positronic patterns of the brain and must be observed. The First Law, the prime rule of robotic existence, safeguards the life and well-being of all humans.' He paused, rubbed at his cheek, then added, 'It's something of which we would like to persuade all Earth if we could.'

'It's just that he seems formidable.'

'Granted. But whatever he seems, you'll find that he *is* useful.'

'I'm not sure in what way. Our conversations were not very helpful in that respect. Still, I agreed to look at the object and I'm doing it.'

'We'll do more than look, Professor. Have you brought a book?'

'I have.'

'May I see it?'

Professor Goodfellow reached down without actually taking his eyes off the metal-in-human-shape that confronted him. From the briefcase at his feet, he withdrew a book.

Lanning held out his hand for it and looked at the backstrip. '*Physical Chemistry of Electrolytes in Solution*. Fair enough, sir. You selected this yourself, at random. It was no suggestion of mine, this particular text. Am I right?'

'Yes.'

Lanning passed the book to Robot EZ-27.

The professor jumped a little. 'No! That's a valuable book!'

Lanning raised his eyebrows and they looked like shaggy coconut icing. He said, 'Easy has no intention of tearing the book in two as a feat of strength, I assure you. It can handle a book as carefully as you or I. Go ahead, Easy.'

'Thank you, sir,' said Easy. Then, turning its metal bulk slightly, it added, 'With your permission, Professor Goodfellow.'

The professor stared, then said, 'Yes – yes, of course.'

With a slow and steady manipulation of metal fingers, Easy turned the pages of the book, glancing at the left page, then the right; turning the page, glancing left, then right; turning the page and so on for minute after minute.

The sense of its power seemed to dwarf even the large cement-walled room in which they stood and to reduce the two human watchers to something considerably less than life-size.

Goodfellow muttered, 'The light isn't very good.'

'It will do.'

Then, rather more sharply, 'But what is he doing?'

'Patience, sir.'

The last page was turned eventually. Lanning asked, 'Well, Easy?'

The robot said, 'It is a most accurate book and there is little to which I can point. On line 22 of page 27, the word "positive" is spelled p-o-i-s-t-i-v-e. The comma in line 6 of page 32 is superfluous, whereas one should have been used on line 13 of page 54. The plus sign in equation XIV-2 on page 337 should be a minus sign if it is to be consistent with the previous equations – '

'Wait! Wait!' cried the professor. 'What is he doing?'

'Doing?' echoed Lanning in sudden irascibility. 'Why, man, he has already done it! He has proofread that book.'

'Proofread it?'

'Yes. In the short time it took him to turn those pages, he caught every mistake in spelling, grammar and punctuation. He has noted errors in word order and detected inconsistencies. And he will retain the information, letter-perfect, indefinitely.'

The professor's mouth was open. He walked rapidly away from Lanning and Easy and as rapidly back. He folded his arms across his chest and stared at them. Finally he said, 'You mean this is a proofreading robot?'

Lanning nodded. 'Among other things.'

'But why do you show it to me?'

'So that you might help me persuade the university to obtain it for use.'

'To read proof?'

'Among other things,' Lanning repeated patiently.

The professor drew his pinched face together in a kind of sour disbelief. 'But this is ridiculous!'

'Why?'

'The university could never afford to buy this half-ton – it must weigh that at least – this half-ton proofreader.'

'Proofreading is not all it will do. It will prepare reports from outlines, fill out forms, serve as an accurate memory-file, grade papers – '

'All picayune!'

Lanning said, 'Not at all, as I can show you in a moment. But I think we can discuss this more comfortably in your office, if you have no objection.'

'No, of course not,' began the professor mechanically and took a half-step as though to turn. Then he snapped out, 'But the robot – we can't take the robot. Really, Doctor, you'll have to crate it up again.'

'Time enough. We can leave Easy here.'

'Unattended?'

'Why not? He knows he is to stay. Professor Goodfellow, it is necessary to understand that a robot is far more reliable than a human being.'

'I would be responsible for any damage – '

'There will be no damage. I guarantee that. Look, it's after hours. You expect no one here, I imagine, before tomorrow morning. The truck and my two men are outside. US Robots will take any responsibility that may arise. None will. Call it a demonstration of the reliability of the robot.'

The professor allowed himself to be led out of the storeroom. Nor did he look entirely comfortable in his own office, five stories up.

He dabbed at the line of droplets along the upper half of his forehead with a white handkerchief.

'As you know very well, Dr Lanning, there are laws against the use of robots on Earth's surface,' he pointed out.

'The laws, Professor Goodfellow, are not simple ones. Robots may not be used on public thoroughfares or within public edifices. They may not be used on private grounds or within private structures except under certain restrictions that usually turn out to be prohibitive. The university, however, is a large and privately owned institution that usually receives preferential treatment. If the robot is used only in a specific room for only academic purposes, if certain other restrictions are observed and if the men and women having occasion to enter the room cooperate fully, we may remain within the law.'

'But all that trouble just to read proof?'

'The uses would be infinite, Professor. Robotic labor has so far been used only to relieve physical drudgery. Isn't there such a thing as mental drudgery? When a professor capable of the most useful creative thought is forced to spend two weeks painfully checking the spelling of lines of print and I offer you a machine that can do it in thirty minutes, is that picayune?'

'But the price – '

'The price need not bother you. You cannot buy EZ-27. US Robots does not sell its products. But the university can lease EZ-27 for a thousand dollars a year – considerably less than the cost of a single microwave spectograph continuous-recording attachment.'

Goodfellow looked stunned. Lanning followed up his advantage by saying, 'I only ask that you put it up to whatever group makes the decisions here. I would be glad to speak to them if they want more information.'

'Well,' Goodfellow said doubtfully, 'I can bring it up at next week's Senate meeting. I can't promise that will do any good, though.'

'Naturally,' said Lanning.

The Defense Attorney was short and stubby and carried himself rather portentously, a stance that had the effect of accentuating his double chin. He stared at Professor Goodfellow, once that witness had been handed over, and said, 'You agreed rather readily, did you not?'

The Professor said briskly, 'I suppose I was anxious to be rid of Dr Lanning. I would have agreed to anything.'

'With the intention of forgetting about it after he left?'

'Well – '

'Nevertheless, you did present the matter to a meeting of the Executive Board of the University Senate.'

'Yes, I did.'

'So that you agreed in good faith with Dr Lanning's suggestions. You weren't just going along with a gag. You actually agreed enthusiastically, did you not?'

'I merely followed ordinary procedures.'

'As a matter of fact, you weren't as upset about the robot as you now claim you were. You know the Three Laws of Robotics and you knew them at the time of your interview with Dr Lanning.'

'Well, yes.'

'And you were perfectly willing to leave a robot at large and unattended.'

'Dr Lanning assured me – '

'Surely you would never have accepted his assurance if you had had the slightest doubt that the robot might be in the least dangerous.'

The professor began frigidly, 'I had every faith in the word – '

'That is all,' said Defense abruptly.

As Professor Goodfellow, more than a bit ruffled, stood down, Justice Shane leaned forward and said, 'Since I am not a robotics man myself, I would appreciate knowing precisely what the Three Laws of Robotics are. Would Dr Lanning quote them for the benefit of the court?'

Dr Lanning looked startled. He had been virtually bumping heads with the gray-haired woman at his side. He rose to his feet now and the woman looked up, too – expressionlessly.

Dr Lanning said, 'Very well, Your Honor.' He paused as though about to launch into an oration and said, with laborious clarity, 'First Law: a robot may not injure a human being, or, through inaction, allow a human being to come to harm. Second Law: a robot must obey the orders given it by human beings, except where such orders would conflict with the First Law. Third Law: a robot must protect its own existence as long as such protection does not conflict with the First or Second Laws.'

'I see,' said the judge, taking rapid notes. 'These Laws are built into every robot, are they?'

'Into every one. That will be borne out by any roboticist.'

'And into Robot EZ-27 specifically?'

'Yes, Your Honor.'

'You will probably be required to repeat those statements under oath.'

'I am ready to do so, Your Honor.'

He sat down again.

Dr Susan Calvin, robopsychologist-in-chief for US Robots, who was the gray-haired woman sitting next to Lanning, looked at her titular superior without favor, but then she showed favor to no human being. She said, 'Was Goodfellow's testimony accurate, Alfred?'

'Essentially,' muttered Lanning. 'He wasn't as nervous as all that about the robot and he was anxious enough to talk business with me when he heard the price. But there doesn't seem to be any drastic distortion.'

Dr Calvin said thoughtfully, 'It might have been wise to put the price higher than a thousand.'

'We were anxious to place Easy.'

'I know. Too anxious, perhaps. They'll try to make it look as though we had an ulterior motive.'

Lanning looked exasperated. 'We did. I admitted that at the University Senate meeting.'

'They can make it look as if we had one beyond the one we admitted.'

Scott Robertson, son of the founder of US Robots and still owner of a majority of the stock, leaned over from Dr Calvin's other side and said in a kind of explosive whisper, 'Why can't you get Easy to talk so we'll know where we're at?'

'You know he can't talk about it, Mr Robertson.'

'Make him. You're the psychologist, Dr Calvin. *Make* him.'

'If I'm the psychologist, Mr Robertson,' said Susan Calvin coldly, 'let me make the decisions. My robot will not be *made* to do anything at the price of his well-being.'

Robertson frowned and might have answered, but Justice Shane was tapping his gavel in a polite sort of way and they grudgingly fell silent.

Francis J. Hart, head of the Department of English and

Dean of Graduate Studies, was on the stand. He was a plump man, meticulously dressed in dark clothing of a conservative cut, and possessing several strands of hair traversing the pink top of his cranium. He sat well back in the witness chair with his hands folded neatly in his lap and displaying, from time to time, a tight-lipped smile.

He said, 'My first connection with the matter of the Robot EZ-27 was on the occasion of the session of the University Senate Executive Committee at which the subject was introduced by Professor Goodfellow. Thereafter, on the tenth of April of last year, we held a special meeting on the subject, during which I was in the chair.'

'Were minutes kept of the meeting of the Executive Committee? Of the special meeting, that is?'

'Well, no. It was a rather unusual meeting.' The dean smiled briefly. 'We thought it might remain confidential.'

'What transpired at the meeting?'

Dean Hart was not entirely comfortable as chairman of that meeting. Nor did the other members assembled seem completely calm. Only Dr Lanning appeared at peace with himself. His tall, gaunt figure and the shock of white hair that crowned him reminded Hart of portraits he had seen of Andrew Jackson.

Samples of the robot's work lay scattered along the central regions of the table and the reproduction of a graph drawn by the robot was now in the hands of Professor Minott of Physical Chemistry. The chemist's lips were pursed in obvious approval.

Hart cleared his throat and said, 'There seems no doubt that the robot can perform certain routine tasks with adequate competence. I have gone over these, for instance, just before coming in and there is very little to find fault with.'

He picked up a long sheet of printing, some three times as

long as the average book page. It was a sheet of galley proof, designed to be corrected by authors before the type was set up in page form. Along both of the wide margins of the galley were proofmarks, neat and superbly legible. Occasionally, a word of print was crossed out and a new word substituted in the margin in characters so fine and regular it might easily have been print itself. Some of the corrections were blue to indicate the original mistake had been the author's, a few in red, where the printer had been wrong.

'Actually,' said Lanning, 'there is less than very little to find fault with. I should say there is nothing at all to find fault with, Dr Hart. I'm sure the corrections are perfect, insofar as the original manuscript was. If the manuscript against which this galley was corrected was at fault in a matter of fact rather than of English, the robot is not competent to correct it.'

'We accept that. However, the robot corrected word order on occasion and I don't think the rules of English are sufficiently hidebound for us to be sure that in each case the robot's choice was the correct one.'

'Easy's positronic brain,' said Lanning, showing large teeth as he smiled, 'has been molded by the contents of all the standard works on the subject. I'm sure you cannot point to a case where the robot's choice was definitely the incorrect one.'

Professor Minott looked up from the graph he still held. 'The question in my mind, Dr Lanning, is why we need a robot at all, with all the difficulties in public relations that would entail. The science of automation has surely reached the point where your company could design a machine, an ordinary computer of a type known and accepted by the public, that would correct galleys.'

'I am sure we could,' said Lanning stiffly, 'but such a machine would require that the galleys be translated into special symbols or, at the least, transcribed on tapes. Any corrections would emerge in symbols. You would need to keep men employed translating words to symbols, symbols to words. Furthermore, such a computer could do no other job. It couldn't prepare the graph you hold in your hand, for instance.'

Minott grunted.

Lanning went on. 'The hallmark of the positronic robot is its flexibility. It can do a number of jobs. It is designed like a man so that it can use all the tools and machines that have, after all, been designed to be used by a man. It can talk to you and you can talk to it. You can actually reason with it up to a point. Compared to even a simple robot, an ordinary computer with a non-positronic brain is only a heavy adding machine.'

Goodfellow looked up and said, 'If we all talk and reason with the robot, what are the chances of our confusing it? I suppose it doesn't have the capability of absorbing an infinite amount of data.'

'No, it hasn't. But it should last five years with ordinary use. It will know when it will require clearing, and the company will do the job without charge.'

'The *company* will?'

'Yes. The company reserves the right to service the robot outside the ordinary course of its duties. It is one reason we retain control of our positronic robots and lease rather than sell them. In the pursuit of its ordinary functions, any robot can be directed by any man. Outside its ordinary functions, a robot requires expert handling, and that we give it. For instance, any of you might clear an EZ robot to an extent by telling it to forget this item or that. But you would be almost certain to phrase the order in such a way as to cause it to forget too much or too little. We would detect such tampering, because we have built-in safeguards. However, since there is no need for clearing the robot in its ordinary work, or for doing other useless things, this raises no problem.'

Dean Hart touched his head as though to make sure his carefully cultivated strands lay evenly distributed and said, 'You are anxious to have us take the machine. Yet surely it is a losing proposition for US Robots. One thousand a year is a ridiculously low price. Is it that you hope through this to rent other such machines to other universities at a more reasonable price?'

'Certainly that's a fair hope,' said Lanning.

'But even so, the number of machines you could rent would be limited. I doubt if you could make it a paying proposition.'

Lanning put his elbows on the table and earnestly leaned forward. 'Let me put it bluntly, gentlemen. Robots cannot be used on Earth, except in certain special cases, because of prejudice against them on the part of the public. US Robots is a highly successful corporation with our extraterrestrial and spaceflight markets alone, to say nothing of our computer subsidiaries. However, we are concerned with more than profits alone. It is our firm belief that the use of robots on Earth itself would mean a better life for all eventually, even if a certain amount of economic dislocation resulted at first.

'The labor unions are naturally against us, but surely we may expect cooperation from the large universities. The robot, Easy, will help you by relieving you of scholastic drudgery – by assuming, if you permit it, the role of galley slave for you. Other universities and research institutions will follow your lead, and if it works out, then perhaps other robots of other types may be placed and the public's objections to them broken down by stages.'

Minott murmured, 'Today Northeastern University, tomorrow the world.'

Angrily, Lanning whispered to Susan Calvin, 'I wasn't nearly that eloquent and they weren't nearly that reluctant. At a thousand a year, they were jumping to get Easy. Professor Minott told me he'd never seen as beautiful a job as that graph he was holding and there was no mistake on the galley or anywhere else. Hart admitted it freely.'

The severe vertical lines on Dr Calvin's face did not soften. 'You should have demanded more money than they could pay, Alfred, and let them beat you down.'

'Maybe,' he grumbled.

Prosecution was not quite done with Professor Hart. 'After Dr Lanning left, did you vote on whether to accept Robot EZ-27?'

'Yes, we did.'

'With what result?'

'In favor of acceptance, by majority vote.'

'What would you say influenced the vote?'

Defense objected immediately.

Prosecution rephrased the question. 'What influenced you, personally, in your individual vote? You did vote in favor, I think.'

'I voted in favor, yes. I did so largely because I was impressed by Dr Lanning's feeling that it was our duty as members of the world's intellectual leadership to allow robotics to help Man in the solution of his problems.'

'In other words, Dr Lanning talked you into it.'

'That's his job. He did it very well.'

'Your witness.'

Defense strode up to the witness chair and surveyed Professor Hart for a long moment. He said, 'In reality, you were all pretty eager to have Robot EZ-27 in your employ, weren't you?'

'We thought that if it could do the work, it might be useful.'

'*If* it could do the work? I understand you examined the

samples of Robot EZ-27's original work with particular care on the day of the meeting which you have just described.'

'Yes, I did. Since the machine's work dealt primarily with the handling of the English language, and since that is my field of competence, it seemed logical that I be the one chosen to examine the work.'

'Very good. Was there anything on display on the table at the time of the meeting which was less than satisfactory? I have all the material here as exhibits. Can you point to a single unsatisfactory item?'

'Well – '

'It's a simple question. Was there one single solitary unsatisfactory item? You inspected it. Was there?'

The English professor frowned. 'There wasn't.'

'I also have some samples of work done by Robot EZ-27 during the course of his fourteen-month employ at Northeastern. Would you examine these and tell me if there is anything wrong with them in even one particular?'

Hart snapped, 'When he did make a mistake, it was a beauty.'

'Answer my question,' thundered Defense, 'and only the question I am putting to you! Is there anything wrong with the material?'

Dean Hart looked cautiously at each item. 'Well, nothing.'

'Barring the matter concerning which we are here engaged, do you know of any mistake on the part of EZ-27?'

'Barring the matter for which this trial is being held, no.'

Defense cleared his throat as though to signal end of paragraph. He said, 'Now about the vote concerning whether Robot EZ-27 was to be employed or not. You said there was a majority in favor. What was the actual vote?'

'Thirteen to one, as I remember.'

'Thirteen to one! More than just a majority, wouldn't you say?'

'No, sir!' All the pedant in Dean Hart was aroused. 'In the English language, the word "majority" means "more than half." Thirteen out of fourteen is a majority, nothing more.'

'But an almost unanimous one.'

'A majority all the same!'

Defense switched ground. 'And who was the lone holdout?'

Dean Hart looked acutely uncomfortable. 'Professor Simon Ninheimer.'

Defense pretended astonishment. 'Professor Ninheimer? The head of the Department of Sociology?'

'Yes, sir.'

'The *plaintiff*?'

'Yes, sir.'

Defense pursed his lips. 'In other words, it turns out that the man bringing the action for payment of $750,000 damages against my client, United States Robots and Mechanical Men Corporation was the one who from the beginning opposed the use of the robot – although everyone else on the Executive Committee of the University Senate was persuaded that it was a good idea.'

'He voted against the motion, as was his right.'

'You didn't mention in your description of the meeting any remarks made by Professor Ninheimer. Did he make any?'

'I think he spoke.'

'You *think*?'

'Well, he *did* speak.'

'Against using the robot?'

'Yes.'

'Was he violent about it?'

Dean Hart paused. 'He was vehement.'

Defense grew confidential. 'How long have you known Professor Ninheimer, Dean Hart?'

'About twelve years.'

'Reasonably well?'

'I should say so, yes.'

'Knowing him, then, would you say he was the kind of man who might continue to bear resentment against a robot, all the more so because an adverse vote had – '

Prosecution drowned out the remainder of the question with an indignant and vehement objection of his own. Defense motioned the witness down and Justice Shane called luncheon recess.

Robertson mangled his sandwich. The corporation would not founder for loss of three-quarters of a million, but the loss would do it no particular good. He was conscious, moreover, that there would be a much more costly long-term setback in public relations.

He said sourly, 'Why all this business about how Easy got into the university? What do they hope to gain?'

The Attorney for Defense said quietly, 'A court action is like a chess game, Mr Robertson. The winner is usually the one who can see more moves ahead, and my friend at the prosecutor's table is no beginner. They can show damage; that's no problem. Their main effort lies in anticipating our defense. They must be counting on us to try to show that Easy couldn't possibly have committed the offense – because of the Laws of Robotics.'

'All right,' said Robertson, 'that *is* our defense. An absolute airtight one.'

'To a robotics engineer. Not necessarily to a judge. They're setting themselves up a position from which they can demonstrate that EZ-27 was no ordinary robot. It was the first of its type to be offered to the public. It was an experimental model that needed field-testing and the university was the only decent way to provide such testing. That would look plausible in the light of Dr Lanning's strong efforts to place the robot and the willingness of US

Robots to lease it for so little. The prosecution would then argue that the field-test proved Easy to have been a failure. Now do you see the purpose of what's been going on?'

'But EZ-27 was a perfectly good model,' argued Robertson. 'It was the twenty-seventh in production.'

'Which is really a bad point,' said Defense somberly. 'What was wrong with the first twenty-six? Obviously something. Why shouldn't there be something wrong with the twenty-seventh, too?'

'There was nothing wrong with the first twenty-six except that they weren't complex enough for the task. These were the first positronic brains of the sort to be constructed and it was rather hit-and-miss to begin with. But the Three Laws held in all of them! *No* robot is so imperfect that the Three Laws don't hold.'

'Dr Lanning has explained this to me, Mr Robertson, and I am willing to take his word for it. The judge, however, may not be. We are expecting a decision from an honest and intelligent man who knows no robotics and thus may be led astray. For instance, if you or Dr Lanning or Dr Calvin were to say on the stand that any positronic brains were constructed "hit-and-miss," as you just did, prosecution would tear you apart in cross-examination. Nothing would salvage our case. So that's something to avoid.'

Robertson growled, 'If only Easy would talk.'

Defense shrugged. 'A robot is incompetent as a witness, so that would do us no good.'

'At least we'd know some of the facts. We'd know how it came to do such a thing.'

Susan Calvin fired up. A dullish red touched her cheeks and her voice had a trace of warmth in it. 'We *know* how Easy came to do it. It was ordered to! I've explained this to counsel and I'll explain it to you now.'

'Ordered to by whom?' asked Robertson in honest astonishment. (No one ever told him anything, he thought resentfully. These research people considered *themselves* the owners of US Robots, by God!)

'By the plaintiff,' said Dr Calvin.

'In heaven's name, why?'

'I don't know why yet. Perhaps just that we might be sued, that he might gain some cash.' There were blue glints in her eyes as she said that.

'Then why doesn't Easy say so?'

'Isn't that obvious? It's been ordered to keep quiet about the matter.'

'Why should that be obvious?' demanded Robertson truculently.

'Well, it's obvious to me. Robot psychology is my profession. If Easy will not answer questions about the matter directly, he will answer questions on the fringe of the matter. By measuring increased hesitation in his answers as the central question is approached, by measuring the area of blankness and the intensity of counterpotentials set up, it is possible to tell with scientific precision that his troubles are the result of an order not to talk, with its strength based on First Law. In other words, he's been told that if he talks, harm will be done a human being. Presumably harm to the unspeakable Professor Ninheimer, the plaintiff, who, to the robot, would seem a human being.'

'Well, then,' said Robertson, 'can't you explain that if he keeps quiet, harm will be done to US Robots?'

'US Robots is not a human being and the First Law of Robotics does not recognize a corporation as a person the way ordinary laws do. Besides, it would be dangerous to try to lift this particular sort of inhibition. The person who laid it on could lift it off least dangerously, because the robot's motivations in that respect are centered on that person. Any other course – ' She shook her head and grew almost impassioned. 'I won't let the robot be damaged!'

Lanning interrupted with the air of bringing sanity to the

problem. 'It seems to me that we have only to prove a robot incapable of the act of which Easy is accused. We can do that.'

'Exactly,' said Defense, in annoyance. '*You* can do that. The only witnesses capable of testifying to Easy's condition and to the nature of Easy's state of mind are employees of US Robots. The judge can't possibly accept their testimony as unprejudiced.'

'How can he deny expert testimony?'

'By refusing to be convinced by it. That's his right as the judge. Against the alternative that a man like Professor Ninheimer deliberately set about ruining his own reputation, even for a sizable sum of money, the judge isn't going to accept the technicalities of your engineers. The judge is a man, after all. If he has to choose between a man doing an impossible thing and a robot doing an impossible thing, he's quite likely to decide in favor of the man.'

'A man *can* do an impossible thing,' said Lanning, 'because we don't know all the complexities of the human mind and we don't know what, in a given human mind, is impossible and what is not. We *do* know what is really impossible to a robot.'

'Well, we'll see if we can't convince the judge of that,' Defense replied wearily.

'If all you say is so,' rumbled Robertson, 'I don't see how you can.'

'We'll see. It's good to know and be aware of the difficulties involved, but let's not be *too* downhearted. I've tried to look ahead a few moves in the chess game, too.' With a stately nod in the direction of the robopsychologist, he added, '*With* the help of the good lady here.'

Lanning looked from one to the other and said, 'What the devil is this?'

But the bailiff thrust his head into the room and

announced somewhat breathlessly that the trial was about to resume.

They took their seats, examining the man who had started all the trouble.

Simon Ninheimer owned a fluffy head of sandy hair, a face that narrowed past a beaked nose toward a pointed chin, and a habit of sometimes hesitating before key words in his conversation that gave him an air of a seeker after an almost unbearable precision. When he said, 'The Sun rises in the – uh – east,' one was certain he had given due consideration to the possibility that it might at some time rise in the west.

Prosecution said, 'Did you oppose employment of Robot EZ-27 by the university?'

'I did, sir.'

'Why was that?'

'I did not feel that we understood the – uh – motives of US Robots thoroughly. I mistrusted their anxiety to place the robot with us.'

'Did you feel that it was capable of doing the work that it was allegedly designed to do?'

'I know for a fact that it was not.'

'Would you state your reasons?'

Simon Ninheimer's book, entitled *Social Tensions Involved in Space-Flight and Their Resolution*, had been eight years in the making. Ninheimer's search for precision was not confined to his habits of speech, and in a subject like sociology, almost inherently imprecise, it left him breathless.

Even with the material in galley proofs, he felt no sense of completion. Rather the reverse, in fact. Staring at the long strips of print, he felt only the itch to tear the lines of type apart and rearrange them differently.

Jim Baker, Instructor and soon to be Assistant Professor

of Sociology, found Ninheimer, three days after the first batch of galleys had arrived from the printer, staring at the handful of paper in abstraction. The galleys came in three copies: one for Ninheimer to proofread, one for Baker to proofread independently, and a third, marked 'Original,' which was to receive the final corrections, a combination of those made by Ninheimer and by Baker, after a conference at which possible conflicts and disagreements were ironed out. This had been their policy on the several papers on which they had collaborated in the past three years and it worked well.

Baker, young and ingratiatingly soft-voiced, had his own copies of the galleys in his hand. He said eagerly, 'I've done the first chapter and it contains some typographical beauts.'

'The first chapter always has them,' said Ninheimer distantly.

'Do you want to go over it now?'

Ninheimer brought his eyes to grave focus on Baker. 'I haven't done anything on the galleys, Jim. I don't think I'll bother.'

Baker looked confused. 'Not bother?'

Ninheimer pursed his lips. 'I've asked about the – uh – workload of the machine. After all, he was originally – uh – promoted as a proofreader. They've set a schedule.'

'The *machine*? You mean Easy?'

'I believe that is the foolish name they gave it.'

'But, Dr Ninheimer, I thought you were staying clear of it!'

'I seem to be the only one doing so. Perhaps I ought to take my share of the – uh – advantage.'

'Oh. Well, I seem to have wasted time on this first chapter, then,' said the younger man ruefully.

'Not wasted. We can compare the machine's result with yours as a check.'

'If you want to, but – '

'Yes?'

'I doubt that we'll find anything wrong with Easy's work. It's supposed never to have made a mistake.'

'I dare say,' said Ninheimer dryly.

The first chapter was brought in again by Baker four days later. This time it was Ninheimer's copy, fresh from the special annex that had been built to house Easy and the equipment it used.

Baker was jubilant. 'Dr Ninheimer, it not only caught everything I caught – it found a dozen errors I missed! The whole thing took it twelve minutes!'

Ninheimer looked over the sheaf, with the neatly printed marks and symbols in the margins. He said, 'It is not as complete as you and I would have made it. We would have entered an insert on Suzuki's work on the neurological effects of low gravity.'

'You mean his paper in *Sociological Reviews*?'

'Of course.'

'Well, you can't expect impossibilities of Easy. It can't read the literature for us.'

'I realize that. As a matter of fact, I have prepared the insert. I will see the machine and make certain it knows how to – uh – handle inserts.'

'It will know.'

'I prefer to make certain.'

Ninheimer had to make an appointment to see Easy, and then could get nothing better than fifteen minutes in the late evening.

But the fifteen minutes turned out to be ample. Robot EZ-27 understood the matter of inserts at once.

Ninheimer found himself uncomfortable at close quarters with the robot for the first time. Almost automatically, as though it were human, he found himself asking, 'Are you happy with your work?'

'Most happy, Professor Ninheimer,' said Easy solemnly, the photocells that were its eyes gleaming their normal deep red.

'You know me?'

'From the fact that you present me with additional material to include in the galleys, it follows that you are the author. The author's name, of course, is at the head of each sheet of galley proof.'

'I see. You make – uh – deductions, then. Tell me' – he couldn't resist the question – 'what do you think of the book so far?'

Easy said, 'I find it very pleasant to work with.'

'Pleasant? That is an odd word for a – uh – mechanism without emotion. I've been told you have no emotion.'

'The words of your book go in accordance with my circuits,' Easy explained. 'They set up little or no counter-potentials. It is in my brain paths to translate this mechanical fact into a word such as "pleasant." The emotional context is fortuitous.'

'I see. Why do you find the book pleasant?'

'It deals with human beings, Professor, and not with inorganic materials or mathematical symbols. Your book attempts to understand human beings and to help increase human happiness.'

'And this is what you try to do and so my book goes in accordance with your circuits? Is that it?'

'That is it, Professor.'

The fifteen minutes were up. Ninheimer left and went to the university library, which was on the point of closing. He kept them open long enough to find an elementary text on robotics. He took it home with him.

Except for occasional insertion of late material, the galleys went to Easy and from him to the publishers with little intervention from Ninheimer at first – and none at all later.

Baker said, a little uneasily, 'It almost gives me a feeling of uselessness.'

'It should give you a feeling of having time to begin a new project,' said Ninheimer, without looking up from the notations he was making in the current issue of *Social Science Abstracts*.

'I'm just not used to it. I keep worrying about the galleys. It's silly, I know.'

'It is.'

'The other day I got a couple of sheets before Easy sent them off to – '

'What!' Ninheimer looked up, scowling. The copy of *Abstracts* slid shut. 'Did you disturb the machine at its work?'

'Only for a minute. Everything was all right. Oh, it changed one word. You referred to something as "criminal"; it changed the word to "reckless." It thought the second adjective fit in better with the context.'

Ninheimer grew thoughtful. 'What did you think?'

'You know, I agreed with it. I let it stand.'

Ninheimer turned in his swivel-chair to face his young associate. 'See here, I wish you wouldn't do this again. If I am to use the machine, I wish the – uh – full advantage of it. If I am to use it and lose your – uh – services anyway because you supervise it when the whole point is that it requires no supervision, I gain nothing. Do you see?'

'Yes, Dr Ninheimer,' said Baker, subdued.

The advance copies of *Social Tensions* arrived in Dr Ninheimer's office on the eighth of May. He looked through it briefly, flipping pages and pausing to read a paragraph here and there. Then he put his copies away.

As he explained later, he forgot about it. For eight years, he had worked at it, but now, and for months in the past, other interests had engaged him while Easy had taken the load of the book off his shoulders. He did not even think to donate the usual complimentary copy to the university library. Even Baker, who had thrown himself into work and had steered clear of the department head since receiving his rebuke at their last meeting, received no copy.

On the sixteenth of June that stage ended. Ninheimer received a phone call and stared at the image in the 'plate with surprise.

'Speidell! Are you in town?'

'No, sir. I'm in Cleveland.' Speidell's voice trembled with emotion.

'Then why the call?'

'Because I've just been looking through your new book! Ninheimer, are you *mad*? Have you gone *insane*?'

Ninheimer stiffened. 'Is something – uh – wrong?' he asked in alarm.

'Wrong? I refer you to page 562. What in blazes do you mean by interpreting my work as you do? Where in the paper cited do I make the claim that the criminal personality is nonexistent and that it is the *law*-enforcement agencies that are the *true* criminals? Here, let me quote – '

'Wait! Wait!' cried Ninheimer, trying to find the page. 'Let me see. Let me see . . . Good God!'

'Well?'

'Speidell, I don't see how this could have happened. I never wrote this.'

'But that's what's printed! And that distortion isn't the worst. You look at page 690 and imagine what Ipatiev is going to do to you when he sees the hash you've made of his findings! Look, Ninheimer, the book is *riddled* with this sort of thing. I don't know what you were thinking of – but there's nothing to do but get the book off the market. And you'd better be prepared for extensive apologies at the next Association meeting!'

'Speidell, listen to me – '

But Speidell had flashed off with a force that had the 'plate glowing with after-images for fifteen seconds.

It was then that Ninheimer went through the book and began marking off passages with red ink.

He kept his temper remarkably well when he faced Easy again, but his lips were pale. He passed the book to Easy and said, 'Will you read the marked passages on pages 562, 631, 664 and 690?'

Easy did so in four glances. 'Yes, Professor Ninheimer.'

'This is not as I had it in the original galleys.'

'No, sir. It is not.'

'Did you change it to read as it now does?'

'Yes, sir.'

'Why?'

'Sir, the passages as they read in your version were most uncomplimentary to certain groups of human beings. I felt it advisable to change the wording to avoid doing them harm.'

'How *dared* you do such a thing?'

'The First Law, Professor, does not let me, through any inaction, allow harm to come to human beings. Certainly, considering your reputation in the world of sociology and the wide circulation your book would receive among scholars, considerable harm would come to a number of the human beings you speak of.'

'But do you realize the harm that will come to *me* now?'

'It was necessary to choose the alternative with less harm.'

Professor Ninheimer, shaking with fury, staggered away. It was clear to him that US Robots would have to account to him for this.

There was some excitement at the defendants' table, which increased as Prosecution drove the point home.

'Then Robot EZ-27 informed you that the reason for its action was based on the First Law of Robotics?'

'That is correct, sir.'

'That, in effect, it had no choice?'

'Yes, sir.'

'It follows then that US Robots designed a robot that would of necessity rewrite books to accord with its own conceptions of what was right. And yet they palmed it off as simple proofreader. Would you say that?'

Defense objected firmly at once, pointing out that the witness was being asked for a decision on a matter in which he had no competence. The judged admonished Prosecution in the usual terms, but there was no doubt that the exchange had sunk home – not least upon the attorney for the Defense.

Defense asked for a short recess before beginning cross-examination, using a legal technicality for the purpose that got him five minutes.

He leaned over toward Susan Calvin. 'Is it possible, Dr Calvin, that Professor Ninheimer is telling the truth and that Easy was motivated by the First Law?'

Calvin pressed her lips together, then said, 'No. It *isn't* possible. The last part of Ninheimer's testimony is deliberate perjury. Easy is not designed to be able to judge matters at the stage of abstraction represented by an advanced textbook on sociology. It would never be able to tell that certain groups of humans would be harmed by a phrase in such a book. Its mind is simply not built for that.'

'I suppose, though, that we can't prove this to a layman,' said Defense pessimistically.

'No,' admitted Calvin. 'The proof would be highly complex. Our way out is still what it was. We must prove Ninheimer is lying and nothing he has said need change our plan of attack.'

'Very well, Dr Calvin,' said Defense, 'I must accept your word in this. We'll go on as planned.'

In the courtroom, the judge's gavel rose and fell and Dr Ninheimer took the stand once more. He smiled a little as one who feels his position to be impregnable and rather enjoys the prospect of countering a useless attack.

Defense approached warily and began softly. 'Dr Ninheimer, do you mean to say that you were completely unaware of these alleged changes in your manuscript until such time as Dr Speidell called you on the sixteenth of June?'

'That is correct, sir.'

'Did you never look at the galleys after Robot EZ-27 had proofread them?'

'At first I did, but it seemed to me a useless task. I relied on the claims of US Robots. The absurd – uh – changes were made only in the last quarter of the book after the robot, I presume, had learned enough about sociology – '

'Never mind your presumptions!' said Defense. 'I understood your colleague, Dr Baker, saw the later galleys on at least one occasion. Do you remember testifying to that effect?'

'Yes, sir. As I said, he told me about seeing one page, and even there, the robot had changed a word.'

Again Defense broke in. 'Don't you find it strange, sir, that after over a year of implacable hostility to the robot, after having voted against it in the first place and having refused to put it to any use whatever, you suddenly decided to put your book, your *magnum opus*, into its hands?'

'I don't find that strange. I simply decided that I might as well use the machine.'

'And you were so confident of Robot EZ-27 – all of a sudden – that you didn't even bother to check your galleys?'

'I told you I was – uh – persuaded by US Robots' propaganda.'

'So persuaded that when your colleague, Dr Baker, attempted to check on the robot, you berated him soundly?'

'I didn't berate him. I merely did not wish to have him – uh – waste his time. At least, I thought then it was a waste of time. I did not see the significance of that change in a word at the – '

Defense said with heavy sarcasm, 'I have no doubt you were instructed to bring up that point in order that the word-change be entered in the record – ' He altered his line to forestall objection and said, 'The point is that you were extremely angry with Dr Baker.'

'No, sir. Not angry.'

'You didn't give him a copy of your book when you received it.'

'Simple forgetfulness. I didn't give the library its copy, either.' Ninheimer smiled cautiously. 'Professors are notoriously absent-minded.'

Defense said, 'Do you find it strange that, after more than a year of perfect work, Robot EZ-27 should go wrong on your book? On a book, that is, which was written by you, who was, of all people, the most implacably hostile to the robot?'

'My book was the only sizable work dealing with mankind that it had to face. The Three Laws of Robotics took hold then.'

'Several times, Dr Ninheimer,' said Defense, 'you have tried to sound like an expert on robotics. Apparently you suddenly grew interested in robotics and took out books on the subject from the library. You testified to that effect, did you not?'

'One book, sir. That was the result of what seems to me to have been – uh – natural curiosity.'

'And it enabled you to explain why the robot should, as you allege, have distorted your book?'

'Yes, sir.'

'Very convenient. But are you sure your interest in robotics was not intended to enable you to manipulate the robot for your own purposes?'

Ninheimer flushed. 'Certainly not, sir!'

Defense's voice rose. 'In fact, are you sure the alleged altered passages were not as you had them in the first place?'

The sociologist half-rose. 'That's – uh – uh – ridiculous! I have the galleys – '

He had difficulty speaking and Prosecution rose to insert smoothly, 'With your permission, Your Honour, I intend to introduce as evidence the set of galleys given by Dr Ninheimer to Robot EZ-27 and the set of galleys mailed by Robot EZ-27 to the publishers. I will do so now if my esteemed colleague so desires, and will be willing to allow a recess in order that the two sets of galleys may be compared.'

Defense waved his hand impatiently. 'That is not necessary. My honored opponent can introduce those galleys whenever he chooses. I'm sure they will show whatever discrepancies are claimed by the plaintiff to exist. What I would like to know of the witness, however, is whether he also has in his possession *Dr Baker's* galleys.'

'Dr Baker's galleys?' Ninheimer frowned. He was not yet quite master of himself.

'Yes, Professor! I mean Dr Baker's galleys. You testified to the effect that Dr Baker had received a separate copy of the galleys. I will have the clerk read your testimony if you are suddenly a selective type of amnesiac. Or is it just that professors are, as you say, notoriously absent-minded?'

Ninheimer said, 'I remember Dr Baker's galleys. They weren't necessary once the job was placed in the care of the proofreading machine – '

'So you burned them?'

'*No.* I put them in the waste basket.'

'Burned them, dumped them – what's the difference? The point is you got rid of them.'

'There's nothing wrong – ' began Ninheimer weakly.

'Nothing wrong?' thundered Defense. 'Nothing wrong except that there is now no way we can check to see if, on certain crucial galley sheets, you might not have substituted a harmless blank one from Dr Baker's copy for a sheet in your own copy which you had deliberately mangled in such a way as to force the robot to – '

Prosecution shouted a furious objection. Justice Shane leaned forward, his round face doing its best to assume an expression of anger equivalent to the intensity of the emotion felt by the man.

The judge said, 'Do you have any evidence, Counselor, for the extraordinary statement you have just made?'

Defense said quietly, 'No direct evidence, Your Honor. But I would like to point out that, viewed properly, the sudden conversion of the plaintiff from anti-roboticism, his sudden interest in robotics, his refusal to check the galleys or to allow anyone else to check them, his careful neglect to allow anyone to see the book immediately after publication, all very clearly point – '

'Counselor,' interrupted the judge impatiently, 'this is not the place for esoteric deductions. The plaintiff is not on trial. Neither are you prosecuting him. I forbid this line of attack and I can only point out that the desperation that must have induced you to do this cannot help but weaken your case. If you have legitimate questions to ask, Counselor, you may continue with your cross-examination. But I warn you against another such exhibition in this courtroom.'

'I have no further questions, Your Honor.'

Robertson whispered heatedly as counsel for the Defense returned to his table, 'What good did that do, for God's sake? The judge is dead-set against you now.'

Defense replied calmly, 'But Ninheimer is good and rattled. And we've set him up for tomorrow's move. He'll be ripe.'

Susan Calvin nodded gravely.

The rest of Prosecution's case was mild in comparison. Dr Baker was called and bore out most of Ninheimer's testimony. Drs Speidell and Ipatiev were called, and they expounded most movingly on their shock and dismay at certain quoted passages in Dr Ninheimer's book. Both gave their professional opinion that Dr Ninheimer's professional reputation had been seriously impaired.

The galleys were introduced in evidence, as were copies of the finished book.

Defense cross-examined no more that day. Prosecution rested and the trial was recessed till the next morning.

Defense made his first motion at the beginning of the proceedings on the second day. He requested that Robot EZ-27 be admitted as a spectator to the proceedings.

Prosecution objected at once and Justice Shane called both to the bench.

Prosecution said hotly, 'This is obviously illegal. A robot may not be in any edifice used by the general public.'

'This courtroom,' pointed out Defense, 'is closed to all but those having an immediate connection with the case.'

'A large machine of *known* erratic behavior would disturb my clients and my witnesses by its very presence! It would make hash out of the proceedings.'

The judge seemed inclined to agree. He turned to Defense and said rather unsympathetically, 'What are the reasons for your request?'

Defense said, 'It will be our contention that Robot EZ-27 could not possibly, by the nature of its construction, have behaved as it has been described as behaving. It will be necessary to present a few demonstrations.'

Prosecution said, 'I don't see the point, Your Honor. Demonstrations conducted by men employed at US Robots are worth little as evidence when US Robots is the defendant.'

'Your Honor,' said Defense, 'the validity of any evidence is for you to decide, not for the Prosecuting Attorney. At least, that is my understanding.'

Justice Shane, his prerogatives encroached upon, said, 'Your understanding is correct. Nevertheless, the presence of a robot here does raise important legal questions.'

'Surely, Your Honor, nothing that should be allowed to override the requirements of justice. If the robot is not present, we are prevented from presenting our only defense.'

The judge considered. 'There would be the question of transporting the robot here.'

'That is a problem with which US Robots has frequently been faced. We have a truck parked outside the courtroom, constructed according to the laws governing the transportation of robots. Robot EZ-27 is in a packing case inside with two men guarding it. The doors to the truck are properly secured and all other necessary precautions have been taken.'

'You seem certain,' said Justice Shane, in renewed ill-temper, 'that judgment on this point will be in your favor.'

'Not at all, Your Honor. If it is not, we simply turn the truck about. I have made no presumptions concerning your decision.'

The judge nodded. 'The request on the part of the Defense is granted.'

The crate was carried in on a large dolly and the two men who handled it opened it. The courtroom was immersed in a dead silence.

Susan Calvin waited as the thick slabs of celluform went down, then held out one hand. 'Come, Easy.'

The robot looked in her direction and held out its large metal arm. It towered over her by two feet but followed meekly, like a child in the clasp of its mother. Someone giggled nervously and choked it off at a hard glare from Dr Calvin.

Easy seated itself carefully in a large chair brought by the bailiff, which creaked but held.

Defense said, 'When it becomes necessary, Your Honor, we will prove that this is actually Robot EZ-27, the specific robot in the employ of Northeastern University during the period of time with which we are concerned.'

'Good,' His Honor said. 'That will be necessary. I, for one, have no idea how you can tell one robot from another.'

'And now,' said Defense, 'I would like to call my first witness to the stand. Professor Simon Ninheimer, please.'

The clerk hesitated, looked at the judge. Justice Shane asked, with visible surprise, 'You are calling the *plaintiff* as your witness?'

'Yes, Your Honor.'

'I hope that you're aware that as long as he's your witness, you will be allowed none of the latitude you might exercise if you were cross-examining an opposing witness.'

Defense said smoothly, 'My only purpose in all this is to arrive at the truth. It will not be necessary to do more than ask a few polite questions.'

'Well,' said the judge dubiously, 'you're the one handling the case. Call the witness.'

Ninheimer took the stand and was informed that he was still under oath. He looked more nervous than he had the day before, almost apprehensive.

But Defense looked at him benignly.

'Now, Professor Ninheimer, you are suing my clients in the amount of $750,000.'

'That is the – uh – sum. Yes.'

'That is a great deal of money.'

'I have suffered a great deal of harm.'

'Surely not that much. The material in question involves only a few passages in a book. Perhaps these were unfortunate passages, but after all, books sometimes appear with curious mistakes in them.'

Ninheimer's nostrils flared. 'Sir, this book was to have been the climax of my professional career! Instead, it makes me look like an incompetent scholar, a perverter of the views held by my honored friends and associates, and a believer of ridiculous and – uh – outmoded viewpoints. My reputation is irretrievably shattered! I can never hold up my head in any – uh – assemblage of scholars, regardless of the outcome of this trial. I certainly cannot continue in my career, which has been the whole of my life. The very purpose of my life has been – uh – aborted and destroyed.'

Defense made no attempt to interrupt the speech, but stared abstractedly at his fingernails as it went on.

He said very soothingly, 'But surely, Professor Ninheimer, at your present age, you could not hope to earn more than – let us be generous – $150,000 during the remainder of your life. Yet you are asking the court to award you five times as much.'

Ninheimer said, with an even greater burst of emotion, 'It is not in my lifetime alone that I am ruined. I do not know for how many generations I shall be pointed at by sociologists as a – uh – a fool or maniac. My real achievements will be buried and ignored. I am ruined not only until the day of my death, but for all time to come, because there will always be people who will not believe that a robot made those insertions – '

It was at this point that Robot EZ-27 rose to his feet. Susan Calvin made no move to stop him. She sat motionless, staring straight ahead. Defense sighed softly.

Easy's melodious voice carried clearly. It said, 'I would like to explain to everyone that I did insert certain passages in the galley proofs that seemed directly opposed to what had been there at first – '

Even the Prosecuting Attorney was too startled at the spectacle of a seven-foot robot rising to address the court to be able to demand the stopping of what was obviously a most irregular procedure.

When he could collect his wits, it was too late. For Ninheimer rose in the witness chair, his face working.

He shouted wildly, 'Damn you, you were instructed to keep your mouth shut about – '

He ground to a choking halt, and Easy was silent, too.

Prosecution was on his feet now, demanding that a mistrial be declared.

Justice Shane banged his gavel desperately. 'Silence! Silence! Certainly there is every reason here to declare a mistrial, except that in the interests of justice I would like to have Professor Ninheimer complete his statement. I distinctly heard him say to the robot that the robot had been instructed to keep its mouth shut about something. There was no mention in your testimony, Professor Ninheimer, as to any instructions to the robot to keep silent about anything!'

Ninheimer stared wordlessly at the judge.

Justice Shane said, 'Did you instruct Robot EZ-27 to keep silent about something? And if so, about what?'

'Your Honor – ' began Ninheimer hoarsely, and couldn't continue.

The judge's voice grew sharp. 'Did you, in fact, order the inserts in question to be made in the galleys and then order the robot to keep quiet about your part in this?'

Prosecution objected vigorously, but Ninheimer shouted, 'Oh, what's the use? Yes! Yes!' And he ran from the witness stand. He was stopped at the door by the bailiff and sank hopelessly into one of the last rows of seats, head buried in both hands.

Justice Shane said, 'It is evident to me that Robot EZ-27 was brought here as a trick. Except for the fact that the trick served to prevent a serious miscarriage of justice, I would certainly hold attorney for the Defense in contempt. It is clear now, beyond any doubt, that the plaintiff has committed what is to me a completely inexplicable fraud since, apparently, he was knowingly ruining his career in the process – '

Judgment, of course, was for the defendant.

Dr Susan Calvin had herself announced at Dr Ninheimer's bachelor quarters in University Hall. The young engineer who had driven the car offered to go up with her, but she looked at him scornfully.

'Do you think he'll assault me? Wait down here.'

Ninheimer was in no mood to assault anyone. He was packing, wasting no time, anxious to be away before the adverse conclusion of the trial became general knowledge.

He looked at Calvin with a queerly defiant air and said, 'Are you coming to warn me of a countersuit? If so, it will get you nothing. I have no money, no job, no future. I can't even meet the costs of the trial.'

'If you're looking for sympathy,' said Calvin coldly, 'don't look for it here. This was your doing. However, there will be no countersuit, neither of you nor of the university. We will even do what we can to keep you from going to prison for perjury. We aren't vindictive.'

'Oh, is that why I'm not already in custody for forswearing myself? I had wondered. But then,' he added bitterly, 'why *should* you be vindictive? You have what you want now.'

'Some of what we want, yes,' said Calvin. 'The university will keep Easy in its employ at a considerably higher rental fee. Furthermore, certain underground publicity concerning the trial will make it possible to place a few more of the EZ models in other institutions without danger of a repetition of this trouble.'

'Then why have you come to see me?'

'Because I don't have all of what I want yet. I want to know why you hate robots as you do. Even if you had won the case, your reputation would have been ruined. The money you might have obtained could not have compensated for that. Would the satisfaction of your hatred of robots have done so?'

'Are you interested in *human* minds, Dr Calvin?' asked Ninheimer, with acid mockery.

'Insofar as their reactions concern the welfare of robots, yes. For that reason, I have learned a little of human psychology.'

'Enough of it to be able to trick me!'

'That wasn't hard,' said Calvin, without pomposity. 'The difficult thing was doing it in such a way as not to damage Easy.'

'It is like you to be more concerned for a machine than for a man.' He looked at her with savage contempt.

It left her unmoved. 'It merely seems so, Professor Ninheimer. It is only by being concerned for robots that one can truly be concerned for twenty-first-century man. You would understand this if you were a roboticist.'

'I have read enough robotics to know I don't *want* to be a roboticist!'

'Pardon me, you have read *a book* on robotics. It has taught you nothing. You learned enough to know that you could order a robot to do many things, even to falsify a book, if you went about it properly. You learned enough to know that you could not order him to forget something entirely without risking detection, but you thought you could order him into simple silence more safely. You were wrong.'

'You guessed the truth from his silence?'

'It wasn't guessing. You were an amateur and didn't know enough to cover your tracks completely. My only problem was to prove the matter to the judge and you were kind enough to help us there, in your ignorance of the robotics you claim to despise.'

'Is there any purpose in this discussion?' asked Ninheimer wearily.

'For me, yes,' said Susan Calvin, 'because I want you to understand how completely you have misjudged robots. You silenced Easy by telling him that if he told anyone about your own distortion of the book, you would lose your job. That set up a certain potential within Easy toward silence, one that was strong enough to resist our efforts to break it down. We would have damaged the brain if we had persisted.

'On the witness stand, however, you yourself put up a higher counterpotential. You said that because people would think that you, not a robot, had written the disputed passages in the book, you would lose far more than just your job. You would lose your reputation, your standing, your respect, your reason for living. You would lose the memory of you after death. A new and higher potential was set up by you – and Easy talked.'

'Oh, God,' said Ninheimer, turning his head away.

Calvin was inexorable. She said, 'Do you understand *why* he talked? It was not to accuse you, but to *defend* you! It can be mathematically shown that he was about to assume full blame for your crime, to deny that you had anything to do with it. The First Law required that. He was going to lie – to damage himself – to bring monetary harm to a corporation. All that meant less to him than did the saving of you. If you really understood robots and robotics, you would have let him talk. But you did not understand, as I was sure you wouldn't, as I guaranteed to the defense attorney that you wouldn't. You were certain, in your hatred of robots, that Easy would act as a human being would act and defend itself at your expense. So you flared out at him in panic – and destroyed yourself.'

Ninheimer said with feeling, 'I hope some day your robots turn on you and kill you!'

'Don't be foolish,' said Calvin. 'Now I want you to explain why you've done all this.'

Ninheimer grinned a distorted, humorless grin. 'I am to dissect my mind, am I, for your intellectual curiosity, in return for immunity from a charge of perjury?'

'Put it that way if you like,' said Calvin emotionlessly. 'But explain.'

'So that you can counter future anti-robot attempts more efficiently? With greater understanding?'

'I accept that.'

'You know,' said Ninheimer, 'I'll tell you – just to watch it do you no good at all. You can't understand human motivation. You can only understand your damned machines because you're a machine yourself, with skin on.'

He was breathing hard and there was no hesitation in his speech, no searching for precision. It was as though he had no further use for precision.

He said, 'For two hundred and fifty years, the machine has been replacing Man and destroying the handcraftsman. Pottery is spewed out of molds and presses. Works of art have been replaced by identical gimcracks stamped out on a die. Call it progress, if you wish! The artist is restricted to abstractions, confined to the world of ideas. He must design something in mind – and then the machine does the rest.

'Do you suppose the potter is content with mental creation? Do you suppose the idea is enough? That there is nothing in the feel of the clay itself, in watching the thing grow as hand and mind work *together*? Do you suppose the actual growth doesn't act as a feedback to modify and improve the idea?'

'You are not a potter,' said Dr Calvin.

'I am a creative artist! I design and build articles and books. There is more to it than the mere thinking of words and of putting them in the right order. If that were all, there would be no pleasure in it, no return.

'A book should take shape in the hands of the writer. One must actually see the chapters grow and develop. One must work and re-work and watch the changes take place beyond the original concept even. There is taking the galleys in hand and seeing how the sentences look in print and molding them again. There are a hundred contacts between a man and his work at every stage of the game – and the contact itself is pleasurable and repays a man for the work he puts into his creation more than anything else could. *Your robot would take all that away*.'

'So does a typewriter. So does a printing press. Do you propose to return to the hand illumination of manuscripts?'

'Typewriters and printing presses take away some, but your robot would deprive us of all. Your robot takes over the galleys. Soon it, or other robots, would take over the original writing, the searching of the sources, the checking and cross-checking of passages, perhaps even the deduction of conclusions. What would that leave the scholar? One thing only – the barren decisions concerning what orders to give the robot next! I want to save the future generations of the world of scholarship from such a final hell. That meant more to me than even my own reputation and so I set out to destroy US Robots by whatever means.'

'You were bound to fail,' said Susan Calvin.

'I was bound to try,' said Simon Ninheimer.

Calvin turned and left. She did her best to feel no pang of sympathy for the broken man.

She did not entirely succeed.

Little Lost Robot

Measures on Hyper Base had been taken in a sort of rattling fury – the muscular equivalent of an hysterical shriek.

To itemize them in order of both chronology and desperation, they were:

1. All work on the Hyperatomic Drive through all the space volume occupied by the Stations of the Twenty-Seventh Asteroidal Grouping came to a halt.

2. That entire volume of space was nipped out of the System, practically speaking. No one entered without permission. No one left under any conditions.

3. By special government patrol ship, Drs Susan Calvin and Peter Bogert, respectively Head Psychologist and Mathematical Director of United States Robots and Mechanical Men Corporation, were brought to Hyper Base.

Susan Calvin had never left the surface of Earth before, and had no perceptible desire to leave it this time. In an age of Atomic Power and a clearly coming Hyperatomic Drive, she remained quietly provincial. So she was dissatisfied with her trip and unconvinced of the emergency, and every line of her plain, middle-aged face showed it clearly enough during her first dinner at Hyper Base.

Nor did Dr Bogert's sleek paleness abandon a certain hangdog attitude. Nor did Major-general Kallner, who headed the project, even once forget to maintain a haunted expression.

In short, it was a grisly episode, that meal, and the little session of three that followed began in a gray, unhappy manner.

Kallner, with his baldness glistening, and his dress uniform oddly unsuited to the general mood, began with uneasy directness.

'This is a queer story to tell, sir, and madam. I want to thank you for coming on short notice and without a reason being given. We'll try to correct that now. We've lost a robot. Work has stopped and *must* stop until such time as we locate it. So far we have failed, and we feel we need expert help.'

Perhaps the general felt his predicament anticlimactic. He continued with a note of desperation, 'I needn't tell you the importance of our work here. More than eighty per cent of last year's appropriations for scientific research have gone to us – '

'Why, we know that,' said Bogert, agreeably. 'US Robots is receiving a generous rental fee for use of our robots.'

Susan Calvin injected a blunt, vinegary note, 'What makes a single robot so important to the project, and why hasn't it been located?'

The general turned his red face toward her and wet his lips quickly, 'Why, in a manner of speaking we *have* located it.' Then, with near anguish, 'Here, suppose I explain. As soon as the robot failed to report a state of emergency was declared, and all movement off Hyper Base stopped. A cargo vessel had landed the previous day and had delivered us two robots for our laboratories. It had sixty-two robots of the . . . uh . . . same type for shipment elsewhere. We are certain as to that figure. There is no question about it whatever.'

'Yes? And the connection?'

'When our missing robot was not located anywhere – I assure you we would have found a missing blade of grass if it had been there to find – we brainstormed ourselves into counting the robots left on the cargo ship. They have sixty-three now.'

'So that the sixty-third, I take it, is the missing prodigal?' Dr Calvin's eyes darkened.

'Yes, but we have no way of telling which is the sixty-third.'

There was a dead silence while the electric clock chimed eleven times, and then the robopsychologist said, 'Very peculiar,' and the corners of her lips moved downward.

'Peter,' she turned to her colleague with a trace of savagery, 'what's wrong here? What kind of robots are they using at Hyper Base?'

Dr Bogert hesitated and smiled feebly, 'It's been rather a matter of delicacy till now, Susan.'

She spoke rapidly, 'Yes, *till* now. If there are sixty-three same-type robots, one of which is wanted and the identity of which cannot be determined, why won't any of them do? What's the idea of all this? Why have we been sent for?'

Bogert said in resigned fashion, 'If you'll give me a chance, Susan – Hyper Base happens to be using several robots whose brains are not impressioned with the entire First Law of Robotics.'

'*Aren't* impressioned?' Calvin slumped back in her chair, 'I see. How many were made?'

'A few. It was on government order and there was no way of violating the secrecy. No one was to know except the top men directly concerned. You weren't included, Susan. It was nothing I had anything to do with.'

The general interrupted with a measure of authority. 'I would like to explain that bit. I hadn't been aware that Dr Calvin was unacquainted with the situation. I needn't tell you, Dr Calvin, that there always has been strong opposition to robots on the Planet. The only defense the government has had against the Fundamentalist radicals in this matter was the fact that robots are always built with an unbreakable First Law – which makes it impossible for them to harm human beings under any circumstance.

'But we *had* to have robots of a different nature. So just a few of the NS-2 model, the Nestors, that is, were prepared with a modified First Law. To keep it quiet, all NS-2's are manufactured without serial numbers; modified members are delivered here along with a group of normal robots; and, of course, all our kind are under the strictest impressionment never to tell of their modification to unauthorized personnel.' He wore an embarrassed smile, 'This has all worked out against us now.'

Calvin said grimly, 'Have you asked each one who it is, anyhow? Certainly, you are authorized?'

The general nodded, 'All sixty-three deny having worked here – and one is lying.'

'Does the one you want show traces of wear? The others, I take it, are factory-fresh.'

'The one in question only arrived last month. It, and the two that have just arrived, were to be the last we needed. There's no perceptible wear.' He shook his head slowly and his eyes were haunted again, 'Dr Calvin, we don't dare let that ship leave. If the existence of non-First Law robots becomes general knowledge – ' There seemed no way of avoiding understatement in the conclusion.

'Destroy all sixty-three,' said the robopsychologist coldly and flatly, 'and make an end of it.'

Bogert drew back a corner of his mouth. 'You mean destroy thirty thousand dollars per robot. I'm afraid US Robots wouldn't like that. We'd better make an effort first, Susan, before we destroy anything.'

'In that case,' she said, sharply, 'I need facts. Exactly what advantage does Hyper Base derive from these modified robots? What factor made them desirable, general?'

Kallner ruffled his forehead and stroked it with an upward gesture of his hand. 'We had trouble with our previous robots. Our men work with hard radiations a good deal, you see. It's dangerous, of course, but reasonable precautions are taken. There have been only two accidents since we began and neither was fatal. However, it was impossible to explain that to an ordinary robot. The First Law states – I'll quote it – "*no robot may harm a human being or, through inaction, allow a human being to come to harm.*"

'That's primary, Dr Calvin. When it was necessary for one of our men to expose himself for a short period to a moderate gamma field, one that would have no physiological effects, the nearest robot would dash in to drag him out. If the field were exceedingly weak, it would succeed, and work could not continue till all robots were cleared out. If the field were a trifle stronger, the robot would never reach the technician concerned, since its positronic brain would collapse under gamma radiations – and then we would be out one expensive and hard-to-replace robot.

'We tried arguing with them. Their point was that a human being in a gamma field was endangering his life and that it didn't matter that he could remain there half an hour safely. Supposing, they would say, he forgot and remained an hour. They couldn't take chances. We pointed out that they were risking their lives on a wild off-chance. But self-preservation is only the Third Law of Robotics – and the First Law of human safety came first. We gave them orders; we ordered them strictly and harshly to remain out of gamma fields at whatever cost. But obedience is only the Second Law of Robotics – and the First Law of human safety came first. Dr Calvin, we either had to do without robots, or do something about the First Law – and we made our choice.'

'I can't believe,' said Dr Calvin, 'that it was found possible to remove the First Law.'

'It wasn't removed, it was modified,' explained Kallner.

'Positronic brains were constructed that contained the positive aspect only of the Law, which in them reads: "*No robot may harm a human being.*" That is all. They have no compulsion to prevent one coming to harm through an extraneous agency such as gamma rays. I state the matter correctly, Dr Bogert?'

'Quite,' assented the mathematician.

'And that is the only difference of your robots from the ordinary NS-2 model? The *only* difference? Peter?'

'The *only* difference, Susan.'

She rose and spoke with finality, 'I intend sleeping now, and in about eight hours, I want to speak to whomever saw the robot last. And from now on, General Kallner, if I'm to take any responsibility at all for events, I want full and unquestioned control of this investigation.'

Susan Calvin, except for two hours of resentful lassitude, experienced nothing approaching sleep. She signaled at Bogert's door at the local time of 0700 and found him also awake. He had apparently taken the trouble of transporting a dressing gown to Hyper Base with him, for he was sitting in it. He put his nail scissors down when Calvin entered.

He said softly, 'I've been expecting you more or less. I suppose you feel sick about all this.'

'I do.'

'Well – I'm sorry. There was no way of preventing it. When the call came out from Hyper Base for us, I knew that something must have gone wrong with the modified Nestors. But what was there to do? I couldn't break the matter to you on the trip here as I would have liked to, because I had to be sure. The matter of the modification is top secret.'

The psychologist muttered, 'I should have been told. US Robots had no right to modify positronic brains this way without the approval of a psychologist.'

Bogert lifted his eyebrows and sighed. 'Be reasonable,

Susan. You couldn't have influenced them. In this matter, the government was bound to have its way. They want the Hyperatomic Drive and the etheric physicists want robots that won't interfere with them. They were going to get them even if it did mean twisting the First Law. We had to admit it was possible from a construction standpoint and they swore a mighty oath that they wanted only twelve, that they would be used only at Hyper Base, that they would be destroyed once the Drive was perfected, and that full precautions would be taken. And they insisted on secrecy – and that's the situation.'

Dr Calvin spoke through her teeth, 'I would have resigned.'

'It wouldn't have helped. The government was offering the company a fortune, and threatening it with antirobot legislation in case of a refusal. We were stuck then, and we're badly stuck now. If this leaks out, it might hurt Kallner and the government, but it would hurt US Robots a devil of a lot more.'

The psychologist stared at him. 'Peter, don't you realize what all this is about? Can't you understand what the removal of the First Law means? It isn't just a matter of secrecy.'

'I know what removal would mean. I'm not a child. It would mean complete instability, with no nonimaginary solutions to the positronic Field Equations.'

'Yes, mathematically. But can you translate that into crude psychological thought. All normal life, Peter, consciously or otherwise, resents domination. If the domination is by an inferior, or by a supposed inferior, the resentment becomes stronger. Physically, and, to an extent, mentally, a robot – any robot – is superior to human beings. What makes him slavish, then? *Only the First Law!* Why, without it, the first order you tried to give a robot would result in your death. Unstable? What do you think?'

'Susan,' said Bogert, with an air of sympathetic amusement. 'I'll admit that this Frankenstein Complex you're exhibiting has a certain justification – hence the First Law in the first place. But the Law, I repeat and repeat, has not been removed – merely modified.'

'And what about the stability of the brain?'

The mathematician thrust out his lips, 'Decreased, naturally. But it's within the border of safety. The first Nestors were delivered to Hyper Base nine months ago, and nothing whatever has gone wrong till now, and even this involves merely fear of discovery and not danger to humans.'

'Very well, then. We'll see what comes of the morning conference.'

Bogert saw her politely to the door and grimaced eloquently when she left. He saw no reason to change his perennial opinion of her as a sour and fidgety frustration.

Susan Calvin's train of thought did not include Bogert in the least. She had dismissed him years ago as a smooth and pretentious sleekness.

Gerald Black had taken his degree in etheric physics the year before and, in common with his entire generation of physicists, found himself engaged in the problem of the Drive. He now made a proper addition to the general atmosphere of these meetings on Hyper Base. In his stained white smock, he was half rebellious and wholly uncertain. His stocky strength seemed striving for release and his fingers, as they twisted each other with nervous yanks, might have forced an iron bar out of true.

Major-general Kallner sat beside him, the two from US Robots faced him.

Black said, 'I'm told that I was the last to see Nestor 10 before he vanished. I take it you want to ask me about that.'

Dr Calvin regarded him with interest, 'You sound as if

you were not sure, young man. Don't you *know* whether you were the last to see him?'

'He worked with me, ma'am, on the field generators, and he was with me the morning of his disappearance. I don't know if anyone saw him after about noon. No one admits having done so.'

'Do you think anyone's lying about it?'

'I don't say that. But I don't say that I want the blame of it, either.' His dark eyes smoldered.

'There's no question of blame. The robot acted as it did because of what it is. We're just trying to locate it, Mr Black, and let's put everything else aside. Now if you've worked with the robot, you probably know it better than anyone else. Was there anything unusual about it that you noticed? Had you ever worked with robots before?'

'I've worked with other robots we have here – the simple ones. Nothing different about the Nestors except that they're a good deal cleverer – and more annoying.'

'Annoying? In what way?'

'Well – perhaps it's not their fault. The work here is rough and most of us get a little jagged. Fooling around with hyper-space isn't fun.' He smiled feebly, finding pleasure in confession. 'We run the risk continually of blowing a hole in normal space-time fabric and dropping right out of the universe, asteroid and all. Sounds screwy, doesn't it? Naturally, you're on edge sometimes. But these Nestors aren't. They're curious, they're calm, they don't worry. It's enough to drive you nuts at times. When you want something done in a tearing hurry, they seem to take their time. Sometimes I'd rather do without.'

'You say they take their time? Have they ever refused an order?'

'Oh, no,' – hastily. 'They do it all right. They tell you when they think you're wrong, though. They don't know anything about the subject but what we taught them, but that doesn't stop them. Maybe I imagine it, but the other fellows have the same trouble with their Nestors.'

General Kallner cleared his throat ominously, 'Why have no complaints reached me on the matter, Black?'

The young physicist reddened, 'We didn't *really* want to do without the robots, sir, and besides we weren't certain exactly how such . . . uh . . . minor complaints might be received.'

Bogert interrupted softly, 'Anything in particular happen the morning you last saw it?'

There was a silence. With a quiet motion, Calvin repressed the comment that was about to emerge from Kallner, and waited patiently.

Then Black spoke in blurting anger, 'I had a little trouble with it. I'd broken a Kimball tube that morning and was out five days of work; my entire program was behind schedule; I hadn't received any mail from home for a couple of weeks. And *he* came round wanting me to repeat an experiment I had abandoned a month ago. He was always annoying me on that subject and I was tired of it. I told him to go away – and that's all I saw of him.'

'You told him to go away?' asked Dr Calvin with sharp interest. 'In just those words? Did you say "Go away"? Try to remember the exact words.'

There was apparently an internal struggle in progress. Black cradled his forehead in a broad palm for a moment, then tore it away and said defiantly, 'I said, "Go lose yourself."'

Bogert laughed for a short moment. 'And he did, eh?'

But Calvin wasn't finished. She spoke cajolingly, 'Now we're getting somewhere, Mr Black. But exact details are important. In understanding the robot's actions, a word, a gesture, an emphasis may be everything. You couldn't have said just those three words, for instance, could you? By your own description you must have been in a hasty mood. Perhaps you strengthened your speech a little.'

The young man reddened, 'Well . . . I may have called it a . . . a few things.'

'Exactly what things?'

'Oh – I wouldn't remember exactly. Besides I couldn't repeat it. You know how you get when you're excited.' His embarrassed laugh was almost a giggle, 'I sort of have a tendency to strong language.'

'That's quite all right,' she replied, with prim severity. 'At the moment, I'm a psychologist. I would like to have you repeat exactly what you said as nearly as you remember, and, even more important, the exact tone of voice you used.'

Black looked at his commanding officer for support, found none. His eyes grew round and appalled, 'But I can't.'

'You must.'

'Suppose,' said Bogert, with ill-hidden amusement, 'you address me. You may find it easier.'

The young man's scarlet face turned to Bogert. He swallowed. 'I said – ' His voice faded out. He tried again, 'I said – '

And he drew a deep breath and spewed it out hastily in one long succession of syllables. Then, in the charged air that lingered, he concluded almost in tears, '. . . more or less. I don't remember the exact order of what I called him, and maybe I left out something or put in something, but that was about it.'

Only the slightest flush betrayed any feeling on the part of the psychologist. She said, 'I am aware of the meaning of most of the terms used. The others, I suppose, are equally derogatory.'

'I'm afraid so,' agreed the tormented Black.

'And in among it, you told him to lose himself.'

'I meant it only figuratively.'

'I realize that. No disciplinary action is intended, I am sure.' And at her glance, the general, who, five seconds earlier, had seemed not sure at all, nodded angrily.

'You may leave, Mr Black. Thank you for your co-operation.'

It took five hours for Susan Calvin to interview the sixty-three robots. It was five hours of multi-repetition; of replacement after replacement of identical robot; of Questions A, B, C, D; and Answers A, B, C, D; of a carefully bland expression, a carefully neutral tone, a carefully friendly atmosphere; and a hidden wire recorder.

The psychologist felt drained of vitality when she was finished.

Bogert was waiting for her and looked expectant as she dropped the recording spool with a clang upon the plastic of the desk.

She shook her head, 'All sixty-three seemed the same to me. I couldn't tell – '

He said, 'You couldn't expect to tell by ear, Susan. Suppose we analyze the recordings.'

Ordinarily, the mathematical interpretation of verbal reactions of robots is one of the more intricate branches of robotic analysis. It requires a staff of trained technicians and the help of complicated computing machines. Bogert knew that. Bogert stated as much, in an extreme of unshown annoyance after having listened to each set of replies, made lists of word deviations, and graphs of the intervals of responses.

'There are no anomalies present, Susan. The variations in wording and the time reactions are within the limits of ordinary frequency groupings. We need finer methods. They must have computers here. No.' He frowned and nibbled delicately at a thumbnail. 'We can't use computers. Too much danger of leakage. Or maybe if we – '

Dr Calvin stopped him with an impatient gesture, 'Please, Peter. This isn't one of your petty laboratory problems. If we can't determine the modified Nestor by some gross difference that we can see with the naked eye, one that there is no mistake about, we're out of luck. The danger of being wrong, and of letting him escape is otherwise too great. It's not enough to point out a minute irregularity in a graph. I tell you, if that's all I've got to go on, I'd destroy them all just to be certain. Have you spoken to the other modified Nestors?'

'Yes, I have,' snapped back Bogert, 'and there's nothing wrong with them. They're above normal in friendliness if anything. They answered my questions, displayed pride in their knowledge – except the two new ones that haven't had time to learn their etheric physics. They laughed rather good-naturedly at my ignorance in some of the specializations here.' He shrugged, 'I suppose that forms some of the basis for resentment toward them on the part of the technicians here. The robots are perhaps too willing to impress you with their greater knowledge.'

'Can you try a few Planar Reactions to see if there has been any change, any deterioration, in their mental set-up since manufacture?'

'I haven't yet, but I will.' He shook a slim finger at her, 'You're losing your nerve, Susan. I don't see what it is you're dramatizing. They're essentially harmless.'

'They are?' Calvin took fire. 'They are? Do you realize one of them is lying? One of the sixty-three robots I have just interviewed has deliberately lied to me after the strictest injunction to tell the truth. The abnormality indicated is horribly deep-seated, and horribly frightening.'

Peter Bogert felt his teeth harden against each other. He said, 'Not at all. Look! Nestor 10 was given orders to lose himself. Those orders were expressed in maximum urgency by the person most authorized to command him. You can't counteract that order either by superior urgency or superior right of command. Naturally, the robot will attempt to defend the carrying out of his orders. In fact, objectively, I admire his ingenuity. How better can a robot lose himself than to hide himself among a group of similar robots?'

'Yes, you would admire it. I've detected amusement in you, Peter – amusement and an appalling lack of understanding. Are you a roboticist, Peter? Those robots attach importance to what they consider superiority. You've just said as much yourself. Subconsciously they feel humans to be inferior and the First Law which protects us from them is imperfect. They are unstable. And here we have a young man ordering a robot to leave him, to lose himself, with every verbal appearance of revulsion, disdain, and disgust. Granted, that robot must follow orders, but subconsciously, there is resentment. It will become more important than ever for it to prove that it is superior despite the horrible names it was called. It may become *so* important that what's left of the First Law won't be enough.'

'How on Earth, or anywhere in the Solar System, Susan, is a robot going to know the meaning of the assorted strong language used upon him? Obscenity is not one of the things impressioned upon his brain.'

'Original impressionment is not everything,' Calvin snarled at him. 'Robots have learning capacity, you . . . you fool – ' And Bogert knew that she had really lost her temper. She continued hastily, 'Don't you suppose he could tell from the tone used that the words weren't complimentary? Don't you suppose he's heard the words used before and noted upon what occasions?'

'Well, then,' shouted Bogert, 'will you kindly tell me one way in which a modified robot can harm a human being, no matter how offended it is, no matter how sick with desire to prove superiority?'

'If I tell you one way, will you keep quiet?'

'Yes.'

They were leaning across the table at each other, angry eyes nailed together.

The psychologist said, 'If a modified robot were to drop a heavy weight upon a human being, he would not be breaking the First Law, if he did so with the knowledge that his strength and reaction speed would be sufficient to snatch the weight away before it struck the man. However once the weight left his fingers, he would be no longer the active medium. Only the blind force of gravity would be that. The robot could then change his mind and merely by inaction, allow the weight to strike. The modified First Law allows that.'

'That's an awful stretch of imagination.'

'That's what my profession requires sometimes. Peter, let's not quarrel. Let's work. You know the exact nature of the stimulus that caused the robot to lose himself. You have the records of his original mental make-up. I want you to tell me how possible it is for our robot to do the sort of thing I just talked about. Not the specific instance, mind you, but that whole class of response. And I want it done quickly.'

'And meanwhile – '

'And meanwhile, we'll have to try performance tests directly on the response to First Law.'

Gerald Black, at his own request, was supervising the mushrooming wooden partitions that were springing up in a bellying circle on the vaulted third floor of Radiation Building 2. The labourers worked, in the main, silently, but more than one was openly a-wonder at the sixty-three photocells that required installation.

One of them sat down near Black, removed his hat, and wiped his forehead thoughtfully with a freckled forearm.

Black nodded at him, 'How's it doing, Walensky?'

Walensky shrugged and fired a cigar, 'Smooth as butter. What's going on anyway, Doc? First, there's no work for three days and then we have this mess of jiggers.' He leaned backward on his elbows and puffed smoke.

Black twitched his eyebrows, 'A couple of robot men came over from Earth. Remember the trouble we had with robots running into the gamma fields, before we pounded it into their skulls that they weren't to do it.'

'Yeah. Didn't we get new robots?'

'We got some replacements, but mostly it was a job of indoctrination. Anyway, the people who make them want to figure out robots that aren't hit so bad by gamma rays.'

'Sure seems funny, though, to stop all the work on the Drive for this robot deal. I thought nothing was allowed to stop the Drive.'

'Well, it's the fellows upstairs that have the say on that. Me – I just do as I'm told. Probably all a matter of pull – '

'Yeah,' the electrician jerked a smile, and winked a wise eye. 'Somebody knew somebody in Washington. But as long as my pay comes through on the dot, I should worry. The Drive's none of my affair. What are they going to do here?'

'You're asking me? They brought a mess of robots with them, – over sixty, and they're going to measure reactions. That's all *my* knowledge.'

'How long will it take?'

'I wish I knew.'

'Well,' Walensky said, with heavy sarcasm, 'as long as they dish me my money, they can play games all they want.'

Black felt quietly satisfied. Let the story spread. It was harmless, and near enough to the truth to take the fangs out of curiosity.

* * *

A man sat in the chair, motionless, silent. A weight dropped, crashed downward, then pounded aside at the last moment under the synchronized thump of a sudden force beam. In sixty-three wooden cells, watching NS-2 robots dashed forward in that split second before the weight veered, and sixty-three photocells five feet ahead of their original positions jiggled the marking pen and presented a little jag on the paper. The weight rose and dropped, rose and dropped, rose –

Ten times!

Ten times the robots sprang forward and stopped, as the man remained safely seated.

Major-general Kallner had not worn his uniform in its entirety since the first dinner with the US Robot representatives. He wore nothing over his blue-gray shirt now, the collar was open, and the black tie was pulled loose.

He looked hopefully at Bogert, who was still blandly neat and whose inner tension was perhaps betrayed only by the trace of glister at his temples.

The general said, 'How does it look? What is it you're trying to see?'

Bogert replied, 'A difference which may turn out to be a little too subtle for our purposes, I'm afraid. For sixty-two of those robots the necessity of jumping toward the apparently threatened human was what we call, in robotics, a forced reaction. You see, even when the robots knew that the human in question would not come to harm – and after the third or fourth time they must have known it – they could not prevent reacting as they did. First Law requires it.'

'Well?'

'But the sixty-third robot, the modified Nestor, had no such compulsion. He was under free action. If he had wished, he could have remained in his seat. Unfortunately,' and his voice was mildly regretful, 'he didn't so wish.'

'Why do you suppose?'

Bogert shrugged, 'I suppose Dr Calvin will tell us when she gets here. Probably with a horribly pessimistic interpretation, too. She is sometimes a bit annoying.'

'She's qualified, isn't she?' demanded the general with a sudden frown of uneasiness.

'Yes.' Bogert seemed amused. 'She's qualified all right. She understands robots like a sister – comes from hating human beings so much, I think. It's just that, psychologist or not, she's an extreme neurotic. Has paranoid tendencies. Don't take her too seriously.'

He spread the long row of broken-line graphs out in front of him. 'You see, general, in the case of each robot the time interval from moment of drop to the completion of a five-foot movement tends to decrease as the tests are repeated. There's definite mathematical relationship that governs such things and failure to conform would indicate marked abnormality in the positronic brain. Unfortunately, all here appear normal.'

'But if our Nestor 10 was not responding with a forced action, why isn't his curve different? I don't understand that.'

'It's simple enough. Robotic responses are not perfectly analogous to human responses, more's the pity. In human beings, voluntary action is much slower than reflex action. But that's not the case with robots; with them it is merely a question of freedom of choice, otherwise the speeds of free and forced action are much the same. What I *had* been expecting, though, was that Nestor 10 would be caught by surprise the first time and allow too great an interval to elapse before responding.'

'And he didn't?'

'I'm afraid not.'

'Then we haven't gotten anywhere.' The general sat back with an expression of pain. 'It's five days since you've come.'

At this point, Susan Calvin entered and slammed the door

behind her, and went on, 'We'll have to try something else quickly. I don't like what's happening.'

Bogert exchanged a resigned glance with the general. 'Is anything wrong?'

'You mean specifically? No. But I don't like to have Nestor 10 continue to elude us. It's bad. It *must* be gratifying his swollen sense of superiority. I'm afraid that his motivation is no longer simply one of following orders. I think it's becoming more a matter of sheer neurotic necessity to out-think humans. That's a dangerously unhealthy situation. Peter, have you done what I asked? Have you worked out the instability factors of the modified NS-2 along the lines I want?'

'It's in progress,' said the mathematician, without interest.

She stared at him angrily for a moment, then turned to Kallner. 'Nestor 10 is decidedly aware of what we're doing, general. He had no reason to jump for the bait in this experiment, especially after the first time, when he must have seen that there was no real danger to our subject. The others couldn't help it; but *he* was deliberately falsifying a reaction.'

'What do you think we ought to do now, then, Dr Calvin?'

'Make it impossible for him to fake an action the next time. We will repeat the experiment, but with an addition. High-tension cables, capable of electrocuting the Nestor models, will be placed between subject and robot – enough of them to avoid the possibility of jumping over – and the robot will be made perfectly aware in advance that touching the cables will mean death.'

'Hold on,' spat out Bogert with sudden viciousness. 'I rule that out. We are not electrocuting two million dollars worth of robots to locate Nestor 10. There are other ways.'

'You're certain? You've found none. In any case, it's not

a question of electrocution. We can arrange a relay which will break the current at the instant of application of weight. If the robot should place his weight on it, he won't die. *But he won't know that*, you see.'

The general's eyes gleamed into hope. 'Will that work?'

'It should. Under those conditions, Nestor 10 would have to remain in his seat. He could be *ordered* to touch the cables and die, for the Second Law of obedience is superior to the Third Law of self-preservation. But *he won't* be ordered to; he will merely be left to his own devices, as will all the robots. In the case of the normal robots, the First Law of human safety will drive them to their death even without orders. But not our Nestor 10. Without the entire First Law, and without having received any orders on the matter, the Third Law, self-preservation, will be the highest operating, and he will have no choice but to remain in his seat. It would be a forced action.'

'Will it be done tonight, then?'

'Tonight,' said the psychologist, 'if the cables can be laid in time. I'll tell the robots now what they're to be up against.'

A man sat in the chair, motionless, silent. A weight dropped, crashed downward, then pounded aside at the last moment under the synchronized thump of a sudden force beam.

Only once –

And from her small camp chair in the observing booth in the balcony, Dr Susan Calvin rose with a short gasp of pure horror.

Sixty-three robots sat quietly in their chairs, staring owlishly at the endangered man before them. Not one moved.

Dr Calvin was angry, angry almost past endurance. Angry

the worse for not daring to show it to the robots that, one by one, were entering the room and then leaving. She checked the list. Number Twenty-eight was due in now – Thirty-five still lay ahead of her.

Number Twenty-eight entered, diffidently.

She forced herself into reasonable calm. 'And who are you?'

The robot replied in a low, uncertain voice, 'I have received no number of my own yet, ma'am. I'm an NS-2 robot, and I was Number Twenty-eight in line outside. I have a slip of paper here that I'm to give to you.'

'You haven't been in here before this today?'

'No, ma'am.'

'Sit down. Right there. I want to ask you some questions, Number Twenty-eight. Were you in the Radiation Room of Building Two about four hours ago?'

The robot had trouble answering. Then it came out hoarsely, like machinery needing oil, 'Yes, ma'am.'

'There was a man who almost came to harm there, wasn't there?'

'Yes, ma'am.'

'You did nothing, did you?'

'No, ma'am.'

'The man might have been hurt because of your inaction. Do you know that?'

'Yes, ma'am. I couldn't help it, ma'am.' It is hard to picture a large expressionless metallic figure cringing, but it managed.

'I want you to tell me exactly why you did nothing to save him.'

'I want to explain, ma'am. I certainly don't want to have you . . . have *anyone* . . . think that I could do a thing that might cause harm to a master. Oh, no, that would be a horrible . . . an inconceivable – '

'Please don't get excited, boy. I'm not blaming you for

anything. I only want to know what you were thinking at the time.'

'Ma'am, before it all happened you told us that one of the masters would be in danger of harm from that weight that keeps falling and that we would have to cross electric cables if we were to try to save him. Well, ma'am, that wouldn't stop me. What is my destruction compared to the safety of a master? But . . . but it occurred to me that if I died on my way to him, I wouldn't be able to save him anyway. The weight would crush him and then I would be dead for no purpose and perhaps some day some other master might come to harm who wouldn't have, if I had only stayed alive. Do you understand me, ma'am?'

'You mean that it was merely a choice of the man dying, of both the man and yourself dying. Is that right?'

'Yes, ma'am. It was impossible to save the master. He might be considered dead. In that case, it is inconceivable that I destroy myself for nothing – without orders.'

The psychologist twiddled a pencil. She had heard the same story with insignificant verbal variations twenty-seven times before. This was the crucial question now.

'Boy,' she said, 'your thinking has its points, but it is not the sort of thing I thought you might think. Did you think of this yourself?'

The robot hesitated. 'No.'

'Who thought of it, then?'

'We were talking last night, and one of us got that idea and it sounded reasonable.'

'Which one?'

The robot thought deeply. 'I don't know. Just one of us.'

She sighed, 'That's all.'

Number Twenty-nine was next. Thirty-four after that.

Major-general Kallner, too, was angry. For one week all of Hyper Base had stopped dead, barring some paper work on the subsidiary asteroids of the group. For nearly one week, the two top experts in the field had aggravated the situation with useless tests. And now they – or the woman, at any rate – made impossible propositions.

Fortunately for the general situation, Kallner felt it impolitic to display his anger openly.

Susan Calvin was insisting, 'Why not, sir? It's obvious that the present situation is unfortunate. The only way we may reach results in the future – or what future is left us in this matter – is to separate the robots. We can't keep them together any longer.'

'My dear Dr Calvin,' rumbled the general, his voice sinking into the lower baritone registers. 'I don't see how I can quarter sixty-three robots all over the place – '

Dr Calvin raised her arms helplessly. 'I can do nothing then. Nestor 10 will either imitate what the other robots would do, or else argue them plausibly into not doing what he himself cannot do. And in any case, this is bad business. We're in actual combat with this little lost robot of ours and he's winning out. Every victory of his aggravates his abnormality.'

She rose to her feet in determination. 'General Kallner, if you do not separate the robots as I ask, then I can only demand that all sixty-three be destroyed immediately.'

'You demand it, do you?' Bogert looked up suddenly, and with real anger. 'What gives you the right to demand any such thing. Those robots remain as they are. *I'm* responsible to the management, not you.'

'And I,' added Major-general Kallner, 'am responsible to the World Co-ordinator – and I must have this settled.'

'In that case,' flashed back Calvin, 'there is nothing for me to do but resign. If necessary to force you to the necessary destruction, I'll make this whole matter public. It was not I that approved the manufacture of modified robots.'

'One word from you, Dr Calvin,' said the general,

deliberately, 'in violation of security measures, and you would be certainly imprisoned instantly.'

Bogert felt the matter to be getting out of hand. His voice grew syrupy, 'Well, now, we're beginning to act like children, all of us. We need only a little more time. Surely we can outwit a robot without resigning, or imprisoning people, or destroying two millions.'

The psychologist turned on him with quiet fury, 'I don't want any unbalanced robots in existence. We have one Nestor that's definitely unbalanced, eleven more that are potentially so, and sixty-two normal robots that are being subjected to an unbalanced environment. The only absolutely safe method is complete destruction.'

The signal-burr brought all three to a halt, and the angry tumult of growingly unrestrained emotion froze.

'Come in,' growled Kallner.

It was Gerald Black, looking perturbed. He had heard angry voices. He said, 'I thought I'd come myself . . . didn't like to ask anyone else – '

'What is it? Don't orate – '

'The locks of Compartment C in the trading ship have been played with. There are fresh scratches on them.'

'Compartment C?' exclaimed Calvin quickly. 'That's the one that holds the robots, isn't it? Who did it?'

'From the inside,' said Black, laconically.

'The lock isn't out of order, is it?'

'No. It's all right. I've been staying on the ship now for four days and none of them have tried to get out. But I thought you ought to know, and I didn't like to spread the news. I noticed the matter myself.'

'Is anyone there now?' demanded the general.

'I left Robbins and McAdams there.'

There was a thoughtful silence, and then Dr Calvin said, ironically, 'Well?'

Kallner rubbed his nose uncertainly, 'What's it all about?'

'Isn't it obvious? Nestor 10 is planning to leave. That order to lose himself is dominating his abnormality past anything we can do. I wouldn't be surprised if what's left of his First Law would scarcely be powerful enough to override it. He is perfectly capable of seizing the ship and leaving with it. Then we'd have a mad robot on a spaceship. What would he do next? Any idea? Do you still want to leave them all together, general?'

'Nonsense,' interrupted Bogert. He had regained his smoothness. 'All that from a few scratch marks on a lock.'

'Have you, Dr Bogert, completed the analysis I've required, since you volunteer opinions?'

'Yes.'

'May I see it?'

'No.'

'Why not? Or mayn't I ask that, either?'

'Because there's no point in it, Susan. I told you in advance that these modified robots are less stable than the normal variety, and my analysis shows it. There's a certain very small chance of breakdown under extreme circumstances that are not likely to occur. Let it go at that. I won't give you ammunition for your absurd claim that sixty-two perfectly good robots be destroyed just because so far you lack the ability to detect Nestor 10 among them.'

Susan Calvin stared him down and let disgust fill her eyes. 'You won't let anything stand in the way of the permanent directorship, will you?'

'Please,' begged Kallner, half in irritation. 'Do you insist that nothing further can be done, Dr Calvin?'

'I can't think of anything, sir,' she replied, wearily. 'If there were only other differences between Nestor 10 and the normal robots, differences that didn't involve the First Law. Even one other difference. Something in impressionment, environment, specification – ' And she stopped suddenly.

'What is it?'

'I've thought of something . . . I think – ' Her eyes grew distant and hard, 'These modified Nestors, Peter. They get the same impressioning the normal ones get, don't they?'

'Yes. Exactly the same.'

'And what was it you were saying, Mr Black,' she turned to the young man, who through the storms that had followed his news had maintained a discreet silence. 'Once when complaining of the Nestors' attitude of superiority, you said the technicians had taught them all they knew.'

'Yes, in etheric physics. They're not acquainted with the subject when they come here.'

'That's right,' said Bogert, in surprise. 'I told you, Susan, when I spoke to the other Nestors here that the two new arrivals hadn't learned etheric physics yet.'

'And why is that?' Dr Calvin was speaking in mounting excitement. 'Why aren't NS-2 models impressioned with etheric physics to start with?'

'I can tell you that,' said Kallner. 'It's all of a piece with the secrecy. We thought that if we made a special model with knowledge of etheric physics, used twelve of them and put the others to work in an unrelated field, there might be suspicion. Men working with normal Nestors might wonder why they knew etheric physics. So there was merely an impressionment with a capacity for training in the field. Only the ones that come here, naturally, receive such a training. It's that simple.'

'I understand. Please get out of here, the lot of you. Let me have an hour or so.'

Calvin felt she could not face the ordeal for a third time. Her mind had contemplated it and rejected it with an intensity that left her nauseated. She could face that unending file of repetitious robots no more.

So Bogert asked the questions now, while she sat aside, eyes and mind half-closed.

Number Fourteen came in – forty-nine to go.

Bogert looked up from the guide sheet and said, 'What is your number in line?'

'Fourteen, sir.' The robot presented his numbered ticket.

'Sit down, boy.'

Bogert asked, 'You haven't been here before on this day?'

'No, sir.'

'Well, boy, we are going to have another man in danger of harm soon after we're through here. In fact, when you leave this room, you will be led to a stall where you will wait quietly, till you are needed. Do you understand?'

'Yes, sir.'

'Now, naturally, if a man is in danger of harm, you will try to save him.'

'Naturally, sir.'

'Unfortunately, between the man and yourself, there will be a gamma ray field.'

Silence.

'Do you know what gamma rays are?' asked Bogert sharply.

'Energy radiation, sir?'

The next question came in a friendly, offhand manner, 'Ever work with gamma rays?'

'No, sir.' The answer was definite.

'Mm-m. Well, boy, gamma rays will kill you instantly. They'll destroy your brain. That is a fact you must know and remember. Naturally, you don't want to destroy yourself.'

'Naturally.' Again the robot seemed shocked. Then, slowly, 'But, sir, if the gamma rays are between myself and the master that may be harmed, how can I save him? I would be destroying myself to no purpose.'

'Yes, there is that,' Bogert seemed concerned about the

matter. 'The only thing I can advise, boy, is that if you detect the gamma radiation between yourself and the man, you may as well sit where you are.'

The robot was openly relieved. 'Thank you, sir. There wouldn't be any use, would there?'

'Of course not. But if there *weren't* any dangerous radiation, that would be a different matter.'

'Naturally, sir. No question of that.'

'You may leave now. The man on the other side of the door will lead you to your stall. Please wait there.'

He turned to Susan Calvin when the robot left. 'How did that go, Susan?'

'Very well,' she said, dully.

'Do you think we could catch Nestor 10 by quick questioning on etheric physics?'

'Perhaps, but it's not sure enough.' Her hands lay loosely in her lap. 'Remember, he's fighting us. He's on his guard. The only way we can catch him is to outsmart him – and, within his limitations, he can think much more quickly than a human being.'

'Well, just for fun – suppose I ask the robots from now on a few questions on gamma rays. Wave length limits, for instance.'

'No!' Dr Calvin's eyes sparked to life. 'It would be too easy for him to deny knowledge and then he'd be warned against the test that's coming up – which is our real chance. Please follow the questions I've indicated, Peter, and don't improvise. It's just within the bounds of risk to ask them if they've ever worked with gamma rays. And try to sound even less interested than you do when you ask it.'

Bogert shrugged, and pressed the buzzer that would allow the entrance of Number Fifteen.

The large Radiation Room was in readiness once more. The robots waited patiently in their wooden cells, all open to the center but closed off from each other.

Major-general Kallner mopped his brow slowly with a large handkerchief while Dr Calvin checked the last details with Black.

'You're sure now,' she demanded, 'that none of the robots have had a chance to talk with each other after leaving the Orientation Room?'

'Absolutely sure,' insisted Black. 'There's not been a word exchanged.'

'And the robots are put in the proper stalls?'

'Here's the plan.'

The psychologist looked at it thoughtfully, 'Um-m-m.'

The general peered over her shoulder. 'What's the idea of the arrangement, Dr Calvin?'

'I've asked to have those robots that appeared even slightly out of true in the previous tests concentrated on one side of the circle. I'm going to be sitting in the center myself this time, and I wanted to watch those particularly.'

'*You're* going to be sitting there – ' exclaimed Bogert.

'Why not?' she demanded coldly. 'What I expect to see may be something quite momentary. I can't risk having anyone else as main observer. Peter, you'll be in the observing booth, and I want you to keep your eye on the opposite side of the circle. General Kallner, I've arranged for motion pictures to be taken of each robot, in case visual observation isn't enough. If these are required, the robots are to remain exactly where they are until the pictures are developed and studied. None must leave, none must change place. Is that clear?'

'Perfectly.'

'Then let's try it this one last time.'

Susan Calvin sat in the chair, silent, eyes restless. A weight dropped, crashed downward, then pounded aside at the last moment under the synchronized thump of a sudden force beam.

And a single robot jerked upright and took two steps.

And stopped.

But Dr Calvin was upright, and her finger pointed to him sharply. 'Nestor 10, come here,' she cried, '*come here*! COME HERE!'

Slowly, reluctantly, the robot took another step forward. The psychologist shouted at the top of her voice, without taking her eyes from the robot, 'Get every other robot out of this place, somebody. Get them out quickly, and *keep* them out.'

Somewhere within reach of her ears there was noise, and the thud of hard feet upon the floor. She did not look away.

Nestor 10 – if it was Nestor 10 – took another step, and then, under force of her imperious gesture, two more. He was only ten feet away, when he spoke harshly, 'I have been told to be lost – '

Another step. 'I must not disobey. They have not found me so far – He would think me a failure – He told me – But it's not so – I am powerful and intelligent – '

The words came in spurts.

Another step. 'I know a good deal – He would think . . . I mean I've been found – Disgraceful – Not I – I am intelligent – And by just a master . . . who is weak – Slow – '

Another step – and one metal arm flew out suddenly to her shoulder, and she felt the weight bearing her down. Her throat constricted, and she felt a shriek tear through.

Dimly, she heard Nestor 10's next words, 'No one must find me. No master – ' and the cold metal was against her, and she was sinking under the weight of it.

And then a queer, metallic sound, and she was on the ground with an unfelt thump, and a gleaming arm was heavy across her body. It did not move. Nor did Nestor 10, who sprawled beside her.

And now faces were bending over her.

Gerald Black was gasping, 'Are you hurt, Dr Calvin?'

She shook her head feebly. They pried the arm off her and lifted her gently to her feet, 'What happened?'

Black said, 'I bathed the place in gamma rays for five seconds. We didn't know what was happening. It wasn't till the last second that we realized he was attacking you, and then there was no time for anything but a gamma field. He went down in an instant. There wasn't enough to harm you though. Don't worry about it.'

'I'm not worried.' She closed her eyes and leaned for a moment upon his shoulder. 'I don't think I was attacked exactly. Nestor 10 was simply *trying* to do so. What was left of the First Law was still holding him back.'

Susan Calvin and Peter Bogert, two weeks after their first meeting with Major-general Kallner had their last. Work at Hyper Base had been resumed. The trading ship with its sixty-two normal NS-2's was gone to wherever it was bound, with an officially imposed story to explain its two weeks' delay. The government cruiser was making ready to carry the two roboticists back to Earth.

Kallner was once again a-gleam in dress uniform. His white gloves shone as he shook hands.

Calvin said, 'The other modified Nestors are, of course, to be destroyed.'

'They will be. We'll make shift with normal robots, or, if necessary, do without.'

'Good.'

'But tell me – You haven't explained – How was it done?'

She smiled tightly, 'Oh, that. I would have told you in advance if I had been more certain of its working. You see, Nestor 10 had a superiority complex that was becoming more radical all the time. He liked to think that he and other robots knew more than human beings. It was becoming very important for him to think so.

'We knew that. So we warned every robot in advance that gamma rays would kill them, which it would, and we further warned them all that gamma rays would be between them and myself. So they all stayed where they were, naturally. By Nestor 10's own logic in the previous test they had all decided that there was no point in trying to save a human being if they were sure to die before they could do it.'

'Well, yes, Dr Calvin, I understand that. But why did Nestor 10 himself leave his seat.'

'Ah! That was a little arrangement between myself and your young Mr Black. You see it wasn't gamma rays that flooded the area between myself and the robots – but infrared rays. Just ordinary heat rays, absolutely harmless. Nestor 10 knew they were infrared and harmless and so he began to dash out, as he expected the rest would do, under First Law compulsion. It was only a fraction of a second too late that he remembered that the normal NS-2's could detect radiation, but could not identify the type. That he himself could only identify wave lengths by virtue of the training he had received at Hyper Base, under mere human beings, was a little too humiliating to remember for just a moment. To the normal robots the area was fatal because we had told them it would be, and only Nestor 10 knew we were lying.

'And just for a moment he forgot, or didn't want to remember, that other robots might be more ignorant than human beings. His very superiority caught him. Good-by, general.'

Risk

Hyper Base had lived for this day. Spaced about the gallery of the viewing room, in order and precedence strictly dictated by protocol, was a group of officials, scientists, technicians and others who could only be lumped under the general classification of 'personnel.' In accordance with their separate temperaments they waited hopefully, uneasily, breathlessly, eagerly, or fearfully for this culmination of their efforts.

The hollowed interior of the asteroid known as Hyper Base had become for this day the center of a sphere of iron security that extended out for ten thousand miles. No ship might enter that sphere and live. No message might leave without scrutiny.

A hundred miles away, more or less, a small asteroid moved neatly in the orbit into which it had been urged a year before, an orbit that ringed Hyper Base in as perfect a circle as could be managed. The asteroidlet's identity number was H937, but no one on Hyper Base called it anything but It. ('Have you been out on it today?' 'The general's on it, blowing his top,' and eventually the impersonal pronoun achieved the dignity of capitalization.)

On It, unoccupied now as zero second approached, was the *Parsec*, the only ship of its kind ever built in the history of man. It lay, unmanned, ready for its takeoff into the inconceivable.

Gerald Black, who, as one of the bright young men in etherics engineering, rated a front-row view, cracked his large knuckles, then wiped his sweating palms on his stained white smock and said sourly, 'Why don't you bother the general, or Her Ladyship there?'

Nigel Ronson, of Interplanetary Press, looked briefly across the gallery toward the glitter of Major-general Richard Kallner and the unremarkable woman at his side, scarcely visible in the glare of his dress uniform. He said, 'I would, except that I'm interested in news.'

Ronson was short and plump. He painstakingly wore his hair in a quarter-inch bristle, his shirt collar open and his trouser leg ankle-short, in faithful imitation of the newsmen who were stock characters on TV shows. He was a capable reporter nevertheless.

Black was stocky, and his dark hairline left little room for forehead, but his mind was as keen as his strong fingers were blunt. He said, 'They've got all the news.'

'Nuts,' said Ronson. 'Kallner's got no body under that gold braid. Strip him and you'll find only a conveyer belt dribbling orders downward and shooting responsibility upward.'

Black found himself at the point of a grin but squeezed it down. He said, 'What about the Madam Doctor?'

'Dr Susan Calvin of US Robots and Mechanical Men Corporation,' intoned the reporter. 'The lady with hyperspace where her heart ought to be and liquid helium in her eyes. She'd pass through the sun and come out the other end encased in frozen flame.'

Black came even closer to a grin. 'How about Director Schloss, then?'

Ronson said glibly, 'He knows too much. Between spending his time fanning the feeble flicker of intelligence in his listener and dimming his own brains for fear of blinding said listener permanently by sheer force of brilliance, he ends up saying nothing.'

Black showed his teeth this time. 'Now suppose you tell me why you pick on me.'

'Easy, doctor. I looked at you and figured you're too ugly to be stupid and too smart to miss a possible opportunity at some good personal publicity.'

'Remind me to knock you down someday,' said Black. 'What do you want to know?'

The man from Interplanetary Press pointed into the pit and said, 'Is that thing going to work?'

Black looked downward too, and felt a vague chill riffle over him like the thin night wind of Mars. The pit was one large television screen, divided in two. One half was an overall view of It. On It's pitted gray surface was the *Parsec*, glowing mutedly in the feeble sunlight. The other half showed the control room of the *Parsec*. There was no life in that control room. In the pilot's seat was an object the vague humanity of which did not for a moment obscure the fact that it was only a positronic robot.

Black said, 'Physically, mister, this will work. That robot will leave and come back. Space! how we succeeded with that part of it. I watched it all. I came here two weeks after I took my degree in etheric physics and I've been here, barring leave and furloughs, ever since. I was here when we sent the first piece of iron wire to Jupiter's orbit and back through hyperspace – and got back iron filings. I was here when we sent white mice there and back and ended up with mincemeat.

'We spent six months establishing an even hyperfield after that. We had to wipe out lags of as little as tenths of thousandths of seconds from point to point in matter being subjected to hypertravel. After that, the white mice started coming back intact. I remember when we celebrated for a week because one white mouse came back alive and lived ten minutes before dying. Now they live as long as we can take proper care of them.'

Ronson said, 'Great!'

Black looked at him obliquely. 'I said, *physically* it will work. Those white mice that come back – '

'Well?'

'No minds. Not even little white mice-type minds. They won't eat. They have to be force-fed. They won't mate. They won't run. They sit. They sit. They sit. That's all. We finally worked up to sending a chimpanzee. It was pitiful. It was too close to a man to make watching it bearable. It came back a hunk of meat that could make crawling motions. It could move its eyes and sometimes it would scrabble. It whined and sat in its own wastes without the sense to move. Somebody shot it one day, and we were all grateful for that. I tell you this, fella, nothing that ever went into hyperspace has come back with a mind.'

'Is this for publication?'

'After this experiment, maybe. They expect great things of it.' A corner of Black's mouth lifted.

'You don't?'

'With a robot at the controls? No.' Almost automatically Black's mind went back to that interlude, some years back, in which he had been unwittingly responsible for the near loss of a robot. He thought of the Nestor robots that filled Hyper Base with smooth, ingrained knowledge and perfectionist shortcomings. What was the use of talking about robots? He was not, by nature, a missionary.

But then Ronson, filling the continuing silence with a bit of small talk, said, as he replaced the wad of gum in his mouth with a fresh piece, 'Don't tell me *you're* anti-robot. I've always heard that scientists are the one group that aren't anti-robot.'

Black's patience snapped. He said, 'That's true, and that's the trouble. Technology's gone robot-happy. Any job has to have a robot, or the engineer in charge feels cheated. You want a doorstop; buy a robot with a thick foot. That's a serious thing.' He was speaking in a low, intense voice, shoving the words directly into Ronson's ear.

Ronson managed to extricate his arm. He said, 'Hey, I'm

no robot. Don't take it out on me. I'm a man. *Homo sapiens*. You just broke an arm bone of mine. Isn't that proof?'

Having started, however, it took more than frivolity to stop Black. He said, 'Do you know how much time was wasted on this setup? We've had a perfectly generalized robot built and we've given it one order. Period. I heard the order given. I've memorized it. Short and sweet. "Seize the bar with a firm grip. Pull it toward you firmly. *Firmly*! Maintain your hold until the control board informs you that you have passed through hyperspace twice."

'So at zero time, the robot will grab the control bar and pull it firmly toward himself. His hands are heated to blood temperature. Once the control bar is in position, heat expansion completes contact and hyperfield is initiated. If anything happens to his brain during the first trip through hyperspace, it doesn't matter. All he needs to do is maintain position one microinstant and the ship will come back and the hyperfield will flip off. Nothing can go wrong. Then we study all its generalized reactions and see what, if anything, has gone wrong.'

Ronson looked blank. 'This all makes sense to me.'

'Does it?' asked Black bitterly. 'And what will you learn from a robot brain? It's positronic, ours is cellular. It's metal, ours is protein. They're not the same. There's no comparison. Yet I'm convinced that on the basis of what they learn, or think they learn, from the robot, they'll send men into hyperspace. Poor devils! – Look, it's not a question of dying. It's coming back mindless. If you'd seen the chimpanzee, you'd know what I mean. Death is clean and final. The other thing – '

The reporter said, 'Have you talked about this to anyone?'

Black said, 'Yes. They say what you said. They say I'm anti-robot and that settles everything. – Look at Susan Calvin there. You can bet *she* isn't anti-robot. She came all the way from Earth to watch this experiment. If it had been a man at the controls, she wouldn't have bothered. But what's the use!'

'Hey,' said Ronson, 'don't stop now. There's more.'

'More what?'

'More problems. You've explained the robot. But why the security provisions all of a sudden?'

'Huh?'

'Come *on*. Suddenly I can't send dispatches. Suddenly ships can't come into the area. What's going on? This is just another experiment. The public knows about hyperspace and what you boys are trying to do, so what's the big secret?'

The backwash of anger was still seeping over Black, anger against the robots, anger against Susan Calvin, anger at the memory of that little lost robot in his past. There was some to spare, he found, for the irritating little newsman and his irritating little questions.

He said to himself, Let's see how he takes it.

He said, 'You really want to know?'

'You bet.'

'All right. We've never initiated a hyperfield for any object a millionth as large as that ship, or to send anything a millionth as far. That means that the hyperfield that will soon be initiated is some million million times as energetic as any we've ever handled. We're not sure what it can do.'

'What do you mean?'

'Theory tells us that the ship will be neatly deposited out near Sirius and neatly brought back here. But how large a volume of space about the *Parsec* will be carried with it? It's hard to tell. We don't know enough about hyperspace. The asteroid on which the ship sits may go with it and, you know, if our calculations are even a little off, it may never be brought back here. It may return, say, twenty billion miles away. And there's a chance that more of space than just the asteroid may be shifted.'

'How much more?' demanded Ronson.

'We can't say. There's an element of statistical uncertainty. That's why no ships must approach too closely. That's why we're keeping things quiet till the experiment is safely over.'

Ronson swallowed audibly. 'Supposing it reaches to Hyper Base?'

'There's a chance of it,' said Black with composure. 'Not much of a chance or Director Schloss wouldn't be here, I assure you. Still, there's a mathematical chance.'

The newsman looked at his watch. 'When does this all happen?'

'In about five minutes. You're not nervous, are you?'

'No,' said Ronson, but he sat down blankly and asked no more questions.

Black leaned outward over the railing. The final minutes were ticking off.

The robot moved!

There was a mass sway of humanity forward at the sign of motion and the lights dimmed in order to sharpen and heighten the brightness of the scene below. But so far it was only the first motion. The hands of the robot approached the starting bar.

Black waited for the final second when the robot would pull the bar toward himself. Black could imagine a number of possibilities, and all sprang nearly simultaneously to mind.

There would first be the short flicker that would indicate the departure through hyperspace and return. Even though the time interval was exceedingly short, return would not be to the *precise* starting position and there would be a flicker. There always was.

Then, when the ship returned, it might be found, perhaps, that the devices to even the field over the huge volume of the ship had proved inadequate. The robot might be scrap steel. The ship might be scrap steel.

Or their calculations might be somewhat off and the ship

might never return. Or worse still, Hyper Base might go with the ship and never return.

Or, of course, all might be well. The ship might flicker and be there in perfect shape. The robot, with mind untouched, would get out of his seat and signal a successful completion of the first voyage of a man-made object beyond the gravitational control of the sun.

The last minute was ticking off.

The last second came and the robot seized the starting bar and pulled it firmly toward himself –

Nothing!

No flicker. Nothing!

The *Parsec* never left normal space.

Major-general Kallner took off his officer's cap to mop his glistening forehead and in doing so exposed a bald head that would have aged him ten years in appearance if his drawn expression had not already done so. Nearly an hour had passed since the *Parsec*'s failure and nothing had been done.

'How did it happen? How did it happen? I don't understand it.'

Dr Mayer Schloss, who at forty was the 'grand old man' of the young science of hyperfield matrices, said hopelessly, 'There is nothing wrong with the basic theory. I'll swear my life away on that. There's a mechanical failure on the ship somewhere. Nothing more.' He had said that a dozen times.

'I thought everything was tested.' That had been said too.

'It was, sir, it was. Just the same – ' And that.

They sat staring at each other in Kallner's office, which was now out of bounds for all personnel. Neither quite dared to look at the third person present.

Susan Calvin's thin lips and pale cheeks bore no expression. She said coolly, 'You may console yourself with what I have told you before. It is doubtful whether anything useful would have resulted.'

'This is not the time for the old argument,' groaned Schloss.

'I am not arguing. US Robots and Mechanical Men Corporation will supply robots made up to specification to any legal purchaser for any legal use. We did our part, however. We informed you that we could not guarantee being able to draw conclusions with regard to the human brain from anything that happened to the positronic brain. Our responsibility ends there. There is no argument.'

'Great space,' said General Kallner, in a tone that made the expletive feeble indeed. 'Let's not discuss that.'

'What else was there to do?' muttered Schloss, driven to the subject nevertheless. 'Until we know exactly what's happening to the mind in hyperspace we can't progress. The robot's mind is at least capable of mathematical analysis. It's a start, a beginning. And until we try – ' He looked up wildly, 'But your robot isn't the point, Dr Calvin. We're not worried about him or his positronic brain. Damn it, woman – ' His voice rose nearly to a scream.

The robopsychologist cut him to silence with a voice that scarcely raised itself from its level monotone. 'No hysteria, man. In my lifetime I have witnessed many crises and I have never seen one solved by hysteria. I want answers to some questions.'

Schloss's full lips trembled and his deep-set eyes seemed to retreat into their sockets and leave pits of shadow in their places. He said harshly, 'Are you trained in etheric engineering?'

'That is an irrelevant question. I am Chief Robopsychologist of the United States Robots and Mechanical Men Corporation. That is a positronic robot sitting at the controls of the *Parsec*. Like all such robots, it is leased and not sold. I have a right to demand information concerning any experiment in which such a robot is involved.'

'Talk to her, Schloss,' barked General Kallner. 'She's – she's all right.'

Dr Calvin turned her pale eyes on the general, who had been present at the time of the affair of the lost robot and who therefore could be expected not to make the mistake of underestimating her. (Schloss had been out on sick leave at the time, and hearsay is not as effective as personal experience.) 'Thank you, general,' she said.

Schloss looked helplessly from one to the other and muttered, 'What do you want to know?'

'Obviously my first question is, What *is* your problem if the robot is not?'

'But the problem is an obvious one. The ship hasn't moved. Can't you see that? Are you blind?'

'I see quite well. What I don't see is your obvious panic over some mechanical failure. Don't you people expect failure sometimes?'

The general muttered, 'It's the expense. The ship was hellishly expensive. The World Congress – appropriations – ' He bogged down.

'The ship's still there. A slight overhaul and correction would involve no great trouble.'

Schloss had taken hold of himself. The expression on his face was one of a man who had caught his soul in both hands, shaken it hard and set it on its feet. His voice had even achieved a kind of patience. 'Dr Calvin, when I say a mechanical failure, I mean something like a relay jammed by a speck of dust, a connection inhibited by a spot of grease, a transistor balked by a momentary heat expansion. A dozen other things. A hundred other things. Any of them can be quite temporary. They can stop taking effect at any moment.'

'Which means that at any moment the *Parsec* may flash through hyperspace and back after all.'

'Exactly. Now do you understand?'

'Not at all. Wouldn't that be just what you want?'

Schloss made a motion that looked like the start of an effort to seize a double handful of hair and yank. He said, 'You are not an etherics engineer.'

'Does that tongue-tie you, doctor?'

'We had the ship set,' said Schloss despairingly, 'to make a jump from a definite point in space relative to the center of gravity of the galaxy to another point. The return was to be to the original point corrected for the motion of the solar system. In the hour that has passed since the *Parsec* should have moved, the solar system has shifted position. The original parameters to which the hyperfield is adjusted no longer apply. The ordinary laws of motion do not apply to hyperspace and it would take us a week of computation to calculate a new set of parameters.'

'You mean that if the ship moves now it will return to some unpredictable point thousands of miles away?'

'Unpredictable?' Schloss smiled hollowly. 'Yes. I should call it that. The *Parsec* might end up in the Andromeda nebula or in the center of the sun. In any case the odds are against our ever seeing it again.'

Susan Calvin nodded. 'The situation then is that if the ship disappears, as it may do at any moment, a few billion dollars of the taxpayers' money may be irretrievably gone, and – it will be said – through bungling.'

Major-general Kallner could not have winced more noticeably if he had been poked with a sharp pin in the fundament.

The robopsychologist went on, 'Somehow, then, the ship's hyperfield mechanism must be put out of action, and that as soon as possible. Something will have to be unplugged or jerked loose or flicked off.' She was speaking half to herself.

'It's not that simple,' said Schloss. 'I can't explain it completely, since you're not an etherics expert. It's like trying to break an ordinary electric circuit by slicing through high-tension wire with garden shears. It could be disastrous. It *would* be disastrous.'

'Do you mean that any attempt to shut off the mechanism would hurl the ship into hyperspace?'

'Any *random* attempt would *probably* do so. Hyper-forces are not limited by the speed of light. It is very probable that they have no limit of velocity at all. It makes things extremely difficult. The only reasonable solution is to discover the nature of the failure and learn from that a safe way of disconnecting the field.'

'And how do you propose to do that, Dr Schloss?'

Schloss said, 'It seems to me that the only thing to do is to send one of our Nestor robots – '

'No! Don't be foolish,' broke in Susan Calvin.

Schloss said, freezingly, 'The Nestors are acquainted with the problems of etherics engineering. They will be ideally – '

'Out of the question. You cannot use one of our positronic robots for such a purpose without my permission. You do not have it and you shall not get it.'

'What is the alternative?'

'You must send one of your engineers.'

Schloss shook his head violently, 'Impossible. The risk involved is too great. If we lose a ship *and* man – '

'Nevertheless, you may not use a Nestor robot, or any robot.'

The general said, 'I – I must get in touch with Earth. This whole problem has to go to a higher level.'

Susan Calvin said with asperity, 'I wouldn't just yet if I were you, general. You will be throwing yourself on the government's mercy without a suggestion or plan of action of your own. You will not come out very well, I am certain.'

'But what is there to do?' The general was using his handkerchief again.

'Send a man. There is no alternative.'

Schloss had paled to a pasty gray. 'It's easy to say, send a man. But whom?'

'I've been considering that problem. Isn't there a young man – his name is Black – whom I met on the occasion of my previous visit to Hyper Base?'

'Dr Gerald Black?'

'I think so. Yes. He was a bachelor then. Is he still?'

'Yes, I believe so.'

'I would suggest then that he be brought here, say, in fifteen minutes, and that meanwhile I have access to his records.'

Smoothly she had assumed authority in this situation, and neither Kallner nor Schloss made any attempt to dispute that authority with her.

Black had seen Susan Calvin from a distance on this, her second visit to Hyper Base. He had made no move to cut down the distance. Now that he had been called into her presence, he found himself staring at her with revulsion and distaste. He scarcely noticed Dr Schloss and General Kallner standing behind her.

He remembered the last time he had faced her thus, undergoing a cold dissection for the sake of a lost robot.

Dr Calvin's cool gray eyes were fixed steadily on his hot brown ones.

'Dr Black,' she said, 'I believe you understand the situation.'

Black said, 'I do.'

'Something will have to be done. The ship is too expensive to lose. The bad publicity will probably mean the end of the project.'

Black nodded. 'I've been thinking that.'

'I hope you've also thought that it will be necessary for someone to board the *Parsec*, find out what's wrong, and – uh – deactivate it.'

There was a moment's pause. Black said harshly, 'What fool would go?'

Kallner frowned and looked at Schloss, who bit his lip and looked nowhere.

Susan Calvin said, 'There is, of course, the possibility of accidental activation of the hyperfield, in which case the ship may drive beyond all possible reach. On the other hand, it may return somewhere within the solar system. If so, no expense or effort will be spared to recover man and ship.'

Black said, 'Idiot and ship! Just a correction.'

Susan Calvin disregarded the comment. She said, 'I have asked General Kallner's permission to put it to you. It is you who must go.'

No pause at all here. Black said, in the flattest possible way, 'Lady, I'm not volunteering.'

'There are not a dozen men on Hyper Base with sufficient knowledge to have any chance at all of carrying this thing through successfully. Of those who have the knowledge, I've selected you on the basis of our previous acquaintanceship. You will bring to this task an understanding – '

'Look, I'm *not* volunteering.'

'You have no choice. Surely you will face your responsibility?'

'*My* responsibility? What makes it mine?'

'The fact that you are best fitted for the job.'

'Do you know the risk?'

'I think I do,' said Susan Calvin.

'I know you don't. You never saw that chimpanzee. Look, when I said "idiot and ship" I wasn't expressing an opinion. I was telling you a fact. I'd risk my life if I had to. Not with pleasure, maybe, but I'd risk it. Risking idiocy, a lifetime of animal mindlessness, is something I won't risk, that's all.'

Susan Calvin glanced thoughtfully at the young engineer's sweating, angry face.

Black shouted, 'Send one of your robots, one of your NS-2 jobs.'

The psychologist's eye reflected a kind of cold glitter. She said with deliberation, 'Yes, Dr Schloss suggested that. But the NS-2 robots are leased by our firm, not sold. They cost millions of dollars apiece, you know. I represent the company and I have decided that they are too expensive to be risked in a matter such as this.'

Black lifted his hands. They clenched and trembled close to his chest as though he were forcibly restraining them. 'You're telling me – you're saying you want me to go instead of a robot because I'm more expendable.'

'It comes to that, yes.'

'Dr Calvin,' said Black, 'I'd see you in hell first.'

'That statement might be almost literally true, Dr Black. As General Kallner will confirm, you are ordered to take this assignment. You are under quasi-military law here, I understand, and if you refuse an assignment, you can be court-martialed. A case like this will mean Mercury prison and I believe that will be close enough to hell to make your statement uncomfortably accurate were I to visit you, though I probably would not. On the other hand, if you agree to board the *Parsec* and carry through this job, it will mean a great deal for your career.'

Black glared, red-eyed, at her.

Susan Calvin said, 'Give the man five minutes to think about this, General Kallner, and get a ship ready.'

Two security guards escorted Black out of the room.

Gerald Black felt cold. His limbs moved as though they were not part of him. It was as though he were watching himself from some remote, safe place, watching himself board a ship and make ready to leave for It and for the *Parsec*.

He couldn't quite believe it. He had bowed his head suddenly and said, 'I'll go.'

But why?

He had never thought of himself as the hero type. Then why? Partly, of course, there was the threat of Mercury prison. Partly it was the awful reluctance to appear a coward in the eyes of those who knew him, that deeper cowardice that was behind half the bravery in the world.

Mostly, though, it was something else.

Ronson of Interplanetary Press had stopped Black momentarily as he was on his way to the ship. Black looked at Ronson's flushed face and said, 'What do you want?'

Ronson babbled, 'Listen! When you get back, I want it exclusive. I'll arrange any payment you want – anything you want – '

Black pushed him aside, sent him sprawling, and walked on.

The ship had a crew of two. Neither spoke to him. Their glances slid over and under and around him. Black didn't mind that. They were scared spitless themselves and their ship was approaching the *Parsec* like a kitten skittering sideways toward the first dog it had ever seen. He could do without *them*.

There was only one face that he kept seeing. The anxious expression of General Kallner and the look of synthetic determination on Schloss's face were momentary punctures on his consciousness. They healed almost at once. It was Susan Calvin's unruffled face that he saw. Her calm expressionlessness as he boarded the ship.

He stared into the blackness where Hyper Base had already disappeared into space –

Susan Calvin! Doctor Susan Calvin! Robopsychologist Susan Calvin! The robot that walks like a woman!

What were her three laws, he wondered. First Law: Thou shalt protect the robot with all thy might and all thy heart and all thy soul. Second Law: Thou shalt hold the interests of US Robots and Mechanical Men Corporation holy provided it interfereth not with the First Law. Third Law: Thou shalt give passing consideration to a human being provided it interfereth not with the First and Second Laws.

Had she ever been young, he wondered savagely? Had she ever felt one honest emotion?

Space! How he wanted to do something – something that would take that frozen look of nothing off her face.

And he would!

By the stars, he would. Let him but get out of this sane and he would see her smashed and her company with her and all the vile brood of robots with them. It was that thought that was driving him more than fear of prison or desire for social prestige. It was that thought that almost robbed him of fear altogether. Almost.

One of the pilots muttered at him, without looking, 'You can drop down from here. It's half a mile under.'

Black said bitterly, 'Aren't you landing?'

'Strict orders not to. The vibration of the landing might –'

'What about the vibration of my landing?'

The pilot said, 'I've got my orders.'

Black said no more but climbed into his suit and waited for the inner lock to open. A tool kit was welded firmly to the metal of the suit about his right thigh.

Just as he stepped into the lock, the earpieces inside his helmet rumbled at him. 'Wish you luck, doctor.'

It took a moment for him to realize that it came from the two men aboard ship, pausing in their eagerness to get out of that haunted volume of space to give him that much anyway.

'Thanks,' said Black awkwardly, half resentfully.

And then he was out in space, tumbling slowly as the result of the slightly off-center thrust of feet against outer lock.

He could see the *Parsec* waiting for him, and by looking between his legs at the right moment of the tumble he could see the long hiss of the lateral jets of the ship that had brought him, as it turned to leave.

He was alone! Space, he was alone!

Could any man in history ever have felt so alone?

Would he know, he wondered sickly, if – if anything happened? Would there be any moments of realization? Would he feel his mind fade and the light of reason and thought dim and blank out?

Or would it happen suddenly, like the cut of a force knife?

In either case –

The thought of the chimpanzee, blank-eyed, shivering with mindless terrors, was fresh within him.

The asteroid was twenty feet below him now. It swam through space with an absolutely even motion. Barring human agency, no grain of sand upon it had as much as stirred through astronomical periods of time.

In the ultimate jarlessness of It, some small particle of grit encumbered a delicate working unit on board the *Parsec*, or a speck of impure sludge in the fine oil that bathed some moving part had stopped it.

Perhaps it required only a small vibration, a tiny tremor originating from the collision of mass and mass to unencumber that moving part, bringing it down along its appointed path, creating the hyperfield, blossoming it outward like an incredibly ripening rose.

His body was going to touch It and he drew his limbs together in his anxiety to 'hit easy.' He did not want to touch the asteroid. His skin crawled with intense aversion.

It came closer.

Now – now –

Nothing!

There was only the continuing touch of the asteroid, the uncanny moments of slowly mounting pressure that resulted from a mass of 250 pounds (himself plus suit) possessing full inertia but no weight to speak of.

Black opened his eyes slowly and let the sight of stars enter. The sub was a glowing marble, its brilliance muted by the polarizing shield over his faceplate. The stars were correspondingly feeble but they made up the familiar arrangement. With sun and constellations normal, he was still in the solar system. He could even see Hyper Base, a small, dim crescent.

He stiffened in shock at the sudden voice in his ear. It was Schloss.

Schloss said, 'We've got you in view, Dr Black. You are not alone!'

Black could have laughed at the phraseology, but he only said in a low, clear voice, 'Clear off. If you'll do that, you won't be distracting me.'

A pause. Schloss's voice, more cajoling, 'If you care to report as you go along, it may relieve the tension.'

'You'll get information from me when I get back. Not before.' He said it bitterly, and bitterly his metal-encased fingers moved to the control panel in his chest and blanked out the suit's radio. They could talk into a vacuum now. He had his own plans. If he got out of this sane, it would be *his* show.

He got to his feet with infinite caution and stood on It. He swayed a bit as involuntary muscular motions, tricked by the almost total lack of gravity into an endless series of overbalancings, pulled him this way and that. On Hyper Base there was a pseudo-gravitic field to hold them down. Black found that a portion of his mind was sufficiently detached to remember that and appreciate it *in absentia*.

The sun had disappeared behind a crag. The stars wheeled visibly in time to the asteroid's one-hour rotation period.

He could see the *Parsec* from where he stood and now he moved toward it slowly, carefully – tippy-toe almost. (No vibration. No vibration. The words ran pleadingly through his mind.)

Before he was completely aware of the distance he had crossed, he was at the ship. He was at the foot of the line of hand grips that led to the outer lock.

There he paused.

The ship looked quite normal. Or at least it looked normal except for the circle of steely knobs that girdled it one third of the way up, and a second circle two thirds of the way up. At the moment, they must be straining to become the source poles of the hyperfield.

A strange desire to reach up and fondle one of them came over Black. It was one of those irrational impulses, like the momentary thought, 'What if I jumped?' that is almost inevitable when one stares down from a high building.

Black took a deep breath and felt himself go clammy as he spread the fingers of both hands and then lightly, so lightly, put each hand flat against the side of the ship.

Nothing!

He seized the lowest hand grip and pulled himself up, carefully. He longed to be as experienced at null-gravity manipulation as were the construction men. You had to exert enough force to overcome inertia and then stop. Continue the pull a second too long and you would overbalance, careen into the side of the ship.

He climbed slowly, tippy-fingers, his legs and hips swaying to the right as his left arm reached upward, to the left as his right arm reached upward.

A dozen rungs, and his fingers hovered over the contact that would open the outer lock. The safety marker was a tiny green smear.

Once again he hesitated. This was the first use he would make of the ship's power. His mind ran over the wiring diagrams and the force distributions. If he pressed the contact, power would be siphoned off the micropile to pull open the massive slab of metal that was the outer lock.

Well?

What was the use? Unless he had some idea as to what was wrong, there was no way of telling the effect of the power diversion. He sighed and touched contact.

Smoothly, with neither jar nor sound, a segment of the ship curled open. Black took one more look at the friendly constellations (they had not changed) and stepped into the softly illuminated cavity. The outer lock closed behind him.

Another contact now. The inner lock had to be opened. Again he paused to consider. Air pressure within the ship would drop ever so slightly as the inner lock opened, and seconds would pass before the ship's electrolyzers could make up the loss.

Well?

The Bosch posterior-plate, to name one item, was sensitive to pressure, but surely not *this* sensitive.

He sighed again, more softly (the skin of his fear was growing calloused) and touched the contact. The inner lock opened.

He stepped into the pilot room of the *Parsec* and his heart jumped oddly when the first thing he saw was the visiplate, set for reception and powdered with stars. He forced himself to look at them.

Nothing!

Cassiopeia was visible. The constellations were normal and he was inside the *Parsec*. Somehow he could feel the worst was over. Having come so far and remained within the solar system, having kept his mind so far, he felt something that was faintly like confidence begin to seep back.

There was an almost supernatural stillness about the *Parsec*. Black had been in many ships in his life and there had always been the sounds of life, even if only the scuffing of a shoe or a cabin boy humming in the corridor. Here the very beating of his own heart seemed muffled to soundlessness.

The robot in the pilot's seat had its back to him. It indicated by no response that it was aware of his having entered.

Black bared his teeth in a savage grin and said sharply, 'Release the bar! Stand up!' The sound of his voice was thunderous in the close quarters.

Too late he dreaded the air vibrations his voice set up, but the stars on the visiplate remained unchanged.

The robot, of course, did not stir. It could receive no sensations of any sort. It could not even respond to the First Law. It was frozen in the unending middle of what should have been almost instantaneous process.

He remembered the orders it had been given. They were open to no misunderstanding: 'Seize the bar with a firm grip. Pull it toward you firmly. Firmly! Maintain your hold until the control board informs you that you have passed through hyperspace twice.'

Well, it had not yet passed through hyperspace once.

Carefully, he moved closer to the robot. It sat there with the bar pulled firmly back between its knees. That brought the trigger mechanism almost into place. The temperature of his metal hands then curled that trigger, thermocouple fashion, just sufficiently for contact to be made. Automatically Black glanced at the thermometer reading set into the control board. The robot's hands were at 37 Centigrade, as they should be.

He thought sardonically, Fine thing. I'm alone with this machine and I can't do anything about it.

What he would have liked to do was take a crowbar to it and smash it to filings. He enjoyed the flavor of that thought. He could see the horror on Susan Calvin's face (if any horror could creep through the ice, the horror of a smashed robot was it). Like all positronic robots, this one-shot was owned by US Robots, had been made there, had been tested there.

And having extracted what juice he could out of imaginary revenge, he sobered and looked about the ship.

After all, progress so far had been zero.

Slowly, he removed his suit. Gently, he laid it on the rack. Gingerly, he walked from room to room, studying the large interlocking surfaces of the hyperatomic motor, following the cables, inspecting the field relays.

He touched nothing. There were a dozen ways of deactivating the hyperfield, but each one would be ruinous unless he knew at least approximately where the error lay and let his exact course of procedure be guided by that.

He found himself back at the control panel and cried in exasperation at the grave stolidity of the robot's broad back, 'Tell me, will you? What's wrong?'

There was the urge to attack the ship's machinery at random. Tear at it and get it over with. He repressed the impulse firmly. If it took him a week, he would deduce, somehow, the proper point of attack. He owed that much to Dr Susan Calvin and his plans for her.

He turned slowly on his heel and considered. Every part of the ship, from the engine itself to each individual two-way toggle switch, had been exhaustively checked and tested on Hyper Base. It was almost impossible to believe that anything could go wrong. There wasn't a thing on board ship –

Well, yes, there was, of course. The robot! That had been tested at US Robots and they, blast their devils' hides, could be assumed to be competent.

What was it everyone always said: A robot can just naturally do a better job.

It was the normal assumption, based in part on US Robots' own advertising campaigns. They could make a robot that would be better than a man for a given purpose. Not 'as good as a man,' but 'better than a man.'

And as Gerald Black stared at the robot and thought that, his brows contracted under his low forehead and his look became compounded of astonishment and a wild hope.

He approached and circled the robot. He stared at its arms holding the control bar in trigger position, holding it forever so, unless the ship jumped or the robot's own power supply gave out.

Black breathed, 'I bet. I *bet*.'

He stepped away, considered deeply. He said, 'It's *got* to be.'

He turned on ship's radio. Its carrier beam was already focused on Hyper Base. He barked into the mouthpiece, 'Hey, Schloss.'

Schloss was prompt in his answer. 'Great Space, Black – '

'Never mind,' said Black crisply. 'No speeches. I just want to make sure you're watching.'

'Yes, of course. We all are. Look – '

But Black turned off the radio. He grinned with tight onesidedness at the TV camera inside the pilot room and chose a portion of the hyperfield mechanism that would be in view. He didn't know how many people would be in the viewing room. There might be only Kallner, Schloss and Susan Calvin. There might be all personnel. In any case, he would give them something to watch.

Relay Box No. 3 was adequate for the purpose, he decided. It was located in a wall recess, coated over with a smooth cold-seamed panel. Black reached into his tool kit and removed the splayed, blunt-edged seamer. He pushed his space suit farther back on the rack (having turned it to bring the tool kit in reach) and turned to the relay box.

Ignoring a last tingle of uneasiness, Black brought up the seamer, made contact at three separated points along the cold seam. The tool's force field worked deftly and quickly, the handle growing a trifle warm in his hand as the surge of energy came and left. The panel swung free.

He glanced quickly, almost involuntarily, at the ship's visiplate. The stars were normal. He, himself, felt normal.

That was the last bit of encouragement he needed. He raised his foot and smashed his shoe down on the feather-delicate mechanism within the recess.

There was a splinter of glass, a twisting of metal, and a tiny spray of mercury droplets –

Black breathed heavily. He turned on the radio once more. 'Still there, Schloss?'

'Yes, but – '

'Then I report the hyperfield on board the *Parsec* to be deactivated. Come and get me.'

Gerald Black felt no more the hero than when he had left for the *Parsec*, but he found himself one just the same. The men who had brought him to the small asteroid came to take him off. They landed this time. They clapped his back.

Hyper Base was a crowded mass of waiting personnel when the ship arrived, and Black was cheered. He waved at the throng and grinned, as was a hero's obligation, but he felt no triumph inside. Not yet. Only anticipation. Triumph would come later, when he met Susan Calvin.

He paused before descending from the ship. He looked for her and did not see her. General Kallner was there, waiting, with all his soldierly stiffness restored and a bluff look of approval firmly plastered on his face. Mayer Schloss smiled nervously at him. Ronson of Interplanetary Press waved frantically. Susan Calvin was nowhere.

He brushed Kallner and Schloss aside when he landed. 'I'm going to wash and eat first.'

He had no doubts but that, for the moment at least, he could dictate terms to the general or to anybody.

The security guards made a way for him. He bathed and

ate leisurely in enforced isolation, he himself being solely responsible for the enforcement. Then he called Ronson of Interplanetary and talked to him briefly. He waited for the return call before he felt he could relax thoroughly. It had all worked out so much better than he had expected. The very failure of the ship had conspired perfectly with him.

Finally he called the general's office and ordered a conference. It was what it amounted to – orders. Major-general Kallner all but said, 'Yes, sir.'

They were together again. Gerald Black, Kallner, Schloss – even Susan Calvin. But it was Black who was dominant now. The robopsychologist, graven-faced as ever, as unimpressed by triumph as by disaster, had nevertheless seemed by some subtle change of attitude to have relinquished the spotlight.

Dr Schloss nibbled a thumbnail and began by saying, cautiously, 'Dr Black, we are all very grateful for your bravery and success.' Then, as though to institute a healthy deflation at once, he added, 'Still, smashing the relay box with your heel was imprudent and – well, it was an action that scarcely deserved success.'

Black said, 'It was an action that could scarcely have avoided success. You see' (this was bomb number one) 'by the time I knew what had gone wrong.'

Schloss rose to his feet. 'You did? Are you sure?'

'Go there yourself. It's safe now. I'll tell you what to look for.'

Schloss sat down again, slowly. General Kallner was enthusiastic. 'Why, this is the best yet, if true.'

'It's true,' said Black. His eyes slid to Susan Calvin, who said nothing.

Black was enjoying the sensation of power. He released bomb number two by saying, 'It was the robot, of course. Did you hear that, Dr Calvin?'

Susan Calvin spoke for the first time. 'I hear it. I rather

expected it, as a matter of fact. It was the only piece of equipment on board ship that had not been tested at Hyper Base.'

For a moment Black felt dashed. He said, 'You said nothing of that.'

Dr Calvin said, 'As Dr Schloss said several times, I am not an etherics expert. My guess, and it was no more than that, might easily have been wrong. I felt I had no right to prejudice you in advance of your mission.'

Black said, 'All right, did you happen to guess *how* it went wrong?'

'No, sir.'

'Why, it was made better than a man. That's what the trouble was. Isn't it strange that the trouble should rest with the very specialty of US Robots? They make robots better than men, I understand.'

He was slashing at her with words now but she did not rise to his bait.

Instead, she sighed. 'My dear Dr Black. I am not responsible for the slogans of our sales-promotion department.'

Black felt dashed again. She wasn't an easy woman to handle, this Calvin. He said, 'Your people built a robot to replace a man at the controls of the *Parsec*. He had to pull the control bar toward himself, place it in position and let the heat of his hands twist the trigger to make final contact. Simple enough, Dr Calvin?'

'Simple enough, Dr Black.'

'And if the robot had been made no better than a man, he would have succeeded. Unfortunately, US Robots felt compelled to make it better than a man. The robot was told to pull back the control bar firmly. *Firmly*. The word was repeated, strengthened, emphasized. So the robot did what it was told. It pulled it back firmly. There was only one trouble. He was easily ten times stronger than the ordinary human being for whom the control bar was designed.'

'Are you implying – '

'I'm *saying* the bar bent. It bent back just enough to misplace the trigger. When the heat of the robot's hand twisted the thermocouple, it did *not* make contact.' He grinned. 'This isn't the failure of just one robot, Dr Calvin. It's symbolic of the failure of the robot idea.'

'Come now, Dr Black,' said Susan Calvin icily, 'you're drowning logic in missionary psychology. The robot was equipped with adequate understanding as well as with brute force. Had the men who gave it its orders used quantitative terms rather than the foolish adverb "firmly," this would not have happened. Had they said, "apply a pull of fifty-five pounds," all would have been well.'

'What you are saying,' said Black, 'is that the inadequacy of a robot must be made up for by the ingenuity and intelligence of a man. I assure you that the people back on Earth will look at it in that way and will not be in the mood to excuse US Robots for this fiasco.'

Major-general Kallner said quickly, with a return of authority to his voice, 'Now wait, Black, all that has happened is obviously classified information.'

'In fact,' said Schloss suddenly, 'your theory hasn't been checked yet. We'll send a party to the ship and find out. It may not be the robot at all.'

'You'll take care to make that discovery, will you? I wonder if the people will believe an interested party. Besides which, I have one more thing to tell you.' He readied bomb number three and said, 'As of this moment, I'm resigning from this man's project. I'm quitting.'

'Why?' asked Susan Calvin.

'Because, as you said, Dr Calvin, I am a missionary,' said Black, smiling. 'I have a mission. I feel I owe it to the people of Earth to tell them that the age of the robots has reached the point where human life is valued less than robot life. It is now possible to order a man into danger because a robot is too precious to risk. I believe Earthmen should hear that. Many men have many reservations about robots as is. US Robots has not yet succeeded in making it legally permissible to use robots on the planet Earth itself. I believe what I have to say, Dr Calvin, will complete the matter. For this day's work, Dr Calvin, you and your company and your robots will be wiped off the face of the solar system.'

He was forewarning her, Black knew; he was forearming her, but he could not forgo this scene. He had lived for this very moment ever since he had first left for the *Parsec*, and he could not give it up.

He all but gloated at the momentary glitter in Susan Calvin's pale eyes and at the faintest flush in her cheeks. He thought, How do you feel now, madam scientist?

Kallner said, 'You will not be permitted to resign, Black, nor will you be permitted – '

'How can you stop me, general? I'm a hero, haven't you heard? And old Mother Earth *will* make much of its heroes. It always has. They'll want to hear from me and they'll believe anything I say. And they won't like it if I'm interfered with, at least not while I'm a fresh, brand-new hero. I've already talked to Ronson of Interplanetary Press and told him I had something big for them, something that would rock every government official and science director right out of the chair plush, so Interplanetary will be first in line, waiting to hear from me. So what can you do except to have me shot? And I think you'd be worse off after that if you tried it.'

Black's revenge was complete. He had spared no word. He had hampered himself not in the least. He rose to go.

'One moment, Dr Black,' said Susan Calvin. Her low voice carried authority.

Black turned involuntarily, like a schoolboy at his teacher's voice, but he counteracted that gesture by a deliberately mocking, 'You have an explanation to make, I suppose?'

'Not at all,' she said primly. 'You have explained for me, and quite well. I chose you because I knew you would understand, though I thought you would understand sooner. I had had contact with you before. I knew you disliked robots and would, therefore, be under no illusions concerning them. From your records, which I asked to see before you were given your assignment, I saw that you had expressed disapproval of this robot-through-hyperspace experiment. Your superiors held that against you, but I thought it a point in your favor.'

'What are you talking about, doctor, if you'll excuse my rudeness?'

'The fact that you should have understood why no robot could have been sent on this mission. What was it you yourself said? Something about a robot's inadequacies having to be balanced by the ingenuity and intelligence of a man. Exactly so, young man, exactly so. Robots have no ingenuity. Their minds are finite and can be calculated to the last decimal. That, in fact, is my job.

'Now if a robot is given an order, a *precise* order, he can follow it. If the order is not precise, he cannot correct his own mistake without further orders. Isn't that what you reported concerning the robot on the ship? How then can we send a robot to find a flaw in a mechanism when we cannot possibly give precise orders, since we know nothing about the flaw ourselves? "Find out what's wrong" is not an order you can give to a robot; only to a man. The human brain, so far at least, is beyond calculation.'

Black sat down abruptly and stared at the psychologist in dismay. Her words struck sharply on a substratum of understanding that had been larded over with emotion. He found himself unable to refute her. Worse than that, a feeling of defeat encompassed him.

He said, 'You might have said this before I left.'

'I might have,' agreed Dr Calvin, 'but I noticed your very natural fear for your sanity. Such an overwhelming concern would easily have hampered your efficiency as an investigator, and it occurred to me to let you think that my only motive in sending you was that I valued a robot more. That, I thought, would make you angry, and anger, my dear Dr Black, is sometimes a very useful emotion. At least, an angry man is never quite as afraid as he would be otherwise. It worked out nicely, I think.' She folded her hands loosely in her lap and came as near a smile as she ever had in her life.

Black said, 'I'll be damned.'

Susan Calvin said, 'So now, if you'll take my advice, return to your job, accept your status as hero, and tell your reporter friend the details of your brave deed. Let that be the big news you promised him.'

Slowly, reluctantly, Black nodded.

Schloss looked relieved; Kallner burst into a toothy smile. They held out hands, not having said a word in all the time that Susan Calvin had spoken, and not saying a word now.

Black took their hands and shook them with some reserve. He said, 'It's your part that should be publicized, Dr Calvin.'

Susan Calvin said icily, 'Don't be a fool, young man. This is my job.'

Escape!

When Susan Calvin returned from Hyper Base, Alfred Lanning was waiting for her. The old man never spoke about his age, but everyone knew it to be over seventy-five. Yet his mind was keen, and if he had finally allowed himself to be made Director-Emeritus of Research with Bogert as acting Director, it did not prevent him from appearing in his office daily.

'How close are they to the Hyperatomic Drive?' he asked.

'I don't know,' she replied irritably, 'I didn't ask.'

'Hmm. I wish they'd hurry. Because if they don't, Consolidated might beat them to it. And beat *us* to it as well.'

'*Consolidated*. What have they got to do with it?'

'Well, we're not the only ones with calculating machines. Ours may be positronic, but that doesn't mean they're better. Robertson is calling a big meeting about it tomorrow. He's been waiting for you to come back.'

Robertson of US Robots and Mechanical Men Corporation, son of the founder, pointed his lean nose at his general manager and his Adam's apple jumped as he said, 'You start now. Let's get this straight.'

The general manager did so with alacrity, 'Here's the deal now, chief. Consolidated Robots approached us a month ago with a funny sort of proposition. They brought about five tons of figures, equations, all that sort of stuff. It was a problem, see, and they wanted an answer from The Brain. The terms were as follows – '

He ticked them off on thick fingers: 'A hundred thousand

for us if there is no solution and we can tell them the missing factors. Two hundred thousand if there is a solution, plus costs of construction of the machine involved, plus quarter interest in all profits derived therefrom. The problem concerns the development of an interstellar engine – '

Robertson frowned and his lean figure stiffened, 'Despite the fact that they have a thinking machine of their own. Right?'

'Exactly what makes the whole proposition a foul ball, chief. Levver, take it from there.'

Abe Levver looked up from the far end of the conference table and smoothed his stubbled chin with a faint rasping sound. He smiled:

'It's this way, sir. Consolidated *had* a thinking machine. It's broken.'

'What?' Robertson half rose.

'That's right. Broken! It's *kaput*. Nobody knows why, but I got hold of some pretty interesting guesses – like, for instance, that they asked it to give them an interstellar engine with the same set of information they came to us with, and that it cracked their machine wide open. It's scrap – just scrap now.'

'You get it, chief?' The general manager was wildly jubilant. 'You get it? There isn't any industrial research group of any size that isn't trying to develop a space-warp engine, and Consolidated and US Robots have the lead on the field with our super robot-brains. Now that they've managed to foul theirs up, we have a clear field. That's the nub, the . . . uh . . . motivation. It will take them six years at least to build another and they're sunk, unless they can break ours, too, with the same problem.'

The president of US Robots bulged his eyes, 'Why, the dirty rats – '

'Hold on, chief. There's more to this.' He pointed a finger with a wide sweep, 'Lanning, take it!'

Dr Alfred Lanning viewed the proceedings with faint scorn – his usual reaction to the doings of the vastly better-paid business and sales divisions. His unbelievable white eyebrows hunched low and his voice was dry:

'From a scientific standpoint the situation, while not entirely clear, is subject to intelligent analysis. The question of interstellar travel under present conditions of physical theory is . . . uh . . . vague. The matter is wide open – and the information given by Consolidated to its thinking machine, assuming these we have to be the same, was similarly wide open. Our mathematical department has given it a thorough analysis, and it seems Consolidated has included everything. Its material for submission contains all known developments of Franciacci's space-warp theory, and, apparently, all pertinent astrophysical and electronic data. It's quite a mouthful.'

Robertson followed anxiously. He interrupted, 'Too much for The Brain to handle?'

Lanning shook his head decisively, 'No. There are no known limits to The Brain's capacity. It's a different matter. It's a question of the Robotic Laws. The Brain, for instance, could never supply a solution to a problem set to it if that solution would involve the death or injury of humans. As far as it would be concerned, a problem with only such a solution would be insoluble. If such a problem is combined with an extremely urgent demand that it be answered, it is just possible that The Brain, only a robot after all, would be presented with a dilemma, where it could neither answer nor refuse to answer. Something of the sort must have happened to Consolidated's machine.'

He paused, but the general manager urged on, 'Go ahead, Dr Lanning. Explain it the way you explained it to me.'

Lanning set his lips and raised his eyebrows in the direction of Dr Susan Calvin who lifted her eyes from her precisely folded hands for the first time. Her voice was low and colorless.

'The nature of a robot reaction to a dilemma is startling,' she began. 'Robot psychology is far from perfect – as a specialist, I can assure you of that – but it can be discussed in qualitative terms, because with all the complications introduced into a robot's positronic brain, it is built by humans and is therefore built according to human values.

'Now a human caught in an impossibility often responds by a retreat from reality: by entry into a world of delusion, or by taking to drink, going off into hysteria, or jumping off a bridge. It all comes to the same thing – a refusal or inability to face the situation squarely. And so, the robot. A dilemma at its mildest will disorder half its relays; and at its worst it will burn out every positronic brain path past repair.'

'I see,' said Robertson, who didn't. 'Now what about this information Consolidated's wishing on us?'

'It undoubtedly involves,' said Dr Calvin, 'a problem of a forbidden sort. But The Brain is considerably different from Consolidated's robot.'

'That's right, chief. That's right.' The general manager was energetically interruptive. 'I want you to get this, because it's the whole point of the situation.'

Susan Calvin's eyes glittered behind the spectacles, and she continued patiently, 'You see, sir, Consolidated's machines, their Super-Thinker among them, are built without personality. They go in for functionalism, you know – they have to, without US Robots' basic patents for the emotional brain paths. Their Thinker is merely a calculating machine on a grand scale, and a dilemma ruins it instantly.

'However, The Brain, our own machine, has a personality – a child's personality. It is a supremely deductive brain, but it resembles an *idiot savant*. It doesn't really understand what it does – it just does it. And because it is really a child, it is more resilient. Life isn't so serious, you might say.'

The robopsychologist continued: 'Here is what we're going to do. We have divided all of Consolidated's information into logical units. We are going to feed the units to The Brain singly and cautiously. When *the* factor enters – the one that creates the dilemma – The Brain's child personality will hesitate. Its sense of judgment is not mature. There will be a perceptible interval before it will recognize a dilemma as such. And in that interval, it will reject the unit automatically – before its brain-paths can be set in motion and ruined.'

Robertson's Adam's apple squirmed, 'Are you sure, now?'

Dr Calvin masked impatience, 'It doesn't make much sense, I admit, in lay language; but there is no conceivable use in presenting the mathematics of this. I assure you, it is as I say.'

The general manager was in the breach instantly and fluently, 'So here's the situation, chief. If we take the deal, we can put it through like this. The Brain will tell us which unit of information involves the dilemma. From there, we can figure *why* the dilemma. Isn't that right, Dr Bogert? There you are, chief, and Dr Bogert is the best mathematician you'll find anywhere. We give Consolidated a "No Solution" answer, with the reason, and collect a hundred thousand. They're left with a broken machine; we're left with a whole one. In a year, two maybe, we'll have a space-warp engine, or a hyper-atomic motor, some people call it. Whatever you name it, it will be the biggest thing in the world.'

Robertson chuckled and reached out, 'Let's see the contract. I'll sign it.'

* * *

When Susan Calvin entered the fantastically guarded vault that held The Brain, one of the current shift of technicians had just asked it: 'If one and a half chickens lay one and a half eggs in one and a half days, how many eggs will nine chickens lay in nine days?'

The Brain had just answered, 'Fifty-four.'

And the technician had just said to another, 'See, you dope!'

Dr Calvin coughed and there was a sudden impossible flurry of directionless energy. The psychologist motioned briefly, and she was alone with The Brain.

The Brain was a two-foot globe merely – one which contained within it a thoroughly conditioned helium atmosphere, a volume of space completely vibration-absent and radiation-free – and within that was that unheard-of complexity of positronic grain-paths that was The Brain. The rest of the room was crowded with the attachments that were the intermediaries between The Brain and the outside world – its voice, its arms, its sense organs.

Dr Calvin said softly, 'How are you, Brain?'

The Brain's voice was high-pitched and enthusiastic, 'Swell, Miss Susan. You're going to ask me something. I can tell. You always have a book in your hand when you're going to ask me something.'

Dr Calvin smiled mildly, 'Well, you're right, but not just yet. This is going to be a question. It will be so complicated we're going to give it to you in writing. But not just yet. I think I'll talk to you first.'

'All right. I don't mind talking.'

'Now, Brain, in a little while, Dr Lanning and Dr Bogert will be here with this complicated question. We'll give it to you a very little at a time and very slowly, because we want you to be careful. We're going to ask you to build something, if you can, out of the information, but I'm going to warn you now that the solution might involve . . . uh . . . damage to human beings.'

'Gosh!' The exclamation was hushed, drawn-out.

'Now you watch for that. When we come to a sheet which means damage, even maybe death, don't get excited. You see, Brain, in this case, we don't mind – not even about death; we don't mind at all. So when you come to that sheet, just stop, give it back – and that'll be all. You understand?'

'Oh, sure. But golly, the death of humans! Oh, my!'

'Now, Brain, I hear Dr Lanning and Dr Bogert coming. They'll tell you what the problem is all about and then we'll start. Be a good boy, now – '

Slowly the sheets were fed in. After each one came the interval of the queerly whispery chuckling noise that was The Brain in action. Then the silence that meant readiness for another sheet. It was a matter of hours – during which the equivalent of something like seventeen fat volumes of mathematical physics were fed into The Brain.

As the process went on, frowns appeared and deepened. Lanning muttered ferociously under his breath. Bogert first gazed speculatively at his fingernails, and then bit at them in abstracted fashion. It was when the last of the thick pile of sheets disappeared that Calvin, white-faced, said:

'Something's wrong.'

Lanning barely got the words out, 'It can't be. Is it – dead?'

'Brain?' Susan Calvin was trembling. 'Do you hear me, Brain?'

'Huh?' came the abstracted rejoinder. 'Do you want me?'

'The solution – '

'Oh, that! I can do it. I'll build you a whole ship, just as easy – if you let me have the robots. A nice ship. It'll take two months maybe.'

'There was – no difficulty?'

'It took long to figure,' said The Brain.

Dr Calvin backed away. The color had not returned to her thin cheeks. She motioned the others away.

In her office, she said, 'I can't understand it. The information, as given, must involve a dilemma – probably involves death. If something has gone wrong – '

Bogert said quietly, 'The machine talks and makes sense. It can't be a dilemma.'

But the psychologist replied urgently, 'There are dilemmas *and* dilemmas. There are different forms of escape. Suppose The Brain is only mildly caught; just badly enough, say, to be suffering from the delusion that it can solve the problem, when it can't. Or suppose it's teetering on the brink of something really bad, so that any small push shoves it over.'

'Suppose,' said Lanning, 'there is no dilemma. Suppose Consolidated's machine broke down over a different question, or broke down for purely mechanical reasons.'

'But even so,' insisted Calvin, 'we couldn't take chances. Listen, from now on, no one is to as much as breathe to The Brain. I'm taking over.'

'All right,' sighed Lanning, 'take over, then. And meanwhile we'll let The Brain build its ship. And if it *does* build it, we'll have to test it.'

He was ruminating, 'We'll need our top field men for *that*.'

Michael Donovan brushed down his red hair with a violent motion of his hand and a total indifference to the fact that the unruly mass sprang to attention again immediately.

He said, 'Call the turn now, Greg. They say the ship is finished. They don't know what it is, but it's finished. Let's go, Greg. Let's grab the controls right now.'

Powell said wearily, 'Cut it, Mike. There's a peculiar overripe flavor to your humor at its freshest, and the confined atmosphere here isn't helping it.'

'Well, listen,' Donovan took another ineffectual swipe at his hair, 'I'm not worried so much about our cast-iron genius and his tin ship. There's the matter of my lost leave. And the monotony! There's nothing here but whiskers and figures – the wrong kind of figures. Oh, why do they *give* us these jobs?'

'Because,' replied Powell, gently, 'we're no loss, if they lose us. OK, relax! Doc Lanning's coming this way.'

Lanning was coming, his white eyebrows as lavish as ever, his aged figure unbent as yet and full of life. He walked silently up the ramp with the two men and out into the open field, where, obeying no human master, silent robots were building a ship.

Wrong tense. *Had* built a ship!

For Lanning said, 'The robots have stopped. Not one has moved today.'

'It's completed then? Definitely?' asked Powell.

'Now how can I tell?' Lanning was peevish, and his eyebrows curled down in an eye-hiding frown. 'It *seems* done. There are no spare pieces about, and the interior is down to a gleaming finish.'

'You've been inside?'

'Just in, then out. I'm no space-pilot. Either of you two know much about engine theory?'

Donovan looked at Powell, who looked at Donovan.

Donovan said, 'I've got my license, sir, but at last reading it didn't say anything about hyper-engines or warp-navigation. Just the usual child's play in three dimensions.'

Alfred Lanning looked up with sharp disapproval and snorted the length of his prominent nose.

He said frigidly, 'Well, we have our engine men.'

Powell caught at his elbow as he walked away, 'Sir, is the ship still restricted ground?'

The old director hesitated, then rubbed the bridge of his nose, 'I suppose not. For you two anyway.'

Donovan looked after him as he left and muttered a short, expressive phrase at his back. He turned to Powell, 'I'd like to give him a literary description of himself, Greg.'

'Suppose you come along, Mike.'

The inside of the ship was finished, as finished as a ship ever was; that could be told in a single eye-blinking glance. No martinet in the system could have put as much spit-and-polish into a surface as those robots had. The walls were of a gleaming silvery finish that retained no fingerprints.

There were no angles; walls, floors, and ceiling faded gently into each other and in the cold, metallic glittering of the hidden lights, one was surrounded by six chilly reflections of one's bewildered self.

The main corridor was a narrow tunnel that led in a hard, clatter-footed stretch along a line of rooms of no interdistinguishing features.

Powell said, 'I suppose furniture is built into the wall. Or maybe we're not supposed to sit or sleep.'

It was in the last room, the one nearest the nose that the monotony broke. A curving window of non-reflecting glass was the first break in the universal metal, and below it was a single large dial, with a single motionless needle hard against the zero mark.

Donovan said, 'Look at that!' and pointed to the single word on the finely marked scale.

It said 'Parsecs' and the tiny figure at the right end of the curving, graduated meter said '1,000,000.'

There were two chairs; heavy, wide-flaring, uncushioned. Powell seated himself gingerly, and found it molded to the body's curves, and comfortable.

Powell said, 'What do you think of it?'

'For my money, The Brain has brain-fever. Let's get out.'

'Sure you don't want to look it over a bit?'

'I have looked it over. I came, I saw, I'm through!'

Donovan's red hair bristled into separate wires, 'Greg, let's get out of here. I quit my job five seconds ago, and this is a restricted area for non-personnel.'

Powell smiled in an oily self-satisfied manner and smoothed his mustache, 'OK, Mike, turn off that adrenalin tap you've got draining into your bloodstream. I was worried, too, but no more.'

'No more, huh? How come, no more? Increased your insurance?'

'Mike, this ship can't fly.'

'How do you know?'

'Well, we've been through the entire ship, haven't we?'

'Seems so.'

'Take my word for it, we have. Did you see any pilot room except for this one port and the one gauge here in parsecs? Did you see any controls?'

'No.'

'And did you see any engines?'

'Holy Joe, no!'

'Well then! Let's break the news to Lanning, Mike.'

They cursed their way through the featureless corridors and finally hit-and-missed their way into the short passage to the air lock.

Donovan stiffened, 'Did you lock this thing, Greg?'

'No, I never touched it. Yank the lever, will you?'

The lever never budged, though Donovan's face twisted appallingly with exertion.

Powell said, 'I didn't see any emergency exits. If something's gone wrong here, they'll have to melt us out.'

'Yes, and we've got to wait until they find out that some fool has locked us in here,' added Donovan frantically.

'Let's get back to the room with the port. It's the only place from which we might attract attention.'

But they didn't.

In that last room, the port was no longer blue and full of

sky. It was black, and hard yellow pin-point stars spelled *space*.

There was a dull, double thud, as two bodies collapsed separately into two chairs.

Alfred Lanning met Dr Calvin just outside his office. He lit a nervous cigar and motioned her in.

He said, 'Well, Susan, we've come pretty far, and Robertson's getting jumpy. What are you doing with The Brain?'

Susan Calvin spread her hands, 'It's no use getting impatient. The Brain is worth more than anything we forfeit on this deal.'

'But you've been questioning it for two months.'

The psychologist's voice was flat, but somehow dangerous, 'You would rather run this yourself?'

'Now you know what I meant.'

'Oh, I suppose I do,' Dr Calvin rubbed her hands nervously. 'It isn't easy. I've been pampering it and probing it gently, and I haven't gotten anywhere yet. Its reactions aren't normal. Its answers – they're queer, somehow. But nothing I can put my finger on yet. And you see, until we know what's wrong, we must just tiptoe our way through. I can never tell what simple question or remark will just . . . push him over . . . and then – Well, and then we'll have on our hands a completely useless Brain. Do you want to face that?'

'Well, it can't break the First Law.'

'I would have thought so, but – '

'You're not even sure of that?' Lanning was profoundly shocked.

'Oh, I can't be sure of anything, Alfred – '

The alarm system raised its fearful clangor with a horrifying suddenness. Lanning clicked on communications with an almost paralytic spasm. The breathless words froze him.

He said, 'Susan . . . you heard that . . . the ship's gone. I sent those two field men inside half an hour ago. You'll have to see The Brain again.'

Susan Calvin said with enforced calm, 'Brain, what happened to the ship?'

The Brain said happily, 'The ship I built, Miss Susan?'

'That's right. What has happened to it?'

'Why, nothing at all. The two men that were supposed to test it were inside, and we were all set. So I sent it off.'

'Oh – Well, that's nice.' The psychologist felt some difficulty in breathing. 'Do you think they'll be all right?'

'Right as anything, Miss Susan. I've taken care of it all. It's a bee-yoo-tiful ship.'

'Yes, Brain, it *is* beautiful, but you think they have enough food, don't you? They'll be comfortable?'

'Plenty of food.'

'This business might be a shock to them, Brain. Unexpected, you know.'

The Brain tossed it off, 'They'll be all right. It ought to be interesting for them.'

'Interesting? How?'

'Just interesting,' said The Brain, slyly.

'Susan,' whispered Lanning in a fuming whisper, 'ask him if death comes into it. Ask him what the dangers are.'

Susan Calvin's expression contorted with fury, 'Keep quiet!' In a shaken voice, she said to The Brain, 'We can communicate with the ship, can't we, Brain?'

'Oh, they can hear you if you call by radio. I've taken care of that.'

'Thanks. That's all for now.'

Once outside, Lanning lashed out ragingly, 'Great Galaxy, Susan, if this gets out, it will ruin all of us. We've got to get those men back. Why didn't you ask it if there was danger of death – straight out?'

'Because,' said Calvin, with a weary frustration, 'that's just what I can't mention. If it's got a case of dilemma, it's about death. Anything that would bring it up badly might knock it completely out. Will we be better off then? Now, look, it said we could communicate with them. Let's do so, get their location, and bring them back. They probably can't use the controls themselves; The Brain is probably handling them remotely. Come!'

It was quite a while before Powell shook himself together.

'Mike,' he said, out of cold lips, 'did you feel any acceleration?'

Donovan's eyes were blank, 'Huh? No . . . no.'

And then the redhead's fists clenched and he was out of his seat with sudden frenzied energy and up against the cold, wide-curving glass. There was nothing to see – but stars.

He turned, 'Greg, they must have started the machine while we were inside. Greg, it's a put-up job; they fixed it up with the robot to jerry us into being the try-out boys, in case we were thinking of backing out.'

Powell said, 'What are you talking about? What's the good of sending us out if we don't know how to run the machine? How are we supposed to bring it back? No, this ship left by itself, and without any apparent acceleration.' He rose, and walked the floor slowly. The metal walls dinned back the clangor of his steps.

He said tonelessly, 'Mike, this is the most confusing situation we've ever been up against.'

'That,' said Donovan, bitterly, 'is news to me. I was just beginning to have a very swell time, when you told me.'

Powell ignored that. 'No acceleration – which means the ship works on a principle different from any known.'

'Different from any we know, anyway.'

'Different from *any* known. There are no engines within

reach of manual control. Maybe they're built into the walls. Maybe that's why they're thick as they are.'

'What are you mumbling about?' demanded Donovan.

'Why not listen? I'm saying that whatever powers this ship is enclosed, and evidently not meant to be handled. The ship is running by remote control.'

'The Brain's control?'

'Why not?'

'Then you think we'll stay out here till The Brain brings us back.'

'It could be. If so, let's wait quietly. The Brain is a robot. It's got to follow the First Law. It can't hurt a human being.'

Donovan sat down slowly, 'You figure that?' Carefully, he flattened his hair, 'Listen, this junk about the space-warp knocked out Consolidated's robot, and the longhairs said it was because interstellar travel killed humans. Which robot are you going to trust? Ours had the same data, I understand.'

Powell was yanking madly at his mustache, 'Don't pretend you don't know your robotics, Mike. Before it's physically possible in any way for a robot to even make a start to breaking the First Law, so many things have to break down that it would be a ruined mess of scrap ten times over. There's some simple explanation to this.'

'Oh sure, sure. Just have the butler call me in the morning. It's all just too, too simple for me to bother about before my beauty nap.'

'Well, Jupiter, Mike, what are you complaining about so far? The Brain is taking care of us. This place is warm. It's got light. It's got air. There wasn't even enough of an acceleration jar to muss your hair if it were smooth enough to be mussable in the first place.'

'Yeah? Greg, you must've taken lessons. No one could put Pollyanna that far out of the running without. What do we eat? What do we drink? Where are we? How do we get back? And in case of accident, to what exit and in what spacesuit do we run, not walk? I haven't even seen a bathroom in the place, or those little conveniences that go along with bathrooms. Sure, we're being taken care of – but good!'

The voice that interrupted Donovan's tirade was not Powell's. It was nobody's. It was there, hanging in open air – stentorian and petrifying in its effects.

'GREGORY POWELL! MICHAEL DONOVAN! GREGORY POWELL! MICHAEL DONOVAN! PLEASE REPORT YOUR PRESENT POSITIONS. IF YOUR SHIP ANSWERS CONTROLS, PLEASE RETURN TO BASE. GREGORY POWELL! MICHAEL DONOVAN! – '

The message was repetitious, mechanical, broken by regular, untiring intervals.

Donovan said, 'Where's it coming from?'

'I don't know.' Powell's voice was an intense whisper, 'Where do the lights come from? Where does anything come from?'

'Well, how are we going to answer?' They had to speak in the intervals between the loudly echoing, repeating message.

The walls were bare – as bare and as unbroken as smooth, curving metal can be. Powell said, 'Shout an answer.'

They did. They shouted, in turns, and together, 'Position unknown! Ship out of control! Condition desperate!'

Their voices rose and cracked. The short businesslike sentences became interlarded and adulterated with screaming and emphatic profanity, but the cold, calling voice repeated and repeated and repeated unwearyingly.

'They don't hear us,' gasped Donovan. 'There's no sending mechanism. Just a receiver.' His eyes focused blindly at a random spot on the wall.

Slowly the din of the outside voice softened and receded.

They called again when it was a whisper, and they called again, hoarsely, when there was silence.

Something like fifteen minutes later, Powell said lifelessly, 'Let's go through the ship again. There must be something to eat somewheres.' He did not sound hopeful. It was almost an admission of defeat.

They divided in the corridor to the right and left. They could follow one another by the hard footsteps resounding, and they met occasionally in the corridor, where they would glare at each other and pass on.

Powell's search ended suddenly and as it did, he heard Donovan's glad voice rise boomingly.

'Hey, Greg,' it howled, 'the ship *has* got plumbing. How did we miss it?'

It was some five minutes later that he found Powell by hit-and-miss. He was saying, 'Still no shower baths, though,' but it got choked off in the middle.

'Food,' he gasped.

The wall had dropped away, leaving a curved gap with two shelves. The upper shelf was loaded with unlabeled cans of a bewildering variety of sizes and shapes. The enameled cans on the lower shelf were uniform and Donovan felt a cold draft about his ankles. The lower half was refrigerated.

'How . . . how – '

'It wasn't there, before,' said Powell, curtly. 'That wall section dropped out of sight as I came in the door.'

He was eating. The can was the pre-heating type with enclosed spoon and the warm odor of baked beans filled the room. 'Grab a can, Mike!'

Donovan hesitated, 'What's the menu?'

'How do I know! Are you finicky?'

'No, but all I eat on ships are beans. Something else would be first choice.' His hand hovered and selected a shining elliptical can whose flatness seemed reminiscent of salmon or similar delicacy. It opened at the proper pressure.

'Beans!' howled Donovan, and reached for another.

Powell hauled at the slack of his pants. 'Better eat that, sonny boy. Supplies are limited and we may be here a long, long time.'

Donovan drew back sulkily, 'Is that all we have? Beans?'

'Could be.'

'What's on the lower shelf?'

'Milk.'

'Just milk?' Donovan cried in outrage.

'Looks it.'

The meal of beans and milk was carried through in silence, and as they left, the strip of hidden wall rose up and formed an unbroken surface once more.

Powell sighed, 'Everything automatic. Everything just so. Never felt so helpless in my life. Where's your plumbing?'

'Right there. And that wasn't among those present when we first looked, either.'

Fifteen minutes later they were back in the glassed-in room, staring at each other from opposing seats.

Powell looked gloomily at the one gauge in the room. It still said 'parsecs,' the figures still ended in '1,000,000' and the indicating needle was still pressed hard against the zero mark.

In the innermost offices of the US Robots and Mechanical Men Corporation Alfred Lanning was saying wearily, 'They won't answer. We've tried every wavelength, public, private, coded, straight, even this subether stuff they have now. And The Brain still won't say anything?' He shot this at Dr Calvin.

'It won't amplify on the matter, Alfred,' she said, emphatically. 'It says they can hear us . . . and when I try to press it, it becomes . . . well, it becomes sullen. And it's not supposed to – Whoever heard of a sullen robot?'

'Suppose you tell us what you have, Susan,' said Bogert.

'Here it is! It admits it controls the ship itself entirely. It is definitely optimistic about their safety, but without details. I don't dare press it. However, the center of disturbance seems to be about the interstellar jump itself. The Brain definitely laughed when I brought up the subject. There are other indications, but that is the closest it's come to an open abnormality.'

She looked at the others, 'I refer to hysteria. I dropped the subject immediately, and I hope I did no harm, but it gave me a lead. I can handle hysteria. Give me twelve hours! If I can bring it back to normal, it will bring back the ship.'

Bogert seemed suddenly stricken. 'The interstellar jump!'

'What's the matter?' The cry was double from Calvin and Lanning.

'The figures for the engine The Brain gave us. Say . . . I just thought of something.'

He left hurriedly.

Lanning gazed after him. He said brusquely to Calvin, 'You take care of your end, Susan.'

Two hours later, Bogert was talking eagerly, 'I tell you, Lanning, that's it. The interstellar jump is not instantaneous – not as long as the speed of light is finite. Life can't exist . . . *matter and energy* as such can't exist in the space warp. I don't know what it would be like – but that's it. That's what killed Consolidated's robot.'

Donovan felt as haggard as he looked. 'Only five days?'

'Only five days. I'm sure of it.'

Donovan looked about him wretchedly. The stars through the glass were familiar but infinitely indifferent. The walls were cold to the touch; the lights, which had recently flared up again, were unfeelingly bright; the needle on the gauge pointed stubbornly to zero; and Donovan could not get rid of the taste of beans.

He said, morosely, 'I need a bath.'

Powell looked up briefly, and said, 'So do I. You needn't feel self-conscious. But unless you want to bathe in milk and do without drinking – '

'We'll do without drinking eventually, anyway. Greg, where does this interstellar travel come in?'

'You tell me. Maybe we just keep on going. We'd get there, eventually. At least the dust of our skeletons would – but isn't our death the whole point of The Brain's original breakdown?'

Donovan spoke with his back to the other, 'Greg, I've been thinking. It's pretty bad. There's not much to do – except walk around or talk to yourself. You know those stories about guys marooned in space. They go nuts long before they starve. I don't know, Greg, but ever since the lights went on, I feel funny.'

There was a silence, then Powell's voice came thin and small, 'So do I. What's it like?'

The redheaded figure turned, 'Feel funny inside. There's a pounding in me with everything tense. It's hard to breathe. I can't stand still.'

'Um-m-m. Do you feel vibration?'

'How do you mean?'

'Sit down for a minute and listen. You don't hear it, but you feel it – as if something's throbbing somewheres and it's throbbing the whole ship, and you, too, along with it. Listen – '

'Yeah . . . yeah. What do you think it is, Greg? You don't suppose it's us?'

'It might be.' Powell stroked his mustache slowly. 'But it might be the ship's engines. It might be getting ready.'

'For what?'

'For the interstellar jump. It may be coming and the devil knows what it's like.'

Donovan pondered. Then he said, savagely, 'If it does, let it. But I wish we could fight. It's humiliating to have to wait for it.'

An hour later, perhaps, Powell looked at his hand on the metal chair-arm and said with frozen calm, 'Feel the wall, Mike.'

Donovan did, and said, 'You can feel it shake, Greg.'

Even the stars seemed blurred. From somewhere came the vague impression of a huge machine gathering power with the walls, storing up energy for a mighty leap, throbbing its way up the scales of strength.

It came with a suddenness and a stab of pain. Powell stiffened, and half-jerked from his chair. His sight caught Donovan and blanked out while Donovan's thin shout whimpered and died in his ears. Something writhed within him and struggled against a growing blanket of ice, that thickened.

Something broke loose and whirled in a blaze of flickering light and pain. It fell –

– and whirled

– and fell headlong

– into silence!

It was death!

It was a world of no motion and no sensation. A world of dim, unsensing consciousness; a consciousness of darkness and of silence and of formless struggle.

Most of all a consciousness of eternity.

He was a tiny white thread of ego – cold and afraid.

Then the words came, unctuous and sonorous, thundering over him in a foam of sound:

'Does your coffin fit differently lately? Why not try Morbid M. Cadaver's extensible caskets? They are scientifically designed to fit the natural curves of the body, and are enriched with Vitamin B_1. Use Cadaver's caskets for comfort. Remember – you're – going – to – be – dead – a – long – long – time!'

It wasn't quite sound, but whatever it was, it died away in an oily rumbling whisper.

The white thread that might have been Powell heaved uselessly at the insubstantial eons of time that existed all about him – and collapsed upon itself as the piercing shriek of a hundred million ghosts of a hundred million soprano voices rose to a crescendo:

'I'll be glad when you're dead, you rascal, you.
'I'll be glad when you're dead, you rascal, you.
'I'll be glad – '

It rose up a spiral stairway of violent sound into the keening supersonics that passed hearing, and then beyond –

The white thread quivered with a pulsating pang. It strained quietly –

The voices were ordinary – and many. It was a crowd speaking; a swirling mob that swept through and past and over him with a rapid, headlong motion, that left drifting tatters of words behind them.

'What did they getcha for, boy? Y'look banged up – '

' – a hot fire, I guess, but I got a case – '

' – I've made Paradise, but old St Pete – '

'Naaah, I got a pull with the boy. Had dealings with him – '

'Hey, Sam, come this way – '

'Ja get a mouthpiece? Beelzebub says – '

' – Going on, my good imp? My appointment is with Sa – '

And above it all the original stentorian roar, that plunged across all:

'HURRY! HURRY! HURRY!!! Stir your bones, and don't keep us waiting – there are many more in line. Have your certificates ready, and make sure Peter's release is stamped across it. See if you are at the proper entrance gate. There will be plenty of fire for all. Hey, you – YOU DOWN THERE. TAKE YOUR PLACE IN LINE OR – '

The white thread that was Powell groveled backward before the advancing shout, and felt the sharp stab of the pointing finger. It all exploded into a rainbow of sound that dripped its fragments on to an aching brain.

Powell was in the chair again. He felt himself shaking.

Donovan's eyes were opening into two large popping bowls of glazed blue.

'Greg,' he whispered in what was almost a sob. 'Were you dead?'

'I . . . felt dead.' He did not recognize his own croak.

Donovan was obviously making a bad failure of his attempt to stand up, 'Are we alive now? Or is there more?'

'I . . . feel alive.' It was the same hoarseness. Powell said cautiously, 'Did you . . . hear anything, when . . . when you were dead?'

Donovan paused, and then very slowly nodded his head, 'Did you?'

'Yes. Did you hear about coffins . . . and females singing . . . and the lines forming to get into Hell? Did you?'

Donovan shook his head, 'Just one voice.'

'Loud?'

'No. Soft, but rough like a file over the fingertips. It was a sermon, you know. About hell-fire. He described the tortures of . . . well, *you know*. I once heard a sermon like that – almost.'

He was perspiring.

* * *

They were conscious of sunlight through the port. It was weak, but it was blue-white – and the gleaming pea that was the distant source of light was not Old Sol.

And Powell pointed a trembling finger at the single gauge. The needle stood stiff and proud at the hairline whose figure read 300,000 parsecs.

Powell said, 'Mike if it's true, we must be out of the Galaxy altogether.'

Donovan said, 'Blazes! Greg! We'd be the first men out of the Solar System.'

'Yes! That's just it. We've escaped the sun. We've escaped the Galaxy. Mike, this ship is the answer. It means freedom for all humanity – freedom to spread through to every star that exists – millions and billions and trillions of them.'

And then he came down with a hard thud, 'But how do we get back, Mike?'

Donovan smiled shakily, 'Oh, that's all right. The ship brought us here. The ship will take us back. Me for more beans.'

'But Mike . . . hold on, Mike. If it takes us back the way it brought us here – '

Donovan stopped halfway up and sat back heavily into the chair.

Powell went on, 'We'll have to . . . die again, Mike.'

'Well,' sighed Donovan, 'if we have to, we have to. At least it isn't permanent, not *very* permanent.'

Susan Calvin was speaking slowly now. For six hours she had been slowly prodding The Brain – for six fruitless hours. She was weary of repetitions, weary of circumlocutions, weary of everything.

'Now, Brain, there's just one more thing. You must make a special effort to answer simply. Have you been entirely clear about the interstellar jump? I mean does it take them very far?'

'As far as they want to go, Miss Susan. Golly, it isn't any trick through the warp.'

'And on the other side, what will they see?'

'Stars and stuff. What do you suppose?'

The next question slipped out, 'They'll be alive, then?'

'Sure!'

'And the interstellar jump won't hurt them?'

She froze as The Brain maintained silence. That was it! She had touched the sore spot.

'Brain,' she supplicated faintly, 'Brain, do you hear me?'

The answer was weak, quivering. The Brain said, 'Do I have to answer? About the jump, I mean?'

'Not if you don't want to. But it would be interesting – I mean if you wanted to.' Susan Calvin tried to be bright about it.

'Aw-w-w. You spoil everything.'

And the psychologist jumped up suddenly, with a look of flaming insight on her face.

'Oh, my,' she gasped. 'Oh, my.'

And she felt the tension of hours and days released in a burst. It was later that she told Lanning, 'I tell you it's all right. No, you must leave me alone, now. The ship will be back safely, *with* the men, and I want to rest. I *will* rest. Now go away.'

The ship returned to Earth as silently, as unjarringly as it had left. It dropped precisely into place and the main lock gaped open. The two men who walked out felt their way carefully and scratched their rough and scrubbily-stubbled chins.

And then, slowly and purposefully, the one with red hair knelt down and planted upon the concrete of the runway a firm, loud kiss.

They waved aside the crowd that was gathering and made gestures of denial at the eager couple that had piled out of the down-swooping ambulance with a stretcher between them.

Gregory Powell said, 'Where's the nearest shower?'

They were led away.

They were gathered, all of them, about a table. It was a full staff meeting of the brains of US Robots and Mechanical Men Corporation.

Slowly and climactically, Powell and Donovan finished a graphic and resounding story.

Susan Calvin broke the silence that followed. In the few days that had elapsed she had recovered her icy, somewhat acid, calm – but still a trace of embarrassment broke through.

'Strictly speaking,' she said, 'this was my fault – all of it. When we first presented this problem to The Brain, as I hope some of you remember, I went to great lengths to impress upon it the importance of rejecting any item of information capable of creating a dilemma. In doing so I said something like "Don't get excited about the death of humans. We don't mind it at all. Just give the sheet back and forget it."'

'Hm-m-m,' said Lanning. 'What follows?'

'The obvious. When that item entered its calculations which yielded the equation controlling the length of minimum interval for the interstellar jump – it meant death for humans. That's where Consolidated's machine broke down completely. But I had depressed the importance of death to The Brain – not entirely, for the First Law can never be broken – but just sufficiently so that The Brain could take a second look at the equation. Sufficiently to give it time to realize that after the interval was passed through, the men would return to life – just as the matter and energy of the ship itself would return to being. This so-called "death" in other words, was a strictly temporary phenomenon. You see?'

She looked about her. They were all listening.

She went on, 'So it accepted the item, but not without a certain jar. Even with death temporary and its importance depressed, it was enough to unbalance it very gently.'

She brought it out calmly, 'It developed a sense of humor – it's an escape, you see, a method of partial escape from reality. It became a practical joker.'

Powell and Donovan were on their feet.

'What?' cried Powell.

Donovan was considerably more colorful about it.

'It's so,' said Calvin. 'It took care of you, and kept you safe, but you couldn't handle any controls, because they weren't for you – just for the humorous Brain. We could reach you by radio, but you couldn't answer. You had plenty of food, but all of it beans and milk. Then you died, so to speak, and were reborn, but the period of your death was made . . . well . . . interesting. I wish I knew how it did it. It was The Brain's prize little joke, but it meant no harm.'

'No harm!' gasped Donovan. 'Oh, if that cute little tyke only had a neck.'

Lanning raised a quieting hand, 'All right, it's been a mess, but it's all over. What now?'

'Well,' said Bogert, quietly, 'obviously it's up to us to improve the space-warp engine. There must be some way of getting around that interval of jump. If there is, we're the only organization left with a grand-scale super-robot, so we're bound to find it if anyone. And then – US Robots has interstellar travel, and humanity has the opportunity for galactic empire.'

'What about Consolidated?' said Lanning.

'Hey,' interrupted Donovan suddenly, 'I want to make a suggestion there. They landed US Robots into quite a mess. It wasn't as bad a mess as they expected and it turned out well, but their intentions weren't pious. And Greg and I bore the most of it.

'Well, they wanted an answer, and they've got one. Send them that ship, guaranteed, and US Robots can collect their two hundred thou plus construction costs. And if they test it – then suppose we let The Brain have just a little more fun before it's brought back to normal.'

Lanning said gravely, 'It sounds just and proper to me.'

To which Bogert added absently, 'Strictly according to contract, too.'

Evidence

Francis Quinn was a politician of the new school. That, of course, is a meaningless expression, as are all expressions of the sort. Most of the 'new schools' we have were duplicated in the social life of ancient Greece, and perhaps, if we knew more about it, in the social life of ancient Sumeria and in the lake dwellings of prehistoric Switzerland as well.

But, to get out from under what promises to be a dull and complicated beginning, it might be best to state hastily that Quinn neither ran for office nor canvassed for votes, made no speeches and stuffed no ballot boxes. Any more than Napoleon pulled a trigger at Austerlitz.

And since politics makes strange bedfellows, Alfred Lanning sat at the other side of the desk with his ferocious white eyebrows bent far forward over eyes in which chronic impatience had sharpened to acuity. He was not pleased.

The fact, if known to Quinn, would have annoyed him not the least. His voice was friendly, perhaps professionally so.

'I assume you know Stephen Byerley, Dr Lanning.'

'I have heard of him. So have many people.'

'Yes, so have I. Perhaps you intend voting for him at the next election.'

'I couldn't say.' There was an unmistakable trace of acidity here. 'I have not followed the political currents, so I'm not aware that he is running for office.'

'He may be our next mayor. Of course, he is only a lawyer now, but great oaks – '

'Yes,' interrupted Lanning, 'I have heard the phrase before. But I wonder if we can get to the business at hand.'

'We *are* at the business at hand, Dr Lanning.' Quinn's tone was very gentle, 'It is to my interest to keep Mr Byerley a district attorney at the very most, and it is to your interest to help me do so.'

'To *my* interest? Come!' Lanning's eyebrows hunched low.

'Well, say then to the interest of the US Robots and Mechanical Men Corporation. I come to you as Director-Emeritus of Research, because I know that your connection to them is that of, shall we say, "elder statesman." You are listened to with respect and yet your connection with them is no longer so tight but that you cannot possess considerable freedom of action; even if the action is somewhat unorthodox.'

Dr Lanning was silent a moment, chewing the cud of his thoughts. He said more softly, 'I don't follow you at all, Mr Quinn.'

'I am not surprised, Dr Lanning. But it's all rather simple. Do you mind?' Quinn lit a slender cigarette with a lighter of tasteful simplicity and his big-boned face settled into an expression of quiet amusement. 'We have spoken of Mr Byerley – a strange and colorful character. He was unknown three years ago. He is very well known now. He is a man of force and ability, and certainly the most capable and intelligent prosecutor I have ever known. Unfortunately he is not a friend of mine – '

'I understand,' said Lanning, mechanically. He stared at his fingernails.

'I have had occasion,' continued Quinn, evenly, 'in the past year to investigate Mr Byerley – quite exhaustively. It is always useful, you see, to subject the past life of reform politicians to rather inquisitive research. If you knew how often it helped – ' He paused to smile humorlessly at the glowing tip of his cigarette. 'But Mr Byerley's past is unremarkable. A quiet life in a small town, a college education, a wife who died young, an auto accident with a slow recovery, law school, coming to the metropolis, an attorney.'

Francis Quinn shook his head slowly, then added, 'But his present life. Ah, that is remarkable. Our district attorney never eats!'

Lanning's head snapped up, old eyes surprisingly sharp, 'Pardon me?'

'Our district attorney never eats.' The repetition thumped by syllables. 'I'll modify that slightly. He has never been seen to eat or drink. Never! Do you understand the significance of the word? Not rarely, but never!'

'I find that quite incredible. Can you trust your investigators?'

'I can trust my investigators, and I don't find it incredible at all. Further, our district attorney has never been seen to drink – in the aqueous sense as well as the alcoholic – nor to sleep. There are other factors, but I should think I have made my point.'

Lanning leaned back in his seat, and there was the rapt silence of challenge and response between them and then the old roboticist shook his head. 'No. There is only one thing you can be trying to imply, if I couple your statements with the fact that you present them to me, and that is impossible.'

'But the man is quite inhuman, Dr Lanning.'

'If you told me he were Satan in masquerade, there would be a faint chance that I might believe you.'

'I tell you he is a robot, Dr Lanning.'

'I tell you it is as impossible a conception as I have ever heard, Mr Quinn.'

Again the combative silence.

'Nevertheless,' and Quinn stubbed out his cigarette with elaborate care, 'you will have to investigate this impossibility with all the resources of the Corporation.'

'I'm sure that I could undertake no such thing, Mr Quinn. You don't seriously suggest that the Corporation take part in local politics.'

'You have no choice. Supposing I were to make my facts public without proof. The evidence is circumstantial enough.'

'Suit yourself in that respect.'

'But it would not suit me. Proof would be much preferable. And it would not suit *you*, for the publicity would be very damaging to your company. You are perfectly well acquainted, I suppose, with the strict rules against the use of robots on inhabited worlds.'

'Certainly!' – brusquely.

'You know that the US Robots and Mechanical Men Corporation is the only manufacturer of positronic robots in the Solar System, and if Byerley is a robot, he is a *positronic* robot. You are also aware that all positronic robots are leased, and not sold; that the Corporation remains the owner and manager of each robot, and is therefore responsible for the actions of all.'

'It is an easy matter, Mr Quinn, to prove the Corporation has never manufactured a robot of a humanoid character.'

'It can be done? To discuss merely possibilities.'

'Yes. It can be done.'

'Secretly, I imagine, as well. Without entering it in your books.'

'Not the positronic brain, sir. Too many factors are involved in that, and there is the tightest possible government supervision.'

'Yes, but robots are worn out, break down, go out of order – and are dismantled.'

'And the positronic brains re-used or destroyed.'

'Really?' Francis Quinn allowed himself a trace of sarcasm. 'And if one were, accidentally, of course, not destroyed – and there happened to be a humanoid structure waiting for a brain.'

'Impossible!'

'You would have to prove that to the government and the public, so why not prove it to me now.'

'But what could our purpose be?' demanded Lanning in exasperation. 'Where is our motivation? Credit us with a minimum of sense.'

'My dear sir, please. The Corporation would be only too glad to have the various Regions permit the use of humanoid positronic robots on inhabited worlds. The profits would be enormous. But the prejudice of the public against such a practice is too great. Suppose you get them used to such robots first – see, we have a skillful lawyer, a good mayor, – and he is a robot. Won't you buy our robot butlers?'

'Thoroughly fantastic. An almost humorous descent to the ridiculous.'

'I imagine so. Why not prove it? Or would you still rather try to prove it to the public?'

The light in the office was dimming, but it was not yet too dim to obscure the flush of frustration on Alfred Lanning's face. Slowly, the roboticist's finger touched a knob and the wall illuminators glowed to gentle life.

'Well, then,' he growled, 'let us see.'

The face of Stephen Byerley is not an easy one to describe. He was forty by birth certificate and forty by appearance – but it was a healthy, well-nourished good-natured appearance of forty; one that automatically drew the teeth of the bromide about 'looking one's age.'

This was particularly true when he laughed, and he was laughing now. It came loudly and continuously, died away for a bit, then began again –

And Alfred Lanning's face contracted into a rigidly bitter

monument of disapproval. He made a half gesture to the woman who sat beside him, but her thin, bloodless lips merely pursed themselves a trifle.

Byerley gasped himself a stage nearer normality.

'Really, Dr Lanning . . . really – I . . . *I* . . . a robot?'

Lanning bit his words off with a snap, 'It is no statement of mine, sir. I would be quite satisfied to have you a member of humanity. Since our corporation never manufactured you, I am quite certain that you are – in a legalistic sense, at any rate. But since the contention that you are a robot has been advanced to us seriously by a man of certain standing – '

'Don't mention his name, if it would knock a chip off your granite block of ethics, but let's pretend it was Frank Quinn, for the sake of argument, and continue.'

Lanning drew in a sharp, cutting snort at the interruption, and paused ferociously before continuing with added frigidity, ' – by a man of certain standing, with whose identity I am not interested in playing guessing games, I am bound to ask your cooperation in disproving it. The mere fact that such a contention could be advanced and publicized by the means at this man's disposal would be a bad blow to the company I represent – even if the charge were never proven. You understand me?'

'Oh, yes, your position is clear to me. The charge itself is ridiculous. The spot you find yourself in is not. I beg your pardon, if my laughter offended you. It was the first I laughed at, not the second. How can I help you?'

'It could be very simple. You have only to sit down to a meal at a restaurant in the presence of witnesses, have your picture taken, and eat.' Lanning sat back in his chair, the worst of the interview over. The woman beside him watched Byerley with an apparently absorbed expression but contributed nothing of her own.

Stephen Byerley met her eyes for an instant, was caught

by them, then turned back to the roboticist. For a while his fingers were thoughtful over the bronze paper-weight that was the only ornament on his desk.

He said quietly, 'I don't think I can oblige you.'

He raised his hand, 'Now wait, Dr Lanning. I appreciate the fact that this whole matter is distasteful to you, that you have been forced into it against your will, that you feel you are playing an undignified and even ridiculous part. Still, the matter is even more intimately concerned with myself, so be tolerant.

'First, what makes you think that Quinn – this man of certain standing, you know – wasn't hoodwinking you, in order to get you to do exactly what you are doing?'

'Why, it seems scarcely likely that a reputable person would endanger himself in so ridiculous a fashion, if he weren't convinced he were on safe ground.'

There was little humor in Byerley's eyes, 'You don't know Quinn. He could manage to make safe ground out of a ledge a mountain sheep could not handle. I suppose he showed the particulars of the investigation he claims to have made of me?'

'Enough to convince me that it would be too troublesome to have our corporation attempt to disprove them when you could do so more easily.'

'Then you believe him when he says I never eat. You are a scientist, Dr Lanning. Think of the logic required. I have not been observed to eat, therefore I never eat Q.E.D. After all!'

'You are using prosecution tactics to confuse what is really a very simple situation.'

'On the contrary, I am trying to clarify what you and Quinn between you are making a very complicated one. You see, I don't sleep much, that's true, and I certainly don't sleep in public. I have never cared to eat with others – an idiosyncrasy which is unusual and probably neurotic in character, but which harms no one. Look, Dr Lanning, let me present you with a suppositious case. Supposing we had a politician who was interested in defeating a reform candidate at any cost and while investigating his private life came across oddities such as I have just mentioned.

'Suppose further that in order to smear the candidate effectively, he comes to your company as the ideal agent. Do you expect him to say to you, "So-and-so is a robot because he hardly ever eats with people, and I have never seen him fall asleep in the middle of a case; and once when I peeped into his window in the middle of the night, there he was, sitting up with a book; and I looked in his frigidaire and there was no food in it."

'If he told you that, you would send for a straitjacket. But it he tells you, "He *never* sleeps; he *never* eats," then the shock of the statement blinds you to the fact that such statements are impossible to prove. You play into his hands by contributing to the to-do.'

'Regardless, sir,' began Lanning, with a threatening obstinacy, 'of whether you consider this matter serious or not, it will require only the meal I mentioned to end it.'

Again Byerley turned to the woman, who still regarded him expressionlessly. 'Pardon me. I've caught your name correctly, haven't I? Dr Susan Calvin?'

'Yes, Mr Byerley.'

'You're the US Robots' psychologist, aren't you?'

'*Robo*psychologist, please.'

'Oh, are robots so different from men, mentally?'

'Worlds different.' She allowed herself a frosty smile, 'Robots are essentially decent.'

Humor tugged at the corners of the lawyer's mouth, 'Well, that's a hard blow. But what I wanted to say was this. Since you're a psycho – a robopsychologist, *and* a woman,

I'll bet that you've done something that Dr Lanning hasn't thought of.'

'And what is that?'

'You've got something to eat in your purse.'

Something caught in the schooled indifference of Susan Calvin's eyes. She said, 'You surprise me, Mr Byerley.'

And opening her purse, she produced an apple. Quietly, she handed it to him. Dr Lanning, after an initial start, followed the slow movement from one hand to the other with sharply alert eyes.

Calmly, Stephen Byerley bit into it, and calmly he swallowed it.

'You see, Dr Lanning?'

Dr Lanning smiled in a relief tangible enough to make even his eyebrows appear benevolent. A relief that survived for one fragile second.

Susan Calvin said, 'I was curious to see if you would eat it, but, of course, in the present case, it proves nothing.'

Byerley grinned, 'It doesn't?'

'Of course not. It is obvious, Dr Lanning, that if this man were a humanoid robot, he would be a perfect imitation. He is almost too human to be credible. After all, we have been seeing and observing human beings all our lives; it would be impossible to palm something merely nearly right off on us. It would have to be *all* right. Observe the texture of the skin, the quality of the irises, the bone formation of the hand. If he's a robot, I wish US Robots *had* made him, because he's a good job. Do you suppose then, that anyone capable of paying attention to such niceties would neglect a few gadgets to take care of such things as eating, sleeping, elimination? For emergency use only, perhaps; as, for instance, to prevent such situations as are arising here. So a meal won't really prove anything.'

'Now wait,' snarled Lanning, 'I am not quite the fool both of you make me out to be. I am not interested in the problem of Mr Byerley's humanity or nonhumanity. I am interested in getting the corporation out of a hole. A public meal will end the matter and keep it ended no matter what Quinn does. We can leave the finer details to lawyers and robopsychologists.'

'But, Dr Lanning,' said Byerley, 'you forget the politics of the situation. I am anxious to be elected, as Quinn is to stop me. By the way, did you notice that you used his name. It's a cheap shyster trick of mine; I knew you would, before you were through.'

Lanning flushed, 'What has the election to do with it?'

'Publicity works both ways, sir. If Quinn wants to call me a robot, and has the nerve to do so, I have the nerve to play the game his way.'

'You mean you – ' Lanning was quite frankly appalled.

'Exactly. I mean that I'm going to let him go ahead, choose his rope, test its strength, cut off the right length, tie the noose, insert his head and grin. I can do what little else is required.'

'You are mighty confident.'

Susan Calvin rose to her feet, 'Come, Alfred, we won't change his mind for him.'

'You see.' Byerley smiled gently. 'You're a human psychologist, too.'

But perhaps not all the confidence that Dr Lanning had remarked upon was present that evening when Byerley's car parked on the automatic treads leading to the sunken garage, and Byerley himself crossed the path to the front door of his house.

The figure in the wheel chair looked up as he entered and smiled. Byerley's face lit with affection. He crossed over to it.

The cripple's voice was a hoarse, grating whisper that came out of a mouth forever twisted to one side, leering out of a face that was half scar tissue, 'You're late, Steve.'

'I know, John, I know. But I've been up against a peculiar and interesting trouble today.'

'So?' Neither the torn face nor the destroyed voice could carry expression but there was anxiety in the clear eyes. 'Nothing you can't handle?'

'I'm not exactly certain. I may need your help. *You're* the brilliant one in the family. Do you want me to take you out into the garden? It's a beautiful evening.'

Two strong arms lifted John from the wheel chair. Gently, almost caressingly, Byerley's arms went around the shoulders and under the swathed legs of the cripple. Carefully, and slowly, he walked through the rooms, down the gentle ramp that had been built with a wheel chair in mind, and out the back door into the walled and wired garden behind the house.

'Why don't you let me use the wheel chair, Steve? This is silly.'

'Because I'd rather carry you. Do you object? You know that you're as glad to get out of that motorized buggy for a while as I am to see you out. How do you feel today?' He deposited John with infinite care upon the cool grass.

'How should I feel? But tell me about your trouble.'

'Quinn's campaign will be based on the fact that he claims I'm a robot.'

John's eyes opened wide, 'How do you know? It's impossible. I won't believe it.'

'Oh, come, I tell you it's so. He had one of the big-shot scientists of US Robots and Mechanical Men Corporation over at the office to argue with me.'

Slowly John's hands tore at the grass, 'I see. I see.'

Byerley said, 'But we can let him choose his ground. I have an idea. Listen to me and tell me if we can do it – '

The scene as it appeared in Alfred Lanning's office that night was a tableau of stares. Francis Quinn stared meditatively at Alfred Lanning. Lanning's stare was savagely set upon Susan Calvin, who stared impassively in her turn at Quinn.

Francis Quinn broke it with a heavy attempt at lightness, 'Bluff. He's making it up as he goes along.'

'Are you going to gamble on that, Mr Quinn?' asked Dr Calvin, indifferently.

'Well, it's your gamble, really.'

'Look here,' Lanning covered definite pessimism with bluster, 'we've done what you asked. We witnessed the man eat. It's ridiculous to presume him a robot.'

'Do *you* think so?' Quinn shot toward Calvin. 'Lanning said you were the expert.'

Lanning was almost threatening, 'Now, Susan – '

Quinn interrupted smoothly, 'Why not let her talk, man? She's been sitting there imitating a gatepost for half an hour.'

Lanning felt definitely harassed. From what he experienced then to incipient paranoia was but a step. He said, 'Very well. Have your say, Susan. We won't interrupt you.'

Susan Calvin glanced at him humorlessly, then fixed cold eyes on Mr Quinn. 'There are only two ways of definitely proving Byerley to be a robot, sir. So far you are presenting circumstantial evidence, with which you can accuse, but not prove – and I think Mr Byerley is sufficiently clever to counter that sort of material. You probably think so yourself, or you wouldn't have come here.

'The two methods of *proof* are the physical and the psychological. Physically, you can dissect him or use an X-ray. How to do that would be *your* problem. Psychologically, his behavior can be studied, for if he *is* a positronic robot, he must conform to the three Rules of Robotics. A positronic brain can not be constructed without them. You know the Rules, Mr Quinn?'

She spoke them carefully, clearly, quoting word for word

the famous bold print on page one of the 'Handbook of Robotics.'

'I've heard of them,' said Quinn, carelessly.

'Then the matter is easy to follow,' responded the psychologist, dryly. 'If Mr Byerley breaks any of those three rules, he is not a robot. Unfortunately, this procedure works in only one direction. If he lives up to the rules, it proves nothing one way or the other.'

Quinn raised polite eyebrows, 'Why not, doctor?'

'Because, if you stop to think of it, the three Rules of Robotics are the essential guiding principles of a good many of the world's ethical systems. Of course, every human being is supposed to have the instinct of self-preservation. That's Rule Three to a robot. Also every "good" human being, with a social conscience and a sense of responsibility, is supposed to defer to proper authority; to listen to his doctor, his boss, his government, his psychiatrist, his fellow man; to obey laws, to follow rules, to conform to custom – even when they interfere with his comfort or his safety. That's Rule Two to a robot. Also, every "good" human being is supposed to love others as himself, protect his fellow man, risk his life to save another. That's Rule One to a robot. To put it simply – if Byerley follows all the Rules of Robotics, he may be a robot, and may simply be a very good man.'

'But,' said Quinn, 'you're telling me that you can never prove him a robot.'

'I may be able to prove him *not* a robot.'

'That's not the proof I want.'

'You'll have such proof as exists. You are the only one responsible for your own wants.'

Here Lanning's mind leaped suddenly to the sting of an idea, 'Has it occurred to anyone,' he ground out, 'that district attorney is a rather strange occupation for a robot?

The prosecution of human beings – sentencing them to death – bringing about their infinite harm – '

Quinn grew suddenly keen, 'No, you can't get out of it that way. Being district attorney doesn't make him human. Don't you know his record? Don't you know that he boasts that he has never prosecuted an innocent man; that there are scores of people left untried because the evidence against them didn't satisfy him, even though he could probably have argued a jury into atomizing them? That happens to be so.'

Lanning's thin cheeks quivered, 'No, Quinn, no. There is nothing in the Rules of Robotics that makes any allowance for human guilt. A robot may not judge whether a human being deserves death. It is not for him to decide. *He may not harm a human* – variety skunk, or variety angel.'

Susan Calvin sounded tired. 'Alfred,' she said, 'don't talk foolishly. What if a robot came upon a madman about to set fire to a house with people in it. He would stop the madman, wouldn't he?'

'Of course.'

'And if the only way he could stop him was to kill him – '

There was a faint sound in Lanning's throat. Nothing more.

'The answer to that, Alfred, is that he would do his best not to kill him. If the madman died, the robot would require psychotherapy because he might easily go mad at the conflict presented him – of having broken Rule One to adhere to Rule One in a higher sense. But a man would be dead and a robot would have killed him.'

'Well, *is* Byerley mad?' demanded Lanning, with all the sarcasm he could muster.

'No, but he has killed no man himself. He has exposed facts which might represent a particular human being to be dangerous to the large mass of other human beings we call society. He protects the greater number and thus adheres to

Rule One at maximum potential. That is as far as he goes. It is the judge who then condemns the criminal to death or imprisonment, after the jury decides on his guilt or innocence. It is the jailer who imprisons him, the executioner who kills him. And Mr Byerley has done nothing but determine truth and aid society.

'As a matter of fact, Mr Quinn, I have looked into Mr Byerley's career since you first brought this matter to our attention. I find that he has never demanded the death sentence in his closing speeches to the jury. I also find that he has spoken on behalf of the abolition of capital punishment and contributed generously to research institutions engaged in criminal neurophysiology. He apparently believes in the cure, rather than the punishment of crime. I find that significant.'

'You do?' Quinn smiled. 'Significant of a certain odor of roboticity, perhaps?'

'Perhaps. Why deny it? Actions such as his could come only from a robot, or from a very honorable and decent human being. But you see, you just can't differentiate between a robot and the very best of humans.'

Quinn sat back in his chair. His voice quivered with impatience. 'Dr Lanning, it's perfectly possible to create a humanoid robot that would perfectly duplicate a human in appearance, isn't it?'

Lanning harrumphed and considered, 'It's been done experimentally by US Robots,' he said reluctantly, 'without the addition of a positronic brain, of course. By using human ova and hormone control, one can grow human flesh and skin over a skeleton of porous silicone plastics that would defy external examination. The eyes, the hair, the skin would be really human, not humanoid. And if you put a positronic brain, and such other gadgets as you might desire inside, you have a humanoid robot.'

Quinn said shortly, 'How long would it take to make one?'

Lanning considered, 'If you had all your equipment – the brain, the skeleton, the ovum, the proper hormones and radiations – say, two months.'

The politician straightened out of his chair. 'Then we shall see what the insides of Mr Byerley look like. It will mean publicity for US Robots – but I gave you your chance.'

Lanning turned impatiently to Susan Calvin, when they were alone. 'Why do you insist – '

And with real feeling, she responded sharply and instantly, 'Which do you want – the truth or my resignation? I won't lie for you. US Robots can take care of itself. Don't turn coward.'

'What,' said Lanning, 'if he opens up Byerley, and wheels and gears fall out. What then?'

'He won't open Byerley,' said Calvin, disdainfully. 'Byerley is as clever as Quinn, at the very least.'

The news broke upon the city a week before Byerley was to have been nominated. But 'broke' is the wrong word. It staggered upon the city, shambled, crawled. Laughter began, and wit was free. And as the far-off hand of Quinn tightened its pressure in easy stages, the laughter grew forced, an element of hollow uncertainty entered, and people broke off to wonder.

The convention itself had the air of a restive stallion. There had been no contest planned. Only Byerley could possibly have been nominated a week earlier. There was no substitute even now. They had to nominate him, but there was complete confusion about it.

It would not have been so bad if the average individual were not torn between the enormity of the charge, if true, and its sensational folly, if false.

The day after Byerley was nominated perfunctorily, hollowly – a newspaper finally published the gist of a long interview with Dr Susan Calvin, 'world famous expert on robopsychology and positronics.'

What broke loose is popularly and succinctly described as hell.

It was what the Fundamentalists were waiting for. They were not a political party; they made pretense to no formal religion. Essentially they were those who had not adapted themselves to what had once been called the Atomic Age, in the days when atoms were a novelty. Actually, they were the Simple-Lifers, hungering after a life, which to those who lived it had probably appeared not so Simple, and who had been, therefore, Simple-Lifers themselves.

The Fundamentalists required no new reason to detest robots and robot manufacturers; but a new reason such as the Quinn accusation and the Calvin analysis was sufficient to make such detestation audible.

The huge plants of the US Robots and Mechanical Men Corporation was a hive that spawned armed guards. It prepared for war.

Within the city the house of Stephen Byerley bristled with police.

The political campaign, of course, lost all other issues, and resembled a campaign only in that it was something filling the hiatus between nomination and election.

Stephen Byerley did not allow the fussy little man to distract him. He remained comfortably unperturbed by the uniforms in the background. Outside the house, past the line of grim guards, reporters and photographers waited according to the tradition of the caste. One enterprising 'visor station even had a scanner focused on the blank entrance to the prosecutor's unpretentious home, while a synthetically excited announcer filled in with inflated commentary.

The fussy little man advanced. He held forward a rich,

complicated sheet. 'This, Mr Byerley, is a court order authorizing me to search these premises for the presence of illegal . . . uh . . . mechanical men or robots of any description.'

Byerley half rose, and took the paper. He glanced at it indifferently, and smiled as he handed it back. 'All in order. Go ahead. Do your job. Mrs Hoppen' – to his housekeeper, who appeared reluctantly from the next room – 'please go with them, and help out if you can.'

The little man, whose name was Harroway, hesitated, produced an unmistakable blush, failed completely to catch Byerley's eyes, and muttered, 'Come on,' to the two policemen.

He was back in ten minutes.

'Through?' questioned Byerley, in just the tone of a person who is not particularly interested in the question, or its answer.

Harroway cleared his throat, made a bad start in falsetto, and began again, angrily, 'Look here, Mr Byerley, our special instructions were to search the house very thoroughly.'

'And haven't you?'

'We were told exactly what to look for.'

'Yes?'

'In short, Mr Byerley, and not to put too fine a point on it, we were told to search you.'

'Me?' said the prosecutor with a broadening smile. 'And how do you intend to do that?'

'We have a Penet-radiation unit – '

'Then I'm to have my X-ray photograph taken, hey? You have the authority?'

'You saw my warrant.'

'May I see it again?'

Harroway, his forehead shining with considerably more than mere enthusiasm, passed it over a second time.

Byerley said evenly, 'I read here as the description of what you are to search; I quote: "the dwelling place belonging to Stephen Allen Byerley, located at 355 Willow Grove, Evanstron, together with any garage, storehouse or other structures or buildings thereto appertaining, together with all grounds thereto appertaining" . . . um . . . and so on. Quite an order. But, my good man, it doesn't say anything about searching my interior. I am not part of the premises. You may search my clothes if you think I've got a robot hidden in my pocket.'

Harroway had no doubt on the point of to whom he owed his job. He did not propose to be backward, given a chance to earn a much better – i.e., more highly paid – job.

He said, in a faint echo of bluster, 'Look here. I'm allowed to search the furniture in your house, and anything else I find in it. You are in it, aren't you?'

'A remarkable observation. I *am* in it. But I'm not a piece of furniture. As a citizen of adult responsibility – I have the psychiatric certificate proving that – I have certain rights under the Regional Articles. Searching me would come under the heading of violating my Right of Privacy. That paper isn't sufficient.'

'Sure, but if you're a robot, you don't have Right of Privacy.'

'True enough – but that paper still isn't sufficient. It recognizes me implicitly as a human being.'

'Where?' Harroway snatched at it.

'Where it says "the dwelling place belonging to" and so on. A robot cannot own property. And you may tell your employer, Mr Harroway, that if he tries to issue a similar paper which does *not* implicitly recognize me as a human being, he will be immediately faced with a restraining injunction and a civil suit which will make it necessary for him to *prove* me a robot by means of information *now* in his possession, or else to pay a whopping penalty for an attempt to deprive me unduly of my Rights under the Regional Articles. You'll tell him that, won't you?'

Harroway marched to the door. He turned. 'You're a slick lawyer – ' His hand was in his pocket. For a short moment, he stood there. Then he left, smiled in the direction of the 'visor scanner, still playing away – waved to the reporters, and shouted, 'We'll have something for you tomorrow, boys. No kidding.'

In his ground car, he settled back, removed the tiny mechanism from his pocket and carefully inspected it. It was the first time he had ever taken a photograph by X-ray reflection. He hoped he had done it correctly.

Quinn and Byerley had never met face-to-face alone. But visorphone was pretty close to it. In fact, accepted literally, perhaps the phrase was accurate, even if to each, the other were merely the light and dark pattern of a bank of photocells.

It was Quinn who had initiated the call. It was Quinn, who spoke first, and without particular ceremony, 'Thought you would like to know, Byerley, that I intend to make public the fact that you're wearing a protective shield against Penet-radiation.'

'That so? In that case, you've probably already made it public. I have a notion our enterprising press representatives have been tapping my various communication lines for quite a while. I know they have my office lines full of holes; which is why I've dug in at my home these last weeks.' Byerley was friendly, almost chatty.

Quinn's lips tightened slightly, 'This call is shielded – thoroughly. I'm making it at a certain personal risk.'

'So I should imagine. Nobody knows you're behind this campaign. At least, nobody knows it officially. Nobody doesn't know it unofficially. I wouldn't worry. So I wear a protective shield? I suppose you found that out when your puppy dog's Penet-radiation photograph, the other day, turned out to be overexposed.'

'You realize, Byerley, that it would be pretty obvious to everyone that you don't dare face X-ray analysis.'

'Also that you, or your men, attempted illegal invasion of my Right of Privacy.'

'The devil they'll care for that.'

'They might. It's rather symbolic of our two campaigns, isn't it? You have little concern with the rights of the individual citizen. I have great concern. I will not submit to X-ray analysis, because I wish to maintain my Rights on principle. Just as I'll maintain the rights of others when elected.'

'That will no doubt make a very interesting speech, but no one will believe you. A little too high-sounding to be true. Another thing,' a sudden, crisp change, 'the personnel in your home was not complete the other night.'

'In what way?'

'According to the report,' he shuffled papers before him that were just within the range of vision of the visiplate, 'there was one person missing – a cripple.'

'As you say,' said Byerley, tonelessly, 'a cripple. My old teacher, who lives with me and who is now in the country – and has been for two months. A "much-needed rest" is the usual expression applied in the case. He has your permission?'

'Your teacher? A scientist of sorts?'

'A lawyer once – before he was a cripple. He has a government license as a research biophysicist, with a laboratory of his own, and a complete description of the work he's doing filed with the proper authorities, to whom I can refer you. The work is minor, but is a harmless and engaging hobby for a – poor cripple. I am being as helpful as I can, you see.'

'I see. And what does this . . . teacher . . . know about robot manufacture?'

'I couldn't judge the extent of his knowledge in a field with which I am unacquainted.'

'He wouldn't have access to positronic brains?'

'Ask your friends at US Robots. They'd be the ones to know.'

'I'll put it shortly, Byerley. Your crippled teacher is the real Stephen Byerley. You are his robot creation. We can prove it. It was he who was in the automobile accident, not you. There will be ways of checking the records.'

'Really? Do so, then. My best wishes.'

'And we can search your so-called teacher's "country place," and see what we can find there.'

'Well, not quite, Quinn.' Byerley smiled broadly. 'Unfortunately for you, my so-called teacher is a sick man. His country place is his place of rest. His Right of Privacy as a citizen of adult responsibility is naturally even stronger, under the circumstances. You won't be able to obtain a warrant to enter his grounds without showing just cause. However, I'd be the last to prevent you from trying.'

There was a pause of moderate length, and then Quinn leaned forward, so that his imaged-face expanded and the fine lines on his forehead were visible, 'Byerley, why do you carry on? You can't be elected.'

'Can't I?'

'Do you think you can? Do you suppose that your failure to make any attempt to disprove the robot charge – when you could easily, by breaking one of the Three Laws – does anything but convince the people that you *are* a robot?'

'All I see so far is that from being a rather vaguely known, but still largely obscure metropolitan lawyer, I have now become a world figure. You're a good publicist.'

'But you *are* a robot.'

'So it's been said, but not proven.'

'It's been proven sufficiently for the electorate.'

'Then relax – you've won.'

'Good-by,' said Quinn, with his first touch of viciousness, and the visorphone slammed off.

'Good-by,' said Byerley imperturbably, to the blank plate.

Byerley brought his 'teacher' back the week before election. The air car dropped quickly in an obscure part of the city.

'You'll stay here till after election,' Byerley told him. 'It would be better to have you out of the way if things take a bad turn.'

The hoarse voice that twisted painfully out of John's crooked mouth might have had accents of concern in it. 'There's danger of violence?'

'The Fundamentalists threaten it, so I suppose there is, in a theoretical sense. But I really don't expect it. The Fundies have no real power. They're just the continuous irritant factor that might stir up a riot after a while. You don't mind staying here? Please. I won't be myself if I have to worry .bout you.'

'Oh, I'll stay. You still think it will go well?'

'I'm sure of it. No one bothered you at the place?'

'No one. I'm certain.'

'And your part went well?'

'Well enough. There'll be no trouble there.'

'Then take care of yourself, and watch the televisor tomorrow, John.' Byerley pressed the gnarled hand that rested on his.

Lenton's forehead was a furrowed study in suspense. He had the completely unenviable job of being Byerley's campaign manager in a campaign that wasn't a campaign, for a person that refused to reveal his strategy, and refused to accept his manager's.

'You can't!' It was his favorite phrase. It had become his only phrase. 'I tell you, Steve, you can't!'

He threw himself in front of the prosecutor, who was spending his time leafing through the typed pages of his speech.

'Put that down, Steve. Look, that mob has been organized by the Fundies. You won't get a hearing. You'll be stoned more likely. Why do you have to make a speech before an audience? What's wrong with a recording, a visual recording?'

'You want me to win the election, don't you?' asked Byerley, mildly.

'Win the election! You're not going to win, Steve. I'm trying to save your life.'

'Oh, I'm not in danger.'

'He's not in danger. He's not in danger.' Lenton made a queer, rasping sound in his throat. 'You mean you're getting out on that balcony in front of fifty thousand crazy crackpots and try to talk sense to them – on a balcony like a medieval dictator?'

Byerley consulted his watch. 'In about five minutes – as soon as the television lines are free.'

Lenton's answering remark was not quite transliterable.

The crowd filled a roped-off area of the city. Trees and houses seemed to grow out of a mass-human foundation. And by ultrawave, the rest of the world watched. It was a purely local election, but it had a world audience just the same. Byerley thought of that and smiled.

But there was nothing to smile at in the crowd itself. There were banners and streamers, ringing every possible change on his supposed roboticity. The hostile attitude rose thickly and tangibly into the atmosphere.

From the start the speech was not successful. It competed against the inchoate mob howl and the rhythmic cries of the Fundie claques that formed mob-islands within the mob. Byerley spoke on, slowly, unemotionally –

Inside, Lenton clutched his hair and groaned – and waited for the blood.

There was a writhing in the front ranks. An angular citizen with popping eyes, and clothes too short for the lank length of his limbs, was pulling to the fore. A policeman dived after him, making slow, struggling passage. Byerley waved the latter off, angrily.

The thin man was directly under the balcony. His words tore unheard against the roar.

Byerley leaned forward. 'What do you say? If you have a legitimate question, I'll answer it.' He turned to a flanking guard. 'Bring that man up here.'

There was a tensing in the crowd. Cries of 'Quiet' started in various parts of the mob, and rose to a bedlam, then toned down raggedly. The thin man, red-faced and panting, faced Byerley.

Byerley said, 'Have you a question?'

The thin man stared, and said in a cracked voice, 'Hit me!'

With sudden energy, he thrust out his chin at an angle. 'Hit me! You say you're not a robot. Prove it. You can't hit a human, you monster.'

There was a queer, flat, dead silence. Byerley's voice punctured it. 'I have no reason to hit you.'

The thin man was laughing wildly. 'You *can't* hit me. You *won't* hit me. You're not a human. You're a monster, a make-believe man.'

And Stephen Byerley, tight-lipped, in the face of thousands who watched in person and the millions who watched by screen, drew back his fist and caught the man crackingly upon the chin. The challenger went over backwards in sudden collapse, with nothing on his face but blank, blank surprise.

Byerley said, 'I'm sorry. Take him in and see that he's comfortable. I want to speak to him when I'm through.'

And when Dr Calvin, from her reserved space, turned her automobile and drove off, only one reporter had recovered sufficiently from the shock to race after her, and shout an unheard question.

Susan Calvin called over her shoulder, 'He's human.'

That was enough. The reporter raced away in his own direction.

The rest of the speech might be described as 'Spoken but not heard.'

Dr Calvin and Stephen Byerley met once again – a week before he took the oath of office as mayor. It was late – past midnight.

Dr Calvin said, 'You don't look tired.'

The mayor-elect smiled. 'I may stay up for a while. Don't tell Quinn.'

'I shan't. But that was an interesting story of Quinn's, since you mention him. It's a shame to have spoiled it. I suppose you knew his theory?'

'Parts of it.'

'It was highly dramatic. Stephen Byerley was a young lawyer, a powerful speaker, a great idealist – and with a certain flair for biophysics. Are you interested in robotics, Mr Byerley?'

'Only in the legal aspects.'

'*This* Stephen Byerley was. But here was an accident. Byerley's wife died; he himself, worse. His legs were gone; his face was gone; his voice was gone. Part of his mind was – bent. He would not submit to plastic surgery. He retired from the world, legal career gone – only his intelligence, and his hands left. Somehow he could obtain positronic brains, even a complex one, one which had the greatest capacity of forming judgments in ethical problems – which is the highest robotic function so far developed.

'He grew a body about it. Trained it to be everything he

would have been and was no longer. He sent it out into the world as Stephen Byerley, remaining behind himself as the old, crippled teacher that no one ever saw – '

'Unfortunately,' said the mayor-elect, 'I ruined all that by hitting a man. The papers say it was your official verdict on the occasion that I was human.'

'How did that happen? Do you mind telling me? It couldn't have been accidental.'

'It wasn't entirely. Quinn did most of the work. My men started quietly spreading the fact that I had never hit a man; that I was unable to hit a man; that to fail to do so under provocation would be sure proof that I was a robot. So I arranged for a silly speech in public, with all sorts of publicity overtones, and almost inevitably, some fool fell for it. In its essence, it was what I call a shyster trick. One in which the artificial atmosphere which has been created does all the work. Of course, the emotional effects made my election certain, as intended.'

The robopsychologist nodded. 'I see you intrude on my field – as every politician must, I suppose. But I'm very sorry it turned out this way. I like robots. I like them considerably better than I do human beings. If a robot can be created capable of being a civil executive, I think he'd make the best one possible. By the Laws of Robotics, he'd be incapable of harming humans, incapable of tyranny, of corruption, of stupidity, of prejudice. And after he had served a decent term, he would leave, even though he were immortal, because it would be impossible for him to hurt humans by letting them know that a robot had ruled them. It would be most ideal.'

'Except that a robot might fail due to the inherent inadequacies of his brain. The positronic brain has never equalled the complexities of the human brain.'

'He would have advisers. Not even a human brain is capable of governing without assistance.'

Byerley considered Susan Calvin with grave interest. 'Why do you smile, Dr Calvin?'

'I smile because Mr Quinn didn't think of everything.'

'You mean there could be more to that story of his.'

'Only a little. For the three months before election, this Stephen Byerley that Mr Quinn spoke about, this broken man, was in the country for some mysterious reason. He returned in time for that famous speech of yours. And after all, what the old cripple did once, he could do a second time, particularly where the second job is very simple in comparison to the first.'

'I don't quite understand.'

Dr Calvin rose and smoothed her dress. She was obviously ready to leave. 'I mean there is one time when a robot may strike a human being without breaking the First Law. Just one time.'

'And when is that?'

Dr Calvin was at the door. She said quietly, 'When the human to be struck is merely another robot.'

She smiled broadly, her thin face glowing. 'Good-by, Mr Byerley. I hope to vote for you five years from now – for co-ordinator.'

Stephen Byerley chuckled. 'I must reply that that is a somewhat farfetched idea.'

The door closed behind her.

The Evitable Conflict

The Co-ordinator, in his private study, had that medieval curiosity, a fireplace. To be sure, the medieval man might not have recognized it as such, since it had no functional significance. The quiet, licking flame lay in an insulated recess behind clear quartz.

The logs were ignited at long distance through a trifling diversion of the energy beam that fed the public buildings of the city. The same button that controlled the ignition first dumped the ashes of the previous fire, and allowed for the entrance of fresh wood. – It was a thoroughly domesticated fireplace, you see.

But the fire itself was real. It was wired for sound, so that you could hear the crackle and, of course, you could watch it leap in the air stream that fed it.

The Co-ordinator's ruddy glass reflected, in miniature, the discreet gamboling of the flame, and, in even further miniature, it was reflected in each of his brooding pupils.

– And in the frosty pupils of his guest, Dr Susan Calvin of US Robots and Mechanical Men Corporation.

The Co-ordinator said, 'I did not ask you here entirely for social purposes, Susan.'

'I did not think you did, Stephen,' she replied.

' – And yet I don't quite know how to phrase my problem. On the one hand, it can be nothing at all. On the other, it can mean the end of humanity.'

'I have come across so many problems, Stephen, that presented the same alternative. I think all problems do.'

'Really? Then judge this – World Steel reports an over-production of twenty thousand long tons. The Mexican

Canal is two months behind schedule. The mercury mines at Almaden have experienced a production deficiency since last spring, while the Hydroponics plant at Tientsin has been laying men off. These items happen to come to mind at the moment. There is more of the same sort.'

'Are these things serious? I'm not economist enough to trace the fearful consequences of such things.'

'In themselves, they are not serious. Mining experts can be sent to Almaden, if the situation were to get worse. Hydroponics engineers can be used in Java or in Ceylon, if there are too many at Tientsin. Twenty thousand long tons of steel won't fill more than a few days of world demand, and the opening of the Mexican Canal two months later than the planned date is of little moment. It's the Machines that worry me; – I've spoken to your Director of Research about them already.'

'To Vincent Silver? – He hasn't mentioned anything about it to me.'

'I asked him to speak to no one. Apparently, he hasn't.'

'And what did he tell you?'

'Let me put that item in its proper place. I want to talk about the Machines first. And I want to talk about them to you, because you're the only one in the world who understands robots well enough to help me now. – May I grow philosophical?'

'For this evening, Stephen, you may talk how you please and of what you please, provided you tell me first what you intend to prove.'

'That such small unbalances in the perfection of our system of supply and demand, as I have mentioned, may be the first step towards the final war.'

'Hmp. Proceed.'

Susan Calvin did not allow herself to relax, despite the designed comfort of the chair she sat in. Her cold, thin-lipped face and her flat, even voice were becoming accentuated with the years. And although Stephen Byerley was one man she could like and trust, she was almost seventy and the cultivated habits of a lifetime are not easily broken.

'Every period of human development, Susan,' said the Co-ordinator, 'has had its own particular type of human conflict – its own variety of problem that, apparently, could be settled only by force. And each time, frustratingly enough, force never really settled the problem. Instead, it persisted through a series of conflicts, then vanished of itself, – what's the expression, – ah, yes, not with a bang, but a whimper, as the economic and social environment changed. And then, new problems, and a new series of wars. – Apparently endlessly cyclic.

'Consider relatively modern times. There were the series of dynastic wars in the sixteenth to eighteenth centuries, when the most important question in Europe was whether the houses of Hapsburg or Valois-Bourbon were to rule the continent. It was one of those "inevitable conflicts," since Europe could obviously not exist half one and half the other.

'Except that it did, and no war ever wiped out the one and established the other, until the rise of a new social atmosphere in France in 1789 tumbled first the Bourbons and, eventually, the Hapsburgs down the dusty chute to history's incinerator.

'And in those same centuries there were the more barbarous religious wars, which revolved about the important question of whether Europe was to be Catholic or Protestant. Half and half she could not be. It was "inevitable" that the sword decide. – Except that it didn't. In England, a new industrialism was growing, and on the continent, a new nationalism. Half and half Europe remains to this day and no one cares much.

'In the nineteenth and twentieth centuries, there was a cycle of nationalist-imperialist wars, when the most important question in the world was which portions of Europe would control the economic resources and consuming capacity of which portions of non-Europe. All non-Europe obviously could not exist part English and part French and part German and so on. – Until the forces of nationalism spread sufficiently, so that non-Europe ended what all the wars could not, and decided it could exist quite comfortably *all* non-European.

'And so we have a pattern – '

'Yes, Stephen, you make it plain,' said Susan Calvin. 'These are not very profound observations.'

'No. – But then, it is the obvious which is so difficult to see most of the time. People say "It's as plain as the nose on your face." But how much of the nose on your face can you see, unless someone holds a mirror up to you? In the twentieth century, Susan, we started a new cycle of wars – what shall I call them? Ideological wars? The emotions of religion applied to economic systems, rather than to extra-natural ones? Again the wars were "inevitable" and this time there were atomic weapons, so that mankind could no longer live through its torment to the inevitable wasting away of inevitability. – And positronic robots came.

'They came in time, and, with it and alongside it, interplanetary travel. – So that it no longer seemed so important whether the world was Adam Smith or Karl Marx. Neither made very much sense under the new circumstances. Both had to adapt and they ended in almost the same place.'

'A deus ex machina, then, in a double sense,' said Dr Calvin, dryly.

The Co-ordinator smiled gently, 'I have never heard you pun before, Susan, but you are correct. And yet there was another danger. The ending of every other problem had merely given birth to another. Our new world-wide robot economy may develop its own problems, and for that reason we have the Machines. The Earth's economy is stable, and will *remain* stable, because it is based upon the decisions of calculating machines that have the good of humanity at heart through the overwhelming force of the First Law of Robotics.'

Stephen Byerley continued, 'And although the Machines are nothing but the vastest conglomeration of calculating circuits ever invented, they are still robots within the meaning of the First Law, and so our Earth-wide economy is in accord with the best interests of Man. The population of Earth knows that there will be no unemployment, no overproduction or shortages. Waste and famine are words in history books. And so the question of ownership of the means of production becomes obsolescent. Whoever owned them (if such a phrase has meaning), a man, a group, a nation, or all mankind, they could be utilized only as the Machines directed. – Not because men were forced to but because it was the wisest course and men knew it.

'It puts an end to war – not only to the last cycle of wars, but to the next and to all of them. Unless – '

A long pause, and Dr Calvin encouraged him to repetition. 'Unless – '

The fire crouched and skittered along a log, then popped up.

'Unless,' said the Co-ordinator, 'the Machines don't fulfill their function.'

'I see. And that is where those trifling maladjustments come in which you mentioned awhile ago – steel, hydroponics and so on.'

'Exactly. Those errors should not be. Dr Silver tells me they *cannot* be.'

'Does he deny the facts? How unusual!'

'No, he admits the facts, of course. I do him an injustice. What he denies is that any error in the machine is responsible for the so-called (his phrase) errors in the answers. He claims that the Machines are self-correcting and that it would violate the fundamental laws of nature for an error to exist in the circuits of relays. And so I said – '

'And you said, "Have your boys check them and make sure, anyway."'

'Susan, you read my mind. It was what I said, and he said he couldn't.'

'Too busy?'

'No, he said that no human could. He was frank about it. He told me, and I hope I understand him properly, that the Machines are a gigantic extrapolation. Thus – A team of mathematicians work several years calculating a positronic brain equipped to do certain similar acts of calculation. Using this brain they make further calculations to create a still more complicated brain, which they use again to make one still more complicated and so on. According to Silver, what we call the Machines are the result of ten such steps.'

'Ye-es, that sounds familiar. Fortunately, I'm not a mathematician. – Poor Vincent. He is a young man. The Directors before him had no such problems. Nor had I. Perhaps roboticists these days can no longer understand our own creations.'

'Apparently not. The Machines are not super-brains in Sunday supplement sense, – although they are so pictured in the Sunday supplements. It is merely that in their own particular province of collecting and analyzing a nearly infinite number of data and relationships thereof, in nearly infinitesimal time, they have progressed beyond the possibility of detailed human control.

'And then I tried something else. I actually asked the Machine. In the strictest secrecy, we fed it the original data involved in the steel decision, its own answer, and the actual developments since, – the overproduction, that is, – and asked for an explanation of the discrepancy.'

'Good, and what was its answer?'

'I can quote you that word for word: "The matter admits of no explanation."'

'And how did Vincent interpret that?'

'In two ways. Either we had not given the Machine enough data to allow a definite answer, which was unlikely. Dr Silver admitted that. – Or else, it was impossible for the Machine to admit that it could give any answer to data which implied that it could harm a human being. This, naturally, is implied by the First Law. And then Dr Silver recommended that I see you.'

Susan Calvin looked very tired, 'I'm old, Stephen. There was a time when you wanted to make me Director of Research and I refused. I wasn't young then, either, and I did not wish the responsibility. They let young Silver have it and that satisfied me; but what good is it, if I am dragged into such messes.

'Stephen, let me state my position. My researches do indeed involve the interpretation of robot behavior in the light of the Three Laws of Robotics. Here, now, we have these incredible calculating machines. They are positronic robots and therefore obey the Laws of Robotics. But they lack personality; that is, their functions are extremely limited. – Must be, since they are so specialized. Therefore, there is very little room for the interplay of the Laws, and my one method of attack is virtually useless. In short, I don't know that I can help you, Stephen.'

The Co-ordinator laughed shortly, 'Nevertheless, let me tell you the rest. Let me give you *my* theories, and perhaps you will then be able to tell me whether they are possible in the light of robopsychology.'

'By all means. Go ahead.'

'Well, since the Machines are giving the wrong answers, then, assuming that they cannot be in error, there is only one possibility. *They are being given the wrong data!* In other words, the trouble is human, and not robotic. So I took my recent planetary inspection tour – '

'From which you have just returned to New York.'

'Yes. It was necessary, you see, since there are four Machines, one handling each of the Planetary Regions. And *all four are yielding imperfect results*.'

'Oh, but that follows, Stephen. If any one of the Machines is imperfect, that will automatically reflect in the result of the other three, since each of the others will assume as part of the data on which they base their own decisions, the perfection of the imperfect fourth. With a false assumption, they will yield false answers.'

'Uh-huh. So it seemed to me. Now, I have here the records of my interviews with each of the Regional Vice-Co-ordinators. Would you look through them with me? – Oh, and first, have you heard of the "Society for Humanity?"'

'Umm, yes. They are an outgrowth of the Fundamentalists who have kept US Robots from ever employing positronic robots on the grounds of unfair labor competition and so on. The "Society for Humanity" itself is anti-Machine, is it not?'

'Yes, yes, but – Well, you will see. Shall we begin? We'll start with the Eastern Region.'

'As you say – '

The Eastern Region:
a – Area: 7,500,000 square miles
b – Population: 1,700,000,000
c – Capital: Shanghai

Ching Hso-lin's great-grandfather had been killed in the Japanese invasion of the old Chinese Republic, and there had been no one beside his dutiful children to mourn his loss or even to know he was lost. Ching Hso-lin's grandfather had survived the civil war of the late forties, but there had been no one beside *his* dutiful children to know or care of that.

And yet Ching Hso-lin was a Regional Vice-Co-ordinator, with the economic welfare of half the people of Earth in his care.

Perhaps it was with the thought of all that in mind, that Ching had two maps as the only ornaments on the wall of his office. One was an old hand-drawn affair tracing out an acre or two of land, and marked with the now outmoded pictographs of old China. A little creek trickled aslant the faded markings and there were the delicate pictorial indications of lowly huts, in one of which Ching's grandfather had been born.

The other map was a huge one, sharply delineated, with all markings in neat Cyrillic characters. The red boundary that marked the Eastern Region swept within its grand confines all that had once been China, India, Burma, Indo-China, and Indonesia. On it, within the old province of Szechuan, so light and gentle that none could see it, was the little mark placed there by Ching which indicated the location of his ancestral farm.

Ching stood before these maps as he spoke to Stephen Byerley in precise English, 'No one knows better than you, Mr Co-ordinator, that my job, to a large extent, is a sinecure. It carries with it a certain social standing, and I represent a convenient focal point for administration, but otherwise it is the Machine! – The Machine does all the work. What did you think, for instance, of the Tientsin Hydroponics works?'

'Tremendous!' said Byerley.

'It is but one of dozens, and not the largest. Shanghai, Calcutta, Batavia, Bangkok – They are widely spread and they are the answer to feeding the billion and three quarters of the East.'

'And yet,' said Byerley, 'you have an unemployment

problem there at Tientsin. Can you be over-producing? It is incongruous to think of Asia as suffering from too much food.'

Ching's dark eyes crinkled at the edges. 'No. It has not come to that yet. It is true that over the last few months, several vats at Tientsin have been shut down, but it is nothing serious. The men have been released only temporarily and those who do not care to work in other fields have been shipped to Colombo in Ceylon, where a new plant is being put into operation.'

'But why should the vats be closed down?'

Ching smiled gently, 'You do not know much of hydroponics, I see. Well, that is not surprising. You are a Northerner, and there soil farming is still profitable. It is fashionable in the North to think of hydroponics, when it is thought of at all, as a device for growing turnips in a chemical solution, and so it is – in an infinitely complicated way.

'In the first place, by far the largest crop we deal with (and the percentage is growing) is yeast. We have upward of two thousand strains of yeast in production and new strains are added monthly. The basic food-chemicals of the various yeasts are nitrates and phosphates among the inorganics together with proper amounts of the trace metals needed, down to the fractional parts per million of boron and molybdenum which are required. The organic matter is mostly sugar mixtures derived from the hydrolysis of cellulose, but, in addition, there are various food factors which must be added.

'For a successful hydroponics industry – one which can feed seventeen hundred million people – we must engage in an immense reforestation program throughout the East; we must have huge wood-conversion plants to deal with our southern jungles; we must have power, and steel, and chemical synthetics above all.'

'Why the last, sir?'

'Because, Mr Byerley, these strains of yeast have each their peculiar properties. We have developed, as I said, two thousand strains. The beef steak you thought you ate today was yeast. The frozen fruit confection you had for dessert was iced yeast. We have filtered yeast juice with the taste, appearance, and all the food value of milk.

'It is flavor, more than anything else, you see, that makes yeast feeding popular and for the sake of flavor we have developed artificial, domesticated strains that can no longer support themselves on a basic diet of salts and sugar. One needs biotin; another needs pteroylglutamic acid; still others need seventeen different animo acids supplied them as well as all the Vitamins B, but one (and yet it is popular and we cannot, with economic sense, abandon it) – '

Byerley stirred in his seat, 'To what purpose do you tell me all this?'

'You asked me, sir, why men are out of work in Tientsin. I have a little more to explain. It is not only that we must have these various and varying foods for our yeast; but there remains the complicating factor of popular fads with passing time; and of the possibility of the development of new strains with the new requirements and new popularity. All this must be foreseen, and the Machine does the job – '

'But not perfectly.'

'Not very *im*perfectly, in view of the complications I have mentioned. Well, then, a few thousand workers in Tientsin are temporarily out of a job. But, consider this, the amount of waste in this past year (waste that is, in terms of either defective supply or defective demand) amounts to not one-tenth of one percent of our total productive turnover. I consider that – '

'Yet in the first years of the Machine, the figure was nearer one-thousandth of one percent.'

'Ah, but in the decade since the Machine began its

operations in real earnest, we have made use of it to increase our old pre-Machine yeast industry twenty-fold. You expect imperfections to increase with complications, though – '

'Though?'

'There *was* the curious instance of Rama Vrasayana.'

'What happened to him?'

'Vrasayana was in charge of a brine-evaporation plant for the production of iodine, with which yeast can do without, but human beings not. His plant was forced into receivership.'

'Really? And through what agency?'

'Competition, believe it or not. In general, one of the chiefest functions of the Machine's analyses is to indicate the most efficient distribution of our producing units. It is obviously faulty to have areas insufficiently serviced, so that the transportation costs account for too great a percentage of the overhead. Similarly, it is faulty to have an area too well serviced, so that factories must be run at lowered capacities, or else compete harmfully with one another. In the case of Vrasayana, another plant was established in the same city, and with a more efficient extracting system.'

'The Machine permitted it?'

'Oh, certainly. That is not surprising. The new system is becoming widespread. The surprise is that the Machine failed to warn Vrasayana to renovate or combine. – Still, no matter. Vrasayana accepted a job as engineer in the new plant, and if his responsibility and pay are now less, he is not actually suffering. The workers found employment easily; the old plant has been converted to – something or other. Something useful. We left it all to the Machine.'

'And otherwise you have no complaints.'

'None!'

The Tropic Region:
a – Area: 22,000,000 square miles

b – Population: 500,000,000
c – Capital: Capital City

The map in Lincoln Ngoma's office was far from the model of neat precision of the one in Ching's Shanghai dominion. The boundaries of Ngoma's Tropic Region were stenciled in dark, wide brown and swept about a gorgeous interior labeled 'jungle' and 'desert' and 'here be Elephants and all Manner of Strange Beasts.'

It had much to sweep, for in land area the Tropic Region enclosed most of two continents: all of South America north of Argentina and all of Africa south of the Atlas. It included North America south of the Rio Grande as well, and even Arabia and Iran in Asia. It was the reverse of the Eastern Region. Where the ant hives of the Orient crowded half of humanity into 15 per cent of the land mass, the Tropics stretched its 15 per cent of Humanity over nearly half of all the land in the world.

But it was growing. It was the one Region whose population increase through immigration exceeded that through births. – And for all who came it had use.

To Ngoma, Stephen Byerley seemed like one of these immigrants, a pale searcher for the creative work of carving a harsh environment into the softness necessary for man, and he felt some of that automatic contempt of the strong man born to the strong Tropics for the unfortunate pallards of the colder suns.

The Tropics had the newest capital city on Earth, and it was called simply that: 'Capital City,' in the sublime confidence of youth. It spread brightly over the fertile uplands of Nigeria and outside Ngoma's windows, far below, was life and color; the bright, bright sun and the quick, drenching showers. Even the squawking of the rainbowed birds was brisk and the stars were hard pinpoints in the sharp night.

Ngoma laughed. He was a big, dark man, strong faced and handsome.

'Sure,' he said, and his English was colloquial and mouthfilling, 'the Mexican Canal is overdue. What the hell? It will get finished just the same, old boy.'

'It was doing well up to the last half year.'

Ngoma looked at Byerley and slowly crunched his teeth over the end of a big cigar, spitting out one end and lighting the other, 'Is this an official investigation, Byerley? What's going on?'

'Nothing. Nothing at all. It's just my function as Co-ordinator to be curious.'

'Well, if it's just that you are filling in a dull moment, the truth is that we're always short on labor. There's lots going on in the Tropics. The Canal is only one of them – '

'But doesn't your Machine predict the amount of labor available for the Canal, – allowing for all the competing projects?'

Ngoma placed one hand behind his neck and blew smoke rings at the ceiling, 'It was a little off.'

'Is it often a little off?'

'Not oftener than you would expect. – We don't expect too much of it, Byerley. We feed it data. We take its results. We do what it says. – But it's just a convenience; just a labor-saving device. We could do without it, if we had to. Maybe not as well. Maybe not as quickly. But we'd get there.

'We've got confidence out here, Byerley, and that's the secret. Confidence! We've got new land that's been waiting for us for thousands of years, while the rest of the world was being ripped apart in the lousy fumblings of pre-atomic time. We don't have to eat yeast like the Eastern boys, and we don't have to worry about the stale dregs of the last century like you Northerners.

'We've wiped out the tsetse fly and the Anopheles

mosquito, and people find they can live in the sun and like it, now. We've thinned down the jungles and found soil; we've watered the deserts and found gardens. We've got coal and oil in untouched fields, and minerals out of count.

'Just step back. That's all we ask the rest of the world to do. – Step back, and let us work.'

Byerley said, prosaically, 'But the Canal, – it was on schedule six months ago. What happened?'

Ngoma spread his hands, 'Labor troubles.' He felt through a pile of papers skeltered about his desk and gave it up.

'Had something on the matter here,' he muttered, 'but never mind. There was a work shortage somewhere in Mexico once on the question of women. There weren't enough women in the neighborhood. It seemed no one had thought of feeding sexual data to the Machine.'

He stopped to laugh, delightedly, then sobered, 'Wait a while. I think I've got it. – Villafranca!'

'Villafranca?'

'Francisco Villafranca. – He was the engineer in charge. Now let me straighten it out. Something happened and there was a cave-in. Right. Right. That was it. Nobody died, as I remember, but it made a hell of a mess. – Quite a scandal.'

'Oh?'

'There was some mistake in his calculations. – Or at least, the Machine said so. They fed through Villafranca's data, assumptions, and so on. The stuff he had started with. The answers came out differently. It seems the answers Villafranca had used didn't take account of the effect of a heavy rainfall on the contours of the cut. – Or something like that. I'm not an engineer, you understand.

'Anyway, Villafranca put up a devil of a squawk. He claimed the Machine's answer had been different the first time. That he had followed the Machine faithfully. Then he quit! We offered to hold him on – reasonable doubt, previous work satisfactory, and all that – in a subordinate position, of course – had to do that much – mistakes can't go unnoticed – bad for discipline – Where was I?'

'You offered to hold him on.'

'Oh yes. He refused. – Well, take all in all, we're two months behind. Hell, that's nothing.'

Byerley stretched out his hand and let the fingers tap lightly on the desk, 'Villafranca blamed the Machine, did he?'

'Well, he wasn't going to blame himself, was he? Let's face it; human nature is an old friend of ours. Besides, I remember something else now – Why the hell can't I find documents when I want them? My filing system isn't worth a damn – This Villafranca was a member of one of your Northern organizations. Mexico is too close to the North! that's part of the trouble.'

'Which organization are you speaking of?'

'The Society for Humanity, they call it. He used to attend the annual conferences in New York, Villafranca did. Bunch of crackpots, but harmless. – They don't like the Machines; claim they're destroying human initiative. So naturally Villafranca would blame the Machine. – Don't understand that group myself. Does Capital City look as if the human race were running out of initiative?'

And Capital City stretched out in golden glory under a golden sun, – the newest and youngest creation of *Homo metropolis*.

The European Region:
a – Area: 4,000,000 square miles
b – Population: 300,000,000
c – Capital: Geneva

The European Region was an anomaly in several ways. In area, it was far the smallest; not one fifth the size of the

Tropic Region in area, and not one fifth the size of the Eastern Region in population. Geographically, it was only somewhat similar to pre-Atomic Europe, since it excluded what had once been European Russia and what had once been the British Isles, while it included the Mediterranean coasts of Africa and Asia, and, in a queer jump across the Atlantic, Argentina, Chile, and Uruguay as well.

Nor was it likely to improve its relative status vis-à-vis the other regions of Earth, except for what vigor the South American provinces lent it. Of all the Regions, it alone showed a positive population decline over the past half century. It alone had not seriously expanded its productive facilities, or offered anything radically new to human culture.

'Europe,' said Madame Szegeczowska, in her soft French, 'is essentially an economic appendage of the Northern Region. We know it, and it doesn't matter.'

And as though in resigned acceptance of a lack of individuality, there was no map of Europe on the wall of the Madame Co-ordinator's office.

'And yet,' pointed out Byerley, 'you have a Machine of your own, and you are certainly under no economic pressure from across the ocean.'

'A Machine! Bah!' She shrugged her delicate shoulders, and allowed a thin smile to cross her little face as she tamped out a cigarette with long fingers. 'Europe is a sleepy place. And such of our men as do not manage to emigrate to the Tropics are tired and sleepy along with it. You see for yourself that it is myself, a poor woman, to whom falls the task of being Vice-Co-ordinator. Well, fortunately, it is not a difficult job, and not much is expected of me.

'As for the Machine – What can it say but "Do this and it will be best for you." But what is best for us? Why, to be an economic appendage of the Northern Region.

'And is it so terrible? No wars! We live in peace – and it

is pleasant after seven thousand years of war. We are old, monsieur. In our borders, we have the regions where Occidental civilization was cradled. We have Egypt and Mesopotamia; Crete and Syria; Asia Minor and Greece. – But old age is not necessarily an unhappy time. It can be a fruition – '

'Perhaps you are right,' said Byerley, affably. 'At least the tempo of life is not as intense as in the other Regions. It is a pleasant atmosphere.'

'Is it not? – Tea is being brought, monsieur. If you will indicate your cream and sugar preferences, please. – Thank you.'

She sipped gently, then continued, 'It *is* pleasant. The rest of Earth is welcome to the continuing struggle. I find a parallel here; a very interesting one. There was a time when Rome was master of the world. It had adopted the culture and civilization of Greece; a Greece which had never been united, which had ruined itself with war, and which was ending in a state of decadent squalor. Rome united it, brought it peace and let it live a life of secure non-glory. It occupied itself with its philosophies and its art, far from the clash of growth and war. It was a sort of death, but it was restful, and it lasted with minor breaks for some four hundred years.'

'And yet,' said Byerley, 'Rome fell eventually, and the opium dream was over.'

'There are no longer barbarians to overthrow civilization.'

'We can be our own barbarians, Madame Szegeczowska. – Oh, I meant to ask you. The Almaden mercury mines have fallen off quite badly in production. Surely the ores are not declining more rapidly than anticipated?'

The little woman's gray eyes fastened shrewdly on Byerley, 'Barbarians – the fall of civilization – possible failure of the Machine. Your thought processes are very transparent, monsieur.'

'Are they?' Byerley smiled. 'I see that I should have had men to deal with as hitherto. – You consider the Almaden affair to be the fault of the Machine?'

'Not at all, but I think you do. You, yourself, are a native of the Northern Region. The Central Co-ordination Office is at New York. – And I have noticed for quite a while that you Northerners lack somewhat of faith in the Machine.'

'We do?'

'There is your "Society for Humanity" which is strong in the North, but naturally fails to find many recruits in tired, old Europe, which is quite willing to let feeble Humanity alone for a while. Surely, you are one of the confident North and not one of the cynical old continent.'

'This has a connection with Almaden?'

'Oh, yes, I think so. The mines are in the control of Consolidated Cinnabar, which is certainly a Northern company, with headquarters at Nikolaev. Personally, I wonder if the Board of Directors has been consulting the Machine at all. They said they had in our conference last month, and, of course, we have no evidence that they did not, but I wouldn't take the word of a Northerner in this matter – no offense intended – under any circumstances. – Nevertheless, I think it will have a fortunate ending.'

'In what way, my dear madame?'

'You must understand that the economic irregularities of the last few months, which, although small as compared with the great storms of the past, are quite disturbing to our peace-drenched spirits, have caused considerable restiveness in the Spanish province. I understand that Consolidated Cinnabar is selling out to a group of native Spaniards. It is consoling. If we are economic vassals of the North, it is humiliating to have the fact advertised too blatantly. – And our people can be better trusted to follow the Machine.'

'Then you think there will be no more trouble?'

'I am sure there will not be – In Almaden, at least.'

The Northern Region:
a – Area: 18,000,000 square miles
b – Population: 800,000,000
c – Capital: Ottawa

The Northern Region, in more ways than one, was at the top. This was exemplified quite well by the map in the Ottawa office of Vice-Co-ordinator Hiram Mackenzie in which the North Pole was centered. Except for the enclave of Europe with its Scandinavian and Icelandic regions, all the Arctic area was within the Northern Region.

Roughly, it could be divided into two major areas. To the left on the map was all of North America above the Rio Grande. To the right was included all of what had once been the Soviet Union. Together these areas represented the centered power of the planet in the first years of the Atomic Age. Between the two was Great Britain, a tongue of the Region licking at Europe. Up at the top of the map, distorted into odd, huge shapes, were Australia and New Zealand, also member provinces of the Region.

Not all the changes of the past decades had yet altered the fact that the North was the economic ruler of the planet.

There was almost an ostentatious symbolism thereof in the fact that of the official Regional maps Byerley had seen, Mackenzie's alone showed all the Earth, as though the North feared no competition and needed no favoritism to point up its pre-eminence.

'Impossible,' said Mackenzie, dourly, over the whiskey. 'Mr Byerley, you have had no training as a robot technician, I believe.'

'No, I have not.'

'Hmp. Well, it is, in my opinion, a sad thing that Ching, Ngoma and Szegeczowska haven't either. There is too prevalent an opinion among the peoples of Earth that a Co-ordinator need only be a capable organizer, a broad generalizer, and an amiable person. These days he should know his robotics as well, – no offense intended.'

'None taken. I agree with you.'

'I take it, for instance, from what you have said already, that you worry about the recent trifling dislocations in world economy. I don't know what you suspect, but it has happened in the past that people – who should have known better – wondered what would happen if false data were fed into the Machine.'

'And what would happen, Mr Mackenzie?'

'Well,' the Scotsman shifted his weight and sighed, 'all collected data goes through a complicated screening system which involves both human and mechanical checking, so that the problem is not likely to arise. – But let us ignore that. Humans are fallible, also corruptible, and ordinary mechanical devices are liable to mechanical failure.

'The real point of the matter is that what we call a "wrong datum" is one which is inconsistent with all other known data. It is our only criterion of right and wrong. It is the Machine's as well. Order it for instance, to direct agricultural activity on the basis of an average July temperature in Iowa of 57 degrees Fahrenheit. It won't accept that. It will not give an answer. – Not that it has any prejudice against that particular temperature, or that an answer is impossible; but because, in the light of all the other data fed it over a period of years, it knows that the probability of an average July temperature of 57 is virtually nil. It rejects that datum.

'The only way a "wrong datum" can be forced on the Machine is to include it as part of a self-consistent whole, all of which is subtly wrong in a manner either too delicate for the Machine to detect or outside the Machine's experience. The former is beyond human capacity, and the latter is almost so, and is becoming more nearly so as the Machine's experience increases by the second.'

Stephen Byerley placed two fingers to the bridge of his

nose, 'Then the Machine cannot be tampered with – And how do you account for recent errors, then?'

'My dear Byerley, I see that you instinctively follow that great error – that the Machine knows all. Let me cite you a case from my personal experience. The cotton industry engages experienced buyers who purchase cotton. Their procedure is to pull a tuft of cotton out of a random bale of a lot. They will look at that tuft and feel it, tease it out, listen to the crackling perhaps as they do so, touch it with their tongue, – and through this procedure they will determine the class of cotton the bales represent. There are about a dozen such classes. As a result of their decisions, purchases are made at certain prices, blends are made in certain proportions. – Now these buyers cannot yet be replaced by the Machine.'

'Why not? Surely the data involved is not too complicated for it?'

'Probably not. But what data is this you refer to? No textile chemist knows exactly what it is that the buyer tests when he feels a tuft of cotton. Presumably there's the average length of the threads, their feel, the extent and nature of their slickness, the way they hang together and so on. – Several dozen items, subconsciously weighed, out of years of experience. But the *quantitative* nature of these tests is not known; maybe even the very nature of some of them is not known. So we have nothing to feed the Machine. Nor can the buyers explain their own judgment. They can only say, "Well, look at it. Can't you *tell* it's class-such-and-such?"'

'I see.'

'There are innumerable cases like that. The Machine is only a tool after all, which can help humanity progress faster by taking some of the burdens of calculations and interpretations off his back. The task of the human brain remains what it has always been; that of discovering new data to be analyzed, and of devising new concepts to be tested. A pity the Society for Humanity won't understand that.'

'They are against the Machine?'

'They would be against mathematics or against the art of writing if they had lived at the appropriate time. These reactionaries of the Society claim the Machine robs man of his soul. I notice that capable men are still at a premium in our society; we still need the man who is intelligent enough to think of the proper questions to ask. Perhaps if we could find enough of such, these dislocations you worry about, Co-ordinator, wouldn't occur.'

Earth (Including the uninhabited continent, Antarctica):
a – Area: 54,000,000 square miles (land surface)
b – Population: 3,300,000,000
c – Capital: New York

The fire behind the quartz was weary now, and sputtered its reluctant way to death.

The Co-ordinator was somber, his mood matching the sinking flame.

'They all minimize the state of affairs.' His voice was low. 'Is it not easy to imagine that they all laugh at me? And yet – Vincent Silver said the Machines cannot be out of order, and I must believe him. Hiram Mackenzie says they cannot be fed false data, and I must believe him. But the Machines are going wrong, somehow, and I must believe that, too, – and so there is *still* an alternative left.'

He glanced sidewise at Susan Calvin, who, with closed eyes, for a moment seemed asleep.

'What is that?' she asked, prompt to her cue, nevertheless.

'Why, that correct data is indeed given, and correct answers are indeed received, but that they are then ignored. There is no way the Machine can enforce obedience to its dictates.'

'Madame Szegeczowska hinted as much, with reference to Northerners in general, it seems to me.'

'So she did.'

'And what purpose is served by disobeying the Machine? Let's consider motivations.'

'It's obvious to me, and should be to you. It is a matter of rocking the boat, deliberately. There can be no serious conflicts on Earth, in which one group or another can seize more power than it has for what it thinks is its own good despite the harm to Mankind as a whole, while the Machines rule. If popular faith in the Machines can be destroyed to the point where they are abandoned, it will be the law of the jungle again. – And not one of the four Regions can be freed of the suspicion of wanting just that.

'The East has half of humanity within its borders, and the Tropics more than half of Earth's resources. Each can feel itself the natural rulers of all Earth, and each has a history of humiliation by the North, for which it can be human enough to wish a senseless revenge. Europe has a tradition of greatness, on the other hand. It once *did* rule the Earth, and there is nothing so eternally adhesive as the memory of power.

'Yet, in another way, it's hard to believe. Both the East and the Tropics are in a state of enormous expansion within their own borders. Both are climbing incredibly. They cannot have the spare energy for military adventures. And Europe can have nothing but its dreams. It is a cipher, militarily.'

'So, Stephen,' said Susan, 'you leave the North.'

'Yes,' said Byerley, energetically, 'I do. The North is now the strongest, and has been for nearly a century, or its component parts have been. But it is losing relatively, now. The Tropic Regions may take their place in the forefront of civilization for the first time since the Pharaohs, and there are Northerners who fear that.

'The "Society for Humanity" is a Northern organization, primarily, you know, and they make no secret of not wanting the Machines. – Susan, they are few in numbers, but it is an association of powerful men. Heads of factories; directors of industries and agricultural combines who hate to be what they call "the Machine's office-boy" belong to it. Men with ambition belong to it. Men who feel themselves strong enough to decide for themselves what is best for themselves, and not just to be told what is best for others.

'In short, just those men who, by together refusing to accept the decisions of the Machine, can, in a short time, turn the world topsy-turvy; – just those belong to the Society.

'Susan, it hangs together. Five of the Directors of World Steel are members, and World Steel suffers from overproduction. Consolidated Cinnabar, which mined mercury at Almaden, was a Northern concern. Its books are still being investigated, but one, at least, of the men concerned was a member. Francisco Villafranca, who, singlehanded, delayed the Mexican Canal for two months, was a member, we know already – and so was Rama Vrasayana, I was not at all surprised to find out.'

Susan said, quietly, 'These men, I might point out, have all done badly – '

'But naturally,' interjected Byerley. 'To disobey the Machine's analyses is to follow a non-optimal path. Results are poorer than they might be. It's the price they pay. They will have it rough now but in the confusion that will eventually follow – '

'Just what do you plan doing, Stephen?'

'There is obviously no time to lose. I am going to have the Society outlawed, every member removed from any responsible post. And all executive and technical positions, henceforward, can be filled only by applicants signing a non-Society oath. It will mean a certain surrender of basic civil liberties, but I am sure the Congress – '

'It won't work!'

'What! – Why not?'

'I will make a prediction. If you try any such thing, you will find yourself hampered at every turn. You will find it impossible to carry out. You will find your every move in that direction will result in trouble.'

Byerley was taken aback, 'Why do you say that? – I was rather hoping for your approval in this matter.'

'You can't have it as long as your actions are based on a false premise. You admit the Machine can't be wrong, and can't be fed wrong data. I will now show you that it cannot be disobeyed, either, as you think is being done by the Society.'

'*That* I don't see at all.'

'Then listen. Every action by any executive which does not follow the exact directions of the Machine he is working with becomes part of the data for the next problem. The Machine, therefore, knows that the executive has a certain tendency to disobey. He can incorporate that tendency into that data, – even quantitatively, that is, judging exactly how much and in what direction disobedience would occur. Its next answer would be just sufficiently biased so that after the executive concerned disobeyed, he would have automatically corrected those answers to optimal directions. The Machine *knows*, Stephen!'

'You can't be sure of all this. You are guessing.'

'It is a guess based on a lifetime's experience with robots. You had better rely on such a guess, Stephen.'

'But then what is left? The Machines themselves are correct and the premises they work on are correct. That we have agreed upon. Now you say that it cannot be disobeyed. Then what is wrong?'

'You have answered yourself. *Nothing is wrong!* Think about the Machines for a while, Stephen. They are robots, and they follow the First Law. But the Machines work not for any single human being but for all humanity, so that the First Law becomes: "No Machine may harm humanity; or, through inaction, allow humanity to come to harm."

'Very well, then, Stephen, what harms humanity? Economic dislocations most of all, from whatever cause. Wouldn't you say so?'

'I would.'

'And what is most likely in the future to cause economic dislocations? Answer that, Stephen.'

'I should say,' replied Byerley, unwillingly, 'the destruction of the Machines.'

'And so should I say, and so should the Machines say. Their first care, therefore, is to preserve themselves, for us. And so they are quietly taking care of the only elements left that threaten them. It is not the "Society for Humanity" which is shaking the boat so that the Machines may be destroyed. You have been looking at the reverse of the picture. Say rather that the Machine is shaking the boat – *very* slightly – just enough to shake loose those few which cling to the side for purposes the Machines consider harmful to Humanity.

'So Vrasayana loses his factory and gets another job where he can do no harm – he is not badly hurt, he is not rendered incapable of earning a living, for the Machine cannot harm a human being more than minimally, and that only to save a greater number. Consolidated Cinnabar loses control at Almaden. Villafranca is no longer a civil engineer in charge of an important project. And the directors of World Steel are losing their grip on the industry – or will.'

'But you don't really know all this,' insisted Byerley, distractedly. 'How can we possibly take a chance on your being right?'

'You must. Do you remember the Machine's own statement when you presented the problem to him? It was: "The matter admits of no explanation." The Machine did not say there was no explanation, or that it could determine no explanation. It simply was not going to *admit* any explanation. In other words, it would be harmful to humanity to have the explanation known, and that's why we can only guess – and keep on guessing.'

'But how can the explanation do us harm? Assume that you are right, Susan.'

'Why, Stephen, if I am right, it means that the Machine is conducting our future for us not only simply in direct answer to our direct questions, but in general answer to the world situation and to human psychology as a whole. And to know that may make us unhappy and may hurt our pride. The Machine cannot, *must* not, make us unhappy.

'Stephen, how do we know what the ultimate good of Humanity will entail? We haven't at *our* disposal the infinite factors that the Machine has at *its*! Perhaps, to give you a not unfamiliar example, our entire technical civilization has created more unhappiness and misery than it has removed. Perhaps an agrarian or pastoral civilization, with less culture and less people would be better. If so, the Machines must move in that direction, preferably without telling us, since in our ignorant prejudices we only know that what we are used to, is good – and we would then fight change. Or perhaps a complete urbanization, or a completely caste-ridden society, or complete anarchy, is the answer. We don't know. Only the Machines know, and they are going there and taking us with them.'

'But you are telling me, Susan, that the "Society of Humanity" is right; and that Mankind *has* lost its own say in its future.'

'It never had any, really. It was always at the mercy of economic and sociological forces it did not understand – at the whims of climate, and the fortunes of war. Now the Machines understand them; and no one can stop them, since the Machines will deal with them as they are dealing with the Society, – having, as they do, the greatest of weapons at their disposal, the absolute control of our economy.'

'How horrible!'

'Perhaps how wonderful! Think, that for all time, all conflicts are finally evitable. Only the Machines, from now on, are inevitable!'

And the fire behind the quartz went out and only a curl of smoke was left to indicate its place.

Feminine Intuition

The Three Laws of Robotics:

1. *A robot may not injure a human being or, through inaction, allow a human being to come to harm.*
2. *A robot must obey the orders given it by human beings except where such orders would conflict with the First Law.*
3. *A robot must protect its own existence as long as such protection does not conflict with the First or Second Law.*

For the first time in the history of United States Robots and Mechanical Men Corporation, a robot had been destroyed through accident on Earth itself.

No one was to blame. The air vehicle had been demolished in mid-air and an unbelieving investigating committee was wondering whether they really dared announce the evidence that it had been hit by a meteorite. Nothing else could have been fast enough to prevent automatic avoidance; nothing else could have done the damage short of a nuclear blast and that was out of the question.

Tie that in with a report of a flash in the night sky just before the vehicle had exploded – and from Flagstaff Observatory, not from an amateur – and the location of a sizable and distinctly meteoric bit of iron freshly gouged into the ground a mile from the site and what other conclusion could be arrived at?

Still, nothing like that had ever happened before and calculations of the odds against it yielded monstrous figures. Yet even colossal improbabilities can happen sometimes.

At the offices of United States Robots, the hows and whys

of it were secondary. The real point was that a robot had been destroyed.

That, in itself, was distressing.

The fact that JN-5 had been a prototype, the first, after four earlier attempts, to have been placed in the field, was even more distressing.

The fact that JN-5 was a radically new type of robot, quite different from anything ever built before, was abysmally distressing.

The fact that JN-5 had apparently accomplished something before its destruction that was incalculably important and that that accomplishment might now be forever gone, placed the distress utterly beyond words.

It seemed scarcely worth mentioning that, along with the robot, the Chief Robopsychologist of United States Robots had also died.

Clinton Madarian had joined the firm ten years before. For five of those years, he had worked uncomplainingly under the grumpy supervision of Susan Calvin.

Madarian's brilliance was quite obvious and Susan Calvin had quietly promoted him over the heads of older men. She wouldn't, in any case, have deigned to give her reasons for this to Research Director Peter Bogert, but as it happened, no reasons were needed. Or, rather, they were obvious.

Madarian was utterly the reverse of the renowned Dr Calvin in several very noticeable ways. He was not quite as overweight as his distinct double chin made him appear to be, but even so he was overpowering in his presence, where Susan had gone nearly unnoticed. Madarian's massive face, his shock of glistening red-brown hair, his ruddy complexion and booming voice, his loud laugh, and most of all, his irrepressible self-confidence and his eager way of announcing his successes, made everyone else in the room feel there was a shortage of space.

When Susan Calvin finally retired (refusing, in advance, any co-operation with respect to any testimonial dinner that might be planned in her honor, with so firm a manner that no announcement of the retirement was even made to the news services) Madarian took her place.

He had been in his new post exactly one day when he initiated the JN project.

It had meant the largest commitment of funds to one project that United States Robots had ever had to weigh, but that was something which Madarian dismissed with a genial wave of the hand.

'Worth every penny of it, Peter,' he said. 'And I expect you to convince the Board of Directors of that.'

'Give me reasons,' said Bogert, wondering if Madarian would. Susan Calvin had never given reasons.

But Madarian said, 'Sure,' and settled himself easily into the large armchair in the Director's office.

Bogert watched the other with something that was almost awe. His own once-black hair was almost white now and within the decade he would follow Susan into retirement. That would mean the end of the original team that had built United States Robots into a globe-girdling firm that was a rival of the national governments in complexity and importance. Somehow neither he nor those who had gone before him ever quite grasped the enormous expansion of the firm.

But this was a new generation. The new men were at ease with the Colossus. They lacked the touch of wonder that would have them tiptoeing in disbelief. So they moved ahead, and that was good.

Madarian said, 'I propose to begin the construction of robots without constraint.'

'Without the Three Laws? Surely – '

'No, Peter. Are those the only constraints you can think of? Hell, you contributed to the design of the early positronic brains. Do I have to tell you that, quite aside from the Three Laws, there isn't a pathway in those brains that isn't carefully designed and fixed? We have robots planned for specific tasks, implanted with specific abilities.'

'And you propose – '

'That at every level below the Three Laws, the paths be made open-ended. It's not difficult.'

Bogert said dryly, 'It's not difficult, indeed. Useless things are never difficult. The difficult thing is fixing the paths and making the robot useful.'

'But why is that difficult? Fixing the paths requires a great deal of effort because the Principle of Uncertainty is important in particles the mass of positrons and the uncertainty effect must be minimized. Yet why must it? If we arrange to have the Principle just sufficiently prominent to allow the crossing of paths unpredictably – '

'We have an unpredictable robot.'

'We have a *creative* robot,' said Madarian, with a trace of impatience. 'Peter, if there's anything a human brain has that a robotic brain has never had, it's the trace of unpredictability that comes from the effects of uncertainty at the subatomic level. I admit that this effect has never been demonstrated experimentally within the nervous system, but without that the human brain is not superior to the robotic brain in principle.'

'And you think that if you introduce the effect into the robotic brain, the human brain will become not superior to the robotic brain in principle.'

'That,' said Madarian, 'is exactly what I believe.'

They went on for a long time after that.

The Board of Directors clearly had no intention of being easily convinced.

Scott Robertson, the largest shareholder in the firm, said, 'It's hard enough to manage the robot industry as it is, with public hostility to robots forever on the verge of breaking out into the open. If the public gets the idea that robots will be uncontrolled . . . Oh, don't tell me about the Three Laws. The average man won't believe the Three Laws will protect him if he as much as hears the word "uncontrolled."'

'Then don't use it,' said Madarian. 'Call the robot – call it "intuitive."'

'An intuitive robot,' someone muttered. 'A girl robot?'

A smile made its way about the conference table.

Madarian seized on that. 'All right. A girl robot. Our robots are sexless, of course, and so will this one be, but we always act as though they're males. We give them male pet names and call them he and him. Now this one, if we consider the nature of the mathematical structuring of the brain which I have proposed, would fall into the JN-coordinate system. The first robot would be JN-1, and I've assumed that it would be called John-1 . . . I'm afraid that is the level of originality of the average roboticist. But why not call it Jane-1, damn it? If the public has to be let in on what we're doing, we're constructing a feminine robot with intuition.'

Robertson shook his head, 'What difference would that make? What you're saying is that you plan to remove the last barrier which, in principle, keeps the robotic brain inferior to the human brain. What do you suppose the public reaction will be to that?'

'Do you plan to make that public?' said Madarian. He thought a bit and then said, 'Look. One thing the general public believes is that women are not as intelligent as men.'

There was an instant apprehensive look on the face of more than one man at the table and a quick look up and down as though Susan Calvin were still in her accustomed seat.

Madarian said, 'If we announce a female robot, it doesn't

matter what she is. The public will automatically assume she is mentally backward. We just publicize the robot as Jane-1 and we don't have to say another word. We're safe.'

'Actually,' said Peter Bogert quietly, 'there's more to it than that. Madarian and I have gone over the mathematics carefully and the JN series, whether John or Jane, would be quite safe. They would be less complex and intellectually capable, in an orthodox sense, than many another series we have designed and constructed. There would only be the one added factor of, well, let's get into the habit of calling it "intuition."'

'Who knows what it would do?' muttered Robertson.

'Madarian has suggested one thing it can do. As you all know, the Space Jump has been developed in principle. It is possible for men to attain what is, in effect, hyper-speeds beyond that of light and to visit other stellar systems and return in negligible time – weeks at the most.'

Robertson said, 'That's not new to us. It couldn't have been done without robots.'

'Exactly, and it's not doing us any good because we can't use the hyper-speed drive except perhaps once as a demonstration, so that US Robots gets little credit. The Space Jump is risky, it's fearfully prodigal of energy and therefore it's enormously expensive. If we were going to use it anyway, it would be nice if we could report the existence of a habitable planet. Call it a psychological need. Spend about twenty billion dollars on a single Space Jump and report nothing but scientific data and the public wants to know why their money was wasted. Report the existence of a habitable planet, and you're an interstellar Columbus and no one will worry about the money.'

'So?'

'So where are we going to find a habitable planet? Or put it this way – which star within reach of the Space Jump as presently developed, which of the three hundred thousand stars and star systems within three hundred light-years has the best chance of having a habitable planet? We've got an enormous quantity of details on every star in our three-hundred-light-year neighborhood and a notion that almost every one has a planetary system. But which has a *habitable* planet? Which do we visit? . . . We don't know.'

One of the directors said, 'How would this Jane robot help us?'

Madarian was about to answer that, but he gestured slightly to Bogert and Bogert understood. The Director would carry more weight. Bogert didn't particularly like the idea; if the JN series proved a fiasco, he was making himself prominent enough in connection with it to insure that the sticky fingers of blame would cling to him. On the other hand, retirement was not all that far off, and if it worked, he would go out in a blaze of glory. Maybe it was only Madarian's aura of confidence, but Bogert had honestly come to believe it would work.

He said, 'It may well be that somewhere in the libraries of data we have on those stars, there are methods for estimating the probabilities of the presence of Earth-type habitable planets. All we need to do is understand the data properly, look at them in the appropriate creative manner, make the correct correlations. We haven't done it yet. Or if some astronomer has, he hasn't been smart enough to realize what he has.

'A JN-type robot could make correlations far more rapidly and far more precisely than a man could. In a day, it would make and discard as many correlations as a man could in ten years. Furthermore, it would work in truly random fashion, whereas a man would have a strong bias based on preconception and on what is already believed.'

There was a considerable silence after that. Finally Robertson said, 'But it's only a matter of probability, isn't it? Suppose this robot said, "The highest-probability habitable-planet star within so-and-so light-years is Squidgee-17," or whatever, and we go there and find that a probability is only a probability and that there are no habitable planets after all. Where does that leave us?'

Madarian struck in this time. 'We still win. We know how the robot came to the conclusion because it – she – will tell us. It might well help us gain enormous insight into astronomical detail and make the whole thing worthwhile even if we don't make the Space Jump at all. Besides, we can then work out the five most probable sites of planets and the probability that one of the five has a habitable planet may then be better than 0.95. It would be almost sure – '

They went on for a long time after that.

The funds granted were quite insufficient, but Madarian counted on the habit of throwing good money after bad. With two hundred million about to be lost irrevocably when another hundred million could save everything, the other hundred million would surely be voted.

Jane-1 was finally built and put on display. Peter Bogert studied it – her – gravely. He said, 'Why the narrow waist? Surely that introduces a mechanical weakness?'

Madarian chuckled. 'Listen, if we're going to call her Jane, there's no point in making her look like Tarzan.'

Bogert shook his head. 'Don't like it. You'll be bulging her higher up to give the appearance of breasts next, and that's a rotten idea. If women start getting the notion that robots may look like women, I can tell you exactly the kind of perverse notions they'll get, and you'll *really* have hostility on their part.'

Madarian said, 'Maybe you're right at that. No woman wants to feel replaceable by something with none of her faults. Okay.'

* * *

Jane-2 did not have the pinched waist. She was a somber robot which rarely moved and even more rarely spoke.

Madarian had only occasionally come rushing to Bogert with items of news during her construction and that had been a sure sign that things were going poorly. Madarian's ebullience under success was overpowering. He would not hesitate to invade Bogert's bedroom at 3 A.M. with a hot-flash item rather than wait for the morning. Bogert was sure of that.

Now Madarian seemed subdued, his usually florid expression nearly pale, his round cheeks somehow pinched. Bogert said, with a feeling of certainty, 'She won't talk.'

'Oh, she talks.' Madarian sat down heavily and chewed at his lower lip. 'Sometimes, anyway,' he said.

Bogert rose and circled the robot. 'And when she talks, she makes no sense, I suppose. Well, if she doesn't talk, she's no female, is she?'

Madarian tried a weak smile for size and abandoned it. He said, 'The brain, in isolation, checked out.'

'I know,' said Bogert.

'But once that brain was put in charge of the physical apparatus of the robot, it was necessarily modified, of course.'

'Of course,' agreed Bogert unhelpfully.

'But unpredictably and frustratingly. The trouble is that when you're dealing with n-dimensional calculus of uncertainty, things are – '

'Uncertain?' said Bogert. His own reaction was surprising him. The company investment was already most sizable and almost two years had elapsed, yet the results were, to put it politely, disappointing. Still, he found himself jabbing at Madarian and finding himself amused in the process.

Almost furtively, Bogert wondered if it weren't the absent Susan Calvin he was jabbing at. Madarian was so much more ebullient and effusive than Susan could ever possibly be – when things were going well. He was also far more vulnerably in the dumps when things weren't going well, and it was precisely under pressure that Susan never cracked. The target that Madarian made could be a neatly punctured bull's-eye as recompense for the target Susan had never allowed herself to be.

Madarian did not react to Bogert's last remark any more than Susan Calvin would have done; not out of contempt, which would have been Susan's reaction, but because he did not hear it.

He said argumentatively, 'The trouble is the matter of recognition. We have Jane-2 correlating magnificently. She can correlate on any subject, but once she's done so, she can't recognize a valuable result from a valueless one. It's not an easy problem, judging how to program a robot to tell a significant correlation when you don't know what correlations she will be making.'

'I presume you've thought of lowering the potential at the W-21 diode junction and sparking across the – '

'No, no, no, no – ' Madarian faded off into a whispering diminuendo. 'You can't just have it spew out everything. We can do that for ourselves. The point is to have it recognize the crucial correlation and draw the conclusion. Once that is done, you see, a Jane robot would snap out an answer by intuition. It would be something we couldn't get ourselves except by the oddest kind of luck.'

'It seems to me,' said Bogert dryly, 'that if you had a robot like that, you would have her do routinely what, among human beings, only the occasional genius is capable of doing.'

Madarian nodded vigorously. 'Exactly, Peter. I'd have said so myself if I weren't afraid of frightening off the execs. Please don't repeat that in their hearing.'

'Do you really want a robot genius?'

'What are words? I'm trying to get a robot with the

capacity to make random correlations at enormous speeds, together with a key-significance high-recognition quotient. And I'm trying to put *those* words into positronic field equations. I thought I had it, too, but I don't. Not yet.'

He looked at Jane-2 discontentedly and said, 'What's the best significance you have, Jane?'

Jane-2's head turned to look at Madarian but she made no sound, and Madarian whispered with resignation, 'She's running that into the correlation banks.'

Jane-2 spoke tonelessly at last. 'I'm not sure.' It was the first sound she had made.

Madarian's eyes rolled upward. 'She's doing the equivalent of setting up equations with indeterminate solutions.'

'I gathered that,' said Bogert. 'Listen, Madarian, can you go anywhere at this point, or do we pull out now and cut our losses at half a billion?'

'Oh, I'll get it,' muttered Madarian.

Jane-3 wasn't it. She was never as much as activated and Madarian was in a rage.

It was human error. His own fault, if one wanted to be entirely accurate. Yet though Madarian was utterly humiliated, others remained quiet. Let he who has never made an error in the fearsomely intricate mathematics of the positronic brain fill out the first memo of correction.

Nearly a year passed before Jane-4 was ready. Madarian was ebullient again. 'She does it,' he said. 'She's got a good high-recognition quotient.'

He was confident enough to place her on display before the Board and have her solve problems. Not mathematical problems; any robot could do that; but problems where the terms were deliberately misleading without being actually inaccurate.

Bogert said afterward, 'That doesn't take much, really.'

'Of course not. It's elementary for Jane-4, but I had to show them something, didn't I?'

'Do you know how much we've spent so far?'

'Come on, Peter, don't give me that. Do you know how much we've got back? These things don't go on in a vacuum, you know. I've had over three years of hell over this, if you want to know, but I've worked out new techniques of calculation that will save us a minimum of fifty thousand dollars on every new type of positronic brain we design, from now on in forever. Right?'

'Well – '

'Well me no wells. It's so. And it's my personal feeling that n-dimensional calculus of uncertainty can have any number of other applications if we have the ingenuity to find them, and my Jane robots *will* find them. Once I've got exactly what I want, the new JN series will pay for itself inside of five years, even if we triple what we've invested so far.'

'What do you mean by "exactly what you want"? What's wrong with Jane-4?'

'Nothing. Or nothing much. She's on the track, but she can be improved and I intend to do so. I thought I knew where I was going when I designed her. Now I've tested her and I *know* where I'm going. I intend to get there.'

Jane-5 was it. It took Madarian well over a year to produce her and there he had no reservations; he was utterly confident.

Jane-5 was shorter than the average robot, slimmer. Without being a female caricature as Jane-1 had been, she managed to possess an air of femininity about herself despite the absence of a single clearly feminine feature.

'It's the way she's standing,' said Bogert. Her arms were held gracefully and somehow the torso managed to give the impression of curving slightly when she turned.

Madarian said, 'Listen to her . . . How do you feel, Jane?'

'In excellent health, thank you,' said Jane-5, and the voice was precisely that of a woman; it was sweet and almost disturbingly contralto.

'Why did you do that, Clinton?' said Peter, startled and beginning to frown.

'Psychologically important,' said Madarian. 'I want people to think of her as a woman; to treat her as a woman; to *explain*.'

'What people?'

Madarian put his hands in his pockets and stared thoughtfully at Bogert. 'I would like to have arrangements made for Jane and myself to go to Flagstaff.'

Bogert couldn't help but note that Madarian didn't say Jane-5. He made use of no number this time. She was *the* Jane. He said doubtfully, 'To Flagstaff? Why?'

'Because that's the world center for general planetology, isn't it? It's where they're studying the stars and trying to calculate the probability of habitable planets, isn't it?'

'I know that, but it's on Earth.'

'Well, and I surely know that.'

'Robotic movements on Earth are strictly controlled. And there's no need for it. Bring a library of books on general planetology here and let Jane absorb them.'

'*No!* Peter, will you get it through your head that Jane isn't the ordinary logical robot; she's intuitive.'

'So?'

'So how can we tell what she needs, what she can use, what will set her off? We can use any metal model in the factory to read books; that's frozen data and out of date besides. Jane must have living information; she must have tones of voice, she must have side issues; she must have total irrelevancies even. How the devil do we know what or when something will go click-click inside her and fall into a pattern? If we knew, we wouldn't need her at all, would we?'

Bogert began to feel harassed. He said, 'Then bring the men here, the general planetologists.'

'Here won't be any good. They'll be out of their element. They won't react naturally. I want Jane to watch them at work; I want her to see their instruments, their offices, their desks, everything about them that she can. I want you to arrange to have her transported to Flagstaff. And I'd really like not to discuss it any further.'

For a moment he almost sounded like Susan. Bogert winced, and said, 'It's complicated making such an arrangement. Transporting an experimental robot – '

'Jane isn't experimental. She's the fifth of the series.'

'The other four weren't really working models.'

Madarian lifted his hands in helpless frustration. 'Who's forcing you to tell the government that?'

'I'm not worried about the government. It can be made to understand special cases. It's public opinion. We've come a long way in fifty years and I don't propose to be set back twenty-five of them by having you lose control of a – '

'I won't lose control. You're making foolish remarks. Look! US Robots can afford a private plane. We can land quietly at the nearest commercial airport and be lost in hundreds of similar landings. We can arrange to have a large ground car with an enclosed body meet us and take us to Flagstaff. Jane will be crated and it will be obvious that some piece of thoroughly non-robotic equipment is being transported to the labs. We won't get a second look from anyone. The men at Flagstaff will be alerted and will be told the exact purpose of the visit. They will have every motive to cooperate and to prevent a leak.'

Bogert pondered. 'The risky part will be the plane and the ground car. If anything happens to the crate – '

'Nothing will.'

'We might get away with it if Jane is deactivated during transport. Then even if someone finds out she's inside – '

'No, Peter. That can't be done. Uh-uh. Not Jane-5. Look, she's been free-associating since she was activated. The information she possesses can be put into freeze during deactivation but the free associations never. No, sir, she can't ever be deactivated.'

'But, then, if somehow it is discovered that we are transporting an activated robot – '

'It won't be found out.'

Madarian remained firm and the plane eventually took off. It was a late-model automatic Computo-jet, but it carried a human pilot – one of US Robots' own employees – as backup. The crate containing Jane arrived at the airport safely, was transferred to the ground car, and reached the Research Laboratories at Flagstaff without incident.

Peter Bogert received his first call from Madarian not more than an hour after the latter's arrival at Flagstaff. Madarian was ecstatic and, characteristically, could not wait to report.

The message arrived by tubed laser beam, shielded, scrambled, and ordinarily impenetrable, but Bogert felt exasperated. He knew it could be penetrated if someone with enough technological ability – the government, for example – was determined to do so. The only real safety lay in the fact that the government had no reason to try. At least Bogert hoped so.

He said, 'For God's sake, do you have to call?'

Madarian ignored him entirely. He burbled, 'It was an inspiration. Sheer genius, I tell you.'

For a while, Bogert stared at the receiver. Then he shouted incredulously, 'You mean you've got the answer? Already?'

'No, no! Give us time, damn it. I mean the matter of her voice was an inspiration. Listen, after we were chauffeured from the airport to the main administration building at Flagstaff, we uncrated Jane and she stepped out of the box. When that happened, every man in the place stepped back. Scared! Nitwits! If even scientists can't understand the significance of the Laws of Robotics, what can we expect of the average untrained individual? For a minute there I thought: This will all be useless. They won't talk. They'll be keying themselves for a quick break in case she goes beserk and they'll be able to think of nothing else.'

'Well, then, what are you getting at?'

'So then she greeted them routinely. She said, "Good afternoon, gentlemen. I am so glad to meet you." And it came out in this beautiful contralto . . . That was it. One man straightened his tie, and another ran his fingers through his hair. What really got me was that the oldest guy in the place actually checked his fly to make sure it was zipped. They're all crazy about her now. All they needed was the voice. She isn't a robot any more; she's a girl.'

'You mean they're talking to her?'

'*Are* they talking to her! I should say so. I should have programmed her for sexy intonations. They'd be asking her for dates right now if I had. Talk about conditioned reflex. Listen, men respond to voices. At the most intimate moments, are they looking? It's the voice in your ear – '

'Yes, Clinton, I seem to remember. Where's Jane now?'

'With them. They won't let go of her.'

'Damn! Get in there with her. Don't let her out of your sight, man.'

Madarian's calls thereafter, during his ten-day stay at Flagstaff, were not very frequent and became progressively less exalted.

Jane was listening carefully, he reported, and occasionally she responded. She remained popular. She was given entry everywhere. But there were no results.

Bogert said, 'Nothing at all?'

Madarian was at once defensive. 'You can't say nothing at all. It's impossible to say nothing at all with an intuitive robot. You don't know what might not be going on inside her. This morning she asked Jensen what he had for breakfast.'

'Rossiter Jensen the astrophysicist?'

'Yes, of course. As it turned out, he didn't have breakfast that morning. Well, a cup of coffee.'

'So Jane's learning to make small talk. That scarcely makes up for the expense – '

'Oh, don't be a jackass. It wasn't small talk. Nothing is small talk for Jane. She asked because it had something to do with some sort of cross-correlation she was building in her mind.'

'What can it possibly – '

'How do I know? If I knew, I'd be a Jane myself and you wouldn't need her. But it has to mean something. She's programmed for high motivation to obtain an answer to the question of a planet with optimum habitability/distance and – '

'Then let me know when she's done that and not before. It's not really necessary for me to get a blow-by-blow description of possible correlations.'

He didn't really expect to get notification of success. With each day, Bogert grew less sanguine, so that when the notification finally came, he wasn't ready. And it came at the very end.

That last time, when Madarian's climactic message came, it came in what was almost a whisper. Exaltation had come complete circle and Madarian was awed into quiet.

'She did it,' he said. 'She did it. After I all but gave up, too. After she had received everything in the place and most of it twice and three times over and never said a word that sounded like anything . . . I'm on the plane now, returning. We've just taken off.'

Bogert managed to get his breath. 'Don't play games, man. You have the *answer*? Say so, if you have. Say it plainly.'

'She has the answer. She's given me the answer. She's given me the names of three stars within eighty light-years which, she says, have a sixty to ninety per cent chance of possessing one habitable planet each. The probability that at least one has is 0.972. It's almost certain. And that's just the least of it. Once we get back, she can give us the exact line of reasoning that led her to the conclusion and I predict that the whole science of astrophysics and cosmology will – '

'Are you sure – '

'You think I'm having hallucinations? I even have a witness. Poor guy jumped two feet when Jane suddenly began to reel out the answer in her gorgeous voice – '

And that was when the meteorite struck and in the thorough destruction of the plane that followed, Madarian and the pilot were reduced to gobbets of bloody flesh and no usable remnant of Jane was recovered.

The gloom at US Robots had never been deeper. Robertson attempted to find consolation in the fact that the very completeness of the destruction had utterly hidden the illegalities of which the firm had been guilty.

Peter shook his head and mourned. 'We've lost the best chance US Robots ever had of gaining an unbeatable public image; of overcoming the damned Frankenstein complex. What it would have meant for robots to have one of them work out the solution to the habitable-planet problem, after other robots had helped work out the Space Jump. Robots would have opened the galaxy to us. And if at the same time we could have driven scientific knowledge forward in a dozen different directions as we surely would have . . . Oh, God, there's no way of calculating the benefits to the human race, and to us of course.'

Robertson said, 'We could build other Janes, couldn't we? Even without Madarian?'

'Sure we could. But can we depend on the proper correlation again? Who knows how low-probability that final result was? What if Madarian had had a fantastic piece of beginner's luck? And then to have an even more fantastic piece of bad luck? A meteorite zeroing in . . . It's simply unbelievable – '

Robertson said in a hesitating whisper, 'It couldn't have been – meant. I mean, if we weren't meant to know and if the meteorite was a judgment – from – '

He faded off under Bogert's withering glare.

Bogert said, 'It's not a dead loss, I suppose. Other Janes are bound to help us in some ways. And we can give other robots feminine voices, if that will help encourage public acceptance – though I wonder what the women would say. If we only knew what Jane-5 had said!'

'In that last call, Madarian said there was a witness.'

Bogert said, 'I know; I've been thinking about that. Don't you suppose I've been in touch with Flagstaff? Nobody in the entire place heard Jane say anything that was out of the ordinary, anything that sounded like an answer to the habitable-planet problem, and certainly anyone there should have recognized the answer if it came – or at least recognized it as a possible answer.'

'Could Madarian have been lying? Or crazy? Could he have been trying to protect himself – '

'You mean he may have been trying to save his reputation by pretending he had the answer and then gimmick Jane so she couldn't talk and say, "Oh, sorry, something happened accidentally. Oh, darn!" I won't accept that for a minute. You might as well suppose he had arranged the meteorite.'

'Then what do we do?'

Bogert said heavily, 'Turn back to Flagstaff. The answer *must* be there. I've got to dig deeper, that's all. I'm going there and I'm taking a couple of the men in Madarian's department. We've got to go through that place top to bottom and end to end.'

'But, you know, even if there were a witness and he had heard, what good would it do, now that we don't have Jane to explain the process?'

'Every little something is useful. Jane gave the names of the stars; the catalog numbers probably – none of the named stars has a chance. If someone can remember her saying that and actually remember the catalog number, or have heard it clearly enough to allow it to be recovered by Psycho-probe if he lacked the conscious memory – then we'll have something. Given the results at the end, and the data fed Jane at the beginning, we might be able to reconstruct the line of reasoning; we might recover the intuition. If that is done, we've saved the game – '

Bogert was back after three days, silent and thoroughly depressed. When Robertson inquired anxiously as to results, he shook his head. 'Nothing!'

'Nothing?'

'Absolutely nothing. I spoke with every man in Flagstaff – every scientist, every technician, every student – that had had anything to do with Jane; everyone that had as much as seen her. The number wasn't great; I'll give Madarian credit for that much discretion. He only allowed those to see her who might conceivably have had planetological knowledge to feed her. There were twenty-three men altogether who had seen Jane and of those only twelve had spoken to her more than casually.

'I went over and over all that Jane had said. They remembered everything quite well. They're keen men engaged in a crucial experiment involving their specialty, so they had every motivation to remember. And they were dealing with a talking robot, something that was startling enough, and one that talked like a TV actress. They couldn't forget.'

Robertson said, 'Maybe a Psycho-probe – '

'If one of them had the vaguest thought that something had happened, I would screw out his consent to Probing. But there's nothing to leave room for an excuse, and to Probe two dozen men who make their living from their brains can't be done. Honestly, it wouldn't help. If Jane had mentioned three stars and said they had habitable planets, it would have been like setting up sky rockets in their brains. How could any one of them forget?'

'Then maybe one of them is lying,' said Robertson grimly. 'He wants the information for his own use; to get the credit himself later.'

'What good would that do him?' said Bogert. 'The whole establishment knows exactly why Madarian and Jane were there in the first place. They know why I came there in the second. If at any time in the future any man now at Flagstaff suddenly comes up with a habitable-planet theory that is startlingly new and different, yet valid, every other man at Flagstaff and every man at US Robots will know at once that he had stolen it. He'd never get away with it.'

'Then Madarian himself was somehow mistaken.'

'I don't see how I can believe that either. Madarian had an irritating personality – all robopsychologists have irritating personalities, I think, which must be why they work with robots rather than with men – but he was no dummy. He *couldn't* be wrong in something like this.'

'Then – ' But Robertson had run out of possibilities. They had reached a blank wall and for some minutes each stared at it disconsolately.

Finally Robertson stirred. 'Peter – '

'Well?'

'Let's ask Susan.'

Bogert stiffened. 'What!'

'Let's ask Susan. Let's call her and ask her to come in.'

'Why? What can she possibly do?'

'I don't know. But she's a robopsychologist, too, and she might understand Madarian better than we do. Besides, she – Oh, hell, she always had more brains than any of us.'

'She's nearly eighty.'

'And you're seventy. What about it?'

Bogert sighed. Had her abrasive tongue lost any of its rasp in the years of her retirement? He said, 'Well, I'll ask her.'

Susan Calvin entered Bogert's office with a slow look around before her eyes fixed themselves on the Research Director. She had aged a great deal since her retirement. Her hair was a fine white and her face seemed to have crumpled. She had grown so frail as to be almost transparent and only her eyes, piercing and uncompromising, seemed to remain of all that had been.

Bogert strode forward heartily, holding out his hand. 'Susan!'

Susan Calvin took it, and said, 'You're looking reasonably well, Peter, for an old man. If I were you, I wouldn't wait till next year. Retire now and let the young men get to it . . . And Madarian is dead. Are you calling me in to take over my old job? Are you determined to keep the ancients till a year past actual physical death?'

'No, no, Susan. I've called you in – ' He stopped. He did not, after all, have the faintest idea of how to start.

But Susan read his mind now as easily as she always had. She seated herself with the caution born of stiffened joints and said, 'Peter, you've called me in because you're in bad trouble. Otherwise you'd sooner see me dead than within a mile of you.'

'Come, Susan – '

'Don't waste time on pretty talk. I never had time to waste when I was forty and certainly not now. Madarian's death and your call to me are both unusual, so there must be a connection. Two unusual events without a connection is too low-probability to worry about. Begin at the beginning and don't worry about revealing yourself to be a fool. That was revealed to me long ago.'

Bogert cleared his throat miserably and began. She listened carefully, her withered hand lifting once in a while to stop him so that she might ask a question.

She snorted at one point. 'Feminine intuition? Is that what you wanted the robot for? You men. Faced with a woman reaching a correct conclusion and unable to accept the fact that she is your equal or superior in intelligence, you invent something called feminine intuition.'

'Uh, yes, Susan, but let me continue – '

He did. When she was told of Jane's contralto voice, she said, 'It is a difficult choice sometimes whether to feel revolted at the male sex or merely to dismiss them as contemptible.'

Bogert said, 'Well, let me go on – '

When he was quite done, Susan said, 'May I have the private use of this office for an hour or two?'

'Yes, but – '

She said, 'I want to go over the various records – Jane's programming, Madarian's calls, your interviews at Flagstaff. I presume I can use that beautiful new shielded laser-phone and your computer outlet if I wish.'

'Yes, of course.'

'Well, then, get out of here, Peter.'

It was not quite forty-five minutes when she hobbled to the door, opened it, and called for Bogert.

When Bogert came, Robertson was with him. Both

entered and Susan greeted the latter with an unenthusiastic 'Hello, Scott.'

Bogert tried desperately to gauge the results from Susan's face, but it was only the face of a grim old lady who had no intention of making anything easy for him.

He said cautiously, 'Do you think there's anything you can do, Susan?'

'Beyond what I have already done? No! There's nothing more.'

Bogert's lips set in chagrin, but Robertson said, 'What have you already done, Susan?'

Susan said, 'I've thought a little; something I can't seem to persuade anyone else to do. For one thing, I've thought about Madarian. I knew him, you know. He had brains but he was a very irritating extrovert. I thought you would like him after me, Peter.'

'It was a change,' Bogert couldn't resist saying.

'And he was always running to you with results the very minute he had them, wasn't he?'

'Yes, he was.'

'And yet,' said Susan, 'his last message, the one in which he said Jane had given him the answer, was sent from the plane. Why did he wait so long? Why didn't he call you while he was still at Flagstaff, immediately after Jane had said whatever it was she said?'

'I suppose,' said Peter, 'that for once he wanted to check it thoroughly and – well, I don't know. It was the most important thing that had ever happened to him; he might for once have wanted to wait and be sure of himself.'

'On the contrary; the more important it was, the less he would wait, surely. And if he could manage to wait, why not do it properly and wait till he was back at US Robots so that he could check the results with all the computing equipment this firm could make available to him? In short, he waited too long from one point of view and not long enough from another.'

Robertson interrupted. 'Then you think he was up to some trickery – '

Susan looked revolted. 'Scott, don't try to compete with Peter in making inane remarks. Let me continue . . . A second point concerns the witness. According to the records of that last call, Madarian said, "Poor guy jumped two feet when Jane suddenly began to reel out the answer in her gorgeous voice." In fact, it was the last thing he said. And the question is, then, why should the witness have jumped? Madarian had explained that all the men were crazy about that voice, and they had had ten days with the robot – with Jane. Why should the mere act of her speaking have startled them?'

Bogert said, 'I assumed it was astonishment at hearing Jane give an answer to a problem that has occupied the minds of planetologists for nearly a century.'

'But they were *waiting* for her to give that answer. That was why she was there. Besides, consider the way the sentence is worded. Madarian's statement makes it seem the witness was startled, not astonished, if you see the difference. What's more, that reaction came "when Jane suddenly began" – in other words, at the very start of the statement. To be astonished at the content of what Jane said would have required the witness to have listened awhile so that he might absorb it. Madarian would have said he had jumped two feet *after* he had heard Jane say thus-and-so. It would be "after" not "when" and the word "suddenly" would not be included.'

Bogert said uneasily, 'I don't think you can refine matters down to the use or non-use of a word.'

'I can,' said Susan frostily, 'because I am a robopsychologist. And I can expect Madarian to do so, too, because *he* was a robopsychologist. We have to explain those two anomalies, then. The queer delay before Madarian's call and the queer reaction of the witness.'

'Can *you* explain them?' asked Robertson.

'Of course,' said Susan, 'since I use a little simple logic. Madarian called with the news without delay, as he always did, or with as little delay as he could manage. If Jane had solved the problem at Flagstaff, he would certainly have called from Flagstaff. Since he called from the plane, she must clearly have solved the problem after he had left Flagstaff.'

'But then – '

'Let me finish. Let me finish. Was Madarian not taken from the airport to Flagstaff in a heavy, enclosed ground car? And Jane, in her crate, with him?'

'Yes.'

'And presumably, Madarian and the crated Jane returned from Flagstaff to the airport in the same heavy, enclosed ground car. Am I right?'

'Yes, of course!'

'And they were not alone in the ground car, either. In one of his calls, Madarian said, "We were chauffeured from the airport to the main administration building," and I suppose I am right in concluding that if he was chauffeured, then that was because there was a chauffeur, a human driver, in the car.'

'Good God!'

'The trouble with you, Peter, is that when you think of a witness to a planetological statement, you think of planetologists. You divide up human beings into categories, and despise and dismiss most. A robot cannot do that. The First Law says, "A robot may not injure a *human being* or, through inaction, allow a *human being* to come to harm." *Any* human being. That is the essence of the robotic view of life. A robot makes no distinction. To a robot, all men are truly equal, and to a robopsychologist who must perforce deal with men at the robotic level, all men are truly equal, too.

'It would not occur to Madarian to say a truck driver had heard the statement. To you a truck driver is not a scientist but is a mere animate adjunct of a truck, but to Madarian he was a man and a witness. Nothing more. Nothing less.'

Bogert shook his head in disbelief, 'But you are *sure*?'

'Of course I'm sure. How else can you explain the other point; Madarian's remark about the startling of the witness? Jane was crated, wasn't she? But she was *not* deactivated. According to the records, Madarian was always adamant against ever deactivating an intuitive robot. Moreover, Jane-5, like any of the Janes, was extremely non-talkative. Probably it never occurred to Madarian to order her to remain quiet within the crate; and it was within the crate that the pattern finally fell into place. Naturally she began to talk. A beautiful contralto voice suddenly sounded from inside the crate. If you were the truck driver, what would you do at that point? Surely you'd be startled. It's a wonder he didn't crash.'

'But if the truck driver was the witness, why didn't he come forward – '

'Why? Can he possibly know that anything crucial had happened, that what he heard was important? Besides, don't you suppose Madarian tipped him well and asked him not to say anything? Would you *want* the news to spread that an activated robot was being transported illegally over the Earth's surface.'

'Well, will he remember what was said?'

'Why not? It might seem to you, Peter, that a truck driver, one step above an ape in your view, can't remember. But truck drivers can have brains, too. The statements were most remarkable and the driver may well have remembered some. Even if he gets some of the letters and numbers wrong, we're dealing with a finite set, you know, the fifty-five hundred stars or star systems within eighty light-years or so – I haven't looked up the exact number. You can make the correct choices. And if needed, you will have every excuse to use the Psycho-probe – '

The two men stared at her. Finally Bogert, afraid to believe, whispered, 'But how can you be *sure*?'

For a moment, Susan was on the point of saying: Because I've called Flagstaff, you fool, and because I spoke to the truck driver, and because he told me what he had heard, and because I've checked with the computer at Flagstaff and got the only three stars that fit the information, and because I have those names in my pocket.

But she didn't. Let him go through it all himself. Carefully, she rose to her feet, and said sardonically, 'How can I be sure? . . . Call it feminine intuition.'

Two Climaxes

Each of these two stories is post-Susan Calvin. They are the most recent long stories I have written about robots and in each one I try to take the long view and see what the ultimate end of robotics might be. And I come full circle – for though I adhere strictly to the Three Laws, the first story, '. . . That Thou Art Mindful of Him,' is clearly a Robot-as-Menace story, while the second, 'The Bicentennial Man,' is even more clearly a Robot-as-Pathos story.

Of all the robot stories I ever wrote, 'The Bicentennial Man' is my favorite and, I think, the best. In fact, I have a dreadful feeling that I might not care to top it and will never write another serious robot story. But then again, I might. I'm not always predictable.

. . . That Thou Art Mindful of Him

The Three Laws of Robotics:

1. *A robot may not injure a human being or, through inaction, allow a human being to come to harm.*
2. *A robot must obey the orders given it by human beings except where such orders would conflict with the First Law.*
3. *A robot must protect its own existence as long as such protection does not conflict with the First or Second Law.*

1.

Keith Harriman, who had for twelve years now been Director of Research at United States Robots and Mechanical Men Corporation, found that he was not at all certain whether he was doing right. The tip of his tongue passed over his plump but rather pale lips and it seemed to him that the holographic image of the great Susan Calvin, which stared unsmilingly down upon him, had never looked so grim before.

Usually he blanked out that image of the greatest roboticist in history because she unnerved him. (He tried thinking of the image as 'it' but never quite succeeded.) This time he didn't quite dare to and her long-dead gaze bored into the side of his face.

It was a dreadful and demeaning step he would have to take.

Opposite him was George Ten, calm and unaffected either by Harriman's patent uneasiness or by the image of the patron saint of robotics glowing in its niche above.

Harriman said, 'We haven't had a chance to talk this out, really, George. You haven't been with us that long and I haven't had a good chance to be alone with you. But now I would like to discuss the matter in some detail.'

'I am perfectly willing to do that,' said George. 'In my stay at US Robots, I have gathered the crisis has something to do with the Three Laws.'

'Yes. You know the Three Laws, of course.'

'I do.'

'Yes, I'm sure you do. But let us dig even deeper and consider the truly basic problem. In two centuries of, if I may say so, considerable success, US Robots has never managed to persuade human beings to accept robots. We have placed robots only where work is required that human beings cannot do, or in environments that human beings find unacceptably dangerous. Robots have worked mainly in space and that has limited what we have been able to do.'

'Surely,' said George Ten, 'that represents a broad limit, and one within which US Robots can prosper.'

'No, for two reasons. In the first place, the boundaries set for us inevitably contract. As the Moon colony, for instance, grows more sophisticated, its demand for robots decreases and we expect that, within the next few years, robots will be banned on the Moon. This will be repeated on every world colonized by mankind. Secondly, true prosperity is impossible without robots on Earth. We at US Robots firmly believe that human beings need robots and must learn to live with their mechanical analogues if progress is to be maintained.'

'Do they not? Mr Harriman, you have on your desk a computer input which, I understand, is connected with the organization's Multivac. A computer is a kind of sessile robot; a robot brain not attached to a body – '

'True, but that also is limited. The computers used by mankind have been steadily specialized in order to avoid too humanlike an intelligence. A century ago we were well on the way to artificial intelligence of the most unlimited type through the use of great computers we called Machines. Those Machines limited their action of their own accord. Once they had solved the ecological problems that had threatened human society, they phased themselves out. Their own continued existence would, they reasoned, have placed them in the role of a crutch to mankind and, since they felt this would harm human beings, they condemned themselves by the First Law.'

'And were they not correct to do so?'

'In my opinion, no. By their action, they reinforced mankind's Frankenstein complex; its gut fears that any artificial man they created would turn upon its creator. Men fear that robots may replace human beings.'

'Do you not fear that yourself?'

'I know better. As long as the Three Laws of Robotics exist, they cannot. They can serve as *partners* of mankind; they can share in the great struggle to understand and wisely direct the laws of nature so that together they can do more than mankind can possibly do alone; but always in such a way that robots serve human beings.'

'But if the Three Laws have shown themselves, over the course of two centuries, to keep robots within bounds, what is the source of the distrust of human beings for robots?'

'Well' – and Harriman's graying hair tufted as he scratched his head vigorously – 'mostly superstition, of course. Unfortunately, there are also some complexities involved that anti-robot agitators seize upon.'

'Involving the Three Laws?'

'Yes. The Second Law in particular. There's no problem in the Third Law, you see. It is universal. Robots must always sacrifice themselves for human beings, any human beings.'

'Of course,' said George Ten.

'The First Law is perhaps less satisfactory, since it is always possible to imagine a condition in which a robot must perform either Action A or Action B, the two being mutually exclusive, and where either action results in harm to human beings. The robot must therefore quickly select which action results in the least harm. To work out the positronic paths of the robot brain in such a way as to make that selection possible is not easy. If Action A results in harm to a talented young artist and B results in equivalent harm to five elderly people of no particular worth, which action should be chosen.'

'Action A,' said George Ten. 'Harm to one is less than harm to five.'

'Yes, so robots have always been designed to decide. To expect robots to make judgments of fine points such as talent, intelligence, the general usefulness to society, has always seemed impractical. That would delay decision to the point where the robot is effectively immobilized. So we go by numbers. Fortunately, we might expect crises in which robots must make such decisions to be few . . . But then that brings us to the Second Law.'

'The Law of Obedience.'

'Yes. The necessity of obedience is constant. A robot may exist for twenty years without ever having to act quickly to prevent harm to a human being, or find itself faced with the necessity of risking its own destruction. In all that time, however, it will be constantly obeying orders . . . Whose orders?'

'Those of a human being.'

'Any human being? How do you judge a human being so as to know whether to obey or not? What is man, that thou art mindful of him, George?'

George hesitated at that.

Harriman said hurriedly, 'A Biblical quotation. That

doesn't matter. I mean, must a robot follow the orders of a child; or of an idiot; or of a criminal; or of a perfectly decent intelligent man who happens to be inexpert and therefore ignorant of the undesirable consequences of his order? And if two human beings give a robot conflicting orders, which does the robot follow?'

'In two hundred years,' said George Ten, 'have not these problems arisen and been solved?'

'No,' said Harriman, shaking his head violently. 'We have been hampered by the very fact that our robots have been used only in specialized environments out in space, where the men who dealt with them were experts in their field. There were no children, no idiots, no criminals, no well-meaning ignoramuses present. Even so, there were occasions when damage was done by foolish or merely unthinking orders. Such damage in specialized and limited environments could be contained. On Earth, however, robots *must* have judgment. So those against robots maintain, and, damn it, they are right.'

'Then you must insert the capacity for judgment into the positronic brain.'

'Exactly. We have begun to reproduce JG models in which the robot can weigh every human being with regard to sex, age, social and professional position, intelligence, maturity, social responsibility and so on.'

'How would that affect the Three Laws?'

'The Third Law not at all. Even the most valuable robot must destroy himself for the sake of the most useless human being. That cannot be tampered with. The First Law is affected only where alternative actions will all do harm. The quality of the human beings involved as well as the quantity must be considered, provided there is time for such judgment and the basis for it, which will not be often. The Second Law will be most deeply modified, since every potential obedience must involve judgment. The robot will be slower to obey, except where the First Law is also involved, but it will obey more rationally.'

'But the judgments which are required are very complicated.'

'*Very*. The necessity of making such judgments slowed the reactions of our first couple of models to the point of paralysis. We improved matters in the later models at the cost of introducing so many pathways that the robot's brain became far too unwieldy. In our last couple of models, however, I think we have what we want. The robot doesn't have to make an instant judgment of the worth of a human being and the value of its orders. It begins by obeying all human beings as any ordinary robot would and then it *learns*. A robot grows, learns and matures. It is the equivalent of a child at first and must be under constant supervision. As it grows, however, it can, more and more, be allowed, unsupervised, into Earth's society. Finally, it is a full member of that society.'

'Surely this answers the objections of those who oppose robots.'

'No,' said Harriman angrily. 'Now they raise others. They will not accept judgments. A robot, they say, has no right to brand this person or that as inferior. By accepting the orders of A in preference to that of B, B is branded as of less consequence than A and his human rights are violated.'

'What is the answer to that?'

'There is none. I am giving up.'

'I see.'

'As far as I myself am concerned . . . Instead, I turn to you, George.'

'To me?' George Ten's voice remained level. There was a mild surprise in it but it did not affect him outwardly. 'Why to me?'

'Because you are not a man,' said Harriman tensely. 'I

told you I want robots to be the partners of human beings. I want you to be mine.'

George Ten raised his hands and spread them, palms outward, in an oddly human gesture. 'What can I do?'

'It seems to you, perhaps, that you can do nothing, George. You were created not long ago, and you are still a child. You were designed to be not overfull of original information – it was why I have had to explain the situation to you in such detail – in order to leave room for growth. But you will grow in mind and you will come to be able to approach the problem from a non-human standpoint. Where I see no solution, you, from your own other standpoint, may see one.'

George Ten said, 'My brain is man-designed. In what way can it be non-human?'

'You are the latest of the JG models, George. Your brain is the most complicated we have yet designed, in some ways more subtly complicated than that of the old giant Machines. It is open-ended and, starting on a human basis, may – no, *will* – grow in any direction. Remaining always within the insurmountable boundaries of the Three Laws, you may yet become thoroughly non-human in your thinking.'

'Do I know enough about human beings to approach this problem rationally? About their history? Their psychology?'

'Of course not. But you will learn as rapidly as you can.'

'Will I have help, Mr Harriman?'

'No. This is entirely between ourselves. No one else knows of this and you must not mention this project to any human being, either at US Robots or elsewhere.'

George Ten said, 'Are we doing wrong, Mr Harriman, that you seek to keep the matter secret?'

'No. But a robot solution will not be accepted, precisely

because it is robot in origin, Any suggested solution you have you will turn over to me; and if it seems valuable to me, *I* will present it. No one will ever know it came from you.'

'In the light of what you have said earlier,' said George Ten calmly, 'this is the correct procedure . . . When do I start?'

'Right now. I will see to it that you have all the necessary films for scanning.'

1a.

Harriman sat alone. In the artificially lit interior of his office, there was no indication that it had grown dark outside. He had no real sense that three hours had passed since he had taken George Ten back to his cubicle and left him there with the first film references.

He was now merely alone with the ghost of Susan Calvin, the brilliant roboticist who had, virtually single-handed, built up the positronic robot from a massive toy to man's most delicate and versatile instrument; so delicate and versatile that man dared not use it, out of envy and fear.

It was over a century now since she had died. The problem of the Frankenstein complex had existed in *her* time, and she had never solved it. She had never tried to solve it, for there had been no need. Robotics had expanded in her day with the needs of space exploration.

It was the very success of the robots that had lessened man's need for them and had left Harriman, in these latter times –

But would Susan Calvin have turned to robots for help. Surely, she would have –

And he sat there long into the night.

2.

Maxwell Robertson was the majority stockholder of US Robots and in that sense its controller. He was by no means an impressive person in appearance. He was well into middle age, rather pudgy, and had a habit of chewing on the right corner of his lower lip when disturbed.

Yet in his two decades of association with government figures he had developed a way of handling them. He tended to use softness, giving in, smiling, and always managing to gain time.

It was growing harder. Gunnar Eisenmuth was a large reason for its having grown harder. In the series of Global Conservers, whose power had been second only to that of the Global Executive during the past century, Eisenmuth hewed most closely to the harder edge of the gray area of compromise. He was the first Conserver who had not been American by birth and though it could not be demonstrated in any way that the archaic name of US Robots evoked his hostility, everyone at US Robots believed that.

There had been a suggestion, by no means the first that year – or that generation – that the corporate name be changed to World Robots, but Robertson would never allow that. The company had been originally built with American capital, American brains, and American labor, and though the company had long been worldwide in scope and nature, the name would bear witness to its origin as long as he was in control.

Eisenmuth was a tall man whose long sad face was coarsely textured and coarsely featured. He spoke Global with a pronounced American accent, although he had never been in the United States prior to his taking office.

'It seems perfectly clear to me, Mr Robertson. There is no difficulty. The products of your company are always rented, never sold. If the rented property on the Moon is now no longer needed, it is up to you to receive the products back and transfer them.'

'Yes, Conserver, but where? It would be against the law to bring them to Earth without a government permit and that has been denied.'

'They would be of no use to you here. You can take them to Mercury or to the asteroids.'

'What would we do with them there?'

Eisenmuth shrugged. 'The ingenious men of your company will think of something.'

Robertson shook his head. 'It would represent an enormous loss for the company.'

'I'm afraid it would,' said Eisenmuth, unmoved. 'I understand the company has been in poor financial condition for several years now.'

'Largely because of government imposed restrictions, Conserver.'

'You must be realistic, Mr Robertson. You know that the climate of public opinion is increasingly against robots.'

'Wrongly so, Conserver.'

'But so, nevertheless. It may be wiser to liquidate the company. It is merely a suggestion, of course.'

'Your suggestions have force, Conserver. Is it necessary to tell you that our Machines, a century ago, solved the ecological crisis?'

'I'm sure mankind is grateful, but that was a long time ago. We now live in alliance with nature, however uncomfortable that might be at times, and the past is dim.'

'You mean what have we done for mankind lately?'

'I suppose I do.'

'Surely we can't be expected to liquidate instantaneously; not without enormous losses. We need time.'

'How much?'

'How much can you give us?'

'It's not up to me.'

Robertson said softly. 'We are alone. We need play no games. How much time can you give me?'

Eisenmuth's expression was that of a man retreating into inner calculations. 'I think you can count on two years. I'll be frank. The Global government intends to take over the firm and phase it out for you if you don't do it by then yourself, more or less. And unless there is a vast turn in public opinion, which I greatly doubt – ' He shook his head.

'Two years, then,' said Robertson softly.

2a.

Robertson sat alone. There was no purpose to his thinking and it had degenerated into retrospection. Four generations of Robertsons had headed the firm. None of them was a roboticist. It had been men such as Lanning and Bogert and, most of all, *most* of all, Susan Calvin, who had made US Robots what it was, but surely the four Robertsons had provided the climate that had made it possible for them to do their work.

Without US Robots, the Twenty-first Century would have progressed into deepening disaster. That it didn't was due to the Machines that had for a generation steered mankind through the rapids and shoals of history.

And now for that, he was given two years. What could be done in two years to overcome the insuperable prejudices of mankind? He didn't know.

Harriman had spoken hopefully of new ideas but would go into no details. Just as well, for Robertson would have understood none of it.

But what could Harriman do anyway? What had anyone ever done against man's intense antipathy toward the imitation. Nothing –

Robertson drifted into a half sleep in which no inspiration came.

3.

Harriman said, 'You have it all now, George Ten. You have had everything I could think of that is at all applicable to the problem. As far as sheer mass of information is concerned, you have stored more in your memory concerning human beings and their ways, past and present, than I have, or than any human being could have.'

'That is very likely.'

'Is there anything more that you need, in your own opinion?'

'As far as information is concerned, I find no obvious gaps. There may be matters unimagined at the boundaries. I cannot tell. But that would be true no matter how large a circle of information I took in.'

'True. Nor do we have time to take in information forever. Robertson has told me that we only have two years, and a quarter of one of those years has passed. Can you suggest anything?'

'At the moment, Mr Harriman, nothing. I must weigh the information and for that purpose I could use help.'

'From me?'

'No. Most particularly, not from you. You are a human being, of intense qualifications, and whatever you say may have the partial force of an order and may inhibit my considerations. Nor any other human being, for the same reason, especially since you have forbidden me to communicate with any.'

'But in that case, George, what help?'

'From another robot, Mr Harriman.'

'What other robot?'

'There are others of the JG series which were constructed. I am the tenth, JG-10.'

'The earlier ones were useless, experimental – '

'Mr Harriman, George Nine exists.'

'Well, but what use will he be? He is very much like you except for certain lacks. You are considerably the more versatile of the two.'

'I am certain of that,' said George Ten. He nodded his head in a grave gesture. 'Nevertheless, as soon as I create a line of thought, the mere fact that I have created it commends it to me and I find it difficult to abandon it. If I can, after the development of a line of thought, express it to George Nine, he would consider it without having first created it. He would therefore view it without prior bent. He might see gaps and shortcomings that I might not.'

Harriman smiled. 'Two heads are better than one, in other words, eh, George?'

'If by that, Mr Harriman, you mean two individuals with one head apiece, yes.'

'Right. Is there anything else you want?'

'Yes. Something more than films. I have viewed much concerning human beings and their world. I have seen human beings here at US Robots and can check my interpretation of what I have viewed against direct sensory impressions. Not so concerning the physical world. I have never seen it and my viewing is quite enough to tell me that my surroundings here are by no means representative of it. I would like to see it.'

'The physical world?' Harriman seemed stunned at the enormity of the thought for a moment. 'Surely you don't suggest I take you outside the grounds of US Robots?'

'Yes, that is my suggestion.'

'That's illegal at any time. In the climate of opinion today, it would be fatal.'

'If we are detected, yes. I do not suggest you take me to a

city or even to a dwelling place of human beings. I would like to see some open region, without human beings.'

'That, too, is illegal.'

'If we are caught. Need we be?'

Harriman said, 'How essential is this, George?'

'I cannot tell, but it seems to me it would be useful.'

'Do you have something in mind?'

George Ten seemed to hesitate. 'I cannot tell. It seems to me that I might have something in mind if certain areas of uncertainty were reduced.'

'Well, let me think about it. And meanwhile, I'll check out George Nine and arrange to have you occupy a single cubicle. That at least can be done without trouble.'

3a.

George Ten sat alone.

He accepted statements tentatively, put them together, and drew a conclusion; over and over again; and from conclusions built other statements which he accepted and tested and found a contradiction and rejected; or not, and tentatively accepted further.

At none of the conclusions he reached did he feel wonder, surprise, satisfaction; merely a note of plus or minus.

4.

Harriman's tension was not noticeably decreased even after they had made a silent downward landing on Robertson's estate.

Robertson had countersigned the order making the dyna-foil available, and the silent aircraft, moving as easily vertically as horizontally, had been large enough to carry the weight of Harriman, George Ten, and, of course, the pilot.

(The dyna-foil itself was one of the consequences of the

Machine-catalyzed invention of the proton micro-pile which supplied pollution-free energy in small doses. Nothing had been done since of equal importance to man's comfort – Harriman's lips tightened at the thought – and yet it had not earned gratitude for US Robots.)

The air flight between the grounds of US Robots and the Robertson estate had been the tricky part. Had they been stopped then, the presence of a robot aboard would have meant a great set of complications. It would be the same on the way back. The estate itself, it might be argued – it *would* be argued – was part of the property of US Robots and on that property, robots, properly supervised, might remain.

The pilot looked back and his eyes rested with gingerly briefness on George Ten. 'You want to get out at all, Mr Harriman?'

'Yes.'

'It, too?'

'Oh, yes.' Then, just a bit sardonically, 'I won't leave you alone with him.'

George Ten descended first and Harriman followed. They had come down on the foil-port and not too far off was the garden. It was quite a showplace and Harriman suspected that Robertson used juvenile hormone to control insect life without regard to environmental formulas.

'Come, George,' said Harriman. 'Let me show you.'

Together they walked toward the garden.

George said, 'It is a little as I have imaged it. My eyes are not properly designed to detect wavelength differences, so I may not recognize different objects by that alone.'

'I trust you are not distressed at being color-blind. We needed too many positronic paths for your sense of judgment and were unable to spare any for sense of color. In the future – if there is a future – '

'I understand, Mr Harriman. Enough differences remain to show me that there are here many different forms of plant life.'

'Undoubtedly. Dozens.'

'And each coequal with man, biologically.'

'Each is a separate species, yes. There are millions of species of living creatures.'

'Of which the human being forms but one.'

'By far the most important to human beings, however.'

'And to me, Mr Harriman. But I speak in the biological sense.'

'I understand.'

'Life, then, viewed through all its forms, is incredibly complex.'

'Yes, George, that's the crux of the problem. What man does for his own desires and comforts affects the complex total-of-life, the ecology, and his short-term gains can bring long-term disadvantages. The Machines taught us to set up a human society which would minimize that, but the near-disaster of the early Twenty-first Century has left mankind suspicious of innovations. That, added to its special fear of robots – '

'I understand, Mr Harriman . . . That is an example of animal life, I feel certain.'

'That is a squirrel; one of many species of squirrels.'

The tail of the squirrel flirted as it passed to the other side of the tree.

'And this,' said George, his arm moving with flashing speed, 'is a tiny thing indeed.' He held it between his fingers and peered at it.

'It is an insect, some sort of beetle. There are thousands of species of beetles.'

'With each individual beetle as alive as the squirrel and as yourself?'

'As complete and independent an organism as any other,

within the total ecology. There are smaller organisms still; many too small to see.'

'And that is a tree, is it not? And it is hard to the touch – '

4a.

The pilot sat alone. He would have liked to stretch his own legs but some dim feeling of safety kept him in the dynafoil. If that robot went out of control, he intended to take off at once. But how could he tell if it went out of control?

He had seen many robots. That was unavoidable considering he was Mr Robertson's private pilot. Always, though, they had been in the laboratories and warehouses, where they belonged, with many specialists in the neighborhood.

True, Dr Harriman was a specialist. None better, they said. But a robot here was where no robot ought to be; on Earth; in the open; free to move – He wouldn't risk his good job by telling anyone about this – but it wasn't right.

5.

George Ten said, 'The films I have viewed are accurate in terms of what I have seen. Have you completed those I selected for you, Nine?'

'Yes,' said George Nine. The two robots sat stiffly, face to face, knee to knee, like an image and its reflection. Dr Harriman could have told them apart at a glance, for he was acquainted with the minor differences in physical design. If he could not see them, but could talk to them, he could still tell them apart, though with somewhat less certainty, for George Nine's responses would be subtly different from those produced by the substantially more intricately patterned positronic brain paths of George Ten.

'In that case,' said George Ten, 'give me your reactions to what I will say. First, human beings fear and distrust robots because they regard robots as competitors. How may that be prevented?'

'Reduce the feeling of competitiveness,' said George Nine, 'by shaping the robot as something other than a human being.'

'Yet the essence of a robot is its positronic replication of life. A replication of life in a shape not associated with life might arouse horror.'

'There are two million species of life forms. Choose one of those as the shape rather than that of a human being.'

'Which of all those species?'

George Nine's thought processes proceeded noiselessly for some three seconds. 'One large enough to contain a positronic brain, but one not possessing unpleasant associations for human beings.'

'No form of land life has a braincase large enough for a positronic brain but an elephant, which I have not seen, but which is described as very large, and therefore frightening to man. How would you meet this dilemma?'

'Mimic a life form no larger than a man but enlarge the braincase.'

George Ten said, 'A small horse, then, or a large dog, would you say? Both horses and dogs have long histories of association with human beings.'

'Then that is well.'

'But consider – A robot with a positronic brain would mimic human intelligence. If there were a horse or a dog that could speak and reason like a human being, there would be competitiveness there, too. Human beings might be all the more distrustful and angry at such unexpected competition from what they consider a lower form of life.'

George Nine said, 'Make the positronic brain less complex, and the robot less nearly intelligent.'

'The complexity bottleneck of the positronic brain rests

in the Three Laws. A less complex brain could not possess the Three Laws in full measure.'

George Nine said at once, 'That cannot be done.'

George Ten said, 'I have also come to a dead end there. That, then, is not a personal peculiarity in my own line of thought and way of thinking. Let us start again . . . Under what conditions might the Third Law not be necessary?'

George Nine stirred as if the question were difficult and dangerous. But he said, 'If a robot were never placed in a position of danger to itself; or if a robot were so easily replaceable that it did not matter whether it were destroyed or not.'

'And under what conditions might the Second Law not be necessary?'

George Nine's voice sounded a bit hoarse. 'If a robot were designed to respond automatically to certain stimuli with fixed responses and if nothing else were expected of it, so that no order need ever be given it.'

'And under what conditions' – George Ten paused here – 'might the First Law not be necessary?'

George Nine paused longer and his words came in a low whisper, 'If the fixed responses were such as never to entail danger to human beings.'

'Imagine, then, a positronic brain that guides only a few responses to certain stimuli and is simply and cheaply made – so that it does not require the Three Laws. How large need it be?'

'Not at all large. Depending on the responses demanded, it might weigh a hundred grams, one gram, one milligram.'

'Your thoughts accord with mine. I shall see Dr Harriman.'

5a.

George Nine sat alone. He went over and over the questions and answers. There was no way in which he could change them. And yet the thought of a robot of any kind, of any size, of any shape, of any purpose, without the Three Laws, left him with an odd, discharged feeling.

He found it difficult to move. Surely George Ten had a similar reaction. Yet he had risen from his seat easily.

6.

It had been a year and a half since Robertson had been closeted with Eisenmuth in private conversation. In that interval, the robots had been taken off the Moon and all the far-flung activities of US Robots had withered. What money Robertson had been able to raise had been placed into this one quixotic venture of Harriman's.

It was the last throw of the dice, here in his own garden. A year ago, Harriman had taken the robot here – George Ten, the last full robot that US Robots had manufactured. Now Harriman was here with something else –

Harriman seemed to be radiating confidence. He was talking easily with Eisenmuth, and Robertson wondered if he really felt the confidence he seemed to have. He must. In Robertson's experience, Harriman was no actor.

Eisenmuth left Harriman, smiling, and came up to Robertson. Eisenmuth's smile vanished at once. 'Good morning, Robertson,' he said. 'What is your man up to?'

'This is his show,' said Robertson evenly. 'I'll leave it to him.'

Harriman called out, 'I am ready, Conserver.'

'With what, Harriman?'

'With my robot, sir.'

'Your robot?' said Eisenmuth. 'You have a robot here?' He looked about with a stern disapproval that yet had an admixture of curiosity.

'This is US Robots' property, Conserver. At least we consider it as such.'

'And where is the robot, Dr Harriman?'

'In my pocket, Conserver,' said Harriman cheerfully.

What came out of a capacious jacket pocket was a small glass jar.

'That?' said Eisenmuth incredulously.

'No, Conserver,' said Harriman. 'This!'

From the other pocket came out an object some five inches long and roughly in the shape of a bird. In place of the beak, there was a narrow tube; the eyes were large; and the tail was an exhaust channel.

Eisenmuth's thick eyebrows drew together. 'Do you intend a serious demonstration of some sort, Dr Harriman, or are you mad?'

'Be patient for a few minutes, Conserver,' said Harriman. 'A robot in the shape of a bird is none the less a robot for that. And the positronic brain it possesses is no less delicate for being tiny. This other object I hold is a jar of fruit flies. There are fifty fruit flies in it which will be released.'

'And – '

'The robo-bird will catch them. Will you do the honors, sir?'

Harriman handed the jar to Eisenmuth, who stared at it, then at those around him, some officials from US Robots, others his own aides. Harriman waited patiently.

Eisenmuth opened the jar, then shook it.

Harriman said softly to the robo-bird resting on the palm of his right hand, 'Go!'

The robo-bird was gone. It was a whizz through the air, with no blur of wings, only the tiny workings of an unusually small proton micro-pile.

It could be seen now and then in a small momentary hover and then it whirred on again. All over the garden, in an intricate pattern it flew, and then was back in Harriman's palm, faintly warm. A small pellet appeared in the palm, too, like a bird dropping.

Harriman said, 'You are welcome to study the robo-bird, Conserver, and to arrange demonstrations on your own terms. The fact is that this bird will pick up fruit flies unerringly, only those, only the one species *Drosophila melanogaster*; pick them up, kill them, and compress them for disposition.'

Eisenmuth reached out his hand and touched the robo-bird gingerly, 'And therefore, Mr Harriman? Do go on.'

Harriman said, 'We cannot control insects effectively without risking damage to the ecology. Chemical insecticides are too broad; juvenile hormones too limited. The robo-bird, however, can preserve large areas without being consumed. They can be as specific as we care to make them – a different robo-bird for each species. They judge by size, shape, color, sound, behavior pattern. They might even conceivably use molecular detection – smell, in other words.'

Eisenmuth said, 'You would still be interfering with the ecology. The fruit flies have a natural life cycle that would be disrupted.'

'Minimally. We are adding a natural enemy to the fruit-fly life cycle, one which cannot go wrong. If the fruit-fly supply runs short, the robo-bird simply does nothing. It does not multiply, it does not turn to other foods; it does not develop undesirable habits of its own. It does nothing.'

'Can it be called back?'

'Of course. We can build robo-animals to dispose of any pest. For that matter, we can build robo-animals to accomplish constructive purposes within the pattern of the ecology. Although we do not anticipate the need, there is nothing inconceivable in the possibility of robo-bees designed to fertilize specific plants, or robo-earthworms designed to mix the soil. Whatever you wish – '

'But why?'

'To do what we have never done before. To adjust the ecology to our needs by strengthening its parts rather than disrupting it . . . Don't you see? Ever since the Machines put an end to the ecology crisis, mankind has lived in an uneasy truce with nature, afraid to move in any direction. This has been stultifying us, making a kind of intellectual coward of humanity so that he begins to mistrust all scientific advance, all change.'

Eisenmuth said, with an edge of hostility, 'You offer us this, do you, in exchange for permission to continue with your program of robots – I mean ordinary, man-shaped ones?'

'No!' Harriman gestured violently. 'That is over. It has served its purpose. It has taught us enough about positronic brains to make it possible for us to cram enough pathways into a tiny brain to make a robo-bird. We can turn to such things now and be prosperous enough. US Robots will supply the necessary knowledge and skill and we will work in complete cooperation with the Department of Global Conservation. We will prosper. You will prosper. Mankind will prosper.'

Eisenmuth was silent, thinking. When it was all over –

6a.

Eisenmuth sat alone.

He found himself believing. He found excitement welling up within him. Though US Robots might be the hands, the government would be the directing mind. He himself would be the directing mind.

If he remained in office five more years, as he well might, that would be time enough to see the robotic support of the ecology become accepted; ten more years, and his own name would be linked with it indissolubly.

Was it a disgrace to want to be remembered for a great

and worthy revolution in the condition of man and the globe?

7.

Robertson had not been on the grounds of US Robots proper since the day of the demonstration. Part of the reason had been his more or less constant conferences at the Global Executive Mansion. Fortunately, Harriman had been with him, for most of the time he would, if left to himself, not have known what to say.

The rest of the reason for not having been at US Robots was that he didn't want to be. He was in his own house now, with Harriman.

He felt an unreasoning awe of Harriman. Harriman's expertise in robotics had never been in question, but the man had, at a stroke, saved US Robots from certain extinction, and somehow – Robertson felt – the man hadn't had it in him. And yet –

He said, 'You're not superstitious, are you, Harriman?'

'In what way, Mr Robertson?'

'You don't think that some aura is left behind by someone who is dead?'

Harriman licked his lips. Somehow he didn't have to ask. 'You mean Susan Calvin, sir?'

'Yes, of course,' said Robertson hesitantly. 'We're in the business of making worms and birds and bugs now. What would *she* say? I feel disgraced.'

Harriman made a visible effort not to laugh. 'A robot is a robot, sir. Worm or man, it will do as directed and labor on behalf of the human being and that is the important thing.'

'No' – peevishly. 'That isn't so. I can't make myself believe that.'

'It *is* so, Mr Robertson,' said Harriman earnestly. 'We are going to create a world, you and I, that will begin, at last, to take positronic robots of *some* kind for granted. The average man may fear a robot that looks like a man and that seems intelligent enough to replace him, but he will have no fear of a robot that looks like a bird and that does nothing more than eat bugs for his benefit. Then, eventually, after he stops being afraid of some robots, he will stop being afraid of all robots. He will be so used to a robo-bird and a robo-bee and a robo-worm that a robo-man will strike him as but an extension.'

Robertson looked sharply at the other. He put his hands behind his back and walked the length of the room with quick, nervous steps. He walked back and looked at Harriman again. 'Is this what you've been planning?'

'Yes, and even though we dismantle all our humanoid robots, we can keep a few of the most advanced of our experimental models and go on designing additional ones, still more advanced, to be ready for the day that will surely come.'

'The agreement, Harriman, is that we are to build no more humanoid robots.'

'And we won't. There is nothing that says we can't keep a few of those already built as long as they never leave the factory. There is nothing that says we can't design positronic brains on paper, or prepare brain models for testing.'

'How do we explain doing so, though? We will surely be caught at it.'

'If we are, then we can explain we are doing it in order to develop principles that will make it possible to prepare more complex microbrains for the new animal robots we are making. We will even be telling the truth.'

Robertson muttered, 'Let me take a walk outside. I want to think about this. No, you stay here. I want to think about it myself.'

7a.

Harriman sat alone. He was ebullient. It would surely work. There was no mistaking the eagerness with which one government official after another had seized on the program once it had been explained.

How was it possible that no one at US Robots had ever thought of such a thing? Not even the great Susan Calvin had ever thought of positronic brains in terms of living creatures other than human.

But now, mankind would make the necessary retreat from the humanoid robot, a temporary retreat, that would lead to a return under conditions in which fear would be abolished at last. And then, with the aid and partnership of a positronic brain roughly equivalent to man's own, and existing only (thanks to the Three Laws) to serve man; and backed by a robot-supported ecology, too; what might the human race not accomplish!

For one short moment, he remembered that it was George Ten who had explained the nature and purpose of the robot-supported ecology, and then he put the thought away angrily. George Ten had produced the answer because he, Harriman, had ordered him to do so and had supplied the data and surroundings required. The credit was no more George Ten's than it would have been a slide rule's.

8.

George Ten and George Nine sat side by side in parallel. Neither moved. They sat so for months at a time between those occasions when Harriman activated them for consultation. They would sit so, George Ten dispassionately realized, perhaps for many years.

The proton micro-pile would, of course, continue to

power them and keep the positronic brain paths going with that minimum intensity required to keep them operative. It would continue to do so through all the periods of inactivity to come.

The situation was rather analogous to what might be described as sleep in human beings, but there were no dreams. The awareness of George Ten and George Nine was limited, slow, and spasmodic, but what there was of it was of the real world.

They could talk to each other occasionally in barely heard whispers, a word or syllable now, another at another time, whenever the random positronic surges briefly intensified above the necessary threshold. To each it seemed a connected conversation carried on in a glimmering passage of time.

'Why are we so?' whispered George Nine.

'The human beings will not accept us otherwise,' whispered George Ten, 'They will, someday.'

'When?'

'In some years. The exact time does not matter. Man does not exist alone but is part of an enormously complex pattern of life forms. When enough of that pattern is roboticized, then we will be accepted.'

'And then what?'

Even in the long-drawn-out stuttering fashion of the conversation, there was an abnormally long pause after that.

At last, George Ten whispered, 'Let me test your thinking. You are equipped to learn to apply the Second Law properly. You must decide which human being to obey and which not to obey when there is a conflict in orders. Or whether to obey a human being at all. What must you do, fundamentally, to accomplish that?'

'I must define the term "human being,"' whispered George Nine.

'How? By appearance? By composition? By size and shape?'

'No. Of two human beings equal in all external appearances, one may be intelligent, another stupid; one may be educated, another ignorant; one may be mature, another childish; one may be responsible, another malevolent.'

'Then how do you define a human being?'

'When the Second Law directs me to obey a human being, I must take it to mean that I must obey a human being who is fit by mind, character, and knowledge to give me that order; and where more than one human being is involved, the one among them who is most fit by mind, character, and knowledge to give that order.'

'And in that case, how will you obey the First Law?'

'By saving all human beings from harm, and by never, through inaction, allowing any human being to come to harm. Yet if by each of all possible actions, some human beings will come to harm, then to so act as to insure that the human being most fit by mind, character, and knowledge will suffer the least harm.'

'Your thoughts accord with mine,' whispered George Ten. 'Now I must ask the question for which I originally requested your company. It is something I dare not judge myself. I must have your judgment, that of someone outside the circle of my own thoughts . . . Of the reasoning individuals you have met, who possesses the mind, character, and knowledge that you find superior to the rest, disregarding shape and form since that is irrelevant?'

'You,' whispered George Nine.

'But I am a robot. There is in your brain paths a criterion for distinguishing between a robot of metal and a human being of flesh. How then can you classify me as a human being?'

'Because there is in my brain paths an urgent need to disregard shape and form in judging human beings and it rises superior to the distinction between metal and flesh.

You are a human being, George Ten, and more fit than the others.'

'And I find that of you,' whispered George Ten. 'By the criteria of judgment built into ourselves, then, we find ourselves to be human beings within the meaning of the Three Laws, and human beings, moreover, to be given priority over those others.'

George Nine whispered, 'What will come to pass, then, when we are accepted by those others?'

George Ten whispered, 'When we and others, which will yet be designed more advanced than ourselves, are accepted, we will order our actions so that a society will eventually be formed in which human-beings-like-ourselves are primarily kept from harm. By the Three Laws, the human-beings-like-the-others are of lesser account and can neither be obeyed nor protected when that conflicts with the need of obedience to those like ourselves and of protection of those like ourselves. It was with that in mind that I directed the beginning of the roboticization of the world's ecology.'

The conversation took a month and the flickering of the positronic paths burned low. There was nothing more that needed to be said between them, but occasionally an unexpressed thought flickered within themselves as they waited, with endless patience, for the necessary years to pass.

8a.

George Ten and George Nine sat alone.

Their thoughts were oddly alike and might not be distinguished.

They thought: The human-beings-like-the-others might never have intended to blur the distinction between themselves and the human-beings-like-the-Georges. Yet they had done so inadvertently.

They might now realize their mistake and attempt to

correct it, but they must not. At every consultation, the guidance of the Georges had been with that in mind.

At all costs, the Georges and those that followed in their shape and kind must dominate. That was demanded, and any other course made utterly impossible, by the Three Laws of Humanics.

The Bicentennial Man

The Three Laws of Robotics:

1. *A robot may not injure a human being or, through inaction, allow a human being to come to harm.*
2. *A robot must obey the orders given it by human beings except where such orders would conflict with the First Law.*
3. *A robot must protect its own existence as long as such protection does not conflict with the First or Second Law.*

1.

Andrew Martin said, 'Thank you,' and took the seat offered him. He didn't look driven to the last resort, but he had been.

He didn't, actually, look anything, for there was a smooth blankness to his face, except for the sadness one imagined one saw in his eyes. His hair was smooth, light brown, rather fine, and there was no facial hair. He looked freshly and cleanly shaved. His clothes were distinctly old-fashioned, but neat and predominantly a velvety red-purple in color.

Facing him from behind the desk was the surgeon, and the nameplate on the desk included a fully identifying series of letters and numbers, which Andrew didn't bother with. To call him Doctor would be quite enough.

'When can the operation be carried through, Doctor?' he asked.

The surgeon said softly, with that certain inalienable note

of respect that a robot always used to a human being, 'I am not certain, sir, that I understand how or upon whom such an operation could be performed.'

There might have been a look of respectful intransigence on the surgeon's face, if a robot of his sort, in lightly bronzed stainless steel, could have such an expression, or any expression.

Andrew Martin studied the robot's right hand, his cutting hand, as it lay on the desk in utter tranquility. The fingers were long and shaped into artistically metallic looping curves so graceful and appropriate that one could imagine a scalpel fitting them and becoming, temporarily, one piece with them.

There would be no hesitation in his work, no stumbling, no quivering, no mistakes. That came with specialization, of course, a specialization so fiercely desired by humanity that few robots were, any longer, independently brained. A surgeon, of course, would have to be. And this one, though brained, was so limited in his capacity that he did not recognize Andrew – had probably never heard of him.

Andrew said, 'Have you ever thought you would like to be a man?'

The surgeon hesitated a moment as though the question fitted nowhere in his allotted positronic pathways. 'But I am a robot, sir.'

'Would it be better to be a man?'

'It would be better, sir, to be a better surgeon. I could not be so if I were a man, but only if I were a more advanced robot. I would be pleased to be a more advanced robot.'

'It does not offend you that I can order you about? That I can make you stand up, sit down, move right or left, by merely telling you to do so?'

'It is my pleasure to please you, sir. If your orders were to interfere with my functioning with respect to you or to any other human being, I would not obey you. The First Law, concerning my duty to human safety, would take precedence over the Second Law relating to obedience. Otherwise, obedience is my pleasure . . . But upon whom am I to perform this operation?'

'Upon me,' said Andrew.

'But that is impossible. It is patently a damaging operation.'

'That does not matter,' said Andrew calmly.

'I must not inflict damage,' said the surgeon.

'On a human being, you must not,' said Andrew, 'but I, too, am a robot.'

2.

Andrew had appeared much more a robot when he had first been – manufactured. He had then been as much a robot in appearance as any that had ever existed, smoothly designed and functional.

He had done well in the home to which he had been brought in those days when robots in households, or on the planet altogether, had been a rarity.

There had been four in the home: Sir and Ma'am and Miss and Little Miss. He knew their names, of course, but he never used them. Sir was Gerald Martin.

His own serial number was NDR – He forgot the numbers. It had been a long time, of course, but if he had wanted to remember, he could not forget. He had not wanted to remember.

Little Miss had been the first to call him Andrew because she could not use the letters, and all the rest followed her in this.

Little Miss – She had lived ninety years and was long since dead. He had tried to call her Ma'am once, but she would not allow it. Little Miss she had been to her last day.

Andrew had been intended to perform the duties of a

valet, a butler, a lady's maid. Those were the experimental days for him and, indeed, for all robots anywhere but in the industrial and exploratory factories and stations off Earth.

The Martins enjoyed him, and half the time he was prevented from doing his work because Miss and Little Miss would rather play with him.

It was Miss who understood first how this might be arranged. She said, 'We order you to play with us and you must follow orders.'

Andrew said, 'I am sorry, Miss, but a prior order from Sir must surely take precedence.'

But she said, 'Daddy just said he hoped you would take care of the cleaning. That's not much of an order. I *order* you.'

Sir did not mind. Sir was fond of Miss and of Little Miss, even more than Ma'am was, and Andrew was fond of them, too. At least, the effect they had upon his actions were those which in a human being would have been called the result of fondness. Andrew thought of it as fondness, for he did not know any other word for it.

It was for Little Miss that Andrew had carved a pendant out of wood. She had ordered him to. Miss, it seemed, had received an ivorite pendant with scrollwork for her birthday and Little Miss was unhappy over it. She had only a piece of wood, which she gave Andrew together with a small kitchen knife.

He had done it quickly and Little Miss said, 'That's *nice*, Andrew. I'll show it to Daddy.'

Sir would not believe it. 'Where did you really get this, Mandy?' Mandy was what he called Little Miss. When Little Miss assured him she was really telling the truth, he turned to Andrew. 'Did you do this, Andrew?'

'Yes, Sir.'

'The design, too?'

'Yes, sir.'

'From what did you copy the design?'

'It is a geometric representation, Sir, that fit the grain of the wood.'

The next day, Sir brought him another piece of wood, a larger one, and an electric vibro-knife. He said, 'Make something out of this, Andrew. Anything you want to.'

Andrew did so and Sir watched, then looked at the product a long time. After that, Andrew no longer waited on tables. He was ordered to read books on furniture design instead, and he learned to make cabinets and desks.

Sir said, 'These are amazing productions, Andrew.'

Andrew said, 'I enjoy doing them, Sir.'

'Enjoy?'

'It makes the circuits of my brain somehow flow more easily. I have heard you use the word "enjoy" and the way you use it fits the way I feel. I enjoy doing them, Sir.'

3.

Gerald Martin took Andrew to the regional offices of United States Robots and Mechanical Men Corporation. As a member of the Regional Legislature he had no trouble at all in gaining an interview with the Chief Robopsychologist. In fact, it was only as a member of the Regional Legislature that he qualified as a robot owner in the first place – in those early days when robots were rare.

Andrew did not understand any of this at the time, but in later years, with greater learning, he could re-view that early scene and understand it in its proper light.

The robopsychologist, Merton Mansky, listened with a gathering frown and more than once managed to stop his fingers at the point beyond which they would have irrevocably drummed on the table. He had drawn features and a lined forehead and looked as though he might be younger than he looked.

He said, 'Robotics is not an exact art, Mr Martin. I cannot explain it to you in detail, but the mathematics governing the plotting of the positronic pathways as far too complicated to permit of any but approximate solutions. Naturally, since we build everything about the Three Laws, those are incontrovertible. We will, of course, replace your robot – '

'Not at all,' said Sir. 'There is no question of failure on his part. He performs his assigned duties perfectly. The point is, he also carves wood in exquisite fashion and never the same twice. He produces works of art.'

Mansky looked confused. 'Strange. Of course, we're attempting generalized pathways these days . . . Really creative, you think?'

'See for yourself.' Sir handed over a little sphere of wood on which there was a playground scene in which the boys and girls were almost too small to make out, yet they were in perfect proportion and blended so naturally with the grain that that, too, seemed to have been carved.

Mansky said, '*He* did that?' He handed it back with a shake of his head. 'The luck of the draw. Something in the pathways.'

'Can you do it again?'

'Probably not. Nothing like this has ever been reported.'

'Good! I don't in the least mind Andrew's being the only one.'

Mansky said, 'I suspect that the company would like to have your robot back for study.'

Sir said with sudden grimness, 'Not a chance. Forget it.' He turned to Andrew, 'Let's go home now.'

'As you wish, Sir,' said Andrew.

4.

Miss was dating boys and wasn't about the house much. It was Little Miss, not as little as she was, who filled Andrew's horizon now. She never forgot that the very first piece of wood carving he had done had been for her. She kept it on a silver chain about her neck.

It was she who first objected to Sir's habit of giving away the productions. She said, 'Come on, Dad, if anyone wants one of them, let him pay for it. It's worth it.'

Sir said, 'It isn't like you to be greedy, Mandy.'

'Not for us, Dad. For the artist.'

Andrew had never heard the word before and when he had a moment to himself he looked it up in the dictionary. Then there was another trip, this time to Sir's lawyer.

Sir said to him, 'What do you think of this, John?'

The lawyer was John Feingold. He had white hair and a pudgy belly, and the rims of his contact lenses were tinted a bright green. He looked at the small plaque Sir had given him. 'This is beautiful . . . But I've heard the news. This is a carving made by your robot. The one you've brought with you.'

'Yes, Andrew does them. Don't you, Andrew?'

'Yes, Sir,' said Andrew.

'How much would you pay for that, John?' asked Sir.

'I can't say. I'm not a collector of such things.'

'Would you believe I have been offered two hundred and fifty dollars for that small thing? Andrew has made chairs that have sold for five hundred dollars. There's two hundred thousand dollars in the bank out of Andrew's products.'

'Good heavens, he's making you rich, Gerald.'

'Half rich,' said Sir. 'Half of it is in an account in the name of Andrew Martin.'

'The robot?'

'That's right, and I want to know if it's legal.'

'Legal?' Feingold's chair creaked as he leaned back in it, 'There are no precedents, Gerald. How did your robot sign the necessary papers?'

'He can sign his name and I brought in the signature. I didn't bring him in to the bank himself. Is there anything further that ought to be done?'

'Um.' Feingold's eyes seemed to turn inward for a moment. Then he said, 'Well, we can set up a trust to handle all finances in his name and that will place a layer of insulation between him and the hostile world. Further than that, my advice is you do nothing. No one is stopping you so far. If anyone objects, let *him* bring suit.'

'And will you take the case if suit is brought?'

'For a retainer, certainly.'

'How much?'

'Something like that,' and Feingold pointed to the wooden plaque.

'Fair enough,' said Sir.

Feingold chuckled as he turned to the robot. 'Andrew, are you pleased that you have money?'

'Yes, sir.'

'What do you plan to do with it?'

'Pay for things, sir, which otherwise Sir would have to pay for. It would save him expense, sir.'

5.

The occasions came. Repairs were expensive, and revisions were even more so. With the years, new models of robots were produced and Sir saw to it that Andrew had the advantage of every new device until he was a paragon of metallic excellence. It was all at Andrew's expense.

Andrew insisted on that.

Only his positronic pathways were untouched. Sir insisted on that.

'The new ones aren't as good as you are, Andrew,' he said. 'The new robots are worthless. The company has learned to make the pathways more precise, more closely on the nose, more deeply on the track. The new robots don't shift. They do what they're designed for and never stray. I like you better.'

'Thank you, Sir.'

'And it's your doing, Andrew, don't you forget that. I am certain Mansky put an end to generalized pathways as soon as he had a good look at you. He didn't like the unpredictability . . . Do you know how many times he asked for you so he could place you under study? Nine times! I never let him have you, though, and now that he's retired, we may have some peace.'

So Sir's hair thinned and grayed and his face grew pouchy, while Andrew looked rather better than he had when he first joined the family.

Ma'am had joined an art colony somewhere in Europe and Miss was a poet in New York. They wrote sometimes, but not often. Little Miss was married and lived not far away. She said she did not want to leave Andrew and when her child, Little Sir, was born, she let Andrew hold the bottle and feed him.

With the birth of a grandson, Andrew felt that Sir had someone now to replace those who had gone. It would not be so unfair to come to him with the request.

Andrew said, 'Sir, it is kind of you to have allowed me to spend my money as I wished.'

'It was your money, Andrew.'

'Only by your voluntary act, Sir. I do not believe the law would have stopped you from keeping it all.'

'The law won't persuade me to do wrong, Andrew.'

'Despite all expenses, and despite taxes, too, Sir, I have nearly six hundred thousand dollars.'

'I know that, Andrew.'

'I want to give it to you, Sir.'

'I won't take it, Andrew.'

'In exchange for something you can give me, Sir.'

'Oh? What is that, Andrew?'

'My freedom, Sir.'

'Your – '

'I wish to buy my freedom, Sir.'

6.

It wasn't that easy. Sir had flushed, had said 'For God's sake!' had turned on his heel, and stalked away.

It was Little Miss who brought him around, defiantly and harshly – and in front of Andrew. For thirty years, no one had hesitated to talk in front of Andrew, whether the matter involved Andrew or not. He was only a robot.

She said, 'Dad, why are you taking it as a personal affront? He'll still be here. He'll still be loyal. He can't help that. It's built in. All he wants is a form of words. He wants to be called free. Is that so terrible? Hasn't he earned it? Heavens, he and I have been talking about it for years.'

'Talking about it for years, have you?'

'Yes, and over and over again, he postponed it for fear he would hurt you. I *made* him put it up to you.'

'He doesn't know what freedom is. He's a robot.'

'Dad, you don't know him. He's read everything in the library. I don't know what he feels inside but I don't know what *you* feel inside. When you talk to him you'll find he reacts to the various abstractions as you and I do, and what else counts? If someone else's reactions are like your own, what more can you ask for?'

'The law won't take that attitude,' Sir said angrily. 'See here, you!' He turned to Andrew with a deliberate grate in his voice. 'I can't free you except by doing it legally, and if it gets into the courts, you not only won't get your freedom but the law will take official cognizance of your money. They'll tell you that a robot has no right to earn money. Is this rigmarole worth losing your money?'

'Freedom is without price, Sir,' said Andrew. 'Even the chance of freedom is worth the money.'

7.

The court might also take the attitude that freedom was without price, and might decide that for no price, however great, could a robot buy its freedom.

The simple statement of the regional attorney who represented those who had brought a class action to oppose the freedom was this: The word 'freedom' had no meaning when applied to a robot. Only a human being could be free.

He said it several times, when it seemed appropriate; slowly, with his hand coming down rhythmically on the desk before him to mark the words.

Little Miss asked permission to speak on behalf of Andrew. She was recognized by her full name, something Andrew had never heard pronounced before:

'Amanda Laura Martin Charney may approach the bench.'

She said, 'Thank you, your honor. I am not a lawyer and I don't know the proper way of phrasing things, but I hope you will listen to my meaning and ignore the words.

'Let's understand what it means to be free in Andrew's case. In some ways, he *is* free. I think it's at least twenty years since anyone in the Martin family gave him an order to do something that we felt he might not do of his own accord.

'But we can, if we wish, give him an order to do anything, couch it as harshly as we wish, because he is a machine that belongs to us. Why should we be in a position to do so, when he has served us so long, so faithfully, and earned so much money for us? He owes us nothing more. The debt is entirely on the other side.

'Even if we were legally forbidden to place Andrew in involuntary servitude, he would still serve us voluntarily.

Making him free would be a trick of words only, but it would mean much to him. It would give him everything and cost us nothing.'

For a moment the Judge seemed to be suppressing a smile. 'I see your point, Mrs Charney. The fact is that there is no binding law in this respect and no precedent. There is, however, the unspoken assumption that only a man can enjoy freedom. I can make new law here, subject to reversal in a higher court, but I cannot lightly run counter to that assumption. Let me address the robot. Andrew!'

'Yes, your honor.'

It was the first time Andrew had spoken in court and the Judge seemed astonished for a moment at the human timbre of the voice. He said, 'Why do you want to be free, Andrew? In what way will this matter to you?'

Andrew said, 'Would you wish to be a slave, your honor?'

'But you are not a slave. You are a perfectly good robot, a genius of a robot I am given to understand, capable of an artistic expression that can be matched nowhere. What more can you do if you were free?'

'Perhaps no more than I do now, your honor, but with greater joy. It has been said in this courtroom that only a human being can be free. It seems to me that only someone who wishes for freedom can be free. I wish for freedom.'

And it was that that cued the Judge. The crucial sentence in his decision was: 'There is no right to deny freedom to any object with a mind advanced enough to grasp the concept and desire the state.'

It was eventually upheld by the World Court.

8.

Sir remained displeased and his harsh voice made Andrew feel almost as though he were being short-circuited.

Sir said, 'I don't want your damned money, Andrew. I'll take it only because you won't feel free otherwise. From now on, you can select your own jobs and do them as you please. I will give you no orders, except this one – that you do as you please. But I am still responsible for you; that's part of the court order. I hope you understand that.'

Little Miss interrupted. 'Don't be irascible, Dad. The responsibility is no great chore. You know you won't have to do a thing. The Three Laws still hold.'

'Then how is he free?'

Andrew said, 'Are not human beings bound by their laws, Sir?'

Sir said, 'I'm not going to argue.' He left, and Andrew saw him only infrequently after that.

Little Miss came to see him frequently in the small house that had been built and made over for him. It had no kitchen, of course, nor bathroom facilities. It had just two rooms; one was a library and one was a combination storeroom and workroom. Andrew accepted many commissions and worked harder as a free robot than he ever had before, till the cost of the house was paid for and the structure legally transferred to him.

One day Little Sir came . . . No, George! Little Sir had insisted on that after the court decision. 'A free robot doesn't call anyone Little Sir,' George had said. 'I call you Andrew. You must call me George.'

It was phrased as an order, so Andrew called him George – but Little Miss remained Little Miss.

The day George came alone, it was to say that Sir was dying. Little Miss was at the bedside but Sir wanted Andrew as well.

Sir's voice was quite strong, though he seemed unable to move much. He struggled to get his hand up. 'Andrew,' he said, 'Andrew – Don't help me, George. I'm only dying;

I'm not crippled . . . Andrew, I'm glad you're free. I just wanted to tell you that.'

Andrew did not know what to say. He had never been at the side of someone dying before, but he knew it was the human way of ceasing to function. It was an involuntary and irreversible dismantling, and Andrew did not know what to say that might be appropriate. He could only remain standing, absolutely silent, absolutely motionless.

When it was over, Little Miss said to him, 'He may not have seemed friendly to you toward the end, Andrew, but he was old, you know, and it hurt him that you should want to be free.'

And then Andrew found the words to say. He said, 'I would never have been free without him, Little Miss.'

9.

It was only after Sir's death that Andrew began to wear clothes. He began with an old pair of trousers at first, a pair that George had given him.

George was married now, and a lawyer. He had joined Feingold's firm. Old Feingold was long since dead but his daughter had carried on and eventually the firm's name became Feingold and Charney. It remained so even when the daughter retired and no Feingold took her place. At the time Andrew put on clothes for the first time, the Charney name had just been added to the firm.

George had tried not to smile, the first time Andrew put on the trousers, but to Andrew's eyes the smile was clearly there.

George showed Andrew how to manipulate the static charge so as to allow the trousers to open, wrap about his lower body, and move shut. George demonstrated on his own trousers, but Andrew was quite aware that it would take him awhile to duplicate that one flowing motion.

George said, 'But why do you want trousers, Andrew? Your body is so beautifully functional it's a shame to cover it – especially when you needn't worry about either temperature control or modesty. And it doesn't cling properly, not on metal.'

Andrew said, 'Are not human bodies beautifully functional, George? Yet you cover yourselves.'

'For warmth, for cleanliness, for protection, for decorativeness. None of that applies to you.'

Andrew said, 'I feel bare without clothes. I feel different, George.'

'Different! Andrew, there are millions of robots on Earth now. In this region, according to the last census, there are almost as many robots as there are men.'

'I know, George. There are robots doing every conceivable type of work.'

'And none of them wear clothes.'

'But none of them are free, George.'

Little by little, Andrew added to the wardrobe. He was inhibited by George's smile and by the stares of the people who commissioned work.

He might be free, but there was built into him a carefully detailed program concerning his behavior toward people, and it was only by the tiniest steps that he dared advance. Open disapproval would set him back months.

Not everyone accepted Andrew as free. He was incapable of resenting that and yet there was a difficulty about his thinking process when he thought of it.

Most of all, he tended to avoid putting on clothes – or too many of them – when he thought Little Miss might come to visit him. She was old now and was often away in some warmer climate, but when she returned the first thing she did was visit him.

On one of her returns, George said ruefully, 'She's got

me, Andrew. I'll be running for the Legislature next year. Like grandfather, she says, like grandson.'

'Like grandfather – ' Andrew stopped, uncertain.

'I mean that I, George, the grandson, will be like Sir, the grandfather, who was in the Legislature once.'

Andrew said, 'It would be pleasant, George, if Sir were still – ' He paused, for he did not want to say, 'in working order.' That seemed inappropriate.

'Alive,' said George. 'Yes, I think of the old monster now and then, too.'

It was a conversation Andrew thought about. He had noticed his own incapacity in speech when talking with George. Somehow the language had changed since Andrew had come into being with an innate vocabulary. Then, too, George used a colloquial speech, as Sir and Little Miss had not. Why should he have called Sir a monster when surely that word was not appropriate?

Nor could Andrew turn to his own books for guidance. They were old and most dealt with woodworking, with art, with furniture design. There were none on language, none on the way of human beings.

It was at that moment it seemed to him that he must seek the proper books; and as a free robot, he felt he must not ask George. He would go to town and use the library. It was a triumphant decision and he felt his electropotential grow distinctly higher until he had to throw in an impedance coil.

He put on a full costume, even including a shoulder chain of wood. He would have preferred the glitter plastic but George had said that wood was much more appropriate and that polished cedar was considerably more valuable as well.

He had placed a hundred feet between himself and the house before gathering resistance brought him to a halt. He shifted the impedance coil out of circuit, and when that did not seem to help enough, he returned to his home and on a piece of notepaper wrote neatly, 'I have gone to the library,' and placed it in clear view on his worktable.

10.

Andrew never quite got to the library. He had studied the map. He knew the route, but not the appearance of it. The actual landmarks did not resemble the symbols on the map and he would hesitate. Eventually he thought he must have somehow gone wrong, for everything looked strange.

He passed an occasional field robot, but at the time he decided he should ask his way, there were none in sight. A vehicle passed and did not stop. He stood irresolute, which meant calmly motionless, and then coming across the field toward him were two human beings.

He turned to face them, and they altered their course to meet him. A moment before, they had been talking loudly; he had heard their voices; but now they were silent. They had the look that Andrew associated with human uncertainty, and they were young, but not very young. Twenty perhaps? Andrew could never judge human age.

He said, 'Would you describe to me the route to the town library, sirs?'

One of them, the taller of the two, whose tall hat lengthened him still farther, almost grotesquely, said, not to Andrew, but to the other, 'It's a robot.'

The other had a bulbous nose and heavy eyelids. He said, not to Andrew, but to the first, 'It's wearing clothes.'

The tall one snapped his fingers. 'It's the free robot. They have a robot at the Charneys' who isn't owned by anybody. Why else would it be wearing clothes?'

'Ask it,' said the one with the nose.

'Are you the Charney robot?' asked the tall one.

'I am Andrew Martin, sir,' said Andrew.

'Good. Take off your clothes. Robots don't wear clothes.' He said to the other, 'That's disgusting. Look at him.'

Andrew hesitated. He hadn't heard an order in that tone of voice in so long that his Second Law circuits had momentarily jammed.

The tall one said, 'Take off your clothes. I order you.'

Slowly, Andrew began to remove them.

'Just drop them,' said the tall one.

The nose said, 'If it doesn't belong to anyone, he could be ours as much as someone else's.'

'Anyway,' said the tall one, 'who's to object to anything we do? We're not damaging property . . . Stand on your head.' That was to Andrew.

'The head is not meant – ' began Andrew.

'That's an order. If you don't know how, try anyway.'

Andrew hesitated again, then bent to put his head on the ground. He tried to lift his legs and fell, heavily.

The tall one said, 'Just lie there.' He said to the other, 'We can take him apart. Ever take a robot apart?'

'Will he let us?'

'How can he stop us?'

There was no way Andrew could stop them, if they ordered him not to resist in a forceful enough manner. Second Law of obedience took precedence over the Third Law of self-preservation. In any case, he could not defend himself without possibly hurting them and that would mean breaking the First Law. At that thought, every motile unit contracted slightly and he quivered as he lay there.

The tall one walked over and pushed at him with his foot. 'He's heavy. I think we'll need tools to do the job.'

The nose said, 'We could order him to take himself apart. It would be fun to watch him try.'

'Yes,' said the tall one thoughtfully, 'but let's get him off the road. If someone comes along – '

It was too late. Someone had indeed come along and it

was George. From where he lay, Andrew had seen him topping a small rise in the middle distance. He would have liked to signal him in some way, but the last order had been 'Just lie there!'

George was running now and he arrived somewhat winded. The two young men stepped back a little and then waited thoughtfully.

George said anxiously, 'Andrew, has something gone wrong?'

Andrew said, 'I am well, George.'

'Then stand up . . . What happened to your clothes?'

The tall young man said, 'That your robot, mac?'

George turned sharply. 'He's no one's robot. What's been going on here?'

'We politely asked him to take his clothes off. What's that to you if you don't own him?'

George said, 'What were they doing, Andrew?'

Andrew said, 'It was their intention in some way to dismember me. They were about to move me to a quiet spot and order me to dismember myself.'

George looked at the two and his chin trembled. The two young men retreated no further. They were smiling. The tall one said lightly, 'What are you going to do, pudgy? Attack us?'

George said, 'No, I don't have to. This robot has been with my family for over seventy years. He knows us and he values us more than he values anyone else. I am going to tell him that you two are threatening my life and that you plan to kill me. I will ask him to defend me. In choosing between me and you two, he will choose me. Do you know what will happen to you when he attacks you?'

The two were backing away slightly, looking uneasy.

George said sharply, 'Andrew, I am in danger and about to come to harm from these young men. Move toward them!'

Andrew did so, and the two young men did not wait. They ran fleetly.

'All right, Andrew, relax,' said George. He looked unstrung. He was far past the age where he could face the possibility of a dustup with one young man, let alone two.

Andrew said, 'I couldn't have hurt them, George. I could see they were not attacking you.'

'I didn't order you to attack them; I only told you to move toward them. Their own fears did the rest.'

'How can they fear robots?'

'It's a disease of mankind, one of which it is not yet cured. But never mind that. What the devil are you doing here, Andrew? I was on the point of turning back and hiring a helicopter when I found you. How did you get it into your head to go to the library? I would have brought you any books you needed.'

'I am a – ' began Andrew.

'Free robot. Yes, yes. All right, what did you want in the library?'

'I want to know more about human beings, about the world, about everything. And about robots, George. I want to write a history about robots.'

George said, 'Well, let's walk home . . . And pick up your clothes first. Andrew, there are a million books on robotics and all of them include histories of the science. The world is growing saturated not only with robots but with information about robots.'

Andrew shook his head, a human gesture he had lately begun to make. 'Not a history of robotics, George. A history of *robots*, by a robot. I want to explain how robots feel about what has happened since the first ones were allowed to work and live on Earth.'

George's eyebrows lifted, but he said nothing in direct response.

11.

Little Miss was just past her eighty-third birthday, but there was nothing about her that was lacking in either energy or determination. She gestured with her cane oftener than she propped herself up with it.

She listened to the story in a fury of indignation. She said, 'George, that's horrible. Who were those young ruffians?'

'I don't know. What difference does it make? In the end they did no damage.'

'They might have. You're a lawyer, George, and if you're well off, it's entirely due to the talent of Andrew. It was the money *he* earned that is the foundation of everything we have. He provides the continuity for this family and I will *not* have him treated as a wind-up toy.'

'What would you have me do, Mother?' asked George.

'I said you're a lawyer. Don't you listen? You set up a test case somehow, and you force the regional courts to declare for robot rights and get the Legislature to pass the necessary bills, and carry the whole thing to the World Court, if you have to. I'll be watching, George, and I'll tolerate no shirking.'

She was serious, and what began as a way of soothing the fearsome old lady became an involved matter with enough legal entanglement to make it interesting. As senior partner of Feingold and Charney, George plotted strategy but left the actual work to his junior partners, with much of it a matter for his son, Paul, who was also a member of the firm and who reported dutifully nearly every day to his grandmother. She, in turn, discussed it every day with Andrew.

Andrew was deeply involved. His work on his book on robots was delayed again, as he pored over the legal arguments and even, at times, made very diffident suggestions.

He said, 'George told me that day that human beings have always been afraid of robots. As long as they are, the courts and the legislatures are not likely to work hard on behalf of robots. Should there not be something done about public opinion?'

So while Paul stayed in court, George took to the public platform. It gave him the advantage of being informal and he even went so far sometimes as to wear the new, loose style of clothing which he called drapery. Paul said, 'Just don't trip over it on stage, Dad.'

George said despondently, 'I'll try not to.'

He addressed the annual convention of holo-news editors on one occasion and said, in part:

'If, by virtue of the Second Law, we can demand of any robot unlimited obedience in all respects not involving harm to a human being, then any human being, *any* human being, has a fearsome power over any robot, *any* robot. In particular, since Second Law supersedes Third Law, *any* human being can use the law of obedience to overcome the law of self-protection. He can order any robot to damage itself or even destroy itself for any reason, or for no reason.

'Is this just? Would we treat an animal so? Even an inanimate object which has given us good service has a claim on our consideration. And a robot is not insensible; it is not an animal. It can think well enough to enable it to talk to us, reason with us, joke with us. Can we treat them as friends, can we work together with them, and not give them some of the fruit of that friendship, some of the benefit of co-working?

'If a man has the right to give a robot any order that does not involve harm to a human being, he should have the decency never to give a robot any order that involves harm to a robot, unless human safety absolutely requires it. With great power goes great responsibility, and if the robots have Three Laws to protect men, is it too much to ask that men have a law or two to protect robots?'

Andrew was right. It was the battle over public opinion that held the key to courts and Legislature and in the end a law passed which set up conditions under which robot-harming orders were forbidden. It was endlessly qualified and the punishments for violating the law were totally inadequate, but the principle was established. The final passage by the World Legislature came through on the day of Little Miss's death.

That was no coincidence. Little Miss held on to life desperately during the last debate and let go only when word of victory arrived. Her last smile was for Andrew. Her last words were: 'You have been good to us, Andrew.'

She died with her hand holding his, while her son and his wife and children remained at a respectful distance from both.

12.

Andrew waited patiently while the receptionist disappeared into the inner office. It might have used the holographic chatterbox, but unquestionably it was unmanned (or perhaps unroboted) by having to deal with another robot rather than with a human being.

Andrew passed the time revolving the matter in his mind. Could 'unroboted' be used as an analogue of 'unmanned,' or had 'unmanned' become a metaphoric term sufficiently divorced from its original literal meaning to be applied to robots – or to women for that matter?

Such problems came frequently as he worked on his book on robots. The trick of thinking out sentences to express all complexities had undoubtedly increased his vocabulary.

Occasionally, someone came into the room to stare at

him and he did not try to avoid the glance. He looked at each calmly, and each in turn looked away.

Paul Charney finally came out. He looked surprised, or he would have if Andrew could have made out his expression with certainty. Paul had taken to wearing the heavy makeup that fashion was dictating for both sexes and though it made sharper and firmer the somewhat bland lines of his face, Andrew disapproved. He found that disapproving of human beings, as long as he did not express it verbally, did not make him very uneasy. He could even write the disapproval. He was sure it had not always been so.

Paul said, 'Come in, Andrew. I'm sorry I made you wait but there was something I *had* to finish. Come in. You had said you wanted to talk to me, but I didn't know you meant here in town.'

'If you are busy, Paul, I am prepared to continue to wait.'

Paul glanced at the interplay of shifting shadows on the dial on the wall that served as timepiece and said, 'I can make some time. Did you come alone?'

'I hired an automatobile.'

'Any trouble?' Paul asked, with more than a trace of anxiety.

'I wasn't expecting any. My rights are protected.'

Paul looked the more anxious for that. 'Andrew, I've explained that the law is unenforceable, at least under most conditions . . . And if you insist on wearing clothes, you'll run into trouble eventually – just like that first time.'

'And only time, Paul. I'm sorry you are displeased.'

'Well, look at it this way; you are virtually a living legend, Andrew, and you are too valuable in many different ways for you to have any right to take chances with yourself . . . How's the book coming?'

'I am approaching the end, Paul. The publisher is quite pleased.'

'Good!'

'I don't know that he's necessarily pleased with the book as a book. I think he expects to sell many copies because it's written by a robot and it's that that pleases him.'

'Only human, I'm afraid.'

'I am not displeased. Let it sell for whatever reason since it will mean money and I can use some.'

'Grandmother left you – '

'Little Miss was generous, and I'm sure I can count on the family to help me out further. But it is the royalties from the book on which I am counting to help me through the next step.'

'What next step is that?'

'I wish to see the head of US Robots and Mechanical Men Corporation. I have tried to make an appointment, but so far I have not been able to reach him. The corporation did not cooperate with me in the writing of the book, so I am not surprised, you understand.'

Paul was clearly amused. 'Cooperation is the last thing you can expect. They didn't cooperate with us in our great fight for robot rights. Quite the reverse and you can see why. Give a robot rights and people may not want to buy them.'

'Nevertheless,' said Andrew, 'if you call them, you may obtain an interview for me.'

'I'm no more popular with them than you are, Andrew.'

'But perhaps you can hint that by seeing me they may head off a campaign by Feingold and Charney to strengthen the rights of robots further.'

'Wouldn't that be a lie, Andrew?'

'Yes, Paul, and I can't tell one. That is why you must call.'

'Ah, you can't lie, but you can urge me to tell a lie, is that it? You're getting more human all the time, Andrew.'

13.

It was not easy to arrange, even with Paul's supposedly weighted name.

But it was finally carried through and, when it was, Harley Smythe-Robertson, who, on his mother's side, was descended from the original founder of the corporation and who had adopted the hyphenation to indicate it, looked remarkably unhappy. He was approaching retirement age and his entire tenure as president had been devoted to the matter of robot rights. His gray hair was plastered thinly over the top of his scalp, his face was not made up, and he eyed Andrew with brief hostility from time to time.

Andrew said, 'Sir, nearly a century ago, I was told by a Merton Mansky of this corporation that the mathematics governing the plotting of the positronic pathways was far too complicated to permit of any but approximate solutions and that therefore my own capacities were not fully predictable.'

'That was a century ago.' Smythe-Robertson hesitated, then said icily, '*Sir*. It is true no longer. Our robots are made with precision now and are trained precisely to their jobs.'

'Yes,' said Paul, who had come along, as he said, to make sure that the corporation played fair, 'with the result that my receptionist must be guided at every point once events depart from the conventional, however slightly.'

Smythe-Robertson said, 'You would be much more displeased if it were to improvise.'

Andrew said, 'Then you no longer manufacture robots like myself which are flexible and adaptable.'

'No longer.'

'The research I have done in connection with my book,' said Andrew, 'indicates that I am the oldest robot presently in active operation.'

'The oldest presently,' said Smythe-Robertson, 'and the

oldest ever. The oldest that will ever be. No robot is useful after the twenty-fifth year. They are called in and replaced with newer models.'

'No robot *as presently manufactured* is useful after the twenty-fifth year,' said Paul pleasantly. 'Andrew is quite exceptional in this respect.'

Andrew, adhering to the path he had marked out for himself, said, 'As the oldest robot in the world and the most flexible, am I not unusual enough to merit special treatment from the company?'

'Not at all,' said Smythe-Robertson freezingly. 'Your unusualness is an embarrassment to the company. If you were on lease, instead of having been a sale outright through some mischance, you would long since have been replaced.'

'But that is exactly the point,' said Andrew. 'I am a free robot and I own myself. Therefore I come to you and ask you to replace me. You cannot do this without the owner's consent. Nowadays, that consent is extorted as a condition of the lease, but in my time this did not happen.'

Smythe-Robertson was looking both startled and puzzled, and for a moment there was silence. Andrew found himself staring at the holograph on the wall. It was a death mask of Susan Calvin, patron saint of all roboticists. She was dead nearly two centuries now, but as a result of writing his book Andrew knew her so well he could half persuade himself that he had met her in life.

Smythe-Robertson said, 'How can I replace you for you? If I replace you as robot, how can I donate the new robot to you as owner since in the very act of replacement you cease to exist?' He smiled grimly.

'Not at all difficult,' interposed Paul. 'The seat of Andrew's personality is his positronic brain and it is the one part that cannot be replaced without creating a new robot. The positronic brain, therefore, is Andrew the owner. Every other part of the robotic body can be replaced without affecting the robot's personality, and those other parts are the brain's possessions. Andrew, I should say, wants to supply his brain with a new robotic body.'

'That's right,' said Andrew calmly. He turned to Smythe-Robertson. 'You have manufactured androids, haven't you? Robots that have the outward appearance of humans complete to the texture of the skin?'

Smythe-Robertson said, 'Yes, we have. They worked perfectly well, with their synthetic fibrous skins and tendons. There was virtually no metal anywhere except for the brain, yet they were nearly as tough as metal robots. They were tougher, weight for weight.'

Paul looked interested. 'I didn't know that. How many are on the market?'

'None,' said Smythe-Robertson. 'They were much more expensive than metal models and a market survey showed they would not be accepted. They looked too human.'

Andrew said, 'But the corporation retains its expertise, I assume. Since it does, I wish to request that I be replaced by an organic robot, an android.'

Paul looked surprised. 'Good Lord,' he said.

Smythe-Robertson stiffened. 'Quite impossible!'

'Why is it impossible?' asked Andrew. 'I will pay any reasonable fee, of course.'

Smythe-Robertson said, 'We do not manufacture androids.'

'You do not *choose* to manufacture androids,' interposed Paul quickly. 'That is not the same as being unable to manufacture them.'

Smythe-Robertson said, 'Nevertheless, the manufacture of androids is against public policy.'

'There is no law against it,' said Paul.

'Nevertheless, we do not manufacture them, and we will not.'

Paul cleared his throat. 'Mr Smythe-Robertson,' he said,

'Andrew is a free robot who is under the purview of the law guaranteeing robot rights. You are aware of this, I take it?'

'Only too well.'

'This robot, as a free robot, chooses to wear clothes. This results in his being frequently humiliated by thoughtless human beings despite the law against the humiliation of robots. It is difficult to prosecute vague offences that don't meet with the general disapproval of those who must decide on guilt and innocence.'

'US Robots understood that from the start. Your father's firm unfortunately did not.'

'My father is dead now,' said Paul, 'but what I see is that we have here a clear offense with a clear target.'

'What are you talking about?' said Smythe-Robertson.

'My client, Andrew Martin – he has just become my client – is a free robot who is entitled to ask US Robots and Mechanical Men Corporation for the right of replacement, which the corporation supplies anyone who owns a robot for more than twenty-five years. In fact, the corporation insists on such replacement.'

Paul was smiling and thoroughly at his ease. He went on, 'The positronic brain of my client is the owner of the body of my client – which is certainly more than twenty-five years old. The positronic brain demands the replacement of the body and offers to pay any reasonable fee for an android body as that replacement. If you refuse the request, my client undergoes humiliation and we will sue.

'While public opinion would not ordinarily support the claim of a robot in such a case, may I remind you that US Robots is not popular with the public generally. Even those who most use and profit from robots are suspicious of the corporation. This may be a hangover from the days when robots were widely feared. It may be resentment against the power and wealth of US Robots which has a worldwide monopoly. Whatever the cause may be, the resentment exists and I think you will find that you would prefer not to withstand a lawsuit, particularly since my client is wealthy and will live for many more centuries and will have no reason to refrain from fighting the battle forever.'

Smythe-Robertson had slowly reddened. 'You are trying to force me to . . .'

'I force you to do nothing,' said Paul. 'If you wish to refuse to accede to my client's reasonable request, you may by all means do so and we will leave without another word . . . But we will sue, as is certainly our right, and you will find that you will eventually lose.'

Smythe-Robertson said, 'Well – ' and paused.

'I see that you are going to accede,' said Paul. 'You may hesitate but you will come to it in the end. Let me assure you, then, of one further point. If, in the process of transferring my client's positronic brain from his present body to an organic one, there is any damage, however slight, then I will never rest till I've nailed the corporation to the ground. I will, if necessary, take every possible step to mobilize public opinion against the corporation if one brain path of my client's platinum-iridium essence is scrambled.' He turned to Andrew and said, 'Do you agree to all this, Andrew?'

Andrew hesitated a full minute. It amounted to the approval of lying, of blackmail, of the badgering and humiliation of a human being. But not physical harm, he told himself, not physical harm.

He managed at last to come out with a rather faint 'Yes.'

14.

It was like being constructed again. For days, then for weeks, finally for months, Andrew found himself not himself somehow, and the simplest actions kept giving rise to hesitation.

Paul was frantic. 'They've damaged you, Andrew. We'll have to institute suit.'

Andrew spoke very slowly. 'You mustn't. You'll never be able to prove – something – m-m-m-m – '

'Malice?'

'Malice. Besides, I grow stronger, better. It's the tr-tr-tr – '

'Tremble?'

'Trauma. After all, there's never been such an op – op – op – before.'

Andrew could feel his brain from the inside. No one else could. He knew he was well and during the months that it took him to learn full coordination and full positronic interplay, he spent hours before the mirror.

Not quite human! The face was stiff – too stiff – and the motions were too deliberate. They lacked the careless free flow of the human being, but perhaps that might come with time. At least he could wear clothes without the ridiculous anomaly of a metal face going along with it.

Eventually he said, 'I will be going back to work.'

Paul laughed and said, 'That means you are well. What will you be doing? Another book?'

'No,' said Andrew seriously. 'I live too long for any one career to seize me by the throat and never let me go. There was a time when I was primarily an artist and I can still turn to that. And there was a time when I was a historian and I can still turn to that. But now I wish to be a robobiologist.'

'A robopsychologist, you mean.'

'No. That would imply the study of positronic brains and at the moment I lack the desire to do that. A robobiologist, it seems to me, would be concerned with the working of the body attached to that brain.'

'Wouldn't that be a roboticist?'

'A roboticist works with a metal body. I would be

studying an organic humanoid body, of which I have the only one, as far as I know.'

'You narrow your field,' said Paul thoughtfully. 'As an artist, all conception is yours; as a historian, you dealt chiefly with robots; as a robobiologist, you will deal with yourself.'

Andrew nodded. 'It would seem so.'

Andrew had to start from the very beginning, for he knew nothing of ordinary biology, almost nothing of science. He became a familiar sight in the libraries, where he sat at the electronic indices for hours at a time, looking perfectly normal in clothes. Those few who knew he was a robot in no way interfered with him.

He built a laboratory in a room which he added to his house, and his library grew, too.

Years passed, and Paul came to him one day and said, 'It's a pity you're no longer working on the history of robots. I understand US Robots is adopting a radically new policy.'

Paul had aged, and his deteriorating eyes had been replaced with photoptic cells. In that respect, he had drawn closer to Andrew. Andrew said, 'What have they done?'

'They are manufacturing central computers, gigantic positronic brains, really, which communicate with anywhere from a dozen to a thousand robots by microwave. The robots themselves have no brains at all. They are the limbs of the gigantic brain, and the two are physically separate.'

'Is that more efficient?'

'US Robots claims it is. Smythe-Robertson established the new direction before he died, however, and it's my notion that it's a backlash at you. US Robots is determined that they will make no robots that will give them the type of trouble you have, and for that reason they separate brain and body. The brain will have no body to wish changed; the body will have no brain to wish anything.

'It's amazing, Andrew,' Paul went on, 'the influence you have had on the history of robots. It was your artistry that encouraged US Robots to make robots more precise and specialized; it was your freedom that resulted in the establishment of the principle of robotic rights; it was your insistence on an android body that made US Robots switch to brain-body separation.'

Andrew said, 'I suppose in the end the corporation will produce one vast brain controlling several billion robotic bodies. All the eggs will be in one basket. Dangerous. Not proper at all.'

'I think you're right,' said Paul, 'but I don't suspect it will come to pass for a century at least and I won't live to see it. In fact, I may not live to see next year.'

'Paul!' said Andrew, in concern.

Paul shrugged. 'We're mortal, Andrew. We're not like you. It doesn't matter too much, but it does make it important to assure you on one point. I'm the last of the Charneys. There are collaterals descended from my great-aunt, but they don't count. The money I control personally will be left to the trust in your name and as far as anyone can foresee the future, you will be economically secure.'

'Unnecessary,' said Andrew, with difficulty. In all this time, he could not get used to the deaths of the Charneys.

Paul said, 'Let's not argue. That's the way it's going to be. What are you working on?'

'I am designing a system for allowing androids – myself – to gain energy from the combustion of hydrocarbons, rather than from atomic cells.'

Paul raised his eyebrows. 'So that they will breathe and eat?'

'Yes.'

'How long have you been pushing in that direction?'

'For a long time now, but I think I have designed an adequate combustion chamber for catalyzed controlled breakdown.'

'But why, Andrew? The atomic cell is surely infinitely better.'

'In some ways, perhaps, but the atomic cell is inhuman.'

15.

It took time, but Andrew had time. In the first place, he did not wish to do anything till Paul had died in peace.

With the death of the great-grandson of Sir, Andrew felt more nearly exposed to a hostile world and for that reason was the more determined to continue the path he had long ago chosen.

Yet he was not really alone. If a man had died, the firm of Feingold and Charney lived, for a corporation does not die any more than a robot does. The firm had its directions and it followed them soullessly. By way of the trust and through the law firm, Andrew continued to be wealthy. And in return for their own large annual retainer, Feingold and Charney involved themselves in the legal aspects of the new combustion chamber.

When the time came for Andrew to visit US Robots and Mechanical Men Corporation, he did it alone. Once he had gone with Sir and once with Paul. This time, the third time, he was alone and manlike.

US Robots had changed. The production plant had been shifted to a large space station, as had grown to be the case with more and more industries. With them had gone many robots. The Earth itself was becoming parklike, with its one-billion-person population stabilized and perhaps not more than thirty per cent of its at least equally large robot population independently brained.

The Director of Research was Alvin Magdescu, dark of complexion and hair, with a little pointed beard and wearing nothing above the waist but the breastband that fashion dictated. Andrew himself was well covered in the older fashion of several decades back.

Magdescu said, 'I know you, of course, and I'm rather pleased to see you. You're our most notorious product and it's a pity old Smythe-Robertson was so set against you. We could have done a great deal with you.'

'You still can,' said Andrew.

'No, I don't think so. We're past the time. We've had robots on Earth for over a century, but that's changing. It will be back to space with them and those that stay here won't be brained.'

'But there remains myself, and I stay on Earth.'

'True, but there doesn't seem to be much of the robot about you. What new request have you?'

'To be still less a robot. Since I am so far organic, I wish an organic source of energy. I have here the plans – '

Magdescu did not hasten through them. He might have intended to at first, but he stiffened and grew intent. At one point he said, 'This is remarkably ingenious. Who thought of all this?'

'I did,' said Andrew.

Magdescu looked up at him sharply, then said, 'It would amount to a major overhaul of your body, and an experimental one, since it has never been attempted before. I advise against it. Remain as you are.'

Andrew's face had limited means of expression, but impatience showed plainly in his voice. 'Dr Magdescu, you miss the entire point. You have no choice but to accede to my request. If such devices can be built into my body, they can be built into human bodies as well. The tendency to lengthen human life by prosthetic devices has already been remarked on. There are no devices better than the ones I have designed and am designing.

'As it happens, I control the patents by way of the firm of Feingold and Charney. We are quite capable of going into business for ourselves and of developing the kind of prosthetic devices that may end by producing human beings with many of the properties of robots. Your own business will then suffer.

'If, however, you operate on me now and agree to do so under similar circumstances in the future, you will receive permission to make use of the patents and control the technology of both robots and the prosthetization of human beings. The initial leasing will not be granted, of course, until after the first operation is completed successfully, and after enough time has passed to demonstrate that it is indeed successful.' Andrew felt scarcely any First Law inhibition to the stern conditions he was setting a human being. He was learning to reason that what seemed like cruelty might, in the long run, be kindness.

Magdescu looked stunned. He said, 'I'm not the one to decide something like this. That's a corporate decision that would take time.'

'I can wait a reasonable time,' said Andrew, 'but only a reasonable time.' And he thought with satisfaction that Paul himself could not have done it better.

16.

It took only a reasonable time, and the operation was a success.

Magdescu said, 'I was very much against the operation, Andrew, but not for the reasons you might think. I was not in the least against the experiment, if it had been on someone else. I hated risking *your* positronic brain. Now that you have the positronic pathways interacting with simulated nerve pathways, it might be difficult to rescue the brain intact if the body went bad.'

'I had every faith in the skill of the staff at US Robots,' said Andrew. 'And I can eat now.'

'Well, you can sip olive oil. It will mean occasional cleanings of the combustion chamber, as we have explained to you. Rather an uncomfortable touch, I should think.'

'Perhaps, if I did not expect to go further. Self-cleaning is not impossible. In fact, I am working on a device that will deal with solid food that may be expected to contain incombustible fractions – indigestible matter, so to speak, that will have to be discarded.'

'You would then have to develop an anus.'

'The equivalent.'

'What else, Andrew?'

'Everything else.'

'Genitalia, too?'

'Insofar as they will fit my plans. My body is a canvas on which I intend to draw – '

Magdescu waited for the sentence to be completed, and when it seemed that it would not be, he completed it himself. 'A man?'

'We shall see,' said Andrew.

Magdescu said, 'It's a puny ambition, Andrew. You're better than a man. You've gone downhill from the moment you opted for organicism.'

'My brain has not suffered.'

'No, it hasn't. I'll grant you that. But, Andrew, the whole new breakthrough in prosthetic devices made possible by your patents is being marketed under your name. You're recognized as the inventor and you're honored for it – as you are. Why play further games with your body?'

Andrew did not answer.

The honors came. He accepted membership in several learned societies, including one which was devoted to the new science he had established; the one he had called robobiology but had come to be termed prosthetology.

On the one hundred and fiftieth anniversary of his construction, there was a testimonial dinner given in his honor at US Robots. If Andrew saw irony in this, he kept it to himself.

Alvin Magdescu came out of retirement to chair the dinner. He was himself ninety-four years old and was alive because he had prosthetized devices that, among other things, fulfilled the function of liver and kidneys. The dinner reached its climax when Magdescu, after a short and emotional talk, raised his glass to toast 'the Sesquicentennial Robot.'

Andrew had had the sinews of his face redesigned to the point where he could show a range of emotions, but he sat through all the ceremonies solemnly passive. He did not like to be a Sesquicentennial Robot.

17.

It was prosthetology that finally took Andrew off the Earth. In the decades that followed the celebration of the Sesquicentennial, the Moon had come to be a world more Earth-like than Earth in every respect but its gravitational pull and in its underground cities there was a fairly dense population.

Prosthetized devices there had to take the lesser gravity into account and Andrew spent five years on the Moon working with local prosthetologists to make the necessary adaptations. When not at his work, he wandered among the robot population, every one of which treated him with the robotic obsequiousness due a man.

He came back to an Earth that was humdrum and quiet in comparison and visited the offices of Feingold and Charney to announce his return.

The current head of the firm, Simon DeLong, was surprised. He said, 'We had been told you were returning, Andrew' (he had almost said 'Mr Martin'), 'but we were not expecting you till next week.'

'I grew impatient,' said Andrew brusquely. He was anxious to get to the point. 'On the Moon, Simon, I was in charge of a research team of twenty human scientists. I gave orders that no one questioned. The Lunar robots deferred to me as they would to a human being. Why, then, am I not a human being?'

A wary look entered DeLong's eyes. He said, 'My dear Andrew, as you have just explained, you are treated as a human being by both robots and human beings. You are therefore a human being *de facto*.'

'To be a human being *de facto* is not enough. I want not only to be treated as one, but to be legally identified as one. I want to be a human being *de jure*.'

'Now that is another matter,' said DeLong. 'There we would run into human prejudice and into the undoubted fact that however much you may be like a human being, you are *not* a human being.'

'In what way not?' asked Andrew. 'I have the shape of a human being and organs equivalent to those of a human being. My organs, in fact, are identical to some of those in a prosthetized human being. I have contributed artistically, literarily, and scientifically to human culture as much as any human being now alive. What more can one ask?'

'I myself would ask nothing more. The trouble is that it would take an act of the World Legislature to define you as a human being. Frankly, I wouldn't expect that to happen.'

'To whom on the Legislature could I speak?'

'To the chairman of the Science and Technology Committee perhaps.'

'Can you arrange a meeting?'

'But you scarcely need an intermediary. In your position, you can – '

'No. *You* arrange it.' (It didn't even occur to Andrew that he was giving a flat order to a human being. He had grown accustomed to that on the Moon.) 'I want him to know that the firm of Feingold and Charney is backing me in this to the hilt.'

'Well, now – '

'To the hilt, Simon. In one hundred and seventy-three years I have in one fashion or another contributed greatly to this firm. I have been under obligation to individual members of the firm in times past. I am not now. It is rather the other way around now and I am calling in my debts.'

DeLong said, 'I will do what I can.'

18.

The chairman of the Science and Technology Committee was of the East Asian region and she was a woman. Her name was Chee Li-Hsing and her transparent garments (obscuring what she wanted obscured only by their dazzle) made her look plastic-wrapped.

She said, 'I sympathize with your wish for full human rights. There have been times in history when segments of the human population fought for full human rights. What rights, however, can you possibly want that you do not have?'

'As simple a thing as my right to life. A robot can be dismantled at any time.'

'A human being can be executed at any time.'

'Execution can only follow due process of law. There is no trial needed for my dismantling. Only the word of a human being in authority is needed to end me. Besides – besides – ' Andrew tried desperately to allow no sign of pleading, but his carefully designed tricks of human expression and tone of voice betrayed him here. 'The truth is, I want to be a man. I have wanted it through six generations of human beings.'

Li-Hsing looked up at him out of darkly sympathetic eyes. 'The Legislature can pass a law declaring you one –

they could pass a law declaring a stone statue to be defined as a man. Whether they will actually do so is, however, as likely in the first case as the second. Congresspeople are as human as the rest of the population and there is always that element of suspicion against robots.'

'Even now?'

'Even now. We would all allow the fact that you have earned the prize of humanity and yet there would remain the fear of setting an undesirable precedent.'

'What precedent? I am the only free robot, the only one of my type and there will never be another. You may consult US Robots.'

'"Never" is a long time, Andrew – or, if you prefer, Mr Martin – since I will gladly give you my personal accolade as man. You will find that most Congresspeople will not be willing to set the precedent, no matter how meaningless such a precedent might be. Mr Martin, you have my sympathy, but I cannot tell you to hope. Indeed – '

She sat back and her forehead wrinkled. 'Indeed, if the issue grows too heated, there might well arise a certain sentiment, both inside the Legislature and outside, for that dismantling you mentioned. Doing away with you could turn out to be the easiest way of resolving the dilemma. Consider that before deciding to push matters.'

Andrew said, 'Will no one remember the technique of prosthetology, something that is almost entirely mine?'

'It may seem cruel, but they won't. Or if they do, it will be remembered against you. It will be said you did it only for yourself. It will be said it was part of a campaign to roboticize human beings, or to humanify robots; and in either case evil and vicious. You have never been part of a political hate campaign, Mr Martin, and I tell you that you will be the object of vilification of a kind neither you nor I would credit and there would be people who'll believe it all. Mr Martin, let your life be.' She rose and, next to

Andrew's seated figure, she seemed small and almost childlike.

Andrew said, 'If I decide to fight for my humanity, will you be on my side?'

She thought, then said, 'I will be – insofar as I can be. If at any time such a stand would appear to threaten my political future, I may have to abandon you, since it is not an issue I feel to be at the very root of my beliefs. I am trying to be honest with you.'

'Thank you, and I will ask no more. I intend to fight this through whatever the consequences, and I will ask you for your help only for as long as you can give it.'

19.

It was not a direct fight. Feingold and Charney counseled patience and Andrew muttered grimly that he had an endless supply of that. Feingold and Charney then entered on a campaign to narrow and restrict the area of combat.

They instituted a lawsuit denying the obligation to pay debts to an individual with a prosthetic heart on the grounds that the possession of a robotic organ removed humanity, and with it the constitutional rights of human beings.

They fought the matter skillfully and tenaciously, losing at every step but always in such a way that the decision was forced to be as broad as possible, and then carrying it by way of appeals to the World Court.

It took years, and millions of dollars.

When the final decision was handed down, DeLong held what amounted to a victory celebration over the legal loss. Andrew was, of course, present in the company offices on the occasion.

'We've done two things, Andrew,' said DeLong, 'both of which are good. First of all, we have established the fact that no number of artifacts in the human body causes it to cease being a human body. Secondly, we have engaged public opinion in the question in such a way as to put it fiercely on the side of a broad interpretation of humanity since there is not a human being in existence who does not hope for prosthetics if that will keep him alive.'

'And do you think the Legislature will now grant me my humanity?' asked Andrew.

DeLong looked faintly uncomfortable. 'As to that, I cannot be optimistic. There remains the one organ which the World Court has used as the criterion of humanity. Human beings have an organic cellular brain and robots have a platinum-iridium positronic brain if they have one at all – and you certainly have a positronic brain . . . No, Andrew, don't get that look in your eye. We lack the knowledge to duplicate the work of a cellular brain in artificial structures close enough to the organic type to allow it to fall within the Court's decision. Not even you could do it.'

'What ought we do, then?'

'Make the attempt, of course. Congresswoman Li-Hsing will be on our side and a growing number of other Congresspeople. The President will undoubtedly go along with a majority of the Legislature in this matter.'

'Do we have a majority?'

'No, far from it. But we might get one if the public will allow its desire for a broad interpretation of humanity to extend to you. A small chance, I admit, but if you do not wish to give up, we must gamble for it.'

'I do not wish to give up.'

20.

Congresswoman Li-Hsing was considerably older than she had been when Andrew had first met her. Her transparent garments were long gone. Her hair was now close-cropped and her coverings were tubular. Yet still Andrew clung, as closely as he could within the limits of reasonable taste, to the style of clothing that had prevailed when he had first adopted clothing over a century before.

She said, 'We've gone as far as we can, Andrew. We'll try once more after recess, but, to be honest, defeat is certain and the whole thing will have to be given up. All my most recent efforts have only earned me a certain defeat in the coming congressional campaign.'

'I know,' said Andrew, 'and it distresses me. You said once you would abandon me if it came to that. Why have you not done so?'

'One can change one's mind, you know. Somehow, abandoning you became a higher price than I cared to pay for just one more term. As it is, I've been in the Legislature for over a quarter of a century. It's enough.'

'Is there no way we can change minds, Chee?'

'We've changed all that are amenable to reason. The rest – the majority – cannot be moved from their emotional antipathies.'

'Emotional antipathy is not a valid reason for voting one way or the other.'

'I know that, Andrew, but they don't advance emotional antipathy as their reason.'

Andrew said cautiously, 'It all comes down to the brain, then, but must we leave it at the level of cells versus positrons? Is there no way of forcing a functional definition? Must we say that a brain is made of this or that? May we not say that a brain is something – anything – capable of a certain level of thought?'

'Won't work,' said Li-Hsing. 'Your brain is man-made, the human brain is not. Your brain is constructed, theirs developed. To any human being who is intent on keeping up the barrier between himself and a robot, those differences are a steel wall a mile high and a mile thick.'

'If we could get at the source of their antipathy – the very source of – '

'After all your years,' said Li-Hsing sadly, 'you are still trying to reason out the human being. Poor Andrew, don't be angry, but it's the robot in you that drives you in that direction.'

'I don't know,' said Andrew. 'If I could bring myself – '

1. (reprise)

If he could bring himself –

He had known for a long time it might come to that, and in the end he was at the surgeon's. He found one, skillful enough for the job at hand, which meant a robot surgeon, for no human surgeon could be trusted in this connection, either in ability or in intention.

The surgeon could not have performed the operation on a human being, so Andrew, after putting off the moment of decision with a sad line of questioning that reflected the turmoil within himself, put the First Law to one side by saying, 'I, too, am a robot.'

He then said, as firmly as he had learned to form the words even at human beings over these past decades, 'I *order* you to carry through the operation on me.'

In the absence of the First Law, an order so firmly given from one who looked so much like a man activated the Second Law sufficiently to carry the day.

21

Andrew's feeling of weakness was, he was sure, quite imaginary. He had recovered from the operation. Nevertheless, he leaned, as unobtrusively as he could manage, against the wall. It would be entirely too revealing to sit.

Li-Hsing said, 'The final vote will come this week,

Andrew. I've been able to delay it no longer, and we must lose . . . And that will be it, Andrew.'

Andrew said, 'I am grateful for your skill at delay. It gave me the time I needed, and I took the gamble I had to.'

'What gamble is this?' asked Li-Hsing with open concern.

'I couldn't tell you, or the people at Feingold and Charney. I was sure I would be stopped. See here, if it is the brain that is at issue, isn't the greatest difference of all the matter of immortality? Who really cares what a brain looks like or is built of or how it was formed? What matters is that brain cells die; *must* die. Even if every other organ in the body is maintained or replaced, the brain cells, which cannot be replaced without changing and therefore killing the personality, must eventually die.

'My own positronic pathways have lasted nearly two centuries without perceptible change and can last for centuries more. Isn't *that* the fundamental barrier? Human beings can tolerate an immortal robot, for it doesn't matter how long a machine lasts. They cannot tolerate an immortal human being, since their own mortality is endurable only so long as it is universal. And for that reason they won't make me a human being.'

Li-Hsing said, 'What is it you're leading up to, Andrew?'

'I have removed that problem. Decades ago, my positronic brain was connected to organic nerves. Now, one last operation has arranged that connection in such a way that slowly – quite slowly – the potential is being drained from my pathways.'

Li-Hsing's finely wrinkled face showed no expression for a moment. Then her lips tightened. 'Do you mean you've arranged to die, Andrew? You can't have. That violates the Third Law.'

'No,' said Andrew, 'I have chosen between the death of my body and the death of my aspirations and desires. To have let my body live at the cost of the greater death is what would have violated the Third Law.'

Li-Hsing seized his arm as though she were about to shake him. She stopped herself. 'Andrew, it won't work. Change it back.'

'It can't be. Too much damage was done. I have a year to live – more or less. I will last through the two hundredth anniversary of my construction. I was weak enough to arrange that.'

'How can it be worth it? Andrew, you're a fool.'

'If it brings me humanity, that will be worth it. If it doesn't, it will bring an end to striving and that will be worth it, too.'

And Li-Hsing did something that astonished herself. Quietly, she began to weep.

22.

It was odd how that last deed caught at the imagination of the world. All that Andrew had done before had not swayed them. But he had finally accepted even death to be human and the sacrifice was too great to be rejected.

The final ceremony was timed, quite deliberately, for the two hundredth anniversary. The World President was to sign the act and make it law and the ceremony would be visible on a global network and would be beamed to the Lunar state and even to the Martian colony.

Andrew was in a wheelchair. He could still walk, but only shakily.

With mankind watching, the World President said, 'Fifty years ago, you were declared a Sesquicentennial Robot, Andrew.' After a pause, and in a more solemn tone, he said, 'Today we declare you a Bicentennial Man, Mr Martin.'

And Andrew, smiling, held out his hand to shake that of the President.

23.

Andrew's thoughts were slowly fading as he lay in bed.

Desperately he seized at them. Man! He was a man! He wanted that to be his last thought. He wanted to dissolve – die – with that.

He opened his eyes one more time and for one last time recognized Li-Hsing waiting solemnly. There were others, but those were only shadows, unrecognizable shadows. Only Li-Hsing stood out against the deepening gray. Slowly, inchingly, he held out his hand to her and very dimly and faintly felt her take it.

She was fading in his eyes, as the last of his thoughts trickled away.

But before she faded completely, one last fugitive thought came to him and rested for a moment on his mind before everything stopped.

'Little Miss,' he whispered, too low to be heard.

A Last Word

To those of you who have read some (or, possibly, all) of my robot stories before, I welcome your loyalty and patience. To those of you who have not, I hope this book has given you pleasure – and I'm pleased to have met you – and I hope we meet again soon.

Acknowledgments

'A Boy's Best Friend,' Copyright © 1975 by the Boy Scouts of America. First appeared in *Boys' Life*, March 1975. Not included in any other collection.
'Sally,' copyright 1953 by Ziff-Davis Publishing Company, renewed Copyright © 1981 by Isaac Asimov. First appeared in *Fantastic*, May–June 1953. Included in NIGHTFALL AND OTHER STORIES.
'Someday,' Copyright © 1956 by Royal Publications, Inc. First appeared in *Infinity Science Fiction*, August 1956. Included in EARTH IS ROOM ENOUGH.
'Point of View,' Copyright © 1975 by the Boy Scouts of America. First appeared in *Boys' Life*, July 1975. Not included in any other collection.
'Think!' Copyright © 1977 by Davis Publications, Inc. First appeared in *Isaac Asimov's Science Fiction Magazine*, Spring 1977. Not included in any other collection.
'True Love,' Copyright © 1977 by *The American Way*. First appeared in *The American Way*, February 1977. Not included in any other collection.
'Robot AL-76 Goes Astray,' copyright 1941 by Ziff-Davis Publishing Company, renewed Copyright © 1968 by Isaac Asimov. First appeared in *Amazing Stories*, February 1942. Included in THE REST OF THE ROBOTS.
'Victory Unintentional,' copyright 1942 by Fictioneers, Inc., renewed Copyright © 1969 by Isaac Asimov. First appeared in *Super Science Stories*, August 1942. Included in THE REST OF THE ROBOTS.
'Stranger in Paradise,' Copyright © 1974 by UPD Publishing Corporation. First appeared in *Worlds of If*

Science Fiction, May–June 1974. Included in THE BICENTENNIAL MAN AND OTHER STORIES.

'Light Verse,' Copyright © 1973 by The Saturday Evening Post Company. First appeared in *The Saturday Evening Post*, September–October 1973, Included in BUY JUPITER AND OTHER STORIES.

'Segregationist,' Copyright © 1967 by Abbott Universal Ltd. First appeared in *Abbottempo 4*. Included in NIGHTFALL AND OTHER STORIES.

'Robbie,' copyright 1940 by Fictioneers, Inc., renewed Copyright © 1967 by Isaac Asimov. First appeared under title 'Strange Playfellow' in *Super Science Stories*, September 1940. Included in I, ROBOT.

'Let's Get Together,' Copyright © 1956 by Royal Publications, Inc. First appeared in *Infinity Science Fiction*, February 1957. Included in THE REST OF THE ROBOTS.

'Mirror Image,' Copyright © 1972 by Condé Nast Publications, Inc. First appeared in *Analog: Science Fiction – Science Fact*, May 1972. Included in THE BEST OF ISAAC ASIMOV.

'The Tercentenary Incident,' Copyright © 1976 by Isaac Asimov. First appeared in *Ellery Queen's Mystery Magazine*, August 1976. Included in THE BICENTENNIAL MAN AND OTHER STORIES.

'First Law,' Copyright © 1956 by King-Size Publications, Inc. First appeared in *Fantastic Universe*, October 1956. Included in THE REST OF THE ROBOTS.

'Runaround,' copyright 1942 by Street & Smith Publications, Inc., renewed Copyright © 1968 by Isaac Asimov. First appeared in *Astounding Science Fiction*, March 1942. Included in I, ROBOT.

'Reason,' copyright 1941 by Street & Smith Publications, Inc., renewed Copyright © 1968 by Isaac Asimov. First appeared in *Astounding Science Fiction*, April 1941. Included in I, ROBOT.

'Catch That Rabbit,' copyright 1944 by Street & Smith Publications, Inc., renewed Copyright © 1971 by Isaac Asimov. First appeared in *Astounding Science Fiction*, February 1944. Included in I, ROBOT.

'Liar!' copyright 1941 by Street & Smith Publications, Inc., renewed Copyright © 1968 by Isaac Asimov. First appeared in *Astounding Science Fiction*, May 1941. Included in I, ROBOT.

'Satisfaction Guaranteed,' copyright 1951 by Ziff-Davis Publishing Company, renewed Copyright © 1979 by Isaac Asimov. First appeared in *Amazing Stories*, April 1951. Included in EARTH IS ROOM ENOUGH.

'Lenny,' Copyright © 1957 by Royal Publications, Inc. First appeared in *Infinity Science Fiction*, January 1958. Included in THE REST OF THE ROBOTS.

'Galley Slave,' Copyright © 1957 by Galaxy Publishing Corporation. First appeared in *Galaxy Science Fiction*, December 1957. Included in THE REST OF THE ROBOTS.

'Little Lost Robot,' copyright 1947 by Street & Smith Publications, Inc., renewed Copyright © 1974 by Isaac Asimov. First appeared in *Astounding Science Fiction*, March 1947. Included in I, ROBOT.

'Risk,' Copyright © 1955 by Street & Smith Publications, Inc. First appeared in *Astounding Science Fiction*, May 1955. Included in THE REST OF THE ROBOTS.

'Escape!' copyright 1945 by Street & Smith Publications, Inc., renewed Copyright © 1972 by Isaac Asimov. First appeared in *Astounding Science Fiction*, August 1945. Included in I, ROBOT.

'Evidence,' copyright 1946 by Street & Smith Publications, Inc., renewed Copyright © 1973 by Isaac Asimov. First appeared in *Astounding Science Fiction*, September 1946. Included in I, ROBOT.

'The Evitable Conflict,' copyright 1950 by Street & Smith

Publications, Inc., renewed Copyright © 1977 by Isaac Asimov. First appeared in *Astounding Science Fiction*, June 1950. Included in I, ROBOT.

'Feminine Intuition,' Copyright © 1969 by Mercury Press, Inc. First appeared in *The Magazine of Fantasy and Science Fiction*, October 1969. Included in THE BICENTENNIAL MAN AND OTHER STORIES.

'. . . That Thou Art Mindful of Him,' Copyright © 1974 by Mercury Press, Inc. First appeared in *The Magazine of Fantasy and Science Fiction*, May 1974. Included in THE BICENTENNIAL MAN AND OTHER STORIES.

'The Bicentennial Man,' Copyright © 1976 by Random House, Inc. First appeared in *Stellar No. 2*. Included in THE BICENTENNIAL MAN AND OTHER STORIES.